THE TITANS

"We cannot separate. We cannot remove our re[...] sections from each other . . ."

Abraham Lincoln's words were to resound in the house of Kent, where young Louis Kent, heir to an American dynasty, and his bride Julia were full of dreams and aspirations; and Jephtha Kent, now journalist for the Northern family newspaper *Union,* would see his three sons turn violently against him and take up the Southern cause. As the nation struggled, so would the Kents. . . .

Gideon, the soldier, torn between his consuming desire to serve the new Confederacy and his love for a woman who preaches peace . . . Jephtha, whose one-time wife has married a fanatical Southerner, turned his own sons against him, and seemingly involved herself in a plot to destroy him . . . Louis, for whom the war is not a matter of freedom or slavery, union or disunion, but an opportunity to build a new, richer Kent empire by extracting ruthless profit from the agony of both sides . . . Michael Boyle, family "friend," who finds himself thrust into the heart of the war between the states and the war between the Kents . . . and looming over all, the titanic, tragic figure of Lincoln, Lee, and Davis, locked in a combat that will forever determine the course of the nation.

The Kent Family Chronicles

With all the color and sweep of American history itself, THE TITANS continues The Kent Family Chronicles— a mighty saga of heroism and dedication, patriotism and valor, shining spirit and abiding faith.

Here is the story of our nation—and an amazing family living in the turbulent times that began the American Experience.

This magnificent series of novels is more than absorbing, entertaining reading—it is a resounding affirmation of the greatness of America.

THE TITANS

•

JOHN JAKES

THE KENT FAMILY CHRONICLES • *VOLUME V*

A JOVE / HBJ BOOK

Four previous printings
First Jove/HBJ edition published August 1978
Fourth printing December 1978

Library of Congress Catalog Card Number: 76-17349

Printed in the United States of America

Jove/HBJ books are published by Jove Publications, Inc.
(Harcourt Brace Jovanovich)
757 Third Avenue, New York, N.Y. 10017

For my daughter Victoria

Contents

"Physically speaking, we cannot separate. We cannot remove our respective sections from each other, nor build an impassable wall between them. A husband and wife may be divorced, and go out of the presence, and beyond the reach of each other; but the different parts of our country cannot do this . . .

"We are not enemies, but friends. We must not be enemies. Though passion may have strained, it must not break our bonds of affection. The mystic chords of memory, stretching from every battle-field and patriot grave, to every living heart and hearthstone, all over this broad land, will yet swell the chorus of the Union, when again touched, as surely they will be, by the better angels of our nature."

> March 4, 1861:
> Abraham Lincoln,
> speaking to the nation
> at his first inaugural.

"The political hostilities of a generation were now face to face with weapons instead of words."

> November, 1884:
> P. G. T. Beauregard,
> General, C. S. A.,
> writing on First Manassas
> for the *Century Magazine*.

The Titans

Prologue

The Night of the Rail Splitter

Prologue

AT NINE-THIRTY ON ELECTION NIGHT, 1860, Michael Boyle walked out of the Bull's Head Tavern at Forty-fourth Street and Lexington Avenue in New York City. His carriage was waiting. His driver, Joel, stood talking with a street vendor beside a small iron stove equipped with wheels and pushcart handles. The smell of roasting yams rose from the stove. The coals glowing beneath the grill burnished Joel's black skin with orange highlights.

Michael knotted the ties of his plain woolen cloak. For November, the weather was unusually mild, and the cloak wasn't necessary tonight. Sounds carried on the night breeze: the clatter of a passing brewer's dray; the clang of a bell on a late horsecar over on Third; the lowing of cattle in the stockyard pens immediately behind the hotel.

The Bull's Head served the best beef in town and poured the best lager. Michael liked the unpretentious atmosphere of the crowded taproom where drovers in muddy boots and butchers in red-stained smocks tossed down a last drink before traveling home. All in all, Michael found the Bull's Head more comfortable than the elegant restaurants where a man of his position would be likely to dine. He'd driven this far uptown tonight because he'd hoped dinner at the Bull's Head would relieve his fatigue, his sense of failure and foreboding.

It hadn't.

Joel stepped forward. "Ready, Mr. Michael?" His employer nodded. "We goin' down to the paper to see who won?"

"We're going—though I don't expect there's much doubt about the outcome."

Joel didn't comment. It was obvious Michael was upset.

Michael Boyle was six feet tall and thirty-one years old. He had fair hair and a handsome face. Women said the long horizontal scar on his forehead added to his rakish good looks. But tonight those good looks were marred by dark circles under his golden-brown eyes. One thought kept running through his mind:

Three and a half hours. Three and a half goddamn hours. And I failed.

He had done everything but fall on his knees in front of the board of directors of The Stovall Works, the steel manufacturing firm in which the Kent family held a twenty-five percent interest. He wasn't as upset about having to tell Louis as much as he was by a feeling of personal inadequacy. If Amanda Kent had been alive, she could have overcome the board's conservatism with the natural force of her personality. But he wasn't Mrs. A's equal in turning aside nay-sayers and perhaps never would be.

I don't know why I worry it so, he thought as he walked to the carriage. *There's a much worse problem afoot tonight—*

As he put his boot on the step the sweet-potato seller tapped his arm.

"Yes?"

"A while ago, Mr. Boyle, two roughnecks were standing across the way watching the carriage. We don't get many rigs this fancy up here any more."

"Where'd the men go?"

"Didn't see. Neither did Joel. Just watch yourself for a few blocks."

"We will, thank you." Michael handed him a gold coin and climbed inside. He completely forgot about the warning until the robbers struck.

ii

As the carriage neared the corner of Forty-third Street someone whistled in the dark. Michael was too preoccupied to pay much attention.

Joel turned the carriage west. On the right, cattle pens slipped by, the smell of manure drifting through the open window. Slouched on the seat, Michael wasn't aware of the carriage slowing until he heard someone yell:

"Pull up! There's a man hurt yonder—"

Michael hammered his fist on the ceiling. "Joel, don't stop!"

The order came too late. The driver had already jerked the reins and booted the brake. The carriage lurched to a halt in the rutted side street.

"Somebody's lyin' in the road, Mr. Michael," Joel called. Looks like he—"

"Shut up and raise our hands!"

The shout came from the same man who'd yelled before. He appeared from behind the carriage—a man in a wool cap and worn coat. As Michael started to open the door the man shoved a revolver in Michael's face.

Michael cursed himself for not returning to Madison Square after the board meeting to get a gun. He knew it wasn't safe to travel this far uptown after the sun went down. And Joel was a churchgoer who hated firearms and refused to carry one.

"Climb out," ordered the man at the window. He backed away, his face a blur in the darkness. "Slow an' careful, m'boy—"

Michael obeyed, bending so he could get through the

door without bumping his head. Left boot on the step
and the door half open, he glanced to the right. He saw
a second man scrambling up in front of the carriage—
evidently the fellow who had pretended to be injured.

"They got guns, Mr. Michael," Joel said from the
driver's seat.

"And if we weren't so damn full of Christian virtue
we would too."

"Shut your fuckin' face and get down, lad."

Michael detected a familiar lilt in the man's speech.
He tried to take advantage of it:

"Is that any way for one Irishman to treat another?"

"Irishman, shit," the man said. "You're not a good one
if you got a nigger driving for you. A Black Republican's
what you are, most like. That'll make emptying your pockets twice the pleasure."

Michael was dismayed by the hatred in the man's
voice. But he understood it. Once he'd harbored such
hatred himself.

When he'd first gone to work for Amanda Kent as a
confidential clerk, he'd disliked Negroes; disliked even
more the idea that they were entitled to the same rights
as white men. His prejudice was natural enough. All the
Irish immigrants pouring into New York had a difficult
time finding jobs. Thousands of freed Negroes suddenly added to the labor market only increased the
competition.

Amanda had talked to him about that—at length—
and slowly convinced him that if the principles of liberty for which her grandfather Philip had fought meant
anything at all, those principles had to apply to all
Americans. He'd finally concluded she was right. Now
he thought as she had. He thought as a Kent—

And Kents always objected to intrusions such as rob-
bery. Objected strongly.

"Gonna be a handsome day's work, Paddy," said the
second man, out of sight at the front right side of the

coach. "I voted six times fer the Democracy. An' we're gonna top it off with a nice haul of—"

"Quit your goddamn yap!" The thief beside the coach extended his arm full length. The revolver pointed at Michael's belly. His palms itched. *Yes, he's close enough—*

"An' you! Get off that step!"

"All right."

Michael put both feet on the step and shoved the carriage door—hard. Its edge hit the muzzle of the thief's revolver and knocked it aside.

The gun went off. The horse reared and whinnied as the ball shattered splinters of wood from the left front wheel. Michael jumped.

"Jesus Christ!" the second thief cried, terrified by the rearing horse. Michael crashed against the man outside the coach. Heard the pop of Joel's whip, then a shriek from the other robber.

He fell on top of the man in the cap. They struggled and the robber cursed as he tried to maneuver the revolver for a shot. Michael brought his right hand over and grabbed the man's gun wrist. The muzzle wavered dangerously close to his eyes.

He forced it away. But the robber was strong. He broke Michael's grip and smacked the gun barrel against the left side of Michael's forehead. Pain dizzied Michael and he felt blood running into his eyebrow—

The robber's cap fell off as they struggled. Michael was still half on top of the other man. Dust from the street clouded up, choking him. Joel's whip popped a second time. Michael heard distant yelling from the Bull's Head. The cattle lowed louder, kicking the pens.

The robber lifted his knee toward Michael's groin. Michael twisted away. He shifted his right hand to the robber's throat, his left to the gun wrist, and closed his fingers like claws. The robber began to gag and thrash from side to side.

"Joel?" Michael shouted, nearly out of breath.

"I whupped the other one, Mr. Michael. He run off."

Running footsteps. Joel hurrying to his aid? Michael turned his head—a mistake. The robber wrenched his arm free and shoved the revolver near Michael's cheek. Only a quick reflex—a jerk backward, a wild roll— saved Michael from taking a shot in the head.

The second shot started the horse bucking and lunging even more wildly. "Toss me the whip and grab the reins!" Michael shouted, scrambling up. The robber had gotten to his knees. The darkness hid his gun. But Michael was sure it was aimed straight at him.

The stiff-handled whip struck his shoulder. He fumbled for it, missed. He bent over. The robber's gun roared a third time.

Michael felt the ball stir the air near his head. He found the whip, arced his right arm back, then forward, laying the lash across the robber's face.

The man howled then tried to yank the whip from Michael's hand. Michael flung the handle. The robber flailed, entangled. Stooped over to present a smaller target, Michael lunged forward. At the last instant he straightened. He kicked the robber between the legs, then clamped both hands on the man's right arm. He smashed the arm against his upraised knee. Bone cracked.

The robber dropped his gun, doubling over. Michael kicked him hard in the belly. Ribs snapped. The robber retched, staggered to his feet and fled into a vacant lot on the south side of Forty-third Street.

Enraged and gasping, Michael found the gun. He hurled it after the thief with all his strength. He heard it land in the weeds where the robber had disappeared.

"You all right, Mr. Michael?" Joel asked, struggling to hang onto the reins and soothe the horse.

"Just splendid," Michael lied. "You?"

"That fellow didn't touch me."

"Good."

He was beginning to shake. He threw the whip. Joel caught it with one hand. Men from the Bull's Head were rounding the corner at Lexington.

"Let's get away from here before we have to answer a lot of fool questions."

Michael slammed the door and sprawled on the seat, a kerchief pressed against the gash on his forehead. Joel clambered to his place, popped the whip— *"Giddap!"*—and the carriage left the approaching men behind.

Gradually, Michael's breathing slowed. His head ached. He was filthy with dust. The cut was bleeding. But that was the extent of the damage. Except to his sensibilities. The assault itself hadn't been half so unnerving as the viciousness he remembered in the robber's voice:

You got a nigger driving for you. A Black Republican's what you are.

Hate, that's all there is in the country any more, he thought. And how much worse will it be by the time the sun's up tomorrow?

His failure at the board meeting was forgotten as he asked himself why God had ever permitted the black man to be brought to America. To test her? Well, she showed every sign of failing the test. The black man's presence and the storm of conflict it had created seemed about to cause a disruption greater than anything seen since the Revolution.

You can take part of the blame, he reminded himself. *You voted for Mr. Abraham Lincoln.*

iii

Joel drove down Fifth Avenue, past the high wooden walls of the Croton Reservoir at Forty-second Street, and into the expanding residential district of the well-to-do. The carriage rattled along the west side of Madison Square, but Michael hardly glanced at the lighted windows of the mansion on the east side of the square, where he lived. The rest of the trip took him down Broadway, past City Hall Park, to Printing House Square.

There, Michael climbed out in front of a familiar three-story building. Over its main entrance hung a wooden signboard carrying the design of a stoppered green bottle about a third full of something dark. The brown paint represented tea. This had been the symbol of the Kent family's printing house since the Revolutionary War. The board's gilt lettering spelled out

THE NEW YORK UNION

"You can drive home, Joel Louis and Julia will be joining me later. They'll take me back to Madison Square."

"Sure you aren't hurt, Mr. Michael?"

"No, thanks to your courage and quick action. Good night, Joel."

The Negro slapped the reins over the horse's back and the carriage rumbled off. Michael stood on the walk, tugging gently at the kerchief now stuck to his wound. Finally he gave it a yank and swore. He balled the bloodied fabric in his hand. It was turning out to be a hell of an evening.

He didn't want to go upstairs. He lingered a moment, surveying the square. It was deserted. On the far side, he saw two men dart inside the door of Greeley's *Tribune*. Half a minute later, another man hurried into the *Times*. Reporters, no doubt. Bringing early ballot totals from the telegraph office of the Associated Press. The New York *Union* had money enough to pay for private wires.

Finally he turned and walked in. The small reception lobby was empty. Beyond a closed door, the presses thumped, churning out the inside pages of the morning edition.

Michael climbed the front stair to the second floor editorial office, a huge, gloomy chamber with sparsely scattered gas fixtures, rows of disorderly desks and one private cubicle back in a corner. At the rear of the office an open arch led to a smaller room where the telegraph sounders chattered.

The editorial office was empty save for a copy boy reading a new Beadle dime novel, a clerk washing down a slate board that had been brought in to display the returns and a lone reporter scribbling out an article. Most of the other members of the reportorial staff were scattered throughout the city's wards, or posted at the headquarters of the two major parties.

The three people in the room all noticed Michael's gashed forehead and dusty, disheveled clothes. The reporter seemed about to ask a question. But he didn't—perhaps because the Irishman looked so severe.

An oil lamp glowed behind the wooden wall of the corner cubicle. Michael entered without knocking.

"Lord God, what happened to you?" Theophilus Payne exclaimed from behind his littered desk.

"A minor altercation with two stalwarts of the One and Indivisible Democracy. Not only did they vote several times for Mr. Douglas, they also tried to cap the evening by relieving me of my pocket money up near the Bull's Head."

Payne chuckled. "You do have a penchant for the seamy parts of town."

"My natural habitat," Michael growled, sinking into a chair.

Payne put down his pen, got up and circled the desk to peer at Michael's clotted wound. The *Union*'s editor was only in his middle forties. But overindulgence had lined his face and blotched his thick pink nose. His shirt bore traces of his evening meal. His breath smelled of .

whiskey. If Michael had been standing, Payne's head would barely have reached his shoulder.

"Are you feeling all right?"

"I won't be if I have to answer that tiresome question all evening. Yes, I am. Got any returns yet?"

"Nothing conclusive." Payne showed Michael the foolscap sheet on which he'd been writing. "But I've roughed out tomorrow's headlines anyway."

Michael scanned the series of headlines that would be set in diminishing type sizes and would occupy the position reserved for the day's most important story—the left column of the six that made up the front page:

LINCOLN ELECTED.

———

NEW PARTY WINS IN
SECOND NATIONAL CAMPAIGN.

———

Sweeps Northeast
And Northwest.

———

Victory Also Predicted
In California, Oregon.

———

Adverse Southern Reaction
Reported By Our Correspondents.

———

Michael tossed the foolscap on the desk. "Sure you're not being premature?"

Payne grinned. "My boy, Mr. Lincoln's already won the state elections in Maine, Vermont, Indiana—and most important, Pennsylvania. They were all held weeks ago, remember?" He screwed up his face. "Are you sure that altercation didn't addle your wits? He's *in*!"

"I wonder if it'll be a good thing."

"May I be so bold as to ask what party you voted for, Mr. Boyle?"

"You know I voted Republican."

"And you're already doubting the wisdom of it?"

"Yes, I'm doubtful because—hell, never mind. Hand me that bottle you keep hidden in the desk."

Puzzled, Payne produced the bottle, then bustled away to the telegraph room. Michael tilted his chair against the partition and took a long swallow. Grimaced. Ghastly stuff.

He'd meant what he said to Theo Payne. He *was* doubtful that Abraham Lincoln's election would be beneficial to the country. It might be necessary. But beneficial? No.

Though his Irish background should have put him with the Northern faction of the hopelessly divided Democrats, he'd voted Republican because he believed in the guiding principle of the six-year-old, clearly sectional party formed from a peculiar coalition of rabid abolitionists, more moderate Free-Soilers, antislavery men from the defunct Whig party, anti-Nebraska Democrats and even a few anti-Catholic Know-Nothings.

Little in the Republican platform had excited Michael. He agreed with the party's support of a transcontinental railroad to link the East with the new states on the Pacific. But that plank, and the one expressing a willingness to spend money for internal improvements, wouldn't have been enough to change his traditional allegiance to the other side. Michael had voted Republican principally because the party stood for containing the expansion of slavery.

He'd cast his vote with an awareness of its possible consequences. Some of the Southern states actually wanted the Illinois lawyer elected almost as badly as did the Northern ones. But the reasons were sharply different.

He replaced the whiskey bottle in the desk drawer and went out into the editorial room. Within an hour it would be packed with frantic men writing page one copy for Payne's approval. The pace wouldn't diminish until almost two-thirty in the morning when the last locked form would go to the pressroom. Now, though, the silence seemed almost ominous—

Payne came hurrying up one of the aisles. Gleeful, he thrust a tally sheet into Michael's hand. "Just received reports from some of the upstate counties. Rochester's turned in a majority for Old Abe. The rest of the state's tending the same way."

"Got anything from the men down South?"

"Not yet."

Payne took back the paper. Michael felt increasingly depressed.

Four presidential candidates had emerged from the unsettled summer of 1860. The Southern wing of the Democracy had rejected Douglas—the Little Giant—whose initially appealing popular sovereignty doctrine had plunged the Kansas territory into armed strife several years earlier. Douglas' sincere if ultimately disastrous belief in the supreme power of the people had found expression in the Kansas-Nebraska Act of 1854. In essence, the act had overturned the 1820 Missouri Compromise and re-established a principle of Congressional nonintervention with slavery. The Douglas bill permitted the legislatures of new territories to allow or deny the presence of slaves.

Douglas' opponents had claimed the senator's proposals had shabby political overtones. Even as far back as the early 1850s, Congress had been studying the feasibility of a cross-country railroad. Proponents of a Southern route, led by President Pierce's Secretary of War, the former Senator Jefferson Davis, had finally swung their support to an alternate route running west from Chicago. The Little Giant's enemies took pleasure in noting that he owned a good deal of land along what might become the northern right-of-way. They suggested he'd pushed popular sovereignty legislation to appease the South in return for its endorsement of the rail route that might bring him a huge real estate profit.

The result of the tangled compromising had been "bleeding Kansas"—where pro-slavery settlers battled abolitionists and Free-Soilers supplied with carbines from the East. The carbines were shipped in crates labeled *Contents—Bibles.* Beecher's Bibles, both sides called them. To purchase them, the abolitionist minister Henry Ward Beecher had raised money among his radical friends.

Douglas' populist philosophy rapidly lost its appeal for the Southern extremists. It didn't go far enough. They not only wanted a free choice on slavery but also a guarantee of its protection in new territories. That, the Douglas Democrats wouldn't give. So the dissident Southerners walked out of the April nominating convention in Charleston and two months later put forth their own candidate—Breckenridge of Kentucky.

A third candidate, Bell, hastily formed the Constitutional Union Party. But it was really pledged to little more than what its name suggested—vague support of the Constitution and perpetual union.

The Republicans had also tried to keep their platform moderate. But they'd doggedly refused to compromise on the plank that had persuaded Michael to switch his vote. The Republicans rejected the Douglas doctrine or *any* doctrine that might open new territories to slavery.

Thus, with the nation offered four choices, simple arithmetic suggested the purely sectional Republicans had the strength to win with the generally unknown Illinois politician. Lincoln might not draw a majority of the popular vote. But by carrying the free states, he should be able to accumulate the electoral votes needed to gain him the Presidency.

And although Mr. Lincoln was generally as moderate as his platform, his election could well turn out to be the worst thing that could happen to a country already angered and torn by the violence and unrest over the slave question.

Open warfare had swept back and forth across the Kansas–Missouri border; there had been the inflammatory Dred Scott decision of '57, with which the Supreme Court had in effect denied black men the rights enjoyed by white citizens, including the right to sue for personal liberty in court. Then came the bizarre attempt by the murdering abolitionist, Brown, to seize the Harper's Ferry arsenal the preceding year. There was a constant outpouring of abolitionist propaganda in books and pamphlets, sermons and lectures. The Underground Railroad continued to operate in defiance of the fugitive slave laws. And then physical violence had erupted on the floor of Congress. All these and more had pushed the conflict to the flash point.

Lincoln had gone a certain distance in his attempts to be conciliatory. He made it clear he wouldn't tamper with the "peculiar institution" in the South. But he also wouldn't permit its spread. Southerners knew it. And tonight they were watching his ascendancy to power.

"I think we owe ourselves a drink to celebrate," Payne declared, lurching back to his cubicle and stumbling into his chair. Michael folded his arms and leaned against the door.

"I'm not so sure festivities are called for, Theo. Besides, you look like you've been celebrating all evening."

"So I have, so I have! The editor of an influential newspaper should have a few privileges. Especially when his candidate's winning!"

Payne nearly dropped the bottle as he pulled it out of

the drawer. He wasn't an out-and-out drunkard. But he kept himself perpetually fortified. It never seemed to impair his performance. He was considered a first-class newsman by his employees as well as by his colleagues on New York's rival newspapers. Even the crusty Greeley admired him.

On her deathbed, Amanda had charged Theo Payne with re-establishing a Kent family newspaper opposed to slavery but firm in its support of any reasonable compromise necessary to maintain national union. Even with Amanda gone eight years, Payne had scrupulously adhered to that policy. But Michael knew the editor must be anticipating the future with immense delight.

Payne swigged from the bottle, then raised it to salute Michael: "I give you, sir, the Rail Candidate. The vulgar mobocrat. The illiterate partisan of Negro equality—"

"That can't be Theo Payne you're quoting."

"Hell no. One of those fire-eaters on Mr. Rhett's *Charleston Mercury*. Tonight they're getting what they deserve."

"You're too eager, Theo. Maybe Lincoln can hold things together. He doesn't despise Southerners the way you do. He's made that eminently clear in his speeches."

"Ah, but they don't *listen* to his speeches! They hear only what they want to hear. That slavery will end. Never mind Lincoln thinks it'll die of natural causes— the factory system, the influence of education, religion—never mind that! To our Southern brethren, he's a threat. An *excuse!*"

Somber, Michael said, "Which is the same thing your abolitionist crowd wants. An excuse for a holy crusade. Without scruples and without mercy—and the devil with the country."

Payne grew truculent. "Those may be my personal

opinions. You know damn well I don't expound them in the paper!"

"Of course you don't. If you did, Louis and I would toss you into the street. Then how would you feed Mrs. Payne and that big brood of yours?"

Payne replied to Michael's good-natured needling with a belch. "Gordon Bennett would hire me in a snap. However, I refuse to listen to you when you start blustering like a longshoreman."

"I *was* a longshoreman before Mrs. A took me on."

"Well, you're also sounding like Louis."

There was a touch of dismay in Michael's laugh. "God forbid!"

"Mr. Payne?"

The cry from the rear brought Michael pivoting around. Payne shouted back, "What is it?"

"We're receiving a dispatch from Lucas."

Payne jumped up. "Charleston! The first reaction—come on, Michael. Let's see how the bastards like their new president!"

iv

Michael followed the editor to the small telegraph room at the back of the main office. In a haze of cigar smoke three young men sat before separate sending and receiving stations. As the sounder in the center clacked, the operator hastily transcribed the dispatch. Payne peered over his shoulder, then began to chuckle:

"Precisely what I expected! Bells. Bonfires. An informal business holiday declared for tomorrow—" He read more. "Lucas heard a band on the Battery playing the 'Marseillaise.' Saw half a dozen hotbloods sporting blue cockades—"

"I don't get the significance."

"The blue cockade, Michael, has been the symbol of resistance ever since Andy Jackson backed South Carolina down on Nullification."

Payne turned back to scan the copy.

"Going to be fireworks tomorrow night. Illuminations in private homes—" A pause. "And a call for a state convention in a month or so. A convention to consider—what does he say?"

The editor leaned on the operator's shoulder, almost pushing the young man out of the chair.

The operator read: "To consider the state's relation to the Federal Government."

"Wonderful. *Wonderful*!" Payne looked almost ecstatic. "Secession is finally going to turn into something besides swamp oratory. Michael, my boy, I'll wager fifty dollars that one or more of the states down there will try to pull out."

"If they do, we'll all be in trouble. Lincoln won't let a state just—resign from the nation. He made that clear when he spoke at Cooper Union in February. He said he wouldn't accept the Southern claim that electing a Republican would destroy the Union."

"That's right," Payne agreed as the sounder went silent. "No one can destroy the Union but the Southerners!" He snatched the completed dispatch. "I've decided on the subject of my editorial. A warning to those fine gentlemen not to act precipitously."

"You're a hypocrite, Theo. You hope they will."

The editor feigned innocence. "I follow company policy!" But Michael saw the beginning of a smile as Payne turned back toward his office. "From this point on, I believe events will take care of themselves."

And that, Michael thought, is what we all have to worry about.

v

The secessionist leaders had already decided the
South couldn't prosper, let alone protect its traditional
way of life, under a Republican administration. No
amount of conciliatory rhetoric from the President-to-
be was going to change that attitude nor resolve the fundamental question underlying the trouble: the status of
the black man. That was the stormcenter. Michael had
seen it tonight in the Irish robber's remark about Joel.

Facts and reason no longer counted in the debate. It
didn't matter, for instance, that the majority of the
Southern yeomanry—farmers who worked their own
land with their own hands—couldn't afford black labor-
ers and undoubtedly wouldn't approve of owning them
if they could.

It didn't matter that the South contained a minority
of respected leaders who staunchly opposed secession.

It didn't matter that there were whole areas in which
the idea of slavery was abominated—the mountainous
western counties of Virginia, for example.

Nothing mattered.

The radical spokesmen for the so-called plantation
aristocracy relied on emotionalism—and a few unim-
peachable truths. They kept reminding Southerners that
for thirty years and more the entire region had had its
honor called into question; every aspect of its style of
life degraded and sneered at by Northern radicals; had
been, in short, the target of relentless ideological campaigns that made every Southerner, slaveowner or not, a
party to what the vituperative Senator Sumner had
scorned on the floor of Congress as a system of "harlo-
try."

The Massachusetts legislator had couched that attack
in the most personal terms. He'd aimed it directly

against the distinguished Andrew Butler of South Carolina. Senator Butler, Sumner charged, "has chosen a mistress who, though ugly to others, is always lovely to him—I meant the harlot, Slavery."

The assault on Butler's character had been delivered on a day when the Senator was absent from the chamber, heightening the insult.

In retaliation, Butler's nephew, young Congressman Preston Brooks, had stalked into the Senate and smashed at Sumner's head and back with a gutta-percha cane, leaving Sumner near death at his desk. The poison kept spreading—

The *Union*'s Washington reporter—who had yet to be heard from, Michael realized—had wired a week ago that the Democratic incumbent was growing sicker in spirit by the day.

Buck Buchanan was a decent man. But he was frightened and hopelessly confused by the possible ramifications of what Seward had once rashly referred to as the irrepressible conflict. Buchanan had come to realize there might be no way to reconcile sectional differences short of separation.

And war?

Some of Michael's acquaintances were already talking as if a sectional war—perhaps of short duration, but war nonetheless—was a strong possibility. Among these acquaintances was Colonel Corcoran, commander of the 69th New York Militia, one of several city regiments composed almost entirely of Irishmen.

The 69th was just about ten years old. Prided itself on being a crack unit. The regiment held regular meetings at Hibernian Hall, which Corcoran owned. From time to time Michael dropped in at the hall on meeting nights to visit with men he'd known during his days as a worker and labor organizer on the docks. Of late, Corcoran had been urging him to join up.

Appeals were made to Michael's Irish pride and patriotism. The 69th was honing its military skills because many of its members belonged to the Fenian Brotherhood, the semi-secret, world-wide organization dedicated to one day liberating Ireland from Great Britain. Gaining experience in a militia regiment, even at the price of going to war, would be invaluable.

Michael spiritedly defended his own position. Yes, he was proud of his Irish heritage. But he was an American now. He had no desire to fight for the country from which his parents had emigrated in poverty and despair. Nor did he want to go to war against other Americans.

Corcoran acknowledged his friend's right to his viewpoint. But he didn't agree with it. Corcoran was also the local leader of the Fenians.

Still, he promised that if Michael ever changed his mind, the New York 69th had a place for him.

vi

Theo Payne was in his office composing the morning's editorial. Michael lingered in the telegraph room as returns continued to come in.

New York was going solidly Republican. New Jersey and Massachusetts were tending the same way. A copy boy ran back and forth between the operators and the tally board, where the clerk continually chalked new figures.

The totals were coming in faster now. Two of the telegraphers bet on whether Lincoln would carry sixteen or eighteen free states. Breckenridge appeared to be taking the lead throughout the South. Bell's Constitutional ticket showed initial strength only in Virginia and two of the border states, Kentucky and Tennessee, where pro and antislavery sentiment existed in almost equal amounts. The embattled Douglas would be lucky to pull even one state in the winning column.

"Washington!" one of the operators exclaimed. Michael stepped forward, awaiting the message from Jephtha Kent.

Jephtha, the son of Amanda's cousin Jared, had been a minister of the Methodist Episcopal Church, South, until his views on slavery had gotten him removed from his itinerancy in Virginia. Next had come separation from his wife and children, then an ignominious period of self-inflicted martyrdom in the little town where the family made its home. Finally there had been the involvement with the Underground Railroad that had nearly cost Jephtha his life.

Broken and disillusioned, he'd fled to New York shortly after Amanda's death in 1852. With Michael's help, he had reconstructed his life along completely different lines. He'd been the *Union's* reporter in the nation's capital for the past three and a half years. He was content to let Michael and Louis administer the enormous sums of money that came from the California gold mining properties originally belonging to his father, who had been murdered in San Francisco.

The money would always remain Jephtha's. But with his approval—given while he was still a minister—Amanda Kent had taken over the management of the Ophir Company on his behalf.

The operator transcribed Jephtha's dispatch in less than half a minute. Both he and Michael stared at the sounder, as if expecting more. The message penciled on the foolscap looked stark because it was so short:

SECESSION OF ONE OR MORE SOUTHERN STATES SEEN HERE AS CERTAIN CONSEQUENCE OF LINCOLN ELECTION. PRAY IT WILL NOT LEAD TO WAR.

Staring at the paper, Michael realized how deeply the night's events must be affecting Jephtha.

He hated slavery. At the same time he regarded most Southerners not as evil people, but as misguided ones— a subtle yet important difference that lingered from his years as a preacher of the Christian gospel.

Every few months Jephtha returned to New York for policy discussions with Theo Payne. From those conversations Michael knew Jephtha desperately feared a final confrontation between the two sections. His three sons still lived in the South. Perhaps that explained why, although he no longer professed much religious faith, he had resorted to the word *pray*.

The operator said, "Guess that's all. But I think Mr. Kent's wrong."

Michael picked up the foolscap. "For what reason?"

"The South will never go to war just because Lincoln's President."

"Oh? Then why have the Charleston papers been writing about a 'revolution of 1860'?"

In the cubicle he found Payne taking a nip. He handed him the sheet—"From Jephtha."—and tried to ignore his smile after he read it.

"Y'see, Michael? Jephtha knows what's coming."

"And just what is my cousin's prediction, gentlemen? Biblical apocalypse?"

The strong, faintly sarcastic male voice startled Michael and Payne. The editor's right hand, seeming to move with a life of its own, snatched the whiskey bottle from the desk top, jammed it in the drawer and slid the drawer shut with amazing speed.

The man who'd spoken was Louis Kent.

vii

Louis took the arm of the young woman at his side and guided her into the tiny office. Michael gave him the Washington copy.

"Read it for yourself." He inclined his head to Louis' wife of two and a half years. "Good evening, Julia."

"Good evening, Mi—heaven above! You're cut. And covered with dust!"

"Nothing serious."

Amanda's son, whom Michael had served as legal guardian until he reached his majority, let the dispatch droop in his hand. "You didn't get that pounding from the Stovall board, I hope."

"Not this particular pounding."

"Then where?"

"It's not important, Louis."

The younger man's eyes showed fleeting annoyance. People didn't refuse to answer questions put to them by Louis Kent.

But he stayed calm: "How did the meeting go?"

"Miserably."

Louis scowled.

He was slender and strongly built. And although he was only twenty-three, he already possessed a confidence and maturity that turned feminine heads.

He looked superb in whatever he wore—tonight a conservative black frock coat, open to show a single-breasted waistcoat in a pattern of black and white checks that matched his trousers. His black satin cravat, tied in a bow, all but hid the round starched collar of his shirt.

It was quite a proper costume for a young man of wealth. Yet its subdued blacks and grays represented a kind of negative but unmistakable ostentation.

The tones of the clothing complemented Louis' dark eyes and swarthy skin—a heritage from the Mexican officer who had fathered him during the trouble in Texas in '36. His hair was jet black, worn thick at the back. The hair curled down behind his ears to neatly combed side whiskers reaching to a point just below his earlobes. He hadn't yet adopted the Dundreary look—or the latest male adornment, a flowing mustache.

Louis laid his gray kid gloves alongside his stick on the editor's desk.

"Summarize the meeting for me, Michael."

The order irritated him. But perhaps he was just feeling tense because of the way the election was going. And the cut was throbbing again.

"I began by telling the board we'd sent agents to Great Britain to investigate a radical new process for converting pig iron into wrought iron or steel. I told them the inventor, Mr. Bessemer, was making claims worth our attention. Saying the converting furnace he designed would one day produce five tons of steel in a quarter of an hour instead of the ten days it takes now. I went over the agents' report line by line. I covered every detail. Well, almost. Then I gave the board our recommendation, including the budget for funding an experimental installation in the Pittsburgh plant. I pleaded the case for more than three hours."

Louis blinked. "I should think they'd have accepted the proposal out of sheer relief. Besides, the level of risk is acceptably low."

"They almost agreed. Until Foley asked what Mr. Bessemer's fellow Englishmen thought about him."

"And?"

Michael shrugged. "I was forced to go back and comment on what I'd omitted from the report. That the other steelmakers say Bessemer *and* his process are crazy."

"You told the truth?"

Michael was nonplused. "Of course."

"And that's what defeated us?"

"The proposal was turned down unanimously."

"Why didn't you lie, for God's sake? That vote completely disrupts my plans to make the Stovall operation more competitive."

"If you'd been there would you have lied?"

"You're damn right. And it's damned evident I *should* have been there!"

His fingers were white as he forced himself to look at the dispatch from Jephtha. Disgusted, Michael walked out of the office. Louis' wife followed.

"Michael, won't you let me find some alcohol for that cut?"

"No, thank you." He was still fuming over Louis' anger and contempt. More and more of late, friction was developing between them. It was one more aspect of the future to worry about.

"I'm frightfully sorry you got hurt—" Julia began.

"Just a scrape with a couple of street thugs."

He perched on the edge of an empty desk. She walked around in front of him.

"You could have avoided it if you'd joined us. I was looking forward to your company."

Julia's remark was coupled with the sort of glance other men might have interpreted as very close to sexual invitation. Michael didn't because he'd seen such glances before. He knew they were automatic and impersonal.

Louis Kent's wife was almost as diminutive as Theo Payne. She had glossy dark brown hair and blue eyes whose vividness was exaggerated by her porcelain-pale skin. Her expensive bell-sleeved gown matched the color of her eyes perfectly.

The gown fitted closely over her breasts and was open to the waist, revealing a blouse of immaculate white muslin with a frilled collar. Her voluminous skirt over crinolines was trimmed with dark blue satin edged with pleated taffeta. Her hat was a shallow-crowned straw; the wide brim drooped exactly as far as fashion dictated. A dark blue satin rosette decorated the hat's front. Two matching satin streamers down the back had been carefully draped over her left shoulder. In weather more typical of November, an outer cloak would have completed the outfit.

Julia stepped closer to him. "I can't see how you of all people could resist Delmonico's."

It was a light jibe at his infamous appetite. He consumed huge quantities of food and never gained a pound. He didn't mind the teasing. But he did mind her physical nearness. He rose and stepped away:

"I suppose it shows my slum upbringing, but I prefer the Bull's Head. The waiters shout in English instead of whispering bogus French."

"But you've never met the Commodore!"

"I've seen him driving his buggy along Broadway like a madman. That's enough for me."

"Do you happen to know how old he is?"

"Sixty-seven, sixty-eight—"

"He's certainly spry. And he's a dear. A perfect original!"

Michael wanted to laugh. If Cornelius Vanderbilt had been poor, no doubt she'd have said he was one of the most shabbily dressed, foul-mouthed men in New York. Louis, at least, was more honest—and calm again as he walked out of the office carrying a sheaf of copy for the morning edition:

"That he is. I don't know many who can swear like a dock hand and chew Lorillard plug at the same time."

Proudly, Julia said, "He invited us to Washington Place for cards after dinner."

"We invited him down here instead," Louis added. "He went home."

"Doesn't he care who wins the election?" Michael asked.

"He cares more about playing whist."

Julia pouted. "I did so want to see his house."

"Ordinary," Louis told her.

But the circumstances of its occupancy had been far from ordinary. The wife of the strong-willed Commo-

dore had originally refused to move from Staten Island
to Manhattan. Vanderbilt had committed her to an insane asylum until she "came to her senses."

"By the way, Michael," Louis said. "He does have
some interesting plans concerning railroad shares. If
we're lucky he might let us in on a small basis."

"Papa's already in," Julia declared.

Michael nodded. He knew of Vanderbilt's ambition
to acquire two short-line roads, the New York and Har-
lem and the New York and Hudson. The Kent family's
bankers had told him on a confidential basis that the
Commodore probably wanted to corner freight business
in the state by linking the short lines with a larger
prize—the New York Central connecting Albany with
Buffalo.

Julia kept watching Michael as he said, "Well, I'm sorry
to have missed such a grand occasion. But the afternoon
was a disaster. I needed lager beer more than either you
or the Commodore needed my presence."

Julia understood the remark was meant for her. Anger, then amusement flickered in her eyes. Through
polite but unmistakable rebuffs, Michael had long ago
made it clear he didn't want to play her little game.
Strangely, with him she persisted.

As she did now, moving in his direction again, and
contriving to turn so that her breast brushed his arm
briefly. She laid a gloved hand on his sleeve:

"I'm sure you did your best at the board meeting. I'm
sure you were very persuasive."

"I was out of my class against that pack of moss-
backs."

Julia stood on tiptoe to whisper: "You're a bit of a
mossback yourself. Some day, dear Michael, I'll break
through that shell—"

Louis lifted his head. His wife's whisper hadn't been
all that soft—perhaps on purpose. He frowned when he
saw how close to the Irishman Julia was standing. She

ignored the frown and Louis forced his glance back to his sheaf of copy.

"Break through?" Michael said to her. "I doubt it."

He was smiling. But his words had an edge. Her eyes opened wide with anger. He stared at her until she looked away, her cheeks scarlet.

Julia Sedgwick Kent, twenty-one, was an odd one indeed, Michael thought. In normal social intercourse she only dealt cordially with those whose wealth and influence matched or outstripped the combined wealth and influence she and Louis had achieved by their marriage.

Her acknowledged beauty probably made such behavior acceptable. Yet her beauty was the one characteristic about which Julia was astonishingly—even cruelly—democratic. She wanted men to admire her. All men. From the roughest press worker at the paper to the gentlemen of important families.

Some men were out of reach. William B. Astor, for instance. Wall Street said his fortune was close to twenty-five million now; the total Kent assets were worth only about half that, placing Louis and Julia several rungs down on the millionaires' ladder. And no matter how rich her husband was, Julia would never be socially acceptable to certain of the Whitneys, the Rhinelanders, the Schermerhorns. To those old families, Louis Kent—even Vanderbilt—would always be upstarts.

Anyway, Michael doubted Julia would ever let any man except Louis touch her. It was the ability to attract men—the challenge to win a response—that excited her. Any idiot rash enough to make an overture would probably be stunned by Julia's anger—and by a scathing rebuff that he had misjudged her friendliness in a vulgar and wholly unforgivable way.

That was only speculation, of course. There'd never been the tiniest scrap of gossip to suggest Julia carried the game to conclusion. But he didn't care to find out for himself. It was too risky for a number of reasons, including potential damage to his own self-respect, and the continuing necessity of working with Louis, who hewed to the socially acceptable double standard of male society: What's right for me is not right for my spouse.

Every few months Louis slept with some young shopgirl who happened to catch his fancy. He didn't attempt to conceal these escapades from Michael. But let any man attempt to seduce Julia and Louis would undoubtedly become the very picture of the outraged, vengeful husband.

Michael didn't like to admit he found Julia hellishly good looking, or that he responded unwillingly to the sexual aura surrounding her like the scent of her cologne. Sometimes he wondered if she sensed he was attracted. That might explain why she pursued him with more determination than she did some who signaled that they wanted no part of her flirtations.

Right now she was furious with him for his latest rebuff. He could tell by the stiffness of her posture as she walked a few steps up the aisle and pretended to examine a button on her glove while Louis kept reading.

Quite apart from Julia's beauty, he supposed she had good reason for her haughty attitude. Her father, in his seventies, was indeed a close friend of Cornelius Vanderbilt. Julia and "Papa" had been among the privileged few who had cruised New York harbor after the launching of Vanderbilt's opulent 270-foot steam yacht *North Star*. Julia had only been fourteen, but she vividly recalled the champagne and the lavish fireworks display.

Sedgwick had gotten rich on the bases of this friendship. He'd been permitted to invest in the Commodore's immensely profitable Accessory Transit Company. At the height of the gold rush, the company had shortened the sea route to California by two days via a connection across Nicaragua rather than Panama. Next Sedgwick had pumped money into Vanderbilt's lucrative New York to Le Havre freight and passenger line. He was currently using his connection to share in the Commodore's new passion—railroads—and to help his son-in-law do the same if he wished.

Sedgwick was by no means old New York society. But he was sufficiently wealthy and well placed so that Louis' successful courtship had been something of an accomplishment.

Julia and Louis had married a year and a half after the conclusion of his last term at Harvard. He'd gone there at Michael's insistence but had dawdled through his classes.

Louis had never received his degree. By the time he quit the university to devote himself to running the affairs of the family, he had only finished a year and a half of actual study. He'd developed a pattern of growing disinterested by the end of one term, at which time he would come back to New York and spend half a year with Michael learning the business.

Twice Michael had been able to persuade him to return for a fall term—and twice, when winter arrived in the city, so did Louis, saying he was bored with Cambridge and eager to get on with his practical education. At the end of the third term Michael abandoned any hope of Louis' graduating.

Not that Louis wasn't bright. He'd quickly absorbed the training Michael had given him, as well as that from the Kents' legal and banking advisers. Michael watched Louis grow into a shrewd and capable administrator who weighed every decision in terms of profit or loss.

A year after the wedding Louis succumbed to Julia's constant complaints about the smelly Italians, the quarrelsome Irish, and the stubborn Germans with whom the better classes were increasingly forced to contend in the crowded city. He presented his wife with a second

home—a country retreat—even more lavish than the
Madison Square mansion, which had become the family
seat after Amanda Kent de la Gura had returned east
from the gold fields.

The new house, a great monster of a place near Tarrytown, had been designed in the popular Gothic Revival style. In Michael's opinion, the house well illus-
trated the paradox of Louis Kent. He was jealous of
even a single penny lost from the profits of the diversi-
fied Kent enterprises—and none too scrupulous, sometimes, about how he increased those profits. Yet he
liked personal ostentation. Contrary to all advice, he'd
indulged his liking on an unprecedented scale by building the country place on wooded property overlooking
the Hudson River.

Louis was never at ease when imagination was required—pyramiding wealth excepted—and so he'd been
at a loss for a name for the house. It was Michael who'd
proposed a name tracing back to the man who had sired
Louis' great-grandfather Philip, the first of the Kents.

Philip Kent's father, a British nobleman, had owned
a country estate called Kentland. Although Louis acted
put out because he hadn't thought of it—and because
Michael seemed to know more of his family's history
than he did—the name was finally adopted, and the
American Kentland was surrendered to its new mistress.
Louis and Julia divided their time between Madison
Square, where Michael lived, and the country house, to
which all of the family heirlooms had been removed.

Louis' easy compliance about the house was just one
reason Michael considered the alliance with Julia unfortunate. Another was the way her temperament rein-
forced her husband's. She approved of, and encouraged,
patterns of behavior that were a distortion of what Michael
considered moral—patterns Louis had alread developed in his private life and in business.

Louis' approach to business and life had been

summed up for Michael in a conversation he'd had with Amanda's son several years after she died.

Just prior to her death, Louis had sexually assaulted one of the household girls. Amanda had discovered it. For punishment, she'd beaten her son with a buggy whip and charged him never again to take advantage of anyone of inferior strength or resources.

Over whiskey one evening, Michael asked Louis outright whether the whipping had left a lasting impression. To this day, he recalled the boy's handsome, swarthy face lighting with an almost rapturous smile.

"An impression, Michael? Definitely. It taught me one invaluable lesson. Whatever you do, no matter how bad, the important thing is not to get caught."

"But Mrs. A said you were contrite—"

"Of course I was contrite! I was damn mad that I'd let myself have a second go at that little slut of a housemaid. If I hadn't, I'd never have been found out. But I was. Only an imbecile would have denied being sorry. I pretended, Michael—*pretended*—principally so my mother wouldn't whip me half to death."

The lightly spoken words had tainted their relationship ever since.

As was his right, Amanda's son gradually assumed control of the various family enterprises: the publishing house in Boston; the *Union*; the Kents' partial ownership of the cotton-spinning mill in Rhode Island; the gold mines; and the steel works in which Amanda had acquired a substantial interest during her lifetime. Michael had occupied the Kent seat on the board of The Stovall Works solely as a surrogate; Louis made every decision.

While Michael saw Amanda Kent in her son, it was a subtly warped reflection. Louis possessed much of his mother's strength, but without the innate decency and compassion that had helped temper her occasionally ruthless use of that strength.

Michael believed the lack in Louis to be partly his fault. Whenever he felt the failure most keenly, he consoled himself with the thought that once Louis had reached fifteen—the age at which Michael had assumed guardianship—a fundamental change in the boy's character had probably been impossible to achieve.

If that wasn't true, at least it eased his conscience.

At first, as Louis was learning about the different businesses, he and Michael had been fairly close. When they argued, it was on the merits of a question, with little or no personal rancor. But the more Louis learned, the more he changed. Julia's presence had only accelerated the change—

And opened another gulf.

Michael felt he was part of the family. Louis and Julia saw it otherwise. Louis was the only true Kent.

He finished reading the last piece of copy as Payne emerged from his cubicle. "That has the makings of a good editorial, Theo," Louis said.

Michael detected insincerity. Except for insisting upon no unfavorable stories about industrialists or the factory system, Louis wasn't interested in the paper's position on issues, only its earnings. It was Michael who enforced the policy Amanda had outlined when she lay dying.

Louis added, "I do hope you're wrong about war— you and our family prophet."

"You mean Jephtha?" Payne asked.

"Yes."

Michael's brow hooked up because Louis actually sounded concerned.

"I don't know how many millions the South owes Northern bankers like Joshua Rothman. But I can imagine the panic if all those loans were suddenly to go into default. It would be worse than '57—and that wasn't exactly a banner year."

"That's all that worries you?" Michael asked. "The possible effects of secession on business?"

Half turned toward the tally board where the clerk was chalking new figures, Louis spun back.

"Why else should I be worried? I certainly don't give a damn about a lot of unwashed niggers. It doesn't matter to me whether they're free men or property, so long as they keep supplying the Blackstone mill with cotton. That supply could be drastically cut—or disappear altogether—if we have real trouble with the South."

"But the Stovall Works should prosper if the North needs munitions," Payne put in.

Louis nodded. "Yes, that's a plus."

Michael said, "Apart from the Bessemer proposal, steel for armaments was almost the sole subject of discussion by the board members. They were all licking their chops. Not a one of them seems to care a damn about the possible disruption of the country."

"I do," Louis said.

Sarcastically, Michael asked, "For humanitarian reasons? Or commercial ones?"

Louis' glance was hostile; his tone curt:

"The latter. The Republicans promise to encourage industrialization. That means they favor the high protective tariff, which benefits—"

"Us," Michael cut in. "The North. And the farmers in the West. It's also one more bone sticking in the South's throat."

"Well, you can't blame the Kent family—or New England and New York and Ohio—because shortsighted fools down in Georgia and Mississippi have built their economy on cotton. Did they expect its price to stay high with so many planters growing one crop? Fewer dollars—no factories to speak of—hell, they have to import most of their goods, and it's getting harder and harder for them to come up with the cash. Too bad. I'm interested in *our* welfare. I'd hate to see the

Republicans forced to abandon their promises about tariffs. It could happen—quickly—if that long-armed lawyer drags us all into a war with his moralizing and his endless dirty jokes." Louis had heard Lincoln speak at Cooper Union. He hadn't been impressed.

"His jokes aren't dirty," Payne said. "Just refreshingly crude."

Julia pouted. "Louis, you know discussions like this are over my head, and wearisome besides. I'm growing dreadfully tired—"

"I want to check the returns and then we'll go along," he assured her.

Michael was seething. With a slashing gesture he indicated the board:

"There they are. Bad for business!"

Louis eyed Michael, but controlled himself. "What about reaction from the South, Theo?"

"Did I neglect to hand you the dispatch from Lucas?" He smiled. "In Charleston they're celebrating. Tomorrow will be an informal commercial holiday."

"A *holiday*?" Louis understood. "Damn. It *is* coming—" He suppressed his anger. "But I suppose we're smart enough to weather it. Alert men should be able to find ways to profit from the wants and misfortunes of both sides. It's conceivable we could turn our need for cotton into trading leverage. Even at war, the South would have to purchase goods somewhere. Michael, we should write a confidential letter to the Lacroix brothers in New Orleans—being cotton factors, they'll have a grasp of what may happen to the supply if some of those hotheads pull their states out of the Union."

Michael exploded: "It's a somewhat broader question than supply and demand! It's a question of whether this country can be torn apart at will. Think of what secession could do to this family. Think of Jephtha! He has three sons in Virginia—"

Louis shrugged. "His concern, I'm afraid. Certainly not mine."

"I expect your mother would have considered Jephtha's boys her concern. I think they'd be somewhat more important to her than our balance sheets!"

Michael's cheeks felt hot. Julia inhaled, quickly and loudly. He didn't look at her. Payne fidgeted as Louis abandoned even the pretense of cordiality.

"My mother is *dead*, Michael. I run Kent's according to my lights. And if you don't care for my style of doing business, you're free to disassociate yourself at any time."

Like a disgruntled employee? Michael thought, furious at the way Louis had put him in his place by stating the truth of their relationship: he was the outsider.

No. That wasn't entirely true. Amanda had given him heavy responsibilities because she'd recognized the potential weakness in Louis. And, at the last, they'd loved one another almost as mother and son. Spiritually if not legally, he *was* a Kent.

But he didn't want a scene in front of Theo Payne and the reporters beginning to fill the editorial room. He held his tongue, though doing so only deepened his anger and gloom. One day—maybe quite soon—his differences with Louis could no longer be contained. Then he'd face a crisis.

Whether to keep silent, or fight—

And lose?

He became uncomfortably aware of Julia's cold gaze. She picked up her skirts and hurried to the front windows. For some minutes Michael had been hearing a crowd gathering in Printing House Square. The crowd's murmur was rapidly growing louder. All at once a new sound was added—

Drums.

"Massachusetts looks certain for Lincoln!" the clerk shouted from the board. "Ohio's going the same way."

Louis acknowledged the news with a disgusted nod. He strolled up to join Julia, pushing two reporters out of the way. She pointed:

"It's those dreadful Wide-Awakes. The mobs follow them wherever they go!"

Michael moved up behind them. The reporters let him through—something they hadn't done for Louis.

Louis didn't turn to acknowledge Michael's presence. Julia knew he was there. She adjusted her bonnet. This time she was careful not to touch him.

The rhythm of the snare drums drifted up through the November dark. Michael craned to see out the window. To the north of Printing House Square, an orange light began to flicker. People poured into the square ahead of the elongated shadows torchlight flung on the pavement—

The shadows of marching men.

Four abreast and boots thudding, the first company of Wide-Awakes appeared. The torches put shimmering highlights on black oilcloth capes. Here and there a silver eagle on a glazed black fatigue cap winked like a mirror reflecting the sun.

Companies of the political marching organization had been formed all through the North in the months since Lincoln's tacticians had snatched the nomination from New York's Senator Seward out at the Wigwam in Chicago. The Wide-Awakes always paraded with torches, and with lanterns bobbing from the ends of rails carried on their shoulders.

The split rail had become the political symbol of the Republican candidate. Some cynics claimed the rail was merely an imaginative device meant to enhance Lincoln's aura of strength and Western simplicity. Others insisted the candidate had indeed cut wood for fences to make money when he was younger.

The Wide-Awakes marched with a military precision and fervor that heightened Michael's fear of what the election could mean. A second company followed the first, circling the square. The sticks beating on the drumheads sounded like volleys of gunfire.

"Oh, blast them!" Julia cried suddenly, up on tiptoe again. Michael scented the lilac cologne Louis imported for her from Paris. The sweet smell seemed incongruous against the pandemonium outside.

The marchers executed smart right and left faces, balancing their lantern-hung rails and maneuvering them perfectly. The crowd clapped to the beat of the drums and screamed.

Michael squeezed far enough forward to see the object of Julia's wrath. A group of celebrants surrounded the Kent carriage down at the curb. Some of the more boisterous men were rocking the vehicle on its springs while the helpless driver tried to shoo them off with jabs of his whip.

"If they damage the carriage—" Julia began.

"I'll send an invoice to Thurlow Weed and let the state Republican party pay the bill," Louis said, slipping an arm around her shoulder.

She seemed irritated by the contact. Louis dropped his hand, his mouth petulant.

Michael was standing at the window next to the one from which Louis and his wife were watching. The stale odor of whiskey told him Theo Payne was close by.

His head still throbbed. The drums seemed to snarl. Suddenly all of the day's danger and frustration boiled to the surface. He whirled to face Louis and Julia.

"For Christ's sake, is that all you care about? A damaged carriage? A business slump? Do you know what it means that Lincoln will be going to Washington? Do you have any appreciation of what it *really* means?"

Behind him, Payne chuckled:

"I do."

Louis looked at Michael with emotionless eyes.

"Whatever it means, we'll turn it to our advantage."

"You don't give a goddamn that the country could be blown apart—?"

"I think you'd better go home, Michael. You're growing hysterical. I've no place for a man who loses his head."

He turned his back.

viii

For nearly a minute Michael was too stunned to move. The reporters exchanged startled or puzzled glances. Even Payne had sobered. Finally, Michael walked away from all of them.

Not out of cowardice. Out of despair.

Lord, I'm thankful Mrs. A isn't here. I'm thankful she can't see what the family's become—

He listened to the screaming in the square. And the drums. Thunderous. Thunderous as cannon.

In all his life he'd never felt more pessimistic. God alone knew what would be left of the Kents—or the country—a year from this night.

Book One

Black April

CHAPTER I

"An Oath Registered in Heaven"

WHEN JEPHTHA KENT started across the morass of Pennsylvania Avenue that Monday morning, he wondered if he was the only person in the whole town who was out of step. Washington City was behaving as if a holiday had been declared.

He didn't feel at all like joining the Northerners *or* the Southerners who were celebrating. He was, in fact, upset. He believed it was likely that the interview young Mr. Nicolay had scheduled over three weeks ago would be canceled in view of the calamitous news from Sumter. If it was, he could look forward to trouble. Early that morning he'd received a terse telegraph message from New York. Theo Payne wanted copy on the situation in the nation's capital. Exclusive copy. And, as always, he wanted it at once.

Halfway across the avenue, Jephtha waited until a horse-drawn omnibus bound for Georgetown passed. He dodged back as the hoofs of the horses shot out splatters of mud. The wheels of the omnibus bumped over half-buried cobbles that had long ago broken apart and sunk into the slime.

Aboard the car half a dozen passengers were bellowing a discordant version of "Hail, Columbia!" Jephtha's scowl deepened.

After the omnibus went by, he started on toward the iron fence bordering the south side of the street. His passage was again impeded, this time by a platoon of the

57

Washington Rifles marching at quickstep. He darted
around the rear of the column, avoided a couple of
shabbily dressed blacks bound on some errand, then
jumped out of the way of a barrow-pusher alternately
blowing a battered horn and shrieking his offer of fresh
oysters.

Jephtha hurried through the gate into President's
Park. Two run-down brick buildings stood on his
right—the War and Navy Departments. They faced two
more on his left—State and Treasury. The buildings
flanked the northern end of the tree-covered lawn on
which several of Washington's unpenned hogs were
wandering, ignored by the clerks and functionaries
hurrying back and forth along the walks.

The walks all converged on the Executive Mansion
further down in the park. Jephtha angled toward the
bronze statue of Jefferson in front of the mansion's
north portico. The statue was occasionally criticized because some people believed the sculptor had given the
former president a Negroid look.

Jephtha noted that the outbreak of hostilities hadn't
resulted in the presence of any additional guards. Just
the usual two stood outside the doors, despite the fact
that the man who lived inside had been violently
hated—and threatened—ever since his election.

Prior to the inauguration, the President had been
forced to sneak into Washington disguised in an army
cloak and a cap of Scotch plaid, guarded by railroad
detectives because of a rumored assassination plot.
Jephtha had heard a description of the pathetic disguise
from an elderly Negro porter who had seen it. In hopes
of getting a story, he had been at the depot shortly after
the special train arrived with its mysterious passenger.

And he'd stood in the raw March wind while Lincoln
spoke to the crowd present for the inaugural. Spoke
outdoors, as Army sharpshooters lined the rooftops of

the city's main thoroughfare in case of a murder attempt.

With that kind of atmosphere pervading the capital even before the news from Sumter, what the hell was there to celebrate now?

A familiar smell tainted the air of the park on this Monday in April, 1861. The warm spring weather always brought with it the stench of the garbage and human waste floating in the old city canal running by the far south end of the park. Jephtha paused a moment, glancing in that direction. On the other side of the canal he glimpsed the base of the obelisk dedicated to the memory of the country's first President. But work on it had been abandoned when the subscriptions to pay for it had lagged.

The uncompleted monument, the smell of sewage pervading the Potomac flats, and the rude, graceless outlines of the mansion with its straggle of greenhouses and outbuildings all confirmed the opinion Jephtha had heard often from foreign visitors: As a national capital, Washington City was a disgrace. It lacked identity, it had a distinct feeling of impermanence, and it was filthy to boot.

Of course, it might not continue to be the capital for long.

Major Anderson, in command of the garrison at Fort Sumter in Charleston harbor, had heard General Beauregard's guns open fire at four-thirty in the morning last Friday, April 12. Thirty-four hours later, Anderson and his men surrendered. The long-anticipated clash of arms had come, precipitated by the question of whether the newly formed Confederacy was entitled to take possession of Federal military installations within its boundaries.

Both Northern and Southern factions in Washington had exploded with a macabre enthusiasm when the first telegraphic reports of the surrender had been posted late Saturday evening on the bulletin board of the *Evening Star*, where Jephtha kept a desk. In his opinion, the Northerners particularly had no reason for joy. The city lay directly across the Potomac from one avowedly Southern state, and was hemmed in by another in which Southern sympathy ran high. How long could Washington survive if the rebels decided to attempt to seize it? In view of that question, the city's euphoric mood struck him as insane.

Or am I the only lunatic in the whole town?

He felt no sense of relief because Sumter had been fired on. He was convinced the President's proclamation, made public that morning, was foolishly optimistic; he had a copy of it in his pocket. The man Jephtha was going to attempt to see had declared an "insurrection" existed. To suppress it, he'd only called out seventy-five thousand state militiamen—and those only for a period of three months. Jephtha recalled the fervor of the people he had known, generally respected, and tried to serve in Virginia. He doubted ninety days would see the Southern rebellion to its end.

He walked up the steps of the mansion. Both sentries recognized him. One waved him on. Pushing through the glass doors, he tried not to think of the three sons he hadn't seen in several years. He didn't even know their whereabouts. That worried him most of all.

ii

At the foot of the main staircase, a family that included four children gawked at the elaborate chandeliers. Farm people, to judge from their look. Jephtha caught bits of excited conversation in German as he climbed the stairs two at a time. Sightseers came and went at will in the President's home.

On the second floor he proceeded to the office of John Nicolay, one of the Chief Executive's two personal secretaries. The red-haired, freckled young man was engaged in conversation with a frock-coated gentleman Jephtha recognized as a low-ranking official who worked for Secretary of State Seward. Nicolay, at least, wasn't smiling or capering like some of the imbeciles in the streets:

"—General Scott will be here at eleven for the meeting. Please send messengers to inform the cabinet members."

The visitor nodded and brushed past Jephtha, who stood waiting in the doorway, unnoticed by Nicolay.

Jephtha Kent was a tall, stern-looking man of forty-one. His gray-blue eyes contrasted sharply with the dark, straight hair he tended to forget about combing. His cheap suit of black broadcloth was equally unkempt. His shirt had a distinctly gray cast.

Jephtha's nose was prominent; blade-like. Like his dark hair, it was a trait he'd gotten from his Indian mother, a Shoshoni squaw named Grass Singing. His father had married her during his days as a mountain man in the far western part of the continent. Jephtha's pale, intense eyes were his only physical inheritance from his Virginia forebears. His grandmother on his father's side had come from the Tidewater country. Jephtha often drew stares; at first glance, he looked more Indian than white.

Nicolay was busy sorting papers on his desk. Jephtha cleared his throat.

"Good morning, John."

"Oh—!" Starting, Nicolay glanced up. "Jephtha. Good morning. One minute—I'm trying to find a note the President gave me right after breakfast."

The secretary located it, then uttered a long sigh. "I'm sorry. I completely forgot you were on the calendar."

"I'm not surprised. It's been a hectic weekend, I imagine."

"It's been hell."

"Any further word from Sumter?"

"Nothing beyond what we heard last night."

"Anderson and all his men got aboard the relief vessels?"

"That's right."

"No more casualties reported?"

"Only the one—Anderson's man who got killed when a cannon blew up. General Beauregard was damned civil about the whole business. Allowed Anderson to salute his flag before he and his troops left the fort."

"You'll find that typical of Southern people, I think," Jephtha said. "I hope it doesn't mislead anyone into believing Southerners won't fight. They're hard fighters."

"I realize. We've a lot of 'em in the army, you know. West Point men. Senior officers. I don't doubt a good many will hand in their resignations."

Jephtha nodded. "Emulating Beauregard's example." The commander at Charleston had withdrawn from the superintendency at West Point to return to his native South. "What about news from Richmond?"

"None. But I expect we'll hear by midweek."

"And they'll follow the first seven states out of the Union."

"That's what the President anticipates," Nicolay agreed with a glum expression.

"How many more does he expect to go?"

"North Carolina, Tennessee, and Arkansas look almost certain. Kentucky, Maryland, and Missouri could fall either way."

"I suppose all this turmoil means Mr. Lincoln won't see me this morning."

"Oh, I think he'll see you. He knows the New York *Union* stumped hard for him while Seward's men were still whining about their licking at the Wigwam."

Nicolay slipped into the hall. "Come along and let's find out. I wouldn't expect more than five or ten minutes, though. Or any specific information. Matters are just too uncertain."

Jephtha followed the secretary to the other end of the building. There, a carpeted corridor led from the Lincoln family's living quarters in the southwest corner to the President's office on the southeast. A crowd of jobseekers, contractors and ordinary citizens wanting favors packed the chairs and benches along the corridor. Such crowds always jammed the mansion's upper halls on business days, waiting to pluck the President's arm and dog his steps whenever he appeared.

Cigar fumes and the smell of sweat fouled the air. Jephtha heard some of the petitioners discussing Major Anderson's safe removal from the Charleston fort. He listened to a couple of obscene comments about the character of Jefferson Davis, the former military officer, legislator, and Secretary of War who was now president of the seven-state Confederacy down in Montgomery. Jephtha had been in the Senate gallery in January when Jefferson Davis had submitted his resignation during a sad, moving speech prompted by Mississippi's following South Carolina out of the Union. The Senator had long held out against secession and its inherent promise of violence. But circumstances and principle had finally forced him to a reluctant decision. While he bid his Senatorial colleagues farewell, many of them wept.

Nicolay left Jephtha beside another blue-clad sentry, Lincoln's sole protector. The secretary knocked and disappeared behind the rosewood door. In less than a minute, he returned.

"You may go in for a few minutes. He's almost finished with his other visitor."

"Who is it?"

Nicolay smiled. "The only person in Washington who can come into the office whenever he wants."

"Ah," Jephtha said, understanding.

The secretary started to push the door open, apologetic:

"As I suspected, the President won't give you any specific answers about government policy or our response to the developments at Sumter."

Understandable, Jephtha thought as he thanked Nicolay and stepped inside, struck again by a feeling of pessimism. Who except perhaps the abolitionists and the Southern fire-eaters had ever expected it would come to this? A country less than a hundred years old at war with itself—?

He doubted Mr. Lincoln—or anyone else in the nation—really knew how to find answers for the problems posed by the unprecedented calamity.

iii

A great deal of sport had been made of Abraham Lincoln's peculiar physique: his great height—six feet four inches—coupled with his lankiness; his stooping posture; his huge hands and feet and ears. This morning the President looked even more like a great skinny ogre—though a genial one—hunched as he was in a fragile chair in front of the small desk by the windows. Southeast through those windows the iron base of the uncompleted dome of the Capitol caught the leaden glare of sun trying to break through clouds. A train whistle shrieked twice. The Baltimore and Ohio from the North—

Another train occupied Lincoln's attention. Of wood, and gaudily painted, the toy had evidently developed some problem with one of its yellow driver wheels. The President was trying to repair the difficulty by pressuring the end of an axle nail with his thumb.

Standing next to him and shifting from foot to foot

was the visitor whose identity Jephtha had already guessed. Lincoln's son Thomas, who was eight or so. He and his eleven-year-old brother Willie lived at the mansion. Lincoln's eldest son, Robert, was away, doing university work.

Satisfied, Lincoln put the locomotive on the desk. He ran it back and forth a few inches.

"There, Tadpole. I reckon she's ready to go to Chicago now." His eyes showed affection as he handed the toy to his grinning son.

"Thank you, Papa dear," Tad exclaimed, hugging his father around the neck. Because of the boy's cleft palate, the words *Papa dear* had a thick, distorted sound— more like *puppy day*. It was Tad's affliction, Jephtha had heard Nicolay comment, that made Lincoln love the boy with a special intensity.

Clutching the repaired locomotive, Tad bounded for the door. "Hello, sir. See my engine? Papa fixed it!"

"Looks like a good job, too," Jephtha smiled. "You're a lucky young fellow—it's not every boy who can persuade the President of the United States to repair his train."

The hall door closed. Lincoln chuckled. He removed his spectacles and stood up—a movement resembling that of an ungainly water bird rising on long legs.

"Mr. Kent, good morning to you." Lincoln extended his immense hand and enfolded Jephtha's fingers. "Sorry you were delayed by the breakdown on Tad's railroad. I also regret we're together on such an unfortunate day."

Despite the words, Lincoln's wide, somewhat slack mouth curled at the corners in that country grin Jephtha found so likable. Lincoln dressed like an undertaker— all in black—much as Jephtha did. His coat and his thin string necktie of silk matched the color of his unruly hair and chin whiskers. He looked older than fifty-two. His skin was much more sallow than it had been when Jephtha had seen him last—at a private dinner given by the family for several reporters early in March.

The President's gray eyes appeared unusually sunken. They were odd, arresting eyes; eyes that looked at the world with a touch of sorrow even when Lincoln laughed, as he did often. Perhaps the change had come over him during the weekend, after the Government's refusal to yield Sumter had led to the cannonading by Beauregard and the surrender by Anderson.

Lincoln gestured his guest to a long oak table covered with green baize. The table dominated the large office. In less than an hour, fat, gouty Winfield Scott would be seated at it with members of the cabinet.

"Yes, unfortunate is a good word for it—" Jephtha began.

"For many more reasons than one. Not only do we have this insurrection on our hands, but right after Tad's locomotive broke, Willie lost his favorite top. Breakfast was a perfect disorder—"

Jephtha took a chair at the table. While Lincoln shambled back to the pigeonhole desk littered with papers and books, he said, "I appreciate that you'll take any time at all to see me, Mr. President." He pulled out the copy of Lincoln's proclamation, then a smaller sheet and a pencil.

"Well, after all, Mr. Kent, you helped start this muss with the South."

Jephtha blinked. "I, sir?"

Lincoln waved. Only then, when the President's lips twitched again, did Jephtha realize Lincoln was teasing him:

"Oh, maybe not you personally. But that Boston printing house your family owns—that certainly played a big part. They always say it's the politicians who cause trouble for common folk. But I sometimes wonder if it isn't our authors who set off the firecrackers first."

Still baffled, Jephtha kept silent. As always, Lincoln's voice had that high-pitched, almost shrill quality that caused so many of his enemies to say he spoke in a "low Hoosier style." He slurred some of his words, too. But despite his speech and the impression he gave of somehow having been put together by a Deity trying to use a collection of unwanted parts, Lincoln had always impressed Jephtha. The feeling went back to the first time he'd heard the President speak, at the inaugural. The man might appear to be a bumpkin. Or, as his most vicious critics claimed, the descendant of a gorilla. Yet Jephtha found him possessed of an intelligence and gentle strength that lent him an extraordinary magnetism—even if some of his ideas were more hopeful than realistic.

Lacing his huge hands together—and still teasing—Lincoln went on:

"What I meant is, books helped stir up this war, Mr. Kent. First and foremost, Mrs. Stowe's novel. Then Mr. Douglass' autobiography. Mr. Helper's tract—"

Lincoln was referring to *The Impending Crisis of the South*, a volume even more thoroughly detested in the cotton states than *Uncle Tom's Cabin*. Hinton Helper, an obscure hack, had put forth the theory that the South should abandon slavery because reliance on it was destroying the potential growth of Southern industry. Helper, a Southerner himself, had strong views about the inferiority of black men and women. But adherence to slavery, he said, would ultimately put the South at the mercy of the industrial North.

"—and I count that other slave autobiography from Kent and Son the fourth of the quartet that pushed us toward the current crisis. Is the mulatto who wrote *West to Freedom* still in your employ?"

"Yes, sir," Jephtha nodded. "Israel Hope's in charge of the family mining operations in California." From time to time Jephtha completely forgot that he was heir to his father's considerable fortune. Others in the family—such as young Louis—found his forgetfulness puzzling. And Fan, who had divorced him after he'd fled Lexington, had found it scandalous.

Did she still? He didn't know. Every letter he'd written to her in the past two years had gone unanswered, a source of bitterness and—often—rage.

Abruptly, Jephtha realized he'd been wasting precious moments; Lincoln was repeating a question that had gone unheard while Jephtha's thoughts wandered.

"I'm sorry, sir, I didn't hear what you—"

"I said, do you have some things you want to inquire about?"

"I do, Mr. President. But Mr. Nicolay warned me you probably couldn't speak freely."

"Said it with an apology in his voice, I suppose?"

"Yes."

"John hates to antagonize you fellows from the press. That's because he used to be one of you. Out in Illinois he worked for the *Pike County Sucker*. My, that's a flavorful name, ain't—isn't it?"

Jephtha smiled but said nothing. After a moment's thought, Lincoln went on:

"But John put it to you honestly. I won't comment on very much. The fact is, I've gagged everybody in the administration for the time being. These next few days will be mighty difficult. We can't afford to have the wrong things get into print. So no major statements are to be given out, except from this office or with my express approval. I imagine that'll save you some time, however. You won't have to scurry from department to department, hoping to find one of your sources ready to blab—"

Lincoln's smile became sympathetic. "Hope I haven't spoiled your morning."

"No, sir," Jephtha lied. Theo Payne would be far

from sympathetic when he learned official Washington
had nothing to say.

"All right, then. If you want to go ahead on those
terms, ask your questions."

Trying to conceal his disappointment, Jephtha took a
moment to scan the questions he'd roughed out earlier.

"I heard your chief opponent in the November election
was here yesterday. Has he endorsed your proclamation?"

Lincoln nodded. "Judge Douglas did call—I can
never get used to referring to him as Senator, you know.
He did endorse the proclamation. Without reservation.
He'll be issuing a statement today."

"With your permission?"

"With my full permission, yes, sir. The Judge and I
scrapped long and hard—the debates in Illinois when I
pinned him to the Freeport doctrine, then the campaign.
But he's a good friend. More important, he's a Union
man. I don't know which is the greater boon, the Judge
supporting me now, or the way he got me out of a real
fix on the inauguration platform when I couldn't find a
place for my old stovepipe."

Writing, Jephtha smiled. "I remember how he took
the hat and held it while you spoke—"

The smile faded. *And I remember your closing
words. Eloquent words about the better angels of man's
nature. I don't believe they exist any longer. Not in this
country—*

"Can you say anything about the state of the army?
Before your call for troops, it was only fifteen thousand
men—"

"Sixteen. Most of 'em scattered hither and yon on the
Western borders."

"Will they be able to put down the insurrection with
the help of the militia?"

Lincoln reflected. "Mr. Kent, I won't answer that.
I've already expressed my thinking in the proclamation.

To say anything further might sound overly belligerent. Make matters worse. The truth is, I'm saddened the South has forced war on this government—"

"Some say you maneuvered the events at Sumter. Specifically, by sending Mr. Chew of the War Department to Charleston earlier this month to inform Governor Pickens you intended to reprovision the fort by sea."

Lincoln looked somber, his silence acknowledging a degree of truth in Jephtha's rather bold observation. But the President let him continue:

"In effect, Mr. Chew's mission signaled a repetition of the *Star of the West* incident before you took office. In Charleston they regarded it as a warning that you wouldn't surrender Federal property. That you'd fight instead—and hoped to provoke them into firing the first shots. Which, as it turned out, they did."

"I'm aware of what people are saying," Lincoln sighed. "They can't see the difference between my duty and my personal feelings. I had to take a stand on the matter of the forts—but the last thing I wanted to do was provoke war. The very idea of Americans quarreling is grievous to me, Mr. Kent. I've said repeatedly I bear no ill will toward the Southern states. I've tried to make it plain my policy was not to interfere in the South's domestic institution where it already exists, only to promote its containment. But that didn't satisfy their more extreme spokesmen. So I tried to sue for accord when I gave my inaugural—though my conscience did compel me to be absolutely candid on one point. I said it in March, and I'll say it now—I do believe I have a solemn oath registered in heaven to prevent an unconstitutional act. I mean the destruction of the Union. But believe me, Mr. Kent, I want to end this struggle quickly, not prolong or inflame it."

Trying to write the essence of the President's thoughts, Jephtha nodded again, then said:

"All right, sir. Could we turn for a moment to the high command of the army?"

Lincoln's hairy brows puckered together. "What are you getting at? Scott is general-in-chief—"

"But he's almost seventy-five. In poor health—"

Lincoln grinned. "Fat as a prairie hen, too. His gout wouldn't plague him so severely if he'd stay away from all that rich food and wine." A finger stabbed out. "Don't write that down."

"I realize General Scott's the senior officer in the service. But there have been persistent rumors that the actual command of the Federal army will be offered to Colonel Lee."

Lincoln's quick backward movement—a sort of jerking in his chair—showed Jephtha he'd hit a target. The President's lids drooped a moment. The gaunt, yellowish face grew unreadable:

"I consider Bob Lee the best officer in the United States army, Mr. Kent. That's no secret."

"No, sir. It was evident in March after he came back from Texas and General Scott promoted him to full colonel and command of the First Cavalry."

Hoping to insure Lee's continued loyalty? Jephtha didn't voice the cynical suspicion. He let Lincoln resume at his own pace:

"Bob Lee's served the Union in exemplary fashion. You know he commanded the Marines who captured that lunatic Brown at Harper's Ferry. But Bob Lee is also a Virginian. I reckon I shouldn't say a word about his possible reaction to any overtures. Not that there *are* any overtures—or will be," Lincoln emphasized.

But Jephtha knew Colonel Lee was resting at his mansion across the river in Arlington. If the special convention sitting in Richmond right this moment voted for secession, Lee's reaction would be of inestimable importance to those on both sides of the quarrel.

The President rose.

"I don't wish to be short with you, Mr. Kent. But we've passed the allotted time by several minutes."

Jephtha stood. "Just one or two more questions before I go—"

"Guess I'm trapped," Lincoln said, chuckling. "You do have a reputation as one of the most persistent reporters in the whole town."

"Is the city in any danger at present?"

"Military danger?"

Jephtha nodded.

Lincoln's eyes shifted away. For the first time during the conversation, Jephtha sensed a deliberate evasion coming.

"I think not. Virginia hasn't left the Union—"

"But everyone assumes she will. Congressman Pryor went to Charleston a while back and all but pleaded with the governor to start the attack on Sumter."

"Yes, I'm acquainted with the pleadings of Mr. Pryor of Virginia. 'Strike a blow,' he said. Then his state would surely step into line. Still, even if Virginia does join the insurrection, we'll manage to keep house. Precautions are being taken—"

His tone said the subject was closed. But it wasn't for Jephtha.

"There are very few Federal troops in Washington, sir. Even with more, can it be defended?"

The President hesitated before answering. "I believe General Scott thinks not. But he also feels we won't be attacked. I can't say whether he's right or wrong. But I do know—and I'm sure you do too—the internal threat is just as great as the threat from Virginia. Southern sympathizers are pretty thick in this town. I know from all the gossip I've heard about us folks from the Northwest. The Southern crowd believes we're sour. Puritanical. Can't even enjoy a good party because of our religious principles—oh, I've heard it all," he finished with a weary wave.

Potential danger for city—real? Fancied? Jephtha wrote, cupping the sheet so the President couldn't see. As he finished jotting the final word, he said:

"Even though fighting's broken out, will you attempt any further conciliation with the Confederacy?"

"I'm sorry, but you're tramping forbidden ground again, Mr. Kent. I won't discuss policy before it's decided. Besides, things are moving so fast, policy has to run like the devil just to stay ten yards behind! Any announcements along the lines you mentioned will be official, not informal ones.

"However, speaking in total confidence, I want peace. Soon, if that's possible. But there can be no compromising with rebellion. The first responsibility of this administration is to prove that popular government hasn't become an absurdity."

The intense, deep-set eyes seemed to catch fire and burn a moment. Strangely, Jephtha was conscious of the humanity of the man before him, not the office he represented. Lincoln's clothes were untidy. His speech was nasal, and to some ears, grating. The Congress wouldn't even vote funds to refurbish the building in which he lived and worked under the awesome burdens of the moment. Directly beneath the conference table, there was a large rip in the threadbare carpet—

"We must settle the question *now*," Lincoln went on. "In a free government, does the minority have the right to sunder the whole whenever they choose? I say no. This administration says no. But if we fail in proving our case it will go far to demonstrate the incapability of the people to govern themselves—"

A sharp knock broke the President's concentration. Jephtha finished writing and slipped his paper and pencil back into his pocket as Lincoln accompanied him toward the rosewood door.

"It's the personal price of what we face that disturbs me most," the President said. "My Bob is old enough to fight. And you have boys of your own—in Virginia—didn't you mention that when we dined together?"

"The boys were in Virginia," Jephtha answered, feeling the familiar anger. "I have no idea where they are now. My wife has remarried. Her husband travels—"

He didn't want to reveal that Fan was married to a man who engaged in a profession respectable people considered only a cut above operating saloons or bawdy-houses. He was an actor. It truly baffled Jephtha that his former wife, always a proper sort, had taken up with a man such as Edward Lamont. Jephtha would have been hurt, even angry, no matter whom she'd married. But if Fan had chosen a merchant, or a teacher, it wouldn't have been half so humiliating—

"Well," Lincoln said, "for the sake of your boys, and mine, I hope we can bring the conflict to a speedy end. I sometimes get depressed and conclude Americans can only settle their great disputes with bloodshed. The trouble is, it's never the disputants—the politicians—who shed the blood. They send their sons and your sons and my sons off to do it for them." He shook his head. "Sad—"

As Lincoln reached for the door, it was opened by an impatient Nicolay, watch in hand:

"Mr. President, forgive me, but it's twenty-five past the hour!"

"Can't help it, John. Mr. Kent and I got engaged in a good chat." Lincoln held out his hand. Jephtha shook it. The President had a strong grip.

Nicolay kept fidgeting. But the melancholy eyes looking out from under the black brow made Jephtha blurt one more question:

"Do you ever regret you've taken this office, sir?"

The President leaned against the door frame in a relaxed way. He put one hand in his pocket. The sentry, rifled musket raised, moved down the hall to bar the favor-seekers who had risen from their benches at the sight of the Chief Executive.

"You know, Mr. Kent, once in a while I feel exactly like a fellow I knew back in Springfield. The man committed a public indecency and was promptly covered with tar and chicken feathers and escorted out of town riding on a rail. Someone asked him how it felt."

The pushy throng in the hallway quieted.

"Well, the miscreant said—"

Lincoln's right thumb hooked under his coat and caught his suspender. His eyes twinkled as he lapsed into an exaggerated rural dialect:

"To be honest, fellers, if 't'wasn't for the honor involved, I'd jist as soon walk."

Jephtha smiled, then thanked the President for granting him more time than originally allotted. Nicolay tapped a nail against the case of his watch. Slowly, like a curtain falling, a tired expression came across Lincoln's face. He turned to re-enter the office, ignoring a man down the hall who held up his hand and exclaimed, "Mr. President, if I could just speak to you for a moment—"

Lincoln scuffed his shoes on the carpet. His shoulders slumped. Nicolay followed him inside. The rosewood door closed. The man who'd raised his hand swore.

Jephtha pushed through the fetid petitioners and headed down the staircase. On the ground floor he saw the German family clustered around draperies at one of the windows. With a guilty look, the wife returned a small pair of scissors to her reticule—and then something else. Jephtha noticed a square had been snipped from one of the drapes.

He shook his head as he walked to the doors. Souvenir-stealing at the mansion was nothing new. But he was deeply concerned about the lack of security in the building. Lincoln was passionately hated by a great many people. Those around the President should exercise more caution—insist on more guards—even if the President refused to do so.

Jephtha knew Lincoln had a fatalistic view about his own death. He'd been exposed to repeated threats on his life and dismissed them, feeling his time had not yet come. Jephtha recalled reading a piece in Medill's Chicago *Daily Tribune* written out of Springfield the morning after the election. Lincoln had spoken of a puzzling dream the preceding night. A dream or, his detractors would claim, hallucination; he was known to fall into black, almost suicidal moods.

The story said that as Lincoln started to go to sleep, he glanced in a mirror and saw himself lying full length on a sofa covered with haircloth. His image had one body, but two faces.

When he rose, the vision disappeared. When he lay down a second time, twin faces again shimmered in the glass. One face was chalk-white.

Lincoln's wife Mary, the small, ambitious woman whom many said vexed her husband almost beyond endurance, had circulated the story next day and given it an eerie twist. She maintained the two faces meant her husband would be elected to a second term. The pallor of one face meant he would never complete it.

Thinking of the story as he went down the mansion's outer steps, Jephtha shivered. Enemies of the President were always circulating tales about his wife's mental instability. Whether Mrs. Lincoln had a morbid imagination was beside the point. Lincoln was vulnerable in the too-public presidential residence. Washington was no longer merely a rough-hewn, basically Southern city that came to life for a few months every year when Congress sat. It was the capital of a nation at war with itself. In war, men killed other men—

And not always on the battlefield.

Jephtha headed toward the brick State Department building. He intended to drop in on one of his contacts to learn whether Lincoln's muzzling of all government officials was a reality. As he approached the building, a party of men emerged, headed for the White House.

In the center of the group, with those on either side leaning close to catch his hoarse, whispery voice—a voice ruined by too many cigars—Secretary of State William Seward kept up a nonstop conversation.

Seward was tall, stooped, and in his sixties. Lincoln had scored a coup by persuading his former opponent to join his cabinet. Some said Seward had already attempted to increase his personal power by offering to assume the burdens of presidential decision-making. Jephtha had never seen the provocative memorandum in which the offer had reportedly been made. But he understood Lincoln had thanked Seward and politely said no. Yet as far as Jephtha could learn, Seward and the Chief Executive still respected one another and were becoming close personal friends.

Seward acknowledged Jephtha's presence with a reedy rasp. The actual words were indistinguishable as he rushed past with his entourage. Ten minutes later Jephtha emerged from State, having satisfied himself that his customary sources of rumor and half-truth were indeed no longer talking.

His contact had been exceedingly nervous—and had twice referred to the small number of militia companies guarding Washington. Jephtha began to think the specter of Southern invasion might be more real than anyone wanted to admit.

He neared several Treasury clerks who had paused to shoo a flock of clucking geese. As he passed, he heard one of the clerks growl:

"—damn fools to go after Sumter that way. If they try to fight us we'll have them whipped by the time Old Abe's ninety-day conscripts are due to go home."

Jephtha left through the gate of President's Park and once more started across the traffic-thronged mire of

Pennsylvania Avenue. He didn't believe the clerk was right. He wasn't sure the President held the same opinion either. As he'd told Nicolay, the Southern people could never be accused of cowardice.

That turned his thoughts back to his three sons.

Gideon, the eldest, would be eighteen in June. Matthew was but a year younger. Jeremiah, thank heaven, was not yet fifteen. But what if the older boys decided to enlist in one of the militia units that had been drilling throughout the South for months?

Damn! He wished he knew where the boys were. He wished he and Fan hadn't parted so bitterly. But she was as loyal to her convictions as he was to his.

Fan and the boys were seldom out of Jephtha's mind for more than a few hours. He always thought of his sons with longing—and of his former wife with anger. Her behavior over the past nine years occasionally drove him into violent rages that upset his relationship with Molly, the woman with whom he'd been living for better than twelve months.

No use working himself into a fury now, he decided. He had a problem to solve. What sort of dispatch could he file to satisfy Theo Payne?

As he dodged carriages on the avenue, he peered at his hastily written notes. He had nothing solid to send to New York. Much of what Lincoln had told him in private was already widely known.

Jephtha's lack of copy would infuriate Payne on two counts. The editor wanted only fresh material. And preferably the kind in which Lincoln, or someone in the administration, fulminated against Southern "traitors." Long an abolitionist even more ardent than Jephtha himself, Payne considered the President not sufficiently hostile in his attitude toward the new Confederacy.

The gag order now in force in the government departments made further foraging there almost useless. But Payne would still expect a dispatch late today or early tomorrow. What the hell could he send except the news of the Douglas endorsement—which everyone else would have too?

Feeling increasingly frustrated, he jostled his way along the crowded plank sidewalk on the north side of the avenue. His destination was Willard's Hotel, one of the cockpits for Washington gossip. There, with breakfast and a little liquid refreshment to inspire him, he might find a way out of his professional predicament.

For the riddle of the whereabouts of his sons he saw no answer at all.

iv

The establishment run by the Willard brothers served breakfast to late-rising Washington from eight until eleven. Jephtha was in time. After he bought four cigars, he took a small table in the corner of the bar. He ordered steak and onions with fried oysters on the side, and a double shot of Overholtz 1855, one of the bar's best whiskeys.

The place was crowded. Government men, officials from foreign embassies, and quite a few army and militia officers were all jabbering about Sumter's surrender. Most of the soldiers were already full of liquor and bombast. The goddamned rebels who had been flaunting the threat of secession for decades—and who had finally acted on it, then dared to fire on the Stars and Stripes—would be taught a swift and humiliating lesson! Hunched over his drink, Jephtha grimaced. If he'd gone the other way along Pennsylvania, to the National Hotel at Sixth, he'd have heard equally gaseous rhetoric from the Southern sympathizers who generally gathered there.

He interrupted his meal to dart to the bar and corner a new arrival, a young man named Alfred Hume who was an assistant secretary at the British embassy. He asked Hume whether the ambassador, florid-faced Lord Lyons, had as yet formulated a policy about recognition of the Confederate government.

"Still a bit early for that, old chap," Hume answered in his languid way. "Must await instructions from Whitehall, don't y'know?"

"Come off it, Alf. Jeff Davis was inaugurated over two months ago. Every report out of Montgomery says he and his cabinet are going to stand by a policy of holding Southern cotton off the European markets. They want to use the cotton to bargain for recognition of the South as a sovereign nation, not a section of America in rebellion."

Hume looked bored. "Say it again—nothing official to report." Then he leaned closer. "Tell you this much, though. If the chaps in the Confederacy continue to sail on that course, they're bloody fools."

"Why, Alf?"

"Because the decision's a blunder! A complete misreading of the economic situation. Let jolly old Jeffey try to use his cotton to force Her Majesty—or Nappy the Third over in France—to recognize his so-called government, and I'm afraid he'll find he's aiming an empty weapon. For the first time in years, all the mills back home *and* in Europe have a surplus of cotton. So where's Jeffey going to find recognition? *Or* the money to finance a war? I've heard there's no more than twenty-five millions in bullion in the entire South!"

"True," Jephtha replied. "And it won't go far. There isn't a single first-rate iron mill, rolling mill, or powder mill down there either. Those cost money to build. Big money."

Hume's smile was smug. "Which in turn requires the sale of the only product the South produces in quantity—cotton. See what I mean about an embargo? I repeat—bloody fools."

The assistant secretary hailed the barkeep for a refill. It took him three calls to make himself heard above the din. After he'd been served, he turned to Jephtha, pursed his lips, and said, "God, I despise this town. Chap can't find a proper club anywhere. Just these noisy saloons. You fellows may be our cousins, but damned if you don't have a lot to learn about life's refinements."

"Alf, one more question about—"

"Cheer-o, Kent," the young diplomat said, turning away and waving to another acquaintance further down the bar. Jephtha went back to his table, smiling because Hume was typical of the Europeans on assignment in Washington. They considered the capital raw, raucous—little better than a backwoods village.

Another man Jephtha knew, a sketch artist for *Harper's Weekly,* stopped by as he was finishing his meal. After a few perfunctory words of greeting, the artist passed along a rumor that a political demonstration would take place on the stage of Canterbury Hall, a popular variety theater, the following night.

Jephtha's pale eyes narrowed. "A demonstration for which side?"

"Could be Union, could be secesh. Either way, with the mixed crowd the Canterbury draws, it might be lively."

A cynical look crossed Jephtha's face. "And to what do I owe this journalistic largesse? I don't have many colleagues who'll point me toward a potential story."

The artist shrugged. "I'm just paying a debt. You tipped me about Miss Chase going to see Joe Jefferson in *Rip Van Winkle.* I hired the box opposite and sketched her."

"That's right, I'd forgotten," Jephtha nodded. The eldest daughter of Secretary of the Treasury Chase was Washington's reigning beauty. "Well, knowing she was attending the theater wouldn't have done me much good. I can't draw, and her looks are what everyone's talking

about." He raised his whiskey glass. "Thanks for the
returned favor."

"Sure, Reverend. As the good book says—one good
slap on the cheek deserves another. Or something like
that."

The artist waved and left. Jephtha's face was scarlet.

The twisted allusion to scripture wasn't accidental.
But by now he should have been able to handle the occasional jibes about his background—which was no secret. Somehow, he wasn't able to do it. He hated to be
called Reverend. Perhaps because he sometimes felt guilty
about turning away from the church.

From God—

No. It was the other way around. God had turned
away from him. When he'd taken a stand for Christian
principles as he understood them, he had lost the respect of the congregations to whom he traveled. He'd
lost the right to preach. He'd lost his home. And he'd
lost the love and companionship of his sons. His faith
hadn't been strong enough to withstand that sort of punishment.

Regardless of what it said in the Book of Job, a God
who would do all that to a man wasn't a God worth
serving.

The artist's remark had spoiled his meal. He pushed
his plate away; made a note about the Canterbury Hall
tip. A piece on a sectional scrap in a theater would be
better than no copy at all.

Still, Jephtha prided himself on being a professional.
So he pored over his notes again, hoping to find some
point he'd overlooked. To stimulate his thinking—and
dull the edge of his worry about his sons—he drained
another double shot of Overholtz. Just as he was doing
so, he spied a line that had gotten smudged while the
notes were in his pocket.

R. Lee—Arlington. The words were followed by two
large question marks.

Damn! There it was. Lee was only a half hour away in Virginia—and certainly a man worth talking to, if it was possible.

Anxious that someone might beat him to the source of his inspiration, he paid his bill and hurried toward the entrance of the Willard bar. He was momentarily blocked by two contractors who were discussing their hope that the rebellion would grow into a long war. Fortunes could be made selling the Federal Army everything from buttons to biscuits—

"Damn vultures," Jephtha muttered as he pushed between the two men. One of them whirled; raised a fist. The other snickered:

"Calm down. That's Kent, the reporter who used to be a preacher." The man lowered his voice. "Look, you don't want to fool with him—he's got a hell of a temper. He was thrown out of the Southern Methodist Church for sermons about freeing the niggers. Everyone in town says it left him a little bit crazy."

CHAPTER II

Colonel Lee

JEPHTHA STARTED FOR VIRGINIA shortly after noon, riding a mare hired at a stable near Willard's. The sky was clearing. The pale April sunlight seemed to accentuate the city's raw, unfinished look. And it did precious little to warm his bones or raise his spirits.

Some of the initial bluster of the citizenry was already diminishing. As he jogged along the avenue near President's Park, he saw a sidewalk speaker haranguing a small crowd. He heard the orator shout, "—a dire and misguided insult to the Union! It shall be *punished!*" Little applause greeted the warning. Jephtha suspected the truth of the situation was beginning to sink in. Washington was encircled, if not by the actual Confederacy as yet, then by states sympathetic to it. There could be danger—and soon.

He saw further evidence behind the iron fence of the park. To the rattle of a drum, a local militia company was holding a muster-in on the lawn of the War Department. He recognized the uniforms of the National Rifles, an organization riddled with Southern partisans. How much help they'd be in defending the capital was debatable.

He turned south at Fourteenth Street and crossed the canal on the high iron bridge. He nearly gagged at the stench below. Once across to the Mall, the surroundings were only slightly more pleasant. Through the trees

on his left he glimpsed the red stone towers of the
Smithsonian and the Capitol with its unfinished wings
and dome. Construction sheds, blocks of marble, stacks
of lumber littered the Capitol grounds. He guided the
mare around the maggot-covered corpse of a mongrel
lying in the mud on the Mall's south side.

As he neared the city end of Long Bridge, traffic increased. Farmers bringing milk and produce into town
created a jam with their vehicles. Jephtha managed to
ride through. As he clattered onto the bridge over the
broad river, he saw, at the far end, disheartening proof
of Washington's precarious situation.

Two blue-clad United States cavalrymen sat on their
horses, rifled muskets resting across their thighs. The
cavalrymen watched the continuous flow of wagons and
carts passing over the bridge. Before long, Jephtha
guessed, there would be more than just mounted pickets
on duty. He put down a mental wager that by the end of
the week, Winfield Scott would be protecting the Long
Bridge with cannon.

ii

Passing between the cavalry pickets, Jephtha got an
even greater shock. A powerful-looking man sat on the
ground against the largest of several blossoming cherry
trees growing near the riverbank. Though the man had
his hat brim slanted over his eyes and appeared to be
resting, Jephtha recognized him instantly—and knew he
wasn't resting at all. Like the cavalrymen, he was observing those crossing the bridge; particularly those
headed south.

What the devil was a disreputable bully like that
doing in Washington?

Jephtha kept going. He had no intention of acknowledging the man's presence. The man had other plans.

He tilted up his hat; gave Jephtha a long stare and a faint smile. Then he rose, dusted off the seat of his pants and walked toward the road.

Uneasy, Jephtha reined in. Beneath Samuel Dorn's tight-fitting coat, he noticed a small bulge. A concealed pistol—

Dorn stopped in front of Jephtha's horse. "Hallo, Reverend."

The man was young, with a blocky Teutonic face, blue eyes and yellow hair curling around his ears. None too bright, Jephtha recalled from their first meeting down at the depot on February 23. He'd been wakened that morning by an informant—a boy he paid to keep watch on the comings and goings of notables. The boy breathlessly told him of Lincoln's arrival at six on a regular passenger train, ahead of the Presidential Special due later that day. Jephtha had rushed down to the station and tried to interview Allan Pinkerton and some of his men who had helped smuggle Lincoln into the capital.

"Mr. Dorn," Jephtha returned with a slight nod.

The blue eyes fixed on him. "Visiting Virginia today, are you?"

"I can't see that should concern the Pinkerton detective bureau. Or anyone else, for that matter."

"Hell, it's only a friendly question. I just happened to be resting here—"

"Spying on travelers?"

Dorn's cheeks reddened. "Watching," he snapped. "The word is watching."

"Whatever the word—or the assignment—I'm damned if I know where you get the authority for it."

Dorn struggled to control his anger. "The chief and a few of the operatives are in town on a special job—"

"If I recall, Mr. Pinkerton is under contract to protect the property of the Philadelphia, Washington and Baltimore—and you're a good distance from the railroad's right-of-way. Isn't it up north? Or has there been an extension I don't know about?"

The man didn't like the sarcasm. "We're looking over the security of the railroad facilities *here*. If it's any of your business."

"No, it isn't," Jephtha returned. "But it is my business when you question my right to enter Virginia."

"Nobody's questioning anything," Dorn shrugged. "If you want to mix with a crowd of traitors—"

"See here—"

"—if you have, ah, some special reason for wanting to mingle with them—carrying a little message, maybe—"

"Get out of my way, Mr. Dorn!"

Dorn actually looked pleased. Pinkerton, the shrewd Scot who had built a successful Illinois detective bureau, was at least intelligent. But some of the men he was forced to hire were little more than thugs. An all-too-plain anticipation lit Dorn's eyes:

"That's pretty strong talk for a gospel man."

"I'm a reporter and you know it."

"But the chief told me about your—ah—former job. The one that didn't turn out so well—"

"Get the hell out of my way!"

Suddenly Dorn's right hand shot up, fastening hard on Jephtha's left arm.

"Don't be so goddamn snotty, Kent. We did come down to survey the yards and the trackage. But we're doing some special work for one of the gents in the government, too."

Hoping to startle an admission out of the detective, Jephtha said instantly, "Seward?"

The detective had wits enough to control his tongue:

"Afraid I can't answer that. But I'll warn you—there *is* a close watch being kept on people who come over the bridge."

"Well, you just run back to your chief and tell him

Jephtha Kent went to Arlington. To talk to a man who's given thirty-five years of his life to the United States. And who knows more about good manners, I suspect, than you ever will."

Savagely, Jephtha wrenched his arm free. Dorn started to reach beneath his coat; checked his hand at the last moment. His eyes were venomous:

"Y'know, Reverend, I didn't like you the first time we met. I didn't take to the way you badgered and pushed and asked questions down at the depot—"

Jephtha shrugged. "Happens to be my job."

"May be. But—"

"As I recall, you were doing most of the shoving. *And* making all the threats about a fight."

Dorn rubbed an index finger across his upper lip. "Reverend, you want to climb down from that horse?"

"For what purpose?"

"We're going to finish what I should have finished at the station."

Calmly, Jephtha answered, "No, thank you."

That amused the detective. "Why not? I won't bruise your nice Christian face too much. 'Less of course it's a yella streak that holds you back."

"You damned, ignorant—"

"Or maybe it's your preacher's training. I wouldn't guess a preacher could hold his own against a real man."

Jephtha flushed, ready to jump from the saddle and knock Dorn's insult down his throat. Jephtha's years of itinerating on horseback had kept him lean and well-muscled—characteristics he hadn't lost. But he didn't dismount, though Dorn obviously hoped he would. His task at the moment was to reach Lee.

"I'll oblige you some other time," he promised. "When I feel up to taking on a baboon."

He hammered his heels against the mare. She bolted

forward, giving him a last, blurred impression of Dorn
red in the cheeks and grabbing for the hidden pistol.

Jephtha's face broke out in a sweat. His spine prick-
led as he trotted toward the bend of the road that
would take him safely out of pistol range. He didn't
look back. But he didn't relax until he was certain the
contour of a hill had cut off Dorn's view.

No doubt Samuel Dorn thought he had good reason
for enmity. That morning at the depot, Dorn and the
other Pinkerton men had been forced to shove Jephtha
away repeatedly, while Jephtha attempted to find out
whether the President-elect had indeed been smuggled
into Washington at Pinkerton's insistence and under his
guidance.

Unsettling as the confrontation with the bad-
tempered detective had been, Jephtha was even more
disturbed by his presence on the Virginia side of the
Long Bridge. As far as Jephtha knew, Allan Pinkerton's
agency only served various railroads and had no official
connection with the United States Government, other
than when Lincoln traveled to Washington on the public railroads.

The bearded detective was a protégé of a once-
promising young army officer, Captain George Brinton
McClellan. But McClellan had resigned the service a
few years ago to take up a more lucrative civilian career. He had quickly become vice-president of the Illinois Central Railroad and then had advanced to the
presidency of the eastern division of the Ohio and Mississippi. He kept Pinkerton operatives busy guarding the
property of his lines.

Perhaps the detective and his men had been secretly
summoned to Washington over the weekend, as the
Government's concern at the threat of an invasion
mounted. Of one thing Jephtha was virtually certain.
Dorn could have no official assignment at the Long
Bridge. As he'd admitted, he was simply doing a favor

for someone in high places. The fact that unofficial spying was already underway showed again how deep the mood of distrust and fear had become—

Jephtha had a healthy fear of a brute like Dorn. Such men were drawn to work that permitted them to indulge their fondness for bullying others. They could develop an instant and permanent dislike for anyone who challenged their authority—which was precisely what Jephtha had done with his persistent questioning at the station. He hoped he wouldn't encounter the Pinkerton man again.

With a start, he realized Dorn would probably still be lounging by the tree when he returned from Lee's home. Well, he'd meet that problem later. Right now he wanted a story.

He urged the mare into a canter.

iii

He'd ridden no more than a few hundred yards when another thought drove the memory of Dorn from his mind. He felt the pain born of remembering—

He was on Southern soil.

In Virginia—where he'd lost so much of himself. So much that was precious to him—

Cantering through the pleasant countryside toward Arlington, he thought that very little had actually changed since the day more than fifteen years ago when he'd passed through the northern part of the state, a new pastor bound for the little town of Lexington in the Shenandoah Valley. Yet everything had changed. And change was one cause of the dilemma that had swept the South into secession, and war.

The American nation—the whole world, in fact— was being pounded by the tides of change. The cottage industries were dying, replaced by the huge smoky industrial plants he'd first encountered when he was on his way to Vermont for pastoral training.

Jephtha had been born in the mountains bordering the Pacific, child of the mountain man Jared Kent, who had seen his livelihood disappear along with the demand for beaver pelts. Before wandering down to the California gold fields at the start of the great rush of '49, Jared had struggled unsuccessfully as a farmer in the valleys of Oregon. Jephtha's mother, Grass Singing, had raised her son to have great reverence for a universal Deity. And so, despite his father's objections, he'd offered his life to God with the help of one of the first Methodist missionaries who had come to the Willamette Valley. He'd journeyed east to the Biblical Institute— and had gazed in wonder at the dark, clattering manufactories ushering in a new age.

As a new, young minister, Jephtha had quickly acquired a liking for Virginians—whom he found to be typical of most Southerners. They were hard-working people; devout yet high spirited; honorable; hospitable. Soon, though, his liking had become tainted by a growing moral anguish over the slave question.

Only later, after he'd courted and wed Fan Tunworth and started raising a family, did it occur to him that perhaps industrialization had caught the South in a trap not entirely of its own devising. As the North began to assert its dominance with the factory system, she locked the South into a set of circumstances which prohibited easy change.

The spinning works of the Northeast and Europe demanded huge quantities of cotton. To supply this world market, the South had clung to slave-based agriculture—at a time when it should have been developing its own industrial base. The refusal to acknowledge the need for change was more than saddening. It was disastrous.

To Jephtha, Virginians such as his wife's father, Captain Virgil Tunworth, were pathetically unrealistic about the way industrialization was trapping them. So they blinded themselves to the evils of the system on which they were increasingly dependent. They convinced themselves—in part because they had to—that slavery was altogether right, proper, and immutable. In Jephtha's eyes the sectional crisis was rooted not only in a peculiarly American problem—Constitutional interpretation—but in an issue that was global in scope: change, and the resistance to it.

There was another facet to the problem of change. Since the days when Jephtha's great-grandfather, Philip Kent, had fired his musket against the King's troops at Concord bridge and fought side by side with Southerners to win American liberty, the South had virtually dominated American politics. Now that too was over. The swollen cities of the Northeast and the expanding population of the Northwest had combined to bring forth the first truly successful sectional party—the Republicans. The traditional party of the North and South—the One and Indivisible Democracy as its adherents liked to call it—had been hopelessly divided on ideological grounds.

Change. *Change*—

It backed a man into a corner.

It robbed him of power he'd once savored.

And a man thus trapped often fought to protect or restore the old ways. Fought with desperation; with an almost religious fervor.

No single incident had aroused the South's militant spirit more than the almost totally foredoomed Harper's Ferry raid in October of '59. With twenty-one men, the abolitionist John Brown had attempted to seize the little town's Federal armory—in preparation for exhorting Southern blacks to rise up against their masters. Brown's scheme, many said, was secretly financed by Boston money. During its planning, it had been referred

to by a code phrase—"the speculation in wool." Thanks
to the swift action of Colonel Lee and that detachment
of Marines Lincoln had mentioned, the raid had failed.
And the Virginians who'd brought Brown to justice
had given him an exceptionally fair trial before sending
him to the gallows.

In the jail at Charles Town where he'd awaited hanging, the condemned man had written, *"I, John Brown,
am now quite certain that the crimes of this guilty land
will never be purged away but with blood."*

The words had a special significance for Jephtha.
He'd stood dry-mouthed and trembling among the reporters who'd watched the mad-eyed old man climb the
gallows steps with remarkable composure—then drop
moments later, his neck snapped.

Jephtha knew of Brown's passion for a verse in the
ninth chapter of Paul's epistle to the Hebrews. Time
and again, he was haunted by the realization that, cen-
turies ago, the great Apostle had foretold that the present:

*"And almost all things are by the law purged with
blood; and without shedding of blood is no remission."*

While he was still a preacher, and zealous to the
point of fanaticism, Jephtha had interpreted the passage
as only a condemnation of the slave system; a promise
of punishment for the South, and for those who permitted its peculiar institution to flourish. Now he saw the
verse in broader and more tragic terms. It applied to the
entire nation. It warned of the fate of men of good will
who had failed to reach an accommodation before it
was too late.

That God permitted such a failure was one more reason Jephtha had stayed away from the church. It was
Christ the merciful and forgiving in whom Jephtha had
believed most passionately. Now events were being directed—if indeed there was any controlling hand at
all—by a vengeful God; the God of the Old Testament
who had somehow spoken a prophecy of this hour

through Christ's own disciple—and who now seemed determined to let suffering, not mercy, rule.

Brown's raid had ignited fearful fires of emotionalism in all parts of the country. Throughout the South the scheme to foment an uprising stirred memories of horror that lay at the base of the section's fear of Negro freedom. In the past, black men themselves had made other attempts—grisly ones—to redress the wrongs done to them. Harper's Ferry conjured the ghost of the quasi-preacher, Nat Turner, who had led a mob of his fellow slaves on a rampage in Virginia's Southampton County in 1831, leaving a trail of fifty-seven innocent men, women and children killed and mutilated before he was caught and hanged. That was the ever-present specter. Free blacks turning on those who had used them.

Jephtha saw Brown for what he was: a vicious murderer. But to add to the humiliation and anger of the South, the abolitionists equated him with history's great martyrs. With Socrates. With Christ Himself. Emerson wept over his downfall. The daughter of Amos Bronson Alcott, the reformer, herself a popular writer, Louisa May Alcott, called him "Saint John." In France, Victor Hugo praised him extravagantly—

Factors complex and beyond clear separation had led to this evil time. On both sides, men of narrow mind had fostered the evil. And a God Jephtha no longer trusted had permitted it to happen.

"And without shedding of blood is no remission—"

Well, there would be blood in plenty now, Jephtha thought. Blood and suffering beyond any American's power to predict or comprehend.

Tell me, Mr. Lincoln, he said to himself as he rode. *Where in all the dark that's coming down do you catch sight of those better angels of our nature?*

I see not one.

iv

As Jephtha drew near the heights of Arlington and the splendid house overlooking the river, he wondered whether change ever worked to a man's favor. He himself had undergone profound changes. And although he accepted his current lot, he was often depressed and miserable about it.

After his personal moral torment forced him to speak out against the mistreatment of blacks, he had been denied a pulpit by the Methodist Episcopal Church, South, one of the two bodies left when the Church itself split over the slave question. His outspoken position had led to bitter arguments with his wife, and ultimately to his banishment from their house in Lexington. Strong in her beliefs, Fan had even turned his own sons against him.

Refusing to leave the town, Jephtha hadn't been content with passive martyrdom. He'd involved himself in the business of smuggling runaway slaves north to freedom.

His partner had been a quirky, unpleasant man named Syme. In 1852 they arranged the flight of a young Negro girl who belonged to Captain Tunworth. They sent her to Jephtha's cousin once removed, the wealthy Amanda Kent of New York City. Syme had been caught, then tortured into confessing. Jephtha barely escaped with a few personal belongings, including the copybooks—his journal—in which he'd recorded his most personal thoughts year by year. He fled to Washington, then went on to New York.

When he arrived, he found that Amanda was dead. The interior of her mansion was in ruins. It had been invaded by a mob that had come partly because she'd

been sheltering the runaway girl. Amanda had been
shot during the attack.

What remained of the household was in the care of
Michael Boyle, the young Irish boy from the slums who
had worked as Amanda's clerk and had grown close to
her. As she lay dying, she'd appointed Michael the legal
guardian of her son Louis, Jephtha's second cousin. Today, Louis managed the affairs of the family with Michael's assistance. Jephtha had never liked or trusted
Louis. And the boy had been too young—and too
preoccupied with himself—to be of any assistance when
Jephtha first arrived in New York. It was Michael who
had helped him rebuild his ruined life. Almost by accident.

Throughout 1853 and '54 Jephtha had gone through
a period of almost total despair. His wife informed him
by letter that she was obtaining a divorce, and he would
be denied the privilege of seeing his sons again. Another
letter in '55 announced she had married the actor Edward Lamont, whom she'd met while visiting her father's relatives in Charleston.

During those years Jephtha hadn't lived—merely existed in the rebuilt house in Madison Square. He repaid
Michael's charity as best he could, working as a handy-
man and doing chores the servants found too arduous
or too distasteful.

Of course, Michael reminded him often that he really
didn't need to spend his days doing drudge work. He
was a rich man. Amanda had proved a good steward of
the profits of the Ophir mining operation in California's
Sierra mountains. She had invested those profits in
quality stocks, further compounding the wealth that belonged to the Virginia branch of the family.

But Jephtha had an almost childlike disregard for
money—perhaps a legacy from his Shoshoni mother,
who had taught him to place a higher value on the mind
and the spirit. He had no desire to travel to California

to learn the mining business. Mathematics and all the other associated skills required for successful management of a fortune were foreign to him. He was content to continue the old arrangement; to let the family's financial advisers, and Louis when he came of age, administer his holdings. At his death the accumulated riches would pass directly to Gideon, Matthew and Jeremiah. A document was drawn up by the Kent attorneys guaranteeing it.

Jephtha wasn't sure wealth would benefit his sons. It became increasingly clear that money hadn't improved Louis Kent's character very much. If anything, the young man had grown arrogant because of his wealth. Still, Jephtha knew he had no right to deny his sons their heritage when he died; nor would he ever attempt to do so. One of the stormiest periods of his relationship with his former wife concerned that very point. When he'd signed the paper permitting Amanda to handle the Ophir funds, Fan had accused him of defrauding the boys. It had been one of her most vituperative outbursts. The memory of it could still generate hatred of a most un-Christian sort.

Gradually, Jephtha and Michael formed a strong friendship. They debated endlessly about the slave question. Michael was candid about his own difficult transition from the behavior patterns of a boy growing up in the Five Points slum. There, the immigrant Irish hated black men because black men, freed, would compete for menial jobs—the only kind the immigrant Irish could get.

Amanda had brought Michael a long way from that attitude. He now believed America would have to decide, soon and for all time, whether the principles of equality on which the country was founded did or did not apply to *all* men.

It was during one of their long night chats that Jephtha had first shown the young Irishman a portion of

the record of his own pilgrimage of the soul. His carefully kept journals; eighteen copybooks whose contents
spanned the years since he had come east to attend the
Bible college.

Michael was taken with Jephtha's writing style—
something to which Jephtha had never given any special
notice. Michael grew excited, struck by an idea.
Jephtha ought to use his brain for something more constructive than shoveling up turds in the coach house behind the mansion. Michael made a specific suggestion.

At first Jephtha laughed. But Michael was persuasive. So Jephtha had permitted the younger man to introduce him to Theophilus Payne. Tentatively, and with
a feeling of great trepidation, he'd gone to work for
Payne.

Initially he'd been confined to a desk in Printing
House Square, doing the simplest sort of editing and
proofreading. To his surprise, he found he both liked
the work and had a talent for it. He asked Payne for
more responsibility. Within a year of starting at the *Union,* he was put on his own as a general reporter.

Despite his share of beginner's blunders, he succeeded. Even drew an occasional compliment from the
editor about a particular story. When the *Union*'s
Washington correspondent died of a stroke, Jephtha
was chosen to replace him.

Payne lectured him before he left for the capital. The
assignment had nothing to do with Jephtha's family
connections. He had become a good reporter; an able
writer, aggressive in his search for news. If his performance didn't continue at that high level he'd be recalled.
Fair enough, Jephtha said, excited by the new challenge.

In Washington he'd performed well enough so that
the possibility of recall soon vanished. He took to cigars; to whiskey. Then to a woman whose bed he now
shared without benefit of wedlock. Ten years earlier

such behavior would have struck him as grossly immoral. In terms of biblical absolutes, no doubt it still was. But like the South, he had been faced with an alternative. Change—or suffer as a prisoner of the past. He'd changed. Perhaps not entirely for the better. But at least he'd managed to build a new life out of the wreckage of the old.

He seldom read scripture these days—and never with the full, mystic faith of his youth. That, together with the cigars, the whiskey, and Molly, occasionally produced painful twinges of guilt.

But he *was* free of his yesterdays—

As free, that is, as a father could be. The past still exerted a hold on him because of his sons.

Sometimes he could bring himself to a calm understanding of the reason Fan had turned the boys against him. She believed she was right and he was dangerously wrong on the question of Negro freedom. Still, her actions had left scars. Occasionally, in the darkest part of the night, he would awaken sweating from a nightmare in which he saw himself striking his former wife. He was fearful that if he ever encountered Fan again he might not be able to refrain from doing her injury. His capacity for hate was a harrowing truth about himself that he couldn't wish away, despite the warning of a remembered passage from Proverbs:

"Whoso diggeth a pit shall fall therein: and he that rolleth a stone, it will return upon him."

In his own way, he supposed, he was as wicked as those men, North and South, who had fomented a war out of their hatreds and would now feel the crushing weight of the stone rolling back upon them.

Jephtha jogged the mare up the long sunlit drive to the pillared house familiar to everyone in the capital.

He had no idea where his boys were. Nor did his friend at the Virginia Military Institute in Lexington,

Professor Thomas Jackson, with whom he corresponded occasionally.

Jackson wasn't on good terms with Fan's father, because of the way Tunworth abused his slaves. Consequently he knew nothing about Fan, her children or her new spouse, he wrote. And he doubted Tunworth would give him an answer even if he inquired.

Once, in a moment of extreme despair, Jephtha had asked Jackson whether a visit to Lexington would be safe. He could make inquiries in person—

Bluntly, Jackson warned him to stay away. His name was still remembered. He would certainly get no cooperation. He might even find his life in jeopardy.

From time to time Jephtha saw a reference to Fan's husband in an old issue of a Southern paper. Twice he'd written to theaters where Lamont had been playing. One of the letters had been returned bearing a notation that the troupe had moved on. He'd heard nothing from the second. He supposed the boys might be traveling with their stepfather. But relying on outdated newspapers to verify it proved futile.

Of one thing Jephtha was dismally sure. With Fan to inspire them, the boys might be hurt—die—in the coming war.

He shook his head and slowed the mare to a walk as he approached Arlington House. The mansion had a solid, serene look. Twin wings extended from the massive main building to add a pleasing symmetry and create a façade Jephtha guessed to be something like a hundred and fifty feet wide. The entire building was stuccoed brick, painted over in buff with white trim. Its most imposing feature was its portico—exceptionally deep; at least twenty-five feet. Eight mammoth Doric columns supported the classic pediment.

A savory smell of wood smoke drifted from vine-covered brick outbuildings he'd passed on his ride up the hillside. He dismounted, tied the mare to a ring block below the portico steps, and wiped sweat from his forehead with a pocket kerchief. Across the river below the tree-shaded lawn the sprawling city with its familiar landmarks had a deceptive look of sunlit calm.

Standing with one dark-skinned hand on the neck of the horse, Jephtha suddenly wished he still had enough faith to say a prayer; enough faith to ask God to protect the lives of his sons, even if he never saw them again—

But he didn't.

v

The huge portico was cool with shadow. Jephtha hesitated before touching the great door knocker. The house itself seemed to speak of the sadness of disunion.

Poor arthritic Mary Lee, the colonel's wife—seldom seen in Washington any longer—was the daughter of George Washington's adopted son, George Washington Parke Custis. The colonel's father, Light-Horse Harry, had served the general as a hard-fighting cavalry officer during the Revolution. At the first president's funeral, Light-Horse Harry had spoken the words that had lingered in the common memory ever since: "First in war, first in peace, and first in the hearts of his countrymen." If most Americans felt a sense of despair today, how much deeper it must be for the inhabitants of this mansion; people whose forebears had done so much to create and nurture the nation.

Feeling somewhat like the violator of a shrine, Jephtha let the knocker fall.

Presently an elderly white housekeeper answered.

"Yes, sir?"

"Forgive the intrusion, ma'am. My name is Kent. I'm a journalist with a New York paper—"

The housekeeper's eyes narrowed with suspicion.

"If Colonel Lee's at home, I'd appreciate a few moments of his time."

The woman started to shut the door. "The colonel is not seeing—"

"Who's there, Hattie?" The housekeeper frowned. She was forced to turn and answer:

"Some fellow from a newspaper, Colonel Lee."

Jephtha heard the sound of boots and then the door swung all the way open.

Though Washington was a relatively small city, Jephtha had never seen Robert Edward Lee in person until now. He judged him about fifty-five, not quite six feet, and powerfully built. Because his legs were slender, his chest, shoulders, and head looked huge by comparison.

Lee was dressed in civilian trousers and a loose linen shirt. A full black mustache contrasted with his graying hair. He had a large nose, kindly brown eyes, and an air of quiet assurance that helped explain why he'd been so successful in the army. His expression, though guarded, wasn't unfriendly:

"I'm Colonel Lee, Mr.—?"

"Kent. Jephtha Kent. Washington correspondent for the New York *Union*."

Lee extended his hand. "How do you do? I'm sorry to tell you I have nothing to say for the public record."

Somehow Jephtha felt audacity would be more effective than a meek thank you and goodbye. He took the chance:

"I can understand that, Colonel. However, I did ride a good distance in the hope you'd be home. I realize I'm intruding on your privacy. But you *are* a public figure. You'll forgive me if I say I'll be very unhappy if you send me back to the city empty-handed."

"Why, of all the Yankee gall!" the housekeeper exclaimed.

Lee held up a hand. His eyes sparkled with amusement:

"Come now, Hattie. Mr. Kent's boldness is commendable." He stepped back: "I'm afraid you will go back empty-handed. But you're welcome to step in and refresh yourself with some lemonade."

"Thank you," Jephtha grinned. He was inside in a second. Hattie vanished, harrumphing.

Lee closed the door. He led Jephtha across the spacious, high-ceilinged central hall and into a parlor on the north side. On the walls hung portraits of eighteenth-century women. One Jephtha recognized as Martha Washington. Arlington House was supposedly a museum of George Washington's possessions. Across the hall, in a formal dining room, he spied a cabinet displaying fine china. From Mount Vernon?

Lee showed him to a chair. "Are you surprised I let you in, Mr. Kent?"

"Yes, sir, a little."

"Well, there's no mystery to it. Indecision and fear are the two greatest enemies men face on a battlefield. I've never put much stock in a soldier who was unwilling to gamble everything for a victory. I much prefer a fellow who risks it all, and loses, to the one who risks nothing. Sit down, sit down."

Lee removed some papers from his own chair, laid them on a table along with a pair of reading spectacles, and seated himself.

"I must tell you, sir—you're the first journalist who's had the courage to show up at my front door."

"I am sorry if I disturbed you. But as I said, your name's constantly in the air over in Washington. I've heard General Scott wants to name you commander of the army."

"Mr. Kent, please—I have nothing to say."

Yet it was evident from Lee's expression that Jephtha's remark caused a painful reaction.

There was a pause as Hattie brought in a tray with pitcher and glasses. While the housekeeper poured Jephtha's drink, he had a chance to study the colonel.

Robert Lee's military career had been long and distinguished. He'd been trained in engineering at West Point. Earned commendations in the war with Mexico. Directed several major projects for the Corps of Engineers, including one to widen and improve the Mississippi channel near St. Louis. He'd even spent a period as superintendent of the military academy from which he'd graduated. In February he'd returned from Texas, where he'd been second in command. At that time his superior had peacefully surrendered the San Antonio arsenal and all other Federal posts to the state government.

Lee saluted Jephtha with his lemonade. He sipped, then smiled in a rueful way:

"I'm at a loss as to how we can carry on a conversation, Mr. Kent. I don't want anything I say put into print."

"But people are anxious to hear whether you'd accept command of the army."

Lee shook his head. "No such offer has been made. And you must remember—Virginia is my native state. You realize the convention is meeting in Richmond at this very hour—"

Again Jephtha decided on boldness. He set the frosty glass aside and leaned forward:

"Colonel, let me make a proposal. If you'll talk with me candidly—for the record—I promise you I'll file no dispatch until the Richmond convention acts and you announce your future plans."

"By heaven, Mr. Kent, you do have nerve!"

"Just as you said about soldiers, Colonel—a journalist can't succeed without it."

Lee smiled. "A good journalist." He sobered. "Still, you're asking me to trust you."

"I am."

"To trust a man I've never seen before—"

Jephtha knew that if he avoided Lee's gaze, he was finished. He didn't so much as blink.

"That's right."

Lee scrutinized him a moment longer. Then he laughed.

"Well, sir, you've offered the dearest thing a man owns. His honor. And I assume you've offered it in good faith. I accept your terms."

Jubilant, Jephtha pulled out scraps of paper and a pencil. He pondered his first question before he uttered it:

"You've never been called a partisan of slavery, Colonel. Have you changed that position at all?"

"I haven't." Lee rose and walked to the window overlooking the river. "I don't think the nigras are ready for full emancipation. I believe the time will come eventually, however. Few enlightened Christians would deny slavery is a moral and political evil—" He turned back. "I've also observed that when one man holds another in bondage, it often turns the master into a worse brute than the slave. I'm of the opinion slavery is even more degrading for whites than it is for blacks." He thought a moment. "On the other hand, the South has been sorely aggrieved by the North's constant hostility. In the face of that, my own state has acted with admirable restraint. *And* in a spirit of conciliation. The special convention—"

"The *secession* convention," Jephtha interrupted softly.

"Call it what you will. You know its members are men of impeccable integrity. Former President Tyler, for one. The convention's been deliberating since February—"

"Excuse me, sir, is that restraint or just a symptom of worry about the numerical superiority of the North?"

Jephtha realized he'd said the wrong thing. Lee's mild eyes lit with annoyance:

"We are speaking of a matter of *principle*, Mr. Kent—not courage versus cowardice. I like to think we have very little of the latter here in the Old Dominion."

"My apologies—you're entirely correct. I didn't mean to imply otherwise."

"But you did choose to ignore the record. Who issued a plea for a peace conference with delegates from every state? Virginia did. That nothing came of the conference is not Virginia's fault. But that didn't end our effort. Just last Friday—with the Montgomery Provisional Government already in operation, and General Beauregard's bombardment underway—our convention sent three men to see President Lincoln, hoping to learn whether he really wants war with what some choose to call the departed sisters."

"Yes, I'm aware of the commission."

"Distinguished men, every one. Honorable men—and fairly chosen to represent the spectrum of opinion—"

Lee folded down a finger of his right hand.

"Mr. Stuart of Staunton—an avowed unionist."

He folded down a second finger.

"Ballard Preston—an advocate of compromise."

The third finger.

"Mr. Randolph, who stands foursquare for secession. You know what happened at the meeting on Saturday. The commission got absolutely no concrete assurances. Just some vague statements from our—from the President that naturally he'd never be so imprudent as to attempt to coerce any sovereign state. He said that in the face of Buchanan's blatant attempt to put the *Star of the West* into Charleston harbor with provisions and military reinforcements for Fort Sumter!"

"I'd point out that President Lincoln is not President Buchanan, sir."

"Granted. But both represent Federal authority. We saw Buchanan's true colors in January. This month—in Mr. Chew's message to Charleston—we saw Mr. Lincoln's. Frankly, I can discern little difference."

"But the Southern side opened the fire at Charleston, Colonel."

"And again, if my information from Richmond is correct, a great many of the delegates consider that to have been ill-advised. However—" Lee sighed. "The whole matter is not under any direct control of mine. I will say this. Regardless of the actions of either side— whether correct or misguided is for history to judge—I see no greater calamity than a dissolution of the Union. Right after I came home, I told a friend over in Washington that if I owned four million slaves, I would sell, free, sacrifice every last one of them to preserve the country. Secession *is* anarchy—"

"Then you really don't approve of what the cotton states have done? Or what your own government in Richmond might be doing right now?"

Lee replied crisply, "I believe I've said enough on the subject. More lemonade?"

"No, thank you." Jephtha wrote rapidly. Then: "What will you do if the Richmond convention does declare the state out of the Union?"

Lee rubbed the bridge of his nose. "I detest war, Mr. Kent. It's not a glorious business as some pretend. It's tragic. It's even more tragic now that one section has taken arms against the other. As late as February, when General Twiggs surrendered the Texas garrisons, I had faith in the eventual triumph of reason. I still have faith—"

But it was weakening, Jephtha suspected. Lee's eyes were melancholy as he went on:

"Yet I'm firm on one count." He took a slow breath. "I could never draw my sword against my native state."

"In other words, Virginia's war would be your war?"

"That's correct."

Jephtha shivered. Lee had spoken without bravado; almost with a note of sadness in his voice. But there was no doubt about his determination.

For several seconds Jephtha stared at what he'd jotted down. Then, slowly, he folded the pieces of paper and tucked them in a pocket. Lee looked surprised:

"You've no more questions?"

"No, sir. Your last answer covered almost everything else I could ask. Covered your whole future, you might say—"

Lee frowned. "I imagine it did, didn't it?"

Touched by the gentle courtliness of the man, Jephtha said softly, "It told me what you'll do if and when Virginia votes to secede. You'll resign from Federal service, won't you?"

Lee's shoulder's seemed to slump a little. He rose again; moved back to the window and gazed down through the sunlit parklands sloping to the Potomac. Finally he said:

"Yes."

Jephtha had seldom heard a single syllable convey so much unhappiness. Lee spun back all at once, his voice firmer:

"But I'm relying on your word that you won't print—"

"Colonel, I promised. I won't print it until you've made your decision public."

"That may come soon. This week—next—events are rushing too fast—"

"And I've prevailed on your courtesy long enough." Jephtha stood up. They shook hands a second time.

Lee ushered him through the airy front hall and watched while he mounted the mare. From the shadow cast by one of the pillars, Lee said:

"I compliment you again on your boldness, Mr. Kent. Were you ever a soldier?"

"No, sir. I used to be a minister. Here in Virginia, in fact. Lexington."

"Indeed! Do you know my old comrade Tom Jackson?"

Jephtha smiled. "I certainly do. He was my only friend when the bishop removed me for preaching against slavery. Jackson welcomed me into his home when hardly anyone else in town would speak to me. He found me a job at the Military Institute where he teaches—"

"A good man. A Christian," Lee added by way of endorsement. He took a step into the sunlight. "You spoke out, did you?"

"Yes."

"Well, that seems to fit with your character—" It was meant as a compliment. "Are you an abolitionist?"

"I am—though I'd prefer to see slavery ended without a fight. Too many Southerners have been blamed for the sins of a few. I was married to a Virginia girl for a time. I loved the people to whom I ministered. I wouldn't wish them ill even today. I'd just welcome an end to all the bitterness—and the peculiar institution at the same time."

"I'm afraid there weren't enough men of your persuasion in positions of influence in the North *or* the South," Lee said. "Now it's almost too late. The fools on both sides who pant for the death of their enemies will rue it."

Jephtha shivered. He wondered if Lee, a devoutly religious man, knew John Brown's favorite passage from Hebrews.

"Colonel, thank you again." He forced himself to invoke a power he wasn't sure he believed in. "God be with you whatever your final choice."

With a gentle smile, Lee said, "He will be, Mr. Kent. That's my only rock of salvation in what we've turned into a mad, bloody world."

Jephtha started off, twisting in the saddle when Lee hailed him:

"Mr. Kent—!"

"Yes, Colonel?"

"I just wanted to tell you—I think you'd have made a very good officer."

Jephtha waved and rode on. Lee stepped back and stood watching, once again enfolded by the shadows of the portico.

vi

For the first few moments of his homeward ride, Jephtha was again overcome with gloom.

In the President he'd interviewed this morning and the army officer General Scott valued above all others, he saw the essence of the tragedy that was breaking like a torrential storm. Neither Lincoln nor Lee was a hothead. Both were men of principle; conviction—titanic figures who seemed to loom larger than life because of their prominence on the national scene. Yet both were intensely human; this very day, he'd glimpsed suffering in the eyes of each of them. It seemed a wicked irony that men of such character had been helpless to prevent the storm—and an unspeakable cruelty that they now had to suffer its fury.

He thought of other brave, tragic figures in the drama. Douglas, who had first tried so desperately to bring accord between the antagonistic sections, then gone South in the last hours of the election campaign. His presidential ambitions in ruins, he'd spoken on platform after platform—often at peril of his life—declaring that the Union was more important than the wishes of the violent few. He'd had the courage to stand before hostile crowds and cry into the flaring torchlight that he was in favor of executing in good faith every

clause and provision of the Constitution; in favor of
protecting every right it promised; and in favor of pun-
ishing every man who took up arms against it:

"I would hang every such man higher than Haman!"

He thought of pale, courtly Jefferson Davis. Born in
Kentucky, as Lincoln had been—and with only a few
miles separating the two cabins; another touch of irony.
Year after year Davis had reiterated one theme. Not out
of cowardice—no man would dare attribute cowardice
to the colonel of the Mississippi Rifles who had fought
and bled at Buena Vista—but out of the hope of conciliation. Over and over, in endless variation, Davis had
sounded the central plea of the Southern moderates:

"All we ask is to be let alone."

But it had not been enough for the Northern radicals—nor, obviously, for the secessionist fire-eaters. On
the night Davis had resigned from the Senate, they said
he had prayed on his knees: "May God have us in His
holy keeping, and grant that before it is too late peaceful councils will prevail." To add one more irony, the
fire-eaters had been rejected by the delegates gathered
in Montgomery to form a new government; it was the
moderate who had been chosen for the presidency.

Lincoln and Lee. Douglas and Davis. The names
rang in Jephtha's mind with a sonorous, bell-like quality. Good men—giants in the affairs of the nation. But
powerless, finally, to prevent a war from coming.

The President had perhaps put it best, he thought.
The very concept of popular government was at stake.
Would the Constitution stand the test? Slavery was the
cause of the confrontation. But the Union itself—its fall
or its preservation—was the issue that had finally
brought the storm.

All the way to the approach to the Long Bridge, he
kept remembering the eyes of Robert Lee. With their
mingled strength and sadness, they seemed to sum up
the best and worst of America in this tortured hour.

Grim as it was, what had to be done would be done.
There was no longer any way for men of conscience to
find a clear road out of the storm; nor any place for
them to hide from its onslaught.

vii

Jephtha's palms began to perspire as he neared the
bridge. He followed the road around the low hill and
caught sight of the cherry grove. He breathed out, long
and loud.

A man was posted there, all right. Scrutinizing south-
bound traffic. But it wasn't Samuel Dorn.

The man was feeding something to his tethered horse
as Jephtha passed. He gave Jephtha a glance before
turning his attention to a farmer's wagon rumbling off
the bridge. The wagon had a family name—
Whitefield—painted in crude letters on the side. Jephtha watched the Pinkerton operative jot the name
down on a small pad.

Once across the bridge, he managed to throw off
some of his depression. He was heartened by the papers
in his pocket. He'd pulled off a coup. He looked forward to informing Theo Payne by telegraph. He wanted
to tell Molly, too, when he saw her at the boarding
house later in the day.

He returned the mare to the stable and went directly
to the noisy office of the *Evening Star,* pausing outside
to read the latest bulletin chalked on the board:

> *Governors of 16 states have pledged
> troops in response to the President's
> proclamation.*

Well, at least that promised some improvement in
Washington's military situation. He hoped the troops

would arrive before hotheads on the other side decided to launch an attack. If such an attack came too soon the Federal capital could easily fall.

He entered the busy newsroom, striding down the aisle.

"Afternoon, Mr. Kent."

He jerked his head up, almost colliding with Jim, the *Star*'s sweep boy. Jim was a Negro. Some affliction at birth had left him mentally slow, but his generally sunny nature helped compensate. He was busy with his broom, cleaning up discarded pieces of copy and proof.

"Jim, how are you?"

"Very fine, thanks."

"And staying far away from my desk, I hope."

He didn't say it unkindly. But the youngster was a thorn to the reporters on Mr. Wallach's staff. Parental training had evidently created an almost maniacal devotion to cleanliness; Jim's broom often swept away papers that spilled off the chronically littered desks of the reporters. They complained frequently and bitterly. Editor Wallach lectured Jim once or twice a week, though less profanely, because of the boy's slowness of mind and his eagerness to do well at the only work for which he was suited. None of the complaints or lectures did any good. Jim's broom kept flying day after day; copy was frequently lost in the refuse bins in the alley.

"B-b-but—" When he was upset, the boy developed a stammer. "I'm s-supposed to sweep all the aisles—"

"But if you'd only do it with a little less enthusiasm, all of us would—"

Tears had started in the black boy's eyes. Quickly, Jephtha squeezed his shoulder:

"Here—I'm sorry. Don't feel bad—"

"I—I'm s-s-*supposed* to k-keep the p-place t-t-tidy—"

"I know," Jephtha nodded. "I keep forgetting. I'm just not as smart as you are, Jim." He twisted his mouth into a rueful smile to hide his shame over his thoughtless remarks. Jephtha's exaggerated grimace made Jim laugh. Jephtha ignored scowls from a couple of the reporters and said:

"You do a fine job, too. Fine."

In a moment Jim was calm again. He wiped his eyes and smiled at the older man in a shy way. Jephtha stepped over the handle of the broom as Jim went back to work, whistling.

When Jephtha reached his desk, a quick survey showed him nothing important was missing. On the center of the desk lay another wrathful telegram from Payne. He sat down, lit a cigar and proceeded to draft a reply. He relished this particular bit of writing:

> OBTAINED EXCLUSIVE INTERVIEW WITH COLONEL R. E. LEE. CANNOT PUBLISH SAME UNTIL LEE REACHES DECISION ON HIS FUTURE. REPEAT. WILL NOT FILE COPY UNTIL LEE DECLARES HIMSELF.

That last was added to head off Payne's insistence that he telegraph his copy at once. The editor was a newsman first, and trustworthy second. If Payne had the interview in his hands, he'd print it and let Jephtha worry about the consequences of a broken promise.

He signed the message J. KENT, then set the sheet aside. For the next hour and a half, he transcribed his notes into a story. He locked the finished copy in a lower drawer of the desk and stubbed out his third cigar, ready to leave for the telegraph office. Only then did he recall the information passed along by the sketch artist from *Harper's Weekly*. Something about a potentially violent demonstration—Union or secesh—at the Canterbury variety hall tomorrow night.

He decided he'd go. If something did happen he could write a background story on the divided feelings in the capital. Perhaps that would mollify Payne while he waited for the Lee piece. The presence of Pinkerton detectives in the city also merited some investigation.

From a desk near the street entrance, Jephtha picked up a still-damp copy of the day's edition. He turned to the theatrical notices. Finally he found the advertisement:

*—Entirely New Programme
Commencing Tomorrow Evening—*

A name among the listed performers caught his eye. He stared at the words, his hand trembling. It was impossible—!

No, not at all. Washington was considered just as much a part of the Southern theatrical circuit as Savannah or New Orleans.

With a feeling of dread, Jephtha read the lines again.

*SPECIAL ATTRACTION!
Dramatic Presentations in Prose and Poesy
by the Noted Tragedian
MR. EDWARD LAMONT*

Jephtha let the paper fall to the desk. He pushed his way through the crowd clustered around the outside board. The past had rushed in upon him with unexpected suddenness. He was totally unprepared—

Questions hammered at his mind. If Lamont was in the city had he brought his wife and stepsons with him? And if so, could Jephtha find courage to face them? To face Fan—?

The thought of her started his heart beating faster and brought a dry feeling to his mouth. He fought his emotions. Unsuccessfully. His hand shook again, harder this time—

The hate in him was beyond control.

CHAPTER III

Molly's Hope

THE LAST LOAVES came fragrant from the oven at one o'clock Tuesday morning. Mrs. Molly Emerson set them out in a row to cool, banked the coals in the iron stove and extinguished the gas jets. She'd been in the kitchen almost an hour, finishing up the bread to be served to her boarders at breakfast. She was tired. It showed in her slow step as she walked toward the rectangle of light at the kitchen entrance.

She happened to glance down. Near the edge of the rectangle cast by the gaslight in the front hall, she saw a tangle of twine. Dropped and forgotten when the butcher's boy delivered in the afternoon.

She picked up the twine, carefully unsnarled it, looped it around three fingers of her left hand and placed the finished coil in a drawer already full of bits of string and twine similarly coiled.

Molly's early life had been spent in poverty. Her mother had died bearing her. Her father had been a self-taught and none too successful doctor of horses, cattle and swine. When he passed away, he'd left her no money, just two beliefs. That life was invaluable. And that the world's paramount sin was waste—whether of a nail, or the humblest God-given ability.

She shut the string drawer and left the kitchen, weary but wide awake. She knew her weariness came less from the day's work than from worrying about Jephtha.

He'd been in a strange mood throughout the evening.

116

True, he was a man of moods; she'd lived with him long enough to know that. But tonight, she felt, he'd been holding something back. Denying her access to what was really in his mind.

In the front hall Molly trimmed the gas to its dimmest level. She made certain the street door was locked. After dark Washington City was plagued with roaming thieves, both whites and free blacks. All her boarders had their own keys, and she kept a hand gun in the bureau near her bed.

As she started up the stairs to her suite of rooms at the second floor front, she pondered the problem of what to do about Jephtha. She didn't even know how to begin probing for the cause of the tension that had kept his conversation guarded and his glance evasive since his return home at nine. For a moment she hoped he'd fallen asleep. By morning, his mood might pass—

Suddenly, she felt she was being a coward for wishing him asleep. Obviously something was troubling him. And she cared for him, despite his complex, occasionally infuriating personality.

By turns idealistic, guilt-ridden and bad-tempered, Jephtha Kent was still a welcome companion. Even jolly on occasion. He was a decent man. And he warmed her bed when the fall winds began to riffle the Potomac— a commonplace pleasure, but one that she'd missed deeply until he came into her life.

Now and then Molly felt embarrassed by her feelings for Jephtha. At thirty-eight she was too old for the sort of vaporish thrills younger women experienced in the name of love. Yet Jephtha could make her feel sentimental; even romantic—

Perhaps it was compensation. Her husband, ten years her senior and four years dead, had been a proper, joyless man. Waldo Preston Emerson, a Hoosier as she was, had been an excellent attorney. But he had never been a satisfactory lover, or even a halfway proficient one. She found it funny that a former Methodist minister was far more ardent; sometimes more than a match for her own lusty appetites.

The sexual liaison with Jephtha was gratifying after her months of widowhood. At the same time it was only one part of a total relationship that caused Molly to think now, *Yes, something's definitely gone wrong. Something so bad, he won't tell me about it—*

Mr. Emerson's law practice had involved him in the politics of the Democracy. After Pierce's election, he'd been offered a patronage job in Washington. When Emerson succumbed to a paralytic seizure in the Patent Office one hot summer afternoon, and died before dawn the next day, Molly had been faced with a choice. Return to raw, provincial Indianapolis or stay in the capital and survive as best she could. She had no family and few friends out in the Northwest. She decided to stay.

Fortunately Emerson had been frugal. He'd put savings away every year. With that money she'd been able to meet the mortgage payments on the two-story house located on G Street, north of Pennsylvania Avenue and several blocks west of the Patent Office, in what was considered Washington's one truly respectable section. She'd partitioned four of the second-floor rooms into eight smaller ones, thus adding one more boarding house to the dozens that provided cheap, clean housing for the clerks and minor officials—between fifteen hundred and two thousand of them—who kept the Federal government functioning smoothly.

That is, they *had* kept the government functioning smoothly until the news from Fort Sumter. That very evening at the supper table, Mr. Swampscott who clerked at the Treasury had declared with certainty and panic in his voice that an army of rabid, raping Virginians would be marching on Washington by week's end.

Could that be what was upsetting Jephtha? she wondered as she hitched up the hem of her faded brown night robe. Fear?

She doubted it. He'd told her most everything about his past. However complex and unfathomable he could sometimes be, he was no coward.

His behavior tonight was even more puzzling in view of his accomplishments during the day. He'd scored a march on his fellow reporters. He'd gotten an interview with Colonel Lee at Arlington. Instead of taking supper when he returned, he'd gone upstairs to work on the story, polishing it so it would be ready to submit when Lee made his position known.

His accomplishment should have put him in ebullient spirits. Instead, when he'd come to her rooms around ten o'clock for a whiskey, he'd been in a strange mood. Not sharp with her. Remote; uncommunicative—

I know he's hurting. I've got to find out why.

She turned at the head of the stairs, walking softly. Behind a door on her right, she heard Mr. Swampscott floundering in a nightmare. Somewhere out in the city's dangerous dark, a pistol discharged.

Nervously, she approached the door of her parlor, which had an adjoining bedroom. Ever since Jephtha had moved into the boarding house and their initial friendship had developed into something more intimate—akin to a marriage—he'd insisted on maintaining the fiction of separate quarters. He still paid for his room just as the others did. He worked in his room but slept with her. All the boarders knew. Some, like Mr. Swampscott, a pious Episcopalian, disapproved. Molly didn't care.

She hesitated outside the door. She was a chunky woman, five feet six. But there was no fat on her. The arduous work of running the boarding house kept her solid and in good health.

Her face had an uncultivated prettiness enhanced by large brown eyes and brunette hair faintly streaked with gray. She had always been self-conscious about the fullness of her breasts; they were too large for a woman of her proportions. It was one of her great regrets that she'd never suckled a child, although she and Emerson had tried to conceive one—he, she always felt, performing a moral duty instead of taking pleasure in the act.

She didn't like her smile, either. It revealed too much. Because her mouth was wide, her teeth seemed to dominate her face. Though sound, they were slightly irregular. Her figure and her teeth made her feel unattractive. But Jephtha claimed he admired her appearance. She was no painted belle, he said. She had the look of a real woman.

Finally, overcoming her apprehension, she drew a deep breath and slipped inside the parlor. She closed the door with care, in case he was sleeping—

He wasn't. She smelled the smoke of one of his strong cigars.

The bedroom door was ajar. She crossed the lightless parlor, pushed the door and looked in on almost total darkness. A small orange spot pulsed brilliantly, then faded.

She felt awkward as she said:

"You're still up."

He didn't answer.

She followed the familiar path around the washstand to the bed. She dropped her robe, stepped out of her slippers, smoothed her cotton nightdress and lay down beside him. The bed gave a faint creak.

The cigar burned brightly again; dimmed. She turned on her right side so her breasts pressed his bare left arm. Jephtha always slept without clothes.

Still no word from him. Another moment passed. When she spoke, her voice was soft but firm:

"Jephtha, you'd better tell me. Else neither of us will get any sleep."

ii

For a long moment, there was silence.

"Tell you what?"

"Jephtha Kent, you've shared this bed long enough for me to know when something's bothering you—"

"Don't badger me just because you're tired, Molly."

She sighed. "Sometimes you can be damned exasperating, do you know that?"

No answer.

She sat up, so physically weary her arms ached when she clasped them around her knees.

"I'd stay awake till next Christmas to help you get rid of that ill-tempered look you had all evening."

Silence.

Determined, she put her bare feet on the carpet and walked through the dark to light the gas. The flame hissed in the etched bowl of cobalt glass, filling the plain but comfortable bedroom with a watery, sea-blue light. She turned back, about to speak. Jephtha was sitting up, the sheet tucked up around his waist. He reached for a cracked dish he kept on the bedside table for his cigars. His hand shook.

He didn't look at her. His pale eyes seemed to stare at nothing. Lines furrowed his forehead.

Alarmed, Molly waited. She'd entertained a fleeting thought that he might need a kiss; the warmth of arms around his neck; perhaps even lovemaking—affection. In an instant she realized she was wrong.

Jephtha knocked ash into the dish, at the same time spilling some onto the table, which showed dark spots—burns—left by other cigars.

He clamped the cigar between his teeth and kept staring at her; *through* her. She noticed the glisten of sweat on his shoulders; his forehead; his hairless chest—

God above! she thought. He's afraid. He's *terrified*.

"Jephtha, what on earth's the matter? Is it all the turmoil in town? I know people are saying we'll be invaded. Is that what's upsetting you?" She still didn't believe it.

"No, it has nothing to do with the war—" He puffed on the cigar. "Well, yes it does. In a way."

"What do you mean?"

The words seemed to tear out of him: "It has to do with my boys."

"You think they'll be fighting for the other side?"

"I don't know." Another puff. "I have to find out."

Again her instinct told her to keep quiet. *Give him time. He'll tell you. Then you can help.*

"Molly, you remember what I said about picking up a tip in Willard's bar?"

"About some sort of demonstration at the Canterbury tomorrow night? Yes."

Jephtha's long black hair shone in the gaslight. "The *Star* carried a list of the artists on the bill. One—one of them's Edward Lamont."

"Lamont! You mean your wife's husband is here in—?"

"I wish to hell you'd stop calling her my wife!" He jammed the stub of the cigar into the dish and stood up. Naked, he walked to the far side of the room, raking a hand through his hair.

"I'm sorry," she said. "That's a ridiculous mistake. I make it too often."

Jephtha turned. Hard and lean as he was—and with his nakedness revealing him to be a well-endowed man—there was still a helpless, childlike quality about him just now. When he spoke again, his voice was faint:

"If Lamont's in Washington, I expect Fan might be with him." He stalked back to the bedside, rummaged in a drawer for another cigar, struck a sulphurous-smelling match on the side of the table. The match left a mark. Molly frowned but said nothing.

He lit the cigar, blew the match out from the corner of his mouth, dropped it—missing the dish by half an inch—and sat down on the bed.

"So that's what it is—"

He nodded, his head in a cloud of smoke. "The whole damn thing's thrown me into such a state—well, I can hardly describe it."

"There's no need, Jephtha—"

This was the moment for going to him. Once around the end of the bed, she laid a cool palm on his warm shoulder. How he trembled!

"No need," she repeated. "I watched the way you fidgeted and stared into space after you came home."

He jerked the cigar from his mouth and began talking rapidly, as if he had to:

"At first I thought it was the wildest kind of coincidence. I mean Lamont turning up here just when there's so much trouble. Then I realized Washington *is* a theater town, and I know Lamont tours the major cities. Still, there's one thing I can't fathom. Why the devil would he appear in a cheap variety hall? Granted he's no Joe Jefferson. No Forrest—no Edwin Booth. But he'd be more likely to play the old Washington. Secondary parts in *Lear,* or *King John*—I just don't understand why a variety hall. Doing recitations!"

"Recitations?"

"That's what the paper said. 'Dramatic presentations in prose and poesy.' " Jephtha tainted the words with contempt. A moment later he went on:

"All evening I've been trying to figure out an explanation."

Molly sat down beside him. She rested a hand on his bare leg. Just a touch; gentle; reassuring.

"Have you?"

"Possibly." It had a doubtful sound. "The town's full up with secesh sympathizers. Lamont's certainly one. Maybe he *wanted* to be booked into the Canterbury at this particular time—" Another puff of the cigar. Molly hated the greenish weeds. But she loved Jephtha enough never to speak against the cigars except in a teasing way. "—because he's involved in that demonstration."

"But you don't know whether the demonstration's for or against the government."

"I don't."

"Perhaps it won't take place. Or be of any consequence if it does."

"That's true. It's easy to get carried away with speculation. After I left the *Star,* I went back to Willard's. I've never heard so much talk of plots in all my life. Everybody in the bar was babbling about Southern schemes to cut off the city. Tear down the telegraph lines to the north. Destroy the railroad tracks from Baltimore. I even heard one man swear some members of the local militia—members with Southern leanings—are planning to blow up the Capitol. On the other hand, just because people are hysterical doesn't rule out my first idea. Lamont could be here to cause trouble."

Feeling she was close to the reason for his torment, she asked quietly, "So you're going to the Canterbury to see for yourself?"

He nodded, puffing out smoke. It made her cough.

"Actually, Lamont's only a side issue. The instant I read his name in the paper, I knew I had to find out whether he brought Fan along. Fan and the boys—"

He jumped up, started to pace again. "It's been how many years—five?—since she stopped answering the letters I sent to Lexington—" The cigar dangling from his right hand, he faced her. "I've got to see her if I can, Molly. I've got to find out about the boys, but—" He swallowed. "—the truth is—" He averted his face. "I'm scared to do it."

There was a tension in the room, heightened by the ghostly blue gas light. She thought she knew the answer to her next question:

"Why?"

"Because everything I studied after my conversion in Oregon—everything I preached until the bishop took me out of the pulpit—everything I believed for years—it's all denied by what Fan's done to me!"

His fingers constricted around the cigar, almost breaking it in half. His face had drained of color.

"I despise her, Molly. I despise her more than I've ever despised any human being on this earth."

Molly's nod was slow and sorrowful. "You've never said it aloud. But from the way you've talked about the letters, I guessed a long time ago that's how you felt."

"I don't care what she believes about the nigras, or Mr. Gorilla Lincoln, or that glorious bullshit about states' rights that started this whole business—I don't give a damn about any of it. Let her swallow every bit if she wants! Let her chase after some flash actor! Let her drag from one sleazy theater to another—but by God she has *no* right to deny me word about my sons. That's exactly what she's done. So if she's here I'm going to see her. Even though—"

He stopped. Lifted the bent cigar. Stared at it as if it could somehow release him from his fury. Then he put it in the dish where it continued to fume and foul the bedroom's blue-lit air.

"Even though I'm frightened to death of what I might do."

"To Fan?"

"Yes. I—I don't know whether I can hold my temper. An hour ago, I made up my mind I should stay away. Not risk even one minute in her presence—" He grimaced. "That resolution didn't last long."

"I'm not surprised. I know how much you worry

about your boys. Sometimes you call their names in the middle of the night—"

"Molly, I haven't seen them in almost ten years!"

"I understand."

"I don't care if they speak to me. I don't care if they despise me—*I've just got to know whether they're all right!*"

Suddenly the little strength remaining in him drained away. He flung himself down on one end of the bed, hands jammed against his eyes. Molly slipped one arm around his shoulder while the man vanished and the child wept:

"Got to—and—Fan's the only one who can tell me—that—that's why I'm frightened. Frightened down to the pit of my soul. I'm frightened that if she won't tell me, I'll—"

"Do what?" Molly whispered.

"Hit her. Throttle her—God Himself only knows!" He fisted a hand; struck his knee. "I *hate* the bitch!"

With the hand that had left a white mark on his knee, he reached across for her hand curled on his left shoulder; closed his fingers over hers:

"I'm ashamed of myself."

"Jephtha, no—"

"I am. It isn't fitting for a man to carry on like this."

"Hush! The only way you'll lick the fear is to face it."

"I'm not sure I can lick it, Molly. I really don't know."

They sat together for five minutes, silently, Jephtha peering at the worn carpet, his naked body cold and free of sweat all at once. Molly pressed against his right side, her arm still over his back. Jephtha held her hand at his left shoulder. His tears stopped, but not the tremors in his fingers.

Conscious of how carefully she must pose the only answer that came to mind, Molly finally said:

"Well, I agree you'll probably end up going to see her if she's here with Lamont. You'll have to face it like a battle, Jephtha. A battle you have to win."

"I'm not sure I can!"

"I know. But you have to try. For your own peace of mind. About the boys. And about yourself. You'll need help. Something to—to make you a little more forgiving of your wife—of Fan."

Gently, she separated her fingers from his. She left him huddled on the bed while she donned her robe.

"I don't suppose you'll sleep much tonight," she said. "Maybe that's good. You can prepare yourself for seeing her. I'll take the couch in your room—" He glanced up, puzzled. "I want you to stay here," she said, "and try going back to the past."

"*What?*"

"The past. To see whether anything there can give you the strength you'll need to face her. To control the rage I know you feel. I don't blame you for the rage, Jephtha. But if you let it run wild, things will be worse than ever. You wait here—"

Despite her anxiety, she forced a smile.

"And put on your nightshirt so you don't catch cold."

iii

When she returned in a little over two minutes, Jephtha had donned the long flannel garment. She was carrying a small book with a red pebbled cover.

"Where did you get that?" he demanded.

"In your room, where else? I think it's what you need. I know you haven't read it much during the past year. But you should read it tonight. I've come to know you fairly well, Jephtha. It sometimes happens when a man shares a woman's bed," she added with a little smile. "You're not the same person you were when you

first walked in here hunting a place to stay. But no one
ever changes completely. I know there's as much goodness in you as there is hatred. In Fan, too—no, you
listen to me. There is! You saw it in her once. You
married her."

"I was wrong about her. I don't believe for one damn
minute she's anything but a vicious, vindictive—"

"Hush," Molly said. "You've got to stop thinking of
her that way. Let this help you—"

She laid the Testament in his right palm and cupped
her hand to close his fingers around it.

He gazed at the book, forlorn:

"I don't believe what's in here any more."

"Underneath everything, I think you do. Or you want
to. I know the kind of man you really are."

"Then you know me better than I know myself these
days."

"I think so." She patted the book. "I'm not the most
religious person in the world. But I remember from the
years I went to church as a little girl—there are a great
many words in this book about the virtue of forgiveness."

Almost inaudibly, Jephtha said, "Yes, there are."

"Read them. Let them help you look for the goodness instead of the bad. In yourself *and* in Fan. Pray if
you can. That's the only way you'll be able to go see her
without hurting—well, you understand."

She bent down and kissed his forehead.

He raised his head. A curious curl turned his mouth
up at the corners. He said softly:

"You do have a passion for saving things. String. Paper. People who've outlived their usefulness—"

"Jephtha, I refuse to listen to that sort of talk. You
know how I despise it when you pity yourself."

After a moment, he sighed. "Yes, I do." His eyes
grew bleak. "But I've never amounted to anything since
I left the itinerancy. That's not self-pity. It's a fact."

"Ridiculous. Writing for the paper—informing people—it's a worthwhile occupation. You've always told me the Kents considered publishing more than a means to make a profit. They felt it was a way to make a contribution."

"True." But he was unconvinced.

Because I've turned so far from God—

No.

Because He's turned so far from me.

"I'm certain of one thing, Jephtha. If you give in to your worst feelings about Fan, you *will* be lost. You'll detest yourself—waste yourself in regrets for the rest of your life."

He thought a moment, then stood up. With the Testament in one hand, he put the other on her waist:

"Forgive me. Most of the time you're absolutely right."

She tried to tease him: "Only most of the time?"

He looked at her soberly. "I appreciate what you're trying to do, Molly."

"You're a good man. I care about you."

"And you're a Christian woman."

She made a face. "Regular churchgoers would disagree."

"Sitting in a pew doesn't make you a Christian," Jephtha said. "For that matter, neither does belonging to a Christian church. You know my mother was a Shoshoni. Her understanding of the Bible was rudimentary. But the parts she understood, she understood completely. If anyone ever struggled to follow Christ's example, she did. You can deny it all you want, but you're the same sort of woman. It—it's one of the reasons I love you."

"Well—" With a sudden rush of breath, she shook her head. Wiped at her eyes. "—that's very kind of you, sir, considering I'm an aging widow who's never been able to bear any man a child, or to be content living the

way respectable women are supposed to live. That's—
very kind—"

"Don't joke."

"I'm not."

He stroked her hair. "I wouldn't have said it if I'd
thought it would make you unhappy."

"Unhappy? Oh, no—" Her eyes shone. She buried
her cheek on his shoulder. "No. You've never said it
before, that's all. Not once—"

"I guess you're right."

"Say it again."

"I love you."

She kissed him, quickly. Ashamed of her tears, she
tried to quell them. By some miraculous accident of intuition, she'd given him a chance to wrestle down the
demons the presence of Lamont had brought back to
life. If God did control any of the events in a world that
seemed close to shaking itself apart, He had chosen to
control one tonight. He had looked into this shabby
room; guided her thinking and lent her the words she
needed. She was unbelievably happy.

She drew away. "You read now. You've got to find
out about your boys—and you've got to do it without
hurting the woman who bore them, much as you think
she's wronged you. You've *got* to, Jephtha."

He stood a little straighter. "All right. I'll try."

With a last dab at her eyes, she kissed his mouth a
second time, retrieved her slippers and started for the
door. In his room, she wept out of a curious mixture of
relief and joy.

She didn't sleep well that night. She was uncomfortable on the old leather couch standing amid the clutter of
his books and clothing in the small room filled with the
stale smell of cigars. Three times she stole up the hall
and took a cautious step into her parlor. Each time, she
saw a sliver of gaslight beneath the closed door of the

bedroom. After the third visit, she managed to doze a while.

Exhausted, she rose at six. She went down to meet Bertha, the free black woman who helped her prepare meals and maintain the boarding house. She and Bertha began serving at seven. Jephtha didn't come down with the others. About seven-thirty, he appeared in the hall, dressed and freshly shaved.

"I'm late," he called. "I'll be skipping breakfast."

"Mrs. Emerson, where's the hot coffee?" Mr. Swampscott complained above the chatter of the men at the table. His righteous eye registered his disapproval of her appearance; no Christian woman served breakfast in robe and slippers.

"Bertha will have it here in a minute," Molly said, rushing to Jephtha. They walked toward the front door, out of the view of the boarders. He touched her arm.

"Thank you for last night. I did read. In a different way than I've read in quite a while."

"Are you going to see her?"

"If she's here."

"When?"

"I can't be sure. First I have to find out where Lamont's staying."

"Will that be today?"

"I don't know. There's so much confusion in town, I'll probably be chasing up and down the avenue just trying to find one fact I can put into a story. And I am going to Canterbury Hall this evening, remember. I'll be back late."

"But if you *should* see her today, are—are you all right?"

"Yes." He seemed to smile faintly. Or did she just imagine that, hoping—?

"Yes, I am," he repeated. He kissed her cheek, opened the front door and strode out. She watched until he vanished from sight.

She hurried back into the dining room. Bertha was pouring from the fresh pot of coffee. When breakfast was over, Molly began clearing the dishes. Her mind wasn't on the work. She kept trying to read Jephtha's mood from their brief conversation.

He'd seemed tired; for good reason. But his face no longer had the tormented, fearful look of last night. And he'd walked briskly away on G Street.

She moved toward the kitchen, barely hearing the table talk of three boarders who had lingered over their coffee. The talk seemed nothing more than speculative variations on an incessant theme—war. Well, let the blasted secessionists march across Long Bridge! The only battle she cared about was Jephtha's—

Are you all right?

Yes, I am.

Perhaps—she dared to let hope come brimming up within her—perhaps he did have a chance to win his victory now.

iv

About nine-thirty, with the washing of the breakfast dishes completed and Bertha busy dusting the downstairs, Molly went to her rooms to put on a dress and comb her hair. The bedroom reeked of Jephtha's cigars. The red-covered Testament lay open on the bedside table.

She picked up the book, scanning the two pages. Saint Matthew's Gospel, the fifth chapter—

Closer scrutiny showed her Jephtha had evidently been studying the Beatitudes. The paper just beneath the seventh verse—*"Blessed are the merciful: for they shall obtain mercy"*—bore a faint horizontal indentation, more clearly discernible when she tilted the Testament. The mark had undoubtedly been left by his fingernail. She saw a similar underscore on the second verse following—

"Blessed are the peacemakers: for they shall be called the children of God."

Encouraged, she replaced the Testament in its original position. She turned slowly, surveying the room. She could find nothing out of order in the entire—

Wait.

A sudden dryness in her throat made it difficult to swallow. One drawer of her bureau was open about two inches. Cold, she crossed to it.

Living alone as she had before Jephtha arrived—and with Washington City's heavy complement of thieves operating almost unopposed after nightfall—she'd felt it wise to keep a personal firearm close by. She'd bought a four-barrel pepperbox, .22 caliber, with ivory grips. It was one of the most popular models manufactured by the gunmaker Christian Sharps of Philadelphia. After a few weeks of practice in the back yard, she'd become proficient at loading, aiming and firing the little hide-out gun. She kept it in the drawer—

As Jephtha knew.

Unsteadily, she touched the drawer's handle.

He didn't want to tell me the truth. The Testament did no good. No good at all—

She pulled the drawer out—.

"Oh, *God."* Tears welled in her eyes.

The pepperbox was gone.

CHAPTER IV

Fan's Fear

FAN LAMONT WOKE to the sound of the parlor clock beyond the closed door. She counted the chimes. Ten.

Pale sunlight cast the pattern of the lace curtains onto the end of the bed. The space beside her still felt warm. Edward was up early.

Early. She smiled at that. In her childhood someone who rose at ten would have been considered deranged. Since her second marriage in '55, she'd gradually accustomed herself to the peculiar hours kept by actors. She hoped Jeremiah was busy with his studies in the smaller bedroom on the other side of the suite Edward had rented in a burst of extravagance.

She yawned. Listened to the late morning sounds of the National Hotel. Faint voices. Footsteps on the stairs. Outside, on the avenue, traffic clattered.

All at once she remembered what day it was. Tuesday. The Tuesday following Sumter's fall. She began to breathe a little faster, recalling the day's significance.

She was excited by what little she knew of Edward's plan. Yet it made her apprehensive, too. Washington City *was* the capital of the Yankee government. Though it wouldn't be for long, Edward and his strange friend Josiah Cheever said. Even Leroy Walker, the Secretary of War for the Confederacy, had predicted a new flag would wave beside the Potomac by the first of May.

Edward wanted to help bring it about. He'd turned

134

down a six-week engagement with a troupe going to
Louisiana, Mississippi and Alabama to perform *Mac-
beth*. She knew it was a sacrifice. He'd been offered the
title role—a part he'd never played before.

She continued to lie motionless, savoring the faint
warmth he'd left in the bed. Through the two doors separating her from Jeremiah's room, she thought she
heard her son utter an exclamation of disgust.

She wished Gideon could have been here to attend
the theater tonight. He was old enough. But he'd rented
a horse on Sunday and set off for Richmond, hoping to
join a military unit that would be mobilized the moment
Virginia seceded.

She thought of Matthew. He wouldn't know for
weeks, or perhaps months, about his stepfather's high-
principled action. Two years earlier, Fan and Edward
had given up their efforts to prod Matthew into further
schooling. In his quiet way, he refused to accept the discipline of academic work. Grudgingly, they'd permitted
him to take a mess boy's berth on one of the cotton
packets traveling out of Charleston. Before coming up
to Washington, they'd received a letter from him. He
was in New Orleans.

But Gideon would undoubtedly be back from Richmond soon. At least she could tell him of Edward's cou-
rageous stand. Of all her sons, Gideon would have the
greatest appreciation for Edward's bravery. Among the
three, he believed most strongly what she had taught
them about Jephtha: that his fanaticism was responsible
for the dissolution of the family.

She slipped her hands behind her head as she lay
thinking about her children. Jephtha had given each of
them a markedly independent nature. The Fletcher
blood, he used to call it. Passed down from his grandmother, who had been a Virginian of rebellious and ultimately unstable temperament.

The trait was just beginning to show in Jeremiah. In

Gideon it manifested itself in various ways. His fondness for loud singing. His sudden outbursts of temper. The way he fumed and swore whenever Edward held forth on the abuse, slander and political manipulation the South had suffered for nearly four decades.

And Matthew—there, too, she saw a rebellious streak, though it took a different form.

Matthew had been hard to raise because he was her second; mothers of Fan's acquaintance always said second children presented special problems. They tended to be introspective—sometimes to the point of being wholly uncommunicative—perhaps because the eldest child, at least at first, got the major share of the parents' attention. Matthew fit the pattern.

He'd repeatedly refused to do the lessons Fan had assigned to him when he traveled with the family. And his sources of enjoyment were contradictory. Only two things seemed to interest him—ungentlemanly games, and a hobby whose origin Fan was at a loss to explain. He liked to draw.

He sketched anything that caught his interest, from a gas fixture jutting out of a brick wall backstage to a variety hall dancer with her foot on a chair as she adjusted her tights. Fan had no idea when he'd begun drawing. She'd only seen his first crude efforts when he was eleven. She had to admit he'd improved remarkably since then. In fact, his most recent letter had contained two folded charcoal studies she thought were quite good for a boy who wouldn't be seventeen for another month.

One showed nigras handling bales on a pier. The figures of the black men had a flowing, sinuous quality that vividly suggested the strength and agility required to handle the bales—which he'd drawn with sharp angles, for contrast. He'd labeled that picture "New Orleans Cotton." The other one, smaller, was a portrait of the skipper of his packet, a stern, middle-aged Charleston sailor with full chin whiskers, fierce eyes and a braided cap. The picture was called "Captain McGill, 1861."

Fan's father considered Matthew's pastime ungodly. She had a more practical concern. She'd have been worried about his masculinity if it hadn't been for his other passion. Often when she and Edward were still in bed the morning after a performance, Matthew had sneaked out of their hotel and found a group of boys— sometimes white, sometimes black—in the poor section of the town, and spent hours with them in a vacant field, playing a game with a wooden bat, a ball and opposing teams which tried to score "runs."

Several times Matthew had tried to explain the game, which he said was getting more and more popular. But the explanation never made sense to Fan. He came home from his outings sweating and happy, so Fan had a hard time disciplining him for his day-long disappearances.

His willingness to take part in hard physical activity—first the games, then the work on the packet— offset her fear that he might be developing in the wrong way. Still, of the three, Mathew was the one whose future concerned her the most.

She did thank God that the independence displayed by all the boys had become her responsibility alone to control as best she could. Her efforts weren't perfect, but at least she was spared Jephtha's damaging influence. She thanked God too that she'd chosen a second husband who directed the boys' political thinking properly. They had developed absolute loyalty to the South, which had been too long at the mercy of the damned Northerners—those men who would free the nigras and set them up as the equals of whites.

At which time, Edward insisted, the nigras would unleash their long-buried rage against their former masters. Kill them in their homes. Rape their women.

Torch their farms and plantations. Destroy their entire way of life.

Edward stood against that ever happening. From birth, Fan, too, had stood against it, influenced by her father, Captain Virgil Tunworth. Though she suspected there was considerable risk in what Edward had decided to do, she was immensely proud of him.

Of course her father hadn't been enthusiastic about her marrying an actor. It was still a disreputable profession. Only Fan's insistence—and Edward's fierce partisanship for the South—had overcome Tunworth's objections.

The courtship had been swift and intense. She and her father had gone to Charleston to visit family relatives. One evening they'd attended the Charleston Theater to see the highly acclaimed tragedy *Francesca da Rimini,* written by Boker, an Englishman who regularly turned out successes for the Sadler's Wells Theater of London.

Afterward, Fan and her father had enjoyed a late-evening supper arranged on the stage by a group of culturally minded Charleston ladies. Fan had met Edward at the supper. Though he'd only played a supporting role in the play, she'd been taken with his good looks. She was almost speechless when she was presented to him in the unfamiliar but oddly delightful backstage atmosphere of painted scenery and other theatrical paraphernalia.

A mutual liking developed at once. Two weeks after their introduction, Edward proposed. Fan had been relieved to discover the actor wouldn't have the slightest objection to bringing up another man's sons as his own. When she described the boys' father, he grew angry. No more of that damned nonsense! He'd raise the lads as proper Southerners. If she'd had any lingering doubt about Edward, it disappeared when he said that.

On balance the marriage had been a happy one, although it had required a severe adjustment on Fan's part. The glamour of the post-performance supper and the headiness of the courtship soon vanished. For months, Fan was ill at ease in the strange world in which actors and actresses lived. Edward's colleagues seemed all of a piece. They were colorful, gregarious people. But they were also vain, boastful, and often afflicted with an incredible sense of self-importance she felt must hide deep feelings of unworthiness.

They were generous and amusing; profane and amoral. Reality for them was gaslight, not sunlight. They bubbled with excitement while an audience gathered, and after the fire curtain dropped, argued endlessly to justify the smallest mistake in the performance. They stayed in cheap hotels, strutting through every lobby as if it were a palace foyer. They expressed horror at the idea of ever abandoning their profession, but they complained endlessly about traveling from city to city in lamp-lit passenger cars with soot-blackened cushions and unpleasant human smells fouling the air. How many times had she been roused at two or three in the morning when a train reached the end of its trackage and all the passengers had to stumble out of one car and onto another, equally filthy and poorly illuminated, because the first railroad's gauge was not the same as that of the next? Frequently the change required a coach ride, the gaps between some lines varying from two miles to twenty.

Yet she was content. Edward treated the boys well. If they felt no love for him, at least they were respectful. And Gideon actually expressed admiration for Edward's raffish occupation.

Like most actors, Fan discovered, her husband was subject to extreme swings of emotion. Periods of exuberance alternated with other periods of melancholy. Fortunately Edward's shifts in mood came less frequently than was the case with many of his associates.

He was, of course, continually concerned about his appearance. He could be impulsive. And he was fond of the grand gesture, the breathtaking effect. He insisted they not be punctual at parties to which the visiting troupe was invited, varying their arrival from thirty minutes to an hour after the specified time as the whim struck him. But the late entrance was mandatory.

On their first anniversary, he'd presented her with an immense floral basket—but not in privacy. Just after buying the basket, which he couldn't afford, he'd been struck by a thought—and instantly arranged for the gift to be delivered to their table in a crowded hotel dining room.

Even his appearance in Washington, while not precisely impulsive, fit the pattern of turning the disorder of everyday living into something structured and spectacular; into *theater*.

Fan learned to accept and cope with these quirks of the actor's personality. In only one area did she feel herself incapable of adjusting to Edward's needs. It was the same area in which she'd had problems during her marriage to Jephtha. But Edward was generally kind and tolerant about it.

She never admitted she'd married him for another reason besides love of his looks, his manners and his political opinions. After the humiliating period in which Jephtha had lingered in Lexington, then fled because of his involvement with the Underground Railroad, life in the little town had become intolerable for her. All her friends sympathized with her. But sympathy wasn't enough. The corner of the Shenandoah in which she'd grown up had become too full of bad memories.

Once in a while she was able to confess to herself that she was in part responsible for those memories. Her tongue had sometimes been too vicious. Anger had sometimes driven her beyond reason—as, for example, during the visit of the objectionable Mrs. Amanda Kent.

Afterward, Fan had accused Jephtha of signing away the boys' birthright by permitting Mrs. Kent—or Mrs. de la Gura as she'd called herself then—to administer the California gold holdings that had been owned by Jephtha's dead father. Tension in the household had made it easy to give in to such excesses.

Edward had rescued her from the failure Lexington had come to represent. He offered escape from the despair that followed her filing for divorce. Despite the peculiarities of his profession, she had never regretted saying yes to his proposal—

A murmuring voice caught her attention. It came from the small dressing chamber adjoining the bedroom. She heard the scrape of his razor as he spoke. She made out the words. *Julius Caesar* again.

Edward had toured in the play during the second year of their marriage. Played Brutus to the Marc Antony of Junius Brutus Booth, Junior, one of the three sons of the transplanted English tragedian Junius Booth, Senior. Of late, Edward seldom quoted any other play. She listened to him: .

" '—then, countrymen, what need we any spur, but our own cause, to prick us to redress? What other bond than secret Romans, that have spoke the word, and will not palter—?' "

She smiled. He was, for the moment, Brutus again.

Slowly, she sat up in bed. The coverlet fell away from the bodice of her nightdress. She stretched; luxuriated in another long yawn—

Her fair hair was a loose tangle around her shoulders. Her lips were full, her eyes gray-green and slightly slanted. She was a slender woman, thirty-five, with a body kept supple by gallops along bridle paths in the towns they visited. From her earliest years, one of her greatest pleasures had been riding one of the half-dozen blooded horses her father kept on the farm near Lexington.

Edward's razor rattled, laid aside on the marble stand. She heard a splashing of water. He was humming now. He had a passable singing voice, though it was not nearly so good as Gideon's baritone.

She recognized the melody. "Old Folks at Home," the sentimental ballad by Mr. Foster, who knew next to nothing about the South. Born in Pennsylvania, for a time he had been a bookkeeper in Cincinnati. But his Negro minstrel songs extolling plantation life— songs licensed during the fifties for exclusive performance by E. P. Christy's troupe—were relished by Southerners. She recalled a recent newspaper item saying Foster had fallen on hard times and was living in a rooming house on New York's Bowery—

The humming stopped. In a moment, Edward appeared, wearing his robe of dark green velvet. He'd applied fresh blacking to his temples, she noticed.

Edward Lamont was eleven years Fan's senior. Tall and solid, he moved with the strength and swagger of a man half his age. His eyes might have been too close together for perfect handsomeness. But he was still physically imposing, with curly dark brown hair showing no trace of gray. He blacked his mustache as well.

"Good morning, Edward," she said, getting out of bed.

"Good morning, my dear!" His smile was broad, his face animated by excitement.

He crossed to her. Slipped his arms around her waist. Kissed her throat even though he knew she wasn't fond of physical expressions of passion. Dismayed, she felt the hardness of him thrusting at her lower body.

Any important occasion—signing for a new part; an opening night—stimulated him.

His mouth explored the contours of her neck. "Sleep well?"

"Splendidly. But by rights, I should have had nightmares."

"In heaven's name why?"

She pulled away. "Worrying about tonight."

"Nonsense!"

"But you haven't told me exactly what you're going to do."

"Because I want to surprise you afterward!"

She made a face. "I suppose that's the actor in you. Wringing your audience with suspense. But I'm your wife, not a stranger sitting in a box!"

He laughed and kissed the tip of her nose. "In this case, you're both. Believe me, Fan—" His right hand caressed the small of her back, moved downward to her buttocks. She turned cold.

"—I'm not planning anything criminal. I'm only going to exercise my right of free speech as an American. A right that goddamned baboon in the White House hasn't yet abrogated—though I'm sure he'd like to! It'll be a marvelous evening, darling. Marvelous!"

The word had a sonorous sound. Edward's voice, deep and mellow, was his greatest asset. During years of apprenticeship in the theater, he'd acquired perfect English diction, losing all trace of a regional accent.

Edward Lamont had been born of middling-prosperous merchant people in Alabama. He'd angered and humiliated his Baptist parents when he'd run away from boarding school to join a traveling troupe. Both parents were dead now. But in her last hours, his mother had written a letter admitting she wasn't altogether ashamed that her son had achieved some minor prominence in his profession, disreputable as it was.

Edward's family was opposed to abolitionism—and with good reason. His aunt on his father's side—a woman beloved by dozens of Lamont relatives—had been married to a cotton planter who treated his slaves in a humane way. He refused to let his overseers and drivers use beatings as punishment; he never sold off a buck, a wench or a baby if it would break up a family. But in the long run his kindness had been misguided.

One November morning, Edward's aunt had asked her eighteen-year-old household boy to go outside for stove wood—a daily request which never produced any response but obedience. For no clear reason, that morning the slave screamed a refusal.

His mistress ordered him again. Again he screamed, striking at her with his fists. When she called for help, the boy ran outside, snatched up the firewood ax, lunged back into the kitchen and drove the ax blade into the woman's skull.

Her husband, pulling up his galluses with one hand while he cocked a revolver with the other, arrived in the kitchen a few seconds later. He thrust by the shrieking, weeping trio of household girls who had watched the killing. The planter shot and killed the murderer with one ball.

Afterward, he refused to bury the dead boy. The planter—quite rightly, Edward maintained—had the boy's body dragged to a clump of woods, there to lie in the frosty weather until the animals and carrion birds devoured it.

From that time on, Edward said, the Lamonts worshipped at the altar of an impassioned hatred for the nigger who had taken his aunt's life. The hatred soon expanded to include any whites who believed such monsters should be allowed freedom—

Edward put his lips against Fan's ear. She tried not to shudder at the feel of the tip of his tongue. He was harder, too; larger. When she started to pull back a second time, he held her fast:

"The fact is, darling, things couldn't be better. As soon as Virginia secedes, there'll be ten thousand from that state marching on this city. Perhaps men from Maryland, too. Despite Governor Hicks and his idiotic loyalty to the Union, Marylanders are strong for the cause. Young Johnny Booth—why, he's a hotter sympathizer than old Yancey himself. All I'm going to do is what must be done. Show Virginia and Maryland there are a great many people in Washington who *want* an invasion—and damned quick!"

As he spoke, he continued caressing her. He stroked her cheek, then her breast. His fingertips closed on her nipple through her nightdress. He didn't hurt her. But he wouldn't be denied.

She attempted another diversion:

"If what you're doing isn't illegal, why can't I go to the theater to watch?"

"My dear, we've already discussed that. Canterbury Hall's a vulgar sort of place. Unescorted ladies don't attend—"

"—except at the matinees, when the performers omit the suggestive songs and stories." She sighed. "I think you're just hiding the fact that it could be dangerous."

"Not a bit! We'll have the house packed with our crowd. Josiah promised. You haven't forgotten he's coming here this morning—?"

"Yes, I did forget." Remembering obviously disgusted her.

"Around eleven or so." He kissed her flesh just above the bodice. "We have ample time."

"Jeremiah—" she began.

"Will attend to his studies without you, my dear."

One arm went around her back. He bent, slipping the other behind her legs. With hardly any effort, he lifted her onto the bed.

He flung off his dressing gown and stood above her, proud of his firm, trim body; proud too of his thrusting member. The sight of it made her skin crawl. Sex belonged in darkness.

"It's a great day, Fan. Celebrate with me."

He sat down beside her. His hand moved beneath the hem of her gown, then up along her thigh. He touched her in that intimate way that knotted her belly and filled her with disgust. Her only defense was a mental litany she'd relied on over the years:

He's your husband.

It's his right.

And your duty to endure it—

She let him pull up the nightdress. She let his mouth linger on her breasts; her stomach—while she lay absolutely rigid. Many things had changed since her marriage to Jephtha, but not this.

Edward didn't seem to mind her lack of response. He thrust vigorously as she closed her eyes and pressed her palms against the sheet. Finally, he let out a groan and withdrew. As always, he touched her cheek:

"Thank you. I know how it displeases you."

She turned her head to the side. "I—I do wish I could be a better wife this way—"

"Be still," he said softly. "You're a wonderful wife. What a man needs is only part of a marriage. We share many things more important—" His dark eyes took on a glow that disturbed her.

As the turmoil in the nation had moved steadily toward armed conflict, Edward's acting career had become almost a sideline. He pursued it so they might eat, have shelter, and care for Jeremiah. But he spoke more and more of politics; less and less of roles and bookings—

"Much more important," he repeated. " 'Heaven hath infus'd us with these spirits—' " She knew he was quoting again, but paraphrasing; changing *them* to us. " '—to make us instruments of fear and warning unto some monstrous state.' "

She ran her hand across his smooth, soap-scented cheek. "That's Casca, isn't it?"

"No, Cassius. Act one, scene three. With thunder and lightning. We'll put on a big display of it tonight! When they hear it down south, the boys will come storming across Long Bridge and hang that misbegotten nigger-lover in front of his own executive mansion!"

She studied him. "There isn't much you wouldn't do for the cause, is there, Edward?"

"There is nothing." He kissed her cheek. "But that's why you said yes to me so soon after we met. Isn't it?"

"Yes," she answered; uneasily. Sometimes she wondered whether she was as fervent—as wholly committed—as her husband. Sometimes she was actually fearful about how far his hatred of the nigras, the abolitionists and the Republicans might carry him.

She stared into his eyes. Right now was one of those times.

ii

While they dressed, Edward told her he wanted to go downstairs for a bite of breakfast before his visitor arrived. He'd seen Josiah Cheever daily, in private, since the family's arrival in Washington the preceding Thursday. He claimed to have met Cheever three years ago in Savannah, though Fan didn't recall it. Of course Edward and his fellow actors frequented a great many saloons that a respectable woman would never enter. Cheever, apparently, had played some part in persuading Edward to come to the capital at this particular time. It was clear to Fan that he was a ringleader of Southern sympathizers in the city.

"Do go," she said to Edward. "I'm not especially hungry. And I must see if Jeremiah's doing the work I assigned."

Edward stood in front of the bedroom's pier glass, using a comb and brush to arrange his hair. Finally, after studying the results, he gave an approving nod. Then he blew her a kiss and walked out through the parlor.

She gazed at the open doorway, unable to still her anxiety. She wished he wouldn't be so secretive about his plan. She knew only that in lieu of his scheduled recitations, he intended to make some sort of speech— an appeal to Southerners to stand fast until an invading army captured the city. Edward's friend Cheever *had* promised a house packed with sympathizers. She supposed there could really be no great risk—

Yet Cheever wasn't a free agent in the sense that Edward was. He still worked for the War Department, and now that the gangling Illinois lawyer had declared the existence of an "insurrection," Cheever was technically a traitor. That fact served to intensify her worry.

Standing up for principle was one thing. Associating with men whose activities could be construed as treason was quite another. She didn't want Edward hurt. *Or* arrested—

To take her mind off her fears, she dressed quickly and looked in on Jeremiah. Elbows braced on the desk, palms cupped under his chin, her son was staring out the window with an unhappy look.

Jeremiah Kent would be fifteen in a little less than two months. He was a strong, lean boy with his mother's fair hair and a touch of his father's gauntness in his cheeks. Living an itinerant life for the past six years, Fan had experienced great difficulty educating her sons. She'd taught them the fundamentals of mathematics and science and tried to interest them in reading, which she hoped would prepare them for college study. On the whole, she'd been unsuccessful with Gideon and Matthew. Jeremiah was her last hope.

Books were a continual problem. Much of what was considered good literature was published in the North. Fan refused to expose Jeremiah to any contemporary author even remotely connected with the abolitionist movement. She wouldn't permit him to read Lowell, Whittier or Professor Longfellow. A week ago, she'd

bought a volume called *Poems*, a title even she admitted
deserved a prize for dullness. Its author, however, was
an eminently safe South Carolinian.

She could see the extent of Jeremiah's interest in Mr.
Timrod's verse. The book lay open—and face down—
on the desk.

Stopping next to his chair, she laid a hand on his
shoulder.

"Jeremiah, have you finished the first three selec-
tions?"

"Oh, Ma—" He screwed up his face. "They're dull
as the devil. Nothing but silly blab about trees and
birds—"

"Mr. Timrod has a fine reputation down south. Studying him is well worth your time. I must insist you do
the reading."

Another grimace.

"When you finish, I want you to write a brief sum-
mary of what each poem says—the theme—" He
looked puzzled. "The meaning. I'd like it by early afternoon. Else there'll be no strolling on Pennsylvania Avenue before supper."

He picked up the book as if it would poison him on
contact. "All right, I'll try again—"

"Good."

"But I hate it."

"Now, Jeremiah, don't—"

He turned sideways in his chair. "I can't help it!
There's so much to see outside. Soldiers mustering—"

"Union soldiers," she reminded him.

"I wish I were old enough to soldier. Old enough to
ride off to Richmond like Gideon. Find a troop to
join—"

She cradled his head against her side. She felt his tension; she often forgot such intimacies were embarrassing
to a boy his age.

"Don't wish for that," she said. "War's an awful business. Necessary sometimes. But people get hurt."

"What if Gideon gets hurt?"

"I pray it'll never happen. But I can't stop him from going. Your brother's nearly eighteen. And *this* war must be fought. Thank the Lord you're too young for it." He wriggled as she embraced him again. "You're the last of my three. I want you safe."

"Will Matt be safe on the cotton packet?"

She answered truthfully: "I don't know. I hope so. Enough talk—you concentrate on Mr. Timrod."

She turned to leave, hearing conversation in the parlor. Edward's visitor had evidently arrived early. She recognized Josiah Cheever's high-pitched voice. Whether Edward approved or not, she intended to listen to the discussion—

Jeremiah's voice stopped her near the door:

"Ma?"

"Yes?"

"Is my father in Washington?"

Fan stiffened. That the boy would even express interest aroused her anger. With as much composure as she could summon, she answered:

"I imagine so. He works here. For that filthy Northern newspaper."

"Are you going to see him?"

"Certainly not!" Jeremiah looked downcast. Her voice softened. "Does that upset you?"

Slowly, the boy traced a finger across the lines of Timrod's verse. He spoke hesitantly:

"Some. I know you say he was a bad man—"

Fan shook her head. "Not a bad man. A foolish one. Completely wrong in what he believed. It caused him to do some bad things. Things which made it impossible for us to live with him any longer. I've explained it all before. His misguided ideas about the nigras were more

important to him than keeping our family together—or
seeing you boys raised properly. That's why I insisted
he leave our house. Really, Jeremiah, there's no reason
to bring up the subject again—"

"I know, but—"

The boy stopped. Fidgeted in the chair. Then
blurted:

"I don't remember him very well. I'd like to see how
he looks."

Fan's lips set in a bitter curve. "He looks the same as
ever, I imagine. Eyes the color of yours. Very dark hair.
You'd take him for a Red Indian except for those
eyes—" Unable to control her anger, she snapped, "I've
shown you his picture!"

"That little tin plate you keep in the drawer?"

"Not tin. Copper."

She hadn't seen it herself in months. To examine it
was purposeless—and painful. Jephtha had sat for the
portrait in New York City in 1844 at her request. He'd
gone to New York for the Methodist Conference—the
meeting at which disagreement over slavery had split
the church into Northern and Southern factions.

The picture was a sad reminder of how happy they'd
been in those days. Newly married, with Gideon barely
a year old. She'd hoarded her extra kitchen funds so he
could bring her a souvenir of his visit to the great me-
tropolis—an image of his face transferred to metal by
the remarkable process people now called photography.
She'd never quite been able to throw away the plate and
its small silk-lined box.

Jeremiah still wasn't satisfied:

"But the last time you showed it to me, it was all
blurry—"

"Daguerreotypes fade. Please—don't entertain any
ideas of visiting your father. I'm married to Edward
now. *He's* your fath—"

"Not my real one."

"Jeremiah, get back to your studies!"

With a stunned look, he averted his head and picked up the book. Sadly, she realized he'd probably make a botch of the paper she'd requested. Today's lesson would be a total loss.

She told herself she needed to be tolerant. Understand his curiosity. Blood ties were strong. They exerted an influence despite the countless times she'd discussed Jephtha's errors. So she mustn't be harsh. Just firm—

For a fleeting moment, she herself was tempted. How *did* Jephtha look today? What was his state of mind? Was he more fanatical, or less—?

As she stood watching her son, she was ashamed of her momentary weakness. Jephtha Kent had filled their household with grief. Even though turning him out had brought her shame and confusion, she knew her decision had been right. Fortunately she'd found Edward— and with him, a new life.

Her son glanced at her as if he'd sensed her transient indecision.

"Ma, would it really do any harm if we talked to father for a little whi—?"

"I said *study!*"

She whirled away. Better that Jeremiah be hurt a little by her severity than exposed again to Jephtha's virulent ideas. To emphasize her determination, she slammed the door as she went out.

iii

On the settee near the parlor window, Josiah Cheever was speaking softly:

"—that's the desperate need, Edward. You're in a position—"

He stopped abruptly when Fan appeared.

"We'll discuss it another time," Edward said. He was seated so he faced Fan. Perhaps she imagined it, but he seemed to be giving Cheever a glance of warning. The visitor leaped to his feet and turned.

Josiah Cheever was about thirty. Short, frail, and—as always—untidily dressed. He had poor teeth and small eyes with a furtive, crafty caste. Despite Cheever's unquestionable loyalty to the cause, those eyes were one reason Fan disliked him. Another—apparent as she approached the settee—was his perpetual odor of perspiration and flatulence.

Cheever executed a clumsy bow. "Miz Lamont—how are you this morning?" His faintly nasal speech put his origins somewhere in the mountainous western counties of Virginia, where his sympathies would have been an exception; western Virginia was strongly Unionist.

She forced a smile. "Dying to know what you and my husband are hatching, Josiah." She seated herself in a chair near them. Edward's thick brows drew together in annoyance. She went on, "Edward absolutely refuses to let me go to the Canterbury this evening."

"His caution's wise," Cheever said. "Seventy-five or eighty friends have promised to be in attendance. But we're bound to have a few goddamned—uh—a few Union sympathizers in the audience, too. Can't ask people for political credentials at the ticket booth, I'm afraid."

Edward said, "I've been trying to reassure Fan there's nothing to worry about. We're staging a show of solidarity, that's all."

"It's a worthy purpose, ma'am," Cheever told her.

Edward smiled. "I wouldn't appear on a third-class variety bill if it weren't. We've got to encourage Virginia to start men marching on Washington the moment the state secedes."

"I realize what you're both trying to achieve," Fan

said. "But it still bothers me. Is the government going to permit that sort of activity?"

"The *government*," Cheever said, "is so infernally confused right now, a thousand Virginians could capture it lock, stock, and barrel in half an hour. Of course, confusion's to be expected when the man in charge practically worships niggers. A man like that can't be sane."

Fan shook her head. "I don't like Lincoln any better than you, Josiah. But I know he doesn't believe the nigra is the equal of the white. He's made speeches stating that explicitly."

Cheever restrained his irritation. "Maybe so. But he's the enemy. And we've got to take advantage of his confusion. He and that bloated Scott and the damn fools in the cabinet are still fumbling with the defense of this town—"

Edward interrupted: "You told me downstairs there's talk of troops on the way."

Cheever nodded. "Four, five hundred volunteers coming from Pennsylvania. Nothing to worry about. They're all green. Massachusetts, now—that's different. The Sixth and Eighth Massachusetts regiments are mustering. They're trained militiamen. Brigadier-general Ben Butler's the commander of the Eighth."

"A Democrat, for Christ's sake!" Edward snorted.

Cheever shrugged. "All the Yanks are sleeping in the same dirty bed these days. I suppose Butler expects to be transferred to a regular command once he arrives. Or should I say *if* he arrives?"

The man's sly expression made Fan lean forward. "I don't understand."

"It has to do with the railroads," Edward said.

"What do you mean?"

Cheever explained: "Both lines to Washington—the one from Harrisburg and the one from Philadelphia— lead to Baltimore. But neither runs directly through the city. To reach Washington, relief troops will have to be transferred from the President Street station of the Philadelphia, Wilmington and Baltimore to the Baltimore and Ohio's Camden Street station. The cars have to be horse-drawn between the stations—along the street railway route. There'll be plenty of time for crowds to form. Plenty of time for tempers to get warm—you know how the folks in Maryland feel about Mr. Lincoln and his policies. Why—" Cheever licked his lips; smiled. "—some of those Union lads might never get out of Baltimore alive."

Fan's palms turned cold. Josiah Cheever continued to smile.

"When are the troops due?" she asked.

"Can't imagine they could get here before the end of the week," Cheever said.

"And by then Virginia should be out," Edward added.

"So if the timing's proper—" Cheever's yellowed teeth glistened. "—if the relief regiments should bog down in Baltimore due to the anger of the good citizens of that city—and if there should be a swift march from Richmond—Washington could be ours."

"Edward, I don't like the sound of this," Fan said. "I don't want you involved in stirring up street mobs—"

"Who said anything about stirring up mobs?" he shot back. "We're just having a theoretical discussion."

"Absolutely right—theoretical," Cheever said. "We aren't responsible for what happens in Baltimore. We're merely—ah—hopeful."

"Exactly," Edward agreed.

But both men were smiling, as if enjoying a private joke. Fan felt a stir of dread. An honorable cause seemed to be turning to a game played in shadows—

"Besides," her husband went on, "Josiah can't afford to become entangled in illegal activities." His tone grew sarcastic. "For the present, at least, he's the devoted employee of one of the Union's most vigilant defenders."

"Vigilant my as—my eye," Cheever said. "We're lucky Mr. Lincoln's campaign managers made their little arrangement out at the Wigwam."

"What arrangement?" Fan asked.

"They traded a cabinet post for the Pennsylvania delegate votes controlled by the imbecile for whom I work. Ah—*pretend* to work."

"Simon Cameron—"

"Our beloved Secretary of War." Cheever snickered. "He's so stupid, he won't know there's been an invasion until he looks up from his desk and sees a Virginia squirrel gun aimed right between his eyes. Now, Edward. About that other arrangement—"

Edward reddened. "I told you last evening, and again not ten minutes ago, I'll handle it in my own way. At the proper time."

For a moment, Cheever looked belligerent. "I hope so. Our mutual friends are relying on it."

Edward turned still redder. He jumped up, grasped Cheever's arm. His knuckles were white. Cheever glared. But the actor, taller and stronger, intimidated the younger man. Cheever kept silent.

Finally a smile fixed itself on Edward's face. A totally false smile, Fan knew. He let go of his guest. Spoke calmly:

"Why don't we discuss it downstairs? You arrived so early, I've had no chance to eat."

"Very well." Cheever's expression was truculent. What in God's name was going on? Fan wondered.

"You go ahead," Edward said. "I'll join you shortly."

Cheever settled his soiled hat on his head. He made a show of dusting the spot on his sleeve Edward had gripped so hard. It was obvious to Fan that the two men didn't care for one another. Only their politics united them. And there seemed to be a peculiar competition for dominance between them, though the reason for it eluded her.

"I'll be waiting, Edward," Cheever said. It was more than a casual remark.

He glanced at Fan, his eyes like small brown stones. "Miz Lamont—a pleasure, as always."

But he looked far from pleased as he strode to the door.

iv

The moment he was gone, Fan exclaimed:

"What was all that about? He sounded as if he were threatening you!"

Edward chuckled. "Come, dear, you're reading too much into it. Josiah's a little—you might call it—unstable. He wants everyone to be as loyal to the cause as he is."

"Edward, look me in the eye."

He did.

"What did Cheever mean about another *arrangement*? Is he trying to drag you into whatever they're planning when the soldiers come through Baltimore? Any simpleton can see he knows all about it."

"Yes, that's it," Edward sighed—too quickly. "Certain—combinations of men are being organized to stir up the crowds. Somehow Josiah will manage to get away from the War Department and go to Baltimore to help. He wants me to go, but I told him I'd be recognized." There was something sad about his confidence in his own fame, Fan thought; sad and entirely typical of his profession. She said nothing.

"Josiah's fervor is understandable. A lot of men in Washington who favor the South believe the situation demands absolute commitment."

"And you said there was nothing you wouldn't do for the cause."

"Well—" A studied shrug. "I exaggerated a little. I'll work it out with him, don't fear."

He squeezed her arm. Pecked her cheek. As he did, she thought:

He's lying to me.

Lying in a way he's never lied before—

Why?

With a jaunty wave, Edward started for the door:

"I'll have a drink and some food in the bar. As soon as I send Josiah along, I'll be back. Oh, yes. While I think of it—"

He walked back to her. He was relaxed; smiling in a thoughtful way. She sensed none of the pretense that had alarmed her a moment ago.

"—I did have one thing I wanted to mention. Forgive me, but I wonder if you've given any thought to the fact that your former husband is probably in the city."

Stunned, Fan struggled for words:

"Jephtha? Why, of course, it—it did occur to me."

"Do you suppose it might be wise to look him up?"

"Look him up? For what reason?"

"For the sake of the boys. I know you've assured me he's an honest man—"

"In his own way, yes."

"And the boys are supposed to be the eventual recipients of those funds he controls—"

"You know very well that when Jephtha passes on, the boys will inherit the California gold money. I don't see why you should bring up—"

"Dammit, Fan, don't look so confounded vacant! I'm thinking of the boys' welfare! A whole new set of factors has been inserted in the situation. A war. Gideon's certain to join up. What if that angers your former husband? Angers him so much, he decides to disinherit his sons?"

"That's unthinkable. Jephtha *was* foolish to put the management of the money into Amanda Kent's hands. But it was never done with any intent to defraud the boys."

"I thought you accused him of that very thing."

Now it was Fan who was scarlet. "I did. I—I was furious with him in those days. I said a great many things I shouldn't have."

"You *do* admit he's violently opposed to slavery—"

"But he's not a cheat!"

"That wasn't how you felt when we met six years ago."

"I realize. Even then, I was still angry with him—"

"You've softened toward him?"

"A little." She was surprised at her own admission. Edward's expression remained bland. "Even so, it might be wise to contact him. To—oh—reassure yourself. I've told you over and over, the money means nothing to me. Actors have damn little regard for worldly goods—" The charming smile reappeared. "As long as we eat with reasonable regularity, and get our share of applause, we're content."

"I know," Fan said. "You've always been decent about the money. Some men wouldn't have been, I expect."

Edward caught her hand in his. "I didn't mean to raise an unpleasant subject. It's just an idea that's been in my head for a day or so. You're here—it might not be amiss to get Jephtha to promise in writing that no matter what the boys do in the war, he'll honor their claim to the inheritance."

"In *writing*?"

"It is the safest way."

"Edward, I honestly don't think it's necessary. Jephtha may be a Northerner now. But he cares for his sons. You know how many letters he's written, wanting to know about them. I never answered the letters because you said I shouldn't." That, too, she had begun to regret.

"Perhaps I was in error. The very lack of answers could be another reason for turning against the boys."

"It's possible, but I doubt it."

"Well, if you don't believe it's worth being absolutely sure—"

"Suppose he has changed his feelings about Gideon and Matt and Jeremiah, what could I do? And if he hasn't changed, talking to him would serve no purpose. Besides, I—I'm not sure I'd have the courage to face him."

Edward's smile was almost mocking: "Good God, I hope you're not having second thoughts about the divorce at this late date!"

"Of course not. I *know* I did the right thing."

"All right, let's forget it." He bussed her cheek. "It was only a suggestion. I·do confess I had an ulterior motive for making it, though—"

Again she felt chilled. "What motive?"

He laughed. "Why, I'd really like to get a look at the fellow. A Bible-shouter who flip-flops into a career as a journalist—a man you say bears a strong resemblance to an Indian—you can't blame me for being curious about him."

"You've seen the daguerreotype."

"Oh, but it's ancient. Faded. The truth is—" A gentle chuckle. "—I suppose I'd really like to know how I stack up against him. A normal enough male reaction, wouldn't you say?"

She felt relieved. "There's no comparison. You're the man I love, Edward."

"I'm glad. I'll be back soon—and please, forget the whole thing. The idea was foolish."

He went to the bedroom. Through the open doorway, Fan saw him glancing at his image in the pier glass. He used an index finger to smooth both sides of his mustache, then returned to the parlor. He smiled as he let himself out. But before the door closed, she saw the smile change to a scowl.

Disturbed, she walked to the window bay overlooking the street. She folded her arms across her breast as she stood in the sunlight. The lace curtains cast a blurred pattern on her face. She was ashamed of her thoughts, but she couldn't escape them:

What is *he involved in? Much more than he's telling me, I'm certain—*

Fan had never distrusted nor even questioned her husband before. Of course she was almost sure he occasionally indulged in sexual activity with other women. But that wasn't a matter to be classified under the heading of trust. It was simply a fact she acknowledged and accepted. He was a healthy, virile man. And she recognized her failure to satisfy him.

So it *was* essentially true that she'd never distrusted Edward—nor been worried about any of his activities.

But now, because of his sudden and surprising interest in Jephtha, she was suspicious.

And because of his association with the enigmatic and unpleasant Josiah Cheever, she was afraid.

Her hands moved on the sleeves of her dress. Fingers flexing, she tried to squeeze warmth into her body. Behind the door to the smaller bedroom, she heard a book thud on the floor. Then Jeremiah's voice:

"Oh, *hang!*"

She was too upset to go and speak to him.

CHAPTER V

The Riot

AT SEVEN-FIFTEEN that same evening, Jephtha Kent left the city telegraph office, having just dispatched copy to Theo Payne.

Much like a symphony, the story contained dominant themes; themes that had come to him almost unconsciously while he wrote at his desk in the *Star* office. Terror and haste. He'd seen examples all day long.

At the Capitol the Assistant Adjutant General, Major Irvin McDowell, had already started work crews fortifying the building. The iron plates meant for the base of the unfinished dome were being set up on the ground as temporary breastworks. Inside, men hammered planks over the windows and built covers for valuable paintings.

Wagons kept arriving with lumber. Other wagons brought barrels of stone and hardened cement. The barrels were manhandled into place to barricade main entrances. Two huge drays delivered loads of firewood to be used to heat the Capitol in case some of the relief troops had to be quartered there.

At the same time, stoneworkers continued to chip away at the capitals of the immense Corinthian columns for the porticos of the new Senate and House wings. Eventually, one hundred columns would be erected. But so far, only three had been put in place. Others lay scattered in the mud. The masons seemed cheerful, unaffected by the grim work going on around them.

Terror and haste. He saw it in every one of the government buildings he visited.

Clerks and undersecretaries were clearing their desks and packing their portmanteaus with personal belongings. Although most of Jephtha's sources were still forbidden to talk for the record, he didn't have much trouble finding out that those who had resigned were Southerners. Officers were quitting the Army and Navy as well. He heard that one of the best-regarded Army men in the city, Quartermaster-General Joe Johnston—another Virginian—was preparing his resignation in case his state seceded; the Lee situation all over again.

Terror and haste. He saw it when he made the rounds of the hotels.

At Willard's a hand-written notice announced a special meeting that evening. A volunteer guard unit was to be recruited from hotel guests who were remaining in Washington. The unit's organizer was tough old Cassius M. Clay of Kentucky. Clay's politics—abolitionist Republicanism—had involved him in several duels in his native state. Some of his opponents had lived to regret their challenges; some hadn't.

In the Willard bar, Jephtha heard that another lately arrived Republican, lanky Senator Jim Lane, was putting together a second defense group composed of men like himself—veterans of the factional fighting in Kansas.

In the lobbies of the National, the Kirkwood and several smaller hotels, he saw Senators and Congressmen from states likely to secede settling their bills and supervising the removal of their baggage.

A gold piece slipped to the clerk at the National provided him with the information that Mr. and Mrs. Edward Lamont were registered there. The desk ledger carried the words *and family* after Lamont's name.

At least two of the boys must be with Fan and her spouse. Which ones, the clerk didn't know. He thought one was fourteen or fifteen. Jeremiah. The description of the older boy was vague. It could be either Matthew or Gideon.

Jephtha's spirits soared. He hadn't seen his sons in almost nine years. He *had* to visit Fan—doing his best to keep a rein on his temper. He almost went directly from the desk to the suite occupied by the Lamonts. Then caution—and a practical problem—checked him and spoiled his mood.

What if Fan denied him admittance? What if she even refused to speak to him at the door? The possibility wasn't all that farfetched.

He had to approach her properly. If she was unwilling to talk to him, creating a scene would insure that he'd never see the boys, or find out anything about them.

He couldn't afford the time to sit in the lobby in the hope that he might spot one of them passing through. So he left the hotel, struggling to come up with a plan to guarantee Fan's cooperation. By day's end, he still hadn't thought of one.

He put the problem out of mind deliberately. Sometimes when he was having difficulty with a key phrase in a story, forgetting about it for a few hours provided the quickest solution. His mind often produced the answer unexpectedly. He hoped it would now.

A steamy twilight was settling as Jephtha walked from the telegraph office toward Canterbury Hall. Pedestrians crowded the sidewalks even though night was coming on—another sign of upheaval. Ordinarily, most people hurried indoors at sunset. Washington City provided only minimal police service. A notoriously inefficient force of fifty officers patrolled the capital by day. Their salaries were paid by the municipality. At night fifty others took over. But they worked for the

Federal government and spent most of their time guarding its buildings and grounds.

Events seemed to have overcome fears of being assaulted and robbed after dark. On Seventh, one of the city's main business thoroughfares, a good many respectable-looking people were abroad. But he also noticed plenty of disreputable types. Earlier in the day he'd felt slightly foolish about taking Molly's pepperbox from the drawer of her bureau. He'd taken it on an impulse—neglecting to ask her permission. But now he was glad he had it in the right pocket of his black coat. Several times, usually Sunday afternoons, he and Molly had plinked away at bottles in the back yard of the boarding house. He knew how to shoot. If he had to defend himself, he could.

He reached the intersection of Seventh and Louisiana. A white glare illuminated the entire block to his right; Canterbury Hall's outside calcium lights. Before he could turn the corner, a pair of boys converged on him.

One was selling secessionist cockades, the other a garish broadside featuring the American eagle, the lyrics of "The Star Spangled Banner," and harsh words about the "traitors" of the South. He bought a broadside and stuffed it in his left pocket. Perhaps he could quote some of the copy in tomorrow's dispatch. Of course the story Theo Payne wanted most was the Lee interview. He'd wired Jephtha twice that day, demanding it. Jephtha had thrown both messages on the floor of the *Star* office, for Jim to sweep away.

Moving along Louisiana, he saw a large, rowdy crowd in front of the variety theater that occupied the capital's old Assembly Rooms. He elbowed his way through groups of tipsy militiamen; passed small bands of blacks from Negro Hill out on North Tenth, and unshaven Irishmen from the Swampdoodle district. He was conscious of being eyed by both the blacks and the Irish. He kept walking. He had no intention of being dragged into an alley and knocked out with a slung shot.

Above the loud voices of the vendors, he heard the shrill sound of a whistle from one of the piers at the foot of Sixth or Seventh. Steamers were still carrying passengers down the river to the railroad junctions at Alexandria and Aquia Creek. He imagined they were jammed with departing government employees and their families.

A procession of three open carts rumbled by. The carts stank; he didn't look at the heaped-up contents. The accumulated garbage and human waste of the city—dumped into the streets from slop jars—had to be hauled out every night and deposited in the countryside.

The walk in front of Canterbury Hall was bright as noonday. As he approached, Jephtha noticed a short, heavily bearded man in civilian dress leaning against the building. The man's hat brim was pulled down to his eyebrows, putting much of his face in shadow.

He looked familiar. But it took Jephtha a moment to recognize him. When he did, he instantly thought of Dorn.

He scanned faces. He didn't see Dorn. But he did spot another heavy, gray-haired fellow he remembered from the morning of Lincoln's arrival—the same morning he'd exchanged sharp words with the bearded man.

Jephtha squeezed into a place along the wall of the brick building adjoining the theater. A large carriage drew up. An unescorted woman alighted. The bearded man was immediately alert.

The woman was beautifully groomed and expensively, though heavily, dressed for the mild, humid weather. She wore a pelisse of vivid red velvet with a black fur collar. Her hooped skirt matched the color of the pelisse, and was accented with double vertical stripes of black. The brim of her red velvet hat drooped fashionably front and back. A black-dyed ostrich plume frothed over the crown and trailed down the nape of her neck.

People murmured and pointed. Mrs. Rose O'Neal Greenhow was one of Washington's most familiar figures. And she made no secret of her Southern sympathies.

She'd come to the city years ago from Maryland, a fresh and lovely country girl whose mother had lost her husband. Rose lived with her aunt at the Congressional Boarding House in the old brick Capitol building. She quickly charmed the resident legislators, the most famous of whom was the "South's Sentinel," Calhoun of South Carolina. Many said Calhoun had been the girl's intellectual mentor, instilling in her a strong belief in states' rights and an equally strong antipathy toward abolitionist demagogues. During the term of the bachelor president, Buchanan, her house at First and I Streets became a sort of annex of the executive mansion and the widow, Mrs. Greenhow, was called the unofficial queen of Old Buck's administration.

In her forties now, she was still a lovely woman, with olive skin accented by lively eyes and glossy black hair. As she glided from the carriage to the sidewalk, a drunk lurched in front of her:

"Why, looky who's come! The Wild Rose herself—"

Mrs. Greenhow pointed with her closed parasol. Her eyes glittered with reflections of the calcium lights. The bearded man watched intently as she said:

"Would you step out of the way, sir?"

The crowd quieted. The drunk hiccoughed.

"Maybe I will. Maybe I won't."

"You will, because I intend to take my seat for the performance."

"We gonna have a hall full of secesh sluts, are we?"

Mrs. Greenhow whacked his cheek with the parasol. The man yelped, swore, lunged at her. The widow's Negro driver started to hop down to help, but she didn't need him. She jabbed the ferrule of the parasol in the drunk's neck, then kicked his right shin.

The drunk stumbled. Mrs. Greenhow swept around him, her chin high and her eyes daring anyone else to try to stop her. No one did.

Jephtha's grudging smile was a response to her bravery. He'd never heard it called into question, even by Washington's most malicious gossips.

Her morals, however, were a different matter. She had contacts throughout the government, in both the Democratic and the Republican party. Her detractors claimed she wasn't above using her charm—and her body—to obtain information or arrange political favors for special friends. A number of army officers had also been seen going in and out of her home. In wartime, their knowledge of confidential military matters could be useful to the Southern side. No doubt that was why the bearded man watched her so closely.

Four well-dressed young men, each with a secessionist cockade pinned to his top hat, surrounded the drunk who had accosted Mrs. Greenhow. They began to push and curse him. Frightened, the drunk suddenly darted between two of the men, fled into the street and vanished behind another waste cart.

The young men transferred their hostility to those in the crowd who were applauding the drunk's escape. Glares and taunts were exchanged. One of the Southerners lifted his cane. The bearded man slipped his hand under his coat and kept it there as the four Southerners rearranged themselves, standing back to back, ready for a fight.

No one in the opposition seemed willing to start it, though there was a flurry of fist-shaking and swearing. The young men waited. Two had canes; all looked capable of defending themselves. The arrival of another carriage broke the tension. The quartet casually strolled inside, laughing.

The bearded man pulled his hand from beneath his coat. Jephtha started to work his way toward him. The man didn't notice. His attention was concentrated on the couple who had just climbed down from the carriage.

Jephtha maneuvered to within a couple of feet of the man. He felt the man sensed his presence. But he had to force an acknowledgement:

"Hello, Pinkerton."

The man pivoted as if hit. His eyes, on a level with Jephtha's chin, glared:

"You've made a mistake. My name's Allen. Major E. J. Allen."

Another carriage unloaded three men wearing blue cockades. There were more taunts from the Northerners jamming the walk

"Allen, is it?" Jephtha chuckled. "I realize not many people in the capital know what you look like. But you won't get away with that name for long. Especially if I say your real one again. Perhaps a little louder."

Pinkerton clutched Jephtha's arm. "Don't cause trouble for me, Kent. We're on the same side—"

"I work for a newspaper. I don't know who you're working for—or why you're in Washington. I take that back. One of those thugs you employ told me you're studying the security of the rail lines from Baltimore."

"You mean Dorn."

"Ah, you got a report from him."

"Yes."

"He was watching the Long Bridge pretty closely yesterday. That's a good distance from the rail yards. So is Canterbury Hall."

Pinkerton's eyes were moving again. Noting arrivals; filing away faces. "Take a word of advice. Don't go into the bar."

"Why not?"

"Dorn's there. He doesn't like you." Pinkerton's eyes flicked to Jephtha. "I can't say I do either."

Sourly, Jephtha said. "What a surprise."

"Kent, I'm trying to do you a favor!"

"Oh?"

"The least you can do is reciprocate."

"How?"

"Forget you saw me."

Keeping his voice as low as the other man's, Jephtha answered, "Why should I? You don't have any official government assignment. So I'm wondering why you're spying on citizens who've committed no crime other than coming to a public place."

"You damn hacks are all alike! Pry, pry—!"

"And I'll keep prying until I get answers. *Major*."

Pinkerton's teeth clenched. But Jephtha refused to be stared down. Finally the detective whispered:

"There's going to be a secesh demonstration in the theater. You know that or you wouldn't be here."

"I'm asking why *you're* here."

"I have no comment."

"Well, I do. I don't like my activities reported on because I ride over to Virginia. I don't like being threatened by clods like Dorn. Who's backing your illegal work?"

"There's nothing illegal about taking precautions."

"Considering the kind of bullies you hire, there could be. In fact, I'd say it's more than likely."

"I hire the best men I can get!"

"That doesn't speak very highly of your profession, does it?"

"You're just taking it out on me because of Dorn."

"In part," Jephtha admitted. "But you're evading my questions. Why are you here? And at whose request?"

"Kent, don't you understand? Washington could go up like powder before the relief troops arrive! The government needs to identify potentially dangerous agitators."

"Sounds to me as if the government's suffering an advanced case of hysteria."

"That shows how little you know. There are traitors right here—tonight!"

Jephtha shook his head to show he wasn't convinced:

"If the Confederacy attacks the Union on the battlefield, that's one thing. But making secret lists at a theater—you *are* making lists, I assume—?"

"Mental ones." Pinkerton's belligerent gaze suggested Jephtha might find himself on one of them.

"Well, I call that assigning guilt without proof. I don't like it. I have my doubts that the President would like it, either."

"There's no way the President will find out—unless someone talks too freely."

Jephtha shrugged. "I report the news."

"Merciful Christ! You're not going to—"

"A little softer, Major." Jephtha smiled. "People are noticing you."

Flushed, Pinkerton leaned closer. "You're not going to report any of this?"

"It depends."

"On what?"

"First of all, on what happens the rest of the evening. If your bully boys get out of hand, it'll be in my paper as soon as I can write it and they can set it."

Pinkerton looked trapped. "That's unconscionable! If you have any loyalty to the Union, exercise a little control!" His voice took on a pleading note. "What my men and I are doing is in the national interest—"

"That excuse could cover a multitude of sins. Or should I say crimes?"

Pinkerton wiped his sweating forehead. Droplets of perspiration glistened in his beard. Jephtha savored the moment. During the day, he'd made some inquiries. Some of Allan Pinkerton's operatives had been observed near the railroad yards. Their presence wasn't a secret. But their chief's was.

He didn't doubt the sincerity of Pinkerton's fear of potential violence. Yet the man's presence still alarmed and angered him. Years ago in Lexington he'd thought it his moral duty to conspire with Syme and operate secretly against those who had trusted him when he occupied a pulpit. Tonight he found the idea of covert police surveillance—American turning against American—despicable. It was another indication of how he'd changed.

Pinkerton licked his lips. "Kent?"

"What?"

"Will you or won't you keep quiet?"

"I told you—it depends on what happens tonight. If there *is* a demonstration for the South, we'll see whether you can control your men."

"But I'm not planning to be inside the theater—"

"Afraid someone might recognize you? They haven't so far."

"None of my men will get out of hand."

"I wish I shared your confidence."

"They're under orders to watch, nothing more."

"I'm not sure Mr. Dorn has the mental capacity to understand orders in English or any other language. I hope he remembers nobody's yet revoked the right of free speech. If he forgets, I promise you I'll write a story you won't like."

"Goddamn it, he'll obey orders! But I can't be responsible for what happens between the two of you."

"That's fair warning," Jephtha said. "I've already given you mine."

He turned and started to push his way into the theater, leaving Pinkerton in the glare of the calcium lights.

ii

While Jephtha stood in line to purchase his ticket, he studied the crowd.

Canterbury Hall usually attracted a lower-class audience. Typical of its patrons was the man just in front of him. A mechanic or day laborer; poorly dressed and working a big wad of tobacco in his jaw. The man spat juice on the floor as the line moved forward slowly.

Tonight, tobacco-chewers were in the minority. Young dandies, of the kind who'd threatened the drunk, clustered in small groups throughout the smoky lobby. Almost all of them carried canes and displayed the blue rosette of rebellion on their hats or lapels. Most of them seemed in a festive mood.

Jephtha also recognized a couple of army officers—out of uniform—and several government clerks, including one frail, jittery fellow named Cheever, from War. Cheever stood at the entrance to the bar adjoining the lobby. Jephtha watched three men approach Cheever one at a time. The clerk whispered something to each of them.

He didn't see Rose Greenhow. She'd evidently entered the auditorium. There were only a few other women present. Each was well dressed and escorted. He wondered whether Lamont had urged Fan to remain at the hotel because of potential danger.

Beside the grille of the ticket booth a poster listed the actors in order of appearance. Edward Lamont was third on the bill. Seeing the actor's name in elaborate type momentarily enraged Jephtha.

At last he was able to buy his twenty-five-cent ticket. He shoved his way to the door of the bar. Cheever was gone.

Cigar fumes, loud talk and the smell of beer drifted

out of the bar. The gas was turned low, but Jephtha soon spotted Samuel Dorn's blond head. Over a drink, Dorn was talking with the stout, gray-haired detective he'd seen outside.

Dorn began making nervous little moves, unconsciously aware of being watched. Presently he turned his head; saw Jephtha. His face registered surprise. Then he smiled and raised his schooner in a mock salute. There was no humor in his eyes.

Jephtha turned away, but slowly, as if Dorn's presence didn't bother him. His fear of the young detective wasn't cowardice so much as common sense. He'd learned that there were a few human beings who were wholly and inexplicably cruel.

He was sure Dorn would like to corner him. Jephtha believed he was probably as strong as the detective, though he lacked the advantage of youth. And he knew nothing about fist fighting. Dorn undoubtedly knew a great deal.

Jephtha was quite thankful for the pepperbox in his pocket.

iii

The smoke and noise in the gas-lit auditorium were even worse than in the lobby. He crowded onto one of the center benches halfway back. Pulled out his watch. The performance began at eight. Five minutes to go.

He saw Cheever bustle down to a seat being saved for him by two friends in the fourth row. Mrs. Greenhow sat directly behind, alone and unmolested by the men on either side of her.

All at once Jephtha recognized the fellow immediately to his left. It was the tobacco-chewer from the ticket line.

The man reached into his right pocket as the piano player entered the shallow pit. There was scattered applause; some shouts about the musician's parentage and the state of his genitals. Jephtha saw what the tobacco-chewer had taken from his coat.

A rock.

"Think you'll need that tonight?" Jephtha asked.

"Could be. Some secesh actor's gonna make a speech." He grinned. "Gonna try, anyway." He tossed the rock up and caught it.

The piano player adjusted his stool, fussed with his inked sheets of music, then launched into a clangorous fanfare. Boys carrying long poles moved down the side aisles to adjust the gaslight cocks. In less than a minute the auditorium was dark. The footlight candles shimmered on a painted curtain bearing the hall's name and a badly painted pastoral scene.

Boots thumped in the aisle to Jephtha's left. Samuel Dorn and his gray-haired associate hurried down to the second row. While the fanfare worked to a climax, Dorn tried to sit down on the bench he'd chosen. Two men objected. Dorn bent and said something to one of the complainers. A moment later, he and his companion had seats.

Jephtha's eyes adjusted to the dim light. He didn't see Allan Pinkerton anywhere. He'd apparently stuck to his plan to remain safely outside.

At the conclusion of the long fanfare, the house curtain rolled up to reveal a backdrop from which the paint was flaking. It represented a European palace surrounded by formal gardens. There were whistles and clapping as a busty, pock-marked woman in tights minced from the wings at stage left. She placed a sign on an easel:

THE CANTERBURY GIRLS

The piano player started hammering a gallopade. A half-dozen women in tights, high boots and brief costumes of garish orange velveteen danced on. Arms resting across each other's shoulders, they stared into the darkness with fixed smiles. If one of them was under thirty, Jephtha was St. Paul.

The Canterbury Girls went through a routine of kicks, steps and turns, bending over occasionally to display their covered bottoms. The audience response was predictable:

"Come down here, sweetie!"

"Show us if 'em tits are real, huh—?"

"How much fer a lay afterward, red?"

Mercifully, the Canterbury Girls only performed one number, but they pranced off to loud applause. The management was too frugal to provide a different scenic background for each turn. Only a new placard went on the easel:

The
Agile & Astonishing
ZOLKOS!

A trio of thick-armed, sweating acrobats bounded on stage to exhibit their ability to tumble and walk while contorted into human U's, their palms and feet on the floor and their bellies pointed toward the fly loft. The turn lasted more than ten minutes. It was frequently interrupted by hissing and boos. The act ended with two of the acrobats balancing the third on their shoulders. More boos and obscene shouts—until the piano player started a crescendo and the man at the top of the human pyramid reached under his sweaty singlet to produce a little American flag.

About half the audience leaped up, cheering. Jephtha heard more than one person shout, "Hurrah for the Union!"

A few opposing catcalls rang out. But no more. Jephtha guessed the Southern sympathizers were saving their enthusiasm for—

The Distinguished Tragedian
MR. EDWARD LAMONT

At the sight of the new easel card, Jephtha's throat went dry. He rubbed his palms back and forth over the knees of his trousers as a decrepit stagehand brought on a small tripod table, then a pitcher of water and a glass. After the man shambled off stage right, Lamont appeared on the opposite side. Someone behind Jephtha yelled:

"Stay off the stage, you goddamn traitor!"

Expressionless, Lamont gazed into the dark, then smiled as friendly applause drowned out a second protest. Jephtha saw Mrs. Greenhow clapping.

Lamont continued to smile as he walked to the table at center stage. Unconsciously, Jephtha clenched his right hand. That was the man Fan had chosen in preference to him. The man who now slept in her bed—

As his initial flash of anger cooled, he was able to concede Lamont was a commanding figure. In his mid- to late forties, he was tall and solid. By sixty he might be corpulent. But his tight-fitting tails and waistcoat revealed no paunch. He had curly brown hair and a full mustache. Neither showed any gray.

One hand resting on the edge of the tripod table, he waited for the tumult to die—

It did; abruptly. People sat forward on the benches. When the piano player rearranged his music, the rustle of the sheets was loud in the silence. To Jephtha's left,

the man with the rock tossed it up and down; up and
down—

He was grinning again.

iv

"Ladies and gentlemen, good evening. I am Edward
Lamont." The actor's rich voice projected to the rear of
the hall without a hint of effort.

*"We know who you are! A no-good secesh son of a
bitch!"*

Once more Lamont waited. Jephtha tried to judge
him objectively. He might not be genuinely handsome.
His eyes were too close together. And he seemed to lack
that indefinable but unmistakable quality that marked
the truly great actor.

But neither was he inadequate. When the clapping
and some equally loud jeers faded, he resumed with
flawless diction—and no accent:

"I do not intend to offer the program previously
planned for this appearance. The hour is too late." His
eyes flicked across the audience; reflected the footlight
candles; burned.

"The crimes of the Republican government are already too numerous and heinous for citizens of good
conscience to ignore them and take refuge in light en-
tertainment. The blessed principles of freedom on which
this nation was founded have been attacked. Attacked
in a manner both vile and unprecedented—"

An older man leaped up. "Who the shit fired on
Sumter? Answer me that!"

"Be still or get out, you Yankee clown," a young man
called from the second row at stage left. Angry mur-
murs spread through the auditorium. *It's coming,* Jephtha thought.

Lamont paused a third time. Finally the insults—to

him and to other members of the audience—died away.
Certainly the actor was brave—or would it be more
correct to say insane?—to expose himself to the kind of
ugliness that was loose in the dark hall.

"In view of that attack," he went on, "it behooves
free men to take action. To reaffirm their belief in the
principle of the sovereignty of individual states. To resist the tyranny which reaches out from this very city in
an outrageous attempt to crush liberty in its cruel,
simian grip."

Laughter; hissing. The word *simian* was perfectly understood as an insulting reference to Lincoln's appearance. Voice rising, Lamont continued:

"On the twentieth of December last, the great com-
monwealth of South Carolina dared to be the first to
defy that tyranny. She was soon followed by six other
sovereign states, which, together, dedicated themselves
to the formation of a government designed to represent
the interests of those who always have been, are today
and always shall be the only *true* citizens of this nation.
I mean white Americans."

More applause; more shouts—the ferocity of both
greater than before.

"Less than one hundred years ago, such men joined
in compact to throw off a foreign oppressor, create a
new nation and promote the common good. Today the
descendants of those men have chosen to disavow that
compact—because they have been betrayed by the very
government their forebears fought and bled to establish!"

Stillness. Even Lamont's foes were listening; or perhaps waiting for some signal for an all-out attack.

If the actor was fearful he didn't show it. His eyes
seemed brighter. His brow glistened. He took two quick
steps toward the footlights. His left hand fisted. Then he
lifted it dramatically—

"Yes, my fellow citizens, today there are *two* governments in this tortured land. But only one—the Provisional Government of the Confederate States of America—stands for the right of every person to live his life as he chooses. For decades the patriotic and God-fearing men of the South have been branded villains—brutes—whoremongers!—by the madmen who now manipulate the lewd and illiterate Illinois lawyer like some pathetic puppet—"

A jerky gesture was startling in the way it suggested a puppeteer's hand. Jephtha could almost see a marionette dancing.

"But that evil congeries of conspirators which piously professes to be America's Constitutional government is *not!* It is instead an abomination in the sight of all liberty-loving people. An abomination to be resisted! *Overturned!*

"It surely will be. The flame of freedom within Southern breasts cannot be quenched. Not by threats—not by blockade—not by military force. Each attempted suppression—each feeble and frightened attempt to diminish the brilliance of that flame will only make it shine the brighter—until its cleansing fire consumes the wicked men of Washington City—which will become a *Southern* city within hours of the day noble Virginia joins her brave sisters in secession!"

In the front row at stage right, a man threw something. Lamont sidestepped. The brown, rancid cabbage struck the painted drop, rippled it and fell, splattering apart.

"That, sir, is the kind of act I would expect of a member of Mr. Lincoln's rabble." He faced front. "Make no mistake, ladies and gentlemen. Virginia *will* join the Confederacy. And other states as well. So let us stand—"

He spread his arms, palms upward.

"Stand up together—"

People began rising, including Mrs. Greenhow.

"—and declare our solidarity. Let us send a message to Richmond that her special convention cannot fail to hear. A message that the free men and women of Washington City await the victorious armies of General Beauregard! The armies that will liberate us from the yoke of the crude and perverted Westerner who now sits enthroned only a few blocks from this theater. A message, ladies and gentlemen! To Richmond! To all the South—"

He flung up his arms.

"To the world!"

The man beside Jephtha jumped up, screamed a curse and threw the rock.

Lamont dodged. The rock struck the pitcher and broke it, splashing water on the actor's evening suit. A piece of flying glass nicked his cheek. A little line of blood showed bright against his skin.

He didn't move, even though people all over Canterbury Hall were surging to their feet, friends as well as enemies. Quite against his will, Jephtha found himself admiring Lamont's courage.

"A message of faith and loyalty!" he cried. "Calling them to come—to conquer—*for the Confederacy*—!"

Another rock whizzed near Lamont's head. He ducked, his eyes flashing a cue to the nervous piano player. The first chords produced the loudest clapping yet.

All around, Jephtha saw frenzied faces, some afire with enthusiasm, others twisted with rage. Mouths screamed words he couldn't understand. Madness, he thought. *Madness—*

Somehow, one voice rang out over the din. Lamont was flushed—and singing:

"I wish I was in the land of cotton,
Old times there are not forgotten—"

"No! *No!*" men howled, leaping over benches, pushing forward, clogging the fronts of the aisles. Yet over their protests and their cursing, the lyric Lamont had begun was picked up by a dozen voices—

Then two dozen—

Then a hundred, until the song began to swell, proud and defiant:

> *"Look away! Look away! Look away! Dixie Land.*
> *In Dixie Land, where I was born in,*
> *Early on a frosty mornin'—"*

Men tried to reach the steps to the stage. Others pushed them back. Lamont held his ground, his right hand moving in rhythm, his head thrown back defiantly. The thunder of the song shook the hall:

> *"Look away! Look away! Look away! Dixie Land!"*

Jephtha had to stand on the bench to see what was happening down by the footlights. Fists and canes were being raised. Men began to hit each other. One against one; a group against one or two; group against group.

Stones, rotten fruit—even a Bowie knife—were hurled at Lamont. Each time, he moved just enough to avoid being hit. But he didn't show any sign of alarm, or shift toward the safety of the wings. At the back of the hall a voice wailed:

"Stop this! You're destroying my theater—"

The unseen owner was drowned out:

> *"Then I wish I was in Dixie, hooray! Hooray!*
> *In Dixie Land, I'll take my stand,*
> *To live and die in Dixie—"*

In the aisle nearest Jephtha, a singing man was set on by two others. Thrown down. He shrieked as they stamped on his groin.

Was there no end to the irony? Jephtha thought. The song rousing such hatred was innocent; innocuous—and the work of a Northerner, Dan Decatur Emmett, who had written it for one of Bryant's minstrel shows.

The song had fired the South's imagination after its first performance in 1859. By the time Jefferson Davis had gone to Montgomery to organize the new Confederacy, "Dixie's Land" had been transmuted from a commonplace tune to a holy anthem. The *Union* had carried a story reporting that poor Emmett was a pariah in his native state—

"Away, Away, Away down South in Dixie!
AWAY, AWAY, AWAY DOWN SOUTH IN DIX—"

"Watch out, Lamont!" someone screamed. A pistol went off.

Bedlam.

Men who had been pummeling one another began to fight toward the exits. Benches sailed through the air. Jephtha saw other men fall, faces streaming blood. Edward Lamont clutched the proscenium at stage left. He'd lunged there to escape the shot that had pierced one of the painted fountains on the drop.

The shrieking—the fighting—the sudden panic touched off by the gunshot—they were the signs of mass insanity. Jephtha almost wanted to weep. He struggled toward the aisle, his senses collecting fragmentary impressions:

The scarlet face of a frock-coated dandy bellowing "Dixie's Land" while he drove an older man to his knees and beat the man's temples with his cane. The man pitched over—

A group formed around Mrs. Greenhow. She kept singing as her protectors tried to lead her up the aisle to safety.

The rock-thrower who had sat beside Jephtha had

now reached the third row, found a victim and was using his thumbs to gouge the man's eyes. One socket oozing blood, the victim was on his knees wailing like an
infant.

Lamont still hadn't left the stage. Eight Southerners
formed a human chain in front of the shallow pit from
which the piano player had disappeared. Suddenly two
men charged the line—

Dorn and the other Pinkerton.

With revolvers.

The detectives punched, butted, and broke through.
Dorn scrambled up on the stage, his companion right
behind. Lamont started to back into the wings at stage
left. Dorn grabbed his shoulder, held him till the other
detective caught up.

Five of the men in the pit started to go to Lamont's
assistance. Dorn brandished his gun:

"Stay away! We're friends. We'll protect him!"

The men in the pit hesitated. Another heavy-set fellow tried to bull past them: "The hell you will—!"

Two of the men in the pit wrestled him back. Then,
unbelievably, Dorn aimed at the attacker. Pulled the
trigger—

A spurt of fire. The heavy man sprawled across an
overturned bench, shot in the stomach. That convinced
Lamont's defenders of Dorn's sincerity. The men let
Dorn and his cohort thrust the relieved-looking actor
offstage.

Jephtha gaped like a bumpkin. Where the hell was
Pinkerton? Why was he letting his operatives worry
about the safety of a Southerner—?

Then it struck. He was ashamed of his own stupidity.

Dorn knew Pinkerton had planned to remain outside.
He had no intention of protecting Lamont. And he'd
shot an innocent man just so he could get his hands on
the actor—

Despicable as Edward Lamont might be, Dorn was

infinitely more so. Jephtha leaped across broken benches, heading for the stage.

The riot was losing its ferocity, though there were still crashes and screams; the tinkle of glass from shattered glass fixtures; oaths and the thud of boots as panicked men struggled to squeeze through the doors to the lobby. A solitary tenor still sang "Dixie"—

All at once Jephtha realized his motive for going to Lamont's aid wasn't solely humanitarian. Even before he was aware of it, his mind had produced the answer to the problem that had frustrated him all day. Helping Lamont would make reaching Fan a certainty. She *couldn't* turn him away—

What a cynical bastard you've become, he thought, weaving down the aisle between the eight men who had left the pit once Lamont was hustled offstage. In a faint voice, the man Dorn had shot pleaded for help. No one paid attention.

Jephtha knew his plan offered both risk and ample opportunity for failure. To make the plan work, he had to locate Lamont *and* prevent the Pinkertons from harming him—

Another glass bowl on a gaslight broke, hit by a stone. Jephtha ran up the steps at the end of the stage right aisle, then started across toward the opposite side. He walked rapidly, almost unnoticed now that the theater was emptying.

He was more than a little afraid of what might be waiting in the dark of the wings. He shoved his hand into his pocket and closed his fingers around the ivory grips of the Sharps.

CHAPTER VI

The Detectives

CONSCIOUS OF THE NEED for haste—Dorn and his crony might already be spiriting Lamont out through the alley—Jephtha plunged into the blackness backstage.

Here and there a gas jet cast a pool of light on a prop table or a rolled backdrop. In the surrounding dark, shadow-figures moved; panicked men and women hurrying to escape the theater. A whistle shrilled in the auditorium. Evidently some of Washington's night police had been summoned for the emergency.

He passed two of the Canterbury Girls wearing cloaks. They smelled of sweat and heavy perfume. The alley door slammed a moment later. Footsteps scurried behind him. The door slammed again.

In one of the gas-lit areas, a small perspiring man was hastily putting on his jacket. Jephtha hurried toward him. The man started as Jephtha appeared in the light:

"Are you the stage manager?"

The little man fingered his mustache. "That's right. Who the hell are you?"

"Never mind. Two men brought Lamont offstage. Where did they go?"

"I don't know. I didn't see."

The man's brow glistened under the gas. His eyes showed his fright—and his lie. Jephtha jerked the pepperbox from his pocket.

186

The manager backed against the table, whiter than ever:

"Believe me, I had nothing to do with what happened! I saw Lamont whispering to the piano player. But I don't know anything else, I swear I—"

Jephtha shoved the four-barrel muzzle against the manager's vest:

"I hope your memory improves. I'm with the Pinkerton agency."

The manager reacted with an even more violent start. The detective's name had a terrifying potency.

"I'll ask you again. Where did those men take Lamont?"

"Down—" The manager's hand shook as he pointed. "Down to the cellar—I think."

"Not to the alley? Not outside?"

"For God's sake, I can't be certain! You can see how dark it is back here! As soon as the trouble started, people were running every which way. I *think* the men went down the stairs. You—you wouldn't—do anything just because I'm not sure—"

The little man was on the point of weeping. Jephtha pushed him aside and dashed into the dark.

He collided with two of the Zolkos dressed for the street. The acrobats cursed in some unfamiliar European tongue. Jephtha avoided an angry fist and dodged between them.

He jumped over three rolled drops laid on the floor. Another hooded gas jet high up on a brick wall shed just enough light to reveal a stairway to the basement.

At the top step, he hesitated. He wondered what the stage manager would think if he knew the man who accosted him was nearly as frightened as he had been—

In the auditorium, police whistles shrilled again. The sound faded. Jephtha stole down the iron stairs as silently as possible.

ii

At the bottom he scanned the grimy corridor.

To his left a spot of blue gaslight revealed a man leaning beside a closed door. It was the detective with the gray hair. From behind the door Jephtha heard a pulping sound—a hard blow—followed by a moan. The gray-haired detective smiled.

All at once Jephtha knew he was rash to try this. A fool; out of his depth. But he still slipped the pepperbox into his pocket and stepped from the shadow at the foot of the stairs.

He walked briskly toward the detective. The man straightened up, his hand stabbing under his jacket and staying there. In his pocket Jephtha clutched the butt of Molly's gun. His fingers were slippery with sweat.

Behind the door someone struck a second blow. A third. A harsh voice said something Jephtha couldn't understand. Crying out, another voice blurred the first.

Before the detective drew his gun, Jephtha put him on the defensive:

"Allen wants you. Right away."

The man's small eyes showed confusion. *"Allen*—?"

Jephtha had trouble breathing. His legs shook as he said:

"Doesn't the name Major Allen mean anything to you?"

"Maybe. But—"

Another heavy sound beyond the door. Then the hectoring voice; Jephtha recognized it as Dorn's. On the door, faded white letters spelled the word *Properties*.

"Dorn's prisoner screamed. The gray-haired detective seemed confused by Jephtha's assertive stare. He mumbled the rest of his sentence:

"—but I don't know you."

Jephtha used the first name that came to mind:

"Emerson. Chicago office. You mean to say you're acquainted with every man on the Pinkerton payroll?"

The sarcasm made the other man lick his lips. He was none too bright, Jephtha decided. He pressed his advantage:

"I'll take over here. The major's outside the theater."

The detective glanced at the door, guilty. "But he doesn't know anything about—that is—"

"Maybe that's why he wants you."

For a moment Jephtha was certain he'd failed. The man continued to peer at him. Jephtha grabbed his shoulder. The man grunted angrily as Jephtha jerked him away from the wall:

"He wants you *now,* damn it!"

The detective moved back, his arm rising threateningly, his fist clenched for striking.

"I'm telling you—you'd better step lively or the major's going to be looking for your replacement." Playing the bluff to the limit, he put his back against the door. It was lucky the detective couldn't hear how fast his heart was beating.

In the property room, the blows hadn't stopped. Lamont was whimpering. Jephtha caught a snatch of Dorn's voice:

"—you fucking traitor, who planned your little performance tonight?"

"Will you get moving?"

Jephtha's harsh whisper produced a response. With an uncertain look, the detective wheeled and scuttled up the stairs.

Jephtha closed his eyes, almost faint. With nerve and a faked air of authority, he'd pulled it off.

But the most dangerous part remained.

Once the gray-haired detective was out of sight, he checked the revolving hammer of the Sharps. It was ready to fire. He bent over the door latch, lifting it slowly—slowly and soundlessly—until he was sure it was free.

Then he sucked in a breath and kicked the door open.

iii

At the sound of the door crashing back, Samuel Dorn whirled. Jephtha saw Dorn's startled face against an eerie background.

A short way down an aisle running to the rear of the huge, gloomy prop room, an oil lamp rested on a closed trunk. On either side of the aisle, racks held dozens of dusty costumes. There was theatrical paraphernalia everywhere—gaudy headdresses; a large free-standing mirror; a box of tambourines; another trunk with a yellowed human skull perching on its corner. The old mirror reflected the skull's distorted image.

In the center of the aisle and perhaps three feet beyond the lamp, Samuel Dorn had roped Lamont into an imitation regency chair from which the gilt had long ago disappeared. Lamont's head lolled toward his left shoulder. His bruised face bled from the nose, The blood dripped from his chin to the bosom of his dress shirt.

Dorn was crouched in front of Lamont but facing the door. On the detective's right hand Jephtha saw metal knuckles, smeared red. He pointed the pepperbox at Dorn:

"Don't move."

Lamont heard him. Tried to open his eyes. He couldn't. He rolled his head to the other side, groaning. Mucus leaked from his nose along with the blood.

Dorn's blue eyes bored into Jephtha. "Where the hell did you come from, Reverend? Where's that stupid Miller?"

"The man outside? I sent him away. I told him I worked for the Chicago office."

Dorn's jaw clenched. "The dumb son of a bitch!" He started toward Jephtha, the brass-knuckled hand rising. Jephtha leveled the pepperbox:

"I said stay right there!"

Dorn stopped.

"Untie him, Dorn."

"The hell I will."

"You'd better. I don't think you brought Lamont down here on the orders of Major Allen—Pinkerton."

The front of Dorn's jacket was marked with Lamont's blood. The lamp threw his huge, crooked shadow over the trunk and the yellow-toothed skull a short way up the aisle behind him. The shadow shifted as he shook his head:

"I'll be goddamned if I understand this—unless there really was something behind your trip to Virginia. Are you and this secesh bastard tangled up in what went on upstairs?"

"Dorn, you're stupider than a wild hog. I'm down here for one reason. I don't like private policemen who beat people because of their politics. Beat them without authority—"

Dorn blinked. Jephtha had hit on the truth. Lamont stirred in the chair as Dorn shouted:

"He's an enemy of the government, for Christ's sake! I'm going to find out who planned the show tonight. I'm sure it wasn't just Lamont. For one thing, there were too many Southerners in the audience. That whore Mrs. Greenhow—and a lot more." He tried to sound confident. "I'm doing the job I'm supposed to do."

"I still doubt your employer authorized methods like this."

The big young man was breathing more regularly now. Standing to his full height; in control. Jephtha's hand grew slippery on the gun's ivory grips. Dorn was trapped; knew it; might try to get out of the trap any way he could.

Finally, with a smug grin, Dorn said:

"No, he didn't. But he'll be happy to have the information I get from him—" A gesture to the actor; the elongated shadow of Dorn's arm flickered across racks of costumes at the periphery of the light. "And I *will* get it, Reverend. Soon as I finish with you. Your name's right on the list with Lamont's."

Jephtha felt weary. It was foolish to argue with Dorn. The detective could spout platitudes about defending the city and the Union without believing a word. He enjoyed this kind of work. And Jephtha's presence threatened him. All the more reason to stop wasting time:

"Move back so I can untie him."

Dorn's blue eyes glared in the lamplight. He grinned suddenly.

"Fuck you, Reverend. I doubt you know how to use that gun you've waving around."

Coloring, Jephtha leveled the pepperbox. The muzzles aimed at Dorn's breastbone.

"Let's find out."

Dorn started to snicker. Jephtha's expression cut it short.

"Now wait a minute. If you get nervous—" The detective's smile looked sickly all at once. "Hell, I could get hurt pretty bad—"

"That's very astute of you, Dorn. You're not quite as dumb as you act."

The detective's smile disappeared.

"I'm going to untie him," Jephtha repeated. He couldn't risk having Dorn do it. "Take three steps backward. But keep facing me."

Dorn hesitated.

"You hear me? Three steps. *Move!*"

The rage in Samuel Dorn's eyes was raw and intimidating. He peered into the four muzzles of the Sharps, let out a disgusted breath, and shifted his weight.

"Slowly," Jephtha warned.

Dorn slid his right foot to the rear. Jephtha started forward. Dorn took a second step. Too late, Jephtha noticed the detective's hand close to the prop skull resting on the trunk. Dorn snatched the skull, flung it, ducked just as Jephtha did. Jephtha jerked the trigger.

His shot went wild, chunking a wall far back in the darkness. The skull hit the door behind him and broke. Old bone rattled on the plank floor as Dorn launched himself forward, his movements incredibly fast.

Jephtha was still crouched. The toe of Dorn's boot whipped up and caught him under the chin. His head snapped back. He staggered, jolted with pain.

Dorn belly-punched him. First with his right hand, then his left. The second punch slammed Jephtha against the wall near the open door. He slid downward.

A knee came out of nowhere to crush Jephtha's right wrist against the wall. The pepperbox slipped from his fingers. Dorn kicked him between the legs. Jephtha almost screamed.

"Now," Dorn whispered, his perspiring face very close. "Now, you goddamn traitor—now we'll see whether your muscles are as big as your *mouth!*"

He shot his right fist at Jephtha's jaw. Jephtha jerked his head aside. Dorn's knuckle-dusters raked his chin. The blow banged his head into the wall a second time.

Jephtha started to sag again. Dorn grabbed his coat. Hauled him up. Jephtha had a distorted view of Dorn's blue eyes—

Murderous.

He fought back. Gave Dorn a knee in the genitals. Dorn exhaled hard; warm, stale breath—

He brought his right hand up between Dorn's arms—

the detective was still holding him—and struck for Dorn's eyes.

Dorn tried to twist away. One of Jephtha's nails nicked his left eyeball. Dorn gasped and let go.

Jephtha bowled into the detective with his shoulder. Knocked him off balance. Kicked his leg—

Dorn stumbled and fell. His head struck the corner of a trunk. His eyes seemed to glaze. Jephtha dropped on his belly with both knees.

He hurt. His head rang. His eyes were blurring. He hadn't been in a fight of any consequence since his boyhood in Oregon. But he knew this contest would have only one winner.

Just when Jephtha thought his adversary was weakening, Dorn heaved upward. He'd only been pretending.

Panting, Jephtha sprawled in the aisle. Dorn jumped up. Aimed a boot at Jephtha's ribs. Jephtha rolled away from it. The miss cost Dorn his balance for a few seconds. Jephtha staggered to his feet.

Dorn threw another punch. Jephtha ducked. The metaled fist slashed by his ear. For an instant he thought he saw surprise in Dorn's icy eyes—

Dorn's right arm was still extended. Jephtha slammed his left fist into Dorn's throat.

The detective gagged, his eyes popping. Jephtha ducked under his flailing arms, raced to the door, scrambled on hands and knees until he found the pepperbox. Behind him, he heard Dorn's pained breathing.

A rattle of metal brought Jephtha's head around. Dorn had flung the metal knuckles away. He pulled a clasp knife from his coat.

He bit the edge of the blade and tugged the handle. The knife opened.

He sidled forward, his boots scraping. He'd lost some of his energy. But he seemed to regain it as he came nearer. His right hand arced over and down, driving the knife point at Jephtha's head—

Still on his knees, Jephtha shot him.

The small-caliber ball was fired close enough to Dorn to stop him. He screamed, more in outrage than pain. The ball had hit him in the left side, near the ribs. Jephtha clearly saw the burned black hole in Dorn's coat.

The detective swayed, blinking faster and faster as the wound bled and drained his strength. The knife clattered onto the floor.

Still blinking, Dorn peered at Jephtha. His lips worked but no sound came. His right hand twisted the fabric of his coat where the ball had entered. Blood began to ooze between his fingers, shining in the lamplight.

When he was finally able to speak, he sounded wheezy—and astonished:

"You—you're the—goddamnedest preacher I—ever came up agains—"

Dorn's eyes rolled up in his head as the lids closed. He fell across one of the property trunks, his arms dangling down the far side, his back heaving.

Further up the aisle, Edward Lamont tried to focus his eyes on the source of the noise. He couldn't. His head still bobbed like a drunken man's. The cuts on his face had clotted. The bruises were already darkening.

Shaking, Jephtha thrust the pepperbox in his pocket. He had trouble standing up. He ached. His vision multiplied images. He saw two oil lamps. Then three. He grew uncontrollably dizzy—

His legs gave out. He struck the floor hard, just as someone came running down the hall.

He lay with his cheek against the splintery planks, close to fainting. If Miller had come back to kill him, there was nothing he could do.

iv

"—said his name was Emerson. Emerson from the Chicago office—"

"There's no Emerson in Chicago, you idiot!"

Jephtha struggled to stay conscious. The dizziness subsided a little. He tried to brace his hands on the floor. The first man exclaimed:

"Oh, my God, Dorn's been shot!"

"We've got worse trouble than that. *Damn!*"

Jephtha managed to open his eyes. He recognized the angry voice. He struggled to his hands and knees—and was helped to his feet by Allan Pinkerton.

Pinkerton snarled at Miller:

"I know this man. Kent, are you all right?"

Jephtha weaved on his feet. Alternating waves of heat and cold swept over him. Every blow Dorn had struck still hurt like the devil.

His breathing slowed. He felt a touch of startled pride. He'd held his own against Dorn.

But almost at the price of his life. He started trembling again.

"Kent?" Pinkerton repeated.

"I—I'm all right."

Miller bent over the trunk where the younger man sprawled. "Major Allen, he's bleeding bad—"

"Let him. We were here to watch. That's *all!* Whose idea was it to drag that actor down here and beat him?"

The gray-haired detective kept plucking at Dorn's coat.

"Miller, *answer me!*"

Miller straightened up. He'd bloodied his fingers trying to get a look at Dorn's wound. He wiped his hands on his trousers. His reply was what Jephtha expected:

"Dorn's. He said Lamont could probably tell us whether there's a Southern spy ring operating here in—"

"He didn't have to hammer a man half to death to get that information. Any half-wit would guess it. We know there are Southern sympathizers all over town." Red-faced, he jerked Miller by the shoulders. "But we have no orders to do anything about it—except observe. You knew that!"

Miserable, Miller nodded.

Pinkerton let go of him. Sighed loudly. "It's my fault. I know the way Dorn operates. I should have kept him outside. By God, if he recovers, I'll see he never works again. Not for any police department or railroad force in the whole damn country!"

After a minute, Pinkerton got control of his temper. Turned to Jephtha, who had sat down on a trunk. He was feeling better, though he'd have welcomed a glass of whiskey to numb the pain.

"How did you get involved in this?" Pinkerton asked him.

"You know I—" Jephtha wiped his damp forehead "I was in the audience. I saw Dorn and Miller hustle Lamont off stage. Pretending they were going to protect him. Knowing Dorn, I—let's say I had some doubts about his sincerity. I may not like Southern politics, Pinker—Major—but I made it clear to you earlier that I like police bullying even less. What you permitted tonight was one hundred percent illegal."

Again Pinkerton's face reddened above his beard. "I did *not* permit it. If I'd known about it, I'd have put a stop to it."

Jephtha shrugged. "I said you should be inside the theater."

"Yes, I remember," Pinkerton muttered. "Still—I can't fathom why you risked your neck. Why didn't you fetch me instead?"

Jephtha answered quickly: "There was no time. I

thought Lamont might be dead before I got to him. Dead, or spirited out the back way."

"There's no connection between you and Lamont except your feelings about Dorn?"

Jephtha hesitated; decided:

"Yes, but it's personal, not political. That's all I'm going to say about it."

"That's plenty!" Miller exclaimed. "Chief, he probably is mixed up with the secesh crowd!"

"Shut your mouth. Kent's no more of a secessionist than Abe Lincoln. If he says the connection's personal, I'll take his word."

Miller started to protest.

"I said *drop* it. Mr. Kent happens to be a reporter for the New York *Union*."

Miller understood instantly. "Oh, Jesus."

"Exactly what went on down here?" Pinkerton said to Jephtha.

"After—" A deep breath. "—after I bluffed Mr. Miller into thinking I worked for you, I tried to stop Dorn from beating Lamont. Dorn came at me with a knife and those knuckle-dusters lying there. I think he meant to kill me." Jephtha's mouth quirked, but it was hardly a smile. "I didn't stop to inquire. I shot him instead."

His mind raced ahead to the question of how to get Lamont away. In a bland tone, he added:

"I'll be glad to report the whole story to a magistrate if you feel—"

"*No!*" Pinkerton said.

"I'll certainly put it in my next dispatch to New York. Unless—"

The pause suggested a possible bargain. Pinkerton was quick to respond:

"Unless what?"

"Unless you'd prefer to hush up the whole matter."

"You know I would."

"Then have Mr. Miller call a hack. Oh, yes—and try to find some ammonia salts upstairs. If we can wake Lamont and take him out through the alley without attracting attention I'll see that he gets back to his wif— his hotel. He's staying at the National."

"That's right around the block."

"That's right, Mr. Miller. But I doubt we could protect the major's reputation—or keep his presence in Washington a secret for very long—if I walked Lamont to the hotel in the condition he's in. There'd be too many questions."

Pinkerton nodded: "There are still people all over the place outside."

"Then my solution's the best one, Major. You help me get him out and I'll forget I met you *or* Mr. Dorn."

Pinkerton chewed his lip. "No dispatches?"

"None."

"Can I rely on your word?"

"Do you have any other choice?"

"No."

"Of course I'd like to know who you're working for—"

"That has no part in any bargain we make!"

"I suppose not. I'd still suggest you get out of town and take your agents with you. Even if the man for whom you're doing these little favors is in the cabinet, it can't help your career—or his—if you're found out. The longer you stay, the greater the risk that you *will* be found out. Even if I keep quiet."

After a moment Pinkerton said softly, "I agree." He glanced sharply at Jephtha. "You really must have a powerful reason for wanting to help Lamont."

"I do." It unsettled him to realize he might be facing his former wife within a very short time. He felt the old hatred stir—and fought it down.

He noticed Lamont sitting up straighter. Blinking as if trying to clear his head. He pointed:

"We'd better look after him. Are we agreed?"

"We are," Pinkerton said. "Miller will drive the hack and see you make it safely through the back door of the National."

"Lamont should be seen by a doctor."

"I'll hire a nigger boy in the street to find one. I'll send the doctor to the hotel. Miller, get going! And don't say one unnecessary word if you want to keep working for me."

Still stunned by the bargain, Miller left, shutting the door behind him.

Jephtha walked to one of the costume racks—each step was a little easier now—and drew down a dress shirt. He carried the shirt to the chair where the groggy actor was tied.

"Lamont?"

The brown eyes flickered open. "Wh—what?"

"I've made arrangements to take you back to your hotel."

"Thank—" Lamont's tongue crawled across his cracked lower lip. "Thank you."

"I've got to clean you up so we can leave the theater without arousing too much curiosity. This may hurt."

"Go—ahead."

He winced as Jephtha began to sponge away the blood and mucus on his face. But he made no sound.

Miller returned with a bottle of ammonia salts from one of the dressing rooms. "The coppers cleared the theater," he reported.

"Backstage too?" Pinkerton asked.

"Yes. There are some men in the alley—"

"How many?"

"Eight or ten. About half of 'em are niggers."

"The hack's on the way?"

"It'll be here any minute."

Jephtha unstoppered the ammonia bottle. He passed

it back and forth under Lamont's nose. The actor's head jerked. He snorted, then coughed violently. Jephtha slapped his back. The coughing subsided.

Jephtha untied the knots in the rope. He and Miller lifted the actor to his feet. Allan Pinkerton darted into the corridor and walked rapidly toward the stairs, his footsteps echoing. Jephtha could have embroiled Pinkerton in a scandal and the detective knew it. He was ambitious—probably the main reason Jephtha's suggested trade-off had been accepted. He'd soon know whether the next step of his scheme would be equally successful.

"Hold him, Miller—"

"I've got him."

Jephtha took Lamont's other arm. The actor groaned as they helped him along the dim hall to the stairway.

v

The hackney began to roll. Outside, the alley loungers shouted questions at the mysterious bearded gentleman who had taken charge of loading the carriage. Through the window, Jephtha watched Pinkerton move away from the men and disappear in the dark.

Miller obeyed Jephtha's orders and drove slowly. Even so, the ride would take only a few minutes. The prospect of seeing Fan made Jephtha increasingly nervous. He was afraid of rejection; worried that his temper might betray him—

On the seat facing him, Lamont clung to the wall strap. Though his face was reasonably clean, he looked bleary and sick. Jephtha passed the salts bottle back and forth under his nose.

Lamont's eyes watered. He drew several deep breaths. The hack turned out of the alley. The actor's face was alternately patterned by gaslight and shadow.

"Feeling any better, Lamont?"

"Some. You have me at a disadvantage. I don't know who you are."

"Not one of your crowd, you can count on that. Let's just say I don't like thug tactics."

"Yes, but—" Lamont grimaced. "—I'd like to thank you by name."

A moment's silence.

"My name is Kent. Jephtha Kent."

Lamont's eyes opened wide. Jephtha thought the actor might faint. He didn't. But his mouth hung open a good ten seconds before he spoke.

"Not Fan's—?"

"Yes. I'm no particular friend of yours. But I couldn't stand by and see you killed just for speaking your mind."

Especially when helping you promised to get me where I want to go.

A puzzling thing happened then. Lamont lost his stupefied look—and smiled.

"Kent," he murmured. "Right like that—" A gesture. "Just when I—" A chuckle. "Remarkable."

The smile and the curious words bothered Jephtha. If his position and Lamont's had been reversed—if he'd been the one encountering Fan's first husband—he doubted he'd have been amused, no matter how much the other fellow had helped him.

The light of a saloon washed the interior of the hack. Lamont's face was visible for a moment. He was studying Jephtha.

"Well, Kent, considering my marital status and your politics, what you did was certainly damned decent." He rubbed his curly brown hair. "That bull-shouldered young man worked me over nicely. What happened to him? I was pretty foggy at the time—"

"I got him away from you."

"Do you know who he was?"

Carefully, Jephtha said, "Just someone who didn't care for your choice of music, I expect."

"I vaguely remember a gray-haired chap. And a fellow with a beard—"

"Acquaintances of the man who beat you. They helped me calm him down."

"Devil of a lot of noise, as I recall. A shot or two. It's all damned confused—"

Jephtha kept quiet. Lamont sighed; appeared to relax:

"Well, I owe you a great many thanks. All differences aside, let me offer them. Sincerely."

He extended his hand. Jephtha shook it. Despite what he'd been through, Lamont's grip was strong. His expression was cordial. Yet at that very moment, Jephtha had the feeling Lamont had begun to—

What was the right word for it?

To pretend.

To *act*.

Jephtha admitted to himself that it was irrational for an offer of thanks to arouse suspicion. Yet he *was* suspicious. He couldn't shake off the conviction that the thanks were insincere.

Lamont's lids drooped as if he were drowsing. Again the exterior circumstances were at odds with Jephtha's thoughts:

He's alert. Alert and on edge—

Why?

Because Fan was my wife?

No, she's his wife now. I'm no threat to him.

Then why is he tense—and acting as if he isn't?

Or is it all my imagination? Because I'm the one who's uneasy—?

The unanswered questions only heightened his nervousness as the hack creaked and lurched through the rutted street, bringing him steadily closer to the National Hotel.

CHAPTER VII

O Absalom!

THE BACK DOOR OF the National was well known to Jephtha Kent. The door, and ones like it in other hotels, helped the capital conduct its private business. Jephtha had long ago learned that ten minutes loitering in an alley could produce more news about who was seeing whom than hours spent wandering through the departmental buildings.

He helped Lamont from the carriage and through the door. An elderly black porter dozing on a stool roused and gaped at Lamont's battered face:

"Mr. Kent, that's one of our guests!"

"You're right, Hiram." The stooped Negro shook his head in amazement.

"Lamont, are you certain you can walk?"

The actor's skin was still as pale as parchment. "Yes. Just—let me have your arm." He took hold.

Jephtha turned to the porter. "I'd appreciate it if you didn't tell anyone you saw us come in." To Miller, who was standing in the doorway: "Tip him a dollar. Major Allen won't miss the money."

Scowling, Miller dug in his pocket and paid. Hiram grinned. Jephtha knew the porter could have been well off if he'd saved every tip he received from a backstairs visitor. But Miller's dollar would go where the rest of the tips went—to support Hiram's church. The porter was the ordained pastor of a small congregation of the forty-five-year-old African Methodist Episcopal denomination. He worked at the National six days a week, and on Sunday occupied the pulpit of a cheaply built but scrupulously maintained frame sanctuary in Negro Hill.

Miller went out to the hack as Hiram closed the alley door. Jephtha and Lamont started slowly up the dim back staircase. After just a few steps, Lamont was breathing hard. So was Jephtha. He was feeling his age and the after-effects of the fight with Dorn.

Lamont clung to his arm as the two men negotiated the hundred and eighty degree turn at the first landing. Jephtha decided his suspicions in the hack had been imagination after all. Lamont had behaved oddly because he'd been badly beaten. Jephtha reached that conclusion because he felt none too clear-headed himself.

They stopped by the door to the second floor corridor. "What's your room number?"

"Three-o-six."

"Just one more flight."

"I can make it," Lamont assured him.

On the third floor Lamont let go of his arm while Jephtha eased the door open and studied the hallway. Empty. He motioned Lamont forward. The actor took a step and started to fall.

Jephtha grabbed him in time. Lamont reddened, mumbling an apology. They walked slowly along the gas-lit corridor.

"Got to say it again, Kent. This is—damned white of you. Got to do something to pay you back for—"

"Here's the room," Jephtha interrupted. There was a tight feeling across his chest. He almost wished he'd left the Sharps at the theater—

Don't think that way. Think of why you're here. To learn about your sons. You can't do it unless you hold your temper!

He knocked. Heard footsteps. Then a voice that

made him catch his breath; it sounded exactly as he remembered it:

"Edward?"

Still laboring for breath, Lamont couldn't reply.

"Edward? Are you there?"

"With a friend," Jephtha said.

He heard her stunned intake of breath. He could imagine the incredulous look in her slanted gray-green eyes.

The wait seemed interminable. At last the bolt rattled. The door opened. White-faced, Fan clutched at the bosom of her velvet robe.

"I thought it was your voice. But I couldn't believe—" Her eyes moved to her husband. "Oh, dear God! *Edward*—!"

"He's all right. Help me get him inside."

She stared at Jephtha, numb and motionless.

"I tell you he's all right! We just need to put him to bed—"

Lamont gasped for air. He grabbed Jephtha with both hands, obviously dizzy. Fan's eyes grew ugly:

"Who hurt him? You?"

Caught in the awkward position of trying to support the actor in the doorway, Jephtha's reason deserted him. Except for the burden of Lamont, he would have struck her—

Stupid bitch!

But he didn't say it aloud. At the end of the sleepless night spent reading the Testament, he'd vowed he wouldn't let years of accumulated hatred drive him to one more act he'd regret. He tried to remember Fan was confused and terrified.

"Don't be a damn fool," he said. "If you aren't going to help, at least move out of the way."

She stepped back. Bearing most of Lamont's weight on his forearms, he dragged the actor into the suite's gas-lit parlor. He saw no one besides Fan.

She had sufficient presence of mind to close and bolt the door. Point—

"In there."

But her eyes were riveted on her husband's bruised face. Jephtha breathed loudly from the effort to support Lamont. The actor was nearly unconscious again. He muttered. Spittle drooled from one corner of his mouth.

"What—what happened to him, Jephtha?"

"I'll tell you after we take care of him. Hurry, will you please?"

She rushed into the bedroom, folded the coverlet back and lit the gas as Jephtha hauled Lamont to the bed and lowered him. Lamont groaned; arched his back. Pain wrenched his face.

Jephtha smelled the linen. Fresh; clean—

The conjugal bed.

He fought away the shameful images of Fan and the actor that filled his mind.

He lifted Lamont's legs. Fan arranged the pillows. Her movements had a jerky quality. She wouldn't look at him.

Jephtha eased Lamont's head down. The actor sighed. He knew he was safe.

His eyes opened again. He searched for Jephtha.

"Kent? Got to—make sure you know—how much I appreciate—appreciate—" It trailed off to a mumble.

"Fetch some whiskey if you have any," Jephtha said to Fan.

She disappeared into the parlor. He heard a decanter clink against a glass. Gingerly, he sat on the edge of the bed, staring at his hands. Fan returned. The anger that had burst loose when she accused him was gone. He was able to face her calmly.

Her face was thinner than he remembered. Drawn. He saw a few gray hairs among the fair ones. As she poured the strong-smelling liquor, she spilled some on her robe.

"I was at the theater," Jephtha began to explain as she handed him the glass. "I went on behalf of—just a minute. Lamont? Can you hear me?" He gently raised the actor's head with one hand. "Drink this."

He managed to get most of the whiskey into Lamont's mouth. The actor swallowed rapidly. Jephtha passed the empty glass to Fan and lowered Lamont's head to the pillow. When he pulled his left hand away, he noticed his fingertips bore faint stains. Something in him took pleasure in realizing Lamont dyed his hair.

Conscious of Fan waiting for the rest of the explanation, he resumed:

"I went to Canterbury Hall to get a story for the paper. I'd heard there might be trouble."

"I knew Edward was involved in something. But he wouldn't give me any particulars. Or allow me to go the performance—"

"He was smart. Actually, all he did was ask the Southerners in the hall to stand and sing 'Dixie's Land.' Rowdies from the other side started to tear the place apart. A couple of them dragged him to the basement of the theater to teach him a lesson, but some friends and I got him away before he was hurt too badly."

Fan relaxed a little. "I thank you for that, Jephtha. Of course, I knew you were in Washington—"

He couldn't keep bitterness from his voice:

"And I'm sure you're astonished I helped him at all." Softly: "Yes."

"I didn't do it entirely to be a good Samaritan. I had another reason. I'll tell you about it in the parlor."

He stood up. Lamont was asleep, his face smooth, his breathing regular. Fan's eyes kept moving back to his face.

"I think he looks worse than he feels," Jephtha said. "But there's a doctor coming just to make certain."

"You say he sang 'Dixie's Land'—?"

Jephtha nodded, angered again by the pride that showed in her eyes. Then a new thought jolted her:

"Will the police arrest him for—?"

"I doubt it. Singing has yet to be declared an act of treason. Don't worry yourself." Without thinking, he touched her arm.

The familiarity made her draw away. He took the glass and decanter from her hands and deposited them on the bedside table. As they started for the parlor, he added:

"When he wakes up, I'd advise you to keep him indoors a day or so. He won't be the most popular fellow in town."

"It'll be difficult for me to dictate to Edward," she said. Jephtha closed the bedroom door. On the parlor's far side, he saw another. Were the boys sleeping in there?

He realized Fan was still speaking:

"—he's quite fervent about the cause. So am I."

An awkward pause. This was very hard. How did you speak to a woman with whom you'd lived for the better part of a decade—and from whom you'd parted as an enemy? He caught himself glancing at her robe; remembering the contours of her body on their wedding night. He remembered the way her eyes had shone with joy during the ceremony. He had been equally joyful.

He thought of quiet breakfasts together, before Gideon was born. The feel of her sleeping close to him during chilly autumn nights. He recalled her struggle to overcome her loathing for the sex act in order to conceive the children they both wanted.

Sinking down into a chair—he was still stiff and pain-ridden—he felt sad and empty. He was flawed; so was she. They had both lost much that was good.

But what should he say to her? He was uncertain.

Fan paced, equally uncomfortable. She kept glancing

at Lamont's door. *Do anything you can to make this less difficult,* he thought. *She deserves it.*

He chose his words with care:

"I can understand your comment about restraining your husband. His courage is obvious. Unfortunately, he almost got himself killed because of it."

Fan stared at him. "That was the case when you helped papa's black wench escape."

No, Jephtha prayed. *Not the past.* He made an effort to shrug off the remark:

"Well, I'm not quite so zealous any longer. I still believe slavery's wrong. *And* secession. But——" He tried to smile. "——I'm somewhat less fierce in other ways."

Liar. Last night you were still thinking of hurting her. Even a few minutes ago, you hated her as much as ever——

But he concealed that truth, working to put her at ease:

"I'm not sure why it's happened. Maybe age has worn me away like water wears away a stone." Another tentative smile at his own expense. "I'm not exactly young any longer."

She sat down on the settee in the window bay, her shoulders drooping.

"I'm not either, Jephtha. I—I must say you're looking quite fit."

"Thank you. So are you."

"Working for the family paper apparently agrees with you."

He shrugged again; leaned back. He was tired, and wanted to get on to the central question. But something warned him to go slowly:

"Let's say I've learned how to handle the job. I've picked up some bad habits that go with it. Cigars. Alcohol——"

"And a touch of swearing." It wasn't said unkindly.

"Everything changes. What a person does. How he feels—" He was testing her.

Thankfully, he heard her murmur, "Yes. I—" She leaned forward. "I really am grateful to you. More grateful than I can say. I know how you feel about Edward's beliefs, and mine. What you did this evening— well, it brings back memories. Memories that make me feel extremely guilty."

"Fan, that wasn't the purpose of my helping—"

"I realize," she broke in. "Still, I can't help thinking of things I said in Lexington. I don't feel any less strongly about the—the differences that separated us. But if it's any consolation—"

He saw the pain this cost her. His heart softened. He wanted to cross and sit beside her; comfort her. But it would be improper. She was another man's wife. He stayed where he was and let her finish:

"—what you did for Edward makes me quite ashamed of—of some events in the past."

"Oh—" He looked rueful. "I expect it was inevitable that we'd separate. We only did in our marriage what the country took a bit longer to do."

"I'm particularly ashamed—"

"Fan, there's no need for this. Lexington's gone. We're different people."

She shook her head, defiantly; an echo of the stormy days they'd suffered. "You must let me finish. I *was* cruel. Especially in the things I said about you and your cousin."

"Amanda?"

"Yes. Accusing the two of you of trying to cheat the boys."

For a moment, suspicion deviled him again. Was she sincere—or only trying to find out if her sons were still wealthy?

He was chagrined by the thought. Hadn't he himself schemed deviously, just to gain entrance to this parlor where two strangers sat with their memories and old hurts?

"—I regret those accusations very much, Jephtha."

He was reassured. "You know I'd never deny my sons what's theirs."

"I've come to realize that."

"Each one of them will get a substantial inheritance when I die. In fact I've finally written a will to insure it. And I haven't touched a penny of the income from California. Nor the profits from its investment."

Now they were closer to the reason he was here; so close, he started breathing a little faster. Fan smiled in a wry way:

"Edward, I'm sorry to say, suspects just the opposite. Only yesterday, he wondered whether you'd cut the boys off. I don't know whether you'll believe me, but I told him I was sure you wouldn't. I told him I was wrong in Lexington. I said you were a fair, decent man—"

The gas shone on her carefully combed hair. He noticed more gray. "That was generous of you. But don't paint me as a saint. Tonight, I—" Tension curled his fingers against his palms. "—I also helped your husband because of the boys."

She frowned. "I don't understand."

"When I saw Lamont's name in the *Star*, I assumed you might be with him. But I didn't know whether you'd receive me. Or even speak to me—"

A sad smile. "I can appreciate why you'd think that."

"—and although it's true I wanted to stop the Pinker—the Yankee thugs at the theater, I also believed that if I did it, you'd be—more inclined to give me a few minutes. To tell me—"

He couldn't hold it back:

"Fan, are the boys well? Are they here?"

"They're all quite well."

He squeezed his eyes shut, startled by the feel of tears.

"Only Jeremiah is here, though. He's sleeping in the other bedroom."

"I'm surprised he didn't wake up when I came in."

"You really didn't make much noise. And young boys sleep very soundly. I sometimes think a fourteen year old could sleep through the last judgment."

He shook his head. "Fourteen. I've gotten confused. I'd have sworn Jeremiah was fifteen."

"No, he was born in June, remember?"

Jephtha's pale eyes glistened. "Yes, I do."

A rap on the hall door brought Fan to her feet. "Probably the doctor," Jephtha said. "But I'd better make sure."

He drew the pepperbox from his pocket, noticing her startled expression. He checked the revolving hammer nose to be certain it was in position to fire again, palmed the weapon and walked to the door.

"Who's there?"

A grumbly voice replied, "Doctor Butterfield."

Jephtha slipped the bolt to admit a white-haired, baggy-eyed fellow with a satchel. Judging by the smell, Dr. Butterfield had been summoned from a conference with a bottle. He nearly tripped as he entered.

While Jephtha rebolted the door, Butterfield said, "Something about an actor getting hurt—" He squinted at Jephtha. "You the actor?"

"He's in the bedroom."

"Sorry. Can't tell who's who these days. President looks like a farmer. General of the army looks like a pig with the bloat."

"It's the lady's husband," Jephtha advised him. "He was beaten severely at Canterbury Hall."

"Oh! That secesh fracas. Heard about it while I was drink—uh, before I was called."

"I don't think he's badly injured. But we'd like you to

verify it." Jephtha opened the bedroom door. Lamont lay on his side. He breathed with his mouth open, a raspy sound.

"Fee's one dollar." Butterfield stopped. "In advance."

"I have it, Fan—"

Deftly, Jephtha hid the Sharps in his pocket and hunted for a gold piece while Butterfield peered in at the patient. As Jephtha paid the fee, he noticed the doctor shift his attention to the whiskey decanter beside the bed.

"Thank you," Butterfield said, stifling a slight burp. He smoothed his lapel, a futile gesture to give himself a more professional appearance. It was impossible.

"A dollar for night calls, you understand—" he began, taking a step and tripping over the edge of the bedroom carpet. Somewhat sententiously, he said, "I'll report shortly." He closed the door in Jephtha's face.

Fan paced again. "I hope he's competent."

"I suppose we have to take the luck of the pot this time of night. Fan—"

"Yes?"

He went to her. Even grew bold enough to clasp his hands over hers. They were cold.

"Tell me about the boys."

"Well, let me see—" Self-conscious, she withdrew her hands. "Gideon's in Virginia. He went to Richmond to try to enlist in a military unit." Jephtha was overjoyed at the nearness of his eldest son, but alarmed at the thought of the boy having committed himself to the war so soon.

"He wants to join a cavalry troop," Fan continued. "Gideon started to ride when he was twelve. He's become very accomplished on Papa's horses. I understand volunteers must supply their own mounts. I'm sure Papa will give him one."

Jephtha forced himself to ask, "How is Captain Tunworth?"

"Not in good health. But he's glad the war has finally come."

Old men are always glad young men will fight for them, Jephtha thought.

"Are you glad?"

She looked straight into his eyes and he felt something akin to the old affection they'd shared.

"I don't know how to answer that, Jephtha."

"Why not? It's a simple question."

"No, it isn't. I think the South's been abused far too long. I believe in the doctrine of state sovereignty. The Union was freely created by separate states, and it can be dissolved just as freely. However, Mr. Lincoln's decided the question can only be settled on a battlefield."

"Sumter decided it, Fan."

"You may be right." She brushed at her forehead. "But no matter what the principles are, I'm not glad at all. I don't want anything to happen to my—to our sons."

Again that small, weary smile. "Gideon's a lot like you. He's as enthusiastic about his cause as you are—"

"Were."

"—about yours."

"Eager to fight?"

"Very. The moment he can find a horse troop that'll take him, he'll be coming back to say goodbye."

"Back here?" Jephtha couldn't keep elation from his voice. "How soon do you think that'll be?"

"In a few days I should imagine. He's a marvelous boy, Jephtha. Big. Good-looking—and he loves to sing. He has a very appealing voice. Of the three of them, he's also the one with the hottest temper." She twitted him gently: "I expect you're responsible. There was that Virginia grandmother of yours, on your father's side—"

"Elizabeth Fletcher. Elizabeth Kent," he amended.

"You always spoke of some strain she'd brought into the family—the Fletcher blood, wasn't that the name? Those who inherited it were always a little headstrong, you said. Even rebellious. I noticed it in you. I certainly see it in Gideon."

Jephtha pondered a moment. "I don't know how long the bridges to Virginia will be open. But if Gideon can get back, I'd like to see him."

"Of course."

He wanted to whoop and hug her. "What about Matthew? Is he here?"

She frowned, returning to the settee. "Matt's been a problem."

"How so?"

"He's even less of a scholar than Gideon. I've tried to teach the boys mathematics and science and some literature while they traveled with us. But Matthew simply balked at schooling. Two years ago Edward and I were at a loss to know what to do. We finally gave him permission to try something he said appealed to him."

"What?"

"He's a seaman. Well, actually a mess boy. On a Charleston cotton packet called the *Prince of Carolina*."

"Good God! I'd never have imagined he'd like that sort of life."

"I think he just wanted to get away. I worry about him among all those foul-talking sailors. But he *is* almost seventeen. And he sounds happy. Here—"

Moving to a secretary, she produced two folded sheets.

"This is his last letter. Written a week ago, from New Orleans."

Jephtha took the sheets. The handwriting was clear and bold. "At least his penmanship's passable."

"More than that. He lettered a card for my birthday

that was positively beautiful. In the letter, you'll come across a reference to sketches—"

"He draws?"

"Quite well. He's completely self-taught."

"He certainly doesn't get the ability from me."

Fan shared his smile. "Nor me. Sometimes I suppose talent just—appears in a person. I'll show you two samples of his work when you've finished reading."

The letter was addressed to *Dear Mama and Edward.* Jephtha experienced another moment of malicious pleasure because his son hadn't referred to Lamont as father. He read on:

> *We are docked in New Orlens, which is a prety town and full of nigras and prety dark-skinned girls, Creols the captain calls them. I enjoy looking at them and sketching them but have not met any personly, I supose I am too young.*

"You're right, he's no student," Jephtha smiled. "I've never seen such spelling and punctuation."

Fan laughed. "More a lack of it, I'd say."

> *Mama I know you have urged me to atend worship but we are busy putting on a new load of cotton and admiring those Creol girls and that leaves me very little time to draw so all I have done is visit a Cathedrel which is very famus in town and catholic and very old but full of lovly figurs of church persons, really very prety.*
> *All hands are hapy with Capt. McGill, he makes us work like devils but to a purpose, we have a trim vesel and always offers of more cargo than we can carry. The captain does not talk much with the crew, he is stern I guess you would say. When not on deck he is in his cabin playing a mouth organ, music is something he loves very much. He has*

*been kind to me though, asked me many questions
about our family even the Kents in the north, I
have a feeling he hates the idea of war thinks it is
mad. I cant explain why he seems to be easy with
me when I make mistaks but he is. I dont think he
would have let anyone else draw him though I
may just be showing off my own fethers saying
that.*

*There is a lot of talk of war here they write out the
news from Montgomry on boards in front of the
newspaper ofices, also many picturs of Mr Davis
are displayed. They talk of a new flag and every-
ones whistling or huming "Dixie's Land"—well
that is all my news except to say I have put in two
drawings I hope you will like, I have saved the
ones of Creol girls for when I get lonesom at sea!!
I will write again when we make port in Charleston*

*Your loving son,
Matthew.*

"Thank you for letting me read it." Jephtha handed
the letter back, musing: "McGill—McGill—I remember! I knew it had a familiar sound. When I arrived in
New York, they told me a clipper captain named
McGill attended Amanda's funeral."

"Was he a Southerner?"

"I don't recall."

"I wonder if it could be the same man."

"You saw the reference to questions about the family. It might be."

"Then I'd feel a little less apprehensive. Here—I
want you to see the sketches—"

Jephtha examined the charcoal drawings of the dock
workers and Matthew's skipper. "Fan, the boy has remarkable talent."

"He does. But he's too carefree."

"He's young yet."

"I think he'll be the same way all his life. He's not interested in anything that can lead to a proper career."

"As long as he's content, does it matter?"

"No, I imagine not. With that Fletcher blood, he's very likely to do as he pleases regardless of what anyone says."

"Oh, how I'd love to see him!"

Jephtha laid the sketches aside, his eye drawn toward the door of the other bedroom. "And Jeremiah—?"

She held out her hand. "Come."

Her smile and the outstretched hand made Jephtha ashamed of all the hate he'd harbored; ashamed too of the cruel faultiness of his own thinking. The passage of time had changed him. But he'd never granted that it could do the same for Fan. He took her hand.

She opened the bedroom door quietly. Whispered: "I'll wake him if you wish."

He almost said yes. Then he shook his head:

"It might startle him too much. I mean, being roused and confronted by a father he hasn't seen in years. I doubt if he remembers me well. He was only six or so when I left Lexington. Perhaps you can tell him I was here. I'll speak to him when I meet Gideon. I'll go in for a moment, if I may—"

"He's your son, too, Jephtha."

She stood aside.

ii

Fan left the door halfway open. The parlor gaslight spread dimly across Jeremiah's bed.

Fearing he'd wake his son—and fearful of his own emotions as well—Jephtha stole to the bedside and gazed down at the stocky, ruddy-cheeked boy breathing slowly in deep slumber.

One of Jeremiah's hands rested on top of the cover. Jephtha knelt. He stretched out his right hand, mingled love and pain welling within him.

Jeremiah stirred. Turned his head on the pillow. Spoke a few muffled syllables.

When he was quiet again, Jephtha touched his hand and cried silently, without shame.

iii

He cried from the profound and wondrous joy of touching one of his three earthly links with immortality; one of his three triumphs over the death that waited for every human being.

Then, like an ugly intruder, came the thought that Jeremiah was, in a way, forever lost to him. He could taste the salt of his own tears as he grieved over the unbridgeable chasm created by the past; by his own fanaticism, and Fan's.

He remembered a passage from II Samuel. His lips formed silent words of love and loss; the words of David—

" '*O Absalom, my son, my son!*' "

Slowly, he bent forward. Jeremiah's hand smelled of soap. Jephtha put his lips against the warm skin; the gentlest of kisses.

Restless, the boy moved again. Jephtha rose quickly. He backed toward the door and Fan's waiting shadow. When he emerged, she was stricken silent by the glow of his smile and the pain in his eyes.

"He—he's turned into a fine-looking young man, he—"

The door of the other bedroom opened. Doctor Butterfield lurched out, fumbling with the clasp of his satchel. Jephtha spun and walked to the window bay,

facing the dark outside so the doctor couldn't see his
tears.

iv

"—nothing broken that I can detect," Butterfield
said. "Swabbed his face clean. Also dressed the worst
cut and gave him a drop of a tincture to help him sleep.
He'll be up and about tomorrow. Sore as hell, though.
Poor fellow took quite a pounding. Would you—ah—
care to have me drop back and examine him in the afternoon?"

"Yes, I'd appreciate it," Fan said. Jephtha sniffed.
The doctor smelled like a distillery. During the exami-
nation, the doctor had evidently sharpened his diagnos-
tic skills with the aid of the bedside decanter.

"Happy to—happy!" Butterfield weaved toward the
door. "Physician's sacred duty to look after his patients! Shall we say—" Another belch. "Beg pardon.
Four o'clock?"

"Fine."

The hall door closed. A moment later, they heard a
loud thud and an outpouring of curses. Fan sighed:

"I'm glad we didn't hire him to perform surgery."

Though Jephtha smiled, he felt sorry for the shabby
doctor. A man haunted. But then, what man or woman
wasn't?

"I expect I'd better be going too—" he began.

"I thank you again for your help and compassion."

"And I thank you for letting me see Jeremiah. For
telling me about Gideon, and Matt."

"When we were back in Lexington—"

"Fan, no more. That's over."

"I have to say this to you. So it'll be off my conscience. You know I thought you were a bad influence—"

"Satanic!" His smile faded. "I still could be. I told you I haven't changed my views——"

"Yes, but you're—you're not wicked, and I claimed you were. I'd never deny you the right to see the boys."

Despite his intentions, remembered wrath got the better of him:

"I'll admit it wasn't pleasant when you refused to answer my letters asking about them."

"Edward and I—that is—I accept the responsibility. Not replying was wrong. What can I say except I hope you can forgive me?"

"Completely."

"I *have* changed, Jephtha."

"We both have. That's good."

She couldn't know how fervently he meant those words. Never again would he have to fear his own anger.

At the door, he said, "You've made me very happy tonight. So let me offer what I hope is a helpful word. You and Lamont shouldn't stay in Washington much longer."

"Because we're Southerners?"

"Zealous ones—and after tonight, notorious ones—why are you smiling?"

"Because Edward *is* a zealot. In many ways he reminds me of you twenty years ago." Softly: "I sometimes ask myself if that's one reason I married him——"

She brightened. "In any case, I appreciate your concern. I'll tell Edward what you said, though I'm sure he'll want to express his thanks in person before we go." She thought a second. "The instant Gideon's back from Richmond, I'll send you a note."

"Send it to Mrs. Emerson's boarding house. On G Street. Any of the nigra bootblacks outside the hotel will know where it is."

"Mrs. Emerson's," Fan repeated. "I'll remember."

"One last word. I—" He conquered his jealously. "—I'm pleased you've found some happiness."

Surprisingly, she saddened. "There's not much happiness in thinking of Gideon being drawn into a war. Even a short one."

"I know. But the Kents have always been somewhat pig-headed on one point."

"What's that?"

"Living without principles, or refusing to act on those principles, isn't living, just cowardice. I loathe the thought of Gideon going to war. I don't believe in his cause. But his willingness to risk himself proves he's a Kent. I'm proud of him. And eternally grateful to you—"

Though he knew he shouldn't, he leaned forward to kiss Fan's cheek. For a space of seconds, she pressed her fingertips lightly against his chin.

He drew back. "Good night, Fan."

He hurried down the hall, happy beyond belief. The Sharps pepperbox in his pocket was forgotten. So was Edward Lamont's peculiar behavior in the hack.

He left the National by the main door leading to Pennsylvania Avenue. In a hurry to reach G Street, he failed to see the watchers lurking in front of an unlighted shop a few doors from the hotel.

A hand caught his arm; whirled him around—

"Hold on, Mister!"

The bile of terror welled in his throat. There were three of them. One took a firmer grip on Jephtha's arm. A second shoved the point of a long Bowie knife against his shirt.

The knife-wielder twisted the handle a quarter turn. On the blade, Jephtha saw a dark patch—

Dried blood.

V

"You got any official business on the streets?" the man with the knife demanded.

Anger overcame fear. Jephtha wrenched back from the Bowie:

"Who the hell are you to be asking?"

"Never mind, just answer," said the man all but hidden in the darkness behind the other two. Jephtha recognized the voice:

"Moore? Call off these fools! You know me."

Solomon Moore stepped forward. He was a grizzled Republican from Ohio. He'd come to the city hoping to find a political appointment. Jephtha had spoken with him twice at Willard's.

"Jephtha Kent!" Moore exclaimed. "I didn't make you out right off—sorry. Ease up, boys."

The two men accompanying Moore relaxed. One reached for a cigar. Jephtha thought he spied a holstered revolver under the man's coat.

"What the devil is this, Moore? Where do you get off stopping people on Pennsylvania Avenue?"

The man with the Bowie growled, "We belong to the new Cash Clay battalion. Organized tonight. We're patrolling the avenue and the side streets. Senator Lane's Frontier Guards are watching the grounds of President's Park. You're still going to explain where you're headed—"

"The hell I am! Moore knows I'm no secesh."

"For a fact," Moore confirmed. "Put the knife away, Luther."

Luther didn't respond. Jephtha shuddered. The Dorns of the world were taking over.

The second man said, "We oughta warn him, Solomon."

"Warn me about what?"

"I just wouldn't traipse around after dark," Moore said.

Luther said, "We come across a loudmouth from Alabama half an hour ago. He got feisty. Wouldn't tell us why he was out."

The second man chuckled. "Now he's walkin' around with his cock halfway up his bung."

The man with the Bowie licked his thumb and stroked the dried blood on the blade. "There's boys from the patrol all over. Next time, Moore might be blocks away."

"I'll bear that in mind." Jephtha's tone said just the opposite.

Moore was irked: "If you don't, you're stupid."

The trio drifted back toward the National. Jephtha went the opposite way, his ebullient mood ruined. On both sides, the hatreds were growing worse and worse—

He thought of the bully with the knife. Of the savagery of the Canterbury riot. And of the animal that hid inside every man; even himself.

In wartime, men made allowances. It was permissible to let the animal out of his pen. And if he maimed—slew—well, that was acceptable—

So long as he maimed or slew an enemy.

The night's events made Jephtha think more realistically about his sons. Especially Gideon.

If the war proved to be anything but short and relatively bloodless, Gideon would face other young men who had been told, *Let the animal free. It's your sacred duty.*

When that happened, Gideon could suffer the fate of the Biblical Absalom; could die because of his own dedication; be slain by the beasts a war let loose.

Until now, Jephtha really hadn't accepted the possibility. At last, he did.

Gideon could *die.*

If the war was long, Matt could be drawn in—
Even Jeremiah.

And he might one day find himself repeating the words he'd whispered in Jeremiah's room, but speaking them as King David had—over a still body; the flesh of his flesh.

He walked faster along the deserted avenue, fear for his sons his sole companion.

vi

In a cramped, untidy boarding house room off Seventh Street, Josiah Cheever set to work.

The bolted door protected him from interruption. An oil lamp illuminated the tiny desk. Despite his aching ribs—he'd been punched three times escaping from Canterbury Hall—he smiled as his pen rasped across the sheet, inscribing the date. He thought a moment, then wrote:

> *As you will no doubt read in the Washington newspapers which I understand reach you regularly via trusted messengers similar to the one who will deliver this report, our mutual friend endangered himself and our larger plan this evening. However, his performance at C. H. conclusively demonstrated the depth of his loyalty.*
>
> *I have learned he escaped safely from C. H. after the melee, though I do not know how. I was also advised that the object of our common interest was in the audience. I did not see him—a fact I regret somewhat. The attendant confusion might have presented an opportunity for the quick accomplishment of our objective. There were weapons in evidence. Many persons were hurt. I myself narrowly avoided severe injury at the hands of two*

*who disliked the sentiments our mutual friend de-
livered from the stage. Given those circumstances,
a man might well have perished without undue notice as to whether he had been "helped along."*

Cheever's upper lip glistened as he read over the last
few words. He pressed his legs together beneath the
desk, feeling an almost sexual excitement. He inked the
pen and continued:

*However, I know that if I had acted as suggested
above, our mutual friend would be upset, perhaps
to the point of withdrawing his cooperation. He
insists on proceeding at his own pace, so as not to
unduly arouse his wife's suspicions. He further insists upon superintending all arrangements; takes a
certain pleasure in it, I suspect. Although the delay
is annoying, I believe we must humor him, for he
is on our side; and invaluable. This is especially true
now that I have at last convinced him of the realism
of our position—viz., that confronted as we are by
the superior manpower and resources of the enemy,
we may not win a war in a matter of weeks or
months; the struggle may be long and—most important—costly. Thanks to my efforts, our mutual
friend now shares that view, and is no longer swayed
by the thoughtless fools who claim quick success is
an absolute certainty. I do not mean to imply that
we must not strive for a quick success—or that it is
utterly impossible to achieve. I mean we must always
have an alternate plan. Therefore, we must continue
to allow our mutual friend a certain latitude.
But I can state the following as a fact. With my
assistance and encouragement, he will—*

Cheever paused to slash three underscores beneath
the last word.

—make certain "Parson K" departs this earth accompanied by the everlasting gratitude of all who serve the cause. On my honor I pledge to you that the anticipated departure will take place reasonably soon. At that time we shall reap the benefits; I trust a righteous God has withdrawn Heavenly rewards for damn yankees.

The clerk chewed the end of the pen a moment, admiring the sardonic quality of his phrasing. To heighten the effect, he added his customary code signature:

Cameron.

He laid the pen aside, rose and took a small brass key from the pocket of his soiled trousers. He burrowed in a smelly, two-week-old pile of laundry in the closet. He uncovered a valise and unlocked it with the key.

From a slit in the valise's lining, he removed a small book. The cover measured four by two inches. The book was less than a quarter inch thick.

With the proper rice paper pages open to the lamplight, he readied a clean sheet. He referred to the book frequently as he rewrote the original message using the correct substitution cipher for the week. The emerging translation was a pattern of letter groupings that would make no sense if the courier to Richmond were captured and the hollow heel of his farmer's boot discovered.

CHAPTER VIII

The Bait

WHEN JEPHTHA BURST INTO the kitchen of the boarding house, Bertha screamed and dropped five dinner plates she was pulling from a tub of rinse water. The black woman's temper exploded before the shards of china stopped rattling on the floor:

"Lord God, Mr. Jephtha, you want to give me a seizure? Look what you done!"

"I'll buy a whole new set to replace 'em!"

She squealed as he caught her around the waist, lifted and whirled her.

"Mr. Jephtha, you put me down! You gone completely crazy? Miz Molly'll have a conniption fit when I tell her about the plates!"

"Then don't tell her. I'll slip you the money for the new ones next time I get paid—"

Breathing hard—he was tired, and Bertha was an armful—he set the black woman on the floor. She gasped when he planted a big smacking kiss on her cheek.

She pursed her lips. "I know you take a drop now an' then. But I never seen you skunk drunk before."

"Bertha, I'm not drunk."

"Well, you could fool me."

"Is Molly still up?"

"No. She was worn out from worryin' about you. She went to bed early."

"Then I'll have to wake her."

He dashed out of the kitchen, leaving Bertha staring after him in bewilderment.

She kicked at the litter of dish fragments, then shook her head. Jephtha Kent grinning like a fool and capering like a schoolboy was just one more symptom of the craziness infecting Washington City like a disease.

ii

He stole into the dark of Molly's bedroom. Smelled the familiar, warm scent of her. Slipped to the edge of the bed and sat down carefully.

He found her temple; brushed his palm across her unbound hair:

"Molly? Molly, I'm back—"

She sat up with violent suddenness. "Who is it? *Bertha*—!"

He pressed a hand over her mouth. "Sssh! Nobody's come to rob you."

"*Jephtha?*" Some of the sleepiness was gone from her voice.

"It's me. Safe and whole. Molly, I saw her! She's going to let me talk to the boys. Jeremiah's right in the hotel—he was asleep. Gideon's in Richmond, hoping to enlist on the other side. But he'll be back. She's going to send a note around when he—"

"Jephtha, wait!"

"What?"

"First you wake me up and then you talk so fast I can't make sense of it—" Molly pressed against his arm as she sat up straighter. The warm feel of her soft breast heightened his exhilaration.

"I've been scared to death all day. And it's your fault."

"Why?"

"Right after you left, I discovered my gun was gone.

I thought—I thought you might be planning to use it on—"

She stopped.

"On Fan?" He laughed. "Never. I took it because I thought I should be prepared in case there was a row at the theater. I should have told you, but I was in a hurry—"

It was not quite the truth, he admitted to himself. If things had worked out differently, his anger might have driven him to use the Sharps to force Fan to—

Don't think that way. You were wrong about her.

"You're damn right you should have told me!" Molly leaned her cheek against his. "I fretted the whole day—" More quietly: "You had no trouble with her?"

"None. She's changed, Molly. Mellowed. Oh, she's still partisan. But we had a cordial visit—"

He slipped off his coat and let it fall on the floor, then put his arm around her. "Of course I paved the way by helping her husband out of a little scrape. I suppose you heard about what happened at the Canterbury—?"

He felt her head nod against his stubbled cheek. He needed to wash up. He felt filthy. The aches caused by the fight were hurting again.

"One of the boarders—Mr. Fly—was there," she said. "And white as milk when he got back. He said he didn't show favoritism to either side. But someone nearly bashed his head in anyway. I want you to tell me about it. Right from the beginning."

"Of course. But the most important part relates to what you said last night. About looking for the goodness in Fan. It's there, Molly. It's really there."

Tenderly: "You sound as if you're ready to cry."

"Damn near am—"

He sniffed; cleared his throat. Then he described the evening's events, including the encounter with Dorn, though he minimized the severity of the fight. She reached for the lamp:

"I want to see how badly he hurt you. Jephtha, let go of my wrist!"

"Molly, I'm fine. Couldn't be better—believe me."

She stopped struggling. His voice dropped to a near whisper:

"When I knocked on the door at the National, I still didn't have much hope. But some things do come out right after all—"

He finished telling her about the talk with Fan. She didn't speak immediately. He thumped his boots down beside the bed, unbuttoned his shirt and trousers and slid them off. He added his singlet and underdrawers to the pile and negotiated his way to the washstand. The water was tepid, but he felt better after scrubbing and drying his face and hands. As he was hanging the damp towel on its peg, she said:

"Jephtha?"

"Mmm?"

"I'm thankful you'll get to visit with your boys."

"You? How do you think I feel!"

"I can hear it in your voice. I'm happy for you for another reason, too. Lately, you haven't seen much of—" She sounded hesitant. "—of God's handiwork in anything."

"I know."

Naked, he stretched out beside her, holding back a groan. He worked his left arm under her shoulder, kissed her cheek.

"I know," he repeated. "I'd like to think it was God's work and not just luck." Hugging her, he pulled up the cover with the other hand. "Whichever it was, I haven't felt so good in years."

She kissed the corner of his mouth. "With everyone in Washington so angry and afraid, finding a little goodness in the world is almost a miracle."

"Yes. And you helped it happen. Without you, I'd never have been able to go to her. *Or* keep my temper."

He was troubled that he still wasn't admitting everything. He remembered his rage over Fan's first confused accusations about hurting Lamont. But he didn't mention it, whispering instead:

"I thank you."

"Well—" She was only half teasing. "—saving a good man from a bad impulse is more important than saving string or butcher's paper."

He wrapped her in his arms and drew her tight against him, reveling in the feel of her supple body and soft hair against his face. He found her mouth; kissed her—

Molly murmured. The tension seemed to drain from her. The lovemaking that followed was a celebration; an outpouring of their mutual relief and happiness, and a temporary escape from the anguish of a city and a land growing darker by the hour.

Afterward, they fell asleep in each other's arms.

iii

Next morning—Wednesday—Jephtha rose at sunup. He ignored Molly's plea that he let her treat the purpling marks on his face, snatched a slice of bread for breakfast and went directly to the *Evening Star* office. He spent two hours completing a dispatch describing the riot at Canterbury Hall, pausing only to light a cigar, say good morning to the Negro sweep or fend off sarcastic or bawdy questions about his distinctly unclerical bruises.

As he was gathering up his copy to take it to the telegraph office, one of the *Star*'s reporters, a likable chap named Van Dyne, arrived at his desk across the aisle.

"Abe's gag order isn't holding fast, Jephtha." Van

Dyne waggled a fist full of notes. "I've been to State and War. A few loose tongues are getting looser."

Jephtha stuffed his dispatch in his pocket. "What have you got?" He and Van Dyne had shared sources and information before.

"First, a general impression. The town *is* unprotected. Panic's setting in. For specifics, I picked up these—" He spread the notes on the desk top. "Snippets of some of the telegraph messages from governors who said no to the appeal for troops. Listen to old John Letcher down in Richmond—"

Van Dyne read aloud:

"Militia of Virginia will not be furnished to the powers at Washington—so on and so on—*your object is to subjugate the Southern states*—so on—*an object, in my judgment, not within the purview of the Constitution*—now here's the gut of it. *You have chosen to inaugurate civil war, and having done so, we will meet it in a spirit as determined as the Administration has exhibited toward the South."*

Jephtha whistled. "Pretty stiff."

"But predictable. And mild in comparison to some of the rest—" He picked out another sheet. *"Kentucky will furnish no troops for the wicked purpose of subduing her sister Southern states."*

"Lincoln was hoping Kentucky'd support him."

"Well, Magoffin's a stubborn old bastard. That's probably his final word. It gets worse. Here's Isham Harris. *Tennessee will not furnish a single man for purposes of coercion, but fifty thousand if necessary for the defense of our rights and those of our Southern brethren."* He turned the paper over. "Governor Jackson of Missouri. Note his admirable restraint—" He pointed to the phrases one by one. *"Unholy crusade. Illegal, unconstitutional, and revolutionary in its object, inhuman and diabolica*l . . . Oh, yes. One more—" Van Dyne smiled wearily. *"Cannot be complied with."*

Jephtha shook his head. "If Lincoln loses all the border states, the situation's worse than ever."

"Correct. I'm beginning to wonder if Abe's as smart as they say. Maybe he shouldn't have requested troops from men like Magoffin and Jackson."

"I suppose he was gambling they'd at least stay neutral."

"If he was, he lost the throw. Virginia's the key, though. The state everyone's waiting for—" He spun in his chair and shouted, "Mr. Wallach? Anything from Dennis in Richmond?"

"Not yet, Mr. Van Dyne." The *Star*'s editor was a salty, paradoxical little man. He was a Democrat; strongly sympathetic to the South, yet insistent on the preservation of the Union. He added, "Either the secession convention's still sitting, or the young whelp's malingering in some saloon. Knowing Mr. Dennis, it could be both."

Jephtha said to Van Dyne, "I talked to your man who covers the depot. He said there's still no word on when the Pennsylvania and Massachusetts troops will arrive."

"If they don't get here, we're in bad straits." Van Dyne rubbed his eyes. "I should have stayed in Louisville. I thought working on a Washington paper would promote my career. Instead, I've promoted myself onto a sinking ship. Without lifeboats." He gathered up his notes and started to write.

Jephtha set off for the telegraph office in the glowing sunlight. He wasn't cheered by what he'd learned from Van Dyne. More and more, Washington City had the feel of an enclave surrounded by enemies. Enemies who would strike soon, and hard.

iv

The city's situation deteriorated even further during the rest of the day. Jephtha spent the late morning and early afternoon visiting government departments in search of usable material. Van Dyne hadn't exaggerated. The mood was the same everywhere: anxiety bordering on outright panic.

Talking off the record, a contact at the War Department spoke of two major dangers. First, for communication with the rest of the country, Washington was completely dependent on the telegraph wires and the single B & O line from Baltimore. Second, Federal facilities in the area stood a good chance of being captured if, as reliable sources said, Virginia militiamen were already massing in the state capital. Of chief concern were Fort Monroe guarding the entrance to Chesapeake Bay; Harper's Ferry with its store of arms and valuable tools for the manufacture of rifles; and the huge Gosport Navy Yard down at Norfolk. All three were vulnerable to a swift thrust from Richmond.

Back at the *Star* in the late afternoon, Jephtha described the danger in his second dispatch of the day. While he was writing, a boy brought him a telegraph message from Theo Payne. The editor again demanded the Lee interview.

Jephtha threw Payne's message on the floor and kept writing. Moments later, a reporter dropped a small envelope on his paper-strewn desk:

"Nigger kid just delivered this to the front door."

Jephtha laid his pen aside. The envelope was addressed to *Mr. J. Kent, Esq., c/o Evening Star Offices.* The handwriting was beautiful but unmistakably masculine.

He opened the envelope. When he noted the signature, his brows shot up in surprise.

My dear Kent:
Feeling much better this morning. Thus I am moved to thank you again for your brave action on my behalf. Though you and I, of necessity, can never share the same political views, I respect and admire your courage. I have been wishing I could express my gratitude in a more tangible manner. A new development suggests that perhaps I can. Although information I receive from my fellow Southerners is sketchy in the extreme, one visitor this morning did offer a tidbit you might find useful. I was led to understand that when Union troops bound for this city attempt to pass through Baltimore, certain combinations of men will make the passage difficult if not impossible. I have no idea whether the information is reliable; very possibly not. But if it is reliable, and circulating to a person such as myself, with no official connections whatsoever, it is not precisely secret. Therefore I need not feel guilty about relaying it to you for your professional use.
Last evening I saw proof that you are a man of probity. Therefore, I trust you will not reveal the source of the above information, but only utilize it as you see fit.
Tendering once again my most sincere thanks for your help, I remain

Yours obediently,
Edw. Lamont

Jephtha stared at the large, ostentatious signature. He tried to detect any hint of speciousness in the letter. He couldn't; Washington was indeed flooded with rumors that the divided citizenry of Maryland might interfere

with the soldiers headed for the capital. Lamont had
done little more than provide a confirmation—though a
pretty strong one.

The tip might be worth a follow-up. There was one
problem. As he'd told Van Dyne, no one knew exactly
when the relief regiments would be coming through Baltimore.

He decided to ignore the lead temporarily. He laid
the letter on the desk. It was probably wiser to stay in
Washington than go chasing up to Baltimore after a
story that might or might not materialize.

v

On Thursday the mail trains began to run late. The
Star's man assigned to the depot reported stories of
mobs wandering the Baltimore streets after dark. That
same morning, Jephtha learned, Colonel Lee rode in
across Long Bridge, bound on some mysterious errand.

The clerks and assistant secretaries taking a late
breakfast at Willard's had haggard faces. In the government offices, the lamps had burned until sunrise. The
pattern would continue, as more and more men with
Southern loyalties resigned their posts and left shrinking
staffs to handle increasingly heavier work loads.

Defense planning was made more difficult by a lack
of information, weary men complained to Jephtha. Additional troops were said to be coming from Rhode Island. The elegant and prestigious Seventh New York
was also on the way.

But when would the troops arrive? Where would they
be housed? How would they be fed? No one seemed to
know—

Just as no one seemed prepared to answer the most
crucial question:

Would they come in time?

By late afternoon, Jephtha was starved. He hadn't
eaten anything since breakfast. And he was worn out
from rushing between the hotels and President's Park.

But the effort had finally yielded one piece of important news. John Nicolay had told him that, the preceding evening, the Virginia convention had finally voted
eighty-eight to fifty-five in favor of an ordinance of secession. Governor Letcher had alerted all of the state's
volunteer regiments to be prepared for immediate service.

Jephtha raced back to the *Star* to write his copy. A
sense of obligation made him stop at Wallach's desk
and pass along the information. Instantly, Wallach
yelled a stop-press order.

Reporters streamed toward the editor. Jephtha repeated his news and Wallach began issuing assignments.
Men ran for the door. Others dashed for pens and copy
paper. In the pandemonium Jephtha went to his own
desk, where he discovered another sealed envelope.

It too bore a man's handwriting. But the script wasn't
Lamont's.

He tore the envelope open. When he saw the signature, he grew uneasy.

> *Dear Sir.*
> *As I stated to you on Monday, I have always been
> an admirer of the man who was audacious rather
> than hesitant. Battles are never won by the faint-
> hearted.*
> *Consequently, your unexpected arrival at my resi-
> dence may have generated responses on my part
> which were ill advised.*
> *I have this day come to Washington for private
> conferences with Mr. F. P. Blair, Sr., and my com-
> manding officer.*

.Jephtha knew then something important had happened. Francis P. Blair was the head of one of the most powerful political families in the nation, the Blairs of Maryland. He and his son Montgomery, the Postmaster General, were channels through which Lincoln sometimes spoke when he didn't wish to speak directly.

The conversations were entirely confidential. But they reflected, in part, some of my utterances to you on Monday.

Thus I have concluded I must ask you, as a gentleman, not to discuss, write, or otherwise disseminate what passed between us.

To make certain my request is granted, I appeal to, and depend on, your sense of honor. I deeply regret any inconvenience I may have caused you.

Humbly & faithfully yours,

R. E. Lee

"Damnation!"

Van Dyne turned to stare as Jephtha flung the letter on the floor and sat down to contemplate this latest turn of events.

In the signature, Lee had omitted his rank. Jephtha thought that was significant. From intuition and experience, he could piece together the events leading to the letter.

Virginia was out of the Union, which prompted Lee to come to Washington. Through Blair, the President had probably offered him command of the Federal forces—and Lee, visiting Winfield Scott, had refused. If the colonel hadn't already handed in his resignation, Jephtha was sure he'd do so shortly.

Feeling frustrated, he kicked the locked drawer where he'd put the Lee notes and copy. Some reporters he knew would have cheerfully ignored the colonel's let-

ter. He was tempted—especially when he thought of
Theo Payne.

But he couldn't let Payne's reaction influence him.
The drawer would remain locked.

In twenty minutes he'd prepared his dispatch for
transmission to New York. As he rose to leave, he noticed the arrangement of the papers on his desk. Looking more closely, he found that some notes for the Canterbury Hall dispatch were missing. So was the letter
from Lamont.

He cursed again—unheard this time because of the
uproar in the lamplit room. Jim, the slow-witted sweep
boy, was undoubtedly the culprit. The notes and letters
had probably fallen on the floor. No great loss. But if
they'd been important—

Reluctantly, he decided he'd better interrupt Wallach
and mention it.

He was moving toward the editor's desk when young
Dennis, the reporter assigned to Richmond, burst into
the room:

"We've got a stop-press, Mr. Wallach!"

Wallach jumped up. "About time you came back!
That free nigra you hired to ride up here with your last
story took twice as long as he should have!"

"Sorry, sir," Dennis panted as Jephtha and the other
reporters crowded around. "They weren't—shall we
say—too friendly at the Richmond telegraph office. I
thought a courier was the safest way. I damn near wore
out three horses myself."

"Something big?"

"Yes, sir. I assume you know about the convention
vote—"

"Kent there brought the word from the presidential
mansion. Don't tell me that's all you've got—?"

"No, sir. An exclusive—I don't think it went out on
the Richmond wire. The Virginia militia's on the march."

All around Jephtha, men started talking excitedly. Wallach shouted:

"Let him finish! How many troops, Dennis?"

"At least a thousand. It must have been planned Monday or Tuesday. They started leaving the city the minute the convention voted."

"Heading where?"

Dennis wiped his perspiring face. The trip from Richmond was nearly a hundred miles. The young reporter looked exhausted.

"According to a source I trust, Harper's Ferry."

More commotion. Dennis added:

"I expect the troops are in position by now. Or getting close—"

"We've already got a stop-press going. We'll add that." Mollified, he added a curt, "Good work."

Dennis looked wearily grateful as he sank to the edge of a desk, only to jerk like a puppet when Wallach pointed at him:

"I want half a dozen paragraphs right away. Some of the rest of you help him. Barlow, you know the situation at the armory and the arsenal—"

"Not exactly favorable to the Union side," Barlow drawled. "At last report, Lieutenant Jones commanded forty-two regular infantrymen."

"Jesus!" another man said. "Forty-two against a thousand—"

"Jones will have to pull out," said a third. "Burn the place."

"He'd better do a good job," Barlow commented. "There are three or four thousand rifle barrels and gun locks stored there. Plus the manufacturing tools. If you want a nice irony, Mr. Wallach, Lieutenant Jones is Robert E. Lee's distant cousin."

"I want a story!" Wallach snapped. "Get busy, Dennis. We'll hold the press until we get the report from the depot."

"Some troops finally arriving?" Jephtha asked.

"Hell, don't give the competition any help," someone called sarcastically. "Let the reverend do his own digging."

Wallach spun. "The reverend has two virtues you don't, Mr. Cooper. He shares his information—as you'd know if you'd been here half an hour ago. And when he writes his copy, he's sober. Yes, Kent, a train's bringing in the Pennsylvania volunteers between six and seven. We received a wire from Baltimore."

Jephtha headed for the door, light-headed. His belly ached from emptiness. But it would stay empty for several more hours. The news from Richmond and the depot was more important than his hunger.

Outside the *Star,* he saw several of Cash Clay's special guards patrolling on the other side of the street. They didn't bother to conceal their holstered sidearms or their sheathed Bowies. Two wagons loaded with household goods went by, the first driven by a middle-aged man who had his wife and adolescent daughter on the seat beside him. A black man—the white man's slave?—drove the other wagon. On all the faces, Jephtha saw fear.

He stood a moment in the lowering light of the April afternoon, wondering about Gideon. Could he be among the thousand advancing on Harper's Ferry?

He hoped not. But he knew Gideon's commitment to the cause would lead him into a battle eventually, along with the sons of countless other fathers—

Hurrying toward the telegraph office, he recalled yet another of the hundreds of passages of Scripture that had become a part of him during his years in the ministry. The verse from Isaiah, chapter sixty, seemed to sum up the chaos into which the country was plunging:

"For, behold, the darkness shall cover the earth, and gross darkness the people—"

He found the remainder of the verse—promising that

the light and glory of the Lord would dispel the darkness—impossible to believe.

vi

At the telegraph office, he expanded the Richmond convention story to include four paragraphs about Harper's Ferry. While the clerk was putting the dispatch on the wire, he quickly wrote a second, shorter message. There was no way to soften the news for Payne:

> COLONEL LEE IN WASHINGTON TODAY. SUSPECT HIS RESIGNATION TENDERED OR FORTHCOMING. LEE REQUESTED I WITHHOLD COMMENTS HE GAVE MONDAY. WILL HONOR THE REQUEST. WILL ATTEMPT TO LEARN DETAILS OF HIS VISITS TO BLAIR SENIOR AND GENERAL SCOTT.

While the clerk hovered, Jephtha stared at the words with a rueful smile. What a fool he was. A priceless story—and solely his. Other reporters wouldn't have—

Enough. He'd made up his mind. He added J. KENT and gave the dispatch to the clerk.

Doing so raised another problem. He'd failed to come up with a single solid and exclusive piece since the firing on Sumter. He'd bargained away one—the presence of the Pinkertons—for selfish reasons. The other he'd abandoned because he had to live with himself.

What could he offer Payne instead of the Lee interview? Nothing suggested itself.

Jarred back to reality by a realization that the clerk had spoken, he said, "What's that?"

"I said, do you want to wait for an answer?"

"To the second message?" Jephtha handed over money. "No. When it comes in, just tear it up."

"Tear it up—?"

The clerk scratched his head as Jephtha walked outside into the lengthening shadows, still trying to come up with another idea for a story. He felt defeated. His tired mind was a blank.

vii

Shortly after seven o'clock, Jephtha found his answer—amid chaos.

He was on one of the platforms of the Baltimore & Ohio station between C and D Streets, three blocks north of the Capitol. Steam still hissed from beneath the twenty-two-ton B & O Engine Number 232, just arrived.

The engine was a beautifully symmetrical woodburner of the type the line had begun buying from Mason of Taunton, Massachusetts. In '57 the builder had developed its prototype, *The Phantom,* for the Toledo & Illinois. Knowledgeable travelers always felt lucky to ride behind a Mason locomotive. The *Railway Gazette* called his engines "melodies cast and wrought in metal."

But this evening, neither Jephtha nor the arriving passengers were the least interested in the aesthetic considerations that had located the upper steam dome exactly above the equalizing lever between the sixty-six-inch driving wheels. Nor did they pay the slightest attention to Mason's use of tasteful dark blue paint accented by dark red on the wheels and cowcatcher—a dignified contrast to the rainbow gaudiness of most locomotives and tenders.

Jephtha wanted to talk to some of the four hundred and sixty Pennsylvanians streaming up the platform. The disorderly ranks hardly resembled a military formation.

But there were quite a few signs that the men had seen some fighting.

The blue capes of the soldiers had a crude, homemade look. They wore forage caps modeled after the French kepi. The caps were decorated with small enameled badges Jephtha recognized as the state seal of Pennsylvania: an eagle spreading its wings above two rearing horses, and a rippling ribbon bearing the words *Virtue, Liberty* and *Independence*.

The relief troops carried every conceivable kind of muzzle-loader. Many were rusty antiques. Jephtha saw only half a dozen of the increasingly popular rifled muskets.

Every other reporter in Washington, it seemed, wanted to talk to the Pennsylvanians too. As a result, Jephtha was jostled and shoved by his competitors and ordered aside by this or that officer while being constantly engulfed in hot steam.

The noise was stupefying. Thudding feet. Crude jokes. Continuous shouting:

"Where they gonna to put us up, Charley?"

"Hear tell it's the committee rooms in the Capitol."

"Mighty fancy!"

"Form up, goddamn it. Form up and keep moving!"

"Hope to hell they got food waitin' for us—"

Jephtha felt it prudent not to inform the complainer that he'd only be eating bacon tonight. Early that day, he'd watched greasy slabs of it being unloaded and carried into the Capitol basement. God, how the world had gone awry! Bacon frying in the halls of Congress—and bright-cheeked volunteers sleeping on Brussels carpets under crystal chandeliers!

He managed to fall into step beside a young fellow with a cut forehead. He shouted, "What unit are you?"

"Washington Artillery. Pottsville."

Jephtha scribbled with a pencil stub. A man just behind yelled, "We're gonna lob some shells straight up the ass of Jeff Davis!"

"Looks like you've already done some fighting—"

"In Baltimore," the man behind growled.

The younger man said, "Secesh crowds followed us while we changed stations. They yelled and cussed something fierce. Threw things, too."

"The officers should of let us shoot the sonsabitches," the man behind declared.

Jephtha struggled to write on a scrap of paper, squinting in the glare at the head of the platform. The oil wick in Number 232's headlight box was still lit.

"How big was the mob that harassed you?" Jephtha yelled.

"Three hundred—four hundred," the youth said. The forward progress of the soldiers was stopped momentarily by a jam-up in the terminal. "Who's countin' when you think you're gonna get killed?"

"Was anyone killed?"

"No. But they say it'll be worse tomorrow."

"Tomorrow—? Hammond, quit shoving me!" Jephtha snarled at another reporter. "Go talk to someone else." He faced the young soldier again, back-stepping to keep up as the men started forward. "Why tomorrow?"

"Sixth Massachusetts is due to pass through."

"When?"

"Noon or thereabouts."

"Were you really frightened?"

The young man looked into Jephtha's eyes. His head seemed to float in a cloud of glowing steam.

"Go ask Nick."

"Who's Nick?"

"Our nigger mascot. He come along for the fun. The *fun*. He's back there a ways—"

The man behind caught Jephtha's arm. "You write this down. For every lick they gave us in Baltimore, we'll give the fuckers ten in Virginia. Nobody fires on Old Glory and gets away with it. *You write it down!*"

Barked orders sent the soldiers shambling out of the headlight's glare. Jephtha waited for the black man he'd spied at the rear of the platoon.

The elderly Negro's uniform was just like those of the white volunteers. But his head was wrapped in rags stained reddish-brown.

"Your name Nick?"

"Nick Biddle, yessir. Come along to fight an' free my people."

Jephtha started walking backward again. He pointed his pencil at the bandage. "How'd you get hurt?"

"Brick," Biddle replied, his eyes watering in the steam. "A brick from the crowd. My God, I never heard such filthy taunts. I'm not scared to fight with my boys from Pottsville. But I don't want to go through Baltimore again. I'll walk home first."

A burly sergeant materialized in the steam:

"Biddle, fall in properly! You—out of the way!"

He shoved Jephtha, who stumbled from the plank platform and fell onto the empty tracks adjoining.

The left knee of Jephtha's trousers tore as it ground against the cinders between the ties. Dim lines of men kept shuffling by, spirits dampened by the long journey and the mob antagonism they'd confronted. Gun barrels glinted in the gusting steam. Jephtha shivered. The train shed resembled a picture from hell.

No, not hell.

War.

If there was any difference.

He collected the scraps of note paper scattered by his fall and stood up, dusting himself off. Suddenly he drew in a breath—

They say it'll be worse tomorrow.

He recalled Lamont's letter. His eyes had an intense

look as he followed the Pennsylvanians out of the depot into the April dark.

A small crowd, including families with children, applauded the troops as they assembled. Soon they started marching toward the Capitol—for a welcome by Major McDowell and a sparse meal of bacon in the basement.

viii

"Strangest damn thing—"

Jephtha sat on the edge of Molly's bed, his brow wrinkled in a moody, thoughtful expression. He was exhausted. The time was just past midnight. An hour ago he'd filed another dispatch about the arrival of the troops.

"—most of them were boys. And they were scared. Scared and worn out. But there was a kind of excitement in the air, too. Expecially when they got back into formation outside the depot. It's the sort of feeling I've read about in the New York papers. People are—" He struggled to phrase it. "—on fire. The whole North's on fire. Because someone dared to shoot at the flag."

"Americans have gone to war for the same reason before," Molly said.

"Not against each other. I tell you, it scares hell out of me."

Molly's skirts rustled as she moved closer to him. "What scares me is the idea of your going to Baltimore in the morning."

"Well, I *am* going. First train—"

He pulled off one boot, then the other.

"—seven o'clock sharp." She started to object. "Molly, I told you what happened with the Lee material. I couldn't use it."

"Name me one other newsman with scruples like

that! Are you trying to be a saint or a reporter?" She stroked his forehead, smiling sadly. "I know the answer. A little of both."

"Don't pin any decorations on me. From a job standpoint, what I did was stupid. But I just couldn't ignore Lee's request. He's the kind of man who still believes the word honor means something. He may be old-fashioned, but there are damned few like him any more. At least in these times. Still, I owe Theo Payne a good piece of copy. Lamont's letter corroborated what the soldiers said about tomorrow."

"I'd be curious to see that letter from Mr. Lamont."

"It got lost at the office. He gave me the information because he didn't know any other way to thank me. I think he was sincere."

She still looked concerned. He took hold of her shoulders:

"Stop fretting. Baltimore's only an hour and twenty-five minutes by train. I'll be back before supper."

"I still wish you wouldn't—"

"I have to go where the stories are, Molly. Tomorrow could bring the first casualties of—"

She jerked away. "You sound like a ghoul."

Softly: "I'm sorry. But I do owe Payne."

"Hang Payne! It's you I care about. This *is* a war—you'll admit that much, won't you?"

He pressed his palms against his temples. Thought of Gideon—

"Yes, it's a war. All we can do now is hope it won't last long. Can we go to bed? I'm worn out."

A short while later, when he thought she'd fallen asleep, he turned onto his side. Despite his exhaustion, he couldn't relax.

He punched at his pillow to rearrange it, then gazed toward the curtained windows. Instead of an expanse of darkness, he saw the ragged lines of volunteers shuffling through the steam and glare at the depot. Instead of the night sounds of the house, he heard the ominous tramp of men marching—

"Jephtha?"

He started: "I didn't realize you were still awake."

"I've been thinking about tomorrow."

"What about it?"

"I want you to be careful. I don't want anything to happen to you."

He slipped his arm under her shoulder, drawing her against him. He kept his voice as light as he could:

"I'm not anxious for that either, Mrs. Emerson."

"Be serious. I want you to take my gun."

"All right, if it'll ease your mind. But I don't think I'll be in any danger. It's the troops who have to worry. No one's interested in killing a hack with a low salary and even lower morals."

He kissed her again. "Let's try to get some sleep."

CHAPTER IX

Bloody Baltimore

THE CROWD JAMMED both sides of President Street, watching the passage of the slow-moving railway car.

A red-faced woman next to Jephtha flung a stone. The woman's daughter, no more than ten, cupped her hands around her mouth and screeched:

"You just wait till old Beauregard gets hold of you!" She too found a rock and threw it.

The first stone had landed harmlessly on the tracks of the street railway behind the passenger car, which was being pulled by two lathered horses. The child's rock struck the frame of one of the car windows. The crowd applauded. It was a hostile crowd, spreading for blocks in either direction.

Behind the window where the rock had hit, a blue-clad man shook a fist. People who saw raised their fists in return.

Jephtha's black suit was unbearably hot. His skin felt gritty from the soot that had accumulated during the early morning ride up to Baltimore's Camden Street station. The loaded Sharps was in his pocket. But he hoped there'd be no need to use the gun. He was here to get a story, and from the mood of the mob, he was sure it would be a grim one.

Maryland was an almost perfect example of the country's divided feeling. The state's northern boundary was the Mason and Dixon line. Sentiment in the eastern

253

counties was predominantly Southern. The farm folk in the western part of the state tended to side with their Unionist neighbors across the border in Pennsylvania. Baltimore too reflected the division. With a distinctly Southern style of life, it still had extensive commercial ties with the North because it was industrialized.

But there appeared to be no Northern sympathizers on President Street today. Perhaps fear had kept them at home.

Jephtha pulled off his hat. Wiped his sticky forehead with the back of his hand. Noon had come and gone. The pleasant April weather seemed at odds with the ugly faces all around him.

The railway car packed with men of the Sixth Massachusetts crossed the intersection half a block to Jephtha's left. It was the ninth car to make the slow transfer from the Philadelphia, Wilmington and Baltimore depot. Jephtha had studied the faces of the soldiers behind the smoke-stained windows of the cars. They were frightened and angry. No wonder. The crowd kept growing; its animosity kept erupting in jeers and curses—

Across the street, a man hurled a chunk of brick at the car which was now well out of range. The man's coat flapped open. Jephtha saw a holstered revolver.

He began to scrutinize the crowd more closely. He soon spotted other weapons. Sheathed knives. Even a muzzle-loader thrust up defiantly a few yards to his right—

The red-faced woman tugged his arm. "Mister you got any idea how many more of those damn blue-coats are waiting at the President Street station?"

Jephtha had calculated the approximate number of men each car carried. "I'd guess four or five companies."

"We can't get to 'em as long as they hide in those cars," the woman complained. A white-bearded man heard her:

"They ain't gonna be able to hide much longer." He pointed to the right. "Looky up yonder."

People strained forward to see:

"What're they doin'?"

"What's in those barrels?"

Jephtha stood on tiptoe in the cobbled street. Up the block half a dozen men were manhandling casks to the tracks. Applause and shouts came rippling down both sides of the street.

"It's sand!"

"They're dumpin' sand on the tracks, God bless 'em—"

"No more cars can come through. The sojers are gonna have to walk—"

"It's about time!" the red-faced woman said to Jephtha. She frowned at his appalled expression. "Or are you on their side?"

He was curt: "I'm a newspaperman. I'm not on either side."

Huge mounds of sand were now heaped in the middle of President Street. To guarantee the barrier would be effective, half a dozen small sea anchors were thrown on top of the sandpiles.

More applause. A man nearby brandished a revolver:

"Come on, Yankee! Show your face, I dare you!"

The sun broiled the back of Jephtha's neck. As he reached up to loosen his sticky collar, he was startled by the sight of a familiar face on the other side of the street. A pinched face, with eyes narrowed against the glare—

The man was standing well back from the curb, screened from time to time by people moving in front of him. Jephtha frowned. What the hell was a War Department clerk doing in Baltimore?

Josiah Cheever noticed him. Jephtha nodded.

Cheever stared but gave no sign of recognition. He turned to speak to a man beside him—a huge fellow with a long beard as red and bushy as his mustache. The man's dirty homespun suit made Jephtha think of a saloon derelict.

He had the uneasy feeling Cheever and the red-bearded giant were talking about him.

Down the street, a pistol exploded. Someone cried, *"Three cheers for Jeff Davis!"*

The cheers roared out, echoed by the people around him. Women waved handkerchiefs. Men flaunted pistols. Jephtha counted eight guns just in his immediate vicinity.

The demonstration momentarily distracted him. When he glanced back across the street, Cheever and the red-bearded man had vanished. For no reason he could explain, his palms turned cold and sweaty.

Far to his left, the last car had dwindled to a blur. After a short interval of calm, the people grew restless again. Where were the Yankees? Cowering in the station because the tracks were blocked? Jephtha presumed someone had carried word to the remaining units that no more cars could get through.

Ten minutes passed.

Ten more.

Repeatedly, Jephtha's glance was drawn back to the place where he'd seen Cheever and his unsavory-looking friend. Neither of them reappeared among the elderly men, young matrons, and pink-faced children with angry faces. He was utterly depressed by the sight of Americans waiting with pistols and stones in the hope of hurting other Americans.

An uneasy stillness settled. All around him, Jephtha smelled human sweat. A jungle smell. Suddenly heads began to turn in the direction of the President Street station—

Jephtha elbowed his way into the street a second time. He shielded his eyes; let out a soft, despairing curse—

Several blocks away, he saw men in blue. Sunlight winked on shouldered muskets. The Sixth Massachusetts had decided to march to Camden Station.

The first sound he heard was the rhythmic tramping of feet. Then a louder one drowned it out: a prolonged, hostile screaming from hundreds of voices that sounded like one voice; like the bay of an animal—

"They're coming through!" the red-faced woman squealed. "Oh, the sons-of-bitches are coming through!"

She hugged her little daughter, her eyes moist. Then she shoved the child away:

"Find more stones, Sulene! Stones for both of us—"

The girl darted away, her face shining with joy. Jephtha closed his eyes and shook his head.

ii

The Sixth Massachusetts came on, splitting into two columns to pass around the anchor-topped piles of sand. When the first company was within a block and a half of Jephtha's position, he noticed a man in civilian clothes out in front of the soldiers. The man rushed from one side of the street to the other, pausing to speak and gesture. He bent toward his listeners in an attitude of pleading.

Jephtha asked a man on his left who the civilian might be. The man spat a stream of tobacco juice.

" 'Pears to be Mayor Brown. Looks like he's tryin' to hep the sojers get through, the damn turncoat."

Jephtha watched the frantic mayor run back to the center of the street ahead of the troops. Brown raised his hands over his head, obviously appealing for restraint. The crowd jeered and hissed. The Massachusetts soldiers kept coming, only a block away now.

Unexpectedly, Brown's presence seemed to quiet the spectators. Faces of the soldiers became discernible. Young faces, mostly. Sweating. Nervous. But the soldiers maintained their cadence. They were obviously better trained than the Pennsylvanians Jephtha had seen the evening before. Officers watched the crowd and kept their hands close to their sidearms.

Suddenly the tobacco-chewer whirled to exhort those nearby:

"You gonna let that yella Brown protect those Yanks?"

"Hell, no!"

"Never!"

"By Jesus, we aren't!" the red-faced woman cried. She threw her rock, hard.

The rock arched high and dropped a few feet from the mayor, who was speaking to onlookers on the street's far side. Brown started when the rock struck the cobbles and skittered toward him. He rushed back to the sun-shimmering rails and thrust his hands in the air again. This time, Jephtha could hear him:

"Citizens of Baltimore! I appeal to your decency—"

"Who paid you, Mayor?" a man yelled. "Abe the ape?"

Groans greeted the mention of the president. Brown saw the weapons in the crowd and grew even more alarmed. Counterpointed by the tramp of the marchers, his voice was shrill:

"Please listen to me! Maryland is not a part of the Confederacy! Harassment of Federal soldiers is unlawful and foreign to the hospitable tradition of our city—"

Derisive laughter. Stones flew. One struck a corporal in the leading platoon, knocking off his cap. The corporal jerked his rifled musket to his shoulder.

Jephtha's fists knotted at his sides. The soldier's

weapon appeared to be a late-model .58 caliber that fired the remarkably accurate bullets developed by the French officer, Captain Minié. He assumed the weapon was loaded.

Sun glared on the barrel as the corporal broke ranks and swung toward the crowd. His captain ran up beside him, grabbed his arm, whispered to him. Scowling, the corporal shouldered his weapon and jogged to catch up with his rank.

Across the way, a man howled, "Here's the hospitality we show Yanks!" He hurled a piece of paving block.

The block hit an infantryman almost abreast of Jephtha. The soldier stumbled, dropped his musket. He had to be helped to his feet by those around him—bringing the column to a halt.

Somewhere beyond the soldiers, Brown was practically screaming:

"I beg you to return to your homes! I *demand* you disperse! We'll have police here any minute to enforce—"

Profanity and boos blurred the rest. More rocks were thrown. The men of the Sixth Massachusetts were forced to stand in the street, dodging the missiles as best they could.

The tobacco-chewer next to Jephtha lunged forward. He grabbed a soldier's musket:

"I'll show you how to use that thing!"

The soldier hung on. "Let go, damn you!" Three more men converged on him. Soon a dozen civilians and soldiers were fighting for possession of weapons. The same sort of melee started at other places down the line. Beyond the struggling men, Jephtha glimpsed Mayor Brown standing motionless, hands at his sides and a sick expression on his face.

One of the Massachusetts infantrymen slammed the butt of his musket into the tobacco-chewer's head. The old man sprawled, yelling obscenities. He tried to get to his feet but was too stunned.

To Jephtha's left, there was a sudden flurry of color. Using both hands, a pretty young woman spread the new Confederate flag he had only heard about. The banner had a broad white stripe between two red ones and a blue field in which a circle of six white stars surrounded a seventh.

Other people seized the edges of the flag, raising it. Despite the confusion, Jephtha couldn't help making a professional judgment:

They'll soon want a new design. No matter how many stars they stitch on, that one looks like the Federal flag. Not easy to differentiate in battle—

The appearance of the flag produced thunderous cheering, wave after wave of sound that diverted the soldiers and civilians grappling over the muskets. An officer at the head of the column seized the opportunity:

"For-*aard*! Quick-step! *Quick-step!*"

The soldiers fought free of their assailants and started jogging. The officer had made a wise decision, Jephtha thought. The sooner the Sixth Massachusetts reached the other depot, the better.

A look of rapture lit the face of the pretty woman who had unfurled the flag. She shrieked at the trotting soldiers:

"Cowards!"

"Look at the yellow dogs, Sulene!" the red-faced woman cried. The mob roared louder. Jephtha realized the people had completely misinterpreted an order issued to prevent the confrontation from growing worse. Rocks rained. The screaming intensified:

"Scairt of Marylanders, that's what they are!"

"Run, little boys! *Run!*"

"Cowards!"

"COWARDS!"

The red-faced woman flung another rock. It gashed

the cheek of a soldier trotting by. Across the street, a pistol cracked. Almost simultaneously, the soldier whose cheek streamed blood swung his musket in Jephtha's direction. He fired into the crowd.

The man who'd been chewing tobacco took the Minié ball in his chest. His mouth spewed brown juice as he pitched onto the cobbles. A soldier kicked the side of his head. The man behind struck it with the butt of his rifle—

Civilians on both sides of President Street scattered, screaming. More gunshots. A sudden yelp of pain. Smoke began to drift in the sunlight—

All around Jephtha, people shoved and pushed, afraid of being hit. He was borne back from the edge of the plank walk as two more soldiers fired. He saw little Sulene fall. A man's hobnailed boot tore her face open.

Three or four yards away, separated from her child by the sudden confusion, the red-faced woman was calling, "Sulene? *Sulene*—?"

Jephtha used his fists and elbows to gain room. His dark hair flying, he snatched up the wailing child.

"Here she is! I have her!" he roared over the din of running feet, clattering rocks, shrieks, gunshots.

The red-faced woman fought her way toward him. Some in the crowd were trying to get back to the street; mostly men with hand guns. He braced his boots on the walk, buffeted from every side. He managed to hold his place until the woman reached him and clasped the girl in her arms:

"Thank you, sir, thank you—oh, my God, Sulene—oh, my God, those *butchers*—"

Jephtha wiped sweat from his nose and said nothing. The weeping woman seemed to have forgotten her role in provoking the violence, and that a civilian, not a soldier, had caused the child's injury.

The woman staggered out of sight. Down the street the Sixth Massachusetts was on the run, followed by a large crowd of men with weapons. More shots rang out. Jephtha prayed the officers had ordered the soldiers to fire above the heads of the civilians. Only that way could a slaughter be averted.

Watching the smoke rise on President Street, he was completely unprepared for the attack from behind.

iv

A man hurrying into the street shoved him. He side-stepped, off balance. Something tore the skirt of his black coat. Astonished, he glanced down and saw a length of metal tangled in the fabric.

The metal vanished in an eyeblink; withdrawn. *Someone was behind him; someone who had struck for his spine with a knife.* Only the accidental jostling had saved him—

He spun around, his pale eyes opening wide at the sight of the red-bearded man.

They were *watching me!*

For an instant, the men exchanged astonished stares. Red-beard was stunned because he'd failed; Jephtha because the unexpected assault was the last touch of irrationality on a sunlit day already poisoned with madness—

In that suspended moment while he listened to the bearded man's breath hissing between his teeth, a curious thought struck him. The man bore him no special animosity. No hate showed in his eyes—

But he still held the knife close to his leg, ready to use again.

About two feet separated Jephtha and red-beard. People hurried by on both sides, hardly giving them a glance. The man's hand jerked upward suddenly, his knuckles white around the Bowie's handle—

A woman saw the knife. Screamed; pointed. Redbeard was quick to explain the knife by shouting:

"You cheered for the Yanks one time too many, mister—"

The blade came streaking toward Jephtha's rumpled shirt. His hands felt heavy; immobilized by his surprise. There was no time to reach for the pepperbox—

The fast thud of Jephtha's heart was loud in his ears as he shot both hands toward the man's wrist. He clamped the hard flesh with his fingers and held the knife away by sheer strength.

The red-bearded man grunted, pushing. The knife quivered two inches from Jephtha's belly.

The huge man pushed harder. Already Jephtha's arms ached. Blood oozed from his lower lip as he bit down on it.

He was aware of several people watching. No one interfered. This was a day for violent quarrels.

He felt himself weakening rapidly. He maintained his grip on the bearded man's arm, but the Bowie moved closer and closer. His fingers were slippery with sweat. If he once let go, he'd be dead—

Numbness was spreading through both hands. He couldn't hold on much longer—

Desperate, he kicked the man's left shin.

The man grunted again, seemingly unhurt. But he shifted the weight off the leg Jephtha had kicked. Jephtha yanked the man's arm downward, hammering his wrist over his own raised knee.

The Bowie clattered on the plank walk. Both men bent for it at the same time. Jephtha thumbed redbeard's left eye.

The man yelled; lurched against him. Jephtha crashed to his knees. The man sprawled across his back.

Even under that crushing burden, Jephtha found the Bowie. He drove the point into red-beard's dangling fore-

arm. The point of the knife pierced homespun—
flesh—scraped on bone—

Red-beard screamed.

Jephtha rolled out from under him; let him fall. The
Bowie stuck out of the man's shabby coat, only half its
blade visible.

Panting, Jephtha looked around. The entire struggle
had lasted less than a minute. Something like a dozen
people had gathered. A man in a frock coat and string
tie stepped forward with an air of authority.

"Which side was that fellow on, sir?"

Jephtha jerked out the Sharps. A woman covered her
mouth.

"The wrong one."

There was a wild look in Jephtha's eyes. The man in
the frock coat hesitated, as if waiting for support from
the others. No one said a word. Jephtha began backing
away.

He spun and leaped into the street, running after the
soldiers. They were almost two blocks ahead. He pursued them as fast as he could, driven to escape a trap he
didn't understand. His heart raced. His lungs and his
bladder hurt.

He jumped over a blue bundle lying on the tracks,
catching a distorted glimpse of a Massachusetts boy
with a black hole in his right temple. The boy's eyes
were focused on the cobblestones an inch from his nose.

He ran on. A panicky glance backward showed no
pursuit. There was too much confusion and carnage on
President Street for one fight to attract great attention.

He dodged around another body; a civilian. Still no
one stopped him. Perhaps it was the pepperbox. He
looked as if he were chasing the troops.

His lungs burned now. His legs began to hurt as
badly as his arms had during the nightmare moment
when the Bowie was only inches from his belly. In his

mind, one question repeated itself; a question for which there was no adequate answer:

Why did he try to kill me?

Why?

iv

By the time he reached the Camden Street Station, detachments of Baltimore police had arrived. They formed a cordon and used their batons to beat back a few determined members of the crowd milling in the street. The mob was small now; two or three dozen. Its size had diminished quickly once the firing started.

After showing a frayed card which identified him as a correspondent, Jephtha was passed through the cordon. With a gasp of relief, he pushed open the depot doors.

Inside the dim station the Massachusetts officers were trying to form up their commands and get the men aboard the cars waiting in the train shed. Still short of breath, Jephtha showed his identification a second time:

"Captain, I'm with the New York *Union.* I damn near got killed back there—"

"You're not the only one."

"Can I get on the train?"

The officer scrutinized him, then said, "Last car. There's plenty of room—" Bitterly: "We've lost a hundred or so."

"A hundred dead?"

"Scattered in the confusion. So far as I know, only four of our men were killed. We took care of at least twice that many. Maybe more. Better hurry. We aren't waiting for stragglers, or the band."

"The regimental band?"

"It's still back at the other station. Get going!"

He shoved Jephtha aside, wigwagging to three young soldiers carrying a fourth on a litter improvised from an overcoat. The unconscious boy's trousers showed a bloody bullet hole above the right hip. The captain pointed to the shed:

"Get aboard! We're rolling out before there's more shooting—"

Jephtha dashed into the shed, hauled himself up the steps of the rear car and stopped on the platform. He drew several deep breaths. The pain in his chest lessened.

He leaned out and peered toward the head of the train. Steam was up. Beyond the engine, he glimpsed men gathering where the shed's roof met sunlight.

The men were civilians. Somehow they'd eluded the police. The trouble wasn't over—

Jephtha entered the car and sank down on a hard bench beside a young soldier without a cap. The soldier's uniform was torn and dirty. The butt of his rifled musket was planted on the floor between his feet. He held the muzzle with both hands, as if he might fall without the support.

The boy stared at the head of the soldier in front of him, totally unaware of Jephtha's presence. Tears ran down his cheeks.

More soldiers swarmed into the car. Officers yelled. The locomotive whistle bellowed twice. The engine bell began to clang and didn't stop.

The car lurched. The train was moving.

The sensation roused the young soldier. He blinked. Noticed Jephtha. Still crying, he said:

"They—they killed Ned. He was—right beside me. When he fell, the sergeant wouldn't let me stop to pick him up."

"Was Ned a good friend?"

"My older brother." The soldier blinked again, several times. "Ned always looked out for me, he—"

The words dissolved into a sob. Still gripping the musket, the boy bent his head. His shoulders shook.

Some of his companions looked at him. One stretched out a hand from across the aisle and touched his shoulder.

Abruptly, sunshine spilled through the dirt-speckled windows. The civilians surged at the train from both sides. Several soldiers lifted their muskets. Up and down the car, officers shouted:

"Sit still!"

"No firing!"

"But goddamn it, Lieutenant—"

"No firing!"

Slowly, the car creaked ahead. Jephtha stared at the cursing men running alongside the car. He heard one well-dressed, white-haired fellow shout:

"Give them one more cheer for Jeff Davis before they go!"

The soldier next to Jephtha smashed the window with the muzzle of his musket and pulled the trigger.

Smoke and the smell of powder swirled through the car. The well-dressed man reeled back, hit. Someone near him screamed, "You filthy bastards, this man wasn't on President Street! He just got here!"

Another man yelled, "Mr. Davis is dead."

Jephtha was confused until he realized the well-dressed gentleman evidently bore the same name as the man for whom he'd proposed a cheer. For his zeal, he'd gotten a bullet.

Dry-eyed, the young soldier resettled his musket between his heels. A lieutenant rushed down the aisle to his side:

"Coyle, you heard the order not to fire!"

The boy glanced up. His look was glacial.

"They shot Ned."

"Oh, Jesus, Jimmy. I didn't realize your brother was one of—"

"He was," the boy interrupted. Before Jephtha's eyes, he seemed to age twenty years. "Now what did you have to say about my shooting—sir?"

The lieutenant knuckled his mustache. "Nothing, Jimmy." He faced about and walked up the aisle.

The bell on the locomotive kept clanging. The train gathered speed.

Jephtha stared at young Coyle's sunlit profile. The hatred in the soldier's eyes was ageless and ugly to behold. His own brush with death momentarily forgotten, he thought, *We've shed the first real blood—*

On both sides.

v

The special train chugged through Maryland's rolling green countryside, passing Relay House where the western line from Harper's Ferry met the main track, then Annapolis Junction where an eastern spur came in from Chesapeake Bay. Most of the soldiers sat quietly, numbed by the carnage on President Street. Occasionally someone offered an obscene boast that the Sixth Massachusetts would retaliate harshly when given the chance. No one responded to the boasting. In the silence, the trucks rattled with a forlorn sound.

Jephtha had finally calmed down. He was able to think of his own situation. Of the bearded man who had talked with Cheever. Questions spilled one on top of the next:

Why was Cheever in Baltimore at all? To help stir up the mob?

It was possible. He'd done the same thing at Canterbury Hall.

Assuming that, why had Cheever conspired with some stranger to arrange an attack? Because Jephtha represented a pro-administration newspaper?

Ridiculous. There had been too many other, more important targets along President Street.

Still, the more he pondered, the more he was convinced the attack was anything but accidental. Yet he couldn't get beyond a final wall represented by one word:

Why?

All at once, the wall cracked:

Cheever had been at Canterbury Hall *to support Edward Lamont.*

And Lamont had written him that note suggesting he might find it worthwhile to be in Baltimore when the troops came through.

Lamont—

Could he be the connection?

As he thought of Fan and her husband, his hands began to tremble again. *My God, was I gulled by Lamont?*

If I was, did Fan know?

He didn't want to believe the suspicions. They undercut his struggle with himself; his victory over his own rage. He didn't want to believe Fan's husband could be involved.

But he could find no other explanation. Coincidence—chance—a spur-of-the-moment murder made no sense—

While a carefully planned murder made excellent sense, for one very good reason.

Jephtha Kent, the trusting fool. The stupid ex-preacher. Eager to see virtue where there wasn't any. Easy to convince; to trick—

He realized young Coyle was staring:

"Mister? You sick?"

Jephtha whispered, "No." He hardly saw the boy's face, or the new-leafed trees and the cattle slipping by in the mellow afternoon light. He was consumed by the same fierce hatred he'd felt before Molly begged him to read the Testament again; pleaded with him to find the good in Fan and her husband—

Cheever and Lamont.

Was there a link?

He had to find the answer, no matter how painful and humiliating it might be.

vi

Toward the end of the afternoon, the special arrived at Washington's B & O terminal. The uninjured troops piled off the cars, confronted by reporters already alerted by telegraph. The scene was almost as tumultuous as that in Baltimore—except that here, the crowd on the platform was friendly.

Stretchers had been piled at trackside. The wounded were unloaded with great care. Small bands of women came charging through the tangle of newsmen and soldiers. The women carried scraps of every sort of cloth from petticoat linen to toweling. Watching the determined progress of one such group, Jephtha collided with a small, primly dressed lady. He knew he'd seen her before but couldn't recall where.

"Excuse me—" he began.

"Quite all right, Mr. Kent." She hurried on.

He remembered then. She worked at the Patent Office, where he went occasionally in search of filler material about novel inventions. She was only a clerk, with the look of the perennial spinster.

Somehow, though, she'd undergone a change. Chin up and head tilted back, she glared at an exceptionally tall officer who barred her way:

"See here, sir. I'll appreciate your stepping aside!"

"Sorry, ma'am. There are too many blasted sightseers on the platform already."

"Those women I'm trying to reach are not sightseers.

I am Miss Clara Barton of the Patent Office. The other ladies and I are volunteers. We've come to tend those who were hurt."

For emphasis, she tapped the strips of white gauze draped over the sleeve of her drab dress.

"Tell me how many wounded you have, Lieutenant," she added. "And be quick about it!"

Astonished by the little woman's assertiveness, the lieutenant mumbled, "How many—? Not sure. At least thirty—"

"Thirty! Let me by so I can see to them! We'll ride with them to the E Street Infirmary. We have special hacks waiting outside—*sir, will you move or must I use bodily force?*"

Gaping, the officer stepped back. Jephtha lost sight of Miss Barton as she worked her way toward the injured men being loaded on the stretchers.

He walked through the station, ignoring questions from a couple of reporters who trailed him. There was a ferocious anger building within him; stronger and more savage than anything he'd ever experienced. He kept it under control as best he could, proceeding on foot to the *Evening Star*.

He shared the essential details of the Baltimore killings with Wallach, then wrote out his own copy for the *Union*. His dispatch was short—about two hundred words—but by the time he handed it in at the telegraph office, darkness had fallen.

He hurried to President's Park, up the steps of the War Department and into the office of one of his usual sources, a pudgy undersecretary named Gray.

Gray was frantically stuffing papers into a valise. He goggled at Jephtha's sooty face and ripped clothing:

"Where the devil did you get so dirty, Jephtha?"

"Baltimore."

Gray sat down. "Oh, Christ. The Sixth Massachusetts—"

"Yes. There are at least four dead. Thirty or more injured."

"I heard there was fighting. I had no idea it was so bad."

"Gray, I need information."

Helplessly, the other man pointed to the bulging bag. "I'm overdue for an emergency meeting with State."

"What's happened?"

"The Virginians have surrounded Harper's Ferry."

"Has it fallen?"

"There's no definite word. Yet. But you figure the odds. Jones has hardly any troops. I hope to God he's torched the place and retreated—" He resumed filling the valise. "There's hell popping down at Norfolk, too. That old fossil Commodore McCauley's in a state of absolute panic. Half his staff's Southern. They've talked him out of taking any action. Our biggest and best steam frigate, *Merrimack,* is still there because McCauley didn't obey orders and move her out. He was afraid of offending the Virginia convention! We'll probably lose our ships and the whole damn yard!" He shut the valise. "Sorry I can't stay to answer your—"

Jephtha seized Gray's arm. "If McCauley's losing the yard this minute, all your conferences won't do any good. I told you—*I need information.*"

Gray swallowed, alarmed by Jephtha's ferocity. "I've said too much already."

Jephtha released him. "Nothing that won't be public in the morning."

"But I'm late!"

"I just want a few facts about one of your clerks."

"Who?"

"Cheever."

"Ah, Josiah—" The pale man waved. "Good riddance."

"What do you mean?"

"He's part of the secesh crowd. He resigned late yesterday."

"Left town?"

"So I assume."

"Gray, this is very important. You've just admitted
Cheever had a good many Southern acquaintances." He
pointed at an inkstand. "Write down the name of every
one of them you can remember. You get around a good
deal—Willard's—the National. Surely you've seen
Cheever talking to men you recognized."

"Jephtha, what the hell's going on? You look grimmer than death."

"These are grim days. Write the names."

"No, I won't put anything on paper. I'll *tell* you as
many as I can recall. I *have* seen Cheever at the National. Often—"

Ten minutes later Jephtha left the War Department
and crossed to the north side of Pennsylvania Avenue.
He was glad he was still carrying the loaded Sharps.

Two rough-looking black men started to accost him,
but stepped aside when they saw the expression on his
face.

CHAPTER X

Accusation

"The years creep slowly by, Lorena.
The snow is on the grass again—"

Gideon Kent's baritone boomed from behind the closed door of the bedroom where he'd gone to shave and wash. Fan tried to concentrate on the discussion between her husband and the young guest who had sent up his *carte de visite* a short time ago. But Gideon's exuberant vocalizing made it difficult.

"The sun's low down the sky, Lorena.
The frost gleams where the flowers have been—"

And why on earth was he bellowing the Reverend Webster's sentimental love lyric, five years old but still as popular as ever, instead of the raucous minstrel novelties he generally favored?

There were a great many more questions she wanted to ask her son. She'd had no opportunity. He'd arrived, sweaty and smiling, only moments before the porter presented the visitor's card.

She thought she heard Jeremiah complain about his brother's noise. She'd sent the younger boy into the bedroom with Gideon, who ignored the complaint:

"But the heart throbs on as warmly now
As when the summer days were nigh.

274

> *Oh, the sun can never dip so low*
> *Adown affection's cloudless sky."*

From the settee in the window bay, Fan said:

"Please forgive the noise, Mr. Booth. My son's happy because his visit to Richmond was such a success."

The caller smiled. "I'm glad, Mrs. Lamont. And there's nothing to forgive. Your son has a fine voice."

The caller's chair faced that of her husband. Edward's left foot rested on a stool. A gutta-percha cane leaned against his thigh. He'd recovered rapidly, though a pulled muscle still made him limp a little. That was the reason he'd bought the cane.

The limp and the cane drew sympathetic glances in the hotel dining room. Perhaps Edward really had no need of the cane, but Fan didn't raise the issue. She'd long ago accustomed herself to his harmless vanities. And he *had* risked his life—

The mantel clock chimed half after seven. Young Mr. Wilkes Booth rose and tucked his own cane under the sleeve of his elegant fawn coat. "I really should be leaving so you can go downstairs for dinner."

"The dining room serves until eight-thirty," Fan said.

"Still, I must be on my way."

"I'm delighted you called," Edward said.

"Since I had to ride over from Bel Air on business, I couldn't pass up the opportunity."

"It's certainly a privilege to meet another member of your distinguished family. When I toured with your brother Junius, he told me you might well emerge as the brightest star of the lot."

"Oh, I think my brother Edwin has his eye fixed on that position." Fan detected an undertone of jealousy in the remark.

She had to admit Edward's guest was exceedingly handsome. She guessed him to be in his early twenties. Though he wasn't tall, he had dash and an air of wiry strength. He was much more carefully groomed than many actors she'd met.

Wilkes Booth picked up his fawn top hat and settled it on his dark hair. Both his hair and his mustache glistened with pomade. Fan could discern only one flaw in his appearance. He was bow-legged. But his loosely cut trousers tended to conceal it. No doubt he bought oversized trousers for that express purpose.

"I'm content to let Edwin shine on the stage," the young man went on. "That buffoon in the executive mansion has given us a more important arena in which to perform. Before the curtain rings down on his contemptible reign, every man with courage will rise to the challenge. One way or another."

Fan was bothered by a peculiar look in the actor's eyes. It disappeared as he extended his hand. Edward labored from his chair with an exaggerated grimace. He clasped the younger man's hand.

"You've already done so," Booth went on. "I'm certain posterity will take note of it." He smiled. "That's the disease of our profession, isn't it? Endless fretting about posterity. What we do on the stage is gone so quickly—"

"Too quickly," Edward agreed.

"Believe me, your boldness is an inspiration. You've given all of us who support the cause a mark to emulate. Somehow I shall, I promise you. Again, sir—it's been an honor." He bowed to Fan. "Mrs. Lamont—a pleasure."

"For me as well, Mr. Booth," Fan murmured. In the bedroom, Gideon and Jeremiah were arguing good-naturedly. Edward picked up his cane and hobbled to the door with his visitor:

"Seriously, Booth—you've a first-class reputation. You should think about playing Washington. You haven't thus far, have you?"

"No. But I'd rather make a debut when Washington's

a Confederate town. Perhaps I'll be able to do it soon. The city's sure to be invaded."

"There's every indication," Edward nodded.

"Then both of us have cause for rejoicing." Booth opened the door. "I wish your son success in his military venture, Mrs. Lamont. You did say he'd enlisted in a volunteer unit—?"

"That's right. He hasn't been back long enough to give us the details, though."

Gaslight put pale pinpoints in Booth's eyes. He posed in the doorway like a performer reluctant for the curtain calls to end. "I admire your son—just as I admire your husband."

Edward waved with false modesty. "I'm only sorry my injuries and the cowardice of the management led to my being removed from the bill after my first—and last—appearance."

"One eternally memorable performance is better than a thousand forgotten ones, Mr. Lamont." He touched the brim of his hat. "Good evening."

ii

After the door closed, Fan said, "My, he's certainly good-looking. And glib. An immense ego, though. He seems to have an obsession about posterity."

"Oh, come," Edward chided as he made his way slowly back to his chair. "It's a passion with every actor. You should know that by now. We all wonder whether anyone will remember our names ten minutes after we die—" Leaning on the chair, he added, "I suppose we should think about dinner."

"I'll see whether Gideon's ready."

Before she could reach the bedroom, the door burst open. Jeremiah came running into the parlor—backward:

"Gideon's got a girl! Gideon's got a girl!"

Gideon Kent chased his brother across the room and made a feint with his fist:

"Be quiet or I'll box your ears!" To Fan: "Mama, do you realize you've raised a blabbing brat?" But he said it with a grin.

"He told me, Ma! He met a girl in Richmond. That's why he was bellering that silly love song."

"Nonsense!" Gideon retorted. But his cheeks were flushed. How handsome he is! Fan thought.

Gideon Kent was a tall young man—he'd be eighteen in June—with a lean, supple body, powerful shoulders and merry blue eyes. He'd razored the stubble from his tanned cheeks. Droplets of water glistened in freshly combed hair the color of a lion's mane.

He'd replaced his travel clothing with spotless trousers of white linen duck and a clean shirt dyed nut-brown. His leather boots still gave off little puffs of dust as he moved to the center of the room. There was a touch of swagger in his walk; a hint of the Virginia temperament that had come down to him from his paternal great-grandmother.

Fan had seldom seen him in such good spirits. Though war was hardly the gentleman's sport he imagined it to be, she was grateful he'd finally found something to which he could give himself with enthusiasm. All her past attempts to get him to study had been futile, even though he showed an aptitude for becoming expert at whatever he chose to do. Unfortunately the only things he liked were horseback riding and outdoor work. Physical work. He'd helped her father for months at a time while the rest of the family traveled with Edward. His one term at Washington College in Lexington had been a disaster. He'd failed every subject—though not for lack of intelligence, his letter of dismissal reported. He just had no interest in sedentary activities.

He rubbed his hands together. "Lord, I'm starved. Everyone ready to—? Oh." He turned to Fan. "The letter from Matt. Will you bring it along to the dining room, Mama?"

Edward waved his cane. "We have plenty of time to get to the dining room. At least give us a hint of what happened in Richmond."

Fan smiled. "I also want to hear about this young lady."

Gideon turned scarlet again. "There's nothing to tell." His denial said just the opposite. "She's just a girl who works part time in her aunt's dressmaking shop and part time in a store where I went to buy a book."

"My heavens!" Fan feigned awe. "You bought a book? To *read*?"

"What is it?" Edward asked.

Gideon plopped himself down on the footstool, realizing he'd have to go hungry a little while longer. "*The Trooper's Manual* by Colonel Lucius Davis. The captain in charge of our volunteer company said every recruit needs a copy as much as he needs a horse. The book's all about cavalry operations. It's adapted from the *Pointsett Tactics,* the book the Federals use."

"Ma, he's changing the subject," Jeremiah complained. "He's supposed to tell us about the girl. Make him!"

"All right, I'll tell you—but you keep quite, Jeremiah Kent, or I'll dump you upside down in the jakes."

"Gideon!" Fan exclaimed.

Jeremiah stuck out his tongue. "Dare you!"

Edward laughed. "The girl—the girl!"

Gideon looked embarrassed. "Well, she's pretty and lively and her name's Margaret. She's lived in Richmond at least ten years, though I'm not sure she's a hundred percent behind the South. We got into quite a hot discussion about whether a state has the right to secede. Of course I said yes. But she said—"

"I'm surprised you'd fancy a girl with Union sympathies," Edward interrupted.

"I don't *fancy* her, sir. I just found her—well—pert and pretty and—"

"She sounds like a damned submissionist to me! Ready to give in to Lincoln's threats."

"Let him finish, Edward," Fan said softly.

"If she is a submissionist, I'd like to change her thinking. But—" Flustered, he exclaimed, "Oh, hell."

"Gideon!"

"I'm sorry, Mama. But you're all making more of it than you should." His blue eyes looked angry.

How typical his reaction was, Fan thought with mixed chagrin and pride. That rebellious streak had drawn him to someone who challenged his beliefs. If the young lady had agreed with everything he'd said, no doubt he wouldn't have shown the slightest interest.

And despite his protests, Gideon's pink face revealed that the wondrous, unfathomable chemistry of romance had affected him at last. She mustn't be too harsh. Nor permit Edward to be. She remembered how deliciously giddy she'd felt when she was young and being wooed by Jephtha. A touch, a glance became sublime experiences. The special feelings between a boy and a girl could never be rationally explained, nor should they be openly tampered with by prying parents.

Gideon seemed to feel a further explanation was required, though:

"Actually, I don't expect I'll have much chance to see Margaret. As soon as the Virginia state forces get organized, my troop will probably leave Richmond for training somewhere else. They say Colonel Lee will be in charge of the disposition of the volunteers."

"But he's in the Federal army!" Fan said.

Edward shook his head. "I heard in the bar that he was closeted yesterday with that power-crazy Francis Blair. Then he went to see General Scott. I'll wager he'll resign if he hasn't already."

Jeremiah sat cross-legged at his brother's feet. "This

love stuff isn't as interesting as I thought. Tell us about your horse troop."

Gideon looked relieved. Edward, however, wasn't ready to drop the first subject:

"This young woman's submissionist leanings raise a question. Is there still any support for the Union in Richmond?"

"Some. The secession vote was nowhere near unanimous. Of course, ever since Sumter surrendered, there've been parades—thousands of people tramping the streets with torches and illuminated boxes with pictures of Jeff Davis all over them. There's an orator on practically every corner. A few of them argue against secession. That's how I got into the fight with—"

Abruptly, he stopped.

"The *fight*?" Fan repeated.

"Don't sound so shocked, Mama. It was nothing serious. I punched a loud-mouth cheering for a submissionist speaker. If I hadn't done it, someone else would have. The man on the box said the South couldn't possibly match the North in terms of factories or numbers of people and that we'd all be destroyed. I spoke up and said one Virginian could whip ten abolitionist soldiers. The fellow next to me—uh—disagreed. We settled the question, that's all."

"Settled it how?" Edward asked.

Gideon's eyes sparkled. "In my favor."

Edward whacked his chair with the cane. "Capital!"

Fan wasn't so pleased:

"You shouldn't let that temper of yours get the best of you, Gideon."

"Mama, it's *temper*—spirit—that's going to help us win. Believe me, I didn't get a scratch. Can we go eat?"

"As soon as we hear about your unit," Edward said.

"I could tell you in the dining room—"

"The dining room's too public. Too many strangers

listening. You're not volunteering to serve the local government, after all. How did you find your troop?"

Gideon sighed. "Through the *Examiner*. The papers are full of advertisements from units trying to fill their last vacancies. The ads make it sound as if you might not get in. 'Only a few qualified applicants will be accepted.' What they really mean is, do you own a gun or a horse, or both? I'll be damned—uh—I refuse to go dragging around in the infantry, so I answered the notice published by Captain Macomb."

Fan said, "Captain who?"

"Macomb. The gentleman organizing Macomb's Hussars."

"What's a hussar?" Jeremiah wanted to know.

"A mounted soldier, you ninny!" Gideon drove a soft punch against his younger brother's head.

"Then why don't they call it Macomb's cavalry?"

"Too dull. All the horse troops in Richmond are hussars or lancers or rangers—something fancy. The infantry doesn't go in for plain names either. There are tiger companies, wildcat companies. Hornets. Raccoon Roughs—"

Jeremiah leaned forward. "Have you got a uniform?"

"I will have."

"What's it look like?"

"Haven't seen it. You can bet it'll be magnificent, though. Hussars always wear impressive uniforms."

"Do you have to buy the uniform?" Fan asked.

Gideon shook his head. "Captain Macomb's furnishing them."

Jeremiah whistled. "Sounds like you're in a rich man's outfit."

"No, Macomb said the others are mostly farmer boys. Not from the plantations. From smaller places, like Grandpa Virgil's."

Edward said, "Does this Macomb know anything about soldiering?"

"Yes, he's a former Federal officer. After the Mexican war, he opened a wholesale yard goods business in Richmond. He knows where to get material for the uniforms at very favorable prices."

"Then you're in with a bunch of poor boys," Jeremiah said.

"Will you stop? Macomb's Hussars are good, solid Virginians. We won't be like some of the high-toned horse troops, with every man bringing his own nigra to look after him. But we'll have fine horses—we'll be a great unit!"

Somehow, his ebullience touched a chord of dread in Fan. How gay he made it sound! Obviously he was caught up in the pervading mood of Richmond. But one day, the romance and zest might disappear, replaced by the harsh reality of men fighting and killing each other.

She was proud of his enthusiasm. She prayed reality wouldn't be too disillusioning.

Or lead to injury. To dea—

Don't think about that.

Gideon spoke to her: "Grandpa Virgil will let me have one of his stallions, won't he? If he doesn't, Macomb won't take me."

With a heavy feeling in her breast, Fan replied, "I'm sure Papa will give you one of his finest. Proudly."

"Then I'm in!" Gideon jumped up. "Now can we get some food? I'm damn near as hungry as the poor nag I turned in at the stable."

Fan was disturbed by the profanity that had slipped into his vocabulary while he was away. Another sign of his manhood, she thought; a saddening reminder that he was growing up. Growing away from her—

She decided to say nothing. Another, more delicate subject remained to be broached:

"We'll go in just a moment. First, I have one more bit of news to convey."

"What's that?"

"As you know, your—"

She glanced at Edward. His look seemed to encourage her.

"—your father is here in Washington."

Gideon's face clouded. He was clearly uncertain about what his response should be. She went on:

"He was at the theater Tuesday night when Edward spoke to the crowd."

"Sang 'Dixie's Land,' " Gideon grinned. "Jeremiah told me. That was a brave thing to do, sir." Edward responded with a preening smile.

"I want to tell you everything that happened," Fan said. She described how Jephtha had helped Edward escape from a Union sympathizer who had been trying to punish him for proclaiming his political sympathies. "Your father acted in a brave and humane way, Gideon. He endangered himself to aid Edward. We owe him a debt for that. He very much wants to see you—you and Jeremiah."

Gideon's eyes remained troubled. Fan knew he must be churning inside. As the eldest, he would remember the bitter scenes in Lexington more vividly than the other boys. Hesitantly, he said:

"I've never thought highly of my father, you know—"

"I realize. Much of that's my fault."

"And mine," Edward murmured.

"Even though he's on the other side and always will be, he's an honorable man. I think you should see him." She glanced at Jeremiah. "Both of you."

The younger boy seemed agreeable. To help persuade Gideon, she added:

"Edward doesn't object."

"No, no, not at all!"

"Well—" Gideon shrugged. "I suppose it's all right. Sometimes I *am* curious about him—"

"He's mellowed a good deal since he left Lexington," Fan said. "I mean personally, not politically. He doesn't conceal his feelings about Fort Sumter or secession. If he comes here I wouldn't want you to lose your temper over some chance remark."

Again Gideon shrugged. "I'll do my best. I'll try to remember he's my father, not just one of those damned—those abolitionists."

With a relieved sigh, Fan squeezed his shoulder. "Good. I promised to send him a note as soon as you arrived."

"He might be a long time answering it," Edward mused.

Puzzled, Fan asked, "What do you mean?"

"Oh—" A quick bob of the head; a charming smile. "—only that reporters are busy folk these days. And we should leave Washington City soon—he warned us about that. General Scott's liable to close the bridges at any time."

"I'll write the note as soon as we finish dinner. Shall we go?"

"Yes, before I pass out." Gideon put his arm around her. They started at the sound of a fist hammering on the hall door.

Concerned, Edward struggled to his feet. "Another caller? I'm not expecting anyone—"

Fan hurried to answer. The instant she opened the door, she went rigid:

"Jephtha!"

"How the devil—?" Fan and the boys didn't see the color drain from Edward's cheeks. They were staring at the wild-eyed man in the doorway. He pushed Fan aside and stormed into the room.

What in God's name had happened to him? Fan thought as she closed the door. His black suit was filthy and torn. And his face—

His face was terrifying.

Scowling, Gideon jumped up. Jeremiah stepped behind his brother. Jephtha looked at his youngest son, then at Gideon, who was nearly a match for his own height. Fan thought she saw his stark eyes soften a moment:

"Gideon—Jeremiah—I'm sorry to meet you again under such circumstances. I think it would be better if you both went into the next room."

Confused and red-faced, Gideon shot back, "Why?"

"Because I ask you!"

"See here, Kent!" Edward said. "This is the damnedest, most insulting performance I've ever—"

Jephtha whirled on him. "Is it, now? I don't doubt you're surprised I'm here at all."

"You have no right to speak to him that way!" Gideon shouted. Jephtha blinked twice, stung by his son's rage. But his voice remained stern:

"I have things to say to your mother and stepfather which I'd prefer you didn't hear."

Fighting for control, Gideon gave Jephtha a scornful look:

"I'll thank you not to treat me like some three-day foal. You forget how old I am. Old enough to join a mounted company in Richmond. I think I can bear whatever it is you have to say."

The contempt made Jephtha hesitate:

"Yes, I—I realize you're grown. Nevertheless, I see no point in your staying. My remarks to your mother and Mr. Lamont won't be pleasant."

"Jephtha—" Fan rushed toward him. "What's wrong? Why are you so furious with—?"

"Don't tell me you don't know, Fan. *Don't lie to me one more time!*"

He looked at her with such fury and loathing, she wanted to hide her face.

iii

For several seconds, no one moved. Jephtha's eyes shifted to Edward, accusing. Gideon's scowl deepened. Of them all, only Jeremiah had the good sense to get out of the way. Slowly and soundlessly, he inched toward the settee, his frightened gaze fixed on his father. All of them understood something ugly was loose in the gas lit parlor.

Finally, Jephtha spoke again, this time more quietly, but still with scathing bitterness:

"Fan, I must compliment you on your remarkable performance Tuesday evening. You've become almost as good at acting as this charlatan you married."

"Damn you!" Gideon shouted. "Don't say such things about—"

Edward cut him short with a slashing motion of the gutta-percha cane:

"Be still. Let him rave till we discover what this is all about."

"It's about my trip to Baltimore today." Jephtha paused. The tick of the mantel clock sounded thunderous. "Baltimore, Mr. Lamont. Where the Sixth Massachusetts infantry was attacked by a hostile mob. In the mob I saw a clerk who worked at the War Department until yesterday. A clerk named Josiah Cheever."

Edward's frozen expression never changed. "You're still not making sense."

"Is that so? Then follow me a little further. To the point where I saw Cheever on President Street in Baltimore—just as I saw him in the audience at Canterbury Hall Tuesday. Cheever had a red-bearded roughneck with him today. They were watching me."

Edward sighed; said to Fan:

"My dear, I think your former husband is suffering some sort of persecution mania."

Jephtha whipped the four-barrel pepperbox from his pocket. "Shut your mouth and *listen!*"

The actor's face whitened. Gideon threw his mother a desperate glance: a plea for an explanation; for a hint of what he should do. But Fan's eyes were focused on the gun aimed at Edward.

"When—" Jephtha used his free hand to wipe his perspiring upper lip. "—when the crowd turned on the troops, the red-bearded man sneaked up behind me. Tried to put a knife in my back. Tried to *murder* me, Lamont. Now do you begin to understand?"

Edward shook his head. "Not at all." His voice was calm. But he too watched the pepperbox in Jephtha's unsteady hand.

Jephtha sneered. "You're going to force me to explain in front of the boys? Very well—" He touched the rip in his coat. "This is where the man's knife hit me first. Luckily, he didn't get a second chance. I got away from him. On the train coming back here, certain things became clear—principally that I was an imbecile to accept thanks for what I did Tuesday night. I was completely taken in by your professions of gratitude, Lamont. You're good at your craft. You very ably concealed your hatred of me." He swung to Fan. "Both of you did."

"Jephtha, you've gone insane!" she protested.

"To the contrary. My only moment of insanity was the moment I began to believe your pretty words about forgiveness. Your explanations of how you'd changed. You haven't changed. You're even more vicious and devious than you were when you drove me out of my own house and turned my sons against me."

Gideon took a step forward. "I've had enough of this. Put that gun down."

"Please, Gideon," Jephtha said. "Don't involve your-

self. I'm sure you had no part in their scheming. I don't
want to hurt you accidentally—"

"Then stop making crazy accusations!"

Jephtha shook his head. "I'm afraid that's impossible.
Your stepfather is a very clever fellow. I discovered
conclusive proof tonight, after I saw a contact at the
War Department. He informed me that among those
with whom Josiah Cheever was seen in public this week
was Mr. Lamont here. My contact observed them twice
in the bar of this very hotel. Cheever's presence at Canterbury Hall was no accident. He and your father are
friends. Or should I say conspirators?"

Losing a little of his aplomb, Edward waved his
cane:

"Of course I know Cheever! I know a great number
of local people who share my political views!"

"How many do you know who were also in Baltimore
this noon? Just one, I think."

Fan listened to Jephtha's venomous words, her
mouth dry, her stomach hurting. She'd never seen such
rage in a man's eyes.

"Where I was foolish—" His voice dropped to a
whisper as he faced her. "—where I was monumentally
foolish was to be taken in by your little performance.
Your husband coached you, I don't doubt. I was also a
fool to swallow the note you wrote, Lamont. A note
pouring out your thanks. A note that included a little
token of your deep, deep gratitude!—the suggestion
that I might find it worthwhile to go to Baltimore when
the troops came through. I might witness an important
news event! I took the bait. Cheever then went to Baltimore—perhaps he even followed me. Boarded the same
train I did. I was paying no attention. But I'm sure he
was on President Street for a double purpose. To help
stir up the crowd. And to hire a man to kill me."

Now Edward looked genuinely shaken. Still eyeing
the pepperbox, he said to Fan:

"Of course I wrote him a note. I *did* want to express my thanks. But the rest is a complete fabrication!"

"*Goddamn you for a liar!*" Jephtha shouted.

"Stop it—*stop!*" Fan cried, lunging at him. Edward dragged her back:

"Stay away from him! He's deranged—"

"For a time, I thought so myself," Jephtha nodded. 'Then it fell together. Cheever. The note. The motive—"

"Edward—" Fan's eyes blurred as she looked at him. "You never showed me the note."

"I'd show it to you if I could," Jephtha snarled.

Quietly, Edward asked, "You mean to say you don't have it with you?"

"I left it on my desk at the *Star*. The sweep disposes of anything that falls on the floor. Evidently that happened to the note. But I don't need it. I remember every word. Especially your suggestion about Baltimore."

Fan gripped her husband's arm. "He can't be telling the truth—"

"Spare me the play-acting—!" Jephtha began. Edward interrupted:

"He isn't." He brushed at his dark hair. "I sent the note to his office by a nigger boy. In the note I thanked him. Sincerely. The rest is invented—for Christ knows what malicious purpose. I said nothing about Baltimore. Absolutely nothing."

"He's lying again," Jephtha said. "But then—" A ragged gulp of air. "You both know that."

"No, I don't—*I don't!*" Fan burst into tears. "Dear God, I can't comprehend what's caused all this—!"

"Your hate," Jephtha whispered. "Your hate and the money."

Fan's head jerked up. "*W—what?*"

"The money," Jephtha repeated. "The California mining money Gideon and Matt and Jeremiah will inherit after my death. *The money you've always been so concerned about, Fan.* Surely you haven't forgotten Lexington so soon? Surely you remember saying I'd defrauded my own sons by letting Amanda manage the income? You remembered it Tuesday night—"

His sarcasm made her cringe. "I also told you I regretted every word!"

"You were lying. Acting."

"Jephtha, I swear to heaven—"

"You also told me your precious husband was worried about the money. That was a little slip, I suppose. But it shed light on why you'd try to have me killed. To make sure I don't change my mind about giving the boys their inheritance. Or perhaps you and Lamont want the money yourselves. Well, that's of no consequence. The motive is clear. And it explains everything. Even why you both came to Washington. The Canterbury Hall speech was secondary. I was the real target. You went to a great deal of unnecessary trouble. The boys will still get the money when I die—of natural causes, I trust. I assume there'll be no more little plots now that this one's been dragged into the open. It's you who disappoints me the most, Fan. I—"

His shoulders slumped. "I just wouldn't have thought you could sink so low."

"Kent, Kent—!" Edward sounded like a weary father pleading with a hysterical child. "—don't say such things to her. Every word is false and you know it. I never plotted with Cheever. I never urged you to go to Baltimore—"

Fan tried to steady herself by planting her feet wide apart beneath her skirts. She wiped her tear-reddened cheeks. Tried to talk to Jephtha rationally:

"What's done this to you? What's put all this into your head? If Edward says he's never meant you any harm, believe him! I do."

Silence. Heavy, hideous silence.

Fan glanced at Gideon, alarmed anew by the wrath

in his blue eyes. She hoped her glance would communicate her plea:

Hold your temper. Don't make things worse than they are—

And they were terrible indeed. Somehow Jephtha had been warped by his fears, his political biases, his long-buried animosity—and his derangement had come spilling out in the dreadful, distorted tale of a scheme to murder him.

"So you believe him, do you?"

Jephtha's long black hair shone in the gaslight. His pale eyes glared. He took one swift step and slapped her face.

"You deceiving slut!"

Gideon leaped for his father's throat.

iv

Afterward, she remembered only isolated bits of the rest of it:

Jeremiah wailing in fright.

Jephtha's startled cry as Gideon caught him by the neck:

"A crazy man, that's what you are! A crazy god-damned Yankee fanatic—!"

Staggered by Jephtha's blow, she'd sprawled on the floor. From there, she saw Gideon let go of his father, snatch Edward's cane, whip it down on Jephtha's gun wrist. The pepperbox thudded on the carpet. Edward kicked it away.

Gideon tried to strike his father a second time. Dodging the cane, Jephtha stumbled. Fell to one knee. She remembered the anguish on his face as his tall, blue-eyed son came at him again, cane flailing—

The cane struck Jephtha's neck with a whipping sound.

"Just as crazy-mean as I always heard you were—!"
Whip.

"You can't call my mother filthy names!"
Whip.

Jephtha raised his hands:

"Gideon, I only want to protect what's yours, I—"
Whip. Jephtha cried aloud, his cheek laid open.

Gideon's next blow broke the cane over Jephtha's head. He sprawled face first on the carpet, groaning. Dizzy and sick at her stomach, Fan tried to get to her feet. Edward caught her as she fell and gasped:

"Don't, Gideon!"

But Gideon had his fist tangled in his father's hair. He dragged Jephtha's head up.

"Boy—listen to your mother!" Edward stepped toward him speaking loudly. "You've done enough. Just—get him out of here!"

Then darkness blurred Fan's sight. She felt herself falling again; felt Edward's arms supporting her—

When she awoke, she was in her bed. Edward knelt in the glow of a bedside lamp, mopping her brow with a moistened cloth. Then he pressed a goblet to her lips; forced whiskey down her throat:

"Drink it all. You'll feel better."

"Jephtha. Is Jephtha—?"

"He's gone. Gideon took him out."

"Edward—"

"What is it, sweetheart?"

"You didn't—in the note—mention Baltimore—?"

"My God—" Edward shuddered, squeezing his eyes shut. The lamp flung his huge shadow on the ceiling. "I may hate the Yankees, Fan. But I'm not a murderer. There wasn't a single reference to Baltimore in that note."

He kissed her cheek. His lips were warm; reassuring.

"I—" Fan started to drift off. "—I had no idea he hated me so. No idea he could invent such a—"

She couldn't go on.

"A sick mind," Edward said, his tone deep and sad. "They say it sometimes happens to preachers who give up the cloth."

Another shadow writhed on the ceiling. Boots thumped across the floor. Fan saw Gideon in the lamplight, his tawny hair disarrayed. His face softened as he gazed down at her.

She tried to rise on her elbows. "You didn't—hurt him any more, did you?"

"No, Mama. I'd have liked to. But I didn't. I carried him down the back way, told the nigra porter to mind his own business and left him in the alley."

"Was he—awake?"

"I don't know and care less." Gideon's eyes shone like blue stones. "I dumped him two feet from a mongrel hunting garbage. That's where he belongs. With his own kind. Let him keep his damn money!"

Edward twisted around to stare up at the boy, a frown on his face. His lips opened. But he didn't say whatever had come to mind.

Grateful for the lulling effect of the whiskey, Fan closed her eyes. In her mind, she still saw Jephtha; dirty; foul-talking; poisoned with hatred. She should hate him in turn. But she grieved for him. He was so lost. She was the one who had been deceived on Tuesday. Deceived by his remarkable control; his feigned tenderness—

Face bright as an illuminated coin in the lamplight, Gideon repeated softly:

"Let him keep his goddamn Yankee money, the crazy man."

She didn't hear.

CHAPTER XI

Behold the Darkness

AT FIVE MINUTES PAST MIDNIGHT, a key rattled in the front door.

Molly jumped up from her chair in the sitting room. She heard the key drop on the porch. Then someone cursed.

The key was inserted again. It took another half minute for the door to open.

She smelled him first. The alcohol fumes were overpowering. When he appeared in the hallway, she exclaimed:

"Oh, Lord, Jephtha—I've been worried out of my mind!" She hurried to him. "We heard about the rioting in Baltimore."

Slowly, as if waking, he focused his attention on her. The hall gaslight revealed lash marks on his cheek. A rip in his black coat. His pale eyes were so stark and forlorn, she hesitated to ask what had happened.

His speech was thick: "I got caught in some of it. Horrible business—" He brushed his fingers across the back of his neck, where she saw a livid red line. "Lost your gun, I'm sorry to say."

"The boarders haven't talked of anything but the riot all evening. Half of them are scared as little babies. They say Washington's sure to be invaded over the weekend. Mr. Swampscott's already packed. In the morning he's taking the first northbound train."

"Wise," he mumbled. "Very wise."

She slipped her arms around his waist; pressed her cheek to his shoulder. "Come upstairs and let me dress those cuts."

"Not neces—necessary." He had trouble enunciating. "I stopped at Willard's for a dose of internal medicine."

"I know the special train carrying the Sixth Massachusetts arrived late this afternoon. I couldn't imagine why you'd take so long to come home—"

Sudden anger:

"I had to file my dispatch! For Christ's sake, Molly, I work for a living, remember?"

Her stomach spasmed. It was unbelievable to see him this drunk. Unbelievable to hear him take the name of Jesus in vain. He drank—but seldom to excess. He cursed—but he never invoked God or the Saviour in anger.

He licked his lips. Muttered:

"Cuts aren't bad. I'll wash up by myself. I'm pretty tired—"

"Won't you let me help?"

He flung off her hand. "Leave me alone, Molly. Just leave me alone tonight."

Staggering, he turned to the stairs. He stumbled and swore. Stumbled again halfway up. With her knuckles pressed to her lips, she listened until the door of his room slammed.

Something dreadful had happened to him. Was it seeing the Baltimore riot? Had that caused his vacant, hopeless look?

She could think of no other explanation.

She paced the sitting room for ten minutes. Finally she put out the gas and went upstairs, her mouth set in a determined line. She _had_ to find out what was wrong.

Three times, she knocked on the door of his bedroom, called his name softly and waited.

No answer.

Anxious and miserable, she walked slowly back to her own room.

ii

She slept poorly the rest of the night. Just as a gray, sunless dawn was breaking, she rose wearily and dressed.

Once more she knocked at Jephtha's door. Once more there was no reply.

She tried the knob. Unlocked.

She looked in. The room was empty. The bed hadn't been slept in.

On top of a pile of books, she noticed the red-covered Testament she'd returned after she'd found it by her bedside Tuesday morning. *That's the cause!* she thought suddenly. *I gave him the book. Encouraged him to read it—*

Guilt overwhelmed her as she remembered the underscored passage from the Beatitudes. *"Blessed are the peacemakers: for they shall be called the children of God."*

The violence in Baltimore had made a mockery of those words. It must have been too much for him to bear.

I tried to help prepare him to meet his wife, and this is the result.

I did it to him.

I'M TO BLAME—

She rushed downstairs to search for him, but he was gone.

iii

All that Saturday, Jephtha moved through the turmoil of Washington like a sleepwalker.

He forced himself to unlock the *Evening Star*'s front door with the key Mr. Wallach allowed him. He forced himself to sit down at his desk as the gray dawn brightened. He'd lied to Molly last night. He'd sent no dispatch to New York. This morning, he was obligated to write one.

He tore up a dozen foolscap sheets before he got a satisfactory first sentence. His mind kept replacing the paper with an image of Gideon's wrathful face. He felt the blows of the cane—

Was he mad? Had he imagined the plot against his life?

No! Lamont *had* urged him to go to Baltimore. If he hadn't misplaced the note, he could prove—

Prove it to whom? To Fan? She knew about it! She'd paved the way for his unthinking acceptance of the note. All the forgiving words Tuesday night had been rehearsed, to lull him into accepting Lamont's bait—

The eyes of the boys haunted him.

Jeremiah's—full of fear.

Gideon's—full of venom.

Gideon will believe them, not me. Perhaps if I hadn't lost my temper—or had the note—

Why think about it? Nothing could be changed now. He just hadn't realized how much they despised him. Or how desperately they wanted the money.

He thought of Monday night. Poring over the Testament until dawn. Trying to find the strength to forgive them—

What a waste. What a pathetic waste.

Silently, he damned Fan and her husband again.

Then damned himself for his foolish faith in them—and in the Testament. He ripped the sheet on which he'd finally penciled a decent opening. He threw both halves on the floor.

For about five minutes, he sat motionless. Then, by sheer force of will, he bent and retrieved the pieces of paper. He edged them together with unsteady hands.

He didn't care about Fan any longer. He didn't care about that bastard Lamont. But he cared about his sons.

And he'd lost them.

Forever.

A key clicked in the front door. He rubbed his eyes, hastily located a fresh sheet and began to recopy the lead sentence. Van Dyne hurried in, looking fatigued:

"Hello, Jephtha. Didn't know anyone was here yet. They've burned the bridges."

Jephtha's head jerked up. "To Virginia?"

"The railroad bridges in Baltimore. The city Police Board met around midnight. They don't want any more troops passing through the city. They're afraid of an even worse riot next time—"

The reporter sat down at his desk; scratched his unshaven chin. "Governor Hicks is sending a delegation to report the action to the President."

"How did you find out?"

"I met the early freight at the depot."

"I thought you said the bridges were burned."

"North of Baltimore—*north*."

"Oh."

"The line from Harper's Ferry to Relay House is useless, too. The rebels captured the town and the arsenal."

"So we're really cut off."

"That's right." Van Dyne yawned. Finally he noticed Jephtha's face. "Jesus, who marked you up?"

"I was in Baltimore yesterday."

Enviously: "In the middle of things?"

Jephtha nodded. "I—" Aimlessly, he touched the

halves of the torn sheet. "—I've been trying to put a piece together—"

"How were you lucky enough to be there when it happened?"

"A hunch," Jephtha lied. "Everyone's been saying there'd be trouble."

"That'll be a nice coup for the *Union*."

"Yes, won't it? That's certainly very important now."

The bitter answer made Van Dyne frown. But he refrained from comment. Instead, he offered advice:

"I'd get the piece on the wire as quickly as you can."

"Why?"

"The crew on the freight train said the rebels have gone wild in Baltimore. They're calling yesterday a great victory for the South. There's a lot of talk about seizing the telegraph offices."

"I see. I guess I'd better get to work."

He picked up a pencil and tried to think of a second sentence. Again he was distracted—this time by Van Dyne's news.

Bridges burned. Harper's Ferry gone. The telegraph lines threatened. The darkness falling on Washington was nearly as deep as the darkness in his own soul.

Hunched at the desk, he fought his way through a second sentence. A third. Gradually, the words began to flow a little faster. But his pain and heartbreak didn't lessen.

iv

A quiet madness spread through Washington City that April weekend. To keep busy, Jephtha trudged from department to department; from the Capitol to the Navy Yard; from the B & O station to the hotels—all except the National.

After each foray, he stopped at the *Star* long enough

to scrawl a few paragraphs and rush them to the telegraph office.

On Saturday and Sunday, the hotels emptied of all
but a few die-hards. All the trains for Baltimore were
packed. Seventeenth Street was hub to hub with wagon
traffic during the daylight hours. Families with their
goods swarmed to the presumed safety of what was still,
despite the Baltimore blood-letting, the North.

An exodus was underway in the other direction, too.
Hacks and carriages, farm wagons and drayman's
trucks heaped with furniture rattled over the Long
Bridge, the Navy Yard Bridge, Benning's Bridge, the
Georgetown Aqueduct. About the only people Jephtha
saw on the streets were riffraff and drilling soldiers.

Despite his deteriorated health, General Scott visited
the presidential mansion both days. Jephtha could learn
nothing about the purpose of the visits. All reporters
were denied admittance to the mansion.

Saturday night, he returned quite late to the G Street
boarding house. He went straight to his room without
looking for Molly. He locked his door and pulled the
wrapping paper off a full bottle of bourbon.

Several times during the night, Molly knocked. He
didn't answer. He drank and stared at the Testament.

Sunday, he again rose before dawn. He encountered
Molly downstairs; she was waiting for him. He was
forced to talk to her, but he restricted the conversation
to information he'd picked up on his rounds. He said
nothing about the scene at the National. He couldn't
bring himself to admit he'd been beaten by his own son.

Besides, she'd tried so hard to help him. To tell her
the effort had been wasted would have hurt her. He
cared for her too much to do that.

He suspected she didn't believe his explanation about
why he'd looked so terrible when he came home after
midnight Friday. Mercifully, she didn't press the issue.

Hour by hour, the situation in Washington grew

grimmer. He watched wagons unloading beans, pork, sugar and flour at the Post Office and the Treasury—provisions for the Rhode Island and New York troops, if they ever arrived.

After a brief rain shower, he watched traffic clog the muddy streets again. Women hugged children while their husbands whipped straining animals. Fights broke out when long lines of vehicles stalled because of a breakdown several blocks ahead.

He watched militiamen building sandbag breastworks in President's Park, and he watched a bizarre muster on the Mall. Several dozen old men—a number of whom said they'd served in the War of 1812—had emerged from their boarding house rooms with antique pistols and rusty swords. They were organizing once more—an utterly useless defense unit called, rather sadly and appropriately, the Silver Grays.

When he stopped at the Kirkwood, he found the hotel's dining room empty save for one guest. The man picking at a solitary meal was Mr. Hannibal Hamlin, former Democrat, former Senator from Maine, and now Vice President of the United States.

As Hamlin glanced up, Jephtha darted back out of sight. He wasn't embarrassed about being seen. He was embarrassed for the Vice President, who was dining alone, his company unwanted and his counsel unsought by anyone in the government.

He stopped at Willard's saloon bar. In view of the crisis, the hotel had relaxed its restrictions on Sunday liquor sales. There were more men present than he'd expected; men whose circumstances or loyalties wouldn't permit them to join the flight of those who feared for their lives—or those who were going home to take arms against the government they'd served.

On the faces of the hard-drinking men, Jephtha saw fear. He heard it in the half-truths and speculations they voiced:

"Abe and the Navy Secretary are fiery mad about Davis down in Montgomery."

"What'd he do now?"

"Announced that letters of marque will be issued to ships joining the Confederacy."

Another man snorted. "Trying to float a pirate fleet, is he?"

A fourth was equally scornful: "Welles and Lincoln are damn fools. That proclamation yesterday about a blockade of Southern ports is nonsense. There aren't fifty steam warships in the whole Navy, and most of the best ones were caught on foreign station when Old Bory took Sumter. What'n hell's Abe going to use to enforce a blockade? Dinghys?"

Laughter. Jephtha ordered a second double whiskey as a new speaker said:

"Even with plenty of ships, a blockade's impossible. You've got thirty-five hundred miles of coast from here to the Rio Grande—a hell of a lot more if you count the inland sounds all the way to the Floridas. Throw in rivers and bays and coves—all the navies in the world couldn't make it work!"

Jephtha drifted down the bar, sipping and listening.

"Got it straight from my cousin! A secesh group's gonna start fires all over town tonight. To signal the Virginia army to come on in!"

"Ben Butler's at Annapolis. He landed this afternoon with the Eighth Massachusetts."

"Bullshit! How do you know?"

"I work at the War Department, I ought to know!"

"Well, I don't believe you."

"Dammit, Butler's there! The Seventh New York's coming, too. And the Rhode Island boys."

"I still say bullshit. Annapolis is only forty miles away!"

"But that's forty miles of enemy country now," someone reminded the doubter. "Has General Scott established contact with Butler?"

"I don't think so," the man from War answered. "He can't spare even one company of cavalry from the city."

"It's all *bullshit!* We're done for! No one's coming. No one except the secesh army!"

Back at the *Star* about four in the afternoon, Jephtha tried to compress what he'd heard into a few brief paragraphs. He rushed the copy to the telegraph office, only to find the clerks extinguishing the gas and tacking up a sign that said *Closed*.

Pale, one of the clerks told him, "We're getting nothing in or out of Baltimore. The last message we received said a mob was hammering on the doors of the office. That was two hours ago. The line's been dead ever since."

Jephtha went outside into the low-slanting sunlight. He wadded his copy and flung it in the gutter. He had no further responsibilities until communication with the North was restored.

If it ever was.

                                    v

He returned to Willard's for three more double whiskeys. When he weaved back to the Avenue, twilight had settled. He gaped at a family—father, mother and two small children—slopping through the mud behind a large wheelbarrow piled with clothing.

The whiskey lent him false courage. He started walking toward the National.

At the hotel he laid sweating hands on the marble counter. "Lloyd?"

The clerk looked up from a ledger. "Yes, Mr. Kent?"

"Is the Lamont family still here?"

"They checked out this morning."

"All four of them?"

"Yes. They took a hack. I spent an hour locating one for them. Mr. Lamont paid me twenty dollars just to make the arrangements. They seemed very anxious to leave."

"For Richmond?"

"They didn't say."

Feeling curiously sober, Jephtha started away. "Thank you, Lloyd."

"Mr. Kent?"

He turned back. In the young clerk's eyes, he saw the fear that had become epidemic.

"Have you picked up any word about those relief regiments?"

Jephtha shook his head. "The telegraph's closed down in Baltimore. All the trains from there are late. And empty."

Suddenly the clerk leaned forward:

"For God's sake, when are the troops coming on?"

"I don't know, Lloyd. I'm not sure there are any troops."

vi

That evening, in the kitchen of the boarding house, he told Molly the Lamont entourage had departed. She reached out to grip his hand:

"Oh, Jephtha—I'm sorry. She never sent her note—"

"No."

He was seated at the plank table, his shoulders slumped. He separated his fingers from hers and sipped from a mug of whiskey-laced coffee. Molly resumed wrapping short pieces of twine around a larger ball. At the hearth, Bertha was stirring a kettle of soup. She kept up a continuous monologue of complaint:

"—thieves, that's what every blamed one of 'em's

turned into! Who ever heard of flour selling for fifteen dollars a barrel? Thursday it was four! Ain't no way we can serve bread to the boarders when we got to pay thieves' prices—"

"No," Jephtha repeated. "She never sent it."

"Then she lied to you. She promised."

He kept his expression blank. "So I thought."

"Damn her." Molly's eyes grew moist as she gripped his hand again *"Damn her."*

Jephtha said nothing. Silently, he'd uttered the same damnation a hundred times over.

vii

By Monday morning, Washington had the look of a deserted city. The streets were empty except for a last trickle of people departing; mostly on foot now.

Though he had no means of filing copy, Jephtha felt he should still make his rounds, if only to keep from having to be alone with his thoughts. He went to the Executive Mansion around nine.

Through the iron fence, he saw a dozen reporters lounging under the north portico. He showed his identification card to the civilian in charge of the four men standing watch at the gate. The men were members of Senator Lane's Frontier Guards. Their belts bristled with knives and revolvers.

Putting his foot on a pile of sandbags, the duty officer returned Jephtha's card:

"You fellows are to be admitted to the grounds. But that's all."

Jephtha nodded wearily. Throughout the park, he spied other guards on duty at the entrances to the departmental buildings. He headed up a walk to the mansion.

It was a damp, depressing morning. The sky was

gray. A touch of mist hung in the air, lending the park—and the city—a ghostly quality.

He joined the reporters waiting at the portico. He lit a cigar. The wet breeze blew the smoke away in a blue stream.

"Someone important expected?" he asked a man from the *National Intelligencer*, whose conservative proprietor had written editorials condemning the President's call for volunteers.

"General Scott," the reporter said. "He's late."

"Can't get those damn gouty legs of his into his boots," someone else joked. No one laughed.

Abruptly, a tired-looking John Nicolay came through the doors. The reporters surged forward, shouting questions. Nicolay shouted louder:

"I have no statement. No information! The President's coming down, that's all."

Grumbles; sullen glances. A sarcastic query:

"Just to take the air?"

Nicolay reacted with an uncharacteristic burst of petulance:

"He does it as a courtesy to the general. You know that!"

They did. Lincoln was concerned about the health of the Army commander. He demonstrated his concern by meeting Scott at the door every time the general called.

A correspondent from Greeley's *Tribune* asked:

"What's the President's state of mind, John?"

"I don't know why you're even bothering to ask when the telegraph wires are down."

"Come on, John! Don't dodge the question!" yelled a man from the administration's strongest local supporter, the *National Republican*.

Nicolay's lips whitened. "I'll say nothing for attribution—"

"All right, damn it! Just tell us!"

"The President is calm—"

Groans interrupted him. Then another question:

"John, is that an evasion? Or an outright lie?"

Nicolay fumed: "That's the truth—whether you believe it or not! Of course he's concerned about the military situation. But he's a man of great strength."

That didn't satisfy the newsmen either. Nicolay controlled his anger and tried to offer something more specific:

"He does look out the office window a good deal."

The *Tribune* man: "At what?"

"At the Potomac."

The quiet answer had a peculiar effect. There were no more questions for the moment. Nor any complaints. Inadvertently, Nicolay had captured what must be the essence of the President's mood:

Worry.

Worry that would draw his gaze to the river clouded with mist this morning. The open water represented the capital's one remaining link with the outside world. And across the Potomac, the President would be looking at enemy country—

Finally someone said, "Can you tell us whether any communication has been established with General Butler and the troops supposedly at Annapol—?"

Nicolay cut off the query with an upraised hand. Behind him, the door opened. Lincoln appeared.

The President's ill-fitting black suit was more wrinkled than usual. His deep-set eyes were ringed with heavy shadows. Jephtha experienced a moment of piercing doubt. Was this awkward, nasal-voiced Illinois lawyer really strong enough—bright enough—to deal with the crisis confronting the country?

Lincoln hooked his thumbs in the armholes of his vest and smiled:

"Why, good morning, gentlemen. My, we've a pretty good lot of brains gathered here, eh, John? Especially for a Monday."

"Yes, sir," Nicolay mumbled. "I told them we had no statement to ma—"

The man from the *Intelligencer* interrupted:

"Mr. President, isn't it true Washington's in great danger?"

"Danger?" Lincoln said in that sleepy tone he sometimes affected. He rolled his tongue in his cheek. Jephtha sensed his effort to hide his feelings. He replied courteously to the abrasive question:

"Henry, you know as well as I do—Washington City is well protected."

Someone snickered. Lincoln paid no attention:

"Besides, I haven't seen any Virginia army as yet. If there *is* one lurking across the river, we could be in a bit of a scrape. But an army's not half so fearful as a lot of other things in this world. You know—" The disarming countryman's grin distorted the sallow face. "—there's only one thing I'm *really* afraid of. Even though I know it can't hurt me."

"What's that, sir?"

"A woman."

The laughter was polite, no more. The *Harper's Weekly* man kept up the pressure:

"Sir, I still think the local citizens need reassurance that the troops from the North are on the way."

The smile vanished from Lincoln's face. "I believe they are. We must take it on faith. I do confess that, last night, my own faith lapsed a little. With the telegraph cut, and no trains running through to Philadelphia or New York, I began to believe that maybe there wasn't any North."

The reporters stood still, motionless and silent. The comically high voice carried emotion anything but comic:

"Yes, sir, I began to believe the Seventh New York Regiment was a myth—and the Rhode Island another. But that kind of thinking is a snare. It traps a man into doing nothing because he believes nothing. I spent half an hour with Tad and Willie just to get myself on the right track again. Worked! I have faith that Washington City will survive. I believe the Union will survive, and this terrible rift will be healed, and—"

Abruptly, the sunken eyes darted toward the gate, where hoofs clattered and wheels creaked. General Scott's coupe swung toward the mansion, a military driver and a blue-clad rifleman on the high seat.

Lincoln came down to the bottom step. The reporters drew back. The coupe was reined to a halt. Nicolay and the rifleman helped the hard-breathing general alight.

The sight of Scott only deepened Jephtha's pessimism. The old veteran was a study in obesity and red-faced ruin. He grumbled greetings as Nicolay and the soldier literally lifted him up one step at a time to spare his legs.

Lincoln waved to the reporters and followed the trio inside. The mansion doors closed.

The reporters drifted off, not saying much.

The Union will survive. This terrible rift will be healed.

Walking through the curling mist, Jephtha wished he had Lincoln's faith. But his was gone.

viii

The day grew increasingly dreary, as if the elements had conspired to heighten the city's atmosphere of dread. He felt useless without constructive work.

He went to Willard's for a while. He was the only customer.

He talked with the bartender, who claimed to have a relative on General Scott's staff. Before the day was over, the bartender confided, Scott would receive the resignations of General Joe Johnston and Colonel Robert Lee, to add to scores of others.

Jephtha finished his drink and wandered outside again. The whiskey did little to warm him against the gloom of the day—and nothing to elevate his spirits. He tramped the streets, paying no attention to where he was going. Sometime around noon he found himself at the Long Bridge.

An occasional wagon laden with household goods creaked toward Virginia. To gain the bridge, the wagons had to pass between a pair of twelve-pound smooth-bore Napoleons. The cannon pointed at the Potomac's far shore.

A truculent artillery sergeant scowled as another wagon approached. The young man driving was having trouble with a nervous team. Beside him, his wife rocked a bundled infant.

Something made the left horse shy. The horse nearly dragged the wagon into the nearest Napoleon. The sergeant shouted at the civilian:

"Watch your fucking wagon! That's Federal property you're trying to damage!"

"I'm not trying to damage anything," the young man panted, jerking the reins. He got the team under control. The hubs of the left wheels cleared the cannon by inches. Over his shoulder, the young man called, "All I want to do is get to Virginny—"

"And that's where we're gonna bury you!"

The young man flung down the reins; almost jumped from the seat. His wife held him back.

The infant began to cry. Leaning against the bridge rail, Jephtha stared at the flushed Southerner, then the cold-eyed artilleryman. Somehow the small confrontation summed up the tragedy in which all of them were caught—

Hatred was loose in the land. Because of it, his wife had betrayed him. His sons abominated him. And Gideon might fall, killed, in the holocaust that was surely coming.

He watched the wagon blur and vanish in the mist hiding Virginia. As he turned and trudged back into the encircled city, he thought of the words of the prophet Isaiah.

For, behold, the darkness shall cover the earth, and gross darkness the people."

ix

The voice woke her around eleven that night:

"Miz Molly! *Please, Miz Molly—*"

A hand shook her. Without thinking, she said, "Jephtha—?"

"It's Bertha."

She struggled upright. Saw the whiteness of Bertha's pupils accentuated by the glare of the lamp in her hand. A faint, foul odor permeated the bedroom.

Molly brushed stray hair from her forehead. "Bertha, what's that stench?"

"I don't know. That's why I come to get you. Smells like the place is on fire. Could it be them Virginians—?"

Molly rushed to the windows, tugged the curtains aside. No sign of a fire, nearby or in the distance.

"Will you hand me my wrapper?"

The black woman brought it from the clothes press. Molly slipped into it, increasingly alarmed. The smoky odor came from the first floor.

She patted the black woman's arm. "You wait here. Or in your room if you prefer."

"Don't you go down there, Miz Molly! Might be Virginny soldiers all over the place!"

"I don't think so. There's no noise."

"I heard somebody clumpin' on the stairs not ten minutes ago."

"Well, I'll see about it."

She hurried to Jephtha's room. Started to knock and noticed the door was ajar. She called his name as she shoved the door open. The feeble gaslight showed her the room was empty.

Had he gone out again? Was he the one Bertha had heard on the stairs?

He'd come in around ten. Reeling drunk. He'd gone straight to bed, barely saying a word. She'd retreated to her own room, in despair about her inability to do anything to ease his misery.

She slipped back down the corridor. The gas jets had been trimmed to their lowest level. The light was eerie, and her shadow huge on the wall beside her.

Sweat made her palm slip on the bannister as she went down. She felt a draft on her bare feet. The front door stood open six inches.

Orange light flickered on the carpet at the sitting room entrance. The smell was stronger. Her heartbeat thudded in her ears. Six steps to the bottom.

Four.

Two.

One—

She ran to the sitting room door. Looked in—

No one there.

Wind in the chimney puffed a gray cloud out of the fireplace. Sticks of kindling flamed and snapped apart. She walked slowly toward the hearth; stopped when she saw the source of the stench.

A whisper: "Oh, Jephtha—"

You'd better stick to saving string, Mrs. Emerson. When you try to save someone you love, you're a total failure.

She knelt on the hearthstone, crying. Wisps of smoke curled from the Testament's charred cover. Nothing remained of the pages but ash.

Interlude

The Girl I Left Behind Me

MICHAEL BOYLE'S POCKET WATCH showed four o'clock but the Westchester woods were already dark. Westward, beyond the Hudson, thunder rumbled.

The carriage bumped along the rutted road, banging him from one side to the other. It was the last Friday in April, and he'd been in a bad mood for days. His dark brown broadcloth suit—perhaps chosen unconsciously—

Only his face, his white stock and his shirt bosom relieved the gloom of the carriage interior. Both windows were down. Michael's golden-brown eyes were fixed on the passing forest, but he saw few details. The breeze through the windows carried an aroma of spring earth and the scent of rain.

An old portmanteau rested against his right foot. Inside it were toilet articles and carelessly packed evening wear. Julia insisted on a formal table at Kentland.

Michael was still baffled about the reason Louis had summoned him up to the country. He didn't believe the pretext given in the note of invitation—a dinner party honoring the Kents' western manager, Israel Hope.

Hope and his wife had arrived from California by steamer two days ago and had been whisked to the Westchester estate. Michael hadn't yet been introduced to the mulatto about whom Amanda had spoken at such length—and with much fondness.

314

The invitation was suspect on several counts. First, Hope had a wife of whom Julia disapproved; like Hope himself, the woman was part Negro. And her background, to say the least, lacked refinement. Hope had supposedly met her at a San Francisco theater. Louis always referred to her as a former variety-hall entertainer—a popular euphemism for prostitute.

Beyond that, neither Theophilus Payne nor Dana Hughes, the man who managed the family's book publishing firm in Boston, would be present tonight—even though Israel Hope's narrative of his escape from slavery in Mississippi and his subsequent migration to California, where he'd met Amanda, had been one of the books responsible for the resurgence of Kent and Son after its repurchase from the Stovall estate. *West to Freedom* had been reprinted eighteen times. Read avidly in the North; damned and double-damned in the South.

Since Theo Payne had been charged by the dying Amanda Kent to see that the book was issued, and Dana Hughes had overseen the actual publication, both men should have been included on the guest list. Instead, Louis had mentioned that the Kents' banker, Joshua Rothman of Boston, would be present with his wife. Michael guessed business was the real reason for the party. What business? He had no idea. It was going to take an overnight visit to answer the question.

Despite its mysterious purpose, the excursion was a welcome one. Michael was glad to be away from the city even for a few hours. Everywhere he went in New York, he saw red, white and blue bunting; recruiting offices operating in abandoned stores; men queuing up to answer Lincoln's call for troops.

All of it induced guilt. A guilt born when the Seventh New York militia left for Washington earlier in the month. He remembered the occasion with acute discomfort.

The Seventh had celebrated its departure with a two-mile parade down Broadway. Thousands jammed both sides of the street, out of patriotism and because the Seventh was composed of young men from the city's elite families. Even now, as the carriage lurched and thunder boomed, Michael could clearly recall the incredible spectacle; hear the tumultuous cheering—

The Seventh's little brass howitzers had blazed with a sunlit luster that matched the glow of proud, excited faces. The men of the Seventh wore trim gray uniforms, immaculate pipe-clayed cross belts, kid gloves. Each soldier's knapsack contained sandwiches prepared by the Delmonico kitchens.

Chance placed Michael alongside a thick-lipped woman on the parade route. She applauded and shrieked as the Seventh's band went by, drums keeping the cadence, horns blaring the rousing tune of "The Girl I Left Behind Me."

Flushed, the woman had turned to speak to him:

"All the young men are going, it seems. My son's going with a company of Zouaves from his firehouse."

Michael evaded her eyes. "Commendable."

"Aren't you going?"

"No, madam, I'm not."

She didn't speak to him again.

He remembered thinking, *I'm staying because there's a gentleman named Louis Kent who needs to be watched.* The excuse didn't erase the memory of the woman's scorn.

The Seventh had boarded ships for Annapolis; had landed and tramped overland to a rail junction, helping General Ben Butler's Eighth Massachusetts repair damaged track en route; and had finally reached Washington. According to dispatches sent by Jephtha after the reopening of the Baltimore telegraph service, the arrival of the Seventh had ended a week of fear generated by the specter of invasion from Virginia. The panic dissipated the instant the first squads climbed off the cars in the capital.

Busy preparing a Stovall Works bid for a government steel contract, Michael kept trying to convince himself he was needed in New York. Louis *did* bear watching; he was already engaged in extensive correspondence with the Lacroix brothers in Louisiana—technically enemy territory now. After the sharp exchange on election night, Louis had kept his communication with the Lacroixs completely private. He didn't even employ his male secretary to recopy his letters. He was definitely up to something; perhaps something illegal—

The carriage creaked out of the trees and onto a somewhat smoother road which ran along the bluffs near Tarrytown. Not far to Kentland, thank heaven. He ached from the long, rough ride.

On the west side of the Hudson, trees crowned the heights above the unseen river. Above them, fat black clouds rolled in. The gusty wind rocked the coach.

Storm coming—

Aren't you going?

No matter how he concocted excuses, his guilt wouldn't leave him.

In spite of martial music, Delmonico sandwiches and camp stools covered in velvet, the war showed signs of lasting longer than ninety days. An eighth state had joined the Confederacy. Jephtha's latest dispatches said Tennessee, North Carolina and Arkansas looked virtually certain to follow Virginia's lead within the next month.

The polarized border states—Missouri, Kentucky, Delaware and Maryland—were also danger points. They might go; they might not. In either case, each could become the scene of fierce partisan fighting. Payne had told him Jephtha was trying to confirm a rumor that Lincoln had already granted General Scott permission to suspend the writ of habeas corpus where "treasonous combinations" could be expected to take action against the Federal government. One of those places was surely Maryland.

Something was wrong with Jephtha's recent work, though. Both Michael and the editor noted a new, exceptionally pessimistic tone to his stories. Payne was forced to edit out dour paragraphs of speculation about the potential savagery of a military clash.

Though still pleased that the South had finally forced a war, Payne was tolerant of Jephtha's temporary aberration:

"How can a man with sons in Virginia *not* be depressed by the sight of soldiers and more soldiers?"

How indeed?

Aren't you going?

In truth, Michael had thought quite seriously about enlisting during the days immediately after Sumter's fall. He'd delayed because of Louis—and thus lost his best opportunity.

Following the surrender of the fort, some sixty-five hundred Irishmen had rushed to Hibernian Hall, and Corcoran's 69th New York had closed its rolls. The regiment had embarked from North River on the twenty-third of April and was now camped somewhere in Washington.

Oh, there was one group still being recruited. The officer in charge was Tom Meagher of Fifth Avenue, the Irish expatriate, journalist and lecturer. Meagher had been strongly pro-Southern until General Beauregard's attack at Charleston. Soon after he heard of it, he began organizing a company of Irish Zouaves destined to join the 69th as soon as possible. No doubt Meagher's rolls were already closed too—

Another excuse! He couldn't escape the persistent feeling that he was somehow less than a man because he was hanging back while thousands of others stepped forward to help put down the threat to Constitutional government.

He peered out the window as the carriage dipped through a low place in the road. The great trees on the far bluffs whipped in the rising wind. Deep within the boiling black clouds, he saw occasional flickers of lightning—

AREN'T YOU GOING?

Scowling, he whacked his fist against the carriage door. The entire side vibrated. Misinterpreting it as a signal of impatience, Joel hawed to the horse. The carriage picked up speed, hurling Michael against the opposite wall, then bouncing him upward. His head banged the ceiling. "God*damn* it!"

Joel slowed down. But Michael remained in ill humor. It was hardly a good beginning for his visit.

ii

Kentland had been built of white marble and envy.

Louis Kent had wanted a country home even more splendid and spacious than The Knoll—sometimes referred to as Paulding's Folly—a little further along the river: The Knoll had been the wonder of the countryside ever since Alexander Jackson Davis, one of the prime movers of the Gothic Revival, had designed it for former New York mayor William Paulding in 1838.

Louis had hired one of Davis' best pupils to outdo the baronial magnificence of the Paulding house. This the designer had done. He had placed his creation at the top of a gently sloping hill, which had been cleared to afford an almost uninterrupted view down to the point where the cliffside plunged to the river.

Popular as it was, Michael loathed the architectural style. Kentland was a jumble of turrets, gables and pinnacles, heavy with Tudor ornamentation and stained glass. The house was dominated by a square and massive central tower. The total effect reminded him of drawings of the grandiose new St. Patrick's Cathedral, proposed in 1850 by Archbishop Hughes and still unfinished on upper Fifth Avenue at Fiftieth Street. Kentland was a shrine, not a home.

As the carriage swung up the curving drive, he noticed lamps lit in many of the downstairs rooms. The lights shone behind ruby or aquamarine glass—the only touches of color in a sweep of pale stone, dark land and sky.

The carriage stopped beneath the marble archway protecting the main entrance. The right-hand door jerked open. Michael's normally pleasant face soured again. Not one but two liveried footmen stood outside.

One reached in to take his portmanteau. Both murmured obsequious greetings. He wondered whether Julia coached them on how to be polite and condescending at the same time.

His worn bag was whisked into the vaulted entrance hall. There, a butler stood at attention as Julia came dashing toward him, hoop skirt a-tilt and a disarming smile on her doll's face:

"Dear Michael! I'm so glad you're here—the weather's turning absolutely foul. When it rains, the roads to Kentland are quagmires. I was afraid you might not arrive in time for dinner—"

"I left Madison Square a little early for just that reason."

One footman marched up the immense carpeted staircase with his portmanteau. He and Julia stood beneath a chandelier whose candles were still unlit; gas wasn't available this far from the city.

Julia looked unusually pretty and animated. Her cheeks showed a slight flush. Her blue eyes were warm as she strained up on tiptoe for an obligatory kiss:

"I'm very glad."

There was a moment's awkwardness. As he bent toward her, she tilted her head slightly. Without meaning to, he kissed her full on the mouth.

He drew back quickly. He was unsettled by the sensual quality of the brief contact. Had he imagined it, or had her lips been slightly parted?

He rubbed a nervous finger across his chin. Quite unconsciously, he'd responded to the pressure of her mouth by kissing her harder than he'd intended—

Fortunately the servants were paying no attention. The butler and the other footman had disappeared into the library. The smell of a wood fire drifted from its open doors.

Julia smiled at him. She'd achieved a little victory; the first such victory he could recall. He was furious with her—and with himself. She didn't give a damn for him. But she'd wanted a response, and she'd gotten it.

"Wicks will show you to your room," she said as the butler emerged from the library. "We'll dine at seven. Provided the Rothmans have arrived."

"Mr. Hope and his wife are here, aren't they?"

"Yes. Louis is showing them the stables and the grounds. Clotilde is a lovely woman—for a nigra."

"Can you really tell she's Negro? I'd heard otherwise."

"Oh, there's no doubt," Julia said. He was again annoyed because his eye was drawn to her small, high breasts. "Her lips show it—and all her French mannerisms can't hide it. You'll see."

"Wasn't her home originally New Orleans?"

"Yes, before she went to California to take up her—ah—profession."

"Perhaps she's one of those women they call quadroons or octoroons. I've heard they're lovely creatures. I can't wait to meet her. I'm always more at home with people who were born poor."

That made her angry—as he'd intended. Her smile

froze. His was genuine as he walked toward the staircase. He'd salved the guilt he felt because of his lapse
during the kiss.

A few minutes later, though, as he unpacked in a
second-floor bedroom where he'd stayed before, he no
longer felt quite so pleased. In fact he felt decidedly uneasy.

Maybe it was the gloom of the day. Two glowing oil
lamps did little to dispel it. Even when the sun shone,
the great arched window overlooking the Hudson let in
very little light; the window was a sort of mural
crowded with bits of dark stained glass arranged to represent typical Gothic subjects—ruined churches, mon-
asteries and the like.

But he couldn't blame the weather for very long. In
one swift moment, arrogant, shallow little Julia had
aroused him. He found himself recalling the contours of
her fragile but well-proportioned body as they kissed
beneath the chandelier. He was ashamed she'd touched
a nerve; even more ashamed that he was still thinking of
her.

*Hell, you're giving it more importance than it de-
serves. Any reasonably attractive woman would have
caused that kind of response.*

The thought eased his conscience. It *had* been almost
a year since he'd bedded a girl—a lithe, good-humored
little actress who'd been appearing in Boucicault's *The
Colleen Bawn*—

*Stop lying to yourself, my lad. It was Julia who did it,
no one else.*

He flung his evening suit in the wardrobe and
slammed the door. An unexpected clap of thunder
made him start.

Christ! He was as nervous as a cat cornered by a
mastiff. He didn't like the way the visit had begun. He
didn't like it at all.

iii

In a dazzle of crystal and silver, dinner was served at the scheduled hour. The Rothmans had come down from Boston on a coasting vessel. Their carriage had arrived from the North River piers a little after five.

Louis welcomed the guests in the drawing room shortly before seven. Michael was introduced to Israel Hope, an emaciated man with Negroid features and a yellowish cast to his skin. The mulatto didn't seem the least awed by his surroundings. His formal suit, while obviously not as expensive as his host's, fitted him well. He looked, and acted, as if he'd worn such clothing all his life. Michael took to him instantly.

Hope's wife Clotilde was short, bright-eyed and exceptionally pretty; an altogether winning woman Michael judged to be about thirty—ten or twelve years younger than her husband. Except for the fullness of her lips and her coffee-and-cream skin, she could have passed for white. An octoroon, he decided.

With ingenuous enthusiasm, she described the thrill of the steamer trip from California and spoke of the wonders yet to be discovered in New York. She particularly wanted to visit Barnum's Museum, to see the famous midget, Major Thumb.

The Rothmans, of course, Michael knew well. Joshua was a lean man with a ready smile and delicate hands. Since their last meeting some six months ago, the banker had grown a luxuriant mustache with neatly waxed tips. New, too, were his thick Dundreary whiskers, reaching almost to the point of his chin. The style had been popularized by theater-goers. Similar whiskers had been worn by Lord Dundreary, one of the characters in Tom Taylor's *Our American Cousin,* a hit of the '58 season.

Joshua Rothman and his plump, cheerful wife Miriam were about the same age; in their late thirties. When Julia made her grand entrance—deliberately late, Michael suspected—she went directly to the Boston couple, greeting them warmly. She ignored the Hopes, who were chatting with Michael and Louis.

Again, Michael believed the delay was intentional. Julia wanted the Hopes to understand the relative importance of those present.

Finally, she glided over to speak with the California visitors for about half a minute before Wicks announced dinner.

To start the feast, half a dozen servants poured wine and set a solid silver tureen containing bisque of pheasant in front of each guest. Michael was the odd man. Partnerless, he was uncomfortable. And damnably aware of his hostess.

It was difficult not to admire Julia this evening. From her place at the foot of the long table, she dominated the gathering like a candle in a cave. Her dark hair cascaded over her ears in loose, glistening falls, and was drawn into a low chignon at the nape of her neck. To adorn her hair, she'd chosen an arrangement of white velvet flowers with tiny orange centers and miniature green velvet leaves, the whole draped artfully down the left side of her head to her shoulder.

Her white satin gown had short puffed sleeves and a boat-shaped décolletage, suitably modest yet not so high as to prohibit a glimpse of her cleavage when she leaned over to speak with Rothman, seated on her right. Silver cord fastened another festoon of artificial flowers across her bodice. Similar cording and flowers edged the hem of her skirt. On each wrist she wore a little band of green velvet decorated with one orange-centered bloom.

The Rothmans sat opposite the Hopes, who had Michael between them. He suspected the arrangement was planned to show him his proper place. He spooned up the bisque as Hope replied to a question from across the table:

"You're right, Mrs. Rothman, the Russell, Majors and Waddell service is a boon to California. In view of what's been happening in the East, people are anxious to get the news as soon as possible."

"What's the record time for those pony riders?" Joshua Rothman asked.

"Seven days and seventeen hours—carrying the President's inaugural speech." Fastidiously, Hope touched his lips with a napkin. "Each man rides about seventy-five miles."

Miriam Rothman shook her head. "I had no idea the Express was so fast."

"Normally, the run from Independence to San Francisco takes eight days," Hope told her. "That still beats Butterfield's Overland Stage by eight days."

In her charmingly accented speech, Clotilde Hope said, "We shall soon feel even closer to you thanks to— how do you say it?—*la télégraphie.*"

Michael said, "But I understand that may put the Pony Express out of business by the end of the year."

Louis finished his soup and laid his spoon aside. "You may find you don't want to hear the news from this part of the country."

Clotilde's husband nodded in a rueful way. "We even thought about canceling our trip. We had no trouble, however."

"Of course not," Miriam said. "There's no such thing as a Confederate navy."

"I'm sorry, my dear, but there is now," her husband said. "That fool McCauley didn't do a thorough job of scuttling the ships before the rebels captured the Gosport yard. My contacts in Richmond say *Merrimack,* among others, will be refloated as a Confederate raider."

"You mean to say you have dealings with your enemies?" Clotilde exclaimed. Louis and Julia exchanged amused looks. Israel noticed; frowned. But Rothman answered courteously:

"Yes, Mrs. Hope, we haven't closed off all lines of communication just yet. There's an excellent reason—especially among bankers. The South owes us a substantial amount in loans. We're trying to collect before it becomes totally impossible. Besides—"

Rothman gestured. Reflections of the table candles multiplied in the leaded panes of the windows. The glass was still wet with raindrops. But the storm had passed.

"—much as I detest the philosophies of some of our Southern brethren—and much as I believe we must meet their military challenge—I can't bring myself to dislike Southerners as individuals. They're Americans, after all. Their region has made invaluable contributions to this country."

Israel said quietly, "It also gave me the scars on my back."

"Amen to that," Mrs. Rothman nodded. She was active among the Boston abolitionists, Michael knew. "Lincoln's proved a distinct disappointment."

"You mean regarding slavery?" Michael asked.

She nodded again. "He said he wouldn't interfere with it where it was already established. That's cowardly and immoral! He should issue a proclamation freeing every black man, woman and child in the South. Then those rebels would be so busy protecting themselves against the people they've exploited and abused for two hundred years, they wouldn't have time to go playing at war!"

Joshua Rothman looked dubious. "You continue to misjudge the South, Miriam. Slaveholders are in the minority. We're at war because the South feels the North's infringing on the rights of sovereign states."

"Nonsense, Joshua! We're at war because they feel superior to black people, want to keep them in bondage—and are terrified at the thought of Negro equality!"

Louis began to look displeased with the trend of the conversation. Israel said:

"I happen to believe you're correct, Mrs. Rothman. But even if the South could be coerced into abiding by it, I doubt a proclamation of freedom would produce any basic change."

Snappishly, the banker's wife said, "You don't want to see your own people liberated, Mr. Hope? I find that hard to believe after reading your book!"

"Of course I want to see the Negro free. I'm only saying a piece of paper won't work a miracle. I know how whites feel about people of my race. A proclamation wouldn't necessarily make the black man's lot any easier. Might make it harder, in fact. Enemies who pretend friendship are a hell of—excuse me—a devil of a lot harder to fight than enemies who don't. How would the country—the *North*—treat hundreds of thousands of newly liberated blacks? Welcome them as equals? I sincerely doubt it. I'm in favor of emancipation. But I'm convinced it would only end one struggle and begin another."

"You're right," Michael said, taking a sip of the white wine that had been served with the bisque. "Where I was born in the city, every nigra is a threat to an Irishman's job."

Israel sighed. "Exactly. We'll be a long, long time solving that problem."

Julia pouted. "Then why must we discuss it? Let's stop all this depressing talk of slavery and war and just enjoy ourselves!"

"Hear, hear!" Louis said. "There may be a war, but we're under no obligation to wear hair shirts because of it. In fact, we have good reason to be happy. As an entity, the Kent family's doing well. The war will help us do even better."

Joshua Rothman looked startled; his wife, upset. Apprehensive, Clotilde watched her husband. Louis prodded the suddenly expressionless mulatto:

"Don't you agree, Israel?"

"I suppose so. I don't see how the war will affect the Ophir Company, though. Are you speaking of some new venture?"

Louis smiled. "Of course."

"What is it, Louis?" Rothman asked, rather sharply. "Some scheme to get more business from the government?" As the family banker, he didn't like surprises.

Louis tapped his spoon against the tureen—*tick, tick*—as if to throw Rothman off balance. Affably, he replied:

"Which government do you mean? The one in Washington? Or the one that may move from Montgomery to Richmond in the next few weeks?"

Israel's head snapped around. Miriam Rothman looked equally astonished. Michael detected a sudden change in the atmosphere of the overheated dining room. Something rank had crept in to mingle with the aromas of candle wax and perfume.

Tick, tick—Louis' spoon kept moving. His glance swept the table, ignoring the women but lingering a moment on each of the men. His flame-lit eyes left no doubt about who was in charge. He addressed the continuation of his thought to the banker:

"Don't forget, Joshua—each government has money to spend."

Israel's yellow fingers drummed on the table. Rothman was aghast:

"Good God, you're not suggesting we deal with *both*?"

Louis waved the spoon; a dismissal. "I'm suggesting we honor Julia's request and enjoy our meal." An almost imperceptible nod. The servants appeared, preparing the table for the next course. Louis continued smoothly, "We can discuss particulars later—after the ladies gather in the drawing room." He tried to joke: "Women gossip too much, eh, my dear?"

"About everything except their lovers," she smiled.

His complexion darkened noticeably. Julia's laugh was bright and faintly mocking:

"Come, don't look so thunderous! I'm only teasing."

Michael wasn't so sure. He found himself studying the tableware, the candles—anything but the faces of the guests. The tension he'd sensed was increasing moment by moment.

As he'd feared, business *was* the reason for the party. Hope and his wife were present only for camouflage. The mulatto and the banker both realized that now. Both were visibly unhappy.

Louis, however, seemed relaxed and expansive all at once, lolling in his heavily ornamented chair. He acted pleased with himself. He'd prepared the men for a pronouncement—then left them dangling until he was ready to deliver it. Another little assertion of his authority. Michael had a hard time remembering Amanda's son was only in his mid-twenties. He possessed the labyrinthine mind of a man many years older.

Michael sensed Julia watching him. Glanced up—

Her blue eyes locked with his for an instant. The bodice of her satin gown showed her rapid breathing. Spots of color dotted her cheeks. He wanted to look away; wanted to and couldn't. She was more beautiful than ever, those velvet flowers a colorful splash against the darkness of her hair.

Once she'd caught his attention—to remind him of her remark about women and their lovers?—she turned to whisper to Rothman. He couldn't hear the words. But he was certain she was leaning forward for his benefit.

He caught a tantalizing glimpse of corseted breasts. Beneath the table, his body reacted in a way that startled and appalled him.

His right hand clenched on the table. Julia noticed. Cast one swift, triumphant glance in his direction, then leaned over even further to hear Rothman's whispered reply. She burst out laughing:

"Oh, Joshua!—that's perfectly delightful!"

Again that uncomfortable feeling of being scrutinized—this time by Louis, who hadn't missed the exchange of glances. Michael felt increasingly fearful about the rest of the evening. Too eagerly, he reached for his wine goblet, drank, then signaled a servant for more.

iv

Despite the disturbing undercurrents Louis had set in motion at the table, Michael indulged his slum-born appetite and ate voraciously. He did it not only to fill his belly but to occupy his hands and mind. To the superb Dover sole, the sauces, side dishes and sweet pastries, he added an uncommonly large amount of the various wines served with each course.

Curiously, the alcohol did little to relax him. He still felt tense when the meal ended and the gentlemen separated from the ladies. The former retired to the library, the latter to the drawing room.

As the ladies left, he experienced a touch of malicious pleasure at the sight of Julia flanked by an octoroon and a Jewess. No doubt she found it galling to be gracious to women she'd consider her inferiors. Her laughter sounded shrill as Louis closed the library doors.

Michael walked to the marble fireplace and extended his palms toward the flames. Amanda had often teased him about his tolerance for temperatures others found unbearable. But until she hired him as a confidential clerk, he'd lived most of his life in unheated slum rooms. He wished she were present this evening instead of her son, who was pouring cognac and offering cigars from a rosewood box.

Kentland's library was an enormous rectangular room with another of those gaudy stained glass windows at the far end. At the highest point of the ceiling—twenty feet above the floor—arches of dark wood met. Each arch was cusped, and the tips of the cusps trefoiled. Some called the carvings beautiful. Michael found them fussy, ostentatious and unconscionably expensive.

Louis tapped his shoulder. "Care for a brandy before we talk?"

Michael turned. He detected no anger or jealousy in the younger man's dark eyes.

"Thanks, I would."

He followed a trail of smoke to the liquor cabinet. Louis clenched the fragrant Havana in his teeth as he poured. "Joshua—"

The banker broke off a low-voiced conversation with the mulatto. "Yes?"

"You and Israel might glance through that stack of newspapers on the table."

Though clearly puzzled by the request, the two men did as bidden. Michael took a long swallow from the snifter. The brandy burned his throat.

Just as he sat down in a large chair, Joshua Rothman exclaimed, "These are Richmond papers!"

"From the weeks prior to Sumter," Louis nodded. "Ignore the news columns. Nothing but a lot of gas. It's the advertisements that are provocative."

Sipping cognac, he strolled to the window. The sky had cleared. The clouds were gone. Some of the re-

maining raindrops caught the moonlight and shone
through the colored panes like bright gems.

Michael heard pages rustling as he returned to the
fireplace. At least Louis hadn't discarded the artifacts
the family had collected over the years. Looking at the
objects was never a painless experience. Amanda had
gotten a mortal wound defending them with an old Colt
revolver the night the house in Madison Square had
been invaded by Irish thugs.

Above the mantel hung the scabbarded French sword
which the founder of the family, Philip Kent, had received from a wealthy young nobleman he'd known in
his native province of Auvergne. Later, in America,
Philip had been reunited with the Marquis de Lafayette,
who was serving as a major-general in the Continental
army. They'd remained lifelong friends.

Below the sword was a Kentucky rifle Philip had acquired during his army service. The stock gleamed with
oil. The metalwork was bright and free of rust. A paint-
ing of Philip himself, dark-haired and faintly truculent,
hung in the drawing room.

On the shelves flanking the mantel, two spaces had
been left among the books of Kent and Son. In the
space to Michael's left stood a stoppered green bottle.
The bottle contained a small quantity of tea; the same
tea Philip had found in his shoes after he and a band of
patriots boarded the king's ships in Boston harbor to
conduct what was still referred to as Mr. Adams' tea
party. A rendering of the tea bottle was used as the co-
lophon of the printing house, and appeared on the masthead of every issue of the *Union*.

The right-hand space was occupied by a glass display
case with wooden ends. Inside the case, a slotted velvet
pedestal held a round, tarnished fob medallion. The
medallion had been presented to Amanda's cousin,
Jared Kent, by her father, Gilbert. A worn circlet of
tarred rope leaned against the front of the pedestal: a

bracelet Jared had woven for Amanda from cordage of the frigate *Constitution,* on which he'd sailed in the War of 1812.

Michael gazed at the obverse of the medallion. The partially filled tea bottle had been used as a central decoration, and was surrounded by a Latin motto he knew by heart.

Cape locum et fac vestigium.

Take a stand and make a mark.

The words were an affirmation of the family's personal code—and a promise to the country in which the Kents had prospered. Michael doubted Louis was much influenced by the first half of the motto, though he certainly seemed intent on living up to the second.

Depressing—

He helped himself to more brandy. Ribbons of smoke drifted over Louis' shoulder as he stood gazing at the moonlit lawn leading down to the bluffs. Israel tossed two papers back on the table:

"Louis, this is all a damned mystery to me. What's so interesting about patent medicine claims, information on militia units, or the announcement that someone named Dr. Schlosser is stopping at the Spotswood Hotel, where he'll be happy to treat corns and bunions just as he did for the King of Bavaria?"

Louis chuckled as he turned. "You read only the trivial advertisements. You missed the significant ones. I thought you were a better businessman."

The mildly sarcastic rebuke made Israel stiffen. Rothman, too, was unamused—but for a different reason:

"I know what he's driving at, Israel. The notices placed by industrial firms." He opened a paper and pointed. "Powder for sale by the Du Ponts of Wilmington." His finger kept moving. "Goodyear extolling its India rubber tents. Whitney's of New Haven—" He flung the paper on the pile. "One company's even offering to alter muskets for percussion fire at two dollars apiece."

Louis beamed. "Exactly."

"What do you mean, *exactly*? Those notices appeared *before* Sumter surrendered."

"Joshua, don't be naïve. Naturally there won't be similar advertisements in the future. Not in the public press. But do you honestly think every Northern firm is going to stop doing business with the South?" He clamped the cigar in his teeth again, squinting through the smoke. "Consider a few simple facts. For instance—how many first-class iron manufactures are located in the South? One!"

"The Tredegar in Richmond," Rothman murmured. Israel stared at the floor.

"Correct. The Tredegar—purveyors of heavy guns and boilers for the U.S. Navy's steam frigates—locomotive bodies and boilers—piping for municipal water systems. Not another factory in Dixie can match it. The Tredegar will convert to making military equipment if the war lasts any length of time. For our sake, I sincerely hope it will."

An unnatural silence decended on the library. Rothman looked as if he'd been bludgeoned. Israel stalked to the mantel and leaned there, staring at the Kentucky rifle, rigid with fury.

"The truth is, gentlemen, the South has some industrial facilities, but not nearly enough. I've studied the subject. I can give you specifics—"

Rothman scowled. "Why bother?"

"Because I want to, my friend! To make my case! In the South, about a hundred and ten thousand people are engaged in factory trades. Compare that with a million three hundred thousand in the North. In the South there are approximately eighteen thousand factories—a hundred and ten thousand up here. We have as many plants as the South has workers!"

He spoke directly to the banker: "Don't you see what that means in the event of a lengthy war? Where is the South going to get shoes? Medicines? Those new vul- canized rubber springs for rail cars? And a hundred other items I could name?"

"You've made your point," Rothman snapped.

"Not quite. Southern cotton is vitally important to one of our enterprises. The Blackstone mills in Paw- tucket. But the cotton we need is going to be rotting in the fields or moldering on the wharves. It won't be shipped to Europe—Jeff Davis is going to hold it back to force England and France to recognize the Confeder- acy."

Michael leaped up, slamming his snifter on a table, as he blurted:

"What the hell are you proposing, Louis? That we join hands with that damn Fernando Wood and support his scheme for Manhattan to secede, set itself up as a separate political entity and trade with both sides?"

Louis waved. "Mayor Wood's an idiot. Certainly I'm not proposing we involve ourselves in any plan as stupid as that. In fact, I'm not proposing anything." A pause. "I'm *telling* you what we're going to do."

Israel erupted: "Trade with the slave states?"

"Yes."

"I'll have no part of it!"

"Calm yourself!" Louis said, walking to the mulatto and reaching for his arm. Israel jerked away. Louis kept his temper:

"You're entirely correct—you'll have nothing to do with it. Personally. But we're going to finance our ven- ture with the Ophir profits."

Pandemonium. Rothman shouted the loudest:

"Louis, that's absolutely unthinkable! Every penny of that money goes into the separate account for Jephtha and his sons—along with the earnings from its reinvestment. The California funds are never mixed with the rest of the Kent income. Never!"

"I appreciate that, Joshua. However, you forget one compelling truth. Take any one of our enterprises. The newspaper—the publishing house—or the Stovall Works and the Blackstone Company, in which we hold substantial interests. Our income from each of those sources has demands on it. Operating expenses. Plowback for improvements to plant and equipment. Your bank collects a sizable managerial fee. So do the attorneys at Benbow and Benbow. Add in my salary, and Michael's—"

"Good-sized sums! Hardly to be minimized with the picayune term salary!"

"Well, Michael and I—you, too, I expect—have become accustomed to a certain style of living."

No one smiled. Abruptly, Louis continued:

"I won't put a penny from *any* of the businesses into a high-risk venture. With one exception. Even after deduction of Israel's share of the earnings, and the shares of those partners, Pelham and Nichols, there's a formidable sum left over. I've thought about it a long time. Our sole source of risk capital is the Ophir."

"*No!*" Rothman thundered. "Your mother left explicit instructions! We can only invest the Ophir money in sound, profitable stocks!"

"What I'm talking about can be fantastically profitable."

"And dangerous," Michael said. "Probably illegal."

"Michael's right," Rothman agreed. "I can't go along with it. Your mother insisted—"

"My *mother*, Joshua, is no longer with us."

Rothman's face turned red. Louis hurled his cigar into the fire:

"Jesus God Almighty, what is this, a conclave of saints? Do you think I'm talking about anything hundreds of other Northern businessmen won't be doing? If things work out, we'll make Jephtha and those pups of his fifty times richer than they are already! Every cent of the principal will be returned to them! Hell, I'll even concede some of the profits."

Coldly, Rothman said, "Keeping a certain percentage as compensation for your efforts, of course."

Louis smiled a bland smile. "I'd be entitled to it. But let's get down to the particulars—starting with cotton. I've been in contact with the Lacroix brothers in New Orleans. They agree with me. Opportunities are bound to exist for commerce between the opposing governments—"

"The Confederacy is no damned *government*!" Israel cried. "It's a region in rebellion! Trying to preserve a system that should have been buried two hundred years ago!"

"Israel, your feelings are understandable. But they don't square with the realities of the situation."

"*What* realities?"

"The Confederacy is already a second, sovereign power on this continent. It will be until it's defeated— which is inevitable. I cited one reason a few minutes ago. Industrial resources. Population's another."

"But—"

"I insist you let me finish. If you want to get technical, Lincoln's already acknowledged the Confederacy's a government, not a section engaged in insurrection."

"That's not true!"

"It is! Lincoln did it with his blundering announcement of a blockade. Naval blockades are instruments one government uses against another. Read your maritime law. Apparently neither the President nor Secretary Welles took the trouble."

Israel looked stunned. Louis lit another cigar. "We've gotten too far from the subject—"

Thick-tongued, Michael said, "No, too close."

Louis ignored him. "I've taken the first steps with the

Lacroixs. They're going to establish a dummy firm in a city convenient for—ah—confidential trading. A city far from Washington. Vicksburg, perhaps. Or Natchez. Our base of operations will be Chicago. The name of our firm will be Federal Suppliers. Benbow and Benbow is already doing the preliminary paperwork to set it up."

"I can't believe it," Rothman breathed. Michael felt sick; sick and betrayed. Israel was eyeing the French sword as if he wanted to haul it down and use it on Amanda's son.

Rothman collapsed in a chair. "I can't believe the Benbows would be a party to—"

"Oh, they don't like it much," Louis interrupted as he helped himself to more brandy. His back was turned. He spoke loudly, to be certain they heard him: "However, the Benbows realize one fact—"

He faced them, massaging the snifter between his palms.

"They work for me. If they don't like the arrangement, they're free to withdraw at any time."

He smiled and drank. *The smile of an adder,* Michael thought, his stomach hurting.

"That applies to you gentlemen, too," Louis added. "Of course, if you break off our association, your financial position will suffer. Substantially. Still, the choice is yours. If you haven't the guts to do what dozens of other businessmen—"

"We are not *other businessmen,* goddamn it!" Rothman roared. "We're the representatives of the Kent family!"

"A family I intend to see prosper even more than it's prospered up till now." Louis said it quietly, unwilling to be baited into a shouting match.

"The principles behind this war mean absolutely nothing to you?"

Louis shrugged. "Our public posture should be full

support of the administration. But as you yourself remarked at dinner, Joshua, we *will* be dealing with Americans. Why the devil are you acting so sanctimonious? You've admitted Wall Street hasn't broken its ties with the South—"

"I explained the reason for that! And its no secret from the Federal government!"

"While your arrangement," Michael put in, "can't be anything *but* secret."

Louis remained calm. "True. All goods will be bought for gold or silver. No paper money accepted by either side. Who knows what paper will be worth before the war's over? A couple of men who will eventually manage Federal Suppliers have started using gold—"

"You've *hired* people?" Michael asked.

Louis nodded.

"Who are they?"

"It's not important."

"I think it is."

"Well, you're overruled. As I was saying—the men have started using gold to buy one of the basic commodities in which we'll be dealing."

Rothman leaped to his feet. "What gold? Nothing's been withdrawn from Jephtha's accounts—"

"Not as yet. I've kept a strict accounting, though. I'll ask for a transfer of funds very soon."

"What's this commodity you're stockpiling?" Michael wanted to know.

"One which the Lacroixs suggested. Something very commonplace. But important."

He smiled the adder's smile again, forcing them to wait. Michael felt beaten. Louis was like a brakeless railroad engine running downhill. Unstoppable.

After he'd teased them a few more seconds, Louis uttered one word:

"Salt."

"God help us," Rothman groaned. "You *have* lost your mind."

"Allow me to disagree. I made the decision after careful research. Just like everything else in Mr. Davis' splendid new domain, salt is critically scarce. The only wells of any significance are located in southwestern Virginia. They'll be taxed to capacity if the war continues beyond three or four months. Without salt, meat can't be cured. Without meat, men can't be fed. Without decent food, no army fights effectively. Salt's important to the civilian population, too. Think of the field niggers working the cotton. Their productivity depends on their strength, and their strength depends on an adequate diet. Which includes meat. Federal Suppliers is going into the salt business."

"Jesus." Michael was trembling. "*Jesus.*"

Louis grew unfriendly. "I anticipated that kind of reaction from you, frankly. I've tried to be reasonable. And I'll say it one more time—I'm doing nothing others won't be doing. On both sides of the quarrel."

White-lipped, Michael told him, "I don't believe you."

"That's your error, then. I'll give you an example to prove it. There's already been private communication between Memminger, that Dutchman who runs the Confederate treasury, and two bank note companies, the American and the National, in New York."

While the others stared, Louis exclaimed:

"What's so astonishing? Where's the Confederacy going to get its first paper money? From companies that specialize in engraving and printing bills! Northern companies! The vice president of National told me he'd have to label the bills products of the *Southern* Bank Note Company—which I doubt exists. National has no qualms, I assure you. And profiteering isn't confined to illegal trade—I personally know a Brooklyn clothier who's working on a contract to supply Federal uniforms. He intends to manufacture them of shoddy. Re-processed rags! He's going to charge the same as he would for uniforms of first-quality wool. No qualms there either. Why should we be exceptions?"

"Jesus," Michael said again. "If Mrs. A ever heard such talk—"

"Michael, I am growing goddamned sick and tired of continual references to my mother!"

"Well, you may not like it, but—"

"—who was, I remind you, my mother and *not yours*."

Michael went white. Before he could retort, Rothman stormed toward Louis, shouting again:

"That's the filthiest, most derogatory thing you've ever said!"

"Joshua—"

"Who the hell took care of you when Amanda died? Who sat with you, hour by hour, after you came out of that concussive sleep Stovall caused when he hit you? Who consoled you when you learned your mother was dead and wept like an infant?"

"Yes, yes, I realize—" Momentarily taken aback, Louis softened a little.

"I've never heard such shameful ingratitude!"

"Well, I'm sorry!" Louis retorted—more angry than apologetic.

Bitterly, Michael said, "Let's not debate my humani-tarianism. I accepted the responsibility Mrs. A gave me. I did it without hesitation—" He faced Louis, his look murderous. "Because she was kind to me. Because I loved her. The subject's closed."

Louis tried to smile. "I'm glad. My mother has noth-ing to do with the present discuss—"

"She has everything to do with it!" Rothman in-sisted. "She believed the Kents stood for something. Honor! Principle! Your sole concern seems to be fin-ancial gain."

"Oh?" Louis was contemptuous. "That's different from yours? You don't approve of the Stovall Works supplying steel for Northern armament factories?"

Rothman stammered, "Naturally I believe in supporting—"

"I see. It's making money from your belief that you object to."

"You're twisting my words—"

"Bullshit."

"You—" The banker mopped his forehead. "You just don't understand. The profit's incidental. I'd give Stovall steel away if it would bring the war to a speedy end—"

"I wouldn't."

"That's because the costs you care about show up in a ledger, not a burial ground. *You'll* never face a Confederate musket! You'll stay safe and secluded in this baronial palace—"

"Joshua, you're getting pretty fucking personal!"

"I have a *right* to get personal! My family and yours have been close for almost eighty-five years! I'm not averse to making money—not even by supplying matériel to the Union. I *am* averse to unprincipled speculation that could prolong the war instead of shorten it. I don't want profits at the price of dead bodies!"

Louis didn't answer immediately. He was breathing hard. Michael glanced at Israel, who was still leaning on the mantel, a queer expression on his face. His eyes rested on Amanda's son. He might have been gazing at excrement.

At last Louis collected his thoughts:

"Again, Joshua—your argument's emotional. Based on faulty assumptions. Any student of the Southern temperament knows those people will fight as long and as hard as they can. They're tough. They believe in their cause. Why shouldn't we take advantage of that situation?"

"Because we're supposed to believe in something, too! We—"

Rothman swayed; gasped for air. Michael rushed to catch him. A feeble motion of the banker's hand rebuffed the help. His voice faint, he said:

"I believe I should retire. The discussion has gotten somewhat out of hand."

Louis gripped Rothman's arm. "My fault." The apology sickened Michael because he knew it was false. He turned away.

I failed you, Mrs. A. But you had doubts about him, too. While you were trying to take Kent and Son away from Stovall, you said you'd done some things that set Louis a bad example—

He leaned on the mantel beside the immobile, somehow frightening Israel Hope.

Forgive me if I put part of the blame on you. Taking it all on myself hurts too much.

"Please do retire if you feel like it," Louis went on.

Unsteadily, Rothman started for the door. "—taxing trip. A lot to drink. Trust you gentlemen will forgive me—"

Naturally Louis answered for all of them:

"Of course."

"I—I'll want to think this over—" Rothman's voice kept growing weaker. "I don't know whether—whether I can go along with—"

"Do think it over," Louis interrupted. "The decision's yours." Cordially, he delivered the killing stroke: "I'm sure many other banks would be happy to handle the Kent business."

"I don't have any thinking to do."

The harsh sound of Israel's voice made Rothman stop and peer with watering eyes. What he'd been through—what they'd all realized about Louis in the past few minutes—seemed to add ten years to his age.

"You want a new manager for the Ophir Company," Israel said. "You want him at once. I resign."

Louis shot out his hand. "Oh, Israel, for God's sake—!"

The mulatto stepped back. Michael honestly thought he might attack the younger man. But, very formally, and with immense control, he bowed:

"I thank you for the excellent dinner and the hospitality at your table. My wife and I will go back to the city now. If you'll be so kind as to call the carriage—"

Louis looked thunderstruck. Israel's decision actually broke through his hard veneer. He attempted to save the situation:

"I'll feel very badly if you and Clotilde leave. I'll feel ten times worse if you go ahead with this idiotic resignation—"

Punctilious in spite of his rage, Israel said, "There's no *going ahead*. I *have* resigned. I don't want any more to do with this family—what's left of it, that is. I'll expect to receive my wages and my share of the mine profits to date. You know the correct address in California."

Louis' face darkened again. His mouth twisted:

"What do you plan to do? Become a carpenter again? Grub with your hands?"

"Yes, sir," Israel whispered. "The way I did when I helped your mother put up the tavern in Yerba Buena. The way your great-grandfather did when he dirtied his fingers with ink at his print shop. Dirt on the hands is better than dirt on the soul."

Another polite bow. "Mr. Boyle—Mr. Rothman— it's been a pleasure to meet you." He paused at the door, addressing Louis. "Don't trouble yourself to say goodbye. Just have the carriage ready."

"Of all the stubborn, unrealistic—"

Slam.

The door vibrated. Louis' mouth hung open. He

poured more brandy, then whirled suddenly and hurled the snifter at the hearthstone.

Michael and Rothman dodged the flying splinters. Louis ran a hand over his hair. Tried to relieve the tension with a weak smile:

"Well, that was certainly a mistake. I mean inviting him to be present during our talk. I really did it as a matter of courtesy, since he manages the source of the income we'll be using for the Chicago operation—"

"He *was* the manager," Michael corrected.

Louis waved. "He'll change his mind when he's calmed down."

"No, Louis. Not every man in the world is for sale. You'd better call the carriage."

Rothman wiped his forehead. "I'm going to bed." The words were barely audible.

"And I'm going to have a drink," Michael said. "In my room."

"I'll send Wicks up with bourbon—" Louis began.

The Irishman stared at him. Such a handsome, splendid figure in his evening attire. Composed again, he strolled to the hearth. He kicked at a shard of glass. *The way he kicks aside every bit of opposition,* Michael thought. *I've got to get out of here before I kill him.*

"Please do," he said. "I want to toast the success of Federal Suppliers."

"Oh, Christ! Don't be snide. You two have blown the whole issue out of proportion!" He hit the mantel with his fist. "Why can't you get it through your heads? *Hundreds* of firms will be trading with the South!"

"That may be so," Michael whispered. "But I stand with Joshua. I'll have no part in profiteering at the expense of human lives."

Louis Kent's black eyes pierced him:

"Then you're not for sale either?"

"Not to you. Good night, Louis."

He followed Rothman out, his step almost as erratic as the banker's.

V

The mellow Tennessee bourbon Louis sent to his room didn't help.

Nothing helped.

He drank; paced; drank, swore and kept drinking—an hour and more.

What could he do to stop Louis?

Nothing.

What could Joshua Rothman do except refuse to act as the Kents' banker? For each of them, only an ineffectual, essentially negative response was possible.

For a long time Michael stared out the window at the silver and shadow of the lawn and the moon-tipped trees beyond the Hudson. He heard the carriage depart with Israel and his wife. Finally, sick of the house and aware that he was not only drunk but also miserably wide awake, he left his room, prowled down through the darkened entrance hall and went outside.

With the passing of the storm, the air had cooled. He'd discarded his coat and cravat, though he still wore his vest and starched evening shirt. He wandered toward the end of the gigantic house whose spires and turrets glowed under the high moon.

God, what a relief to escape the poisoned air inside. He savored the wholesome smell of wet earth and grass. He stumbled through a flower bed and made his way around to the back of the mansion to the two-story stable where he caught the scent of straw and manure and the horses.

He walked on, passing a pergola. On the far side, he started down the lawn to the dark trees edging the bluff at one side of the cleared area.

He'd gone only a few steps when he thought he heard a sound.

He looked back. The pergola's diamond-shaped lattices spread their shadows across the silvery grass at the top of the slope. The shadows faded as a cloud crossed the moon. He blinked, fancying he'd seen a different kind of shadow moving behind the pergola just before it darkened—

Only imagination, he decided.

He wandered on to the comforting gloom of the trees. The branches rattled in the light wind. He sank down and rested his back against rough bark. The breeze dried the sweat on his face. The liquor kept him warm—though it did nothing to relieve his feelings of rage and impotence.

Soon the damp ground began to soak the seat of his trousers. He rose, lurched forward, tripped over a root and blundered into a fern that spattered him with water. At the edge of the bluff, he gazed down at the tranquil, faintly iridescent river—

And heard another sound.

He spun to peer through the trees. He wasn't imagining this time. Someone was moving on the lawn—

He sucked in a swift breath. The moving shadow was that of a woman.

Her gown belled around her feet as she ran toward him. Her hair streamed behind her, suddenly moonlit as the cloud passed. Surprised and uneasy, he felt obliged to hail her:

"Julia?"

"Yes. I can't see you, Michael—"

"I'm down by the bluff. Be careful, the grass is slippery."

She made it without a fall, vanishing for a moment among the trees. When she emerged and hurried to his side, she was breathing rapidly.

She'd put on a heavy night robe. Dark fur trimmed

the collar and cuffs. He experienced a sharp sense of danger as Julia's pale face turned up toward his. She clutched his arm for support:

"You're right about the grass. I nearly fell twice."

His mouth tasted stale. His head felt heavy. He was a little dizzy. He'd consumed all the bourbon—half a decanter. He should have been relaxed. But he wasn't. The feeling of danger persisted.

He tried to banter: "Bit damp for a stroll, isn't it?"

"How could I possibly sleep? Louis stormed into his bedroom swearing like old Vanderbilt. He bolted himself in—he wouldn't answer my knocks. Then I heard someone prowling—"

"Me, probably. I couldn't sleep either."

"I gathered as much when I looked into the hall. Your door was open and the lamps were lit. Michael, you must tell me what happened. Why is Louis so upset?"

"Oh—" He was careful; he didn't trust her. "We had a rather heated conversation about business, that's all."

"I should say it must have been heated! When I came downstairs, Wicks was just going back to bed. He said Mr. Hope and his nigger wife had left in a huff."

"No, in the carriage."

She stamped her foot. "Don't try to be clever! I want to know why they left."

He sighed. "Ask Louis. Preferably in the morning. Things always seem more out of joint when it's dark and everyone's tired."

Julia folded her arms across her small breasts. "That won't do. Louis tells me only what he wishes to tell me. You know how stubborn he can be."

"God, yes! Still—any explanations should come from him. He *is* your husband—"

"You sound so bitter."

"Do I? Sincere apologies."

He moved away from her, raking fingers through his rust-colored hair. To be alone with her made him uncomfortable.

All at once a tiny suspicion stole into his thoughts. Leaving the house to follow him was a definite indiscretion. Had she done it solely to find out what had taken place in the library? He studied her eyes. The moon lent them a gem-like luster that stirred his loins.

"Julia, I believe you'd better go back. If you stay here you'll catch grippe or worse."

"My bed clothes are thin, but my cloak's very warm."

Leave, he said to himself. Leave *now*. There is more to it than curiosity about the quarrel—

"Then I'll go." He started past her, fighting the damnable physical reaction her presence caused.

She caught his hand, swept it around her waist, pressed her back against his chest. "Don't leave until you tell me." She leaned back, her head touching his shoulders. Her hair smelled sweeter than the spring grass. Murmuring, she went on:

"Louis won't. You're my only hope. You can't refuse me. You're kind—a quality we both know Louis lacks. I—I've always admired that about you, Michael—"

He wanted to laugh. Game-playing again. *Damn you, Michael Boyle—you know what she's doing. Are you so weak that you'll stand and permit it?*

He was.

Her head was motionless against his shoulder, her eyes fixed on the western sky above the Hudson. "I know you probably don't believe I admire you—"

"Truthfully, no." He still didn't move.

"But it's true!"

She whirled, standing quite close. He sensed the warmth of her body.

"I wish you'd be my friend. I wish you'd do as I ask and explain what—"

"*No!*" Michael said, seizing her arms. Too late, he realized his mistake. The physical contact only roused him all the more.

He hardened his voice:

"Ask Louis."

Her face was tilted up toward his. The moon set her eyes afire, hiding whatever thoughts those eyes might reveal. She seemed so small; fragile; needing protection—

Be careful!

"All right." She sounded sad. "But at least you don't have to speak so roughly. I'm terribly upset because I know there's been trouble and I can't discover the reason. You *are* my only hope. Michael, I—"

She seemed to rise on her toes. Her mouth—the mouth that had pressed his with such surprising passion earlier in the day—was very near. She whispered:

"I need you to be my friend. I have no one else. I don't *want* anyone else—"

Gently, she kissed him. His self-control shattered. He circled her waist with his arms, pulled her against him and kissed her as she was begging to be kissed.

The damp spring air—the interplay of moon and slow-moving tree branches—her seeming sadness all conspired against him. Her lips were warm and wet. Unmistakably, she felt him through her robe.

Her hands stole up to his face. Her palms caressed him. She opened her mouth. Their tongues touched.

Shuddering, she thrust even closer, one of her hands tangled in his hair—

Then, abruptly, she ended it. Her small, surprisingly strong hands closed on his forearms and pushed him back:

"Michael, we mustn't—"

The moonlight showed him her eyes. Not alarmed. *Amused—*

Enraged, he wrenched free, grabbed her and pulled her toward the trees.

She struggled: "No, darling. We've gone too far already—"

"The hell we have."

"Michael—" She wrenched hard, escaping his hands. "I'm a married woman!"

"I see," he said. "The hunt's over. The trophy's claimed."

"What in heaven's name do you mean?"

"You know very well."

"I certainly do not, I—"

Drunk and angry, he lunged and caught her again.

"Let go of me!"

"No, by God. We're not finished just yet. You shouldn't have started the game, Julia, because now we're going to play it to the end."

"Michael, I beg you, let g—*ahh!*"

She cried out as he jerked her up against his body. He took satisfaction from the fright in her eyes; from her wild pleading:

"Michael, I wasn't myself—I didn't intend to lead you on—"

"Of course you did. You got exactly what you wanted. And a bit more than you bargained for—"

"What—what are you going to do?" Her effort at sarcasm was tinged with terror: "What slum boys do when they want a woman? Commit rape—?"

"Call it anything you please." He swept one arm beneath her legs; lifted her. She was no match for his strength. He spun and climbed toward the trees with long, savage strides.

"Oh, God," she whispered against his throat. "You're cruel, you're *an animal*—"

"No more than you, my dear."

Among the trees where no light penetrated, he

slammed her on her feet. Branches clacked in the wind.
A night creature scuttled away in the underbrush.

"Michael, I'm warning you—" He couldn't see her
face. But her voice conveyed her desperation. "I'll tell
Louis."

He chuckled. "I don't think so. He'd give you worse
punishment than you're going to get from me."

Using both hands, he tore her robe outward and
down; tore the flimsy lace-edged fabric beneath at the
same time.

His eyes had accustomed themselves to the dark. Her
face was a dim white oval. Her bared breasts looked
black at the tips.

Breathing hard, he cupped his hands around those
breasts. Closed his fingers slowly. He didn't want to
hurt her—

Not too much.

vi

He took her on the damp ground, her robe thrown
open beneath her and her lace gown a tangle above her
hips.

At first she was rigid. She beat at him with small,
hard fists. He kept his mouth on hers so she wouldn't
cry out.

Then, in the midst of his deliberately brutal assault,
something changed. He felt it first where their bodies
joined.

Her fists opened. One arm curved around his neck.
She tried to match his motion, not fight against it.

He was surprised when he heard her groan. She
strained closer, uttering throaty, pleading cries—

It was too late.

He stood up, attending to his clothing. She twisted
from side to side, moaning still louder:

"Ohhh. *Ohhh*—"

He didn't know whether she was feeling pain or desire. Nor did he care. "Good night, Julia," he said, wheeling away and striding through the grove toward the lawn.

He was vaguely ashamed of what he'd done. The shame lingered and grew sharper when he was back in his room, sobering fast.

But mingled with the shame, there was pleasure.

vii

An hour before dawn, still dressed in his formal suit and lugging his hastily packed portmanteau, Michael left the house a second time.

He encountered no one until he wakened the groom in the stable. By lantern light, the two of them proceeded to the second floor room where Joel was spending the night.

Joel and the groom hitched up the horse. As gray light began to whiten the eastern face of the house, the carriage wheeled from the drive and was soon careening through the muddy ruts in the Westchester forest.

Michael slumped on the seat, drained. His eyes itched. He was unable to get the stale taste out of his mouth—nor the feel of Julia's body out of his thoughts.

Chilly air gusted through the open window. He tried to analyze his confused state of mind.

He hadn't departed suddenly, and without announcement, because he feared repercussions from Louis. He'd meant what he'd told Julia. He doubted she'd ever say anything about the—

What's the term for it? he asked himself sourly. *Semi-*rape?

Even if they'd been detected—if Louis or a servant had accidentally glimpsed one or both of them on the lawn—he wasn't concerned. Suppose Louis did come after him with a cane, a horsewhip—even a pistol. It might be a relief. At least he'd have a chance of winning that kind of contest. Whereas in the battle waged with words in Kentland's library, he'd been defeated and left without further options.

The carriage bounced and jolted him. Completely sober, he finally admitted he was running away from something other than the hopeless struggle with Amanda's son. He was running from himself—and his feelings about Julia.

He knew what kind of woman she was. She'd made that clear again down by the river. He'd hoped to teach her a lesson; show her she couldn't sport with him; lead him just so far, then call a halt.

But she'd won after all. As the terrible light of day revealed the woods, so his own mind revealed the long-buried truth. Even though Julia Kent was despicably flawed, during those moments when they'd moved together in passion—and long before—he'd *wanted* her.

He squinted against the wind. Stared at the woods slipping by. Self-deception wasn't possible any longer. She was beautiful—and he'd envied Louis for possessing her:

All this time you were so careful. Ignoring her sly invitations. Refusing to play her game. Not because you despised her but because, secretly, you wanted *to succumb—*

Added to the rupture that had taken place in the library, it was an impossible situation. So he was fleeing back to New York.

But what peace could he find there? He couldn't persuade Louis to abandon that damned dummy company in Chicago. He had no power to force him to do it.

And he couldn't see Julia again. For the sake of his own sanity, he didn't dare.

Trapped.

Doubly trapped—

With no way out.

The carriage sloshed through standing water. Mud splattered against the side, the sound rousing him a little. The first brilliant orange sunlight speared between the trees. He remembered what day it was—

Saturday.

There *was* something he could do to escape.

viii

Shortly after two o'clock that afternoon, Michael approached the steps of the brownstone residence at 129 Fifth Avenue, between Nineteenth and Twentieth. The April sun shone.

He had made two previous stops. One on Beekman Street and, prior to that, at old St. Patrick's, on Mulberry just north of Prince.

His progress along the row of handsome houses was impeded by a crowd that had gathered for yet another parade. He recognized the uniforms of the rough-looking men marching by. They were Fire Zouaves, recruited from the brawlers who manned the city's volunteer pump companies. A crony of Lincoln's, one Colonel Ellsworth, a patent attorney from Chicago, had set out on a personal campaign to whip up enthusiasm for the type of military uniform the French had copied from the Berbers during some forgotten war in Algeria.

Outside Number 129, Michael paused to watch. The New York Fire Zouaves swaggered along in ballooning red trousers, short, tight-fitting blue jackets and scarlet sashes. Their muskets were canted carelessly over their shoulders. Most of the men carried Bowie knives. Each wore a red fez.

He heard drums. Their band, a block away—

"They gonna ship you boys to Washington by rail?" a spectator shouted.

One of the Fire Zouaves bawled back, "Sure as hell hope so. We'll go through Baltimore like a dose of salts!"

Cheers and applause. Each Zouave walked at his own pace. No one acted concerned, least of all the officers. Many of them were busy conversing with young ladies along the parade route.

The thumping drums grew louder. The horns blared suddenly, brassy and assertive. The melody seemed a cruel comment on his own wretchedness—

The band was playing "The Girl I Left Behind Me."

The crowd went wild as the band drew closer. The music became a painful din. Against it, he heard the words he'd spoken in the shadowy church he hadn't visited in far too long—

Bless me, father, I have sinned.

A mortal sin.

Adultery.

Well, he would do his penance. But he would go beyond the prescribed Hail Marys, the Our Fathers, the Act of Contrition. He'd do a penance that would free him of the futile fight with Louis Kent; a penance that would help absolve him of the guilt springing from the feelings about Julia which he'd finally acknowledged—

And absolve another guilt as well.

"Is the master at home?"

"Mr. Townsend?"

He'd forgotten the man he wanted to see lived with his properous father-in-law. "I'm sorry—I mean Mr. Meagher."

"In the parlor, sir. Who shall I say is—?"

Michael hurried by without answering.

Thirty-eight year old Thomas Meagher rose from his

chair, looking annoyed. Piles of documents surrounded the chair. On the mantel rested a forage cap with the 69th's distinctive metal insignia—a small Irish harp. A stack of circulars lay on a table. Michael had seen them before:

> *YOUNG IRISHMEN TO ARMS!*
> *TO ARMS YOUNG IRISHMEN!*
> *IRISH ZOUAVES*
> *One hundred young Irishmen—healthy,*
> *intelligent and active—wanted at once*
> *to form a Company under the command of*
> *THOMAS FRANCIS MEAGHER.*
> *To be attached to the 69th Regiment,*
> *N.Y.S.M. No applicant under eighteen—*

"I don't believe we're acquainted," Meagher barked.

"My name's Michael Boyle, sir. I'm a friend of Colonel Corcoran's. We were introduced once at Hibernian Hall."

Meagher's stern expression moderated. "Oh, yes. I do recall the meeting. What can I do for you?"

"I wanted to ask whether your company roster's filled. I went to the recruiting office on Beekman—the one mentioned in that circular—but it was closed. I thought perhaps you'd gotten your hundred men—"

"The recruiting hall is never open on Saturday afternoons. I use that time for personal business." Meagher nodded toward the piles of documents, growing more cordial:

"Won't you be seated, Mr.—Boyle, is it? To answer your question—no, the roster is not filled. We still need seven men."

The faint, taunting music of the Zouave band faded down Fifth Avenue. "If you'll have me," Michael said, "now it's only six."

Book Two

Red July

CHAPTER I

City at the Edge of War

THREE O'CLOCK, the normal hour for closing, came and went. At four, the shop still had customers. Margaret began to fret. Would she be free soon enough to meet Gideon?

He'd promised to be at their rendezvous by five-thirty at the latest. If he were on time, they'd have an hour together before he had to rush back to the Fair Grounds. She kept thinking of it as the Fair Grounds even though it had been renamed Camp Lee in honor of the famous colonel who'd come to Richmond as major-general in charge of the state military forces.

Four fifteen. La Mode Shoppe remained busy.

The shop occupied a narrow frontage on Main Street near Tenth, a block and a half from the teeming Spots-wood Hotel, the unofficial center of the town's political activity. Though La Mode had always enjoyed the pa-tronage of a few of the capital's well-to-do ladies, the owner—Margaret's aunt—had never been able to match the scope of the stock at establishments such as Miss Semon's. Miss Semon was prosperous enough to travel to Europe and bring back the latest continental fashions—this season Arabian mantles for women, and suits in the Spanish mode for young gentlemen. At four-fifteen, Eliza Marble was measuring Mrs. Honeyman's surly little boy for just such a suit.

What La Mode lacked in resources, it made up by hard work. Aunt Eliza regularly observed Miss Semon's windows, sketched her latest arrivals from memory, and then showed the four girls who worked evenings in the back how to run up cheaper copies. Customers who couldn't afford originals found Aunt Eliza's imitations satisfactory both in design and price.

Normally, this procedure helped insure a tiny profit at the end of every month. But conditions in Richmond were no longer normal. The city was now part of the Confederacy—a situation Margaret loathed because it meant war. Arkansas had left the Union, followed by Tennessee. Mrs. Honeyman, overseeing Aunt Eliza's measuring of the disagreeable and fidgety Clovis, had reported that everyone up in the elegant Church Hill district was certain North Carolina would secede within seven days.

"—and they've just appointed Brigadier Johnston to take command of the state troops assembling at Harper's Ferry."

Margaret overheard Mrs. Honeyman's remark as she finished writing the order for a uniform. The uniform would be worn by a young man who belonged to one of the volunteer units. Margaret had taken his measurements with considerable embarrassment; she'd turned red as a tomato when she'd knelt and run the tape up his inseam.

But he'd been polite. Hadn't joked or taken advantage of her embarrassment. As she'd performed the unladylike task, Margaret consoled herself by recalling the extra profit Aunt Eliza realized from uniforms. The gentlemen's tailor shops couldn't keep up with the demand—another sign of the disruption in the city Margaret Marble had called home for thirteen of her eighteen years.

Trade in uniforms had become so brisk, Margaret had been forced to resign her part-time position at West & Johnston, the book and music store where she'd formerly clerked three days a week because

Aunt Eliza couldn't afford to pay her full wages. Although Margaret was now working exclusively at La Mode, she received no extra money. Most of the shop's increased income went to purchase additional fabric and decorative materials for the next batch of uniforms.

Margaret didn't object. She owed Eliza Marble more than she could ever repay. She did her work faithfully, even though she disliked the uniform business and all it represented.

Of late, her dislike had changed to outright fear. The transformation had started on that showery afternoon when Gideon Kent had walked into West & Johnston's to buy his book on cavalry tactics. He was tall; boisterous—and the possessor of the most appealing blue eyes she'd ever seen.

Something had happened between them. Something instantaneous and dizzying. Because of him, she feared and loathed the foolish enthusiasm sweeping the city. He had no notion of the real meaning of war. But she did. She saw a devastating reminder when she went home every evening to the dingy suburb of Rockett's.

As she finished writing the instructions for the uniform, a picture of eastern Kentucky came into her thoughts. She saw the green, peaceful mountains. She'd been very small when she'd left Kentucky. But her mind still stored a few images of that sweet time before the Sergeant had gone off to Mexico, leaving a small daughter and an ailing wife who died of influenza the first winter he was away. When he came home—the memory of the first sight of him still had power to terrify her— he was incapable of running the farm. They'd sold it, and ever since, they'd survived on the charity of Eliza Marble, a spare, graying spinster with a pleasantly prunish face.

"Brigadier Johnston? Is that a fact!" Aunt Eliza said. The words were muffled because her mouth was

full of pins. Her brattish customer eyed the pins with
apprehension:

"Mama, she's going to jab me with one of those!"

"Clovis, you hush," Mrs. Honeyman said. "Else I'll
jab you myself!"

The little boy raised a hand in front of his face. From
her position behind a counter, Margaret saw him stick
out his tongue. Chattering on, Mrs. Honeyman didn't
notice:

"I was just as surprised as you, Eliza. Everyone
thought General Lee would get the command. He's such
a gracious, charming man—"

"And a true Christian," Aunt Eliza commented.

"Johnston, you know, was only a general because the
rank went with his job. They say he's a regular little
gamecock about rank. He insisted on taking charge here
because he was higher than Lee in the Federal service.
If Beauregard comes north, Johnston will probably demand to be Bory's superior too—even though Bory's
fought a battle and Johnston hasn't."

Margaret finished her notations and said pleasantly:

"I don't think you can call the bombardment of a
surrounded fort a battle, Mrs. Honeyman."

The well-dressed woman looked startled, then insulted. Aunt Eliza was on her knees again, busying with
the tape and pins. Clovis tried to kick her while his
mother's head was turned. She pinched his leg. He
squealed.

"Oh, dear, Clovis," she said. "The pin slipped."

Clovis reddened. Aunt Eliza gave Margaret a look
conveying her disapproval of the comment to Mrs. Honeyman.

Mrs. Honeyman was more direct:

"You certainly speak your mind, Margaret. Several
of the ladies at St. Paul's have asked why you don't join
your aunt in the evening and help us sew tents and pre-

pare lint and bandages. I've told them you have strong feelings against our cause. Haven't I, Eliza?"

"Frequently," Aunt Eliza said, almost sighing.

St. Paul's, just up by Capitol Square, was an affluent church. Margaret and her aunt were perhaps its poorest members. Still, Eliza Marble had lived in Richmond all her life. When it came to religion, she refused to acknowledge any other resident—or any other Episcopalian—as her better.

But Margaret had challenged a paying customer. The older woman tried to take a bit of the heat out of the situation:

"You know the reason for Margaret's feelings. Her father—"

"Yes, yes!" Mrs. Honeyman interrupted. "But it's no excuse. Not when that black-nigger Republican in Washington has thrown down the glove! The sovereign states of the South have every right to undo a compact into which they entered voluntarily. For Lincoln to say otherwise is illegal. It can't be tolerated!"

"Mrs. Honeyman," Margaret said quietly, "it's all very fine to indulge in such talk. It's all very fine to drive out to Camp Lee with lunch baskets for the boys, and wave the new Stars and Bars and brag about whipping the Yankees in a month—"

Aunt Eliza stood up suddenly. Pudgy-faced Clovis directed a venomous stare at the unpatriotic girl behind the counter. Gently but firmly, Eliza said, "Please, Margaret. You have a right to your opinions—wrong as they are. But do try to remember you're speaking to a patron."

Margaret's eyes blazed. Her head up, her chin thrust forward, she refused to be intimidated by her aunt's request—or Mrs. Honeyman's unfriendly expression:

"Have you ever lost a loved one in a war, Mrs. Honeyman?"

"No. I have not. I can't say the question's of any relevance—"

"But it is. Everyone in Richmond looks on the war as a—a carnival! Wait till you see one of your relatives bleeding—maimed. Fighting Yankees won't be a jolly sport after that!"

"Margaret, I must insist you stop!" There was frost in Aunt Eliza's voice. "Take that dragoon's measurements to the workroom—this instant."

"All right," Margaret said, infuriated but outwardly pliant. She shouldn't embarrass her aunt any further— or cause the loss of an order. She picked up the paper on which she'd been writing. Why *was* she so irritable today?

And every day?

She knew. The larger the reality of war loomed, the more she detested all the posturing. Attempted to withdraw from it; seal off her emotions so as not to be touched by it in any way.

But her emotions *were* touched. For one very special reason.

She walked from the amber of the sun-filled shop into the darker back room. Willa Perkins, an undernourished, poorly dressed white girl bent over a work table, laboriously scissoring pieces of a trousers pattern from butternut cloth. Partially completed garments of every color from dull gray to gaudy azure lay on chairs and cartons. Finished, boxed uniforms jammed wooden shelves along one entire wall.

"Here's another, Willa." She handed the notes to the pinch-faced girl.

"Oh, Lord," Willa sighed. "I'm so far behind, I ain't ever gonna catch up."

"I'll be back this evening to help you and the other girls."

Willa rolled her tongue in her cheek. "Gonna see your young gentleman first?"

"That's right."

"I'm kinda surprised you took up with him. I mean, he *is* a soldier—"

"He's a cavalryman."

And I wish to God he weren't.

"I seen him Monday when he come in. He's mighty handsome in that hoosar suit."

"It's not *hoos*ar, Willa, it's *huss*ar." Margaret tried to be kindly about correcting the girl's pronunciation. Willa too lived out in Rockett's. Her father was a longshoreman at the nearby port.

Despite Willa's lack of education, she had an intuitive intelligence. She knew there was a contradiction in Margaret's choice of a male friend. A contradiction that was making Margaret more miserable by the day.

Margaret Marble was of slender build but with a round and ample bosom. She had a generous mouth, brown hair that matched her animated eyes and a stubby nose she'd always hated because it made her look boyish. And if she had any enemy on this golden afternoon—Wednesday, the fifteenth of May—it wasn't some faceless Yank. It was Gideon Kent himself.

Gideon had charmed her on sight. He'd walked into West & Johnston's and boldly engaged her in conversation after he bought his book. For practically the first time in her life, she'd found her hands tingling; her laugh sounding too shrill; her breast rising and falling too rapidly. She kept telling herself he was a soldier. To no avail.

She'd seen him almost daily for the past month. And of late, she'd frequently asked herself whether it was possible to care for a man and despise him at the same time.

In a way it was a dishonest question. She didn't despise Gideon at all. The mere prospect of meeting him again tonight filled her with excitement. But she *did* despise the abandon with which he was plunging into the preparations for war. She considered that part of his character to be her enemy. An enemy against whom she had to wage her own war—

She'd never known a boy who affected her as deeply as Gideon did. She'd only had a few beaux. Two could be classed as serious. Both had come from good families. She'd finally allowed each to call on her at the flat in Rockett's instead of meeting her in the center of town. Neither boy had ever come back:

Truly, Mama, I had no idea the girl lived in such a squalid place. Certainly I won't see her another time.

Gideon knew where she lived. But she'd never permitted him to escort her home. Nor had she ever spoken a word about her father.

She thought of Gideon almost constantly when she was away from him; thought of him in ways Aunt Eliza would have considered distinctly improper.

Margaret was a virgin. Not from any overwhelming devotion to prudery. Not even because the church she attended with Aunt Eliza on Sundays taught that such restraint was the moral way. She was a virgin by her own choice.

All she had to offer the man she would finally marry was herself. She wanted that self to be as valuable as possible. To her, valuable meant unsullied—unused. She had no money. No social standing. Just herself—

Willa's giggle pulled her back to reality:

"Oh, you really must have a case! You ain't heard a word."

Blushing, Margaret answered, "What did you say?"

In the front of the shop, Aunt Eliza and Mrs. Honeyman were concluding their business.

"I asked if you'd heard any more about the capital comin' here from Montgomery."

"The capital of the Confederacy? Aunt Eliza says the move will take place by the end of the month."

"An' Mr. Davis'll be here, too?"

"Mr. Davis and that whole Western crowd." To the

people of Richmond, deep-South states such as Alabama, Mississippi and Louisiana were practically the
frontier; distinctly cruder than the Old Dominion.
"Then watch this town go topsy-turvy! Goodness
knows what will become of General Lee—"

"He's gonna run the army, ain't he?"

"Probably not, Willa. Mr. Davis has two titles. President and commander-in-chief. Mrs. Tatnall—the lady
who orders yards of lace on all her dresses—" Willa
nodded "—well, she was down in Montgomery for the
inauguration. There was a story going around that
Davis just about wept when he was offered the presidency."

"God's truth?"

"Mrs. Tatnall swore to it."

"Why'd he bawl?"

"I don't know as he actually did it—he just felt like
it. He wanted to be general of all the Confederate armies. More than anything, he fancies himself a soldier.
He'll undoubtedly try to keep General Lee in the background, and make sure Lee knows who's giving the orders. Of course," Margaret added, "nothing's official
until the people go to the polls a week from tomorrow
and ratify the secession vote."

"But they're goin' to—!" Willa exclaimed.

"Everywhere except the western counties. Aunt Eliza
says there are a lot of submissionists out there. But the
majority will approve. Then all of General Lee's troops
will be swallowed up in the Confederate Provisional
Army."

"Includin' your hoos—your hussar?"

Margaret nodded.

"I can see why you'd look sorta glum."

"Was I looking glum?"

"Sure were. I'd think you'd be proud—"

"Proud that he wants a chance to be killed?" Tears
sprang into her eyes. "For that, he's a fool! So is every-

one in Richmond who doesn't count the cost of—oh, never mind!"

"Lord, it must be love to make you bust out cryin' so often," Willa said. Margaret whirled away and hurried toward the front, wiping her eyes. She was ashamed of herself.

"—a deposit of three and a half dollars will be ample, Mrs. Honeyman."

"Very well. Just a moment—"

The woman fumbled in her reticule. Clovis stood by the door, watching pedestrians on the sun-dappled sidewalk. Mrs. Honeyman couldn't locate what she wanted:

"I do declare patriotism has its inconveniences—"

And many more to come, Margaret thought.

Aunt Eliza looked apprehensive about her return. She kept her head down to conceal her reddened eyes and set about straightening bolts of yard goods.

"—I can't get used to these Corporation of Richmond bills flooding the town—well, finally! Here's a two. A one. And a fifty-cent bill." The paper money, engraved on pink stock, crinkled loudly as Mrs. Honeyman paid the deposit. "I'll call for the suit Saturday morning. I want Clovis to wear it for Holy Communion on Sunday."

Clovis looked anything but holy as he stuck out his tongue again and uttered a retching noise.

"Clovis Honeyman, do you want God to strike you dead?"

"Rather He did that than make me go to rotten old church."

"What*ever* am I going to do with you? It's your father's fault! I rue the day I married a godless drinker of alcohol!"

"Amen!" Aunt Eliza said with conviction. "I hope we'll have the suit finished on time. However, you do realize the work for the military takes precedence—"

"Naturally. That's of first importance to everyone."

Her glance at Margaret was meant to make the girl feel
uncomfortable. It did. "Will I see you at church this
evening, Eliza?"

"I'll be there."

"Good day, then. Come along, you ungrateful
child!"

Mrs. Honeyman seized Clovis by the ear lobe and
marched him out. The closing door muffled his squeals
and the laughter of a group from the elite home guard
unit, Company F, just passing.

The moment the door clicked, Eliza Marble charged
toward her niece like an infantryman on the attack.

ii

"Margaret, your comments to Mrs. Honeyman were
entirely out of line! You're making it very difficult for
me to deal with our regular customers."

Margaret bristled. "I try to be courteous. What's
wrong with saying what I believe?"

"Nothing—except when you argue against the war.
This *is* a Southern city—"

"And I was born a Southerner! At least I've always
considered Kentucky part of the South. I just think the
war's foolish. I think it can't be won. I only asked Mrs.
Honeyman an honest question. How will your customers feel when their sons die? Or come home like Papa—?"

Aunt Eliza shook her head. "Despite the regrettable
fact that army life left your father in the thrall of spirits,
I've always been proud of the Sergeant's service to—"

"His *service* destroyed him!"

Though the older woman looked angry for a moment, she said nothing. She pursed her lips; drew a deep
breath. Touched Margaret's hand gently:

"I understand. But try to see my point of view—"

Shame-faced, Margaret said, "I will. I'm sorry I

spoke sharply. It seems that's all I do lately. Fly off the handle—"

"I know one reason. That young man."

Margaret's silence was an admission that Eliza Marble had hit on the truth. The older woman went on:

"I don't blame you for being in a turmoil. Romance does that to young girls. And Mr. Kent's certainly good looking. Quite polite, too. Perhaps—" She paused. "Perhaps it's time I asked one or two questions about him."

Margaret fretted, aware of time hurrying by. But she wanted to make amends:

"All right."

"First of all—and most important—is Mr. Kent a cold-water man?"

"No, he isn't." She glided from the truth to a fib. "I don't believe he takes anything stronger than beer, though."

"No distilled spirits?"

"I've never seen him suffering the effects of spirits."

It was a truth that evaded a lie. Gideon had in fact told her of several occasions when a supply of busthead had been smuggled into camp, and an evening of surreptitious celebrating had been followed by a morning of pounding headaches and bleary vision.

But she didn't consider drinking liquor a sin, as Aunt Eliza did. Regrettable as it was, men sometimes needed liquor to ease their anxiety or their suffering. The Sergeant was a perfect example.

Eliza Marble, however, would never have agreed. She was an ardent member of the temperance movement. Supporting her niece and the Sergeant wasn't the sole reason she was always short of funds. She spent sizable sums to help pay the expenses of reformed drunkards who came to Richmond to lecture to the local Temperance Union.

And she collected books and pamphlets on the evils

of drink. She owned a rare copy of *An Inquiry into the Effect of Spiritous Liquors on the Human Body and Mind*, a classic on the subject even though it was years old. The tract's author was Dr. Benjamin Rush, a signer of the Declaration, surgeon general of the Continental Army, and later professor of medicine at the University of Pennsylvania. Eliza was famous at local temperance meetings for her ability to rise and repeat in ringing tones Dr. Rush's description of the way "ardent spirits" affected an individual:

"'They cause him in folly to resemble a calf. In stupidity, an ass. In roaring, a mad bull. In quarreling and fighting, a dog. In cruelty, a tiger. In fetor, a skunk. In filthiness, a hog. And in obscenity, a he-goat.'" Margaret knew the litany by heart.

Aunt Eliza's library included several other publications of note—among them the six color illustrations prepared by Dr. Sewell of Columbian College, which showed the degeneration of the human stomach from a pale pink—the *"Healthful"* state—to a condition in which bilious purples, browns and blacks demonstrated *"Death by Delirium Tremens."*

She owned an 1855 first edition of Mr. T. S. Arthur's classic work, *Ten Nights in a Barroom and What I Saw There,* as well as a paper-covered copy of the stage dramatization and sheet music for the play's plaintive lament, *"Father, dear father, come home with me now,"* which was sung in the drama by a golden-haired child seeking to rescue Papa from the evils of the Sickle and Sheaf Tavern.

Further, Aunt Eliza possessed rock-like faith in the scientific accuracy of Kittredge's pamphlet recounting horrific stories of tosspots who had exhaled too close to an open flame, caught fire and been incinerated by the alcohol in their systems.

"I trust he doesn't frequent taverns?" Aunt Eliza continued.

"Not that I'm aware."

Another fib for which she felt guilty. But she didn't want her aunt to deny her permission to see Gideon.

"Good. Even John Adams knew the evils of taverns. He called them the spawning ground of diseases, vicious habits, bastards and legislators."

Margaret felt it wiser to refrain from smiling. "Yes," she said soberly, "I remember."

"So Mr. Kent is not a victim of the viper in the bottle—?"

"Oh, definitely not."

"I'm delighted to hear it. Now to a somewhat more delicate subject. Has your relationship with him progressed beyond—that is—has it led to—physical intimacies?"

Margaret flushed again. "Aunt Eliza, we're only friends!"

"Then the answer is no?"

Truthfully this time: "That's right."

"I'm pleased. You understand the reason for my concern. With emotions running so high, it would be easy for a young girl to be carried away into—behavior she would later regret." Never having been married, even a circumlocution pertaining to sex was enough to make Eliza Marble beet-faced.

"Aunt Eliza, you've been very generous to Papa and me—"

The older woman gestured. "Bosh! Weak though he is, the Sergeant is my brother. You two are my only family."

"That's why I wouldn't do anything to hurt you or dishonor you."

Aunt Eliza hugged her. "Thank you. You've answered my questions."

"I have one more thing to say. I truly apologize for offending Mrs. Honeyman. I know I spoke out of turn, but I can't help how I feel. This war *is* wrong. Because it's hopeless. Principles don't win battles. Men and guns win them. And the North has more of both."

"Child, there hasn't even been any fighting yet—!"

"But the Yankees are gathering in Washington. I've heard they'll be across the Potomac by the end of the month."

"It's possible. However—" She looked determined. "The people of Virginia have always been willing to stand up for what they believe. Now is no exception. If there's ever been an hour when Virginians were called on to show courage, that hour has come."

"I appreciate what you're saying, but—" The outburst came against her will: "You've seen what courage did to Papa! It ruined his life!"

"And yours?" Aunt Eliza asked softly.

"No, please—I didn't mean that. I'll always take care of him. I love him. But women like Mrs. Honeyman don't have a notion of what war is going to cost! Poverty instead of prosperity. Mutilations and wounds instead of strength and health. Pain and death instead of happiness and life—"

Aunt Eliza was thin-lipped again. "And for that reason you believe we should be submissionists?"

"No, we—oh, I don't know. *I don't know!*" she cried.

Eliza Marble put her arm around her niece. "We do what we must, child. Former President Quincy Adams once said that if the sections of the country no longer felt a magnetism of common interests and sympathies, then it was better for the sections to go their separate ways. 'Let the disunited states part in friendship'—that's exactly what he said. A Yankee, too. But he was correct. We've suffered too long under the abuse of those Northern mobocrats."

"Aunt Eliza, the war's *our* fault! I'm not averse to the South defending its rights by legal means, but—"

"*Legal* means were exhausted years ago. We were simply too witless to realize it."

"So instead, we chose to start an insurrection."

"Which Old Abe means to put down so he can free the nigras."

"He's never said that! Why, over and over, he's promised he'll never interfere with slavery in the South. He really wishes every black in the country could be shipped over the water and resettled in Liberia."

Eliza scoffed: "Do you really think he won't interfere? Lincoln's going to be controlled by men like that abolitionist he put in charge of his treasury—"

"Chase."

"Yes. And Thad Stevens, the Congressman who keeps a mongrel nigra woman right in his own house in Pennsylvania. No—" An assured shake of her head. "This had to come. Ever since they hung that maniac Brown for trying to start an uprising, you could feel the mood of the state change."

That was true enough. Once the immediate terror of John Brown's aborted raid had passed, militia organization and drill throughout the city had intensified.

"But we mustn't allow ourselves to get depressed, Margaret. Most everyone believes the fighting—if any—will be of very short duration."

"Evidently Mr. Lincoln doesn't feel that way."

"I suspect his call for additional volunteers is just a bluff."

"Forty-two thousand men? To serve for three years—?"

"Or less, if there's a speedy conclusion to—"

"That doesn't sound like a bluff to me! Besides, what difference does it make how long a man serves? It only takes a second for him to become like—like—"

She stopped; turned away. Long ago, she'd vowed to put an end to these arguments. She seemed powerless to do it.

Aunt Eliza sighed again. "You're an admirable girl, Margaret. Spirited. Determined—you know how much I admire the way you took your education into your own hands because we couldn't afford a proper girl's school. I love you like my own. But you do have some peculiar ideas—misguided ones, frankly. I think you'll abandon them when you realize our cause is just. As a church-going woman, I've never approved of slavery. I think it should be abolished—and would be, one day, if left to run its course. Many people in Virginia feel the same way. But it's gone beyond the matter of the nigras now. It's gone to a question of our Constitutional rights. And who's to say Mr. Kent won't come out of it unscathed? Not every young chap who joins an army suffers what the Sergeant—"

She drew a quick breath, realizing her blunder. Awkwardly, she patted her niece's arm:

"Enough glum talk. Neither of us can change what's going to happen. So we might as well take each day's blessings and appreciate them. Go meet your young man. You'd better have something to eat first—"

She went behind a counter and knelt. Margaret heard the rattle of the cashbox lid. In a moment, Eliza pressed a fifty-cent bill into Margaret's hand. The pink paper bore a portrait of balding, bespectacled Governor Letcher.

"Take this. Buy an ice at Pizzini's. You've half an hour until Mr. Kent comes in from Camp Lee, don't you?"

Margaret nodded. She was ashamed of her inability to control her temper. Despite good intentions, she was beginning to be caught up in the city's hysteria.

She held out the bill. "Thank you, Aunt Eliza, but you keep this. I'm not hungry. And the shop needs every penny."

"Nonsense. La Mode has never made so much money."

"Taken in so much, you mean."

"Either way, let's enjoy it while it lasts."

She tucked the bill back into her niece's fingers. "Be thankful you've a young man who likes you. I—" A resigned, almost sad shrug. "—I never had a beau. I was too plain, I suppose. Or too religious. But you're lucky. Mr. Kent seems very upright. Your words about his refusal to drink liquor are most reassuring. I also happen to know he comes of reputable people down in Lexington."

Margaret gasped: "How did you learn that?" She'd told her aunt very little of what she knew about Gideon's family. She feared an adverse reaction on two counts:

His stepfather was a member of a notorious profession. And his true father's history was even more suspect. He was a former Virginia circuit rider who'd been thrown out of his church for pronouncements against slavery, then turned to journalism—Yankee journalism—in Washington.

"When the welfare of my niece is involved, I make it my business to ask questions," Aunt Eliza replied. "Now you do as I say. Stop for an ice at the Palace of Sweets. But avoid the soldiers—except for Mr. Kent."

At last, Margaret laughed. "That's impossible. Six months ago, there were thirty-seven thousand people in Richmond. Now the population's doubled—and most of the new arrivals are military men. They seem to feel wearing a uniform gives them the right to approach any young lady they meet. Even so, most of them are gentlemen—"

But not all. She'd been the target of some ugly, lustful glances from members of out-of-state units. She didn't want Aunt Eliza to worry, though:

"I'm perfectly capable of looking after myself. Besides, I'll be meeting Gideon while it's still daylight."

"Have a good time. Make sure you don't go home alone after dark."

"I'm planning to come back and help Willa and the other girls. Gideon will have drill again this evening."

And I don't want him to see that terrible little place where we live. I don't want him to see that pathetic man who glories in having everyone call him Sergeant—and whose sole friend is another army man he hasn't seen in over a decade.

The man her father revered—the only person with whom he took the trouble to correspond—seemed to share a common misery with the Sergeant. Military service had left him totally unfit for civilian life. He, too, had a drinking problem. He couldn't make a go of any business he tried. Yet Margaret's father reveled in the occasional letters he received from the man in Illinois. He always referred to the man by his old army nickname, Uncle Sam, as if it were something to be proud of, instead of a reminder of the inability to succeed at anything except killing other men while wearing a uniform. What an idol to worship! A sot doomed to failure and obscurity for the rest of his life—

"Then we can ride home together on the horsecar after I finish at St. Paul's," Aunt Eliza said with a satisfied nod. "Hurry along, now. Enjoy this wonderful weather and your soldier's company while you can."

The words meant in kindness lingered in Margaret's mind, a fearful reminder:

While you can.

iii

Margaret returned to the workroom for her spoon bonnet and shawl, though she doubted she'd need either in the mellow May twilight. In fact, she already felt warm under the layers of crinoline that stiffened the skirt of her long-darted walking dress.

Two years ago, when she was just coming into full physical maturity and beginning to have those disturbing thoughts about intimacy with a man after marriage, a lady from Church Hill had ordered the dress, then died of a seizure during a spell of steamy summer weather. Since the woman's measurements matched Margaret's, Aunt Eliza had given her the dress as a birthday present. The gold fabric was still bright, and complemented her brown eyes and hair. But she wished propriety didn't demand all the bulky petticoats, not to mention lace-trimmed underdrawers.

Willa Perkins watched her primping in a speckled mirror. She giggled again. Margaret said, "Jealous!" in a teasing way, and left the shop.

Our Rome, Eliza Marble had called Richmond in those first, dimly remembered weeks after she and her father had arrived from Kentucky. Gradually, Margaret began to appreciate the term. She came to love the genteel, slow-paced city of the hills—Chimborazo, Shockoe, Gamble's and the rest.

Aunt Eliza had shown her all the sights. Walked her past the splendid Georgian homes of mellow brick in Church Hill. Strolled with her to the leafy quiet of Hollywood Cemetery; only three years ago, Margaret and her aunt had watched President Monroe's remains reburied there, returned at last to his native Virginia. An elegant New York militia regiment had accompanied the coffin from the North. The soldiers had been entertained in some of the best homes. Today that sort of hospitality was unthinkable.

Certain things hadn't changed, of course. There were still familiar sounds and smells in the May air as she hurried up the brick walk toward the Spotswood.

Fine carriages traveled Main Street along with huge tobacco wagons drawn by lathered mules hitched four

abreast. The famous illuminated clock in front of the
Meyers and Janke jewelry emporium resonantly struck
the hour of five. Windlass-driven, its powerful chime
could be heard for a mile.

The five strokes were counterpointed by the wail of a
train coming in across the sixty-foot-high Richmond
and Petersburg trestle spanning the James. And, as always, she could hear the soothing murmur of the falls.

Despite the influx of soldiers, certain sections of the
city retained a peaceful air. Capitol Square at the crest
of Shockoe's, for instance. There stood the elegant capitol building President Jefferson had designed. Its rotunda housed Houdon's full-length statue of Washington, as well as a Houdon bust of the Marquis de
Lafayette. Gideon claimed the founder of his family, a
Bostonian named Phillip Kent, had known Lafayette
personally.

With delight, Margaret recalled the public holiday
celebrating completion of a second monument to Washington. Crawford's equestrian statue had been unveiled
in the square in '58. Wags noted the rear of the great
leader's horse pointed North.

The statue's pedestal featured figures of three other
great Virginians. Jefferson. Mason, who had hammered
out the Bill of Rights. And Patrick Henry, who had
stood up in old St. John's on Church Hill and thundered
that he preferred death if he were deprived of liberty.
Capitol Square was a proud reminder that the state was
one of the true wellsprings of American freedom.

Because so much that was good and meaningful had
come from Virginia—and Richmond itself—Margaret
was saddened to see the city transformed. The evidence
of transformation was nowhere more evident than on
Main Street.

True, the lawyers and the businessmen, the fashiona-
ble ladies and the easy-going free blacks still crowded

the walks. But so did the newer arrivals—young men in military costumes of every description.

She recognized members of local units. The Blues. The Howitzers. The Henrico Light Dragoons. Mingled among them, in costumes that were homely or operatic or somewhere between, were men belonging to regiments from other parts of the South. Just in the short distance to the Spotswood, she saw a group of Georgians in full-skirted butternut coats with green trim. She saw half a dozen from Alabama wearing smart blue. She saw towering, long-haired men with out-sized silver spurs and fringed buckskin jackets. They had revolvers and Bowie knives in their wide leather belts and lumps of tobacco bulging in their cheeks. Texans.

She passed two men in shabby Zouave uniforms who were lounging in front of a haberdasher's. One, a wart-faced fellow, whispered something to his companion. She only caught the words, "—like to give that a tumble."

Staring straight ahead, she rushed on, passing two more Texans. She turned at the sound of a commotion.

One of the Texans had hauled the wart-faced man off his feet. Holding the offender by the jacket, the Texan bounced him against the store front:

"You Tigers are gonna have to learn how to speak decent when they's ladies on the street—"

"Put me down, you son-of-a-bitch!" the Zouave howled. The other Zouave pulled out a set of knuckle-dusters. People crowded around Margaret to watch.

The Zouave with the knuckle-dusters crept up behind the first Texan. His companion shoved the point of his Bowie into the Zouave's back.

"No, sir," he said quietly, confiscating the knuckles. The first Texan continued his lecture:

"—else the First Texas will see to it that you're sent back to where you come from. The New Orleans jails."

He set the gulping Tiger on his feet with a jolt. Then

he turned and sought Margaret. He swept off his broad-brimmed, cream-colored hat:

"My apologies for the vulgarity he directed against you, ma'am."

"Thank you," she said with an embarrassed smile. There was brief applause. The small crowd dispersed, the two members of the Tigers departing faster than the rest. The wart-faced one glanced back at Margaret, fury in his eyes.

The Texan marred his gallant behavior by spitting a long stream of tobacco juice toward the curb. As he and his friend sauntered off, he didn't notice that a few drops struck the hem of Margaret's dress, leaving stains.

"Scum—outright scum," she heard a Virginia Military Institute cadet exclaim to another as they passed her going the other way. "Those Louisiana ruffians shouldn't be allowed to fight under the same flag as—"

The voices faded, overlapped by the noise of some citizens gathered outside the Spotswood. They were shouting questions at a handsome officer Margaret recognized instantly. The officer wore a cocked hat with a black plume, a huge saber and a close-fitting roundabout that showed off his well-proportioned figure. John Bankhead Magruder had commanded the First U.S. Artillery until he'd resigned to serve his native state—where the people pridefully referred to him as Prince John.

The crowd was asking about the progress of the artillerymen he was training out on the campus of Richmond College. Magruder smiled:

"Why, my boys are developing into first-class cannoneers. Any Yank who sets foot on Virginia soil will soon find out—and go back to the North multiplied into four or five parts."

Laughter. Whistles. Magruder climbed into a waiting carriage. Several V.M.I. cadets began to lead the others in a chorus of "The Bonnie Blue Flag." The cadets came from Gideon's home town. Because of their experience, they'd been rushed to Richmond to supervise the instruction of the newest recruits. One of their professors was Colonel T. J. Jackson, whom Johnston would soon relieve at Harper's Ferry.

> *"Hurrah! Hurrah! For Southern rights, hurrah!*
> *Hurrah for the Bonnie Blue Flag,*
> *That bears a single star!"*

There was more applause as the discordant version of the popular new song came to an end. Margaret pushed through the crowd, ignoring an inebriated gentleman who tipped his hat and three soldiers who tried to attract her attention.

Her encounter with the crude Louisiana soldiers lingered in her mind as she hurried down the slope of Main Street. Richmond was the same and not the same. Smoke still plumed from the stacks of the Tredegar she glimpsed far down on her left as she crossed Eighth. Gamble's Hill still afforded one of the loveliest and most panoramic views of the city. But the best times were gone—

The times when great men—the novelist Thackeray, for instance—had come to lecture and savor the beauty of old residential streets lined with lindens and maples and tulip trees. Only last October, Lord Renfrew, the nineteen-year-old Prince of Wales, had been received with full civic pomp.

In Richmond Margaret had found a rich intellectual heritage. *The Southern Literary Messenger*, for a time under the assistant editorship of the curious and tormented Mr. Poe, had turned the city into one of the literary centers of the western world. Much of her own self-education had been made possible because the people of Richmond owned and loved books. Customers of her aunt gladly loaned them to her. She'd even read *Un-*

cle Tom's Cabin, though it was disguised with a false
cover declaring the contents to be Gibbon.

Here, too, she'd sampled culture from beyond the
state's borders. Touring troupes played the Marshall
Theater regularly. By hoarding spare coins, she'd been
able to spend a few wondrous evenings in the Marshall's cheapest gallery seats. In the winter of '59 she'd
sighed for weeks over a young, flamboyant supporting
player in a melodrama; a Mr. John W. Booth of the
famous acting family.

The pleasant decade in which she'd come to young
womanhood seemed almost an illusion now. The Tredegar smoke still bannered the sky at evening. The flour
drays still rumbled to the port from the impressive nine-
story Gallego Mill—the largest in the world, people
boasted. Occasionally you could still hear lovely, lilting
Latin speech when the South American coffee ships
came up the James to unload fragrant sacks of beans.

You could hear the work chanties of the blacks in the
tobacco factories. The cadence of a gallop bursting
from a fine house during the height of the social season.

You could hear it all, but less clearly. New sounds
had intruded—

On the night of the news of Sumter's fall, the Fayette
Artillery had fired a hundred rounds in Capitol Square.
Skyrockets had exploded in the heavens. Blazing barrels
of tar sizzled on the corner of every major intersection.
The church bells rang almost until morning. And she'd
walked with Aunt Eliza in the midst of mobs waving the
South Carolina palmetto, screaming oaths against Lincoln, cheering Beauregard's name and howling *"Down
with the old flag!"*

She'd watched, horrified, when people poured
through Rockett's the Sunday night following the secession vote. Wild rumors were sweeping the city. The
Yankee gunboat *Pawnee* was steaming up the river to
menace the port! Mobs turned out with every sort of

weapon, prepared to repel an attack that never materialized.

On the once-drowsy streets, she'd seen other, equally savage mobs hang straw men from the stanchions of the gas lamps. The dummies bore crude placards:

HIS MAJESTY THE ORANG-OUTANG.

HENRY WARD BEECHER, THE MAN WHO HAS DONE MOST TO CAUSE OUR PRESENT TROUBLE.

Garrison, Douglass, other abolitionists—their effigies were hanged as well.

The voices of hate were being heard in Richmond, along with the voices of false prophets. The South's cause was just! The North would be defeated in a swift, relatively bloodless war—

Was she the only person in the city who saw the insanity of that? Who understood it took only one bullet to destroy a man forever?

No matter. She was determined to prove her case to Gideon Kent.

I'll find some way, she thought as she rushed along Main, Pizzini's and the half-dollar note forgotten. *I must.*

If he goes to war thinking it's a grand crusade—a lark—a holiday—

If I can't make him understand what war really means, I could lose him.

I mustn't lose him.

Because I—I love him.

CHAPTER II

The Amateur Cavalier

THEY HAD A SPECIAL meeting place on the canal towpath, at the foot of Gamble's Hill. The spot was equi-distant from the Tredegar Works to the west and the sprawling, long-idle state armory on the east.

Gideon was late.

Margaret paced, stepping aside from time to time and smiling automatically as other couples passed, whispering, laughing, holding hands. Her eyes kept returning to the Tredegar across the canal.

Even at this late hour of the day, workmen swarmed in the yard. They were transferring scrap iron from wagons to barrows and trundling it into the great, sooty buildings. To be melted down to make new iron. Iron for the instruments of war—

Both the Tredegar and the armory stood on a narrow strip of land separating the river from the James River and Kanawha Canal. The river purled, glittering in the gold light of the sinking sun. Further along the path in the canal basin, one of the four-mile-an-hour packets from Lynchburg was tying up.

Somewhere on the wooded slope behind her, she heard loud, lusty singing. "Lorena." One of his favorites—

She spun around, her heartbeat faster. There he was! Running recklessly downhill among the trees.

He waved, so vigorously the white plume bobbed on

his visored leather shako. She waved in return, her emotions all jumbled together. There was excitement; apprehension; even a little amusement. Captain Lester Macomb had outfitted his Hussars in what he thought was the European mode. To a girl brought up around an apparel shop, the captain's taste was highly questionable.

Margaret and her aunt knew the yard goods merchant, of course. Purchased bolts of cloth from him on occasion. La Mode Shoppe hadn't been hired to sew for Macomb's Hussars, however. Had the reverse been true, Gideon would have looked less garish—or Aunt Elzia would have been discharged from the job for her protests.

Gideon's uniform consisted of new and beautifully polished high boots, tight-fitting sky-blue trousers and a matching coat. The coat had a choker collar and an excess of gaudy braid across the front. At a distance, the outfit possessed a certain showy splendor. Up close, its shortcomings were more apparent.

The leather cavalryman's belt and the sabretache attached to it by straps had been crudely cut and laced by someone with no respect for leather or workmanship. And Gideon lacked the final touch—the saber itself. All he'd brought from Lexington were four gifts from his mother's father:

The new boots; a 30-gauge revolving-cylinder percussion shotgun from Colt's of Paterson; a round-tree English saddle; and the absolutely indispensible requirement—his horse Dancer, a handsome and spirited gray stallion.

Most of the seventy-eight men of Macomb's Hussars were no better equipped, save for Gideon's friend Rodney Arbuckle. Rodney hailed from a Peninsula tobacco estate on the Pamunkey River near White House. Rodney had money—though not nearly as much as the dandies in the celebrated Goochland Troop. Not only did the boys from Goochland County dress more splendidly, but the majority had two horses and a black body servant.

Still, Gideon Kent was outrageously proud of his troop and his uniform—including an absolutely ghastly left-shoulder dolman. To spare his feelings, Margaret hadn't told him the dolman was poor-quality rabbit fur.

But it was the man, not the costume, that started a pulse beat in her throat as he came scrambling through the shrubbery at the foot of the hill.

His cheeks were flushed. His smile seemed to glow in the twilight. He called her name as he ran the last hundred yards, waving again.

Why was he so excited? He was always in good spirits when they met. Tonight, though, she sensed a special eagerness in him. His blue eyes shone as he jumped over a low fern and landed on the path with a crunch. He seized her shoulders; hugged her fiercely—

"Margaret, I've got the grandest news! A lot of it!"

The feel of his cheek set off little warm bursts all through her body. Whenever he touched her, she ached in a distinctly unladylike way.

"My Lord, Gideon—" Gasping and laughing, she pulled away and straightened her bonnet. "Such a display in public!"

"Why shouldn't I make a display with my girl?" He caught her hands in his. Despite their frequent meetings, their physical contact had been restrained. First handshakes. Then hand-holding. Next, pecks on the cheek. Finally, kisses on the mouth. They had advanced very properly and cautiously to intimacy of the kind they shared at this moment. They stood close together while he gazed down at her, his shako slightly awry. The slanting sun fired the tawny hair around his ears.

His smile faded to an earnest look. Softly, he said:
"My very favorite."

"Oh, do you have others now?"

"Don't tease me. You've got to hear what we did this afternoon."

A short distance behind them, another couple stopped. The boy, one of the Greys, was whispering in the girl's ear. She slapped his face lightly with her glove. He laughed. The girl joined in. It was clear what sort of suggestion he'd made.

A little embarrassed, Margaret linked her arm with Gideon's and they walked the other way, toward the canal basin, where the packet-handlers were unloading cargo and swearing cheerfully. Shadows were lengthening on the hill above the towpath.

"Exactly what did you do?" she asked.

"We held elections! Of course Macomb kept his captaincy. He organized the troop, and he's still the most popular man."

She knew his pause was deliberate. "Is that all?"

"No, *ma'am*!" Bursting with pride, he turned and laid both hands on her shoulders. "Miss Marble, I have the honor to introduce the new second lieutenant of Macomb's Hussars."

"Oh, Gideon—that's grand."

His face grew a shade less happy. "You really don't sound enthusiastic."

"I am!" She squeezed his arm. Ignored propriety and raised on tiptoe to kiss his cheek. "I'm very proud."

It *was* an accomplishment. Although many people said election of officers was a poor way to establish the command structure in a volunteer unit, it was the custom. Only officers above the rank of regimental commander were appointed by General Lee.

They resumed walking arm in arm. Margaret's breast brushed his sleeve, a deliciously wicked sensation.

"Actually," Gideon said, "I'd hoped for first lieutenant. But Jack Harris got that. He's always paying for rounds at the Spotswood Bar or Mrs. Muller's Lager Beer Saloon. I think he starts his euchre games so he can lose on purpose. I can't afford to buy popularity."

Margaret had met the lean, dark-visaged Harris at Camp Lee. She thought him coarse and shallow:

"Do you think Jack Harris is fit to be first lieutenant?"

"Hell—oh, I'm sorry—"

"Stop. I'm used to your swearing by now."

He chuckled. "Guess I've fallen into the camp habit. Anyway—the men like Jack. He's a fair rider. His papa raises horses on their place down near Petersburg. He's fond of rough language, though. I mean really rough. I don't know why. Maybe it makes him feel more of a man. Trouble is, I doubt cussing will help him when we see action. Men want to be led, not browbeaten."

The last sentences spoiled the moment; reminded Margaret of her fears for this tall, big-shouldered young man from the Shenandoah who seemed so adult at times, so full of boyish bravado at others.

When we see action.

Somehow, *somehow*, she had to convince him he wasn't involved in a game or a pageant—

She hesitated to raise the subject when he was so happy. She'd tried to discuss her viewpoint several times before. He always acted bewildered as well as vaguely annoyed that she'd question his desire to fight for the South. She kept to a safe subject:

"In my opinion your friend Rodney might have made a better first lieutenant."

"Of course. But you know the situation with the boys whose folks have any kind of money. They've got this damned notion it's undemocratic and undignified to be an officer. They'd rather serve in the line than give orders to another gentleman. The boys from the Valley sure don't think that way. But you still haven't heard all the news."

"Tell me."

He grinned. "There's no drill tonight."

"Not at all?"

"No. Captain Macomb's mare took a fall this afternoon. Broke both her forelegs. You should have heard old Lester swear!"

"I should imagine. She was a lovely animal."

"What upset him most is having to rush around town and find another. You know, I sometimes get worried about the cavalry. How can we fight if every man has to provide his own horse? What if we lose half our horses in battle? We'd be at half strength for days. Maybe weeks."

Battle. She tried to keep it from her mind.

"I thought the government owned the horses."

"Technically, they do. They take 'em over. They provide forage, shoes, a smithy—and compensation at forty cents a day per horse—" He was talking rapidly, his arm across her shoulder and his eyes focused somewhere in the delicate blue shadow along the towpath.

So intense, she thought. *The cavalier who has yet to learn what battle really means—*

"—and if a horse is lost in combat, the government's supposed to reimburse the rider for the animal's assessed value. But the man has to go on furlough right away to locate a new one. It's not so much the cost, it's the headache of searching. I expect Macomb will be up all night visiting stables. He'll be lucky if he finds a mount as good as the mare at any price. The government's gobbling the ones around here for artillery caissons, ambulances—"

Though the May breeze was warm against her cheeks, she shuddered. Gideon halted abruptly:

"What's wrong?"

"Nothing."

"Yes, there is." He turned to her again, half his face in sunlight, the other half dark. He touched her chin. "I want to know."

"Well, I can't help shivering when you talk so

blithely about ambulances and—and combat. You sound as if it's nothing but a grand game!"

Puzzled, he answered, "I've never been so happy in my life. Finally, we're going to show the Yanks they've pushed us too hard—for too long."

"You *want* to fight!" she exclaimed, more harshly than she intended.

A sudden frown. "Yes, I do. So does every fellow in the troop. You should have heard the cheering yesterday when Wise came out to look us over."

"Wise? Oh—the former governor—"

Gideon nodded. "He's supposed to be a brigadier before long. He gave a little speech—"

"Don't you mean sermon?"

Gideon's brows quirked up. "Why would you call it that?"

"Well, I assume it's the same pseudo-religious twaddle he's been spouting all over town." Her mouth soured. " 'The fiery baptism—?' "

His zeal was as strong as her contempt: "He did use those words. My God, I've never heard anything so stirring. I can remember almost every sentence. 'You want war, fire, blood to purify you, and the Lord of Hosts has demanded that you should walk through fire and blood. You are called to the fiery baptism, and I call upon you to come up to the altar.' "

Unsmiling, he added, "Wise is right. I have a duty. All of us d—*now* what's the trouble?"

"Your attitude! Are you going to let yourself be influenced by senile old fools? If you're injured, you won't remember a thing about duty—or how glorious it is to go through the *fiery baptism*!"

"Now wait—"

"No! Is there one boy in your troop who's done anything but fist-fight behind a barn?"

"No one except Macomb, probably. What difference does it make?"

"All the difference. War's a horrible business. You don't know how horrible!"

She spun away, rubbing her upper arms and staring at the smoke streaming from the Tredegar stacks. The smoke was black; forbidding in the pale, sweet light of the fading afternoon.

"Why do you keep bringing that up?" Gideon snapped at her. "Joining the troop was my choice."

"A foolish choice!"

"*Hell!*" He kicked stones on the path. "Here I thought we'd have a grand evening together. Go to supper—but you want to argue! That's a fine how-do-you-do when time's so short!"

The rustle of the trees on Gamble's Hill drifted to her in the silence. The falls murmured. Cold clear through, she turned back to him. She found she could barely speak:

"What do you mean, time's so short?"

He dragged off his shako. Slapped it against his blue-clad thigh once—twice—struggling to master his temper. Eventually he did:

"That's the third piece of news. On Sunday we're breaking camp—"

Margaret's hands clenched.

"—provided Captain Macomb finds a horse. We're going up to Harper's Ferry."

"This soon?"

"It's a critical defense point. Joe Johnston's taking over the command there."

Faintly: "I heard that this afternoon."

"He'll be an improvement over that lunatic Presbyterian professor from the Institute!"

"Jackson?"

"The cadets call him Tom Fool." Remembered pain flashed in his eyes. "I guess I never mentioned he was my father's only friend after Mama turned Papa out of the house. Jackson's a fanatic. About discipline—about

observing the Sabbath—I can understand why he'd take
up with my father. Like to like!"

Gideon's face showed that sudden, flushed anger so
characteristic of him. It would probably make him a
good cavalry officer. She knew he was a good rider.
Almost fearless in committing himself and his mount
when he drilled at a gallop.

He seemed to want to say something else. She waited.
At last it came out:

"I didn't tell you I met my father in Washington, did
I?"

Surprised, she shook her head. "When?"

The color faded from his cheeks. He gazed in a somber way at the gold and white riffles on the river. "Last
month. Right after I enlisted and met you. My stepfather—"

"The actor?"

Gideon nodded. "Edward and Mama were in Washington so Edward could appear at a variety hall. Actually, he had a more praiseworthy purpose for being
there—"

He drew her a few steps further along the path. They
reached a large stone. With a gesture, he offered it as a
seat, then squatted on the ground beside it.

She laid a hand on his shoulder, hoping to soothe
away the unhappiness showing in his eyes. She was
thankful for his apparent need to talk about the Washington encounter. The news about Sunday had thrown
her mind into chaos; she needed a chance to think.

Her thoughts sped ahead to what she might say later.
Not to persuade him to resign from the troop; he'd
never do that. But she had to counteract the fatal bravado that could lead him straight to the grave—or to
the kind of living death her father suffered.

He was speaking softly now:

"—he stood up on the stage and led the crowd in

singing "Dixie's Land." There was a bad muss. He got beaten by some thugs. Could have been killed—"

"Then he shouldn't have taken the chance."

"Of course he should have! Edward wanted to prove there's a lot of Southern sympathy in Washington. I admire him for it. But you haven't heard the most peculiar part. My father was in the audience. He helped Edward escape. All that happened while I was here. The night I got back, Papa burst into our hotel room spouting a lot of accusations—"

"That was the first time you saw him?"

"The first time since Lexington."

"Who was he accusing?"

"Edward. He claimed Edward was plotting to have him murdered." There was disgust in his voice: "Mama used to say he was unbalanced. Anyway, things—got out of hand. I hit him with Edward's cane. More than once."

A whisper: "Your own father?"

"I lost my head." His eyes grew defiant. "He called Mama names. Filthy names. I'm not ashamed of what I did. But—I can't explain it, exactly—I was hurt and angry at the same time. I've always respected Edward and his feelings for the South. But it's not the same as loving a father. I guess I hoped all the bad times would be forgotten someday—"

He shook his head. The breeze stirred green branches behind them. Gideon's next words seethed with bitterness:

"It won't happen. Everything Mama said in Lexington is true. I saw it for myself. My father's crazy."

Yet Margaret had the strange feeling the truth made him grieve.

She touched his face. "Gideon—"

His eyes were lost in the Tredegar smoke. "What?"

"You've told me very little about what it was like with your father in Lexington."

"No point. It was miserable." He sat up a bit straighter. "Mama's back there now. With Edward. I had a note from them today."

"Are they going to stay?"

"Not indefinitely. When the capital of the Confederacy moves here, Edward wants to volunteer his services."

"To the army?"

"No, he's too old. No military experience, either. He hopes to find work in some part of the government. If he does, Mama will leave Jeremiah with my grandfather, Captain Tunworth."

"Was it really terrible when your father left home?"

"Bad enough that I'd rather not talk about it."

She hesitated, then plunged on:

"But I don't think we should hold anything back from each other any longer."

He twisted around to look at her, his blue eyes narrowing just a little:

"What do you mean? Why not?"

"Because you're leaving Sunday. It's time for—for candor." She stared at her hands. "I have some things I need to say to you."

A kind of dizziness swept over her; a feeling of racing toward a waterfall. Reckless or not, she must go ahead—

While you can.

"Tell me about Lexington," she said. "I think you want to. And you might feel better. Then I'll talk."

He hesitated, though not for long. She'd gauged his need correctly:

"Maybe I should. Christ knows it hurts keeping it penned inside all the time—"

As they sat beside the canal in the dusk, he began to speak of Jephtha Kent.

ii

He began by telling her the essentials:

His father's religious objections to slavery, which led to the loss of the itinerancy; his mother's growing consternation, then mounting wrath. Jephtha Kent, Gideon said, particularly loathed his wife's father, one of the few farmers around Lexington who kept a substantial number of slaves and—Gideon didn't gloss the truth—made no secret of treating them harshly:

"It was a terrible situation from the beginning. I've always thought Mama might not have turned against Papa if he hadn't despised Captain Tunworth so much. Though I don't think Papa realized it, some of the people in Lexington actually approved of his stand. The Shenandoah isn't the same sort of slave territory as the Tidewater. But Papa made the mistake of picking my grandfather as a special target. Mama ordered him out of the house. She's said since that she regrets doing it, but in view of that damn disgusting scene in Washington, she shouldn't. Papa stayed in Lexington a while. Found a menial job at the Institute. I suspect he liked being a sort of—living conscience for the town."

"An accusing conscience."

"Yes. As I said, only one person befriended him publicly. Colonel Tom Fool Jackson. Then Papa got involved with the Underground Railroad. He helped one of Captain Tunworth's nigra wenches escape, and fled to the North to live with his father's cousin. Mrs. Kent—I've mentioned her, haven't I?"

"The wealthy woman. Yes. Go on."

"She started the paper Papa works for now. She piled up a lot of money out West, too." He described the California gold properties and revealed something new about them—he and his brothers would receive the income when Jephtha Kent died.

"Back in Lexington, Mama also charged Papa with defrauding us by putting control of the mines in Mrs. Kent's hands. She's spoken of regretting that, too. But Edward still thinks my father would like to see Matt and Jeremiah and me disinherited."

"Would he disinherit you?"

"I never believed so until that night in the hotel. Papa actually said Edward was scheming to kill him so *he* could control the money. What rubbish! If he'll say that, he's capable of anything. There were years after Papa was gone when I wished he were with us. I was an idiot. He's a maniac. I never want to set eyes on him again."

Gideon's voice shook. So did his hands. He laced his fingers together to control the tremors. Margaret stroked his arm.

She felt tremors there, too. She'd never realized how much the tangled relationship with his father tormented him.

All at once Gideon's mouth set. "Enough from me. That's the end of the story."

He jumped up. "Come on. I'm starved. While we eat, maybe you'll explain how you got me to blab so much. I've never told half of that to anyone else." He touched her hair as she rose from the rock. "You also mentioned you had something to say—"

A gangling Texan no older than Gideon came strolling along the path, a young belle in rustling crinolines on each arm. The Texas boy gave Gideon a grave nod of greeting—soldier to soldier—and passed on.

"I don't want to wait for supper," she said. "I've got to speak now. You'll think I'm presumptuous, probably. Foolish. But—"

"Nothing you say could be foolish, Margaret." He bent nearer, pink-faced. "Nothing."

"I don't want you to go."

"Sunday?"

"Yes."

He reacted with disbelief, not anger:

"Well, that's not exactly a secret." He laughed. "I guess once in a while, you *might* say something foolish—"

"Gideon—" Her hand constricted on his arm. "You don't know what it'll be like! You think it'll be wonderful—"

"You're damn right. It'll be a privilege and a pleasure to meet up with some Yanks."

"It'll be a disaster! The South's not equipped to fight a war. You've seen our troops. Boys. *Amateurs!*"

"Now just a damn minute—!"

"I'm sorry, it's true."

"Amateur or not, we'll have the Yanks whipped in ninety days."

"Don't you think they're saying the same thing in Washington? The difference is, Lincoln's got hundreds of thousands of men to conscript if he wants to—" Her voice grew shriller. "How can you be so blind to the truth? Look at your own captain. A yard goods merchant!"

"With military experience."

"Years ago!"

"We're going to have a hell of a fine commander at Harper's Ferry. A Virginian from Patrick County—James Ewell Brown Stuart. Jeb, they call him. *He* doesn't lack experience. He resigned from a captaincy in the First Cavalry—one of the best units in the Federal army. He brought his family home from the West and went straight to Lee—"

They were walking again, Gideon more animated; trying to use enthusiasm to overcome her hostility:

"Lee thinks highly of him. Stuart happened to be on leave in Washington in '59. He went with Lee to catch old Ossawatomie Brown. Stuart's been in Arkansas, the Kansas territory—he's fought the meanest Indians on the Plains, the Cheyenne—they say he's a hell of a scrapper. I'm told he sings a lot, too. I'd follow him to perdition if he's a singer. He's at Harper's Ferry right now, starting to whip the state cavalry into shape—*Margaret*!"

"What?"

"Don't look so blasted glum! Your theory about amateurs is all wrong. I couldn't ask for a better commander than Stuart. Why, the top men in the Federal service were all attached to the First or Second cavalry regiments. Joe Johnston was lieutenant colonel in the First, Bob Lee in the Second under Albert Sidney Johnston. Hardee and George Thomas and Hood and that Union dandy, McClellan—the list's a quarter mile long! And we've got the pick of the lot!"

She shook her head. "You just won't—"

"Stuart's young. Twenty-eight or so. But he's smart. A West Pointer."

"Gideon!"

Her ferocity checked his rush of words.

"I don't care how clever he is—or how well he's been trained. *He can still get you killed.*"

"Why, yes," Gideon answered calmly. "But I accepted that risk."

"I don't accept it. I couldn't stand it! Gideon, I—I love you."

Stunned silence.

Awed, he whispered, "Glory be to God." A shout: *"Hallelujah*! I've been wanting to say the same thing, but I was too damn scared."

Laughing and crying at the same time, she flung herself against him, clasping him tight. She experienced a soaring moment of release and joy:

"I don't care if every righteous lady in Richmond

calls me a tart for coming right out with it—" She drew
back. "I love you and I won't see you hurt."

"Glory be to God," he repeated—and let out a
whoop that turned heads in the blue shadows further
down the towpath.

He grabbed her waist, hugging her so tightly her
breasts hurt, a lovely pain. He scooped her up and
whirled her. She gasped as he set her on the ground,
looked at her tenderly a moment, then kissed her.

She put her arms around his neck, without shame.
Pressed against him, she could feel the hardness of his
wanting. It frightened and thrilled her.

She let her lips open just a little. For one abandoned
moment, she caressed his tongue with hers, praying he
wouldn't think her a harlot—

His mouth tasted of tangy clove. He must have been
chewing one to freshen his breath on the walk from the
Fair Grounds. How funny and sad and unbearably
sweet—

They broke apart. She fussed with her bonnet to hide
her embarrassment over the way she'd embraced him;
the way she'd wanted more of him than was proper—

She had to discover his reaction:

"I expect I've acted like a fast woman—"

"Let anybody say that and I'll bust his eye!" He
squeezed her hand. "Lord, Margaret! All the way over
here, I kept wondering if I could work up nerve by Sunday to tell you how I felt. I knew I couldn't work up
nerve tonight—"

His mood changed again; he was no longer the exuberant soldier bragging about his new commanding officer, but boyish; uncertain. He chafed her hands with
almost comical haste:

"We really should talk."

Gravely: "Yes."

"I mean about your—doing me the honor of—
becoming my wife as soon as the fighting's done."

She thought she might faint. But she didn't—because of one word. One detestable word.

Fighting.

"I would, Gideon—"

"Oh, my *God!*" he bellowed, doing a foolish little jig on the path. He lunged for her waist to give her another whirl.

"—except—" She fended him off. Startled, he withdrew his hands.

"Except what?"

She had to say it:

"I don't want to promise myself to a man who may not come home to me."

"Why, honey, I'll be back from Harper's Ferry in no time. We—"

"Gideon, *listen.* You're as crazy as that father of yours if you think you're going on a holiday."

To blunt her savagery, he tried to tease:

"It *will* be a holiday, because you'll be waiting for—"

"Gideon, if you care for me—"

"I *do!* I've told you!"

"Then you must pay attention to what I'm saying. I saw one man go off just like you. A man I loved—"

Jealously: "What man?"

"My father."

"I didn't know anything about—I mean, you never mentioned—" Chagrined, he rubbed his cheek. "I thought he must be dead."

"No. He lives with Aunt Eliza and me."

She was desperate now. Vulnerable because she'd revealed how she felt. He wouldn't leave Captain Macomb's troop. But at least she might save his life by opening his eyes to the reality of what was waiting in some far, unseen place where the gay uniforms would grow stained with dirt and gore—

"He went to war too," she said. "The Mexican war.

He came home, but it might have been better if he hadn't—"

High up on Gamble's Hill, the tops of the tallest maples burned in the setting sun. A cardinal flew from a branch; caught the sunlight, red as blood.

The bird dipped, lost among the shadows of the leaves stirring in the May wind.

She knew the extent of the risk she was contemplating. But there was no other way to open his eyes. She took his hand:

"I don't want to eat supper."

"But I thought we'd talk about—"

"No," she said, tugging him along the path. He reached down to grab the shako that had fallen unnoticed. It took all the courage she possessed to say the rest:

"I want you to come out to where we live in Rockett's. I want you to see my father."

CHAPTER III

The Tigers

MARGARET LEFT GIDEON in front of the Spotswood:

"You have a bite to eat. I'm not the least bit hungry. I'll go along to the shop and leave a note for Aunt Eliza. She worries about me traveling home alone."

Gideon knew he should insist on accompanying her. Even though the distance was short, the walks were still packed with soldiers, as well as with representatives of less respectable professions who emerged after dark. But his stomach was growling.

"All right. I'll meet you here in ten minutes."

Besides food, he wanted a stiff drink and a little time to himself.

He stayed outside the Spotswood until she disappeared in the crowds eddying back and forth in the glow of the gas lamps. As he turned to go into the hotel, a ragged black boy stopped him. Grinning, the boy informed him that the finest fleshy entertainments in Richmond could be obtained at a certain address in Ram Cat Alley.

"Son, I've got the best girl in the whole damn town. Skedaddle!"

He entered the immaculate, marble-floored lobby, passing beneath ornate gas fixtures of polished brass. He was only marginally aware of a white-coated Negro clanging out three strokes on the dinner gong.

He was confused by his own state of mind. He should

405

have been elated. To an extent he was. At last, he'd managed to articulate the feelings for Margaret that shyness and inexperience had kept locked inside him since not long after their first meeting.

But the relationship was marred by her stubborn resistance to the war, and his role in it. The resistance had cropped up before. Only tonight had he gotten a clue as to its cause.

That Margaret's father was living had come as a total surprise. He knew she'd been born in Kentucky; had moved from a failing farm to live with her aunt more than ten years ago. But he'd always imagined she was an orphan.

The prospect of meeting her father out in Rockett's put him on edge. Margaret evidently hoped the encounter would reinforce her views about fighting. He loved her, but she couldn't change his mind about certain things. The trip to Rockett's would probably do nothing but cause trouble.

He shouldered into the noisy, smoky saloon bar. The place was packed with men in civilian dress and uniforms of every description. One man's face bore a slight resemblance to his father's.

He still saw Jephtha Kent in nightmares, his eyes full of pain and bewilderment as he waited for the gutta-percha cane to slash down. Gideon hadn't been wholly truthful with Margaret on one point. No matter how Jephtha had slandered Fan Lamont, he was still the man who'd given life to his sons. It was impossible for Gideon to hate him without guilt and an occasional twinge of sorrow.

Because of his height and obvious strength, he had little trouble forcing his way up to the polished bar. He squeezed in beside a fast-talking man in a cream-colored frock coat. The man was promising a couple of wide-eyed Georgia captains that the stakes were modest at a certain faro bank to which he could lead them. The captains would emerge big winners. They took the lure and followed the gambler out of the bar.

The barkeep approached. "Eat or drink?"

"Both. Haven't got much time, though. Throw a few slabs of that ham on white bread." The bartender proceeded to put the sandwich together, then slid the plate across the mahogany.

"What's your pleasure for drinking?"

"Applejack."

Gideon fished out a Richmond Corporation note. The bartender reached down. Gideon leaned over and caught his arm.

"I don't mean the hard cider you sell to youngsters who can't tell the difference."

The barkeep noted Gideon's size and the unblinking severity of his blue eyes. He admitted his guilt with a grin:

"Yes, sir. You ain't exactly a graybeard yourself."

"But I've been in Richmond long enough to know about gouging. As long as you're going to charge me for it, I want the real goods."

"Coming up."

Shortly, Gideon had a glass of the biting liquid from the unfrozen heart of a hard-cider barrel set out to ice over the winter. The applejack refreshed him after several mouthfuls of coarse bread and salty country ham.

His belly grew comfortably warm. But his apprehension lingered. Margaret's father had to be the one responsible for her hatred of the war. He knew she wasn't entirely in disagreement with the principles for which the South was fighting.

"—don't give a hang what the Ape *says*. He'll wind up interfering with the slave trade, mark my word. All the radicals are pushing him."

The overheard remark came from one of three prosperously dressed men immediately to his left. The speaker opened the pages of a paper whose masthead Gideon recognized at once. The New York *Union*.

He wasn't surprised to see it. Dozens of Northern papers found their way to Richmond. Captain Macomb said General Lee had an aide who did nothing but read the *Tribune*, the *Times*, the *Union* and the sheets published in Washington City. The newspapers generously reported every shift of Federal policy and every major troop movement—numbers of men, their armament, everything.

"They're doing it already," the man with the paper went on. He quoted in a cynical tone:

"*—so let me tell the gentlemen of the South that although the abolition of slavery is not an object of the war—*"

Guffaws.

"*—they may, in their madness and folly and treason—*"

Oaths from both listeners.

"*—make the abolition of slavery one of the results of this war.*"

One of the men snorted. "What Republican fuckhead said that?"

"Senator Henry Lane of Indiana."

"When our boys meet up with the Yanks, they'll show them who's going to abolish what. The only thing abolished will be the Ape's army!"

The man beside Gideon nudged him, as if for endorsement. Gideon smiled and raised his glass and nodded.

The trio rendered a few opinions on the parentage and sexual habits of Senator Lane and those who'd printed his statement. Gideon shoved his glass across the bar. "Another one." What if the gentlemen knew they were standing beside someone with ties to that very newspaper? He supposed there'd never been such a strange war in all of human history.

His next drink reminded him of something else. Alcohol—or the probable absence of same up at Harper's Ferry. He'd been informed James E. B. Stuart was a devout Episcopalian and a total abstainer. He'd heard too many good things about Stuart to be much concerned about his piety. But others might complain.

He hoped to do well when Stuart led the cavalry into battle. He wanted to offer his mother some reason to be proud of him. He knew he'd been a disappointment to her so far. He was wholly uninterested in book learning. His term at Washington College had been a catastrophe. About the only things he honestly enjoyed were hunting, fishing or galloping the roads and meadows around Lexington on one of Grandpa Virgil's horses.

That was one reason he thanked the Almighty the war had come. He'd finally found something to which he could give himself with unstinting enthusiasm. If only Margaret could be proud of him, too—

Dammit, he'd *make* her proud!

He checked the back-bar clock. He still had a couple of minutes. He asked for a third applejack to brace himself for what could be a pretty grim evening.

More opinions and predictions kept spouting from groups waiting for an opening at the bar:

"—old Telegraph Morse is sympathetic—"

"Hell, he's a *Yank!*"

"But he stands with the South. He thinks we were foolish to fire on Sumter, though. Says it's made it impossible for Northerners who want peace to exert any influence in Washington—"

"—want a job, Simeon? There's still a card in the *Enquirer.* The Louisiana State Military Academy's hunting for a superintendent. Some Northerner named Sherman resigned the post—"

"—the paper says the prize in the Royal Havana Lottery's up to half a million dollars—"

"—no more Federal mail service in the Confederacy come the end of the month—"

"Godamighty! My poor mother's ailing in Wisconsin. How'll I find out whether she's recovered?"

"—the Little Giant's down with the typhoid out in Illinois—"

"Well, I hope he pulls out of it. Yankee Democrat or not, he was a friend of ours for a long, long time. How old is he?"

"Forty-eight, forty-nine—but I saw him up in Washington in March and he looked sixty. Sick. Pasty. A worn-out bulldog."

"If any man could have saved this country, he—"

"It isn't *this country*, Neville. It's two countries now. Besides, it's too late. He's dying."

Conversation to his right caught his attention. He couldn't see the man immediately next to him. The fellow had his back turned. But over the man's shoulder, he spied a small, nervous chap whose frock coat bore stains on the lapels and whose hair looked as if it hadn't met up with a comb in weeks. The man was squinting at his companion as he said:

"You can take everything Jeff Davis says and discount it about fifty percent. I mean all that garbage about how we'll mince the Yanks in ninety days because *our* boys are going to war with fire in their bellies."

The man beside Gideon grumbled, "Whose side are you on, Josiah?"

"That's a stupid question. I'm being realistic. All that fire in the belly talk isn't worth a pig's ass if we haven't got decent factories or railroads."

"The crop surpluses will finance those."

"Oh, will they? We sure as hell can't sell cotton up North any longer. Davis won't sell it to Europe either. And may I remind you which ships used to carry our cotton and tobacco and sugar? Ships owned by Yankees! Think they're going to come steaming up the James to do business as usual? I tell you Davis is totally wrong! Fire in the belly's no good without *money*."

For emphasis, the ferret-faced man slammed his shot glass on the bar. He lowered his voice, but Gideon could still hear:

"And if the government can't raise enough—which it can't—then the private citizen has to help. Using any means available, fair or foul."

"Hell, there's nothing you can do about it."

"No? You'd be surprised if you knew—"

Abruptly he noticed Gideon listening. He signaled his friend with a glance. The two huddled closer together, elbows on the bar. Gideon missed the rest of the conversation; no tragedy. Obviously the South had partisans of all kinds. But he didn't like the attitude of that pale little weasel doing most of the talking.

A glance at the clock made him start. Fifteen minutes had gone by. He drained his drink and rushed for the lobby. Outside the hotel, he jerked up short. Turned to the left, then the right. His head felt light from the three fast applejacks.

He should have been able to spot the golden dress easily. The crowds had thinned a little now that it was fully dark. The more timid had retired to their homes, leaving the walks to the soldiers, the sharps, the black urchins pimping for the whore's cribs.

He didn't see Margaret anywhere.

Worried, he began to walk quickly toward the dress shop.

ii

He passed the gilt-leafed doors of a gambling palace. Inside, dim figures moved in a sulphurous light. He walked faster. His head was clearing. The night air dried the sweat on his cheeks and palms.

He reached the corner. A horse-drawn omnibus came clattering along Ninth from one of the depots. He ran around behind it, his left boot flattening a turd. He ignored the stink as he scanned the brick walk down by La Mode.

The area was dim because the shop stood midway between two gas lamps. He thought he spied men clustered around the shop's entrance, though. Two men. No, three—

A few more long strides and he identified the men's clothing. Zouave uniforms. The man nearest him had his right hand against the building. He was talking to his companions—or someone else.

Gideon began to run. Those were New Orleans Tiger Zouaves. The worst riffraff on the streets—

A pedestrian tried to push by the men. One shoved back. Gideon heard a voice ask the intimidated pedestrian for help.

The voice was Margaret's.

He ran faster. His shako fell off. He was dead sober. His boots hammered the bricks as he passed through the glow of one of the gaslights. The Zouaves saw him coming.

"Watch it, Hall," one said.

Gideon dashed around the white-faced pedestrian who'd been pushed off the walk. The man addressed as Hall stepped away from the building. Only half a dozen store fronts separated Gideon from the trio now. He saw Margaret trapped among them, the very instant he realized he had no weapon.

The Zouave named Hall peered at him. The man's face was blotched with warts. He slipped his hand under his vest.

Taking advantage of the diversion, Margaret tried to dash away. Another Zouave caught her; slapped her face; laughed:

"Hold on, Miss Pretty-tits. We ain't done with you yet."

Gideon stopped under the gaslight nearest the shop. He was aware of a couple of people watching across Main Street. A gambler lounged outside his establishment down at the end of the block. He'd get no assistance from either source, he suspected. Nor did he see any Blind Pigs—the guards assigned to patrol Capitol Square; lately they'd expanded their rounds to include major thoroughfares. But a Blind Pig wouldn't be much help either. All were elderly; some, tottering veterans of 1812.

So it was up to him. He started forward again.

Margaret cried out:

"Stay back, Gideon! They're all armed—"

"Get away from her!" he shouted.

"Why, looka this!" the wart-chinned Hall snickered, weaving a step in his direction. "A sojer boy. Dressed up damn near as fancy as the girl!"

"Gideon, be careful!" Margaret was still struggling. But she couldn't free herself from her captor.

"Shit, he ain't gonna interfere," Hall grinned. Even at a distance, Gideon smelled the rum on the man. "If he tries—"

Hall's hand slid from under his vest.

"—we'll just chop his balls off."

Margaret lunged again. The second Zouave caught the point of her chin, shoved her head against the shop's wall. Gideon heard the thump. Red-faced, he charged straight at Hall. The Zouave stood spraddle-legged, his knife pointed at Gideon's belly.

iii

There was anger in Gideon Kent; the uncontrollable anger of which his mother often spoke with weary concern. He launched himself into a long leap.

Hall yelled: "Crazy son of a bitch—!" He jumped back, stumbling into his friends as Gideon caught his knife arm and bent it at the wrist.

Bone popped. Hall shrieked.

Gideon didn't get a firm footing as he landed. He fell on top of Hall. The Zouave dropped the knife.

Kneeling on Hall's chest, Gideon seized his ears, raised his head, bashed it down on the bricks. Then again—

Hall howled on the first crunch; fainted on the second. There was commotion inside the shop. Lamps bobbing. Two or three young women hurrying through the darkened front section—

Gideon leaped up, still shaken from the fall on top of the wart-faced Zouave. He wiped sweat from his forehead, aware of the other two moving at him. They fumbled for concealed weapons.

The shop door opened. Three girls screamed and jabbered. Margaret got free, darting toward him. The second Zouave kicked her. She stumbled. He yanked her out of the way, mouthing filthy words as he lunged at Gideon, his right arm extended at shoulder level. In his fist, a knife.

Gideon twisted sideways to narrow the target. The knife raked the left side of his face. He felt pain; the warmth and wetness of blood. He rammed a fist into the Zouave's stomach.

The man doubled, then tried to grapple Gideon around the waist. The dragging weight threw him off balance—left his face exposed again as metal came streaking out of the shadows. Sharp-edged knuckle-dusters on the hand of the third Zouave—

The knuckle-dusters damn near tore his head off. He staggered. Still on his knees, the second Zouave gut-punched him twice. The punches were clumsy but powerful. Gideon reeled into the street, landed on his back, the wind knocked out of him.

Blinking, he rolled over. Tried to push up. His arms seemed to be made of jelly. A hack came flying around the corner of Ninth, thundering toward the spot where Gideon floundered. Margaret screamed.

A chaos of overlapping sounds then. The grinding wheels. The rattling hoofs. The oath of the driver dragging on his reins and booting his brake. The hack veered. Simultaneously, the second Zouave jumped on Gideon's back.

Gideon's jaw slammed the dirt. Like a gored animal, he bellowed and heaved upward. The Zouave tumbled off. Landed under the hoofs of the rearing hack horse—

Gideon crawled the other way; stumbled up. The hack driver whipped his terrified animal. No use. Fore-hooves slashed down, striking the Zouave's face.

The maddened horse kicked and stamped until his driver got him under control. Clutching his face with both hands, the Zouave gained his feet. He lurched straight up the middle of Main. Blood streamed between his fingers. He almost blundered into another hotel omnibus. The passengers yelled and pointed. The Zouave staggered on, moaning.

Head near to bursting with pain, the showy dolman almost torn in half, Gideon shambled back to the brick walk. The Zouave with the knuckle-dusters was still crouched there. He started backing away. Gideon ran at him.

"Don't!" Margaret exclaimed. He barely heard. Panting, he snagged the Zouave's arm and hurled him against the building.

A small crowd was collecting. People off the omnibus; the hack driver; the gambler from the corner. He puffed a cheroot and watched Gideon with hard, admiring eyes.

Gideon began to punch the Zouave. The man begged; put up the hand with the bloodied knuckle-dusters. Gideon knocked it down, drove a fist into his face, then rammed his knee in the man's groin.

Blood squirted from the Zouave's nose. His eyes rolled up in his head. When he started to slide down the wall, Gideon held him with one hand and battered his face with the other.

Hit him once.

Twice.

Three times—

Margaret tore at his arm: "Let go of him, Gideon!"

"Here, I'll take charge!" A wheezy voice. Gideon glimpsed the white-stubbled cheeks of a Blind Pig. Gaslight winked on the metal letters on the old fellow's cap. P. G. Pig without an i. Blind Pig—

The Public Guard tried to thrust an antiqauted musket between Gideon and the Zouave. The weapon was nearly knocked from his hands when Gideon hit the Zouave again.

"I say, sir, let me take charge!" the elderly man protested. "Young ladies—someone—help me!"

More hands grabbed Gideon. He had his right arm drawn back for another punch. His knuckles bled. All at once, he felt Margaret's nails bite through his sleeve again:

"You've done enough!"

The words seemed to echo and re-echo. The Zouave collapsed. Gideon was shaking. Growing uncontrollably dizzy—

He shot out his free hand; propped himself against the front of the shop. With an arthritic groan, the Blind Pig knelt to examine the man Gideon had beaten.

"Done for. Be in the hospital a week. Ought to send these Louisiana thugs straight home. We don't need their kind."

People swarmed around Gideon, slapping his back, congratulating him. It was safe now that the battle was over.

He realized how close he'd come to being killed. While he was fighting, the thought had never entered his mind. He shook his head. Looked for Margaret. She'd understand.

Suddenly a lamp held by one of the girls illuminated Margaret's face. He couldn't believe what he saw.

His knees gave out. He started to fall. The Blind Pig made a feeble attempt to catch him; failed. Gideon tumbled sideways. The left side of his face—the knifed, bleeding side—smeared against the skirt of Margaret's gown before he hit the walk and sprawled.

The last thing he remembered was Margaret's expression. She looked at the swath of blood on her skirt, then down at him. Even with his eyes watering and things growing grotesquely distorted, he recognized the meaning of the look.

There was no pride on her lamplit face. Only anger.

iv

Voices. Margaret's first, edged with irritation:

"Where did you get that, Willa?"

"Oh, we just keep it hid around here. Do we have to say where?"

"You know how Aunt Eliza feels about liquor. If she realized you had a bottle cached in the shop—"

Another girl broke in: "We're the ones working half the night to finish the uniforms. Shouldn't we have a little something to make the time go faster?"

"And the seams come out crooked?" Margaret snapped back.

He heard grumbles. The first girl spoke again:

"You sound in a fearful temper."

"Do you blame me?"

"Well," Willa sniffed, "we ain't bein' of any help standing around discussin' temperance. This gin will clean up his knuckles and that gash."

Though he hadn't opened his eyes, sensation was returning to Gideon's body. He was seated in a chair, his legs stretched out. He ached like the devil. The left side of his face felt warmer than the right. A lamp close by?

His nose itched. That told him where he was. The back room of La Mode Shoppe. He'd been there before, and he'd sneezed violently every time because of all the thread and lint lying loose.

He probed his lower lip with his tongue. Found a small, clotted cut. Something wet and sweet-smelling pressed his left cheek. His eyes popped open:

"Jesus Christ! That hurts!"

"You sit still, Mr. Kent. I need to swab out the cut. Marcy, hand me a piece of linen."

The girl hovering behind one of the shop's I. M. Singer automatic sewing machines jumped to find the cloth for Willa, who knelt at his side. The reek of the gin and the heat of the lamp started his stomach churning. Vomit rose in his throat.

Finally Willa finished cleaning his face and his raw knuckles. She handed him a fresh, folded square of linen:

"Just hold that to your cheek and I think the bleeding will stop."

"Thank you, ladies," Gideon breathed. He felt stiff, but he'd live. He peered into the shadows beyond the Singers and the cutting table. He couldn't locate Margaret. She must be standing behind him.

Her voice confirmed it: "You should have let me tend to him, Willa."

Willa shrugged. "Would of, except you were nearly as unstrung as he was."

"That's impertinent."

Willa sighed. "Guess so." She didn't apologize.

"You should rest, too," another girl said to Margaret. "Those Tigers treated you pretty rough."

"Mean bastards," said a third.

Gideon managed a grin. "Nothing a Virginian couldn't handle."

The attempt at levity had precisely the wrong result. Margaret exhaled loudly. He tried to crane his head around while still holding the linen to his cheek:

"Where the devil have you got to, Margaret?"

"Here."

She walked to where he could see her. The blood on her gold skirt had turned brown. She looked as if she were ready to cry.

"You all right?" he asked.

"Fine. Perfectly—fine."

"You don't sound so fine."

"You were a fool to throw yourself at those bullies!"

"A *fool*?" He sat up straighter, causing an unexpected and painful throb along his spine. "What the hel—what the devil was I supposed to do? Stand by and give 'em permission to rape you right in public?" A girl tittered. "They acted like they'd seen you before."

"This afternoon. Two of them accosted me on the street. After I left you at the hotel, I noticed them when I was turning into the shop. They were down at the end of the block. And waiting at the door when I came out."

"Two of the Blind Pigs hauled 'em to the lock-up," one of the girls said.

"Wonderful," Margaret said.

Gideon clucked his tongue. "I don't know why you're

so blasted peevish. You were in a bad scrape. Someone
had to get you out!"

"You could have waited for help—" she began.

"*What* help? Ladies and little boys on the hotel omnibus? Old fossils with rusty muskets? Jesus!" He
shook his head. "I don't understand this."

"Oh, you don't?" Fists clenched, she leaned down.
"You attacked those three men without a weapon. You
could have been killed. You were crazy to do it!"

A gasp of astonishment from Willa. Glances of surprise, then derision from the other two girls. Margaret
was aware of the reaction. Nervously, she brushed back
a curl straggling in front of her ear. When she spoke
again, he sensed she was addressing the girls as well:

"Please don't think I'm ungrateful—"

"Why, no! How would I possibly get that idea?"

"Don't be snide. You were too rash. That temper of
yours—"

Willa thumped the gin bottle on the cutting table.
"Lord. I can't stand any more. Margaret Marble, you
can fire me for sayin' so, but you oughta be ashamed.
Mr. Kent pulls you out of a ferocious muss, and instead
of thankin' him, you're jabbin' him about—"

"I *do* thank him!" Margaret blazed. "But it's no
business of yours."

"Sure is, long as he's bein' badgered. Riles me something fierce. Mr. Kent did what any decent young man
would have done—"

The others seconded her loudly. Close to tears, Margaret spun away from them:

"God! Nobody has any sense any more! Nobody!"

She ran to the front of the shop.

Gideon rose, pulled the linen from his cheek and
winced. He dabbed the linen on a spot of blood oozing
from a scraped knuckle.

"I'll try to straighten this out, Miss Willa. Thanks for
your help."

"Least I could do. I'd be proud to have a cavalry soldier lookin' after me."

"Well, Margaret is too. Those Mississippi river rats upset her, that's all."

The girls weren't convinced and neither was he. He was angry, and more than a little insulted by her behavior. Apparently she objected to his attack on the Tiger Zouaves for the same reason she objected to his eagerness to ride off to Harper's Ferry. And even though she'd given him a hint of the reason for her feelings, understanding those feelings wasn't the same as sympathizing.

How to deal with her? How to convince her she was wrong? Especially now, when men had no choice but to defend their homes—and, in the case of scum like the Tigers—their women?

Damned if he knew the answer.

One thing was plain, though. He'd have to find it soon. All of a sudden he and the girl he cared for had confronted a wall that divided them just as surely as long-standing animosities divided the North and South.

In a tired voice, he said, "I'll go talk to her. Maybe she's settled down. I expect you ladies want to go back to work—"

"Don't want to," Willa said. "Got to." She shooed the other girls like a mother hen: "Marcy, hide the gin. Miss Eliza will be back from church before long. Heloise, take those bloody linens out to the scrap bin. Bury 'em—way down in the bottom."

Gideon paused at the curtained doorway. "I'll be seeing Margaret home—"

Willa nodded absently. "She wrote a note for Miss Eliza." The girl pulled her stool up to the cutting table, gave him a pitying look and sat down.

In the darkened front of the store, Margaret stood still as a statue. He touched her arm:

"We can go."

She spun around. "Gideon, you misunderstood every-thing I tried to say back there!"

"No, I didn't. I just didn't care for it much. Come on, let's not squabble."

"But you rush into danger without thinking about—"

"*Enough,* Margaret. I did what any man would do. Now shall I see you home or not?"

There was an instant when he wished she'd say no. With his face throbbing and his body hurting, he was in bad spirits. He had a premonition the trip to Rockett's might only worsen their differences—

He resolved not to let it happen. He loved her too much to see everything spoiled.

It's up to me to change her mind.

In reply to his question, she said, "Yes, I do want you to take me home. It's more important than ever that you meet my father."

Outside, he drew a deep breath of the night air. Scratched his nose and sneezed.

"Could we walk back to Ninth first? I lost my hat someplace."

"Of course. I wouldn't want you to look anything less than splendid when you go riding off to—"

She cut off the sentence; caught his hand:

"Forgive me. I keep saying things I shouldn't."

He squeezed her fingers. "Forgiven."

But he wasn't reassured. Her hand felt frigid.

He managed to locate the shako, dusty but otherwise undamaged. Under a gas lamp, she watched him settle it on his head and stretch the strap beneath his chin. Her eyes were sad.

Hand in hand but awkwardly silent, they went to catch the horsecar.

CHAPTER IV

Lost Love

IRON GRINDING AGAINST IRON, the horsecar rolled through the May dark. The car was pulled by a swaybacked nag in blinders. The animal's hoofs struck the street with a slow clopping rhythm. As the car climbed a slight grade, an oil lantern hooked to the ceiling shifted the shadows of the passengers.

Only three people were aboard besides Gideon and Margaret. Two were bearded, tipsy fellows with huge bellies and the look of dock workers. The third, seated in the rear, was a gaunt young woman in a flamboyant scarlet pelisse. She either lived in Rockett's or was searching for an evening's employment.

The car windows were lowered to admit the mild night air. But the interior still smelled stale. The atmosphere wasn't improved when one of the men passed wind.

The young woman laughed. In a moment she moved to the front of the car and struck up a conversation. The three began whispering. Gideon heard what he thought was haggling over prices.

Since the start of the ride Margaret had been sitting with her hands clasped in her lap and her eyes straight ahead. Several times she seemed on the verge of speaking but held back.

Gideon felt much better. Physically. His mood was growing steadily worse. That was the subject Margaret finally used to end the silence:

"I can tell you're furious with me."

He let out a long sigh. At least the tension was broken. He lied to her:

"I'm more mixed up than anything else. You acted like I committed a sin going after those Tigers."

"You still think I'm ungrateful." She reached for his hand. "Honestly, I'm not. But to throw yourself at three armed and vicious men—"

"Why must we keep going over it, Margaret? I did what was necessary! What happened was my fault. If I hadn't let my belly get the best of my brains I'd have walked you back to the shop."

The two men and the woman in red were talking boisterously now. There was a great deal of patting and pinching going on at the front of the car. Margaret shook her head:

"Necessary. I suppose that's what my father told my mother when he joined up for the Mexican War." Her gaze drifted out the window to a saloon where piano music jangled. "You don't know how much war has cost me. Mama fell ill while Papa was serving with the Kentucky Mounted Volunteers. She died almost a week to the day after he fought at Buena Vista."

"That was a big battle."

"Big and ghastly. It would have been better if he'd died there."

"You said something like that before. Jesus, Margaret—it's cruel."

"You won't think so when you see him."

Her eyes moved from the saloon to passing store fronts, all dark. The white-whiskered driver clanged the bell and shouted at a pair of boys who raced across the track. A second later, half a dozen loud pops—firecrackers—started the horse whinnying and balking.

The driver swore; lashed the reins over the nag's back. The car rolled forward again.

In a solemn voice, Margaret went on, "Papa came

home in the spring of '47. We moved back into the home place—I stayed with some neighbors after Mama was buried. Papa couldn't work the farm. Women who lived close by brought food from time to time. But it wasn't enough. So Papa hired a twelve-year-old boy to come over once a day and kill one of the rabbits."

"Did you raise them?"

"Yes. They were so pretty—soft and white. We had dozens of cages. Mama built most of them before she died. I gave all the rabbits names. That made killing them harder than ever. I bawled every time the neighbor boy showed up. Papa wouldn't pay any attention. He'd just say, Ephraim, you go out and bring us Joseph. Bring us Samantha—I'm not even sure those were the names. But I remember screaming when Ephraim went out to the hutches. I'd wait for the sound. Little as I was, I remember the sound to this day."

She was pale.

He asked, "What sound?"

"The sound when Ephraim broke the rabbit's head with a stone. Papa said that way was quicker and more merciful. For—for a while I wouldn't eat any of the rabbit meat—" Tears filled her eyes. "You see what it cost? My mother's life. The animals. Papa—"

"But he's alive!"

"Not really."

The overhead lamp swayed, flinging her shadow behind her shoulder. Gideon struggled for the proper words:

"Well—your feelings make a little more sense now. Trouble is, sometimes people *have* to fight for what they believe."

"Christ didn't teach that. I don't accept that."

"What are you going to do, then? Just—stand aside from the war? Take no part in it?"

Softly: "That's right."

"You honestly don't believe we've got to fight for the South's independence?"

"Is that what the war's about? I'm not so sure."

"Hell, yes that's what it's about. Freedom to live the way we please. My great-great-grandfather Kent fought for the same thing in the Revolution. So did his grandson —my grandfather Jared. He was aboard Old Ironsides when she got her nickname and we whipped the British once and for all. The Kents have always stood up for what they believed, Margaret. Even my father did in his own crazy way."

"And how many Kents—including your father—have been hurt?"

"That's beside the point."

"It certainly isn't. Life's too precious to squander on—"

"Nobody's *squandering* anything! Nothing worth-while comes cheap, Margaret!"

The red-clad woman and her companions stared. Gideon lowered his voice:

"I still get the feeling you don't believe in the South."

"You're unfair!"

"Why?"

"You imply I'm some sort of traitor because I can't stand to see lives ruined."

"Well, do you believe in the cause or don't you?"

She hesitated. "I can't lie to you. Not after the things we've already said to each other. No, I don't believe in black slavery."

To her surprise, he waved that aside:

"I'm discovering there are a lot of lads in the troop who don't. Growing up, I thought most everyone did. But it's a bigger question than the nigras going free. It's a question of rights."

"If that's all it is, then I'm a Southerner." He looked relieved. "I might even say yes to defending those rights if I thought we could win quickly."

His eyes hardened. "But you don't."

"No. And every statistic about the North says I'm right."

He tried a smile: "I still say one Virginian can lick a dozen Yanks."

"Gideon—*Gideon*—" She clutched his sleeve. "That's what terrifies me so much. Your—little boy attitude. Don't argue, that's what it is. You'll go charging off behind Stuart, having a grand time and singing at the top of your lungs. Until the minute you see one of your friends shot to death, or—"

She bent her head. Her bonnet hid her face.

"Or die yourself."

She turned to plead with him:

"God gave men *life*. They have no right to throw it away, I don't care how holy they think their cause is! Rather than know you were hurt, I'd sooner die myself. Or never see—"

She stopped. Angry again, he finished the sentence for her:

"Never see me again?"

"Gideon, I didn't mean—"

"You did."

"Sweetheart, let's not quarrel—"

His laugh was harsh. "Appears to me we've already done a heap of it, Margaret. And there's no sign we'll be doing any less till you change your mind."

"I won't. But you will, after you meet Papa—"

She broke off again. The car had stopped. The gaunt woman and her two customers were leaving. The driver rapped on the partition between the left and right front doors:

"End of the line."

ii

Margaret glanced outside, startled. "I didn't realize we were here already—"

Gideon rose to let her out, then followed her to the head of the car as the swaying lamp came to rest. The horse stamped and blubbered its lips as the couple emerged on a dark, cobbled street which angled sharply down toward the James. Lanterns gleamed on three small packets tied up at piers.

The neighborhood—mostly warehouses and factories—appeared deserted. And smelled none too savory. The odors of dampness and mold mingled with the stench of garbage.

The driver started unhitching the nag in preparation for the return trip, on which it would pull from the opposite end of the car. As Margaret and Gideon passed, the old man gave them a perfunctory smile:

"Hope you young folks enjoyed the ride. May be one of the last you'll get."

Margaret halted. "Are they going to discontinue service on the line?"

The driver stroked tobacco-stained whiskers. "Could be. The superintendent said work gangs would be ripping up the rails pretty quick now. The metal's valuable, y'know. Every piece of metal in the South's valuable if we're gunna have enough guns to beat the fucki— uh—the damn Yanks."

Margaret looked shaken by this latest evidence of disruption. Perhaps because the driver was embarrassed by his lapse in language, he switched his attention to Gideon:

"You're a sojer, eh?"

"Macomb's Hussars."

"Oh, yeah. Quartered out at Camp Lee."

"We've moving to Harper's Ferry this coming Sunday."

The old man slapped his arm. "Good for you! Wish I was young enough to go. You kill a few of them abolitionists fer me, y'hear?"

"Do my best," Gideon said; but not too loudly. Margaret had already moved away. Her rigid back showed how much she hated that kind of talk.

He caught up with her and took hold of her arm. Their long shadows leaped across the face of a tobacco warehouse, which ended abruptly at a dark, narrow passage he assumed was an alley. To his surprise, Margaret turned into it.

He was astonished to see lamps lit behind curtains in the windows of three rickety frame buildings no better than the New York tenements he'd read about. The buildings formed a U at the end of the cul-de-sac.

His boot slipped on a rotting cabbage. A fat-bellied rat went scurrying by in front of them. The air in the dead end was foul.

She led him to the sagging stoop of the building at the bottom of the U. On the second floor of the one to his left, he heard a profane argument between a man and a woman. Without looking around, Margaret said:

"Welcome to Melton's Court. Not very courtly, is it? I didn't want to bring you here. I've always been ashamed of it."

He hurt for her. Tried to soothe her bitterness:

"There's nothing shameful about living in a poor place—"

She spun on the second step, her face dim in the light filtering through filthy curtains in a first floor window.

"Oh, yes, there is. Especially when the thing that brought us here is the very thing you're so eager to experience. Come inside. I'll show you how splendid it is to be a soldier."

iii

The moment she opened the outer door, he whiffed the vileness of the place. Disinfectant and rotting wood, evening cooking and human filth blended into a sickening miasma. The lower hall was lightless. A feeble gas jet glimmered on the second landing. As if marching to some private battle, Margaret began to climb the stairs with hard, precise steps.

On the second floor, she drew a key from her reticule, unlocked one of three doors and went in. He pulled off his shako as he entered the flat.

Another gas fixture cast slightly brighter light in the parlor. The furnishings were shabby; out of date. The broken leg of a settee was propped up with a small chunk of pine. The carpet was worn and dingy.

Yet the room was immaculate. Furniture and sills showed no dust. The only disorder was a spill of newspapers at the foot of a horsehair chair positioned beneath the gas jet. Margaret and her aunt obviously worked hard to keep the place presentable.

To his right, he observed a narrow hall with two closed doors and light at the end. He could see only a few details of the kitchen. A stained plank floor. A portion of a chipped table. A washboard leaning against a large iron kettle beside the rear door. Back there, a man was muttering to himself.

Margaret took off her bonnet and laid it on an old cherrywood taboret. Sounding tired, she said, "The profits from the shop have always been slim. Aunt Eliza's also inclined to let her Christianity influence her credit policy. She doesn't object if customers wait six or eight months to pay their bills. She'd be able to live in a much nicer section if she weren't so devoted to temperance work—and spent the rest of her money on one person instead of three."

From the kitchen, the man called in a slurry voice: "Who's there? Margaret?"

"Yes, Papa. With a visitor."

"A visitor—? Lord amighty!"

Gideon didn't know precisely what he'd been expecting. But it certainly wasn't the kind of jocular boom he was hearing:

"A lady or a gentleman?"

"Gentleman."

"Then I'll bring a jug—"

A purple oath and a rattle testified to a near calamity with glassware. Next Gideon heard a peculiar scraping. A grotesque figure popped into sight at the end of the hall. It was a man—or half of one—on a small wood platform with rollers affixed to the bottom. Glasses and a bottle gleamed in the man's lap as he propelled himself along the corridor. He pushed against the floor with his palms; strong, vigorous pushes.

The closer he came, the more Gideon smelled whiskey. The parlor reeked by the time the man arrived. The gaslight showed Gideon the pinned-back trouser legs on both sides of the man's crotch. He was too flustered to speak.

At first glance, Margaret's father appeared to be healthy despite his crippled condition. His hair was white, spiky, uncombed. His bleary grin was cordial.

As the moments of strained silence passed, though, more details registered. Even whiskey couldn't mask the man's fetid breath. His cheeks were sunken. His prominent nose was pink, and he had trouble focusing his eyes. His only strength lay in the over-developed shoulders and forearms. Gideon guessed he was forty-five or forty-six. He looked sixty.

"Papa, this is the young man I've mentioned before.

Mister—ah, Lieutenant Gideon Kent. Gideon, this is my father, Willard Marble."

"How do you do, Mr. Marble?"

"Sergeant's the name I go by, Kent." He sounded petulant. "Margaret knows everybody in Melton's Court calls me the Sergeant. That's the rank I held in '47—holy Christ, Margaret, take these things! Here, here—"

He fumbled in his lap. Only Margaret's quick action prevented a glass from breaking.

"Put those on the table." She did. "Now hoist me up so I can meet your friend proper-like—"

Gideon stepped forward to help. Margaret waved him back. Avoiding his eyes, she slipped her hands beneath her father's arms, dragged him off the little platform and supported him with one hand while she pushed the horsehair chair against his back. With the girl lifting and the man pushing—he had huge knuckles—he was soon in the chair. Gaslight showed rust on the pins of his trousers

More cheerful again, he rubbed his watering eyes while he studied Gideon:

"So this is the one. Handsome specimen, Margaret."

"Papa!"

"Well, goddamn it, he is!" A fuzzy grin. "Looks like a horse soldier's outfit, son."

"Yes, sir. I'm with Macomb's Hussars."

Marble gestured to the litter of newspapers. "I've read about 'em. Hell of a bunch."

The man had trouble articulating his words. Bunch sounded like *bunsssh*. His yellowed teeth were too even to be his own. The odor of whiskey and sweat sat on him like a ground fog.

Gideon twisted his shako in his fingers.

"Sit down, young man, sit down! Margaret, where's your hospitality? Pour a dollop for our guest."

Stiffly, she walked to the chipped table where she'd

set the bottle and glasses. "This is really quite unlike you, Papa. I mean drinking before Aunt Eliza or I get home." Straight-faced, Gideon sat down as if he hadn't heard the lie behind her words.

"Unlike—?" Marble scratched his belly. All at once Margaret's strategy registered on his fuddled mind. "Oh—guess it is. Guess it is! Had to celebrate, though."

She poured liquor into two glasses. One drink was scanter than the other. She handed the short one to her father:

"What do you have to celebrate?"

He scowled at the meager drink and didn't take it immediately. He dug in the pocket of his threadbare vest. Drew out folded sheets of paper:

"I heard from Uncle Sam today. He's in the army again. 'Course, it's the wrong army. But at least he's back where he belongs."

"He belongs in a saloon. He's not fit for anything else."

"Hang it, Margaret, don't be so hard on the man! He's the finest friend I ever had. I treasure knowing him." To Gideon: "Uncle Sam's an officer—I mean he was. In Mexico. Picked up his nickname at West Point. 'Count of his initials. There's a picture he sent me when I asked—"

He pointed to the wall. Gideon hadn't noticed the framed photograph before. He crossed to examine it. He could see nothing unusual in the full-length portrait of a somewhat ordinary soldier wearing a long military coat and clamping a cigar in his teeth against the background of a tent. Marble went on:

"After the war, they sent him to California. Away from his family. I guess the loneliness turned him to what a lot of us turn to—"

He dropped the letter in his lap; took the glass from

his daughter's hand. He drank the contents in several quick swallows.

"Uncle Sam served in the Fourth Illinois. He saved my life one night in bivouac. Like a dumb fool I got into a card game with five of his noncoms. One was a cheat. I called him on it. The pack of 'em started to beat the tar out of me. Like to killed me before Uncle Sam come along. He knocked the ringleader down, gagged him with a bayonet tied across his mouth and marched him off smart as you please. I prob'ly wouldn't be here if it wasn't for Uncle Sam. We write each other every chance we get. He's been pretty miserable since he left the service.

"What sort of exalted position does he have now?" Margaret wanted to know.

"This here—" Marbled tapped the letter with his empty glass. "—says he went up from Galena to Springfield—" For Gideon's benefit: "Springfield, Illinois. To enroll. He figured they could use him since he's had so much experience. Eleven years with a regular commission. He caught the governor's eye, and now he's working for the Adjutant General, mustering in militia units. Gets paid three dollars a day!"

"About what he's worth," Margaret said.

"Dammit, girl, you quit speakin' of Uncle Sam that way! He's one of the finest soldiers who ever trod this earth. Fought like a maniac at Chapultepec, he did. General Worth cited him for distinguished service. Major Bob Lee commended him, too. Why, if he was on our side now—"

"We'd lose," Margaret finished.

Marble scowled. "Shows what you know." He turned to Gideon to find a more receptive audience. "Uncle Sam says they may put him in charge of a regular regiment. The 21st Illinois. A bunch of no-goods everybody calls the Mattoon Mob. He'll straighten 'em out! We been good friends 'cause we understand each other. We understand how much soldierin' means—and how a man sometimes can't fit in after he's had a taste of it."

He fingered the letter, regret on his face. "Uncle Sam's pretty strong about the war. Says we got only two p'litical parties left. Traitors an' patriots. I don't expect I'll hear much more from him. But we'll hear plenty *about* him, you count on it. Uncle Sam Grant—you remember his name and see if I ain't right."

Gideon tasted his whiskey. Horrible stuff. He fought to keep from making a face. Margaret looked at him as if to ask whether he'd seen enough.

Marble held out his glass. "Another tot, if you please."

"Papa, I think you've—"

"Another, honey." The man's fixed smile belied his annoyance. Margaret bristled, then gave in and refilled the glass.

"So you're in the cavalry, Lieutenant—?"

"Kent. Yes, I am."

"Mighty fine service. I was a horse soldier myself. Kentucky Mounted Volunteers. We were with Zach Taylor. President Taylor—" He drank. "Old Rough an' Ready. I fought under his command at Buena Vista. Twenty-third of February, 1847. Did Margaret tell you I was at Buena Vista?"

"I believe she did mention—"

"Papa," Margaret broke in, "Lieutenant Kent can't stay long. I doubt he wants to hear about old campaigns—"

"How do you know what he wants to hear about?" He drank again. "Fill this up!"

"No, you shouldn't—"

"For Christ's sake quit arguing. *Fill it.*"

Margaret closed her eyes a moment, then obeyed.

Marble wiped a drop of spittle from his lip. "I went almost the whole way with Zach Taylor. Palo Alto. Resaca de la Palma—my God, what a bunch of fighters

we had in that war! Stalwarts! My friend Uncle Sam
Grant—his ma named him Ulysses after some old
Greek story—I don't know which one, nobody knew
any Greek stories in the Kentucky hills where I was
raised. Uncle Sam could fight like a son-of-a-bitch. He
wasn't the only one, though. There was Lieutenant
Longstreet. Lieutenant Meade. Oh—an' Captain Bragg.
Old Braxton Bragg. He had balls as hard as the shell he
lobbed out of his cannon. You know much about Buena
Vista, Lieutenant?"

Gideon shook his head.

"We fought on a rainy day. Miserable, shitty
weather—"

"Papa."

"Sorry, sweet." But he wasn't. "Old Scott, that damn
turncoat Virginian who's runnin' the army up in Washington, he'd taken a lot of our men for the campaign to
knock out Mexico City. We had only about five thousand effectives left. Know how many Santa Anna had
with him when we tangled?"

"No, sir."

"Twenty thousand! Jesus, Jesus!—we had our work
cut out, we did!" He rocked back and forth. His disco-
lored dentures glistened. Made of animal teeth, Gideon
suspected.

Margaret stood near her father's chair, speaking to
Gideon with her eyes:

You see?

He felt obliged to offer another comment:

"President Davis was with you, wasn't he?"

"He surely was! Why, there wasn't a hotter partisan
the live-long day than Colonel Davis of the Mississippi
Rifles."

Marble drained his drink. He seemed to look through
Gideon to the lost, wintry day of victory.

"Davis took a bad wound. But he never quit fighting.
He kept those Mississippi boys in their red flannel shirts

an' white pants scrappin' like devils—" His voice
dropped to a murmur "We fought near a mountain
pass. La Angostura. The Narrows. A little ways on
where the valley widened out, there was this hacienda
called Buena Vista. That's where ol' General Torrejon
took our measure."

The rheum-filled eyes shone. Without so much as a
glance at his daughter, Marble extended his glass. She
filled it again.

"God, there were brave boys on that field. Bragg
wheeled his light battery hither and yon, going wherever
things were the hottest. And old Rough and Ready—
nobody could ruffle that old fighting cock. He sat there
on that farm plug he rode—Old Whitey—ridic'lous animal—!"

A broad gesture. His hand nearly upset the glass
Margaret was extending. Marble snatched the glass and
gulped.

"—but Taylor, he was cool as a pond in February.
He saw the greaser line crumblin' some, so he says,
'Give them a little more of the grape, Captain Bragg.
Give them a little more of the grape.' Outnumbered or
no, we had an *army*!"

Marble raised his glass to salute the vanished companies. Then he finished the whiskey. A sardonic grin distorted his mouth:

"If you been around Margaret any time to speak of,
Lieutenant Kintz—"

"Kent."

"Oh, tha's right. Sorry. Get a little foggy here—" He
tapped the empty glass against his temple. "Kent, not
Kintz. Mus' remember that."

Once more the ritual of extending the glass, which
Margaret filled to the brim. Gideon wondered why she
pandered to the man's vice. Was she tired of battling
him?

"What was I saying?" Marble belched. "Oh, yeh—

Margaret. She don't cotton to warfare, although it's the most honorable calling a man can have. Serving his country. Serving his flag—she don' understand it because she's a woman."

The careless condescension put fire in Margaret's cheeks. Her hands fisted at her sides as Marble went on:

"She don't know how it felt to be there at the hacienda. General Torrejon's lancers tried to break through from the rear. That's when us mounted boys from Kentucky he'ped carry the day. Us an' Colonel Yell's Arkansas regiment and some Indiana sharpshooters on the roof of the hacienda buildings. I killed four greasers for sure and two more possibles. Then I lost my horse. A greaser caught me on the ground an' hacked my left leg to pieces with his saber. Another one shot me through the right leg before an Indiana boy killed both of 'em. When I woke up, there was a gent with a bloody hacksaw standin' over me. My legs were gone. I'll admit I cried some. But not too much—"

The wrinkles around Marble's eyes deepened. He saw glory in the room's dark corners.

"I stopped soon as I heard we'd sent old Santa Anna runnin' to save his skin. It was the finest day I ever spent. That kind of a day a dumb dirt farmer's privileged to experience once in his life, if God's good to him."

Margaret turned away.

"*Glorious*! So don' you listen to what Margaret says, Lieutenant Kin—uh, Kent." He was blubbering now; submerged in the liquor and the memories. He grew waspish:

"Women don' have any grasp of how it is with a man. A man's got to prove he can stand up to the worst. That's why war can be a glorious thing—"

He sipped and leaned his head back, gazing at the ceiling but seeing bright pennons and the red smear of cannon beneath a drizzling sky. His voice was barely audible:

"Give 'em a little more of the grape, Cap'n Bragg."

Marble kept talking, an unintelligible mumble. His right arm lolled over the side of the chair. The last of the whiskey spilled on the carpet. Gideon caught one more word, pronounced slowly; savored:

"Glorious."

He rose. "I'd better be going. A pleasure to meet you, Mr. Marble."

Margaret's father tried to focus his eyes. "Yessir, Lieutenant Kintz. You come back. Like to tell you the whole story. The whole action, hour by hour. You can be proud you said yes to the cause, it's—"

His head flopped over. A prolonged, wheezing sigh.

"—a glorious thing for a man to do."

Gideon put on his shako as he started out. Margaret hurried after him while the white-haired man dozed and mumbled. Gideon opened the door. Marble roused:

"Forgot to—call me Sergeant. Everyone knows—the Sergeant, he was—at Buena Vista—"

Margaret slammed the door and faced him on the sour landing. Her lips looked bloodless.

"Answer me now, Gideon. Do you still want to be what he was?" She shook both his arms.

"Do you?"

iv

He knew what reply she wanted. He knew he might be able to evade her until she was calmer. He didn't want to hurt her, but he was still annoyed that she'd think him so easily influenced:

"I can see why you hate what happened to your father. But it strikes me Buena Vista's a good memory for him, not a bad one."

"He's too drunk to know the difference. He's been drunk for fourteen years!"

Fatigue and his aches and his inexperience with this sort of ideological fencing drove him to snap at her:

"You don't help much. Whenever he asks for the busthead, you hand it to him."

"If I didn't, someone else would. The neighbors will fetch him whiskey any time he thumps on the wall."

"Where's he get the money?"

"From Aunt Eliza. He's worse when he doesn't have liquor in him. He screams and raves—she can't stand to see him hurting. She hates it more than she hates alcohol."

"He may be hurting, but I'd say he's a proud man. A brave one, too."

"Brave? He's pathetic! Look at that man he worships—"

"Uncle Sam?"

"A sot who failed at *everything* once he left the army. Failed at farming. Failed at peddling real estate—do you know what he was doing before he got that pitiful job papa's so excited about? He was living on his family's charity. Clerking in his father's leather goods store in Galena—but even his own father and brothers couldn't stand him. They wouldn't lend him so much as a penny because they knew he'd throw it away in a saloon. You call that kind of man a worthy friend? Someone to admire?"

"But maybe your father's right. Maybe the man can't be happy anywhere except in the army."

She scoffed: "If he's typical of the new Union troops, I can imagine their behavior. They'll drill in grog shops and parade with rum in their canteens. Contrary to what papa says, nobody's *ever* going to hear of Uncle Sam—unless he's shot down drunk on a battlefield!"

Testily: "Well, if he wants to go out that way—if it makes him happy—why not?"

"Damn you, Gideon Kent! Hasn't it sunk in yet? Papa was just like you before he went to Mexico—" She started to beat at him with her fists. *"Just like you!"*

"Hold on, Margaret. I'm worn out—"

The flying fists hammered his chest. He batted her left hand aside, hard:

"I said hold on!"

Silence. She lowered her fists in defeat:

"I guess bringing you here didn't do any good."

"What did you expect? That I'd offer to quit the troop because I might wind up crippled too? I said it before. That's a risk I accept. We better get a few things straight. I love you. I want to be with you—marry you. But not at the price you're asking."

"I know you won't resign. I just want you to be realistic about what can happen to you."

"What am I supposed to do? Put in a request for duty behind the lines? The hell with that! I want a chance at the Yanks."

"You're angry again—"

"You're damn right. You make me feel like a baby instead of a man. I don't think the war's going to be as bad as you make out. But even if it is—which I doubt—I mean to do my part."

She looked much smaller all at once. "I can't even convince you to—take care of yourself? Be cautious—?"

He grabbed her forearms. "Being *cautious* won't accomplish a blasted thing! Unless we go at the Yanks full tilt—"

"Gideon."

"—there isn't a chance of our win—"

"Gideon!"

Her eyes frightened him. "What is it?"

"Take your hands off me."

Paling, he did. His arms dropped to his sides. His fingertips drummed against his dusty blue trousers. Her voice started loud and grew louder:

"You can call me wrong-headed. You can call me unpatriotic—call me anything you want. I love you. But war has *cost me too much.* I couldn't stand the sight of you coming back hurt. Ruined—the way he is—*no, let me finish*! I'll have nothing to do with this war. Or—"

She closed her eyes. Spoke from her pain:

"Or any man who involves himself in it."

"Then you'll have nothing to do with me, goddamn it!"

A slight nod. "I realized that a few minutes ago." A sad shrug. "I suppose it's better to have a little hurt now than a lot of it later."

She flung an arm around his neck; pressed her wet cheek against his:

"Goodbye, Gideon."

Before he could think of what to say, she rushed back into the flat. He heard the bolt slide home.

"Margaret?" He pounded the door, his temper making him roar. "Open up!"

A man's head poked from a doorway on the first floor. "Who the fire's doin' all the hollerin'—?"

"Shut the hell up!" he bawled, beating the door. The clotted spots on his knuckles began to bleed again. Finally, he gave the door a ferocious kick and ran down the stairs past the goggling tenant.

v

He stormed out of Melton's Court and headed for the end of the horsecar line. A steam whistle sounded on the river, shrill as a cry of pain.

He swore nonstop. Booted anything in his path—a broken vegetable crate; a stone; the putrid-smelling corpse of an immense rat. Damn her for being a soft, scared woman! She'd ruined what had begun as the sweetest night of his life; a night which promised years of—

Never mind. It was over.

Not his fault, either. *She* was the one who'd acted unreasonable—and slammed the door. Let her go hang!

He'd never felt so angry at another human being, with the possible exception of his father that night in Washington.

He saw a horsecar starting its run back toward the center of town. He raced to catch it, swung aboard and yelled at the driver as he paid his fare:

"Give that plug a good slap of the reins! I've got to get back to camp."

He slammed into the lantern-lit car and sank down. He realized he was sitting in the identical spot he and Margaret had occupied on their earlier ride. He moved.

He stared out the window. The iron tires screeched on the rails. He was glad it was over. She was stubborn and wrong. He was a man, fulfilling a man's responsibilities. If she couldn't understand and accept that, he was better off without her.

"Yes, sir," he growled to himself. "Better off."

But if that was true, why did he feel so wretched?

CHAPTER V

With Jeb Stuart

A LITTLE MORE than a month later, Gideon Kent's life had changed to such a remarkable degree that the parting in Rockett's sometimes seemed unreal.

He still thought of Margaret, and usually with regret. But he didn't write her. Nor did she write him.

Occasionally he thought of her father as well. But he never seriously entertained the idea that what had happened to the Sergeant could happen to him. Margaret's father had been an old man—over thirty—when he mustered in for the Mexican War. Age had probably slowed him down at Buena Vista. Gideon had confidence in his own youth and strength. Horror stories from the past had no bearing on his future.

Sometimes he speculated on whether better control of his own temper might have altered the outcome with Margaret. He doubted it. Such introspection became less frequent as the pace of military operations quickened, and events pushed both sides toward a major confrontation.

Douglas was dead in Chicago. Jefferson Davis and his cabinet had arrived in Richmond. The Federals had crossed the Potomac on the twenty-fourth of May and fortified Alexandria. The Union commander, McDowell, had arrogantly appropriated the Lee mansion for his headquarters. General Lee had written him to ask that the property be treated as respectfully as possible.

McDowell replied that he'd do his best. No one believed it.

The Yanks had a martyr now. Some hothead named Colonel Ellsworth had invaded an Alexandria hotel, the Marshall House, to tear down a Confederate banner flying from its roof. In clear weather, the offending flag could be seen in Washington City.

Coming downstairs with the flag, Ellsworth was shotgunned by the hotel owner, who was in turn killed a moment later by one of the colonel's New York Fire Zouaves. The colonel's body lay in state in the presidential mansion. The death heightened Northern hatred.

Runaway slaves had arrived at Fort Monroe. General Benjamin Butler refused to surrender them to their owners. Butler's adamant stand against returning "black contrabands" to their rightful owners thrust the slave issue to the forefront again. Virginians seethed and denounced Butler's illegal behavior.

Lincoln had issued a call for a special Congressional session to convene on July fourth. Northern newspapers issued a call of their own—for a demonstration of Federal power. The chief agitator was Greeley, whose *Tribune* reached the Confederate lines from time to time, smuggled across the Potomac by Southern sympathizers. Angrily, Gideon read the New York editor's repeated exhortation: *"Forward to Richmond!"*

The sloganeering was understandable, Gideon thought in calmer moments. Letters from his mother in Lexington noted the Confederate Congress would assemble in Richmond on the twentieth of July. Greeley and the other journalistic agitators wanted the city in Union hands by that date. They had a practical reason. The three-month volunteers Lincoln had called out in April would be free to go home by July's end.

At Harper's Ferry, Gideon's regiment had been turned over to the Provisional Army of the Confederacy. Term of service—one year. General Joe Johnston relieved the peculiar Colonel Jackson and withdrew from Harper's Ferry. He felt the position could not be properly defended, and its hilly setting made it unsuitable for the constant drill needed to sharpen green recruits.

Before Johnston pulled out, he burned the railroad bridge over the river. Down the Valley, at Winchester, he established the headquarters of the Army of the Shenandoah. Colonel Jackson was posted some nine miles north, at bucolic Bunker Hill.

The army in the Valley was growing; becoming truly representative of the Confederacy. It now included men from both of the Carolinas, and from the deep-South states of Georgia, Alabama and Mississippi. Tennessee volunteers had arrived; even a Maryland battalion.

Johnston was highly visible around the regimental camps. From the first, the soldiers took to him. He was a small, animated man in his middle fifties with a gift for making the lowliest private feel important. Often the general paused to ask a question of a young soldier. Where did he come from? How was he getting on?

Joe Johnston looked and acted like a commanding officer. He sported a carefully trimmed gray goatee and tended to strut. He was a gamecock, all right. Just wait till the Yanks felt his claws!

Johnston was also considered a great improvement over Old Jack, as some of the soldiers had begun calling the odd professor from the Military Institute. Colonel Jackson still refused to dress properly. He went about in worn-out high boots and an old, single-breasted uniform coat. The coat was blue, threadbare and too large. Jackson's headgear consisted of one shabby cadet cap, which he usually wore tilted down over his forehead to hide his stormy, light-colored eyes. Most of the rest of his face was concealed by a bushy beard the color of rusting metal.

Men liked the gamecock, but they laughed at old Old

Jack—probably out of fear. When he was seen, he was
never smiling. At Harper's Ferry he'd acquired a reputation as a harsh disciplinarian. It was whispered that because of his religious convictions, he'd probably refuse
to fight a battle if it should accidentally fall on a Sunday. Altogether, Gideon and a great many others crossed
him off as a fanatical farmer type of whom little could
be expected in the way of intelligent leadership.

In the first week of June, General Beauregard arrived in Richmond where he received a public ovation
and assumed command of the Army of the Potomac on
the so-called Alexandria line. The line's center was
Manassas Junction, some thirty miles below Washington and sixty miles from Johnston's force at Winchester.

Manassas constituted a logical target for the Federal
army because of its strategic location near major high-
ways. It was also a junction point for the little Manassas
Gap Railroad that linked the Valley's rich agricultural
lands with the eastern part of the state via the Bull Run
Mountains. If the Federals could seize Manassas, com-
munications and shipments of food between the two re-
gions could be interrupted. It took no genius to guess
Federal strategy would probably call for two armies—
one to devastate the Valley, another to seize and hold
Manassas, thereby preventing either Johnston or Old
Bory from using the railroad to relieve the other. With
Manassas captured, the Federals would be in a good
position to mount a drive to Richmond.

As couriers shuttled back and forth through the
mountains, Gideon learned that the emerging Union plan
was no secret to Old Bory. He read it in the Washington newspapers he received every day. Indeed, the
North's intentions were soon widely known in Johnston's encampments. Some papers got there as well, and
Gideon read of General Scott's opposition to the whole
Federal concept. Piecemeal attacks—a hasty thrust
here, another there—ran counter to his own master

plan. He wanted to spend the proper amount of time in preparation, then enclose the entire South with naval blockades and military advances on fronts as far apart as Manassas and the Mississippi. He wanted to encircle the enemy like a constricting snake. Scott's Anaconda, the papers called it.

But the helpful newspapers said Lincoln was impatient. The special July fourth Congress would share that impatience—and Lincoln's concern about the ninety-day enlistments. The papers claimed Scott was being overruled, and the double thrust into Virginia would be the plan of choice. Time for the attack—an unspecified date in July.

In June the Confederates began to see the proof. Pickets brought back word of a Federal force massing in Maryland under General Robert Patterson, a relic whose service dated back to 1812. But each passing day helped the Shenandoah army. By the end of the month, staff officers predicted, it would be up to a strength of ten thousand effectives.

Gideon was astonished at the amateurism which seemed to prevail in Washington. He continued to hear that Beauregard knew the specifics of Northern troop strength and tentative dates of departure; Old Bory received daily reports from a Southern sympathizer named Mrs. Rose Greenhow. The Wild Rose was continually wheedling—some said seducing—Federal officers and clerks. Maybe even a Congressman or two. The information she acquired was converted to cipher and slipped across the Potomac by courier.

Gideon couldn't believe Mrs. Greenhow would be allowed to continue her spying, but she was. Though under suspicion, she wasn't arrested. No one in power seemed to think it polite to arrest a lady. So Old Bory continued to read the papers and cipher messages, arrange his defense lines and receive volunteer units from all over the South. He issued a proclamation calling on

Virginians to rally against the unprincipled Federals. Their cry, he said, would be simple and savage. *Beauty and booty.* Rape and destruction—

All of this reached Gideon where he was stationed— Bunker Hill. It was a lovely place. The sweet-smelling meadows and the hazy slopes of the Blue Ridge in the distance created a summery charm that seemed far removed from any danger. Even the few skirmishes that took place had a comic-opera quality.

About a hundred of Lieutenant Colonel Stuart's troopers, for example, rode up to the Potomac and repelled an "invasion" by Maryland canal workers. Several of the enemy were killed. No cavalryman received so much as a scratch.

Gideon's company didn't take part in the foray, which displeased him. He wanted to fight; others were—and setting enviable examples. The camp had celebrated the news of the June tenth engagement at Big Bethel Church, only eight miles from Butler's outposts at Fort Monroe. Twelve hundred Confederates under the general command of Colonel Magruder—Prince John—had routed nearly twice as many Federals. The Yanks had blundered into Magruder's men and fought like schoolboys, losing eighteen dead. There was one Confederate casualty. Did anyone need further proof one Southerner was more than a match for a dozen Pennsylvania farmers and New York ribbon clerks? The Federals would stop squealing, "Forward to Richmond!" after a few more actions like Big Bethel. Gideon just wanted his chance to be part of one of those actions—

He was still feeling impatient on a sunny morning in mid-June when the First Virginia Cavalry Regiment again assembled for instruction by its commander.

The regiment was not yet at full strength. Only ten companies so far. Stuart hoped for at least twelve. But the existing First Virginia still made a splendid if motley sight in the damp meadow.

The men were mounted on every kind of horse from farm plugs to thoroughbreds. The horses stamped while the troopers exchanged whispers and fidgeted in their saddles. Shortly, the regimental staff—Colonel Stuart and several majors appointed by Richmond—cantered along in front of the assembled companies.

The majors looked tired and openly disdainful of the appearance of their men. Stuart, by contrast, seemed in high spirits. He *always* seemed in high spirits. If he ever slept for more than an hour or two, no one knew it.

There was something rakish and grand about Jeb Stuart; a personal aura in no way diminished by his rag-tag uniform. He wore an old Union Army greatcoat and trousers of blue, and ancient boots whose tops reached to his knees. He'd added personal touches to the shabby costume: spotless gauntlets of white buckskin; a fawn-colored hat pinned up on the right and decorated with a white ostrich plume. Beneath the open greatcoat Gideon glimpsed a sash of gold silk that held Stuart's French saber. Small gold spurs decorated his boots.

James Ewell Brown Stuart was almost six feet tall, stocky and long-armed. His huge, flaring beard and luxuriant mustachios glinted with bronze highlights as he jogged by on a blood bay hunter with black points. Stuart's blue eyes were merry but alert. The troopers agreed he looked better riding than walking. When he was afoot, the contrast between his long arms and chunky torso was more apparent. His classmates at West Point had nicknamed him Beauty, for the same reason a man of great height was sometimes called Shorty.

Stuart and his majors completed their inspection and cantered out to a position in front of the regiment. Stuart dismounted. Gideon rubbed Dancer's neck and pressed his lips together to hide a yawn.

Gideon was leaner and more fit than at any time in his life. He was also exhausted. Beside him was First Lieutenant Jack Harris, who looked horrible. Harris had spent the night drinking illegal busthead and playing euchre in the tent, making it impossible for Gideon to sleep.

Gideon's eye wandered to Captain Lester Macomb. The company commander had lost about twenty pounds since their first meeting. He'd developed a nervous tic in his cheek—with good reason. A number of volunteer commissions had already been revoked because the regimental officers believed those holding them were incompetent. Jackson had started it in the infantry. Macomb was afraid he might encounter a similar fate in the cavalry.

As for the Hussars themselves—now I Company—they looked much less presentable than they had in Richmond. Almost to a man, they had discarded the useless rabbit-fur dolmans. A few still wore shakos, but other, more practical types of hats had appeared. Gideon had appropriated a dark, soft-brimmed Union campaign hat from Private Enders. The private had been reassigned to Company Q. "Reassigned" was a euphemism for punishment.

Company Q consisted of incorrigibles plus a few men temporarily without mounts. Like some of the other well-born members of the regiment—including Gideon's lanky, dark-haired friend, Private Rodney Arbuckle III—Enders regarded military discipline as an insult to his status as a gentleman. The preceding week, Jack Harris had assigned Enders to guard duty. Enders had refused. Harris repeated the order, lacing his language with some of his favorite gutter talk. Enders promptly challenged him to a duel.

The duel was fought in a woods well away from camp. Gideon had held his own horse and that of the first lieutenant while the antagonists faced off with revolvers. Enders fired first, narrowly missing his superior. Harris' shot went wild. The ball struck Enders' horse behind the right eye. Minus a mount and charged with insubordination, Private Enders was transferred to Company Q before the day was over.

Gideon took possession of Enders' hat, as well as a forty-two-inch Union light cavalry saber that Enders had brought from home. Enders had enjoyed displaying the sword at the evening cook fire, even though he wasn't entitled to wear it.

Gideon still felt a bit guilty about the quasi-theft. On the other hand, until the duel, he was the only officer in 1 Company lacking a blade. And he doubted Enders would ever be returned to the ranks.

The confiscated saber hung from a white sash around his waist. There were no standardized uniforms as yet, and hence no badges of rank. A sash had to serve.

He glanced at his friend. Private Arbuckle was examining his fingernails, oblivious to Stuart out in the field. Rodney was almost as bad about discipline as Enders, though not nearly as arrogant. Gideon let out a low whistle. Rodney heard it and reluctantly turned his attention to the commander.

Stuart addressed the regiment in a loud but pleasant voice:

"Gentlemen of the First Virginia, let me say I'm well pleased with your progress. A little more drill is in order, however. We can't be satisfied to be second best. We know the resources of the opponent are greater than ours. So we must substitute expertise—and *esprit*—for numbers. Good training and the spirit of the chase will make the difference in battle."

A few cheers broke out among the enlisted men. Stuart held his smile, but his blue eyes ripped from offender to offender, silencing the noise. He knew well the problem of whipping untrained and highly independent men into some semblance of military organization. The troopers of the First Virginia had the spirit he wanted. But they had not yet become soldiers.

"We'll review the fundamentals once more," Stuart continued. Standing on the left side of his mount, he extended a gauntlet toward his reins. Gideon admired the smoothness of the move. Despite the long arms and legs so at odds with his short torso, Stuart possessed a natural grace few could match

"Stand to horse—everything begins from that."

Somewhere to the rear, Gideon heard a rattle of musketry. One of the infantry units sharpshooting. He yearned to wipe a trickle of sweat on the underside of his freshly razored chin.

Far away, artillery caissons rumbled. The meadow was warm beneath the cloudless June sky. Fat yellow jackets buzzed in the long grass. Jack Harris belched, then idly swatted at a fly pestering the ears of his horse. Stuart scowled him. Harris reddened.

"Note again the correct stance." Stuart demonstrated. "Heels together—so. Left hand hanging naturally at the side. Body erect but not stiff—"

Suddenly Gideon heard the creak of leather; the jingle of harness. Turning, he sucked in a breath.

"Rodney!"

The long-jawed private from Peninsula paid no attention to the whisper. He broke ranks and walked his horse several yards in front of the company. Captain Macomb looked apoplectic. But Rodney was well out in front of him, oblivious. Cheerfully, he waved and shouted:

"Colonel? 'Fore we go ahead, wonder if I might bring up a point."

Harris goggled. Gideon was afraid Macomb was going to faint and fall from the saddle. He whispered again:

"Jesus Christ, get back here!"

Astonished that his curiosity met with objection, Rodney Arbuckle swung to glance at his officers.

"I want to speak to the colonel. What's wrong with that?"

He faced Stuart again. The commander's cheeks were flushed. He dropped the reins, rigid beside the blood bay. The fingers of his gauntlets flexed. Rodney stood in his stirrups.

"Colonel, sir? It's about our company smithy. He shod Red Eye here, and I'd like you to look at the piss poor job he did. I'm not the only one with a complaint. A number of the other boys——"

"Trooper," Stuart roared, "return to your position!"

Rodney blinked, hurt. "You mean you don't care if our smith's no damn good?"

"I said return to your position!"

Rodney turned as red as the colonel. "Now wait just a minute, sir. You're talkin' to a gentleman, and I was under the assumption I was doin' the same. I see nothing wrong with askin' a sensible question."

Quivering, Macomb leaned over his mount's neck to plead in a strangled voice:

"For God's sake, Arbuckle, don't say any more or——"

"Trooper," Stuart broke in, "you have sixty seconds to return to your position and shut your mouth or you'll be back in Richmond by tomorrow night."

Rodney clenched his teeth. Gideon thought he might charge the colonel. Stuart began walking toward the private.

"I realize a great many of you *gentlemen* fail to comprehend the need to obey orders—maintain discipline—submit yourselves to the commands of your superiors. I could try to present the case in a reasonable way. I could tell you obedience is necessary for a pretty performance on horseback—being good riders, most of you are doubtless quite interested in a pretty performance."

The sarcasm grew heavier:

"But in combat, gentlemen, there is no time for outpourings of sweet reason. So let me be more direct. Do not break ranks unless instructed. Do your utmost to forget you were formerly able to lord it over your chums back home because you had a little more money or a better horse. Kindly stay where you're supposed to at all times—"

He reached Rodney and glared. Rodney seemed to alternate between rage and cringing terror.

"One more tidbit of advice—private. In battle, I believe you'll notice it's the undisciplined man—the man guilty of breaking ranks—who gets shot first. The veteran knows there's safety in numbers." Stuart drew a deep breath. "Now perhaps we can recommence the drill. I sincerely hope my little explanation of why you should obey orders has satisfied your curiosity—*because your sixty seconds are up!*"

One white gauntlet lashed out to slap Rodney's horse. Stuart jumped back as the animal reared. Rodney fought to keep his seat. Finally, he controlled Red Eye and maneuvered the horse back to the ranks. Stuart faced about and marched off.

Rodney fumed under his breath:

"Goddamn West Pointers! No respect whatsoever for a gentleman's rights!"

Jack Harris rode up beside him. "You pull another stunt like that, you're gonna be exercisin' your fuckin' rights sittin' on your fuckin' ass in Company Q."

"I don't care. Those West Point boys treat us like niggers!"

"Shut *up*," Gideon hissed. Rodney looked deeply injured; even his good friend had turned on him.

Here and there in I Company, others voiced whispered support for Rodney's stand. Gideon suddenly wondered whether even a man of Colonel Stuart's ability could turn this pack of disorderly individualists into a cavalry regiment.

Stuart certainly gave it extra effort that morning. He went through the fundamentals, then kept the companies practicing on their own until noon and beyond. The sun grew broiling. Men began to faint and tumble from the saddle. By three o'clock thirty or forty troopers lay on the ground in various stages of heat prostration.

But the drill kept on.

ii

The horses stirred and tugged at their picket lines as Gideon approached.

The stars were out. Behind him, lanterns glowed in the regiment's tents. He spied a figure strolling among the animals, an old musket cocked over one shoulder.

"Private Arbuckle?"

The sentry halted. Turned. Gideon swore when he saw the dusting of starlight on curly gray hair.

"No, sir, Lieutenant. It's me."

Gideon ducked under one of the ropes. "Damn it, Isom, where's your master?"

The middle-aged black dressed in cast-off clothing tried to blunt Gideon's anger with a smile. "He was feelin' a mite poorly, sir. He asked me—"

"I can imagine why he was feeling poorly!" Gideon broke in. "Because Stuart reamed his butt this morning and I ordered him to stand watch tonight. Stay here, Isom. You'll be relieved in a minute."

"But I don't mind, Lieutenant. Master Rodney brung me along for times like this."

"Colonel Stuart has issued explicit orders. No body-servants are to stand in for their owners. You'll be sent home as soon as we move into the field. Your master won't have anyone to relieve him then. So he'd damn well better start practicing."

"Yes, sir," Isom said in a meek tone. "But master Rodney, he ain't 'customed to bein' ordered around—"

"We're going to fix that!" Gideon stalked back to the tents.

In one of them, someone was plucking a slow version of "Dixie's Land" on a banjo. In another, he heard Harris conducting a euchre game. Harris had undergone a remarkable change of luck since his election. He seldom lost. And he welcomed players without money in their pockets. He handed them kernels of corn, tallied their losses at the end of the game and collected cash once the men received their back pay.

A couple of Rodney's messmates were lounging in front of a small fire outside their tent. One was writing a letter. The other leaned on his elbow and puffed on a cob pipe while reading a worn copy of *The Life and Opinions of Tristram Shandy,* a novel still considered quite racy. With an odd feeling, Gideon noted the design stamped in gold at the bottom of the spine. The partially filled tea bottle of Kent and Son.

The pipe smoker raised his head; started to speak. Gideon gave him no time. He slapped the flap of the tent aside.

Rodney yelped in surprise. He was resting on his cot, bare-chested, a letter in his hand. Shredded wrapping paper, a huge mound of large and small articles and some kind of red bunting lay beside the cot.

"Private Arbuckle, you undisciplined son-of-a-bitch—" Gideon began.

Rodney's dark eyes grew resentful. "Come on, Gideon—!"

"Lieutenant!"

"All right. Lieutenant. Do you have to holler that way? I took enough abuse for one day."

"Stand up."

"*What?*"

"You heard me. Put on your uniform and get to the horse corral double-quick."

Rodney didn't get up. Instead, he laughed. "Boy, with that temper of yours, you'll be a junior Jeb Stuart 'fore you know it. Not me, though," he sighed, relaxing and returning his attention to the letter.

Gideon snatched it away, banging his head on a hanging lantern:

"Ow! *Dammit,* you're making me mad, Rodney."

"You be careful how you handle that letter. It's from my girl Nancy. Miss Nancy Wonderly of White House—"

"I'll tear the damned thing to pieces if you don't get dressed!"

"My. You sure have gone high-ass since you got elected."

"That's right, I got elected. And until you and the rest of the boys decide to put someone else in my place—"

"Lead us not into temptation," Rodney murmured.

"—it's my responsibility to see that orders are carried out. Lord!" He raked a hand through his hair. "If every man in this regiment keeps galloping off on his own, we'll never whip the Yanks. Don't you realize Stuart was right this morning? A man by himself is ten times more likely to get killed than one who stays with the troop and *does what he's told.*"

A shrug. "Maybe so. But I am just not used to bein' ordered about. Do this, do that, piss here, crap there, yes, sir, no, sir, up your West Point bum, sir!"

Rodney's grin failed to mollify his friend. He grabbed the letter, then tried a new tack:

"You can let Isom take over for a while. Lookit all this stuff I got to sort out!"

Gideon surveyed the jumble of articles beside the cot. "Did your girl send you a package?"

"More like the entire contents of the general store. What am I goin' to *do* with all this?" He crouched and began pawing through the shipment. "Extra pair of pants. Extra set of underdrawers—"

"Pretty personal." Gideon smiled in spite of himself.

Rodney spread his fingers and tented the drawers. "Silk! Cost a fortune. Can you imagine what'd happen to me if Jeb found out I not only shoot off my mouth but do it wearin' silk panties?"

Shuddering, he discarded the garment. His face grew forlorn as he fingered through the rest.

"Two pair of boots. Eight pair of stockin's. Four flannel shirts—flannel! In the summertime!"

"Guess she thinks you're cold-blooded."

A foxy grin. "She knows better'n that."

"Then she doesn't want you to catch the grippe."

"Lookin' glass. Six cans of peaches. Cough syrup. Salts for the bowels. Pencils. Paper. Button stick. Sewing kit. New razor and strop—those, I can carry. A Bible. A pocket Shakespeare—she must think I got time to sit around improvin' my mind."

"Maybe the books are supposed to keep you away from wicked companions."

"Could be. For toppers, here's a double wool blanket—*and* a rubber one. I'll need a wagon, not just a horse." He sighed. "She's just tryin' to look after me. 'Course, there's a price for all this generosity—"

"Oh! She wants something in return—"

"Wipe that leer off your face. It isn't what you're thinkin'. Not this time, anyway." He pointed to the letter. "When we finally fight, she wants me to run around afterward an' pick her up some souvenirs."

"Like what?"

"Lord, I don't know. A bayonet. Some Yank's false teeth—anything she can show off, I guess. She's a mighty patriotic girl—even if she's got no notion of how light the cavalry travels." He kicked a good portion of the shipment under the cot. "Want to see her picture? She sent that, too."

"Sure."

"Nancy may not be too quick in the head, but I got to admit she's the prettiest little piece in four counties. Hotter'n a fowling piece after a rabbit hunt, too."

From beneath the cot blanket he drew a small leather presentation case, opened it and showed Gideon a daguerreotype of a plump, pretty young woman with ringlets over her ears.

"Mighty good looking girl," Gideon agreed. He hoped he'd calmed his friend to the point where he could talk sense to him.

"Bet she'll raise a rumpus in bed once we get married." Rodney shut his eyes and let out a grunt of anticipation.

"You haven't—ah—sampled the merchandise yet?"

Gideon's voice had a strangely hoarse quality. The little picture-box in his hand brought Margaret's face to mind. He experienced a sharp feeling of loss, then longing. He hardened himself against it. She wasn't the girl for him and never would be.

Less boisterous all at once, Rodney answered the question in a reflective way:

"Truth is, I haven't. Not that I wouldn't like to, mind. Nancy can put me in a mighty uproar when we fool around. But a gentleman doesn't take advantage of the girl he means to wed. Here, I forgot to show you what else she sent me—"

Gideon was still staring at the daguerreotype.

"Gideon?"

He snapped the case shut and handed it back. Rodney laid it on the blanket, then unfolded the red bunting Gideon had noticed earlier. It turned out to be a Stars and Bars, though of a style he hadn't seen before. On the blue canton, a single large white star was centered in a circle of ten smaller ones.

"Sewed it herself," Rodney declared. "It's the newest design. They call the big one the Virginia star."

He raised the banner by its upper corners. "Measures fifteen by fifteen exactly. Just half the size of a regular cavalry flag. I can carry it under my shirt in battle." With the toe of his boot he nudged the rubber blanket sticking out beneath the cot. "Sure don't know how I can carry the rest."

"I have a notion about how you can get rid of the things you don't want."

"For God's sake tell me."

"Do you play euchre?"

Rodney's face fell. "'Fraid not. I'm not one of those who considers euchre a gentleman's game."

"Do you think you could lower yourself to the level of us common folk for one night?"

"You're makin' sport of me, Gideon."

"I'm sorry. I'm trying to say the solution to your problem is Jack Harris."

"What can that dirty-talkin' horse breeder do for me?"

"Careful. You're speaking of the lieutenant we know, love and elected."

"I didn't elect him. I voted for Hanks."

"Harris is still your answer. Tell him you want to learn euchre."

"I hear he cheats."

"All the better. Join one of his games. For your stake, put up whatever you want to shed—and in three or four hours Jack will have you traveling light again."

"Well—" Rodney looked dubious. "Guess I could be civil to him for that short a time—" An emphatic nod. "All right, I'll give it a go. It's either that or die of the heart failure tryin' to lug this stuff in the field. I might as well go see Jack right now—"

"No, not tonight."

"Why the devil not?"

"We have one more subject to discuss."

Gideon sank down on an empty cot across from his friend's. He rubbed his temples, finally managing to banish thoughts of Margaret:

"It's pretty hard for me to talk to you as a friend one minute and an officer the next. I'm no more experienced as a soldier than you."

"No," Rodney admitted, "you're just more popular at election time. I don't hold that against you."

"Believe me when I say you're only hurting yourself if you refuse to follow orders."

"Gideon, it goes against my grain!"

"But you'll never get that flag into battle—or turn up those souvenirs Miss Nancy wants—unless you change your ways. I imagine your girl's proud of you—"

Rodney pointed to the letter. "That's what she says."

"And you want her to stay proud?"

He thought it over. "Reckon so."

"Then you *don't* want to end up in Company Q. Or be mustered out as unfit. So bend a little!"

"You askin' me? Or tellin'?"

Earnestly, Gideon gazed across the lamp-lit tent. "Asking. As your friend."

Rodney Arbuckle III reflected on that a while, too. Then he shrugged again:

"Well, maybe you're right. Nancy *would* be shamed if I didn't comport myself properly. My mama and papa would be shamed. Even the house niggers would be shamed, I 'magine."

Gideon doubted the last, but said nothing.

"I'll make you a bargain."

Encouraged, Gideon leaned forward.

Rodney picked up the letter. "Nancy gets mighty sentimental in here. I won't read you the exact words. But she says if anything should ever happen to me—you know. A wound—"

The word death crept into Gideon's mind. He sus--
pected it was in Rodney's, too.

"Go on," he said.

"If anything like that did happen, I'd want her to
have the flag and any souvenirs I turn up. She'd also
want to know whether I fought well. Could I ask you to
tell her?"

"Of course."

"She'd appreciate it. So would I."

"You can count on me—*if* anything happens." He
smiled. "Which is unlikely, provided you learn the lessons old Jeb's trying to teach."

"Old!" Rodney snorted. "He's not five years older'n
me, I'll wager."

"But he's experienced." Gideon rose and put an arm
across his friend's shoulder. "Trust that experience and
you'll come through just fine. We all will. It's just like
Stuart says—we have to out-fight the Yanks because we
don't outnumber them. We can't do it unless we pull
together."

A truculent expression crossed Rodney's face. "I
hope nobody's got the idea I'm *scared* to fight."

"No. But you'll never get the opportunity if you keep
disobeying orders. Let's consider the bargain sealed. In
the unlikely event you get your big toe shot off or a
Minié ball in your backside, I'll get the flag and the
souvenirs to Miss Wonderly. I will, that is, provided you
put on your uniform and go stand watch."

Rodney stared at the eleven-star flag draped over his
palms. Let out one more long sigh.

"Fair enough."

He laid the flag on the cot, then pulled on his sweat-
stained coat. Before he buttoned it, he folded the flag
and slipped it inside against his belly. As he started out,
Gideon said:

"Do me one more favor."

"What?"

"Send Isom home. Tomorrow. You'll be a better soldier."

"Really think so?"

"I do."

"All right." He bent to leave, then hesitated again. "Y'know, Gideon, I shouldn't tell you this. But I think you're gonna make a damn fine officer. I'd hate your damn guts if we weren't friends."

He waved, smiled and left.

Gideon relaxed and allowed himself a weary smile. He'd won a small victory. Out of such small victories might emerge a cavalry regiment worthy of the name.

He noticed the presentation box again. He looked at it for nearly half a minute. Then he went out into the darkness, no longer smiling.

iii

Just after dawn the next day, Gideon was yawning over a bitter cup of coffee at the cook fire in front of his tent. He glanced up to see Isom standing a couple of feet away. The graying Negro carried a maple branch with a bandana-wrapped bundle tied to one end.

"Good morning, Isom."

"Morning, sir. Master Rodney—he sending me home today."

Gideon nestled his tin cup at the edge of the coals so the contents would stay warm. He stood up; stretched. The morning air was fragrant and full of sound: men complaining as they turned out of their tents; the whicker of a horse; the tang of woodsmoke and droppings.

"I know. I suggested it. You'll be safer there."

The black nodded sadly. "I 'spose."

"Did Rodney write you a pass so you won't be stopped and locked up as a runaway?"

Isom patted the bundle. "Got it right here. I reckon I'll walk on down to Piedmont an' catch the Gap Railroad. I wanted to ask you somethin' first, though."

"Anything, Isom."

The older man's eyes locked with his. "I know you his bes' friend. He thinks a mighty lot of you—even though you wearin' that officer's sash now. I want you to look after him, please, sir. I love that boy. Been with him since the hour his mama birthed him."

"I'll do everything I can, Isom."

"Thank you, sir. That's welcome news." The black man shook his head. "Wish this whole scrape was over. I feel plumb sorry for them Yanks."

Gideon misunderstood: "I don't blame you. We're going to lick 'em hands down."

"Hope so. I'm gettin' too old to be turned out in the world with no family to look after—and none to look after me. I sure wish everybody'd quit fightin' over us niggers."

"Isom, that's not the issue. It's our right to independence, to—"

Again Isom shook his head. Gideon frowned:

"What is the issue in your opinion?"

"I don't mean to show no disrespect, Lieutenant. But this war *is* about the niggers and what to do with 'em. I can read, sir. The Arbuckles, they good people. They never had that fool notion that a nigger who can read is a dangerous nigger—" Gideon caught a touch of resentment in the words.

"So I know folks up north—old Linkum—they gonna set us all free if they win. Then it's gonna be worse."

"Why do you say that?"

"'Cause I don't think those Yanks know what they're doin'. Sure, things are bad for some of my people who got masters that ain't decent like the Arbuckles. But it won't improve things none if all the niggers are turned loose overnight—free an' equal like it say in that Declaration old President Jefferson wrote. Deep down, I don't b'lieve most of the Yanks really want us free. They just want to punish the South. The Yanks won't know what to do with us if we *are* free—I don't think they'll even want us around. It's a bad war, sir, a bad war. It's goin' places nobody ever dreamed."

Gideon said nothing. The Negro shrugged in a self-conscious way:

"Guess I'm talkin' out of turn. Didn't mean to. Mostly I just wanted to ask you to look out for Master Rodney."

"I will, I promise. I wish you a safe journey, Isom."

"Yes, sir. Thank you. An' you take care of yourself, too."

He turned and walked away with a slow, tired step. Gideon stared after him until he was lost in the blue smoke and the confusion of men stumbling out of their tents.

Isom could be right. Those windy, hate-filled abolitionists would never welcome poor black people into their elegant parlors if the South lost—

Hell, what a ridiculous speculation! They weren't going to lose. They were going to win.

With men like Stuart leading, they couldn't fail.

iv

The hot weather intensified, and with it, the training. But not in camp. The First Virginia spent more and more time on patrol, ranging north toward the Potomac. Gideon kept learning.

He learned how to sleep in the saddle while jogging over some unfamiliar back road. Sleep was an irritant to Jeb Stuart. He needed next to none himself and failed to understand why other men did.

Gideon learned how to prepare a quick meal at a woodland campfire. How to grab his ration of flour; wet it in a handy stream or with water from his canteen; season it if there happened to be a paper twist of salt in his sabretache; fry the putty-like mass in bacon fat and wolf it as bread before jumping into the saddle again.

He learned how to endure.

They rode in fair weather, out before dawn and continuing until long after moonrise. They rode in thunderstorms and the humid aftermath, gradually perfecting their ability to travel in a column of fours—the best way to move masses of mounted men rapidly along a road.

No matter how long the hours or unpleasant the weather, Stuart and his staff always seemed jaunty. Perhaps it was because the commander usually sang in the saddle. Depending on the position of I Company, Gideon could sometimes catch the sound of Stuart's fine, resounding voice tossing "Alabama Gals" to the summer wind. Or, Sundays, "Rock of Ages." Stuart permitted no secular songs on the Sabbath.

Gradually, too, Gideon gained an understanding of why Stuart drove himself and his men so hard. He believed in the cause, of course. But he was goaded by something more personal: a desire to match the reputation of his father-in-law, Colonel Philip St. George Cooke.

Cooke had been commandant of the Second U.S. Dragoons when Stuart had courted and married his daughter Flora out at Fort Leavenworth. But Cooke had remained with the Union—and fancied himself an expert in the relatively new area of cavalry tactics.

"You see, gentlemen," Stuart explained one drizzly night in late June when H, I and J Companies halted briefly during a cross-country ride, "until about seven years ago there was no such animal as a cavalryman.

"In the Federal service we had the dragoons—big,

beefy fellows packing muskets and sabers for fighting on horseback or on foot. We had the mounted rifles—which is where I got my start, in Texas, after coming out of the Point. Mounted riflemen are nothing more than infantry on horseback. The animals are mere transportation to get the men to and from the battlefield.

"It was President Davis who figured out that maybe there should be a new type of horse soldier. A man who could fight on horseback most of the time. That's why Davis organized the First and Second Cavalry when he was Secretary of War for President Pierce. His idea was radical but sound. In seven years it's become clear that cavalry can fulfill one function better than any other branch of service. Moving fast, cavalrymen are the eyes of an army."

He grinned at the soaked men gathered around him. "There's something I like even better. When reinforcements are needed, the cavalry can get to a fire fight faster than anybody else. Well—" He tugged out a pocket watch. "We've spent twenty minutes resting and palavering. That's ten too many. But I wanted to present a little explanation of our purpose for the benefit of you gentlemen—" His glance singled out several troopers, including Rodney. "Especially you gentlemen who insist on explanations along with your orders. All right—stand to horse! Let's see whether any Yank pickets have stuck their noses over the river."

Gideon had never imagined his body could withstand so much physical punishment. He discovered he had almost limitless strength when it was demanded—and Stuart demanded it often, from all the men who rode with him across the upper Shenandoah, hunting for signs of an enemy invasion.

The First Virginia rode with a growing certainty that their state would be the chief theater of war. True, fighting had erupted way out in Missouri, which the

Confederacy had hoped to claim. To counteract the maneuvering of a secession-minded governor, Congressman Blair—a younger member of the powerful Maryland clan—had helped an Army captain named Lyon organize the Missouri Home Guards and secure the city of St. Louis. Promoted to brigadier, Lyon had then defeated an enemy force at a place called Boonville—all but guaranteeing Missouri's presence in the Union.

There were equally ominous developments closer at hand—in Virginia's western counties, where the farmers and mountain folk had never taken to slavery. Troops from both sides were moving into the area, and there was a plan afoot to set up a new government at Wheeling. The damned traitors in that part of the state were actually talking of seceding from the South! Talking of establishing a separate state, possibly called Kanawha. Naturally the devious Mr. Lincoln didn't object. The new state would be on his side.

The First Virginia often covered thirty-five or forty miles a day. Side roads; forest trails; open fields. Despite the grueling pace, the men thrived. Their legs strengthened. Their butts hardened. Their pride grew right along with their muscles.

Gideon accustomed himself to getting by with very little sleep. Even when he did catch a few winks, he heard commands in his dreams—

Prepare to mount.

Mount!

DRAW SABERS!

And he was pleased to see that although Rodney still huffed and complained about the discipline, he'd finally surrendered to it, and was earning marks as a good trooper. Even Captain Macomb had survived the threat of removal.

On Sunday, the thirtieth of June, they were back at the Bunker Hill encampment. The next night, after seeing to the sentries, Gideon retired to his tent to open a letter delivered at evening mail call.

His body throbbed. They'd been in the saddle almost four days. He was growing increasingly impatient to test himself under fire. Stuart's spirit was catching.

With a groan, he lay down on his cot. He had the tent to himself. Jack Harris had opted for euchre with the enlisted men. Curiously, his victims seemed to enjoy being beaten. Respect had an almost endless array of sources among Southerners, Gideon had decided. Rodney was still much admired because he'd dared to ride out and ask Beauty Stuart a question.

Wiping perspiration from his forehead, Gideon studied the envelope. The return address—a street in Richmond—was unfamiliar. But the handwriting was clearly his mother's. He ripped the letter open.

> *My dearest son:*
>
> *I trust this finds you well and in good spirits. As you must have judged from the envelope, we have returned to the capital, leaving Jeremiah in Lexington with Grandfather Virgil—who, I might note, is in a state of outrage. Quartermaster officers for the War Department purchased (his word is stole) all of his remaining horses. Further, he was paid an outrageously low price for each. So guard well that fine mount he gave you.*
>
> *You will guess why we are in Richmond. Edward has taken a position as a copyist-clerk in the Treasury Department. He was welcomed for his patriotic spirit—not to mention his willingness to accept a pittance in wages! The Department makes good use of your stepfather's fine, clear handwriting. He transcribes many important documents and memoranda. His office is one floor below that of the President, in what was formerly the Federal Customs House. Everyone is generally in*

support of the President, and admiration is univer-
sal for his lovely and intelligent spouse, Mrs. Var-
ina Howell Davis. Still, we hear occasional grum-
blings. They say Mr. Davis insists on taking all the
principal decisions, civil as well as military, upon
himself; that he considers anyone who dares disa-
gree with him an enemy; and that his condition—
nervous dyspepsia, which I understand he has suf-
fered for some years—continually aggravates ten-
sions within the government.

Yet hope is high. People are confident "Old Bory"
is more than a match for his pedestrian West Point
classmate, McDowell. Despite Mr. Greeley's shrill
incantations, everyone is certain McDowell will
never come "forward to Richmond!"

Our physical circumstances are not the best. Be-
cause of Edward's low wages, we have been forced
to take a small and rather drab flat. But I am re-
solved to sacrifice, just as so many others are
doing, and would not for a moment question Ed-
ward's wish to serve. I will say his clerkship in the
Treasury has made him a positive maniac on the
subject of finance. He talks of nothing but the
South's need for huge sums to carry a potentially long
war to a successful conclusion. He works long hours.
Perhaps fatigue is the explanation for a curious in-
cident which took place just the other day on Main
Street.

After church, we encountered an old acquaintance
from Washington, Mr. Cheever.

Gideon frowned. Where had he heard that name? He
couldn't recall.

But he neither acknowledged Edward, nor was ac-
knowledged by him. When I mentioned it later,
Edward grew quite sharp and refused to discuss it.

*I take his behavior as a sign of the mounting strain
upon those striving to blend conflicting personali-
ties and urgent priorities into a cohesive and well-
run government.*

Cheever, Gideon thought again. *Where—*?

He remembered. He'd heard the name at the National. His father had mentioned someone named
Cheever being in Baltimore; being involved in that imag-
inary murder plot. Edward had admitted knowing
Cheever while denying everything else.

Why the peculiar turnabout in Richmond? The unanswered question left Gideon puzzled and a bit uneasy.

*I must end this, my dear son, and see to preparing
some supper for Edward. It is well after nine in the
evening, but he is not yet home.*

*We are all earnestly praying the Valley—including
Lexington—will not become a battleground——*

A vain hope, Gideon decided. The Federal and Confederate strategies were emerging on parallel courses:
two armies confronting one another in eastern Virginia;
two more in the Shenandoah. It remained in doubt as to
which area would see the first heavy fighting. Camp
speculation said eastern Virginia.

*—and every night I ask the Almighty to give us a
swift victory so that younger boys like your
brother Jeremiah will never need to experience the
perils of military service.*

*Of Matthew we have heard little. He, like you, is
not a frequent correspondent. But that is understandable given your ages and your devotion to
what you are doing. Matthew's last brief letter said
he was attempting to find a berth on some vessel
in our Navy. Whether he will succeed, I cannot*

*say. I know I cannot stop him, regardless of my
reservations or fears.*
*Gideon, we think constantly of your welfare. I
have often wished that I knew the full name and address of your young lady—*

His eyes grew somber.

*—so that I might call on her and make myself
known. But the two letters we have received from
you made no mention of her. Is something amiss?
Must close now. Write to me when you can. I am
glad you are with "Beauty" Stuart, of whom many
admirable things are said. But I implore God to
keep you safe from harm.*
Please write.

*Your loving
Mother*

Slowly, Gideon refolded the sheets, more upset than
comforted by all Fan had written.

There was that odd incident with Cheever. And the
even more unsettling reference to Margaret—

He must set his mother straight about Margaret. Tell
her in his next letter that the relationship was ended. In
fact, he might as well write tonight. He had time.

He began to search under his cot for the pencil and
precious sheets of foolscap he'd borrowed from Rodney.
He'd barely gotten them out when the sounds outside
intensified.

There was always noise in the camp. Men wandering
about restlessly; singing; joking. But now it was interrupted by distant bugles and drum rolls. Then he heard
horses. Perhaps some of Turner Ashby's Rangers.
Ashby, the son of a prominent Valley family, had refused
to serve under Stuart and insisted on a cavalry com-

mand of his own. Gideon knew of only a few First Virginia patrols on the move tonight.

He laid the writing materials aside and started for the tent entrance. Jack Harris burst in, strewing frayed playing cards behind him.

He flung the rest of the deck over his head. The cards came drifting down as Harris grabbed Gideon and hugged him:

"It's happened! *It's happened*!"

"For God's sake, Jack, what are you talking about?"

"Some of our scouts just galloped in. That old fucker Patterson's over the Potomac."

"For sure?"

"Yessir. He started crossing at Williamsport at four this morning."

"How many Yanks?"

"Fifteen, twenty thousand."

"My God."

"We're gonna see some action at last. Cap'n Macomb says the regiment will be movin' out quick. With Jackson and an infantry brigade."

Gideon let out a whoop, seized Jack Harris' waist and then his right hand. He waltzed Harris around the card-littered tent, both of them yelping and barking at the top of their lungs. All thought of Fan's letter was gone from her son's mind.

CHAPTER VI

"The Ball Is Open"

THE JULY THUNDERSTORM blazed and boomed above the woodland. The shimmering lightning dimmed all too soon, leaving Gideon as hopelessly lost as he'd been for the last hour.

He was soaked and bone-weary. His campaign hat did little to keep the rain out of his eyes. He ran a hand along Dancer's neck as the stallion shied from ruts and rain pools in the road that was rapidly becoming a morass.

At the next lightning flash, he reined in. He tried to decide whether it would be wiser to follow the road—it ran westward, he thought—or to leave it.

Neither alternative seemed very attractive. The road might take a turn in the wrong direction. The woods might stretch on for miles, and he could wander the rest of the night without locating the men of I Company he'd been leading on patrol a few miles southwest of Shepherdstown.

Rain poured over Gideon and his horse. Lord, it seemed like a century since that evening a week ago when Jack Harris had brought the news of the invasion. The very next day, near the little hamlet of Falling Waters, up river from Harper's Ferry, he'd gotten his initial taste of battle—

Stuart's cavalry had been out with Old Jack. The colonel had three hundred and eighty infantrymen and a single battery. Jackson took the brunt of an attack by

musket-armed men in blue. From the cavalry's position
on Jackson's flank, Gideon heard a sound foreign to
him before—cannon fired in combat.

Old Jack's artilleryman was a former preacher named
Pendleton. He'd christened his four pieces Matthew,
Mark, Luke and John. One of those iron apostles
helped hold a road open while Jackson's men retreated
in front of blue-clad hordes who fired, reloaded, kept
firing, kept coming on—

Stuart fretted on the flank with his troopers, waiting
to be put to use. Gideon would never forget the scene—
especially the moment when he saw a Union soldier fall
in the sunlight on the road, hit by a shot from the retreating Confederates. He'd never seen a man die in
battle before.

A bit later he'd heard another new sound—the
screaming of the wounded.

All the while, the apostolic cannon kept *crumphing*.
Smoke billowed across the countryside, obscuring the
Yank companies on the road. Finally Stuart's patience
gave out. He ordered his troopers into action with a
shout—"Fours ahead! *Gallop!*" It was a principle with
Stuart that cavalry always galloped at the enemy, but
trotted away; a gallop was a gait unbecoming to a
mounted man unless he was going toward his foe.

The troopers swept down on the Yanks. Inevitably,
the terrain forced a breakup of the precise formations.
Captain Macomb led I Company into a stand of maples
where he'd spotted a few moving patches of blue he assumed to be infantrymen. The company galloped into
the grove with sabers drawn and side arms ready.

In the dapple of sun and shadow, the leading riders
came on the enemy. A dozen Yanks. Not on foot.
Mounted.

The Northern cavalrymen let go with their muskets.
Gideon ducked, catching another sound completely new

to him: the odd, terrifying whine of a Minié ball passing close by.

Horse to horse and saber to saber, he clashed with a young officer in blue. He was so hard by the Yank, he could see the pupils of the officer's gray eyes, and a yellow down on his chin. The officer was even younger than Gideon.

A lucky saber stroke slashed the officer's wrist. He cried out; fell from his horse. Jack Harris rode up and finished him with a pistol ball. Gideon would never forget the astonished look on the officer's face—or the abrupt blankness in his gray eyes as the ragged black hole in his throat spouted blood.

The clash in the grove lasted no more than three minutes. The outnumbered Yanks scattered, leaving four dead in the shifting shadows of the maples. Captain Macomb lay dead, too, killed by a saber through the belly.

Harris assumed command and reassembled the company. He refused to let anyone stop for Macomb's body. Riding out of the grove, Gideon was more stunned than elated. It had all happened so quickly. Including the dying.

For the rest of the day, the cavalry screened the retreat of Jackson's brigade. By sundown, Gideon had taken part in several more charges, and gone through an almost unconscious transition. The sudden roar of cannon no longer startled him. He was proud of the way he'd adapted to the racket and disorder of battle.

But he couldn't get the memory of that first young officer's glazing gray eyes out of his mind.

Scattered companies of the cavalry fell back in the darkness past the outpost camp Jackson had abandoned to the Federals. Gradually, the regiment reassembled. Stuart was jubilant. He led the men in chorus after cho-

rus of "The Bonnie Blue Flag," accompanied by the
First Virginia's fifers and drummers.

At first Gideon sang with less than full enthusiasm.
Soon, though, he was bellowing. Singing had a tonic effect. It helped erase the memory of the gray-eyed Yank.

The regiment had fared well. There were no losses
except for Macomb. That same night, Harris was brev-
etted to captain and Gideon to first lieutenant. The vacant post of second lieutenant was filled by a quick
election. A sergeant named Sunderlind was elevated to
the rank.

Sunderlind was a foolishly cheerful young man Gideon considered brainless. After the election, he and
Harris met privately and agreed to ignore the feather-
headed farm boy as much as possible.

Falling Waters was scarcely a victory—or even worthy of being called a battle. But the high command was
impressed with the mettle of the officers during the engagement. Johnston recommended Old Jack for promotion to brigadier and Stuart to full colonel.

Gideon learned later that the day had been a personal triumph for the commander of the First Virginia.
Riding alone, he'd encountered a Union company in a
field. The Yanks mistook the man in the blue greatcoat
for one of their own.

Stuart immediately demanded that the company surrender. He told an effective lie: they were covered by
snipers in some nearby trees and would all be massa-
cred if they refused to throw down their arms. Forty-
nine shamed men of the 15th Pennsylvania Volunteers
were now prisoners thanks to Stuart's audacity.

Other stories emerged from the day's fighting. Men
in one of the newer companies described how Stuart
had led them within range of an enemy artillery piece.
He halted the green riders until the cannon fired. The
round shot roared over the heads of the petrified troop-

ers. One of them told Gideon exactly what the commander had said:

"There. I wanted you to learn what a cannon's like. I wanted you to hear it. They fired high. They always do. There's no harm in them."

In the days immediately after the Falling Waters fight, the regiment probed toward the Potomac—and Patterson's camp at Martinsburg. Small units patrolled every road by which the Yankees might advance. Occasionally the Confederate troopers saw blue-coated infantry scouts or horsemen. Occasionally fire was exchanged, but with little effect. Gideon lived in the saddle as the cavalry ranged across a fifty-mile front from Leesburg to Shepherdstown, watching. Riders raced back to Winchester at the slightest sign of a Union movement—

Tonight, just as darkness fell, half of I Company under Gideon's command had encountered an equal number of Federal riders. There was another running skirmish; another inconclusive exchange of fire as the thunderstorm broke. The rain hampered vision. Gideon saw one of his corporals nicked in the arm, but he failed to see a low-hanging branch. It slammed his forehead, flung him out of the saddle and left him floundering.

The rest of his men thundered away in the rain, not even aware of his accident. Despite his dazed condition, he had the presence of mind to whistle three times. Dancer had been trained to recognize the signal. The stallion came trotting back.

Dizzy and sick at his stomach, Gideon struggled to his knees. He caught the reins and wrapped them around his right hand. Then he passed out.

He woke a short time later. His teeth were chattering. The rain beat on his face. He smelled Dancer in the dark. The reins were still wrapped around his fingers.

But he'd lost his command. So here he was an hour later, halted in another wood.

Thunder rumbled down the sky. Wind lashed the leaves. He'd just about decided to cut left, away from the road, when he saw a glimmer of light ahead and to the right.

The light was no more than a quarter of a mile away. A cabin? Cabins were usually located near croplands. Maybe he was closer to the edge of the wood than he imagined.

Wouldn't hurt to stop, he thought. *Dry off. Ask directions.*

"Come on, boy." He nudged Dancer. Reluctantly the stallion started along the treacherous track.

During a lull in the thunder, Gideon caught another sound. Horses.

And more than one.

They were up by the cabin, whickering in the downpour.

He wiped water from his eyes. He teeth started to chatter again. He shifted his weight a little to free the saber on his left hip, then ran his right hand down over the laces of the oilskin sheath hanging from the saddle. The sheath kept the 30-gauge Paterson shotgun dry and ready to fire.

The horses could belong to the cabin's owners. Or even to a couple of his own men. But he advanced cautiously in case he was wrong on both counts.

Dancer's hoofs splashed in puddles of water. Gideon reined him to the left; the shoulder. Muddy, but less noisy. He rode another few yards, then stopped again, listening and watching.

A fresh gust of wind set nearby tree branches clattering. He clenched his teeth to stop their clicking. The anticipated lightning flash finally lit the heavens, showing him what he wanted to see.

The building ahead wasn't a log cabin but a somewhat more substantial plank cottage. Two big horses were tied to a low-hanging branch of a tree growing between the cottage and the road.

Darkness again. Thunder boomed. He waited for more lightning. When it came, he was ready. He concentrated on the saddles of the tethered animals.

He recognized the design instantly. Also the wood stirrups with leather hoods. The saddles were McClellans—of which there were precious few in his regiment, just as there were precious few black horses, even though the Northern press continually referred to Virginia's ferocious "black horse cavalry."

After an inspection trip of European military establishments some years ago, the Union officer now taking charge in western Virginia had recommended that particular type of saddle for the Federal army. His name had been linked to it. Gideon reckoned the odds were about ninety to ten against the owners of the horses being friendly.

He pondered. Capturing a couple of Yanks was a tempting proposition—

No, the attempt would be foolish. There were only two of them; the prize wasn't worth the risk. He'd be wiser to pass by and hunt for his own men.

He was about to turn Dancer ninety degrees to the left, into the trees, when a woman screamed inside the cottage.

ii

The piercing scream canceled any idea of leaving. He dismounted. Rubbed Dancer's muzzle to quiet him. Looped the reins and tied them loosely around a low-hanging limb.

He unlaced the oilskin sheath. Slid out the revolving-cylinder shotgun. Shielding the mechanism under his left arm, he stole onto the road.

The woman shrieked again. Gideon thought he heard a man laugh. He quickened his step. Complete silence was impossible because of the mud and the puddles. But he was reasonably sure the hiss of the rain would cover the sound of his approach.

He couldn't see what was happening in the cottage. Burlap curtains hung inside the oil-paper windows. The tied horses stamped as he crept across the yard, doubled over to protect his weapon from the slash of the storm.

He heard the woman moan; then sounds of struggle. He pressed himself against the warped planks just to the side of the door. Inside, a man growled:

"Lie still, goddamn you. Else Frank's liable to open your skull with that there hogleg."

The man laughed again. He was breathing hard:

"I said *lay still*! This yere's secesh country, and you're a secesh gal, so you might as well give up an' swallow your medicine."

A second voice, somewhat higher: "Watch her hand, Silas!"

Perhaps the woman struck or scratched. Silas yelled, "Goddamn bitch!" A heavy blow landed. The woman cried out.

There were more grunts of effort. More profanity. A sound of cloth ripping—

"There. Now we got your ass bare, you're gonna take some punishment."

"Christ, Silas," the other man protested. "That ain't no way to take a woman."

"She ain't a woman, she's a fuckin' rebel whore. She damn near tore my eye out to boot! You want her the reg'lar way, you can have her when I'm done. I'm gonna hurt you, woman. I'm gonna make you mighty sorry you clawed me like you did—"

Another powerful grunt; another scream. Gideon stepped in front of the door, kicked it open and jumped into the lamplit room.

"*Silas, look out!*" The younger Yank's cap fell off as he spun toward the door, caught with his revolver dangling at his side.

Details of the scene registered in an instant. The men were on Gideon's right, in front of a low, rope-spring bed placed against the wall. The woman lay face down on the bed. Her butternut skirt was hiked above her hips. Torn cotton pantaloons hung around her calves.

The bigger man—bearded; perhaps thirty—had one knee on the bed. His other boot was braced on the floor. The man's trousers and drawers had fallen below his knees. He held his stiffened organ in his right hand.

A plank table stood between Gideon and the soldiers. He booted the near edge as young Frank leveled the revolver. The table skidded into the Yank's thighs, ruining his aim. Gideon ducked a second before the revolver went off.

The ball struck the wall behind him. Before Frank could aim and fire again, Gideon pulled the trigger of his 30-gauge, aiming high so as not to hit the woman. Thunder blended with the boom of the gun.

The shot spread, striking the back of the bearded soldier's head and the wall beyond. Little geysers of blood erupted from the man's hair. He fell forward across the writhing woman, who began to scream hysterically. Blood ran down the soldier's cheek onto her neck.

Frank didn't try a second shot. He raised his hands:

"Don't shoot me, Reb. Jesus, don't! This weren't my idea—"

It was a trick. While Gideon hesitated, the young soldier lunged for the table. Overturned it in Gideon's direction.

Gideon leaped back. But not far enough. The table banged his leg painfully. Frank bolted past and dashed outside.

By the time Gideon reached the door, the young soldier had untied both horses, mounted one and started out of the yard. Gideon knelt, jammed the stock against his shoulder and fired.

His aim was poor. The soldier galloped away, unhurt. The riderless horse followed the first into the dark.

Gideon was shaking with rage. He took a minute to gain control. He staggered to his feet, stepped away from the open door and laid the shotgun on the floor.

The woman sobbed and struggled under the dead man. Gideon walked to the bed, his boots squishing. Vomit rose in his throat at the sight of the Yank's head.

The woman screamed again, unable to free herself from the weight of the corpse. Blood slopped down over her throat, her shoulder—

Gagging, Gideon dug his hands into the Union soldier's armpits; heaved upward. His speech was wheezy:

"I'm with—Colonel Stuart's cavalry, ma'am. I'll get him outside—"

The dead man's head lolled. The woman rolled over, saw the corpse. She covered her mouth and buried her face in the gory blanket. Modesty was forgotten. Her bare buttocks were still in plain sight. Her body was thin; bony. The body of a woman worn by working the land.

Gideon was thankful for the bracing feel of the rain as he hauled the dead man through the yard. He dragged him to the corner of the cottage, then about a half dozen yards into the brush. He let the body fall as lightning burst. He whirled away so as not to see the corpse.

I killed him.

I killed a man.

His hands were shaking.

Back at the cottage door, he braced himself against the frame, staring straight ahead to the dark mud-brick hearth. He didn't want to go in and embarrass the woman, whom he heard stirring on the bed.

"Ma'am?"

Her voice was faint: "What is it?"

"My horse is tied down the road a piece. I'll go fetch him so you'll have time to—to fix up."

"All right." She sounded a little less shaky.

He trudged back to Dancer, wondering why he felt no pride in having killed an enemy soldier—and one bent on rape at that. The image of the man's bloody head lingered in his mind, lapped by a second one— the wide gray eyes of the young officer.

As he led Dancer into the cottage yard, the woman appeared in silhouette in the doorway. She brushed at her straggly hair.

"You'll find a shed 'round to the side. You can put the horse in there if you want. There's some old straw—"

"Thanks."

His teeth started to chatter again. He unsaddled Dancer and pushed him into the shed. The stallion resented the unfamiliar surroundings; kicked hard at the door as Gideon dropped the outside bar into its bracket. Two more sharp kicks and the stallion settled down.

Gideon walked around to the front. He spotted his campaign hat lying in the mud. He hadn't even felt it fall off.

He approached the door but didn't enter. He heard the woman righting the overturned table. He knocked.

"You can come in," the woman said. "I'm fine now."

"Much obliged."

He stepped into the light, easing the door shut. The rain's roar became a quiet rush.

The woman bent to pick up a stool. As she straightened, Gideon noticed she'd wiped the blood from her neck and thrown the blanket and the ragged remains of her pantaloons in a corner. The stains on the shoulder of her blouse were drying.

She set the stool beside the table. Gave another push to the untidy hair hanging over the right side of her face.

She tried to smile. Crossed her arms. Uncrossed them. To ease the tension, Gideon said:

"I got separated from my unit. I was coming along the road when I heard you yell."

"They—" Her shiver left no doubt about who she meant. "—they were lost too. They barged in about ten minutes before you got here. At first they pretended to be courteous." Her mouth wrenched. "I thought all they wanted was food."

Though she was nervous, she still showed admirable composure considering what she'd been through. Her hand jerked toward the stool. "Won't you sit down a moment, Mister—?"

"Kent. Lieutenant Gideon Kent. First Virginia Cavalry."

"Stuart's cavalry, you said. Ours—"

"Yes, ma'am."

He retrieved the shotgun, leaned it against the wall, then sat down on the stool. He felt exhausted; and soiled, somehow. He had no desire to bellow a patriotic song to celebrate the death of the bearded man. He was surprised and a little guilty over his lack of enthusiasm.

"I suppose I should have been better prepared for visitors," the woman said with weary humor. "I've seen Yanks all over the county roads for days."

"I can't imagine they're all as mean as those two."

"I wonder. Oh—my name's Cullen. Mrs. Ida Cullen."

He judged her to be about thirty. Her face had a certain pale prettiness; an echo of prettiness, rather. Hard labor had wasted her figure and carved hollows in her cheeks. Her full mouth and hazel eyes were her most attractive features.

As Mrs. Cullen moved toward a crudely built cabinet beyond the hearth, he said:

"It's a pity your husband wasn't here when the Yanks showed up."

She opened the cabinet. "I've some gooseberry wine left. It's not very good. But it might warm you up."

"Thank you, I'll have some."

Each word was an effort. He was chilled to the bone. He rubbed his cheeks but it didn't help.

Mrs. Cullen set an earthenware jar and a cracked cup in front of him.

He poured half a cup of wine. As she'd predicted, it was thin and sour. But it helped ease his chill.

"Is Mr. Cullen serving with the army?"

She shook her head. She pulled a shawl from a peg, draped it around her shoulders and took some kindling from a box. She scraped a match. It fouled the air with sulphur fumes.

With her back turned, she lit the kindling. "I buried my husband in February. His heart just quit one night when he sat down for supper. He was sixteen years older than I am. He did too much hard work in bad weather. He owned thirty acres of this timber. Cutting and hauling it to Shepherdstown was too big a chore for a man his age."

Gideon set the cup on the table. "You shouldn't be staying here alone. You said it yourself—there are Yank patrols all over the place."

"But I don't have anyplace to go, Lieutenant." She found another cup for herself; poured. "My kin are all dead. My husband was my only—well, you understand."

She drank. The rain drummed on the shake roof. There was a leak above the antique cookstove. A drop of water plopped on the iron every few seconds.

"Then if I might make a suggestion—"

The hazel eyes met his over the rim of her cup.

"Yes?"

"You'd be safer in Winchester or further down the Valley. I could take you with me when I go."

"Behind the lines?"

He nodded, adding silently, *Wherever they are at the moment.* There was no point in telling her that even as they sat talking, an advance from Martinsburg could be in progress, cutting them off.

"I should be on my way soon," he went on. "I need to find my company."

"Not tonight!"

"Yes, I was planning—"

"You're soaked clear through. You ought to rest for a little. Let me hang your jacket up to dry."

"I don't know, Mrs. Cullen. I really should move along—"

"Please," she said, leaning across the table. The hazel eyes pleaded. She didn't want to be left alone in a place that had suddenly become full of poisonous memories.

"Well—I wouldn't mind half an hour's sleep—" He felt like a traitor to Stuart for admitting it.

"Take the bed. I'll curl up by the fire. First get out of your coat."

He was too tired to refuse. He took off the sodden jacket. Mrs. Cullen held it up by the torn choker collar:

"My, your unit must look elegant. This is handsome."

"It was before the fighting started," he grinned.

He helped himself to more wine. Mrs. Cullen's eyes darted to the hard muscles of his chest. Then, pivoting, she drew a chair close to the hearth and draped the jacket over the back.

"It really has started, hasn't it?" she said softly.

"Yes, ma'am. In Colonel Stuart's words—the ball is open."

"People in the neighborhood have seen Colonel Stuart. They say he's a fine-looking man."

"That he is."

"A singer. A dancer—" Her eyes met his for a second. "Fond of the ladies."

"Oh, yes, he's cordial to them. But he has a wife and children."

"Do you?"

"No."

He approached the fire; stood a while absorbing the warmth. Then he went to the bed, so weary it didn't bother him that a man had died there only a short time before.

He dropped his saber and sash on the floor. His teeth were chattering again. Mrs. Cullen brought him a fresh comforter. He bid her good night and turned his face to the wall, asleep a moment after his eyes closed.

iii

"Glorious. *Glorious*!"

He thrashed from side to side, trying to hide from the yellow grin; the wasted face pursuing him, disembodied—

"Glorious, my boy. GLORIOUS!"

He heard screams. Mrs. Cullen's. The Union soldier's. The screaming multiplied:

Two voices.

Ten.

A hundred—

"Lieutenant?"

"Get away from me!" he shrieked, sitting straight up in bed.

Sweat slicked his face. He was trembling violently. "I said get—" He stopped when he saw the woman kneeling on the edge of the bed.

He rubbed his eyesockets with his palms while Mrs. Cullen watched him with a worried expression. She'd put on a cotton gown and wrapped herself in another blanket. Her breath smelled of the wine they'd been drinking.

Wood popped in the fireplace. The rain dripped on the stove. She touched his face.

"Are you all right?"

"Yes."

"You were having a nightmare. Repeating someone's name."

"Whose?"

"Well, not a name, exactly. You kept talking about the sergeant."

It was slipping away so fast, he could barely remember. All of it was dissolving like smoke in the wind—

God, he felt awful.

His teeth rattled. He chafed his arms but couldn't warm them. Mrs. Cullen rushed for the earthenware jar.

She sat down beside him, handing him a cup. Then she slid the blanket from her shoulders and draped it over his. Inadvertently, she pressed against him. He felt her small, hard breast through her nightgown. She drew back quickly.

He drank the wine. It didn't help either. The darkness outside, the forlorn sound of the rain, the killing he'd done—all combined to leave him troubled and full of doubt about his fitness for the war.

"The jug's empty," she said. "I've more put away, though. I'll get it—"

"Don't bother."

"But you're still cold as ice."

"The blanket helps."

It had slipped. He groped for it with his left hand. Simultaneously, she reached out. Their hands touched.

He should have pulled his hand away immediately. He didn't. Without thinking, he closed his fingers around hers.

With a tired sigh—more exhaustion than passion—she leaned against him. Her gray-streaked yellow hair felt soft against his neck.

The cottage was dark except for embers on the

hearth. He shifted away from her just a little. Lifted his right hand toward her chin, his body astonishingly warm all at once—

Suddenly he went rigid, the tips of his fingers an inch from her face.

Some of the pain seemed to drain from her eyes. She tugged his hand until it was touching her skin. She smiled.

"It's all right, Lieutenant. I'm cold too."

iv

He was frightened. He'd never been intimate with a woman before.

But they seemed to communicate without words, she from her loneliness and a need to eradicate the memory of the Union soldiers; he from exhaustion and a feeling of being lost on a dark night that might last till eternity. His first kiss was almost chaste, their lips barely meeting. Her palm rested gently against his cheek.

What a damn fool he was! Having been married, she'd know right off that he'd never had a woman. But his fears didn't stop him. She was patient during his first clumsy tugs at her gown. Then she helped him pull it up over her head. He couldn't help gazing at the small, dark-tipped breasts before they burrowed under the covers together.

They lay facing one another, kissing. He put his arms around her, drawing warmth from her body; the thin, hard legs; the torso so undernourished he could feel her ribs.

But her mouth was pliant and giving, opening against his. If she realized he was inexperienced, she still said nothing.

She drew him to her. Strange new sensations made him forget his anxiety. He lowered himself, feeling the rough brush of hair. An awkward union quickly became a mutual striving for heat; affection; tenderness in a world no longer tender—

When he uttered a long gasp and collapsed on her shoulder, wondrously relieved, she bore his whole weight without complaint. From time to time she stroked the back of his head, or kissed his cheek.

They slept in each other's arms the rest of the night.

v

At first light, she left the bed. He was awakened by the delicious aroma of fatback frying.

She set out a heaping plate—practically the last food she had, she told him. The small sum of money left when her husband died was almost gone.

He ate every morsel, then drank thick, bitter coffee while she packed some clothing and a few personal possessions in a worn valise.

He dressed, collected his saber and shotgun, and went out to saddle Dancer.

It was a beautiful morning. Droplets of moisture glistened on ferns and the pink and blue blossoms of honeysuckle and lupine. The woods steamed after the night's rain. The sun promised intense heat.

She emerged from the cottage just as he mounted. She'd pinned her shawl around her bosom and put on a bonnet. She handed him the valise, smiling:

"There are a lot of things I forgot to ask you, Gideon."

"For instance?" He felt in much better spirits. But he was impatient to be off.

"Where are you from?"

"Lexington, way down the Valley."

"You said you aren't married—"

"No."

"Do you have a young woman you're courting?"

A moment's silence. "I did."

"I don't suppose I'll see you again——"

"Oh, you never can tell. We might run into each other in Winchester."

It was a lie and they both knew it. The ball was open. The patterns of the red dance were shifting too swiftly.

"I hope so," she said. "But if we don't, I want to wish you well. I'll pray you come through the war safely."

A cocky shrug. A little of his old assertiveness had returned; at least outwardly:

"I imagine I will. The war shouldn't last longer than two or three more months. Here——" He extended his hand. "Come on up."

"In a minute. There's one more thing I have to do."

She walked back into the cottage. He heard a loud clang—the stove door opening?—followed by a series of soft thumps. When she emerged into the sunlight, he saw her image upside down in a pool of standing water. He smelled smoke; heard a crackling. A quizzical look in his eyes, he moved his gaze from the water to her face.

"That's right," she said. "I scattered the coals from the stove. It's the only home I have. But I'll be damned if any Yank will ever make himself comfortable in it. Now may I have your hand, please?"

She clambered up behind him, slipping her arms around his waist. He gigged Dancer. The stallion fairly leaped toward the road.

The smell of smoke thickened. He felt her look back once as they took the rutted track through the steaming woods.

His last remark about the war had been a lie, too. He was beginning to doubt whether it would be short after all. If the dead Yank was typical of the roughnecks the

North was sending to do its fighting, the Confederacy could be in for a hard run. Maybe Old Bory's warning about beauty and booty wasn't so far wrong, either.

He felt himself caught in a whirl of change. Not only was the war changing day by day; so was he.

I killed a man.

Loved a woman.

The same night.

And dreamed of Margaret's father, too.

He didn't like the dark tenor of his thoughts. He broke into a chorus of "Lorena" as they jogged along. But the stench of the burning cottage filled the forest. Yes indeed, the ball was surely open.

And even as he sang, he knew he was no longer the same light-hearted dancer who'd waited impatiently in Richmond for the first martial measures.

CHAPTER VII

Ride To Glory

"GIDEON? Bring that goddamn torch over here!"

Gideon slopped through the creek shallows, the rags on the end of the branch trailing smoke and flame. The fire reflected in water nearly as black as the night sky. The creek was about five miles southeast of the ford where they'd crossed the Shenandoah on their way to Manassas this warm Friday, the nineteenth of July.

Bearded and filthy, Jack Harris squatted among the reeds. He watched the water directly in front of him, moving his Bowie knife slowly back and forth.

Gideon came up beside him. "Stand still!" Harris whispered. Seconds later, he stabbed the knife in the water, scattering the reflections.

"Got the son of a bitch!"

Harris yanked the knife out of the creek. A fat bull-frog twitched on the blade. Harris grinned:

"There's our supper. You can douse the torch."

"Can I have it, Lieutenant?" one of the enlisted men called from a few feet away. He started toward them. "Ain't found a thing for myself yet."

Wearily, Gideon handed over the torch and followed Harris up the muddy, tree-lined bank. Harris was whistling and admiring his catch, dead now.

The two officers walked past Second Lieutenant Sunderlind. Knife in hand, he was splashing in the water, hoping to spot a fish below the surface. "Asshole

495

doesn't know enough to be quiet," Harris whispered. Sunderlind gave them a sullen glance as they passed; he'd learned they didn't care for his company.

Gideon and Harris reached the small open place in the brush where they'd piled up dry sticks. Soon they had a fire going. Similar fires burned along the shore for half a mile in either direction. Gideon hunkered down beside I Company's captain, who began to roast the dripping frog on the point of his Bowie.

For a second Gideon thought he saw two frogs. He covered a long yawn; shook his head. He'd been in the saddle almost continuously since the first of the week, pausing only long enough for a short nap, or to forage for berries to supplement a scrap of moldy bread from his sabretache, or to relieve himself, or slop his filthy jacket in a stream and put it back on immediately so it would dry as he rode.

On Monday the Union general the boys had nicknamed Granny Patterson had sent men out from Martinsburg toward Bunker Hill. Gideon encountered some of them in another twilight fight that ranged cross-country through hazy meadows and dim groves. At one point Dancer stepped into an animal burrow and took a spill. Gideon lost his shotgun when he was unhorsed.

Dancer scrambled up, miraculously unhurt. Gideon had no time to search the weeds for the 30-gauge. Four blue-clad horsemen were coming up fast behind him. He jumped into the saddle and rode like hell to escape.

Later that night, his luck reversed itself. He and his patrol came across three Yank bodies. He screwed up his nerve, crouched over the stiffened corpses and walked away with a pair of .44-caliber old model army Colt revolvers, plus ample ammunition.

Toward the end of the following day, Tuesday, the telegraph to Winchester reported General McDowell was at last on the move from the Potomac. Gideon heard varying estimates of the size of the Union force.

One man at staff headquarters said McDowell was coming on with thirty-five thousand effectives—about fifteen thousand more than Old Bory's Manassas army.

It wasn't hard for the First Virginia to guess what was coming. Beauregard would need reinforcements from the Valley. The problem was to keep Granny Patterson from discovering relief troops were on the move. The assignment fell to Stuart's regiment.

The First Virginia saddled and rode toward Patterson's lines. The cavalrymen had no great fear of Granny. He'd already shown himself to be indecisive. He lived up to his reputation that same Tuesday, withdrawing most of his troops to Charleston. For two days and nights, the riders of the First Virginia kept Granny's pickets well occupied. They hallooed back and forth across the countryside, shooting at enemy outposts and generally making a noisy advertisement of their presence.

Behind the screen of this activity, Joe Johnston started nine thousand men from Winchester on Thursday, the eighteenth. Only a rear guard of two thousand and a few men on the sick list were left in place in case Granny suddenly recovered from his case of the indecisives.

On Friday, the First Virginia was back in Winchester to receive new orders. They were to ride to Manassas along with Pendleton's five batteries of artillery. A small contingent of the regiment would remain behind to confuse Patterson as long as possible.

Gideon had no idea how much ground I Company had covered in the past five days. But it was enough to make him feel about a thousand years old as Jack Harris surveyed the spitted frog and declared:

"Little fucker's done. I'll chop him up and we can dig in."

Gideon ripped into a plump leg with lip-smacking gusto. The meat was incredibly delicious; best he'd ever tasted. But he wouldn't have cared if he'd been chewing spoiled beef. Anything to fill his aching belly!

Harris picked bits of bone from his tongue and wiped his hand on his trousers. Beyond the line of fires, the picketed horses cropped what field grass they could find. They had no oats, just as the men had no rations. The regiment's cumbersome commissary wagons had been outdistanced hours ago, together with Pendleton's twenty cannon.

Gideon finished eating and spat out a piece of gristly fiber. He walked down to the creek, knelt and lapped up the muddy water as if it were cold beer. Then he filled his canteen, which was wood, and crudely made. Linen straps were attached to it by iron staples. But the plug fit tightly, and the wood was durable. Sutlers in Winchester sold fragile canteens of glass or clay sheathed in leather or rattan. Gullible newcomers brought them for exorbitant prices and regreted it later.

For Gideon the canteens symbolized the army's makeshift nature. No two men carried the same equipment. No two companies wore identical uniforms. Of course Stuart still said *esprit* counted more than fancy trappings. Sometimes, though, Gideon had his doubts.

He jammed the plug tight, splashed water over his head and stood up to let the breeze dry his stubbled face. Crickets chirped in the brush. The men gathered by the dim fires talked quietly. Everyone realized the regiment was headed for a major engagement. Larger, even, than the recent battles that had led to Confederate defeats in the mountainous western counties.

Gideon knew the forthcoming engagement would be crucial. He recalled a page from that scurrilous *Tribune* which he'd read in Winchester. The paper screamed the same message it had screamed for weeks:

> *Forward to Richmond! Forward to Rich-*
> *mond! The Rebel Congress must not be allowed*

*to meet there on the 20th of July! BY THAT
DATE THE PLACE MUST BE HELD BY
THE NATIONAL ARMY!*

He wasn't sure the Federals would arrive in Richmond on time. But soon after—who could tell?

He trudged back toward Harris, who was urinating to
extinguish the fire. Gideon was angry at himself for his
pessimism. But he couldn't help it. Sometimes the army
did strike him as a collection of amateurs.

He worried because his mother was in Richmond.
And Margaret. He'd thought of Margaret often in the
past few days—just as he thought of the dead men he'd
seen. Once in a while, doubt devilled his mind:

*Maybe she's right. Maybe all this isn't as grand as we
pretend.*

Necessary. But not grand.

A brass bugle played a familiar call in the humid
dark. Other bugles repeated the call along the creek.
Boots kicked at embers. Clouds of ash drifted up. The
troopers walked wearily to claim thier mounts.

Jack Harris buttoned his trousers. "Jesus, that's
mighty white of old Jeb. A whole twenty minutes for
supper."

"More time than we're likely to get at Manassas,"
Gideon said, unsmiling. The very name of the place had
taken on an ominous sound.

He felt neither boisterous nor brave this evening; just
tired and tense. He fought back another yawn as he
went to find Dancer beneath the heat-blurred stars.

ii

They rode on toward Paris in the summer dark.
Really humid weather was on the way. Gideon could
tell from the rank smell of the air.

As the night wore on, they encountered an increasing number of obstacles. Trains of white-topped supply wagons. Infantry companies plodding in the road or resting on the shoulders. Finally Stuart had to lead his regiment into the fields.

"Damn foot-draggers," one of Gideon's privates complained as they trotted through rustling stubble. Suddenly, up ahead, they heard frantic cries:

"Jump—*jump!* They're sleepin' all over the place!"

The cavalry column broke apart in total disorder. Troopers galloped, hunching low and kicking their mounts into long leaps over terrified infantrymen waking in the weeds.

Gideon saw a white face and frantic arms wigwagging directly ahead. "Get out of the way, you lazy bastard!" he screamed as he reined Dancer to the left, just missing the roused sleeper. The stallion galloped at two more men still floundering on the ground. Gideon booted him into a jump—

The horse barely cleared the cowering men. Dancer landed with a ferocious jolt.

Each four-man rank was supposed to be separated from the ranks ahead and behind by at least a yard. As a result, the entire regiment strung out over a good distance even in normal formation. Because of the sleepers in the field, it took almost an hour to restore order and tighten up the formations again. The confusion and all the near-accidents only worsened the mood of the troopers.

They reached the little railhead at Piedmont while it was still dark. Lanterns burned on flatcars along a siding. Gideon had pulled a bandana over his nose. The cavalry raised a hellish dust; the lanterns on the rolling stock shed a pale, diffused light through the billows. Faces peering from the cars might have belonged to ghosts.

"Who are you, boys?" someone called from one of the cars. "Turner Ashby's Rangers?"

A man in I Company screamed back, "Want me to climb up there and brain you? This yere's the First Virginia!"

A couple of shrill yells erupted from the troopers. Harris pulled away from the head of the company:

"Shut up and keep moving! Let the fuckin' babies have their rest."

"Ain't our fault we're stuck here!" someone else protested from one of the flatcars. "Goddamn railroad engineers refuse to work at night." Gideon frankly wouldn't have minded changing places with the foot soldiers.

He passed some boxcars with men hanging from the open doors. He couldn't identify the unit to which the soldiers belonged. They wore blue—as did most of the Yanks, but not all. Some of the enemy wore gray instead. The confusing color schemes reminded him that the Stars and Bars being carried far ahead with the regimental colors looked much like the Federal flag when there was no wind to spread the banner and reveal three bars instead of thirteen.

I Company clattered on through the dust, leaving the cars, the pale lanterns and spectral faces behind. God, Gideon thought wearily, I wonder if any man in this army, excepting a few like Colonel Stuart, understands what war is really like.

Images of Margaret's father troubled his mind. The Sergeant had insisted war was glorious. But Gideon was beginning to accumulate evidence to the contrary. His crotch itched from sweat and dirt. His armpits crawled with some kind of bugs he'd picked up. His tailbone was a mass of pain. His eyes were gritty from dust. He wondered whether they were riding to glory or something far less romantic.

Colonel Stuart can flay me for thinking it, but it strikes me the Sergeant wasn't only drunk, he was crazy.

iii

Saturday's dawn brought no letup in the heat. They followed the railroad line through the gap in the Bull Run mountains. Occasionally they passed a chugging engine pulling a load of flatcars packed with soldiers.

By midday they were out of the mountains and down into rolling wooded hills. Here and there an isolated farmhouse stood against the skyline. To judge from the number of hours they'd been in the saddle, they couldn't be far from their destination.

A courier approached galloping the opposite way. He paused long enough at the head of the column to pass along some news Gideon and the rest of I Company received long after the rider vanished down the railroad line.

Though outnumbered, General Beauregard was already forming battle lines near Bull Run, a meandering stream that ran beneath an arched stone bridge spanning a major highway—the Warrenton Turnpike. A short distance northeast of the bridge lay the village of Centreville, only twenty miles from Washington City. But it had taken McDowell's army two and a half days to cover those twenty miles. There was plenty of joking about that:

"Those Yanks don't move any faster, we'll never meet up with 'em."

"Fella up ahead says they was all the time fallin' out to pick blackberries at the roadside—and never mind how their officers yelled at 'em to get back in line."

Mopping at the grime and sweat on his face, Jack Harris dropped back beside Gideon, who had pulled out of the column to speed the lagging rear ranks—which included Rodney Arbuckle. Occasionally Rodney still had trouble staying in formation. Again he offered the familiar excuse—daydreams about Miss Nancy Wonderly of White House. Unsmiling, Gideon told him to take his place.

For a while Gideon and Harris rode in the choking dust behind their men. Harris looked like a worn-out ghoul. Bad as I must look, Gideon thought.

The captain took a swig from his canteen, then chuckled:

"I just heard the goddamnedest thing, Gideon. Positively can't believe it."

"What'd you hear?"

"That some of the Yanks have already turned around and started back to Washington."

"You're making that up."

Harris raised his right hand. "Swear to God I'm not! C Company got it from the courier when he stopped to fill his canteen. The ninety-day Yanks are keepin' right good track of their enlistment time, it appears. The minute it's up—I mean the *minute*—home they go."

Gideon laughed for the first time in days. "Well, that's a few less to fight. Come on, Jack. Let's get up ahead where we belong."

"Wait. You ain't heard the best. On Thursday, old McDowell sent some of his lads pokin' up that river or whatever it is—"

"Bull Run?"

"Yep. The blue-bellies got their tails kicked by some of General Longstreet's Virginians. They ran like scairt rabbits."

"That's a good start," Gideon agreed. "But what the devil's McDowell been doing since Thursday?"

Harris shrugged. "Fuckin' around, I guess. Reconnaissance—who the hell knows?"

Gideon heard the bell of a locomotive chuffing up

the track behind them. "I bet McDowell wouldn't be wasting time if he knew we had boys coming in on the cars every hour."

"Bet he wouldn't." The two riders swung out around the ranks and trotted forward. " 'Pears this is one time when things a feller don't know *can* hurt him. Bad."

iv

By Saturday night the grueling thirty-six hour ride was nearly over.

The sun was a hazy red disk behind huge dust clouds rolling across fields and groves and hillsides. As the regiment veered away from the rail line, Gideon counted forty-seven cars pulled up, the foremost ones empty, the rear ones still spilling men in gray and blue.

The First Virginia encountered General Johnston at the campsite of an infantry regiment. Gideon spied Colonel Stuart, filthy but cheery as ever, chatting with the little gamecock outside a cluster of headquarters tents. Outranking Beauregard, Johnston had assumed supreme command for the engagement—although it was Beauregard, obviously, who had drawn the plans and deployed the men already in place.

Johnston returned the salutes of the mounted officers. The troopers sat straighter and kept their formations more orderly as they passed by. Harris told Gideon the high command's headquarters were located at a nearby farmhouse called Portici.

Shortly after they left the infantry area, they were plunged into a confusion of food and ammunition wagons. The foul-mouthed teamsters cursed the heat and their balky mules.

Gideon started when a distant cannon boomed. As they labored on to their assigned bivouac area, the noise came again—but not frequently. Only a few isolated batteries were firing. Still, given the confusion of the rear lines, the dust and the promise of worse heat next day, Gideon found the cannon fire profoundly unsettling.

At last they reached the bivouac—a field of broom sedge a little south of the center of the eight-mile-long Confederate line. The field lay between Bull Run and the Sudley-Manassas road. The road ran roughly southeast to northwest, intersecting the Warrenton Turnpike north of their position. The troopers saw to their horses, drew rations and then collapsed to rest.

For the last few hours Gideon's body had been almost totally numb. Stopping didn't relieve the feeling. He limped as he walked, his clothing soggy from foulsmelling sweat.

Finally he settled himself in the sedge, his head on his saddle. He shut his eyes and groaned in sheer relief—only to rouse a moment later at the sound of someone calling his name. Disgusted, he struggled to open his eyes.

He'd slept a little without realizing it. The sedge field was darker.

The new arrival was Harris. He flung his saddle down beside Gideon's.

"Well, I guess it's gonna be tomorrow for sure."

"You woke me up to tell me that?" Gideon covered his mouth to hide a jaw-cracking yawn.

"Thought you'd like to know," Harris replied in a laconic way. "I was talkin' to one of the boys on Jeb's staff. That high-assed Major Duncan, he says there's all kinds of folks comin' out from Washington in the morning."

Gideon lowered his hand from his mouth. Tiny drops of chill sweat moistened the dust on his palm. "You mean more soldiers?"

"Shit, no. *Folks!* Congressmen an' their wives. Ladies and their gentlemen friends. Reporters—"

Gideon thought briefly of his father as Harris went on, "Guess the civilians are rentin' every damn carriage they can find. Even bringin' picnic hampers so they can eat while they watch the fun. 'Course, I doubt they'll get too close to the lines—"

Gideon's head felt like a huge stone. He could barely move it from side to side to express his doubt:

"Sightseers—Yanks who pick blackberries and go home when they take a notion—Jack, this whole war's unbelievable."

"Maybe so, but Major Duncan got the part about the sightseers straight from Bory's staff."

"Bory still receiving information from the Wild Rose, is he?"

"He must be."

"Right now I'd be happy if Jeb sent us in to fight some girls with picnic baskets. I'm too damn worn out to tackle infantry."

"For fuckin' sure," Harris groaned as he sprawled out.

"Unless you've got some other startling news, Captain, request permission to go to sleep."

"Permission granted." Harris put his head on his saddle, curled on his side and was soon snoring.

But there was to be no rest for Gideon. He'd barely dozed off again when someone else touched his shoulder.

Yelping, he sat up. "Dammit, Jack—! Oh." He blinked at the shadowy figure looming between him and the last glimmers of scarlet in the west. "Didn't recognize you, Rodney."

"Hate to bother you, Gid—Lieutenant," Rodney amended when Harris rolled over, peered at him, then rolled back.

"Isn't any bother," Gideon said with feeble humor. "I'm so tired, I can't hear what you're saying anyway."

Crestfallen, Rodney started away. Gideon lumbered up, caught his friend's elbow:

"Listen, I didn't mean that. What's your problem?"

"No problem. I just wanted to remind you of your promise."

Gideon stared blankly. He didn't even catch on when Rodney patted the front of his jacket, though he suspected he should know the significance of the slight bulge. He just couldn't dredge it from his soggy mind.

"The flag," Rodney said.

"Oh, yes. The Stars and Bars your girl gave you—"

"You said you'd get it to her if anything happens to me."

"You're worrying over nothing. Just remember Jeb's warning. Stick with the company all the time and you'll come through just fine. Every one of us will."

He hoped the lie sounded convincing.

"Sure, I know that," Rodney said.

Something about his friend's eyes troubled Gideon. All at once he realized what it was. Despite the attempted reassurance, Rodney was afraid.

In a soft voice, he added, "I'm only asking in case—"

Gideon broke in: "And my promise stands—in case. But you won't be able to look out for yourself tomorrow if you're dead on your feet." He squeezed Rodney's arm. "Go catch some sleep. That's an order."

Rodney checked to be sure Harris was asleep. Then: "Thank you, Gid."

He turned and shambled away in the dusk.

Gideon settled himself on the ground again. He was so exhausted, he wasn't even troubled by a fleeting thought:

Rodney knows. Tomorrow could be the last day of our lives.

Fortunately he had no nightmares about it. Instead, he dreamed an erotic dream of Margaret.

v

At first he thought every Confederate drummer boy
this side of Richmond had taken up his sticks and
slammed them on drumheads simultaneously.

He scratched his left trouser leg. Something was wig-
gling down there. He squashed it. Then he raised his
head.

Jack Harris was already up. Gideon squinted at the
sky. He could barely discern the treetops to the east.

The sound which had penetrated his mind as an
enormous drumbeat took on a deeper, more realistic
tone the second time. Instantly, the sleepiness left him.
Harris peered in the direction of the artillery fire:

"Comin' from up around the Turnpike. We ain't got
anything that big. Bet it's one of them Parrotts."

Gideon had heard of the rifled cannon. All the Confederates could throw against them were outmoded
smoothbores.

In every part of the sedge field, men were waking. A
bugle blared. Gideon scrambled to his feet.

"What time is it, Jack?"

"Five thirty. Quarter to six." Both picked up their
saddles. Gideon sniffed the still air:

"Lord, it's going to be hot today."

"In more ways'n one."

At the edge of the field, Stuart popped out of the tent
where he'd evidently been conferring with his senior officers. The officers looked drowsy but Stuart didn't. He
was grinning, his teeth a brilliant patch of white amid
the luxuriance of his beard and mustache. He faced the
north like a man hearing the sound of heavenly trumpets.

Gideon and Harris roused the sluggards in I Company—including Second Lieutenant Sunderlind, who

listened to the artillery fire with a ridiculous grin on his face.

Quartermaster sergeants converged on a supply wagon that had arrived in sometime during the night. While the cannonading continued, coffee pots were set to boil over hastily built fires. Noncoms supervised the issuing of horse rations from the wagon. Each man tied the nose bag on his mount, then returned to fill his canteen from barrels of tepid water. By the time dawn broke, smoke was drifting above the oak trees screening the regiment from the country to the north.

Perhaps the firing meant the Yanks were already attempting a thrust across the stone bridge over Bull Run.

Gideon was hazy about the local geography. He'd seen no detailed map of the area; maps were in short supply, and reserved for the senior staff. But as he understood it, Beauregard's defense line followed the twisting course of Bull Run, starting down near Manassas Junction and running up to the Turnpike—the spot where everyone anticipated a Federal attack.

He questioned Harris; found out that Beauregard's strategy supposedly called for a sharp thrust against the Union left. It seemed instead that the Federals were launching a similar thrust on the Confederate left— and doing it earlier.

By seven the cannonading was much louder. Confederate batteries were answering, he imagined. The sun was already glaring in the tops of the oaks.

Time dragged. An occasional crackle of muskets blended with the artillery fire. Gideon began to sweat.

Not a single courier came galloping to Stuart with orders. Finally, furious with impatience, the commander had the bugler blow stand to horse.

Gideon's relief was short-lived. Major Duncan rode up and barked at Harris. I Company was to remain behind to hold the position.

With colors and the Stars and Bars out in front, the

rest of the regiment formed into column of fours. The troopers disappeared along a rutted track leading through the heavy stands of oak. Gideon noticed that a few men in I Company looked relieved at being left behind.

An intolerable two hours followed. Toward the end, with the smoke growing heavier and heavier above the trees, Gideon heard cannon booming from a new quarter—more to the northwest. Unless he misunderstood, that was far beyond the end of the Confederate left—

Finally the regiment came thundering back. Gideon saw a few light wounds but nothing worse. They'd pushed to the stone bridge, encountered stiff Federal resistance from Tyler's division and withdrawn. Gideon questioned the excited men. To them, the meaning of the new bombardment was clear:

McDowell's main thrust—a surprise flanking movement that must have gotten underway not long after midnight—was coming down from the north, directly against the left end of the Confederate line concentrated near the Turnpike. Two whole Yank divisions were evidently pouring down from a ford near a place called Sudley Springs.

Gideon asked a lieutenant in B Company to tell him exactly what was happening on the battlefield. The man replied bitterly:

"Confusion, that's what's happening. Damned if I think Old Bory was ready for a roll-up of the flank. They're sending units up from our right flank like fire brigades. May already be too late. Last we saw, Shanks Evans was pulled back from the stone bridge and going into line above the Turnpike."

As the morning dragged on, Stuart stomped back and forth in front of his tent. He paused once in a while to take a report from an incoming scout, and sent each rider out again with a reminder that the First Virginia was awaiting orders. Evidently the battle had grown too hot for anyone to *think* of the First Virginia.

Around noon Stuart finally lost patience and advanced the entire regiment northwestward over low, forested ridges. The long column swung in an arc and doubled back to a thick stand of oak trees overlooking the Sudley-Manassas road.

The Turnpike junction was barely visible up to the left. Due east lay a plateau which was actually the top of a fair-sized hill. A portion of a stream—Young's Branch—could be seen curving away from the side of the hill nearest the Turnpike. As Gideon dismounted and gazed out from the oaks, he understood why the regiment had been forgotten.

Where the Warrenton Turnpike arrowed northeast from the junction to the invisible stone bridge, smoke mingled with blowing dust clouds. North of the road he glimpsed blue uniforms as well as gray ones; glittering bayonets; rank upon rank of men charging and countercharging; artillery in battery, firing—

It was difficult to tell which side some of the blue and gray uniforms belonged to until masses of men clad in the latter color began to fall back across the Turnpike and climb the moderate slope of the hill directly opposite the First Virginia's position. The Henry House Hill, someone said it was called—after the family inhabiting one of two farmhouses visible occasionally through the thickening smoke.

Confederate cannon roared on the eastern edge of the Henry Hill. The batteries of Imboden, Pendleton, Alburtis and Stanard. But their smoothbores were taking more damage than they were giving. Heavy fire poured from Federal guns on the north side of the highway.

More Yanks came streaming from the trees of the Matthews Hill above the Turnpike, obviously intending to cross and assault the Confederate reinforcements appearing all over the Henry House Hill. It was a scene such as Gideon had never witnessed, let alone imagined.

Because of the smoke and dust, the battle had a certain blurred unreality—except for the sudden brilliance of blood when men fell, bayoneted or cut down by musket fire. Those men screamed, and that was real. So was the thunder of the artillery; and the whizzing and crashing of projectiles.

Wave after wave of Federal troops climbed the Henry House Hill, only to be blown back by the Confederate gunners. But the blue ranks kept coming. The Confederate infantry seemed to be in disorder. They held positions for a while, then retreated under the furious cannonading from Matthews Hill.

A scout reported the attackers who had come down at Sudley Springs had been joined by Sherman's brigade, which had stormed across Bull Run not far above the stone bridge. The Union force was growing.

Gideon could see it. There appeared to be thousands of Yanks crossing the highway and climbing the hillside. The Union bombardment intensified. Shot and shell decimated the hill's defenders. Gray-clad foot troops pitched over, or fled to escape the bursts. Gideon saw a cannon and limber hit; wood, iron, horseflesh and human flesh all exploded simultaneously.

Surveying the carnage, he thought of those spectators who were supposed to have ridden out from Washington to watch the fight. He hoped they were safe and comfortable on some distant knoll, enjoying their picnic lunches and titillated by the stutter of the guns. He doubted they'd enjoy watching the battle itself.

He didn't.

The smoke made it impossible to see everything, most of all the grand strategic pattern—if either side had one. What he did see continued to sicken and horrify him.

Stuart was still upset by the regiment's inaction. He

kept riders galloping back and forth between the First
Virginia and the Henry House Hill. The reports they
brought back were discouraging:

Only Colonel Bartow's Georgians, Wade Hampton's
South Carolina Legion and a mixed brigade from Winchester—men of Mississippi, Alabama and North Carolina under General Barnard Bee—were holding off the
utter collapse of the Confederate defenses—

All at once that situation changed.

Stuart jammed his field glasses to his eyes and
pointed through rifts in the smoke. Muskets held by
men lying prone bristled from a heavy growth of pine
trees at the south side of the Henry House Hill. The
word spread along the ranks of men standing beside
their horses: those were Virginians! Five of Brigadier
Jackson's regiments. Sufficiently protected so that the
Federals would have to come all the way to the exposed
hilltop to get at them.

How late was it? Gideon squinted at the yellow-gray
haze hiding the sun. Past noon, certainly—

And hot as a furnace. Humid heat. Rain would fall
by morning.

He took a drink from his canteen. The water was
running low. The pungent stink of fresh droppings told
him Dancer was nervous. But no more than he.

By the hundreds, Yanks came up the Henry slope,
then were blasted back by the fire of Jackson's sharpshooters. Yank batteries were working their way across
the Turnpike, lobbing in more shells and exploding can-
ister that scythed men down with bits of murderous
metal. Corpses lay all over the hill. Except for Jackson's
line, the Confederates weren't holding. Entire companies streamed to the rear in panic.

Another scout arrived from Jackson. The rider's arm
was a tangle of gray fabric, ripped flesh, bloody muscle.
Though Gideon was a good distance from the com-

mander, he heard the courier's almost hysterical shout:

"Colonel—!"

"Calm down, man, what is it?"

"Johnston and Beauregard are on the field, trying to stop the rout. Barnard Bee's dead."

The troopers frowned and muttered. Stuart said, "You're sure?"

"Yes, sir. He was shot from the saddle while he tried to gather his men. I—I saw him fall. He was shouting. Pointing to the Virginians. Telling his men Jackson was standing like a stone wall, so they should rally too—"

"I'm sorry Bee's gone, but I'm not interested in his phrase-making," Stuart snapped with uncharacteristic harshness. "Did you reach Brigadier Jackson?"

"I—did." The man swayed in his saddle, near to fainting. He fought to stay upright. "I reminded him you were ready."

"And?"

"He—requested no assistance. He's been hit."

More groans from the men. Though Jackson was still feared, respect for him had risen rapidly after the Falling Waters fight.

"How badly?" Stuart wanted to know.

"Only a little nick in the finger, he—"

The man swayed and slid off his horse.

Stuart ordered two troopers to carry the scout a hundred yards to the rear and put him in a safe place. There was no medical help nearby.

Harris asked Rodney Arbuckle the time. He'd forgotten to wind his pocket watch. It had stopped at three past one. Gideon never did hear the hour because a shell whined in and burst fifty yards to the south of the regiments, sending oak limbs crashing. Horses bucked and whinnied.

Soon Stuart was pacing again, slamming one gauntleted fist into another. Gideon unstoppered his canteen and drank it. The warm water would be the last he'd get for a while. In the heat, thirst was almost as unbearable as the waiting.

Shouts riveted his attention on four Federal brigades in line massing for another—and perhaps final—assault on the Henry House Hill. Two Union batteries previously across the Turnpike were right behind them.

Another scout came back. Stuart sprang forward to help him dismount. Still more grim news. The Henry farmhouse—lost from view long ago in the smoke—had been hit. The widow Henry, eighty-four years old, had died when an enemy shell burst through the wall of her bedroom. And Jackson's Virginians were threatened on the left.

"I don't want to hear about that!" Stuart roared. "I want *orders!*"

The courier shook his head helplessly. Stuart walked away, the ostrich plume on his hat quivering.

The Yank brigades swept up the hillside. The two artillery batteries followed and unlimbered. Now the enemy had cannon on the hill itself—and up near the Turnpike, Jack Harris pointed out a column advancing southward along the Sudley-Manassas road. Gideon caught flashes of bayonets in the dust.

Finally a courier arrived with the kind of message the commander had been awaiting:

"Are you Colonel Stuart?"

"I am."

"General Jackson's compliments, sir. His left flank is in danger—"

Angrily, Stuart indicated the Union troops on the Sudley road: "That's hardly a secret. If that's all you came to tell me, you wasted your time!"

"It isn't all, sir. General Jackson directs that you bring your command into action to protect the flank."

Stuart's anger cooled. "Thank you. We'll do so immediately."

He ignored the bugler. His bellow could be heard by every man who stood waiting beside his horse:

"*Mount!*"

Heart slamming in his chest, Gideon hoisted himself into the saddle; checked his saber to be sure it was loose in the scabbard; quickly inspected the pair of loaded Colt's revolvers thrust into his sash—

He saw Rodney struggling with his mount as the column of fours formed. He shouted:

"Private Arbuckle—*in formation* where you belong!"

Rodney clenched his teeth, kicked his horse viciously and took his place.

Stuart unsheathed his saber. Raised it in a graceful arc:

"Column of fours—*trot!*"

Some three hundred horsemen began moving out of the oaks. Above the hoofbeats, the musketry, the cannon fire, Gideon heard a voice in his mind:

Glorious, my boy. *Glorious!*

Wrong.

Wrong, by God. It was ugly and frightening as hell; that was the truth Gideon Kent saw in those moments when the First Virginia headed into action.

CHAPTER VIII

The Waters of Wrath

HOT JULY AIR FANNED GIDEON'S FACE as he urged Dancer on. Dust and bitter powder smoke stung his eyes. Up the road the Yank column appeared and disappeared in the rolling yellow-gray clouds. But the regiment would cross well ahead of the enemy.

The First Virginia was entering the battle at a little past two in the afternoon by Gideon's reckoning—thundering straight up to the holocaust on the Henry House Hill. Another command was relayed by the captains in the column:

"Draw sabers!"

"Draw sabers!"

"DRAW SABERS!"

Blades slid out, the metal catching red glints from exploding shells. Gideon's mouth was dry, his eyes slitted. The frantic rhythm of his blood pounded in his ears, loud as Dancer's thudding hoofs. A pain in his midsection seemed to be eating him alive.

He thought of Margaret:

I wish I could tell you again how I loved—

How I do love you.

The regimental colors and the Stars and Bars vanished briefly in a thin stand of oaks at the summit. One by one, the companies negotiated the trees and burst into the open—

Gideon rode past terrified men in gray who were

517

fleeing down to the Sudley Road. On the plateau the smoke was even thicker and more acrid. He caught sight of soldiers in red trousers and fezzes coming up the hillside on the regiment's left. Zouaves. But whose—?

It was impossible to tell. The color bearers carried regimental and company flags and something that resembled the Stars and Bars. But all the banners hung limp.

Stuart halted the regiment well beyond the trees and surveyed the scene. Gideon bent low over Dancer's neck as a stray Minié ball whined by. Suddenly the Zouaves coming onto the hill veered away from the First Virginia. They were heading for the Federal batteries.

Stuart trotted toward the men in red, waving his saber:

"Don't run, boys! We're here to help—"

Major Duncan charged after him, shouting:

"Colonel, are you sure those men are ours?"

Stuart trotted a few yards closer. Abruptly, one Zouave rank knelt and fired at him.

Stuart ducked. Major Duncan was blown out of the saddle. A Zouave color bearer whooped, waving his flag from side to side.

"Son-of-a-fucking-bitch!" Jack Harris yelled. "Thirteen stripes—"

"Lookit the regimental flag, Captain!" another man cried. "It's the 11th New York!"

"*For'aard—gallop!*" Stuart howled, standing in his stirrups with his saber raised, indifferent to the musket balls whizzing around him. His saber slashed down, pointing at the enemy. Every man stood in his stirrups as the First Virginia charged.

Gideon squinted into the yellow smoke, his teeth locked together. He tried to keep Dancer on a straight course, barely hearing the Zouave muskets because of the thundering horses. But he heard Jack Harris shriek, whipped his head around—and saw Harris' mount stumble, riderless—

The First Virginia crashed against the front ranks of the Zouaves, horses rearing, sabers hacking. Men pitched from their saddles as the leading companies broke apart. Some troopers sheathed their swords and resorted to sidearms: shotguns; rifled muskets; pistols. Gideon saw a trooper blast a portly Zouave with a buck-and-ball. The Zouave seemed to lift off the ground, his head bursting apart in a rain of gore and gristle.

Now Gideon's own company was close to the melee. The smiling nonentity, Sunderlind, riding next to Gideon, flourished his saber:

"Get 'em! Kill the bast—"

Abruptly, Sunderlind's eyes bulged. His blade jerked down, nicking Dancer's neck. The stallion lunged to the left, nearly unseating Gideon.

Gideon booted the horse ahead, out of the way of the second lieutenant who was slipping sideways from the saddle, still staring at the fighting but not seeing it. A Zouave ball had torn Sunderlind's neck open. Spurting blood— That was why Gideon's cheek felt wet and warm.

Sunderlind fell, lost amid the charge. The whole right side of Gideon's jacket was stippled red. He twisted around; saw Sunderlind lying in the parched and trampled grass. Troopers of J Company rode right over him, cracking his skull open.

The 11th New York fired another volley. Gideon felt a ball pluck his left sleeve. I Company had reached the enemy; formations on both sides had already disintegrated—

A stubble-faced Zouave lurched against Dancer, cursing. The man tried to jam the muzzle of his musket beneath Gideon's chin. Gideon brought his saber across and down; felt the blade hack cloth and flesh and bone.

He wrenched his head away as the musket discharged barely a foot from his ear.

Then the Zouave dropped it, staring up at Gideon with astonished eyes. All at once the pain in his hacked arm penetrated his mind. He opened his mouth to scream. Gideon ran him through the throat.

The quick charge had broken the Zouaves. They went scrambling away across the hill or back toward the Turnpike. Gideon rallied his men and followed an enemy company fleeing down to the curve of Young's Branch. There was no orderliness to the pursuit. Four troopers rode on Gideon's right flank, three on his left.

Two of the retreating Zouaves threw down their weapons and flung themselves on the ground. One screamed, "We're done. It's their black horse cavalry—!"

Saber in his right hand, Gideon cocked a Colt with his left. He rode close enough to a Zouave to shoot him through the chest. Stupid damn Yanks, he thought as the soldier fell. The First Virginia rode bays and roans and grays.

Disorderly bands from the 11th New York reached the Turnpike and ran in the direction of the stone bridge. The rout was complete. Gideon signaled his men to a halt just this side of Young's Branch; looked back and saw soldiers in gray swarming over the two Federal batteries, shooting and bayoneting horses and men. The 33rd Virginia had charged from the pines where Jackson stood.

He heard bugling. The signal to reassemble. He led his men—perhaps twenty of them—toward a thicket at the western edge of the Henry House Hill. Noise on the battlefield distorted sound, but he thought the bugling had come from there.

He was wrong. Reaching the thicket, he saw no sign of Stuart.

Men on lathered horses crowded around him. A private shouted, "Where's the regiment, Lieutenant?"

"I don't know. I can't see the colors anywhere—"

"How many men lost, Lieutenant?"

"I don't know that either. I saw Sunderlind fall. And Harris—"

"Horses, too. Fifteen or twenty—"

A hand pounded Gideon's shoulder. He looked around at Rodney Arbuckle's grinning, dusty face:

"Hell of a fight, huh?" Rodney's eyes shone as he displayed his revolver. "I got me two for sure."

Gideon had gotten a couple himself. But he felt no joy because of it; and he was too shaken for more than a touch of pride. The First Virginia had prevented the 11th New York from rushing to the defense of the two Federal batteries he glimpsed through the smoke clouds. The 33rd Virginia was swarming all over the Yank artillerymen, locked in vicious hand-to-hand combat. But when Gideon gazed back at the bodies of the Zouaves on the hillside, his eyes were bleak. Those were *men,* not dummies of straw—

A scout galloped past the thicket, halting long enough to shout that President Davis had reached the field; had come on the cars from Richmond because he'd heard the battle was going badly and hoped to rally the men—

Gideon wasn't interested: "We're part of the First Virginia. Have you seen our colors?"

"On the Sudley road," the scout cried, then galloped on.

Gideon sagged in his saddle, aware of the men watching him. The charge and pursuit had separated them from the main part of the regiment, and he was uncertain about what to do. He had no idea whether the scout's information was reliable. In the smoke it was easy to make a wrong identification of flags or uniforms. He hid his indecision by delaying.

He shoved the Colt's back into his sash. Reached for the canteen hanging from his saddle and discovered both sides of the canteen had been drilled through by an enemy ball without his even being aware of it.

"Lieutenant?"

"What?"

"We going back to the Sudley road?"

"I guess we should. Form up. Column of twos—"

The men maneuvered their mounts, congratulating one another. But Gideon knew the Yanks weren't licked yet. On the far side of the Henry House Hill another wave of blue infantry was charging the summit in a rank that seemed half a mile wide.

He tried to close his mind to the sounds of cannonading; musketry; the eerie counterpoint of men moaning and crying out all over the field. No, the Yanks weren't licked by a damn sight. There was still plenty of time left for a man to die—

He wanted to lie down and rest. But Stuart had taught his troopers to call on strength they didn't know they had. Though Gideon's arm felt leaden, he raised his saber:

"For'aard—*trot*!"

Five minutes later, they found the colors.

ii

Holding a position on the Sudley-Manassas road, the First Virginia saw more heavy fighting during the rest of that incredible afternoon. Endless companies and regiments and brigades surged back and forth contesting possession of the Henry House Hill.

The regiment launched a second charge at fresh Union troops on the road, and scattered them. Gideon killed one more Yank, wounded two and narrowly missed being gutted by a bayonet.

As the riders turned back, Stuart brought up a light battery and wheeled it into the trees overlooking the body-littered highway. The cannon blasted Yank brigades from Heintzleman's division attempting to turn the Confederate left. The First Virginia thundered forward in one more short, devastating attack and cleared the road again.

It was impossible to find out what was happening elsewhere, though it seemed to Gideon that more and more Yanks were retreating up the Sudley road or across Young's Branch to the Centreville highway.

Still, there were conflicting reports:

McDowell had been swept from the Henry House Hill.

No, he hadn't. The two Federal batteries—Ricketts' and Griffin's—had been lost and retaken three times. The action was still fierce, the outcome uncertain.

Then Gideon heard Colonel Jubal Early's brigade was quick-marching from the extreme right end of Beauregard's original line. And a last brigade from Winchester—Kirby Smith's—was coming off the cars to reinforce Early. Finally, Early's brigade appeared on the Confederate left, muskets spouting fire and smoke, bayonets at the ready. One of the strangest sounds Gideon had ever heard pierced the smoke pall:

As Early's men charged to secure the Sudley road, they began to wail.

Wail—that was the only word for it. The cry started deep in the throats of a few men, then spread, rising in pitch, growing louder and louder—a terrifying yell of rebel defiance—

Gideon heard it from Early's left flank, where he was galloping through more of those oak trees with eleven men left under his immediate command. He'd again become separated from the regimental colors. He listened to the yell and shivered. It was a savage cry; a defiant bay rising from a thousand throats—

That was the beginning of the end. Early's brigade hit

the Union troops. Shooting, clubbing,, stabbing. The Yanks broke and ran for the Turnpike.

Gideon and his troopers swung back to the road. Caught up with one of Early's companies. Saw exultation on young, bearded faces.

"Where's Stuart?" he shouted. He got more answers than he wanted:

"Chasin' the Yanks up to Sudley Springs."

"Naw, he's runnin' them down the Turnpike. We're gonna have that bridge over Bull Run in half an hour!"

The battle had degenerated into near-leaderless confusion on the Confederate side; total confusion on the other. Lacking reliable information, Gideon decided on pursuit toward Centreville. Soon he was north of the Turnpike, leading his eleven men northeast.

They were reduced to ten by a Confederate marksman in some briars at the foot of Matthews Hill. He had confused the soiled hussar jackets with Union blue and shot one of Gideon's men out of the saddle as they rode by. The troopers wanted to go after the marksman and kill him, but Gideon held them back.

Enemy soldiers were streaming northeastward, their army totally destroyed. Near Bull Run, Gideon and his men caught up with a panting Union corporal. Gideon didn't flinch when Rodney shot the corporal in the back of the head.

The troopers reined in and surveyed the stone bridge. Now the Confederates occupied it, moving artillery up and blasting shells into the smoke clouds hiding the hills where those Washington picnickers were supposed to be gathered. The bridge was impassable. Gideon led his ten up the brown stream to a ford, crossed there and cut back to the Turnpike.

Near the highway they dismounted and holed up in a thicket, to rest and pick off Yanks running wildly toward Centreville by themselves or in groups. The Yanks no longer had any semblance of organization——or even any officers that Gideon could see.

The time in the thicket was a respite and a turkey shoot too. After a while he tired of emptying his revolvers at the demoralized Yanks. He also had an uneasy feeling he'd led his troopers in the wrong direction. He saw no more men from the First Virginia. Perhaps Stuart was up on the Sudley road after all.

Sick of watching the Yanks fall, he ordered his ten to mount. They'd turn west again and try to locate the regiment.

The Turnpike was temporarily clear. Down by the stone bridge, cannon boomed. A shell went screaming overhead, invisible in the murk. Gideon trotted his men out of the thicket. An instant later a Union platoon appeared on the road to the right. Gideon wheeled his riders, drew his saber and shouted the command to charge.

Most of the Yanks scattered to the shoulders of the Turnpike, but kept going. A few stood and fired. Gideon lost three more. The Union soldiers vanished and Gideon's remaining troopers scattered in pursuit. Soon he was alone.

He hallooed into the drifting smoke. Got a faint answer far to his left. He searched the south side of the road for the next ten minutes but found no one.

With a terrible thirst scalding his throat, he headed Dancer back toward the highway. The three men who had fallen were dead.

What to do now? He'd lost his command.

But he still had ammunition for the brace of revolvers. He still had his saber. And he was unharmed.

Since the Yanks were running east, he'd go that way, too. See whether he could find some of his men.

He didn't really want to go. But he felt he had no choice.

iii

As the steaming July Sunday drew to a close, Gideon rode up the Warrenton Turnpike through clouds of smoke hanging between the hills in the still air. Occasionally, out on either side of the highway, he glimpsed men in blue moving in the same direction. Not a one of them paid any attention to him.

The Confederate pursuers seemed almost as disorganized. Frequently Gideon spied groups of them chasing the Union stragglers north and south of the Turnpike. He passed others on their knees beside Yank corpses. The Confederates were manhandling the bodies; stripping them of equipment. Ammunition. Canteens. Even buttons.

Drawing close to a slight curve in the road, he heard screaming up ahead; screaming so raw and full of hurt, the cries of the wounded on the battlefield seemed like lullabies by comparison. Shortly, he jogged by the source of the hideous noise—a tent erected at the roadside.

The canvas facing the highway was pinned back. Inside, hazy lanterns burned. Men thrashed on wood trestle tables. Surgeons with forceps probed for bullets. Others were busy sawing off injured limbs. The arms, faces and aprons of the doctors were slopped with the blood of their shrieking patients.

At the eastern edge of the tent he saw a four-foot-high pile of amputated arms, legs, hands, feet. Fly-covered. Stinking. He kicked Dancer ahead, reined in and leaned to the left, vomiting.

Sour fluid spattered his left leg. It took him some time to stop retching. Afterward he felt faint.

He encountered a band of jubilant Confederates surrounding eight miserable prisoners. One of the men in gray called to him:

"You better hurry up if you want to catch any Yanks, Mr. Cavalry. Most of 'em are in Centreville already. They ain't gonna stop till they're safe in Papa Lincoln's arms—ain't that right, you pig-fucker?"

The man gigged one of his prisoners with a bayonet. The prisoner lowered his head and kept walking; tears trickled down through the dirt on his cheeks.

A little further on, a familiar figure came lurching out of the darkening smoke. Gideon sucked in a breath:

"Jesus—*Rodney!*"

Rodney Arbuckle stopped on the shoulder as Gideon rode to him. Suddenly Gideon's stomach began hurting again. The lower left side of Rodney's hussar jacket showed blood. A corner of the Stars and Bars he carried next to his belly hung down to his crotch.

Rodney had three canteens slung over his right shoulder. He held a rifle in his right hand, and something small in his left. A pair of oddly shaped iron plates connected by a link chain dangled over his left forearm.

Though he was weaving from side to side, Rodney grinned:

"Damnation, Gid. Where'd you come from?"

"From where we hit that Union platoon and got separated." He jumped down and rushed to Rodney's side. "You're hit—"

"Scratch, that's all. Guess Jeb was right. Doesn't pay to lose the rest of your company. Couldn't help it, though. Wanted to chase those Yanks."

"So did I. Wasn't smart." Gideon meant it. He'd permitted his little band to violate the very rule he'd lectured Rodney about.

"Where've you been since we broke up?" he asked.

"Up an' down the fields alongside this road. Hunting souvenirs. Gid, you've never seen such a mess as there is up ahead!"

"Where?"

"That little wood bridge over the next creek. Cub Run, I think it is. A couple of shells hit just as some Yank wagons were crossin'. I was right beside the bridge when all hell tore loose."

"What happened?"

"The Yanks went crazy. Cut their teams free. Left everything—includin' ambulances with wounded inside. Then a lot of buggies started comin' down from the hills and that made the jam all the worse. I had to ford the creek 'cause there was no way to get over the bridge. God, you never saw such a commotion! Our boys started haulin' prisoners in right and left. Not just soldiers, either. Ladies and gents in those fancy rigs—"

"The sightseers."

"Yessir. I heard we even caught a New York Congressman."

Gideon thought his friend was about to fall. He grabbed Rodney's arm. Rodney pried his fingers away:

"I don't need any help, Gid. It's nothin' but a teeny nick in the ribs. I lost Red Eye, though. Some blasted Yank teamster took a shot at me while I was splashin' across Cub Run. Drilled poor Red Eye square in the head. Second shot—"

He lifted his left arm. The peculiar metal plates clanked together.

"—went through here."

With horror, Gideon saw the hole the ball had torn above Rodney's left hip.

"Not bleeding much any more," Rodney added.

"Better let me look at it anyway."

"No, you go on and try to find some of the others."

"You haven't seen any of them?"

"Nope."

"Nor Stuart either?"

"Not a sign."

"Then I did pick the wrong direction. *Damn.*"

Rodney licked his lips. "You go on now, Gid—"

"Not till I take care of you."

"Dammit, it's a scratch, that's all! I feel fit as a spring peeper comin' out to croak in the moonlight."

He didn't look it. His face had broken out in a sweat that streaked the dust on his cheeks. He dropped the rifle on the ground and touched the bit of flag sticking out below his jacket:

"Bled a little on this, though. 'Course, that doesn't hurt. When I send the flag along to Nancy with the rest of this stuff, the blood'll prove I saw the elephant and looked him square in the eye."

"Rodney, you listen to me. There's a field hospital a little ways back. You stop and have a surgeon check you."

Rodney ignored him. "Just feast your eyes on this gear I picked up for Nancy—" He drooped his right shoulder. The canteens rattled and clacked. Then he kicked the rifle. "The Yanks are throwin' it away! Look—"

He opened his left hand. Gideon saw some sort of implement resembling a clasp knife.

"Those blue boys sure travel better'n we do. This here's a knife, fork and spoon all in one. Folds up nice and neat, doesn't it?"

Gideon tapped the other souvenir—the sculptured iron plates. Originally they'd been connected by two link chains. One of the chains was broken.

"What the devil is this thingamajig, Rodney?"

"Don't you know a vest when you see one?"

"A vest—!" Finally the contours of the iron plates made sense.

"Guess someone sold 'em to the Yanks to protect 'em from bullets. Weighs half a ton, but Nancy'll be tickled to have—"

He swallowed. Squeezed his eyes shut. He seemed unsteadier than ever. Gideon grasped both his arms.

"—to have it," Rodney finished, opening his eyes. Again he wriggled free of Gideon's hands. "Maybe I will stop at that hospital and have 'em slap on a dressing. It hurts a little bit."

"Be careful. There are still Yanks moving out there."

"Moving! They're runnin' like hell. We whipped 'em, Gid. We whipped 'em for fair!"

"Yes," Gideon nodded slowly, "it's beginning to seem as if we did."

"See you when the regiment's together again."

Gideon looked sour. "Whenever that is."

Rodney picked up the captured rifle, wincing. Gideon frowned but said nothing.

He watched his friend wave and stagger off. When Rodney finally disappeared, he walked back to Dancer.

Pulling his body into the saddle was an excruciating chore. He felt older than Methusaleh.

iv

At Cub Run, the bridge was still blocked by wagons marked *U.S. Army*. Some were upright, some overturned.

He met soldiers escorting bands of Yankee prisoners. One group consisted of two elegantly dressed young women and a Federal officer whose uniform bore no marks of battle, only dust.

"A few of the picnic crowd?" Gideon asked one of the boys in gray.

"Yes, sir. This here major spent the afternoon explainin' to the young ladies—Miss Partridge and Miss Claire of Washington City—how General McDowell was gonna beat the tar out of us. The major an' the ladies were packin' up the last of their fried chicken when we come across 'em. We ate the chicken an' caught the birds."

Laughter. One of the young women began to weep
The major put his arm around her, staring at his captor
with sullen eyes.

Gideon forded Cub Run upstream from the bridge
He couldn't believe the tangle of overturned carriage
and Federal wagons blocking the road on the other side
One civilian wagon—an odd, oversized wooden box or
wheels—gave off a hideous chemical stench. Wide
pieces of black cloth dangled between splintered rea
doors. The staved-in side bore an arch of lettering—*M
BRADY PHOTOGRAPHY*. A smaller, horizontal line
centered beneath the arch said *Washington City*.

Smoke drifted over the wreckage. A wheel on an
empty Federal ambulance still revolved slowly, squeak
ing.

Gideon tried to guess the time. Five o'clock or later
to judge from the slant of the sun. He heard a fain
rattle of musketry from the direction of Centreville. He
knew it was his duty to continue that way and search
for his remaining men. But he was tired. Tired and
alone and wishing he were standing close to Margaret
touching her; telling her yes, God, yes, she was right, i
was cruel and dirty business, even when a victory was
won.

While Dancer drank from Cub Run, a company of
Confederate infantry came along. The men scrambled
through the shallow water on the other side of the
bridge. The foot soldiers were whistling; joshing; ex
changing obscenities about the Yanks. The first disci
plined gray unit Gideon had seen in hours.

The infantrymen hailed Gideon as he knelt beside the
stallion, scooping water to his parched mouth. He re
turned the hails with a listless wave.

Dancer kept lapping the water; couldn't get enough
The soldiers reassembled beyond the wrecked wagon
and marched away toward Centreville. Suddenly, on the
opposite bank of the creek and some twenty yard

north, a man in blue dashed out of the underbrush. He leaped into the shallows, his rifle clutched in front of his chest. Too late, he saw Gideon.

Gideon reached for one of the Colts in his sash. The Yank stopped in the water, white-lipped.

Gideon pulled the revolver. Drew the hammer back. The Yank's hands whitened on his weapon.

An immense tiredness and a sense of futility overcame Gideon. He couldn't bring himself to fire.

The Yank stared at him a moment longer, then bolted back to the bank and raced upstream. He vanished in the smoke. Presently Gideon heard splashing. The man had crossed.

He didn't care.

v

Riding back toward the stone bridge, he still felt thirsty. He could tell from the foam on Dancer's muzzle that the stallion needed more water, too.

He took to the shoulder as four Confederate ambulances came grinding up from Cub Run. Each canvas-topped two-wheeled vehicle was drawn by a single horse. The uniform of the first driver showed blood from shoulder to knee. The other three drivers were only a little cleaner.

Inside the ambulances Gideon heard the incoherent voices of men in pain. The left front wheel of the leading ambulance hit a large stone, bounced over and down, hard. A man shrieked.

"Godamighty," Gideon whispered. The shriek dwindled away. The ambulances rolled on. He raised one hand to cover his face.

"Godamighty."

vi

About a quarter mile further on, he was riding slowly when he saw a lanky figure in a filthy light blue uniform lying face down, legs on the shoulder, head in the ditch.

He reined Dancer to a halt. A few feet this side of the body, two vest-shaped iron plates lay in the dirt. A foot closer, the rifle and the canteens. Almost under Dancer's muzzle he spied the combination utensil.

Gideon's throat filled with bile as he dismounted and started walking. He could tell Rodney was dead; his back showed no signs of breathing. The little nick hadn't been so little—

Gideon rubbed his eyes. They seemed unusually blurred and wet.

He raised his head at the sound of boots tramping on the road. A disorderly column of Confederate infantry appeared from the direction of the stone bridge.

He wanted to run away. Run as fast and as far as he could. But he clenched his hands and took a step toward the body.

Another—

At last he knelt and reached for Rodney's shoulder. His mind was a jumble:

Souvenirs for Nancy—

Separation means risk—

My fault.

"Hey, you!" a sergeant shouted from the head of the column rapidly drawing abreast of him. "What unit you from?"

Without glancing up, Gideon said, "First Virginia Cavalry."

"Come along an' join the fun. Old Stone Wall says—"

"Who?"

"Old Jackson. He says if he can rally five thousand boys, we can be in Washington City by morning. Wouldn't you like to get to Washington City?"

Gideon stared at the passing faces. An enormous rage was building within him. A rage directed at everything in creation: the marching men with their idiot grins; the heat; the smoke; the slaughter that wasn't glorious, but ghastly—

His fatigued face had the look of a skull. Other soldiers shouted:

"Comin'?"

"Hey, what do you say?"

"I say go to hell. I don't give a goddamn if I never see Washington City."

Several men swore at him before the column disappeared.

To reach the flag under Rodney's jacket, he had to roll him over. Look at his open eyes. At the lips already a little blue and peeled back from his teeth in what might have been a puzzled smile.

Carefully, he pulled the Stars and Bars free. As Rodney had said, the flag was bloodied; still damp. Some of the blood smeared Gideon's fingers.

Clutching the flag against his side, he staggered into the ditch, vomiting up the water he'd swallowed at Cub Run.

vii

The closer he came to the stone bridge, the more traffic he encountered. He rode past couriers; advancing units; ambulances. Rodney's flag was folded over his sash on his right hip.

He was feeling a little better. Less light-headed—

But no less guilty. He'd led Rodney and the rest away from the regiment; away from the safety of numbers.

When he came to Bull Run, he decided to water
Dancer again. And try to drink a little himself. The
spasms in his belly had eased. After the stop, he'd ride
to the junction and search for his regiment northward
on the Sudley Road.

He didn't want to go back to the regiment. It was his
duty. Nothing else would have influenced his decision.
He'd seen too much in the hours since the boom of the
great Parrott gun had awakened him before dawn.

He'd survived the day. He'd fought without letting his
fear get the better of him. But he'd seen too much, and
most of it he loathed.

He cut away from the Turnpike at the bridge, hoping
to go down to the stream near the arches. The way was
blocked.

By dead bodies.

Scores of them—all in Union blue—lay along both
banks. He presumed the men had been shot down while
retreating.

Here and there among the corpses he saw a hand
twitch. A shoulder lift. Beneath a mound of five or six
corpses, someone was crying.

Bodies floated in the stream as well. The water was
more red than brown.

How many more streams would be reddened before
all this was done? How much more wrath would be un-
leashed? How far would it spread? To the Deep South?
Across the West? Into the North? Over the entire country? Would there be death and suffering along the waters of the whole nation before there was an end, and
peace among Americans again?

You've got to remember why you're fighting.

Independence.

The right to be let alone—

He tried to remember. But he only kept thinking of
the price. It was exactly what Margaret had promised.

Angry at his own weakness, he bowed his head and

held Dancer's rein until the worst of the chaotic feelings passed. Then, despite the litter of dead, he found a path to the edge and dismounted.

Bull Run smelled foul. Maybe it was the stench from men whose bowels had loosened as they died. But he knew he couldn't swallow a drop of that scarlet water, even if he perished of thirst.

Dancer shied. Kept backing and bumping against him, as unwilling as his master to taste the tainted stream.

Finally, the gray put his muzzle down. But he kept backing and bumping his hindquarters against Gideon, and twitching his tail as he drank the water and the blood.

viii

About four yards behind Gideon, the Massachusetts boy opened his eyes.

He blinked, puzzled. His genitals felt wet and hurt like fury. He knew he was gone.

Gradually a little feeling returned to his right hand, which was still curled around the muzzle of his rifled musket. His eyes focused. He saw a yellow-haired man and a horse directly in front of him at the water's edge.

The man seemed to be trying to get the balky horse to drink. It would lap a little, then shy and switch its hindquarters, bumping the man—

The boy's tongue edged out between lips stained by the blackberries he'd picked coming down from Centreville. Because he hurt so badly, he knew he had very little time.

And in three more days, his enlistment would have run out. He could have gone home to Massachusetts—

Well, it was too late to think of that.

One fact bothered him. The yellow-haired man wore blue.

Yet it wasn't regular Union blue. It was a queer, light shade, unlike any he'd seen among the Federal divisions. Nor did it carry any insignia he recognized.

Maybe the man was from some cavalry regiment with which he was unfamiliar—

No, he'd seen the cavalry, too. They wore dark blue.

Attempting to quiet the horse, the man turned slightly. His right side was exposed. What the boy saw then told him the man was probably a Reb.

A fly crawled into the mouth of a dead man a foot from the boy's face. The boy didn't stir. He felt a terrible hatred as he stared at the small flag hanging on the man's sash.

He saw only part of a red stripe, and a narrower parallel of white. But the width of the stripes told him it wasn't the flag he followed.

He bit down on his lower lip, fighting pain.

The man turned his back again, speaking to the horse in a tired, almost quarrelsome voice. Very carefully, the boy slid his musket to his shoulder.

Was it loaded?

He thought so. He couldn't remember positively. He believed he'd loaded it just before the retreating company broke at the Turnpike and ran for the stone bridge with the Rebs howling that strange, godawful yell.

He sighted. Vision was difficult. The man and the horse blurred, sharpened, blurred again. He heard wagon wheels on the stone bridge.

He steadied the musket so it was aimed at the yellow-haired man's broad shoulders. He wished the horse would stand still. Quit switching its tail and shifting its hind legs between drinks. The movement kept blocking his target—

Finally he had a clear shot. Again the horse moved, spoiling it.

No time left. Up on the bridge, a wagon driver shouted a warning.

But the horse was drinking again.

The musket pointed straight at the man's back.

The Massachusetts boy pulled the trigger and heard the explosion. His blackberry lips curved into a small, sleepy smile as he died.

CHAPTER IX

The Wounded

"THE SHOP WILL BE CLOSED until further notice," Eliza Marble said, tying her bonnet ribbons under her chin. The roar of rain was punctuated by bursts of thunder, flares of lightning and the howl of the wind.

Dumbfounded, Margaret asked, "Are you serious?" On the counter near her hand lay a stop-press edition of the *Examiner*. She'd been scanning the upsetting headlines when Aunt Eliza came in from the street, soaked.

Margaret had no idea where the older woman had been for the past hour and a quarter. Nor had Aunt Eliza explained. She'd gone directly to the back room to fetch the bonnet, a shawl and her umbrella.

Margaret felt miserable. Yesterday—Sunday—had been bright and warm. Today, a torrential storm was lashing Richmond. But the weather wasn't the sole cause of her distress. She wanted to study the paper again, even though she detested the thought of doing so.

"Perfectly serious," her aunt snapped. "It's nearly four and we haven't had a single customer since we opened."

"You can't expect many shoppers today, Aunt Eliza. I don't suppose a person in the city had more than an hour's sleep last night."

Her aunt's reply was unusually testy:

"I should imagine you slept quite well."

"I didn't."

"How peculiar. I thought you had no concern for the welfare of the troops."

Margaret held back a furious retort. Aunt Eliza was obviously tired. And there was good reason for her remark about Margaret's indifference. She knew her niece hadn't communicated with Gideon Kent since their quarrel in May. Margaret had absolutely refused to discuss the subject—or the reason she'd grown so wan and listless during the intervening weeks.

The truth was, she hadn't slept well for days. Her anxiety had grown to the point where Gideon was seldom out of her thoughts. Worrying about him kept her tossing night after night. Even now, she saw his face; remembered the feel of his caresses that evening on the towpath—

Just as she remembered the bitter words afterward, when her fear had driven him away.

Aunt Eliza walked to the door, preparing to open her umbrella. She gave her niece another unsympathetic look:

"The ladies of St. Paul's don't share your indifference, I'm happy to say. We've been holding a special meeting for the past hour. The cars carrying the casualties from Manassas should start coming in by nightfall. St. Charles and the other two hospitals can't possibly accommodate all the men. People are being asked to go to the depot to help receive them. And to open their homes. We haven't adequate space in Rockett's so I want you and Willa to clear away the cuttings in back. We'll take one or two of the soldiers here—"

"That's really why you're closing the shop, then?"

"Correct. If your sensibilities are too tender to permit you to help care for the men, I'll rely on Willa."

Margaret shook her head. "You're very angry with me, aren't you?"

"It's un-Christian of me, but I am."

"I've felt it for days."

When the older woman spoke again, her tone was less severe:

"Margaret, I have a good idea why you and Lieutenant Kent severed your relationship. Your father talks excessively while under the influence of spirits. You took the lieutenant to Rockett's—"

"Yes," Margaret murmured.

"—for a purpose which some of the Sergeant's subsequent remarks helped me to understand. He overheard your quarrel on the stairs. You tried to discourage your young man from being too ardent about this war."

Margaret's silence was an admission.

"Though I find it hard to sympathize, I can understand that too. What happened to your father hurt you. You're afraid of ever being hurt again. So you've built a kind of wall around yourself—"

"Do you blame me?" Margaret cried. "I can't stand the sight of suffering! I've seen too much. I don't want to see any more!"

"Then you'd better lock yourself in a room, young woman. And hide there for the rest of your life! If you don't have the courage to take the world as it is—to accept its irrational cruelties along with its God-given goodness—"

"I don't," Margaret whispered.

Softly: "Then I suppose you don't deserve anger. Merely pity. However, the decision's yours."

"I appreciate your granting me that much!"

"Margaret—" The older woman still spoke gently. "You must realize it was never mandated in Heaven that our existence on this earth would be easy. Until you understand and accept that fact, you don't deserve to be called an adult. Nor fully conversant with God's plan for man, I might add. I'm not saying this to hurt you—"

Margaret's scornful glance questioned the statement.

"Child, I'm not. I love you. But I can't abide self-centered behavior. Or cowardice. I'm sorry to be harsh, but that's how I feel. I've kept it to myself too long."

Margaret turned away, bitter:

"Thank you so much for telling me."

"*See here!*" The ferrule of Aunt Eliza's umbrella rapped the floor. "I should think you'd at least be pleased President Davis has returned safely. That we've won a victory. I am."

Her niece remained silent, her back turned.

Aunt Eliza jerked the door open and raised her umbrella. Rain gusted into the shop. Wind flapped her bonnet. She was seething:

"Very well. Your attitude's quite clear. After you help Willa prepare the back room, go home. Behind your wall."

Crash.

The closed door lessened the noise of the storm. Margaret bowed her head.

Aunt Eliza was right. She *was* afraid to give herself to Gideon—to the war—to anything that might expose her to suffering of the kind that had made her early years so unhappy. Although she'd thought of Gideon constantly since their parting, and had come close to writing him a dozen times, she'd held back.

But now there was a new and agonizing worry rising within her. She knew from the paper that he had probably been in the fighting yesterday. With an unsteady hand, she spread the front page and forced herself to look at it again.

GLORIOUS TRIUMPH
OF OUR TROOPS AT MANASSAS!

**McDowell's Hirelings Utterly Routed
In The Greatest Battle Ever Fought
On This Continent!**

A Victory Unprecedented On American Soil!
Foe In Wild Retreat To Washington.
A Panic Among Northern Civilians
Present Near Battle Site.

———————

President In The Field
To Inspire The Soldiers.

———————

General Bee And Colonel Bartow Mortally
Wounded. Heavy Casualties On Both
Sides. Lists Of Killed, Injured And
Captured Not Yet Compiled.

———————

The Heroic Exploits Of General Jackson's
Virginia Infantry Defending Strategic Hill.
Rout Of The Ferocious Fire Zouaves
By Colonel Stuart's Cavalry.

———————

Scattered words drew her eye again:

Heavy Casualties—
Lists Of Killed, Injured and Captured—
Colonel Stuart's Cavalry—

Quickly, Margaret turned the paper face down.

She walked to the door, her eyes wet with tears. Main Street was almost as dark as midnight.

Gideon—

No. She mustn't permit herself to think of him. If he were hurt, or dead, it would destroy her—

She'd told herself the same thing for weeks. Repeated

silently that he meant nothing to her. That she was better off never seeing him again.

Then why didn't she believe it now?

Furious at her weakness, she rubbed the stubby nose she disliked so much. She sniffed twice, controlling the tears. Then she squared her shoulders and walked into the back.

Willa was busy removing cloth, pins and other paraphernalia from the cutting table. Without a word, Margaret began to help her. She moved awkwardly; self-conscious. Willa had surely heard the exchange with Aunt Eliza. But she had the good grace not to mention it.

At last, Willa said in a cool voice, "Is it all right if I leave as soon as we're finished?"

"Are you going home?"

"No, to the Spotswood. President Davis is 'sposed to speak from the balcony if the rain lets up. He's gonna talk about the battle yesterday. I'd sort of like to see the manacles, too."

"What manacles?"

"Didn't you read about them in the war news?" Willa's tone implied a failing on Margaret's part.

"I don't read the war news, Willa."

"Well, our boys captured chains and manacles at Manassas. Meant for lockin' up our generals and maybe President Davis himself when the Yanks came on to Richmond. That ain't gonna happen now," Willa finished, her pride obvious. A moment later she blurted, "I don't understand why you ain't happy about the wonderful victory!"

"*Happy*? We may have lost as many as two thousand young men. That's something to be happy about?"

Willa didn't flinch from the hostile gaze. "Yes. Yes, I think so—" A shrewd glint in her eyes then. "How do you know the figures? Thought you didn't read the war news."

"I—"

Scarlet, Margaret stopped. Thunder exploded, loud as the artillery fire she'd dreamed of Saturday night. She knew from the Sergeant's incessant retelling of Buena Vista that exploding shot could tear a man apart—

Gideon!

The rain pounded the roof. A wagon clattered by on Main. Perhaps a farmer's wagon. Earlier in the day, Aunt Eliza had said every farmer in the district was being asked to rush fresh vegetables to the city's hospitals.

Margaret realized Willa was still watching her. In a faintly contemptuous voice, Willa said:

"Do I have permission to leave?"

"Yes. Get out of here!"

"That'll be a *pleasure!*"

Willa flounced out.

Go on! Margaret thought. *Go listen to Davis tell you how splendid it was. Then go down to the depot and look at them. Smell them. Listen to them wailing. Watch the coffins being unloaded—*

"Then come back and tell me how happy you are, damn you!"

She beat her hand on the cutting table, shaking her head savagely.

It didn't help. Nothing helped. Not reason. Not rage. Nothing.

"Gideon," she said to the gathering darkness. "Dear God—*are you safe?*"

ii

For more than an hour, Margaret struggled with her own fear and confusion. She read the *Examiner* dispatches half a dozen times. Finally she extinguished all but one gas lamp, put on her shawl and bonnet and went out, locking the door behind her.

Rain pelted her face and soaked her skirt as she turned up Main. The street was dark. Gaslit windows of shops and saloons had a pale, watery look.

Even with the downpour, the sidewalks were crowded. Most people were going the same direction— up Eighth Street toward the Richmond, Fredericksburg and Potomac depot.

The people around her were quiet; speaking in subdued voices if they spoke at all. She paid little attention to them, or to the driving rain, as she walked the four blocks to the station.

She was terrified. But she had to know about Gideon. She had to see whether he was among the wounded. If she didn't find him, she'd ask some of those returning whether they knew him.

The odds against it were staggering. But any effort was better than the futility and torment of trying to pretend she didn't care.

A huge crowd waited outside the depot. Tonight there were no illuminated banners. No oratory. No rhythmic stamping of feet to the cadence of martial music. The people were still, gathered around the long lines of canvas-topped wagons, farm rigs, private carriages ready to receive the casualties—

Lightning raked across the sky. Off to the north, she heard the whistle of a train.

She began to run, her cheeks streaming rain and tears.

iii

The Public Guards tried to keep worried families and the curious out of the depot and train shed. But the guards were too few and too feeble to accomplish the job.

The depot waiting room was hopelessly clogged with people. But an almost hysterical compulsion was driving Margaret. She twisted, shoved and jabbed her way to the platforms.

She shielded her eyes against the glare of a locomotive lantern. The first train had arrived. A harried man in a white duster caught her arm:

"Ma'am? Please go back. There are too many people out here already. We won't be able to get the boys through—"

She tore away from him. Stepped off the platform to the bed of the track adjoining the one where the train stood. Freight cars stretched out past the last arch of the shed. The rear of the train was lost in the wet darkness.

Doors rolled back. Uniformed men began to climb out. Civilians—children as well as adults—surged down the platform alongside the cars. There were sudden outcries as parents or wives saw familiar faces. Hurrying up the track, Margaret watched a red-haired boy in soiled gray stumble against an older woman. The woman clasped the boy in her arms and pulled his head to her shoulder, weeping. The boy's left leg was wrapped in brown-spotted linen.

They poured off the cars by the dozens, some with exhausted smiles, others grimacing, still others with lost, vacant looks. Most of them had bandaged heads or splinted arms. The walking wounded; leaning on canes; crutches; a piece of a tree branch—

The babble of voices grew louder; almost painful. The shed itself was steamy, and poorly lit by lanterns hanging on wooden pillars beween the tracks. A woman's scream knifed through the din. Margaret saw her—a matron in a fine brocaded dress. She dropped her parasol, swooning onto the tracks several yards ahead. On the platform, a boy on crutches asked someone, anyone, to help his mother. The boy's right leg had been amputated at the knee.

The woman roused; began thrashing from side to side, hands over her face. She screamed again. Leaning on a gray-haired man in a frock coat, the amputee tried to calm her. She kept screaming. Two other men pulled her up and dragged her away.

Now stretchers were being handed down from the cars. Orderlies fought to hold back the crowds. All at once Margaret smelled the stretcher cases. They stank of dirt, sweat, pus, urine. She gagged.

The high sides of one stretcher completely concealed its occupant. But his chalk-white hand was visible, clutching the pole that ran through the canvas. The hand opened and closed; opened and closed—

She could almost feel the unseen soldier's spasms of pain.

As she worked her way down the track, the cars outside the shed became visible. Rough-clad men were hauling off pine boxes. Handling them carelessly. Slamming them on the platform; stacking them like so much cordwood.

At intervals along the platform, small aid stations had been set up: crates with wash basins on them, and casks on adjoining trestles. Women dippered water from the basins, or dampened cloths, then picked out a stretcher and rushed along beside it to offer a wounded man a drink or sponge his face. By the time Margaret had gone halfway down the length of the train, she'd passed three such stations.

Another headlight loomed out in the darkness, growing larger. The second train was chugging in on the track on the extreme left side of the shed. The bellow of the whistle and the clang of the bell only added to the noise.

She moved more slowly now, searching the faces of

the walking wounded. She saw no uniforms resembling Gideon's but she kept looking, her breathing fast and shallow.

A boy with both arms splinted tried to embrace a portly man. The boy burst into tears. "Oh, Pa—I thought I'd never get here. Oh, God, you can't imagine what it was like—"

The press on the platform worsened as more and more civilians crowded into the shed. The frustrated volunteers handling the stretchers began to swear; loud, ugly obscenities. Chuffing and grinding, the huge locomotive pulled in along the far track. Margaret fought an impulse to flee the bedlam of foul odors and maimed bodies and grief.

Not watching her footing, she stumbled on a tie. Gasped loudly. Three women operating an aid station turned to stare—

Aunt Eliza's eyes glared with reflections of the shed lanterns:

"What are you doing here?"

Margaret gained her balance. With a look of shame, the older woman rushed to her niece:

"Are you all right?"

Margaret nodded. Aunt Eliza put both arms around her, pulling her close. Margaret clung to her for warmth and comfort.

"Child, you're soaked through!"

"Don't worry about it, Aunt Eliza, I—"

Over her aunt's shoulder, she saw the pole of a stretcher slip from a volunteer's hand. The head end of the stretcher dropped. A blond boy rolled off the canvas, shrieking. Both his arms were missing.

"Clumsy dumb son of a bitch!" the other volunteer yelled. "Get him up! Goddamn it, woman, *stay back unless you want us to leave him there—!*"

"Oh, Margaret—" Aunt Eliza's voice broke as she

hugged her niece. Margaret's eyes were riveted on the blond boy thrashing his heels on the platform.

"—I said cruel things to you at the shop. I'm sorry."

Margaret wrenched her eyes away from the gruesome sight of the armless boy. "It's all right—"

"No, it isn't. I realized that coming over here. I couldn't rest last night. I'm tired. That's why I said such cruel things. I'm truly sorry. Forgive me?".

"There's nothing to forgive."

"But—"

"No. There isn't. I deserved every word."

Softly, the older woman asked:

"Why did you come here? To help?"

"I came to look for—"

She stopped. The blond amputee was being lifted back to his stretcher. He screamed. Margaret's heart broke. Her nod was as small as her voice:

"Yes. I'll help."

Let the memories hurt forever—I'm not hard enough to turn away from this.

In a stronger voice, she said:

"Tell me what I can do, Aunt Eliza."

iv

A half hour went by. A third train arrived. Margaret lost track of time. Her dress grew filthy. Blood and pus stained her sleeves and collected between her fingers as she hurried along beside stretchers from the train:

"Let me wash your face for you."

A stubbled, boyish face grinned at her. "Well, ma'am, it's been washed four times a'ready. But go ahead if you want to."

As gently as possible, she swabbed his forehead with the cloth. Then his closed eyes; his cheeks; his throat.

As he was carried on, he lifted one hand in a gesture of thanks.

She turned back to the crates where Aunt Eliza and the two other women from St. Paul's were emptying red-tinted basins on the ties next to the platform. The blazing headlight box of the latest train blinded her for a moment. Two empty tracks separated her from the train, and as she stared at it, a new worry tormented her.

Having told Aunt Eliza she'd help, she took the duty seriously. But it had prevented her from watching the arriving soldiers as closely as she wanted. If Gideon came in on one of the trains, she might miss him—

"Clean water, Margaret," one of the women called.

She dodged the elbow of a stretcher bearer and bent to dip her cloth in the freshly filled basin. The doors of the new train's boxcars were clattering open. For some reason the order of the cars had been reversed. Coffins were unloaded from the head end, stretcher cases from the middle, and the walking wounded were climbing down at the rear. She was wringing her cloth when she thought she spied a familiar face in the press of soldiers limping up the platform. She dropped the cloth—

"*Gideon—?*"

She gathered her skirts in her hand and jumped down to the track, running. By the time she reached the next platform, she knew there was no mistake. Laughing and weeping at the same time, she waved. Called to him again. But he didn't hear—

He was *walking*. No bandages visible. No sign of injury. Just dirt and bloodstains on his once-splendid jacket and trousers. He moved slowly, his head down. A saber hung at his hip. Two revolvers jutted from a sash that had once been white. Some sort of flag was folded over the sash.

"Gideon—here! *Here I am!*"

This time, he heard. Raised his head, puzzled. All at

once he saw her across a pile of coffins on the empty track that separated them.

A strange, hesitant smile lifted his mouth. She ran frantically around the coffins, her mind conjuring terrors. *He wants to smile but he can't. He's hurt, but I can't see the wound—*

They literally crashed into one another. He flung his arms around her waist, hugging her so hard she felt her spine would break. She didn't care.

He smelled abominable. She didn't care about that either. "Oh, Jesus," he said. It sounded like a sob and a laugh in one. "Margaret. *Margaret—*"

She kissed his hair. His face. His throat. He hugged her again, his matted beard scraping her skin. Then he kissed her fiercely on the mouth.

Finally they separated. Laughing, he wiped at his eyes:

"I'm acting like some damn fool boy—"

"Are you hurt, Gideon?"

"No."

"Are you sure?"

"Yes. My Lord, what are you doing here? I never expected—"

"I know. I know. But all I could think about was how I sent you away because I was frightened. Too weak to bear the thought of something happening to you. But not hearing from you was worse. So much worse—and tonight, I knew—" The words tumbled out, almost incoherent. "—I knew I couldn't stand back any longer. I couldn't stay away. Not help. Not care—"

His blue eyes took on a stark look.

"Then I guess we've both changed some, Margaret."

"What do you mean?"

"You were right in everything you said before I left. Manassas was—Christ, I can't even begin to tell you. There were brave men there—my God, so brave you wouldn't believe it. I saw them die. Stabbed by bayonets. Blown apart by cannon. You were right, it—" One hand lifted, clumsily. "—it was no holiday. No place for boys who think soldiering's nothing but a grand game—"

She couldn't keep her hands from caressing him; feeling for wounds. She found none—

Except when she looked in his eyes.

V

Aunt Eliza had finally located her vanished niece. She was staring with pop-eyed wonderment at the two young people walking close together, as if to draw strength from one another.

"I don't understand why you were on the train," Margaret said. "There's not a scratch on you."

"Nearly was. I lost Dancer at the river. Bull Run. A Yankee took a shot at me. I didn't see him. My back was turned. Poor old Dancer was nervous. He bumped against me just as the Yank's gun went off. The ball caught him in the belly. I had to shoot him. So I'm just the same as an invalid now. I haven't got a horse. I don't know where I can find another. But I have to look. That's why I got permission to hop the cars and come back to Richmond. It was either that or be detailed to sit in Company Q."

Margaret halted. "So you're going back to the cavalry?"

"Soon as I can. Not that I'm very excited about it. This is going to be a mean war. It may last a lot longer than we expected."

"But the papers said the Yanks ran from the field!"

"Not all of them. I think the ones that did had bad leadership. With better officers, the outcome might have been a lot different. Some of our own did their share of running, too."

She leaned her head against his soiled blue jacket. "I don't want you to go back."

"I have to. But before I do, there's something I'd like to be sure about—"

Awkwardly, he scratched the end of his nose. Under the layer of grime his face was red.

"What's that?" she said.

"You, Margaret."

She kissed him lightly, ignoring Aunt Eliza on the other side of the track.

"Doesn't that tell you?" she whispered.

He grinned, then grew apologetic: "I should have written. I didn't because I thought you were through with—"

She pressed her fingers to his lips. "I was wrong. I hate to see you fight. I don't want to lose you. But I—" She turned red, too. "—I've decided I'd rather run the risk than never—I mean—"

Flustered, she couldn't continue. They stood close together, oblivious to stares. He held both her hands:

"You know what it was like hearing you call to me? It was like a miracle. Margaret—" Scarlet now, he blurted, "One thing would make it a devil of a lot easier to go back—"

"What?"

"Knowing that when it's all over, you'll give me your hand in marriage."

She shook her head. He looked stunned:

"But I thought—"

"I love you, Gideon. I don't want to wait. I want to marry you now. *Before* you go back."

Dawning wonder lit his face. "Oh, my Lord—!" He threw his head back. *"Eeeowww!"*

The whoop made Aunt Eliza start. The two Episcopalian ladies at her side raised their eyebrows. Suddenly Margaret was fearful again. If she married him and he died, the grief would be beyond imagining. Did she have enough love—enough courage—to face the possibility? To live with it day after day—?

Gazing at his face, she knew the answer. She'd known it when she closed the shop and walked all the way to the depot in the rain. As Aunt Eliza said, there was always risk; always the promise of pain—

But the promise of love was stronger. More than anything in the world, she wanted the love of this tired, bedraggled boy who had become a man.

"You really mean it, Margaret?"

"Yes, my darling, I do."

vi

"Come on!" He jerked her hand, practically dragging her off her feet. "I've got to take you to meet my mother—"

"Is your mother here in Richmond?"

He nodded. "My stepfather's working for the Treasury. I've never been to the place they're renting. But I wrote down the address."

"I should stay until Aunt Eliza says it's all right to go. I've been helping her tend the wounded—"

Astonishment: "You have?"

"Yes."

"Lord, things really have changed!"

Gideon turned toward the older woman on the platform. Eliza Marble had gotten over her surprise and looked not a little annoyed by her niece's behavior.

In a whisper, Gideon said, "She looks fierce."

"Just tell her your favorite drink is cold water and she'll melt."

"All right. I guess I'll stay with you. I might as well—I'll have to ask her permission to marry you."

Despite the ugliness in the shed—the maimed men; the coffins; the groans and occasional screaming—Margaret had never felt so happy.

"Yes, I suppose you will," she agreed. "I don't think she'll chop your head off." She grasped his hand. "Let's find out."

"Hell," Gideon grumbled. "Facing the Yanks was easier than this."

vii

At a few minutes past one o'clock that same night, Edward Lamont rocked back in his chair and slapped the page of the late edition that had appeared on the streets at eleven thirty.

"By God," he smiled. "Right here in Richmond!"

"Couldn't believe it myself until I read we'd captured civilians along with the soldiers," Josiah Cheever said.

Mrs. Muller's Lager Beer Saloon was almost empty. A table in a rear corner provided complete privacy for the two men. Cheever's triangular face had a scarlet cast. Above the table a dim gaslight glimmered in a dark red cup.

"Did your wife swallow that message saying there was an emergency at the Treasury?"

"I think so. You picked a pretty convincing nigger boy to deliver it. Besides, she's been upset all day. Not thinking too clearly—"

"Why?"

"Gideon. He was at Manassas with Stuart's cavalry. The papers haven't yet printed the list of casualties."

Lamont smoothed his mustache with a fingertip. Sipped from his stein. Then picked up the paper to re-read the portion of the column Cheever had been so eager to show him:

Among the civilians taken prisoner in the confusion following the enemy retreat were Congressman Ely of Rochester, New York, and a Washington journalist, one of many gathered near the field of battle.

The journalist, a Mr. Jephtha Kent, represents The New York Union, *a paper which has constantly hurled scurrilous accusations of treason at the Confederate States of America.*

Congressman Ely is unharmed. The journalist, however, was injured in the mad melee at Cub Run. His rented buggy overturned, and he was brought on to Richmond unconscious, suffering a possible concussion of the brain.

Despite the repugnant political attitudes of the civilian prisoners, General Johnston's headquarters has issued a statement saying they will be humanely treated and given full medical attention. Similar treatment will be accorded some five hundred enemy officers and enlisted men who are likewise being forwarded to the capital for incarceration—

"Right here," Lamont repeated, chuckling.

"Sounds like he's half dead, too."

Lamont nodded in a thoughtful way. "Makes the task that much easier, Josiah."

"With a concussion he might die naturally."

"Let's take no chances. We'll proceed as if he's going to recover. With a spot of luck, and some medical help, he probably will."

"You have no reservations about going through with it?" Cheever's eyes grew faintly intimidating. "Our mutual friends are still counting on it."

Lamont snorted. "Our *mutual friends*! They're more than willing to funnel money into the Treasury by devious routes. But if anything goes wrong at our end, they won't know us. They'll never admit being parties to—"

"They don't dare admit it," Cheever interrupted. "You know Davis would never use Yank money obtained the way we plan to obtain it. Use it knowingly, I mean."

The actor grimaced. "A gentleman to the end. If the President was on a sinking steamer, he wouldn't jump into a longboat if he discovered it had been built in Boston."

"You haven't answered my question. If you're worried about the personal risk, we can arrange for a third party—"

"Like the idiot who failed in Baltimore? And the one you hired to try to get the job done in Washington? No, thank you. I prefer to do it properly."

He leaned forward, his brow shining in the dark red light.

"Not for gain, understand. I'll kill the first man who says I'm into this for personal gain."

Intimidated himself, Cheever swallowed. "I know you're not, Edward."

"I didn't marry Fan for gain. I didn't give a damn about the money that belongs to her sons until the political situation made it important. I have no second thoughts, Josiah."

"Even though it means deceiving your wife?"

Lamont waved. "I'm fond of Fan. I wouldn't have married her if I weren't. But as to deception—I've done my share. An actress or a saloon girl from time to time—it's never troubled my conscience. Do you imagine this would trouble my conscience? A chance to do something important for the cause—?"

He took a hefty drink of beer; wiped foam from his mustache. "I work for old Memminger, remember? I know the government's financial situation—which won't change because that damn Davis still refuses to sell our cotton abroad. We've got to whip that Northern crowd any way we can—"

His eyes shone. "I lost a beloved aunt to a black boy. I'd do anything rather than see victory go to those bastards who want to foment nigger insurrection." His quiet rage shifted to Cheever. "I frankly resent your doubting my sincerity."

"I didn't mean to suggest—"

"The hell you didn't! *Nothing* is more important than dealing with the reverend. As a matter of fact, I'd say you're the one whose reputation's in question."

"Now just a minute—!"

"Keep your voice down! I'm only reminding you that you chose one bungler in Baltimore, and another one after Fan and I left the capital. Their capital," he amended.

"The man in Washington came well recommended! And it's hard as hell doing business by cipher and courier. I had to hire him sight unseen. It's not my fault he was a sot who couldn't find the end of his arm, let alone one stinking reporter. If he'd been the right sort, Kent would be dea—"

Lamont grabbed his wrist. "*Don't speak that name.* Anytime—anywhere."

Cheever's cheeks darkened. "But you're making accusations—"

"Valid ones."

"Is that why you've been operating behind my back?"

"My." Lamont smiled in a cold way. "There's very little you don't know, is there?"

"Very little. I know you've been writing letters—"

"To more reliable people in Maryland. I started when it became obvious your Washington agent wouldn't come through. I've been discreet. I only contacted one or two men I felt I could trust. Young Wilkes Booth, for instance. But I never got to the point

of revealing what I wanted done. Now we don't need
outside help. The good reverend dutifully went out to
Manassas with all the other reporters, including that
London Times fellow I've been reading about—"

He saluted the ceiling with his beer stein:

"And a benign deity saw fit to come to our aid."

Lamont set the stein on the table. "This time it's
going to work, Josiah. But you've got to help. I'll need
special clothing—used clothing, which I can't be seen
buying. Once we know where the prisoners will be quartered, I'll need a pass."

"Since I'm in Walker's department, that should be no
problem."

"I'll do the—" Lamont smiled again. "—the actual
work."

"You'll be taking a terrible chance."

"What's the alternative?"

"Even with a pass, you can't simply walk in—"

"Of course not. That's why I'm the logical choice. I'll
go as someone else. I'll have no difficulty. But most important, doing it myself will give me immense pleasure."

Cheever pondered, then nodded. "All right. Now
how about your wife? Will she suspect?"

"No. I've been cautious so far, and I'll continue to be
cautious. Afterward, you can be sure I'll appear appropriately grieved. For weeks. And she'll believe it."

"You mean we'll have to wait weeks for—?"

"*Yes.* I'm not going to lick my chops and dip into the
coffers the minute he's gone. She'd catch onto that in an
instant. I have to be particularly careful because of that
one foolish mistake in public—"

"When we met?"

A nod. "We should have acknowledged one another.
We both reacted hastily—and wrongly. I know it
aroused Fan's suspicion. I think she's forgotten about it,
but in case she hasn't, I have to proceed with extreme
care. Lead her along. A hint here, a hint there—until

our goal seems like *her* idea. I can pull it off. She's deeply loyal. Besides, there's no real harm in caution. We both believe the war may last a good while. And once the reverend is no longer with us, putting the money in the proper hands is only a matter of time."

At last Cheever looked satisfied. "Just like the reverend's—ah—departure."

"Yes. It's finally going to happen. Let's drink to it, Josiah—"

He clinked his glass against that of his friend. His handsome face was composed; even cheerful. His dark eyes sparkled with little red highlights as he added:

"The most important performance of my career."

CHAPTER X

The Murderer

FAN'S LETTER had told the truth. The second floor flat the Lamonts had rented was shabby and cramped. The building and the neighborhood—below Main Street east of the canal basin—were correspondingly dingy.

Yet the flat seemed a paradise to grimy and exhausted Gideon Kent. Wood crackling in the tiny hearth generated a warmth he found unbelievably luxurious after exposure to the rainy darkness.

A mantel clock brought from Lexington showed a quarter past three in the morning. Bundled in a dressing gown, Fan looked almost as tired as her son. She'd burst into tears when he knocked at the door, Margaret on his arm. After a lengthy conversation with his mother and his future wife, he'd left to see Margaret home, returning about two.

He wiggled his disgracefully dirty toes in front of the fire, yawning. His saber scabbard, sabretache and two Colts lay on the floor beside his chair.

Edward sat opposite him. Fan's husband had come in a half hour before, having finished his night work at the overburdened Treasury. He said he'd rushed straight home from the office but would have to be back at the regular starting time.

Edward had embraced his stepson when Gideon announced his intention to marry soon, then interjected enthusiastic comments while he listened to Gideon's description of the action at Manassas. In contrast to the other people Gideon had met on the streets, Edward was in unusually high spirits. He seemed unaffected by the city's forlorn atmosphere.

"That's exciting, Gideon," he said when Fan's son finished his account of the battle. "Exciting and heartening. So is your news about marriage." He smiled at his wife. "I haven't found out if your mother approves of this young lady, though."

"We only met this evening, Edward. She seems pleasant and quite intelligent. She's certainly attractive—" With a touch of sadness, Fan gazed at the powerful-looking young man near the fire. "But I wonder if I really have any say in the matter. I look at Gideon and realize he doesn't belong to me any longer."

It was said gently. Gideon took no offense:

"I want your approval."

"A mother gives her approval to a boy, not to a man. I can't get over how much you've changed since we left Washington."

He smiled, but without much humor. "I'd guess everyone who was at Manassas and lived through it looks a few years older."

"Well," Edward said, "I'm damned sorry Davis didn't permit Jackson to push on to the Potomac." He rose and paced to a cracked mirror to smooth his mustache. "The President will take a good deal of fire for that decision, I'll wager."

Edward turned back to mother and son. Gideon wondered why he didn't feel wholly comfortable in his stepfather's presence tonight. Perhaps it was because Edward's joviality struck him as peculiar. Bad humor would have been a more logical mood for someone forced to work until after two in the morning.

"I do regret I didn't meet Miss Marble," Edward continued. "But I will in a day or two. I'm looking forward to it."

Gideon stretched; yawned again. "I'm looking forward to falling into that tin tub."

"I wish we had a second bedroom for you," Fan apologized.

Gideon pointed a big toe at an old settee:

"That'll feel as comfortable as a cloud. I may sleep for two days."

"You deserve it!" Edward said.

Gideon shook his head. "I'm only joking. I have to hunt up a horse. And send a letter to Miss Wonderly. Along with the flag—"

His eye moved to the mantel. The blood-marked Stars and Bars lay folded beside the clock. He'd already explained how he'd come to have it, and why it was to be sent on to White House.

Edward snapped his fingers. He stalked to the table where he'd flung a paper he'd brought home:

"With all this talk of marriage and the battle, I nearly forgot a piece of news I saw in the late edition."

He opened the paper and pointed out a column. Gideon blinked to focus his itching eyes. Suddenly he exclaimed:

"Oh, my God."

Fan leaned forward. "What is it, Gideon?"

He handed the paper across. "The crowd of civilians who came out to watch the fighting included reporters. Some of the civilians were captured near Cub Run. One—" He felt utterly confused; uncertain whether his response should be elation or dejection. "—one of them was father."

White-faced, Fan read the item. Gideon saw a flash of anxiety in her eyes as she whispered one word:

"Concussion—"

She glanced up. "Edward, what will they do with him?"

"Imprison him, naturally. But give him medical assistance, as the story indicates. What difference does it make? I'm certainly not going to fret about his welfare."

Somehow that angered Gideon. He peered at his filthy toes, wondering why he was concerned about a man who had villified his mother; a man he'd struck in rage.

He knew one reason. Ever since Fan had written him about the street encounter with Edward's friend Cheever, doubt had deviled him. Doubt about Edward's honesty.

Edward stepped behind Fan's chair. Reached down to squeeze her shoulders between his palms:

"Neither should you. After his outrageous behavior in Washington, he's entitled to no sympathy from us."

Fan sighed. "I expect you're right. But he *is* hurt—" Gideon felt a new admiration for his mother when she added, "Perhaps we should at least inquire about his condition."

Edward withdrew his hands; shrugged. "Inquire if you wish. I'll have nothing to do with it."

Again Gideon was troubled. Edward's curt words didn't quite fit with his expression. His cheeks were flushed all at once. And Gideon thought he detected a momentary half-smile on the actor's mouth. Fan, gazing at her lap, didn't notice.

"I'm going to bed," Edward announced.

Fan stood up slowly. "We all should. I'll check to see whether the water's boiling—"

"I can pour the bath, Mama."

"No, let me. Oh, Gideon—" She rushed to embrace him. "I'm so thankful you're safe!"

With a vehement nod, Edward said, "Those are my sentiments, too."

When Fan and her son separated, Edward walked to Gideon's side and gripped his arm in a comradely way. "Enjoy your rest. God knows you've earned it forty times over."

"Thank you," Gideon said as Edward turned to

leave. He struggled to keep his face blank. He was startled by an odor he'd whiffed while Edward stood close to him.

The actor bid them good night. On his way out, he paused to touch the flag on the mantel. His fingers caressed it almost reverently. Then he left the parlor. A moment later, a door closed down the hall.

Gideon followed his mother along the dark, lightless corridor. Behind the bedroom door he heard Edward humming softly. Suspicion flared in his mind again. He nearly spoke to Fan but held back at the last instant.

He carried the kettle of boiling water from the stove to a corner of the kitchen. He filled the tin tub while Fan hovered at his elbow. He kissed her cheek and said good night. Presently the bedroom door closed a second time.

He stripped off his filthy clothes and put one foot in the tub. He yelped. The water was scalding.

He clenched his teeth, held the sides of the tub and lowered himself cautiously. After the initial shock, the water was wonderfully relaxing.

Pleasant images of Margaret drifted behind his closed eyelids. If she had her way—and he had no plans to object—they'd be married before the weekend. Tired as he was, the thought of the wedding night aroused him. He deliberately shifted his mind to the pressing and seemingly insoluble problem of finding another mount.

He offered Margaret a mental apology for thinking of horseflesh instead of her. But he was useless to the army without a horse. And they were in short supply. He also had no money to buy one.

No solution suggested itself. He let his mind wander. Thought of Edward again.

He kept remembering Edward's good humor, minus any hint of pique about long hours. The only subject that had annoyed him was the mention of Jephtha Kent.

That didn't seem natural for a man who'd labored at his job well into the night—

But had he?

Gideon wondered. He'd smelled Edward's breath.

I can't imagine the Treasury serves refreshments to clerks who stay late. And he said he came straight home—

So why had Edward's breath carried the faint but unmistakable odor of beer?

ii

At a quarter past nine on Wednesday evening, darkness hid the magnificent statuary of Capitol Square. In the dimly lit rotunda of the Capitol itself a slow procession still moved past the flower-covered biers of Bee and Bartow.

The evening was windy. Thunder muttered in the northwest. Gideon and Margaret had just come from a short visit with the rector of St. Paul's. Yes, he would be glad to solemnize their marriage; he was grateful for the opportunity to preside at a joyous event. Too much sadness lay on Richmond in the wake of the magnificent victory of Sunday past—

Holding Margaret's arm, Gideon walked toward the intersection of Bank and Eleventh. For protection after dark, he'd brought along one of his Colts. The sight of it in his sash had produced an awkward moment with the elderly churchman. But now he noticed a group of scruffy-looking soldiers loitering across the way; not the first they'd seen. He was glad to have the weapon visible.

A hearse was passing as they reached Bank. The horses wore black plumes. Two carriages of mourners followed. The hearse and carriages proceeded west on Bank—just one of dozens that had journeyed to Holly-

wood Cemetery these past two days. To accommodate
the numerous families that had lost loved ones, funerals
were being scheduled from early morning to well after
dark.

Gideon and Margaret paused in front of the granite
bulk of the Treasury Building to watch the cortege. All
the Treasury's windows were dark. Two gray-clad soldiers with muskets guarded the entrance. Boys, Gideon
thought with contempt, even though the guards were
only a year or two younger.

With a sad little shake of her head, Margaret gazed
after the disappearing carriages.

"What's wrong?" Gideon asked.

"I was just thinking about those poor people. I suppose it's shameful for us to be so happy when so many
others are grieving—"

She leaned up to kiss him. "But I can't help it."

"Nor I. And I don't imagine anyone will get after us
for being happy while we can."

"Gideon—"

"Yes?"

"Have you had any word of your father?"

"No. Mama hasn't inquired. She mentioned doing it,
but Edward's against it. I imagine he's right. My father's
a prisoner of war. An enemy."

Something within him still protested the harshness of
that judgment. Earlier in the evening, he'd told Margaret the whole story of the encounter at the Washington hotel. She'd offered no comment until now:

"The fact that he's your father is more important,
don't you think? Perhaps it's not my place to say it, but
I really believe you ought to find out whether he's re-
covering."

"No, Margaret. We owe him nothing. He accused my
mother of scheming with Edward to get hold of the California money. By means of murder—"

"There's no truth in that, of course."

"None," Gideon declared. Yet he couldn't escape certain recollections that crept into his thoughts at unexpected moments—particularly the memory of Edward's pretending not to recognize someone he'd previously admitted knowing. Twice, Gideon had started to discuss the incident with Fan, only to decide it would just upset her. She already had enough problems coping with near-poverty because of Edward's fanatical insistence on serving the cause.

Margaret asked, "Do you know where your father is?"

"The City Almshouse."

"How did you find out?"

"It was in the *Enquirer* this morning. A lot of the military prisoners and some of the civilians are temporarily quartered at the Almshouse."

"If you wanted to, could you get in?"

"Not without a pass. The authorities are taking no chances. There are too many angry people in Richmond. Some of the wagons bringing in prisoners were stoned, you know. Stoned and shot at—I'm sure I wouldn't be allowed past the front door."

They were nearing Main. Gideon intended to leave Margaret at La Mode Shoppe, where she and her aunt would spend the rest of the night watching two wounded Georgia infantrymen who were recuperating on cots in the back room.

Margaret wouldn't drop the subject of Jephtha:

"Of course it's your affair. But I'd certainly go to the Almshouse and ask about him."

Gideon held back a sharp retort. Since Edward had shown him the paper and Fan had suggested the same sort of inquiry Margaret was endorsing, Gideon had in fact come close to attempting to locate his father several times. In spite of the accusations that had led to violence—or perhaps because of them—he felt guilty about ignoring the man who'd given him life. The fact that the man was a Yank, and a maniacal one, didn't alter his feelings, even though he steadfastly said just the opposite. It was a major admission to murmur:

"Maybe you're right. Papa and I can never be close again. But if he's dying, I suppose finding out is the only decent thing to do."

The conflicting pulls—a hatred he couldn't quite sustain; a guilt that grew increasingly sharper—drove him to add:

"Perhaps I'll do it in a day or so."

"For certain?"

"No, I'm not ready to say that."

"You'd feel better if you were."

He didn't answer. He was ashamed to confess she might be correct.

iii

Josiah Cheever occupied a room in a boarding house a block from the Richmond, Fredericksburg and Potomac depot. The room wasn't much different from the squalid place where he'd lived in Washington. At ten past nine that same evening, he closed the filthy curtains and sat down on a cane chair while Edward Lamont unloaded papers from a worn satchel.

"This is the work I'm supposed to be doing tonight," Lamont said as he stacked the papers on the bed. "I'll leave it here and pick it up afterward. Along with this—"

He held up a small milk-glass jar.

"Hair blacking. I'll need it again before I go home."

"You've thought of everything," Cheever said.

"Preparation is the foundation of the actor's craft, Josiah." Lamont stripped off his clean shirt.

Cheever licked his lips. His pointed face shone with sweat. Excitement brightened his eyes.

Under the single pale gas fixture, Lamont went to the

washstand. He bent, cupped water into his hands and spilled it over his head. Within minutes, the basin was stained by the blacking. More of it came off on a ragged towel. Dried, Lamont's hair and mustache showed pronounced streaks of gray.

"Hand me a piece of charcoal."

Cheever scuttled to the cold hearth.

Watching his image in the blurred mirror behind the stand, Lamont daubed charcoal on his upper lip, chin and throat. With the tip of his little finger he applied a touch below each eye. He rubbed the charcoal carefully until it blended with his day's growth of beard. Then he added very light lines to the creases in his forehead and alongside his nose. He blended these, too, so they appeared natural. Cheever marveled at the swift transformation. Lamont's face now belonged to a man who got dirty in his work and didn't bother to clean up. A few more applications of charcoal, and Lamont's hands were equally grubby.

The actor snapped his fingers. "The clothes."

Cheever began pulling parcels from under the bed. He unwrapped them one by one:

"Work boots. Homespun shirt. The duster—"

"What about trousers?"

"I couldn't locate an old pair exactly your size."

"All right. I'll wear my own and smear mud on them."

Proudly, Cheever held up a soft black hat with a wide, floppy brim and a hole in the crown. "This looks seedy enough, don't you think?"

Lamont laughed. "Perfect."

His hard, muscular chest showed his rapid breathing. Like Cheever, his eyes shone with excitement. He buttoned the coarse shirt, donned the duster—"A little tight, but it'll do." —then exchanged his own clean boots for the much older ones. As he tugged on the right boot, he said:

"Were you able to learn anything further about Kent's condition?"

"I confirmed the report I got yesterday. He'll definitely recover. But he's sleeping a good deal."

"I hope your information's reliable."

"It is."

"I assume he'll be sleeping at this time of night."

"Yes, I'd imagine so."

"Where are they keeping him in the Almshouse? I've never been there before."

"The guards will direct you—"

"I like to know the plan of the stage, Josiah! *Where is he?*"

"I—I'm not exactly sure. I only know the soldiers are in wards, and the civilian prisoners in separate cells. I can't be more specific. I've never visited the Almshouse either."

Unsatisfied, Lamont asked, "Will a guard stay right outside the cell all the time?"

"Not according to my source. Naturally they'll search your satchel when you go in. After that, you'll be pretty much on your own. The guards don't much care what happens to the prisoners. They're mostly young recruits— full of piss and anger because the Yanks are being given decent treatment."

"Anything else I should know?"

"You shouldn't encounter any medical personnel. The surgeon in charge only calls in the morning. There are no nurses—although from the number of pass applications we've received at the War Department, it seems dozens of our dear Richmond ladies can't wait to hurry to the Almshouse to help relieve the misery of the poor Yanks."

Lamont looked cynical. "Southern courtesy does have its drawbacks. What about the pass?"

"Right here—" Cheever drew a folded paper from

the pocket of his food-spotted coat. "It's been duly signed by the assistant secretary—"

"You mean forged."

"After a good deal of practice, I don't mind telling you. The countersignature's authentic." He pointed to it. "Secretary Walker's. My work passed the test."

Lamont glanced at the flowery handwriting, nodded and slipped the paper in the pocket of his duster.

"Got the rest of the things?"

One more parcel came from beneath the bed. Lamont opened his satchel to full width and reached down to smooth the cloth in the bottom. The feel of the coarse fabric sent a peculiar stir of anticipation through him; it was almost like the anticipation before bedding a woman.

He really shouldn't have taken the article in the bottom of the satchel. It had only caught his eye at the last moment, as he was leaving the flat. Bringing it along had struck him as the perfect touch of theatrics; and appropriately symbolic as well.

Fan had been out of the parlor when he took it. She might notice its absence. He had no fears about Gideon. He'd be gone all evening with his young woman—

Though he'd acted impulsively, worrying wouldn't change the situation now. Besides, the presence of the stolen item in the satchel did lend the whole proceedings a sharper edge of danger. A bit of nervousness always improved an actor's performance.

Cheever handed him articles from the last parcel:

"Note paper—"

Lamont put it away.

"Pencils."

Again Lamont's hand dipped into the satchel.

"Cigars. I bought cheap ones—"

"Why be extravagant for a dead man?"

"—and a box of creams from Pizzini's."

"Oh, that's a nice fillip." Lamont laid the wrapped

candy away. Cheever reached for the soiled pillow at
the head of the bed. The actor shook his head:

"I don't need that."

"But there are no beds in the Almshouse. No bedding. Will you use the duster?"

"Something else."

He smiled, relishing Cheever's befuddlement. After a
suitable delay, he patted the satchel:

"It's already packed away. I'll hide it under my shirt
before I get to the Almshouse."

"What is it, Edward?"

"I'll tell you afterward."

"You shouldn't vary the plan! We worked out every
detail so nothing would go wrong."

"*Nothing will go wrong!*" Lamont's loud voice
cowed the smaller man. "This item won't be detected.
They'll be hunting pistols and knives—at least that's
what you said."

"I'm fairly certain the search will be cursory,"
Cheever nodded.

"Then don't worry."

"Damn it, Edward, you owe me an explanation of
how you intend—"

"No!" Lamont interrupted. His dark eyes glowed as
he put on the disreputable hat, pulled its brim low over
his forehead and affected a stooping posture. "Like any
good actor, I owe you suspense and a pleasing surprise
at the final curtain. I'll be back within two hours. And
then Mister—"

He pulled out the pass. Studied the name inscribed.
Blinking and twitching his lips, he modulated his voice
until it was shrill; raspy; rustic:

"—Mr. Artemus McAfee of Mechanicsville, Hanover County, will disappear from Richmond forever—
having given a single flawless performance."

Cheever clasped his hand. "I'll be waiting."

Lamont was embarrassed because Cheever felt the sweat on his palm.

He's right about changing the plan. I really shouldn't have surrendered to that impulse and taken—

Nonsense! It would work perfectly. He would *make* it work. Years of training and experience were on his side. The danger was minimal. And the reward—

Breathing hard a moment, he remembered his aunt axed down by that rabid, murdering nigger boy.

The reward was more than worth the risk.

"Good night to ye, sir," Lamont said with a quirky smile. He touched his hat brim with two fingers and slipped out the door carrying his satchel.

From the door, Cheever watched him go. A low, cackling laugh echoed along the sour hallway as Lamont clumped down the stairs in a perfect imitation of a countryman's clumsy gait.

iv

Fan hadn't expected her son home so early.

Gideon explained that Eliza Marble, energetic as she was, had grown exceedingly tired after tending the wounded Georgians for two nights. Margaret had returned to the shop so her aunt could rest. Both women were sleeping on the premises until the visiting physician pronounced it safe for them to leave their charges alone at night.

The Lamont flat was silent except for the wind whining at the windows. Gideon pulled off his boots and flopped in the chair that had become his favorite resting place when he wasn't sleeping or spending time with Margaret. Fan came back from the kitchen where she was heating potato soup—thin, unsatisfying stuff, she'd apologized. But the best she could prepare given Edward's low salary.

She halted in the parlor doorway, stricken silent by her son's odd look.

Gideon was staring into the unlit hearth. Ever since coming in a few minutes ago, he'd sensed something wasn't quite right—

Maybe it's my own behavior, he thought cynically. Margaret's remarks had accentuated his guilt about Jephtha.

He raised his head as Fan approached, her skirts rustling softly. She touched his shoulder:

"Gideon, you look unhappy."

"Not really. Just been thinking."

"About what?"

"Well, I sort of hate to bring it up, but—" After hesitating, he plunged ahead. "—Margaret and I talked about Papa tonight."

Fan didn't seem upset, so he went on:

"Margaret thinks it's my duty to ask about him at the Almshouse."

"You'll recall the same thing occurred to me when I first learned he was a prisoner."

Gideon nodded in a troubled way. "One minute I'm convinced you and Margaret have the right idea. The next, all I can think of is that night in Washington—"

"Have you been thinking a lot about your father?" Fan asked softly.

"More than I like to admit. I keep wondering whether—whether he's dying. Or if he needs anything we could or should provide—"

"I'm a bit surprised at your concern."

"Are you angry?"

"No. I've been feeling the same way."

"Even after what he said about you?"

"Gideon, when a human being's hurt or facing death, very little else matters. Especially not the past."

He pondered that, then said:

"I told Margaret Papa and I could never be close.

He'll always be a stranger. And a deranged one, at that."

Sitting, Fan murmured, "I wonder."

"What?"

She shook her head. "Go on."

Gideon shrugged. "There's nothing more to say. I just can't decide whether Margaret's right."

Fan covered her eyes a moment. "I think she is." A wan smile. "It's rather shameful that an outsider should have to remind us of our responsibilities."

"*If* we have any."

"I believe we do. Margaret strikes me as a very kind and Christian young woman—"

Gideon didn't interrupt to tell his mother that Margaret's willingness to concern herself with others had only surfaced after a hard personal struggle.

"—and you're very fortunate she wants to marry you."

"I'm glad you feel that way." He rubbed his forehead. "If you don't mind, I'd like to settle this business about Papa—"

"We should."

"I know he wouldn't want to see me even if I could get into the Almshouse, which I can't. You need a special pass from the War Department. But I *could* go to the office and ask about him—"

He wanted her to agree. It astonished him, but he did. Perhaps deep inside, there ran a blood-river stronger than any of the divisive currents of their yesterdays. He said suddenly:

"I could do it tomorrow."

"Yes," Fan whispered. "Do. I know he isn't one of us. But he—he *was* my husband and he *is* your father."

"Then I'll go in the morning. I'm glad you approve. While I was walking home, I nearly decided that's what I wanted to do. I hesitated to bring it up because I thought Edward would object—where is he, by the way?"

"Working."

Gideon's palms turned cold. "Where?"

"Why, at the Treasury."

"Mama, Margaret and I passed the Treasury coming back from St. Paul's. There wasn't a light burning in the building. Not one."

Confused, she stammered, "But, Gideon, he—he told me his section had important documents to transcribe for the President's signature first thing in the morning."

"If that's true, his section is working somewhere else tonight."

"He took his satchel—the one he carries every day. I watched him pack it with papers, I—Gideon, what are you thinking?"

Scowling, he waved. "I'm not sure."

"Please—" She hurried to kneel beside him. He was startled by the troubled expression in her gray-green eyes. "For my sake, speak your mind."

"It's probably ridiculous, Mama. But a few times, I've asked myself whether—" He stopped. "No. I don't want to speak ill of Edward—"

"Tell me, Gideon!"

He drew a deep breath. "All right. I'll say this much. Sometimes I ask myself whether Edward's always truthful. Monday night—Tuesday morning—he said he'd been at the Treasury. He claimed he came straight home. But he smelled of beer."

"You noticed that." Her tone said he hadn't been the only one. "Still, I don't suppose it's fair to call a man dishonest because he stops for a drink without telling anyone."

"There are some other reasons. I've thought about Papa's accusations in Washington. I was convinced he was out of his head with that story about a murder plot to get control of the money Matt and Jeremiah and I will inherit. Convinced, that is, until a name cropped up in your letter. Cheever."

"Gideon—" A look of shame flickered in her eyes. "I'm going to confess something to you." He waited. "I've been suspicious of Edward myself."

"Why?"

"It's the sum of a lot of little things. The way Edward and Mr. Cheever ignored one another on the street—as if Cheever had never once set foot in our hotel room—"

"Which he had."

"Of course. I wrote you that Edward lost his temper when I questioned him about the incident. He didn't deny knowing Cheever. How could he? But he's refused to discuss it ever since. I've seen Mr. Cheever a second time, however."

"When?"

"A week ago. Again on Main Street. He didn't see me. I felt dishonorable, but I turned around and followed him. To the War Department. I approached one of the guards and made a discreet inquiry. Cheever's in Richmond on a permanent basis. He's working for the same government that employs Edward—yet Edward saw fit to deny knowing him, and I don't know *why*."

The wind pushed at the windows, setting up an eerie whine. That was the moment when the pattern began to emerge from scattered fragments of the past:

Edward's quiet fury whenever he spoke of the Nergo boy who'd murdered his aunt.

Edward's hatred of the Yanks.

Edward's worry about the financial plight of the Confederacy.

And Edward's professional skill; his ability to simulate virtually any emotion or attitude——

Add to that the apparent lie about working at the Treasury tonight and the fragments formed a dreadful whole. In his mind, Gideon posed the nearly unthinkable question:

What if Papa wasn't lying?

He didn't dare voice the question to Fan. He might still be imagining things. If he could only be *sure*—!

He hid his confusion by feigning a smile and chafing her hands:

"Well, perhaps there's a proper explanation for the business with Cheever. Anyway, visiting the Almshouse is more important—"

She looked disappointed, as if she'd hoped he could answer her questions. But he had too many of his own.

He had to get out of the flat. Think it through. He jerked on his left boot:

"I need a bit of air. Keep the soup warm."

"When you came in, you said you were famished—"

"I am. I'll just take a turn around the block and come right back."

He stamped his foot down in his right boot and stood up. His eyes came level with the mantel. Then he knew why he'd sensed something awry the moment he walked into the parlor.

Fretting over the problem of his father, he hadn't been alert enough to notice the flag he was duty-bound to send to Miss Wonderly at White House. The chore was so freighted with sad memories, he hadn't been able to write the accompanying letter yet—

Now the flag was gone.

"Mama—" He pointed. "Did you move the flag?"

Fan clambered to her feet. "Why, no. It was there early this evening. It was there before Edward went—"

Round-eyed, she stared at him.

"Mama, what the hell is Edward up to?"

"I—I have no idea, Gideon, I—"

"No one else could have taken that flag."

"Certainly not. But why on earth would he—?"

"I don't know!"

"I'll get my shawl. Let me walk with you—"

He shook his head angrily.

"Why not?"

"Because I'm feeling damned uneasy all at once——"
He knew the rest would hurt her. He couldn't help it:

"I'm going to the Almshouse right now."

"Oh, Gideon——"

Tears started in her eyes.

"——you don't imagine Edward——? You don't think
what your father said could possibly——?"

"*I don't know*! But what other explanation is there?
Maybe he really does want us to get control of the California money——"

"He's never shown the slightest interest in that
money! Although——"

"Although what?"

Miserable, she forced out the rest:

"In Washington, he did express fear that your father
would try to deprive you and your brothers of the
inheritance——no! It still doesn't make sense! Edward's
always assured me he wants no part of the money——"

Like a knife, intuition cut through to show Gideon a
motive:

"Maybe he doesn't want it for himself. Or for us, either."

"Then for who——?"

"The government."

"Oh, God."

Her small voice was enough to convince him the idea
wasn't so far-fetched. No longer hesitant, he exclaimed:

"That must be it! You know how strong he is about
the cause. Maybe he has some wild notion about ac-
quiring the money to support the war. He could be
working hand in glove with that Cheever to make himself a hero to the whole damn Confederacy!"

"That's too terrible even to think abou——"

"No, it isn't. Finally it puts all the details in place.
Every one!"

Gideon's heart was beating fast. He despised what he

was saying because of the way it hurt her. He put his arms around her. She was stiff; trembling.

"Mama, we've got to remember two things. First, how much Edward despises the nigras *and* the Northerners waging war for them. Second—before he joined the Treasury, he earned his living deceiving people."

"Deceiving—?"

"Isn't that what an actor does? Isn't that exactly what he does when he takes a part?" Gideon wiped his mouth. "It may all be ridiculous—totally unfair to him—"

"Yes. *Yes.*" Fan said it as if she were praying.

"Just the same, I'm going to the Almshouse."

He left her standing with her head bowed, in tears.

He ran down the stairs into the windy dark. He could be as mad as his own father. Yet the theory he'd proposed to Fan explained so much—

Patriot; actor. Edward was surely those. But perhaps he planned to play one more role as well.

Murderer.

v

The City Almshouse was a sprawling, multistoried building overlooking a weed-grown cemetery where generations of the indigent—and a good number of smallpox victims—had been buried. Strong gusts of wind tugged at Edward Lamont's hat as he climbed the steps of the main entrance.

His shoulders slumped like those of an old man. He feigned nervousness as he presented his pass to a guard—a boy with bad skin, an ill-fitting uniform and a rusty musket. The boy was one of two sentries on duty under the lanterns mounted above the doors.

"I come to visit one of yer prisoners," Lamont said, pleased with the high-pitched quaver he managed to put into his voice. "Didn't want to, but the bastard's related to my wife."

He looked suitably respectful while the boy examined the pass. The boy jerked his head at the doors:

"You'll have to show this to the duty sergeant inside." He indicated the satchel. "And have that searched. Your clothes, too."

"Yessir, 'course. Thank ye much." Lamont shuffled into the building.

Ancient benches lined the yellowing walls of the large, dingy lobby. The old wood floor creaked. From an open door on his left, a voice barked:

"In here."

A sergeant not much older than the guards studied his pass, then handed it back and pushed a ledger across the counter.

"Sign this."

Lamont deliberately dropped the pen, mumbled an apology and scratched the words *Artemus McAfee, Mechanicsville, Hanover County* in handwriting next to illegible. In the appropriate column he added the name of the prisoner he'd come to see.

"It's a little late in the day for visiting," the sergeant complained as he rummaged through the satchel.

"Yessir, I know. Like I told the young man outside, I didn't want to come at all. Them Yanks can die an' go to hell fer all I care. But my wife, she's cousin to one of 'em—"

The sergeant turned the ledger. "Kent—that abolitionist reporter?"

"Yessir."

"I wouldn't go around bragging about it."

"No, *sir*."

The sergeant broke the ribbon on the box of Pizzini creams and helped himself to one before he replaced the lid. While he examined the rest of the articles, Lamont fidgeted in a perfect imitation of a semiliterate man awed by a uniform. At last the sergeant closed the satchel and gestured:

"Come around the counter and raise your arms over your head."

He searched Lamont's duster, then his pants pockets. He thrust a hand carelessly beneath the duster to pat the homespun shirt. That was the moment Lamont sweated the worst. He'd bunched the flag inside his underdrawers—

The sergeant's casual search didn't get that far.

"All right." The sergeant returned the satchel and walked back to his desk on the other side of the counter. "You're allowed fifteen minutes with him. I expect the prisoner'll be sleeping, though."

"I don't even want to talk to the son-of-a-bitch. I'll just leave off these yere things my wife bought for him. I'm sure sorry to rout you fellows out this way. I couldn't come no sooner. Had to finish the evening chores—"

Bored, the sergeant was seated again and turning the pages of a paper. He waved at the door:

"Go up the stairs to the third floor. Kent's in one of the cells in the south wing. The guard on the landing will unlock it for you."

Lamont touched his hat. "Much obliged." The sergeant didn't glance up as he left the office.

The draughty, creaking hall smelled of disinfectant. In case anyone was watching, he clutched the sweat-blackened bannister and breathed loudly as he labored up the staircase. On the second floor landing, a laconic guard sat on a stool. Large arched doorways revealed long, dim rooms lit by a few gas fixtures. In each room, rows of straw pallets were arranged on either side of an aisle. Men lay on the pallets. Lamont heard the sounds of restless slumber; an occasional groan of pain—

The guard inspected his pass. "On upstairs—" In the ward to the left, a prisoner cried out. "*Shut up in there!*"

Lamont had to force himself to go slowly up the final flights. Excitement was mounting within him. It was working perfectly—more perfectly than he'd ever imagined. As Cheever had said, the callow guards didn't care about the prisoners. Would just as soon see them all die, probably—

I'll be happy to oblige. Won't be long till they have one less Yank to worry about.

His confidence increased with every step. So did his contempt for the guards. They were no match for a man who'd played everything from a comic rustic to a Roman senator. He'd be in, out and gone in less than half an hour. The guards probably wouldn't detect the death until morning—

The third floor guard took his pass, leaned his musket against the wall behind his stool and pulled a ring of keys off his belt.

"Follow me."

They walked through another of the shadowy wards. Blue-uniformed men tossed on pallets. Some of the Yanks wore foul-smelling bandages. At the end of the ward the guard led him through a second arch and turned right into another, equally dim corridor. Lamont saw bolted doors along both sides.

The guard stopped at the fourth door on the left. He peered through the small barred window, then slipped a key into the lock and twisted it.

"Used to keep the crazy folks up here," he explained as he unfastened the bolt below the lock. "Did the sergeant tell you fifteen minutes—?"

"Right, sir. I don't aim to be here half that long."

The guard swung the door back. Lamont entered the sour, narrow room lit by one gas fixture.

The furnishings consisted of a stool, a straw pallet and a slop jar in the corner near an unwashed window overlooking the cemetery and the lighted hills of the city. Lamont could barely control his excitement at the sight of the man curled on his side on the pallet. He recognized the black hair; soiled black suit; swarthy skin. There was a length of linen wrapped around Jephtha Kent's head. He was breathing loudly.

Asleep.

"Want me to kick him in the head and wake him up?" the guard asked.

"No, sir. I got no intention of talkin' to him. Like I 'splained to the other officers, he's my wife's kin, not mine. I'm kinda winded from all them stairs, though. I'll set a minute, then unload the stuff my missus bought. After I leave, you hep yourself to whatever you want." He opened the satchel to display the contents. "There's candy. Writin' paper. Some cigars——"

"Why, that's white of you, Mister——"

"McAfee, Artemus McAfee." Lamont whispered it, fearful of waking Jephtha. This was the critical moment. If the guard stayed——

But he didn't:

"Shoot the bolt when you leave, Mr. McAfee. I'll tend to the lock later. That sumbitch ain't goin' no place. He ain't awake more'n four or five hours every day."

Lamont played it for all it was worth:

"Is there any chance he's gonna die?"

"Don't think so. He ain't hurt that bad."

Glumly: "Oh."

"But once he's back on his feet, he still ain't goin' anyplace."

"Good!"

"When you're finished, come back an' see me at the landing. And bring me a couple of them cigars."

"Yessir——" Lamont bobbed his head. "Surely will."

He waited until the guard tramped off down the corridor. Silently, he put the satchel on the floor.

He eased the door shut. Turned. Took two steps.

Lifted the stool and placed it beside the pallet without making a sound.

He sat down. He propped his elbows on his knees and laced his fingers under his chin, gazing down at the injured man. A smile broke the blankness of his dirty face.

He'd never experienced such anticipation. Not even waiting to make his very first professional entrance in a Savannah theater years ago. He'd never felt so fine—or so certain of success.

He sat studying Jephtha for perhaps a minute. Then he reached into the waistband of his trousers and started to pull out the bloody flag Gideon had brought home from Manassas.

vi

"Listen!" the sergeant said from behind the counter. "There's *no* visiting without a pass from Secretary Walker's office!"

Testy, Gideon said, "I don't want to visit Mr. Kent. I just want to find out how he is."

The sergeant eyed Gideon's uniform. "What unit you with?"

"Stuart's First Virginia Cavalry." He touched the sash to make sure the sergeant understood who outranked whom: "First lieutenant."

"You must have been at Manassas—"

"Yes, I was."

"Get hurt?"

"Lost my horse. It's practically the same thing. You're wasting my time, Sergeant."

Gideon's sharpness made the other man more respectful:

"Sorry, sir. You say this Kent is your pa?"

"That's right. I want to know how he's getting alon—"

"Sure a popular fellow, that Kent," the sergeant interrupted. Gideon's blue eyes widened:

"What do you mean?"

"He's already got one visitor."

"Now?"

"Yes, sir, the man's up in Kent's cell this minute."

Shaken, Gideon asked, "Who is he?"

"Some old farmer married to a cousin of the prisoner—"

The sergeant spun the ledger. Gideon's belly began to ache as the sergeant pointed out the signature:

"McAfee of Hanover County. You must know him if Kent's your daddy—"

"My father doesn't have any relatives in Hanover County."

"How—how's that?" Confused, the sergeant tried to grin. "But the old codger told me—"

"He was lying. I don't know who that man is."

But he did. He was sure he did. He spun toward the door:

"Take me up there right now."

The sergeant gnawed his lip. "Lieutenant, I can't do that. The farmer had a proper pass from Walker's office. But you don't. I'm not allowed—"

The sergeant yelped as Gideon's left hand shot across the counter and fastened on his throat. With his right hand, Gideon yanked the revolver from his sash. He shoved the muzzle against the sergeant's chin:

"This says otherwise. Come around that counter and *take me upstairs!*"

"Jesus Christ, Lieutenant, you'll be arrested for pulling something like thi—"

Gideon jerked the man by the throat, slamming his belly against the edge of the counter. The sergeant exclaimed in pain.

Gideon gouged the Colt's barrel into the sergeant's

left cheek. The man's eyes rolled toward the gun. Sweat beaded his face.

"You take me up there," Gideon repeated. "If we meet any guards, you tell them to stay away or I'll blow your head off."

The sergeant started to protest. Then he looked into Gideon's eyes. What he saw there made him draw a loud breath. Slowly, he lifted a quaking hand:

"All right. *All right.* Just don't fire that piece accidentally. You'll have to let go so I can come around the counter—"

vii

Seated on the stool, Lamont watched Jephtha Kent grimace in his sleep; turn his head slightly on the filthy straw.

Time was passing quickly. Lamont knew he'd already stayed longer than necessary. But the moment was too precious to waste. He wanted to savor it; fix it in his mind so he could recall every detail of his accomplishment in the years to come.

He'd succeeded beyond all expectation. Let them search the whole damn South for Mr. Artemus McAfee. Let them search till the trumpets of judgment blew! No one would ever connect Edward Lamont with the elderly farmer—or with the death. God, it had worked *brilliantly*—!

Lamont toyed with the blood-stained Stars and Bars. Stroked it. Kneaded it. He was glad now that he'd given in to the impulse. He couldn't have found a more fitting way to end the life of the man at his feet.

He stood up.

Jephtha Kent stirred. Muttered in his sleep, then shuddered. Tense, Lamont watched Jephtha's eyelids flutter—

Christ! *If he woke up now—*

He inhaled silently and held the breath. Seconds passed—

A half minute.

A minute.

His chest hurt. Suddenly Jephtha uttered a sound that was half sigh, half groan. His restless movement stopped. His eyelids were still.

Lamont expelled the breath in a barely audible hiss. Carefully, he squatted down and laid the flag on his right knee.

He stretched out his left hand. Grasped the satchel standing by the slop jar. Pulled it—

The scrape of the satchel across the floor seemed incredibly loud. But Jephtha didn't rouse.

Dipping his hand into the satchel, he found three cigars. He transferred them to a pocket of his duster. So much for the guard.

Hands perfectly steady, Lamont picked up the flag. Folded it until he had a pad of sufficient thickness. He could feel little lines of sweat running down his cheeks and neck. Still moving with extreme caution, he knelt beside Jephtha's head.

The gaslight flickered. Wind hummed the dirty windowpanes. Thinking of his beloved aunt, he cupped the folded flag in his left hand and closed his right on Jephtha Kent's throat.

viii

Instantly, the man on the pallet woke.

Lamont pressed the folded flag over Jephtha's face, covering his eyes, nose and mouth. Jephtha's right hand groped out. He groaned; thrashed his legs—

Lamont put more pressure on the flag. His other hand gripped Jephtha's neck like a claw.

Not too hard! Mustn't leave marks—

Jephtha couldn't see him; could only feel him. His fingers closed on Lamont's left leg. But feebly. He was still too weak to offer much resistance, even though he must know he was dying—

Thick, croaking sounds came from beneath the flag. Lamont pressed harder.

Jephtha kicked against the straw. Lamont could barely hear the thumping. A roaring filled his ears; like the sound of a powerful, cleansing wind—

Jephtha's nails dug into his trousers. Lamont pressed and choked, breathing in spasmodic gasps. The sweat trickling down his face smeared the blacking and made it run.

He felt exhilarated. Exalted. Almost unaware of Jephtha's legs drumming louder and faster. Odd, how loud the hammer of Jephtha's boots sounded. Lamont didn't look at them. He couldn't pull his eyes from the head he held motionless with the grip of his right hand and the weight of his left.

Jephtha's hand fell away from the actor's leg. *Almost gone,* Lamont thought. *A moment more and he'll stop making that racket with his boots—*

Suddenly a line came to mind. Cinna's line, spoken immediately after Caesar's assassination. Lamont's lips peeled back from his teeth. He whispered joyfully:

" 'Liberty!' "

He pressed harder.

" 'Freedom!' "

Choked harder.

" 'Tyranny is dead! Run hence, proclaim, cry it about the streets!' "

"You murdering son-of-a-bitch!"

With a scream, Lamont tumbled over on his side. Gideon's boot smashed into his ribs a second time.

Lamont's hat fell off. His eyes flared with fear as he

crawled away from that incredible figure looming above him, revolver in hand.

Behind Gideon—*oh, God help me*—Lamont saw the sergeant from the lower floor and the guard from the third floor landing. It was the noise of their coming he'd heard, not Jephtha's boots slamming the floor. He'd been too caught up in the deed; too carried away to realize—

Gideon's blue eyes shone with a pitiless fury. On the pallet, Jephtha Kent rolled his head from side to side. Tried to sit up, gulping air. His eyes were still closed.

Gideon lunged at Lamont. Tore the flag out of his hand. Drew his other arm back and whipped Lamont across the face with the barrel of the Colt. Lamont reeled back, upsetting the slop jar.

"Gideon, please—"

Lamont held up his hands.

"*Please!* Listen to me! I don't know how you got here, but I—I'm only giving him what he deserves—"

Lamont pushed up with both hands, stood unsteadily. Though he was frightened, he managed a little more strength in his voice:

"After he's gone, the money will be yours."

"That *was* it—" Gideon was trembling so hard, he could barely speak. "The money—"

"For you. For your brothers—"

"*Bullshit.*"

Lamont took a step backward, terrified by the yell from the young man with the revolver in one hand and the flag clenched in the other.

"All right!" Lamont screamed. "For the government! That's why I wanted it—to help the cause. Gideon, he's a Yank. A nigger-loving Yank! Think of what the money could do! You know how badly the government needs help—"

He wiped his mouth, watching the muzzle of the revolver. Red-faced, Gideon thrust out the flag:

"And you meant to do it with this? Dishonor this with a murder? It's already got blood on it, you bastard. The blood of a decent man who did his killing openly—good God in heaven! I never realized how sick you are."

Lamont knew he was trapped then. He lost control; screamed like a woman:

"The cause comes before everything!"

"No," Gideon said. "No, that's wrong."

"If you deny it, you're not loyal, you're a traitor!"

Color drained from Gideon's face.

"I'm a *Southerner*," he whispered. "A Southerner, Lamont—not a murderer. You don't understand the difference."

Silence. The actor wanted to cry. He was finished.

Gideon kept staring at him, tall and hot-eyed and vengeful.

Finished. Unless—

In a space of seconds, he began to breathe faster. *Unless*—

He dove for the satchel. Caught the handle and swung the bag with all his strength.

Gideon jerked the trigger. The wild shot plucked at Lamont's duster and tore a long furrow in the stained wall. The satchel smashed against Gideon's head.

The satchel wasn't heavy. But the blow made Gideon stumble. Lamont saw his chance. If he could get past the guards outside the door—

He ran. Gideon dropped the revolver and the flag. Grabbed the hem of Lamont's duster. Fabric tore.

Screeching and kicking, Lamont drove a knee into Gideon's crotch. The younger man yelled, doubling over.

Lamont crowded him to the wall. Shoved his right palm against Gideon's face, slammed his head against the plaster, hard:

I'll kill him if I have to—

Somehow Gideon managed to free his right arm. He pounded his fist into Lamont's stomach.

Gagging, the actor reeled back. He clutched his belly. Gideon's anger was beyond control. He seized the lapels of Lamont's duster; jerked him; hurled him—

Frantically Lamont windmilled his arms. His boots slipped in the mess from the overturned jar. Off balance, he floundered backward. He had a distorted glimpse of Gideon's stunned eyes. Then his spine struck the window.

Glass shattered. His nails scratched for a hold on the frame; found none—

He shrieked as a piece of glass slashed the back of his hand, ripping a vein. Blood spouted—

And there was nothing behind him.

He tumbled into the darkness, the wind howling in his ears as he fell toward the ground three floors below.

CHAPTER XI

"And If a House Be Divided—"

"LIEUTENANT KENT? The President is ready to receive you."

Gideon stood up and stepped away from the bench in the second-floor corridor of the Treasury Building. He'd been fretting there more than two and a half hours while haggard aides shuttled back and forth between their offices and the President's suite.

It was the Friday morning following Edward's death. Gideon was extremely nervous about the forthcoming interview. He'd been summoned to it without prior warning, and given no hint of its purpose. Even if he got through the interview without difficulty, there'd be no respite in the afternoon. Edward's burial service was scheduled to begin at two.

Fan had borne the tragedy with surprising strength. He knew the events of Wednesday night had affected her deeply, however. Not just the death, but the circumstances surrounding it—especially the swift action by the investigating authorities to suppress the truth in the papers. Someone high in the government had reached the press and won cooperation. The published reason for Edward Lamont's death was an accidental slip on the stairs of the building where he lived.

Gideon had explained to his mother that he hadn't meant to kill Edward, only to prevent him from murdering Jephtha and escaping. He spared himself to a certain extent during the explanation. He didn't tell Fan he was furiously angry when he caught Edward and flung him so that he stumbled and crashed through the Almshouse window.

Fan accepted Gideon's story without question. She showed no rancor. Yet he still felt uncomfortable about having to sit through prayers and a sermon at St. Paul's and accompany his mother to the grave already being prepared out at Hollywood. Thank God Margaret had agreed to be at his side during the ordeal.

This morning he'd polished his saber and attempted to clean and repair his uniform for the interview. But he still felt shabby as he followed the man who had summoned him. They entered a gaslit office. Before the man closed the door to an adjoining room, Gideon caught a glimpse of the President's secretary working his way through a gigantic stack of papers.

The man retired via the main corridor, leaving Gideon at attention in front of an imposing desk. Behind it stood the leader of the Confederacy, Jefferson Davis.

Outside the office windows, gray clouds pressed down on Richmond, dulling the day. Davis turned from one of the windows. Gideon gave him a crisp, correct salute.

The President gestured. "Please be seated, Lieutenant."

Awkwardly, Gideon maneuvered his saber and took a chair. He felt awe in the presence of the slim, well-dressed man in his early fifties. Davis had strong features, including a particularly firm-looking mouth. He carried himself with perfect erectness—probably a heritage from his days as a soldier.

The President sat down at his cluttered desk. The desk's only ornamentation was a small miniature in a gold frame; a portrait of a handsome, dark-haired woman at least fifteen years younger than the President.

Gideon recognized Varina Howell Davis instantly. He'd seen her at the Spotswood twice this week. She was the President's second wife; a woman for whom the citizens of Richmond had a high regard. Along with almost everyone else in the city, Gideon knew her background, as well as that of her predecessor.

Jefferson Davis had married his first wife against the protests of her father, Zachary Taylor. The former President had been Davis' commanding officer at the frontier post where the couple met.

Davis had resigned his commission so he and his bride wouldn't be subjected to the personal and professional harassment of an unforgiving father.

Happy though the marriage might have been, it was not a long one. Davis took his wife home to his plantation on the Gulf of Mexico, near Biloxi, Mississippi. There she contracted malarial fever and died. After a suitable period as a widower, he'd courted and wed young Varina Howell.

The second Mrs. Davis came of a fine family of Virginia Whigs; people with important political connections in the North. One of her grandfathers had been governor of New Jersey.

There were frequent jokes about the affectionate relationship of the President and his wife. He called her Winnie; her pet name for him was Banny. And though Mrs. Davis had a romantic streak in her nature, no one questioned her intelligence. Or her courage. She was the one who'd accepted the responsibility of relaying the telegraphed news of widowhood to her close friend Mrs. Bartow.

The President reached for a file buried beneath several others. Gideon crossed and uncrossed his ankles, conscious of scuffs he'd been unable to polish off his boots.

He was surprised at how fit Davis looked. Everyone knew of his nervous dyspepsia. And although his cheeks displayed a certain hollowness, his hair was still quite dark, parted on the side and worn long in back.

Davis opened the file and leafed through its contents for a moment. Then he lifted his gaze to his visitor. It was impossible for Gideon to tell that one of those clear, intense gray eyes—the left, he recalled—was blind.

"Lieutenant Kent, I believe you've already been informed that no charges will be lodged against you— even though you entered the Almshouse at gunpoint, without official permission. As it turns out, there was good and sufficient reason."

"I *was* told there'd be no charges, sir. But I'm relieved to hear you say it. I didn't intend for Mr. Lamont to fall. My first consideration was preventing a killing."

"As you stated in the presence of the guards—" Davis consulted a paper from the file. "Something to the effect that Southerners are not murderers. I applaud you for that. I'm no more fond of the Yankee prisoners than you are. That doesn't condone an attempt to kill one of them, however."

He drew out another sheet. "I'm sure you're wondering why I sent the messenger to your mother's flat, asking you to stop here."

"Yes, sir."

"I felt I owed you a personal report on the disposition of the case. I apologize for making you wait, but I was attending an important conference."

His words had a rather abrupt quality; there was an unmistakable air of authority about the man. He assumed Gideon would accept the explanation without question. Gideon did.

"After Mr. Lamont's death and your deposition for the authorities," Davis went on, "we apprehended and interrogated Mr. Cheever—"

A crudely scrawled paper rustled in Davis' hand:

"He made a full confession. He and Lamont had indeed concocted a scheme to do away with your father.

The scheme dates back at least to April, when a first attempt was carried out during the Baltimore riot. The object of the scheme—as you suspected and Cheever subsequently admitted—was to transfer control of certain financial holdings to you and your brothers. I gather the transfer only becomes effective upon your father's death."

"That's correct," Gideon said. He explained briefly about the California gold properties belonging to the Kents.

"The Kents," Davis mused. "I wondered if the name was a coincidence. Is the prisoner related to the family that publishes that vile newspaper he works for?"

"The New York *Union?*" Reddening, Gideon nodded.

"Mm. Well—to continue. Cheever told us your stepfather intended to persuade you, your mother and your brothers to permit a certain percentage of the inheritance to be funneled into our Treasury—though I fail to understand how he meant to transfer bullion between warring territories."

"I'm not sure he even thought that far—" Gideon began.

"Possibly not. Mr. Lamont was evidently a self-styled patriot—?"

"Yes."

Davis' mouth showed distaste. "Not the sort with whom I care to have this government associated—though God knows I'll take every bit of money we can get." Quietly: "Except blood money."

He cleared his throat. "The two conspirators were evidently aware of my feelings. Cheever admitted the source of this new-found wealth was never to be revealed to the Treasury Department. The money was to be turned over by intermediaries."

"Did Cheever reveal their names?"

"No. He was too terrified to do that—even under the somewhat—ah—rigorous questioning to which he was subjected. In any case, Cheever and your stepfather clearly hoped that within a few months, your family could be persuaded to go along with the plan, at which time they would begin passing funds to the donors whose names would appear on the record. I assume those donors would have to be wealthy men in their own right. Otherwise their sudden generosity would be suspect—"

"Perhaps that's why Cheever was afraid to reveal their names."

"Undoubtedly." Davis closed the file. "That appears to be the essence of the plot. I'm sorry to tell you no formal charges will be filed against Cheever. Thanks to your actions at the Almshouse, no murder was done. And in return for his confession it was agreed he would not be prosecuted as an accessory. But Mr. Cheever *has* been dismissed from Secretary Walker's department. In fact he's left Richmond—under armed escort. He'll never again be permitted to hold any post in this government. Nor any military rank, even noncommissioned. Should he choose to enlist under an assumed name—which I expect is unlikely, given his devious and cowardly character—there's nothing we can do to prevent it. But we don't want his kind serving our new state. Our cause is just, our basis for separation is Constitutional, and I like to believe we are honorable men. For that reason—"

Davis reached to the bottom of the file and withdrew an official-looking paper.

"—I have, this morning, signed your father's parole."

"A parole!" Gideon exclaimed, unable to contain his surprise and pleasure. "I was certain he'd be kept in prison."

"Technically he should be. But he's been grievously

treated. And he's not without a certain degree of influence in Northern newspaper circles—"

Davis tented his fingers. "My motives aren't entirely pure. I feel that if your father's paroled, he may be slightly less inclined to write about us as barbarians—rebellious traitors. We can use a few temperate voices speaking for us in the North. Of course, I hope I've made clear I also consider your stepfather's scheme unforgivable. My sense of fair play demands satisfaction. Cleansing of guilt, if you prefer."

Davis laid the document on top of the file.

"Naturally the parole won't be publicized. And it's conditional to this extent. If your father doesn't pledge his word to withhold the frankly scandalous reasons behind the parole, he'll be detained in Richmond. I don't want a word about Lamont's plot published. It could do us irreparable harm—especially in the European press. All in all—" Davis shrugged. "I believe it's an equitable arrangement, and one to which I hope he'll be a party. All of the civilians will be exchanged eventually. Your father's early release won't cause too much gossip—provided he doesn't create it himself."

"What if he won't cooperate, Mr. President?"

"Then I'll make an exception when the rest of the paroles are arranged, and he'll be kept in Richmond for the duration of the war. I certainly hope that won't be necessary. Of course I have no idea of how he'll react to my proposal."

Gideon was candid: "Neither do I. I tried to speak to him at the Almshouse, but he was only half conscious. He's not fully recovered. I haven't been back to visit him since Wednesday evening. My mother's demanded most of my time—"

"Well, when he is himself again—the physicians assure me it will be within a week or two—and if he agrees to my terms, I intend to assign you the task of transporting him north."

"To Washington City?"

"As close as practicable." Davis smiled. "Our mounted picket lines reach almost to the Potomac thanks to General McDowell's disastrous performance. And you're temporarily detached from Colonel Stuart's cavalry after what I understand was gallant service at Manassas—"

"Detached and horseless," Gideon said.

"I'll arrange for a wagon and a team. That should make the journey a little easier on your father. You'll have to return the wagon, however. And both horses."

Gideon was elated. Davis' clemency, and his disgust with Lamont's scheming, might go a long way toward changing some of Jephtha's ideas about the so-called traitors of the South.

From a personal standpoint too, he was relieved. Jephtha Kent remained on the other side of the conflict. But Gideon was still guilt-ridden because he'd turned on Jephtha; struck him that night at the National Hotel. To balance that act Gideon wanted to see freedom granted to the man who would forever be something of a stranger to him, yet who could never be wholly a stranger because of the blood binding them together—

A tap at the door of the adjoining office turned Davis in his chair. The secretary looked in:

"Excuse me, Mr. President. Just a reminder about your meeting with Attorney General Benjamin."

"Yes. Thank you."

The President's quick nod dismissed the secretary. The door closed. Davis stood up and smiled:

"I hear you plan to be married soon, Lieutenant."

"That's correct, sir." Gideon rose. "To Miss Margaret Marble of this city."

"I told Winnie—Mrs. Davis—" A gesture at the framed miniature. "—about the events at the Almshouse. She was quite taken with your courage and resourcefulness. I believe she'd like to be present for the wedding. Would you favor us with an invitation?"

Flustered, Gideon stammered, "Why—why, yes—naturally I—we—my Lord!" He blushed. "Excuse me, sir. We'd be honored."

"Count on it, then. Now that you've been fortunate enough to find a bride, I hope you'll be equally successful in finding something that's become just as important as a wife." Davis' good eye twinkled. "I'm referring to a horse. Don't tell your fiancée."

"The horse is a definite problem, sir. I haven't solved it yet. I understand there are animals for sale illegally—"

"Yes, the damn profiteers are working in Richmond just as I'm sure they're working up north."

"But I can't afford their prices."

"Well, I do hope you discover some way to secure another mount. Colonel Stuart's cavalry is an admirable unit. Young men like you and the colonel are the bright hope of this government. The North has its millions of people—its immense factories. We have more limited resources, and fewer citizens. But if you are representative of them, and I think you are, I have no doubt of our eventual victory. Not military victory, necessarily. I'd prefer a peaceful acknowledgement of our legal right to exist as a separate nation—"

His expression grew even more sober. "That is the *one* thing I want the North to acknowledge. Our *legal* right."

Gideon nodded much too vehemently. But he wanted to please Davis because he'd been so generous.

"You're entirely correct, sir," he said. "We've got to make them acknowledge we haven't committed treason.

And we don't dare lose in the field before they do, or I expect they'll hang us."

"They'd hang me, certainly," Davis murmured.

He gazed out the window at the gray clouds above Richmond's rooftops. Then, moving slowly, he accompanied Gideon toward the door to the corridor.

"Of course, we're not committing treason at all. We're only doing what our American ancestors did in the last century—" He pondered a moment. "Any people, anywhere, so inclined and having the power, have the right to rise up and shake off the existing government and form a new one that suits them better. That's a most valuable and sacred right—a right which I hope and believe can liberate the world."

With one hand on the filigreed knob of the door, Jefferson Davis looked Gideon in the eye.

"Nor is that right confined to cases in which *all* the people of an existing government may choose to exercise it. Any portion of such people that can, may revolutionize—and make their own of—as much of the territory as they inhabit."

Overwhelmed that he'd been allowed to share the President's thinking to such an extent, and anxious to have Davis know he agreed, Gideon exclaimed:

"I've never heard the argument for our cause put so perfectly, Mr. President."

Davis was amused. "Nor I."

The reply stunned Gideon. He hadn't suspected the chief executive of such blatant egotism.

Davis waved:

"Oh, the words aren't mine. I was merely quoting a certain gentleman who spoke on behalf of the Texas rebellion against Mexico in forty-eight. The gentleman was serving his first term in Congress—"

He clapped Gideon on the shoulder. Yet there was a certain melancholy in his tone when he added:

"His name was Lincoln. Good morning, Lieutenant."

ii

Eight days later, toward four o'clock on a drizzly, humid afternoon, Lieutenant Gideon Kent reined in the team and brought the wagon to a halt at a road junction some three miles southwest of Washington City.

Four Confederate cavalrymen jogged toward the wagon. Gideon recognized two of them. The trooper in charge was a sergeant of K Company, First Virginia.

He examined Gideon's papers, which bore the signature of the President himself. The sergeant's companions were more interested in the black-haired, cigar-puffing civilian seated next to Gideon.

The sergeant seemed displeased by the documents Gideon had presented:

"Lieutenant, this man has the same last name as yours—"

"What about it?"

"He's no kin, is he?"

"He's my father."

The cavalrymen exchanged surprised looks. The sergeant's reply bordered on insolence:

"We got to let him go on your say-so?"

Irked, Gideon pointed to the papers. "Not mine. The President's."

Jephtha reached into the wagon for an old portmanteau he'd been given at the time of his release from the Almshouse. The motion stirred the cloud of cigar smoke around his head. The smoke moved slowly in the damp air. The sergeant sounded even more hostile:

"Says here the wagon stays—"

"I'm taking it back to Richmond."

"Then the prisoner'll have to ride shank's mare the rest of the way."

"He's not a prisoner any longer."

"He'll be lucky if he gets into Washington City," another of the soldiers said. "Them Yanks are so damn scairt of an invasion, they pull up planks on all the bridges ever night."

"Are there enemy troops between here and the river?" Gideon wanted to know.

"No, just a few of ours." Again the sergeant eyed Gideon. "That's an I Company uniform you're wearin', isn't it?"

"Correct."

"You detached from duty?"

"You want to try saying, 'sir' once in a while, Sergeant?"

The other man's cheeks darkened. "Sorry, sir. Just sort of forgot—"

"Hell you did. Yes, I'm detached until I find a horse. I lost mine at Manassas. Are there any other personal questions I can answer for you?"

Scarlet, the sergeant said, "No, sir." He touched his cap and wheeled his men away down the road leading left from the junction.

Gideon sat still, staring past the team toward the mist-covered hills gray as the sky above them. A farmhouse and trees in the distance were dark blurs in a darker world.

The journey up from Richmond had been an uncomfortable one; and not just physically. Gideon and his father had conversed along the way. But always about inconsequential topics. Each acted wary of the other; almost overly polite. Their talk had been the talk of strangers thrown together for a few hours by circumstance.

Jephtha flipped the butt of his cigar into a pool of water at the roadside. "Torn-up planks or not, I'll be in the capital by dark."

Gideon hoped so. His father was still weak, and looked it. His normally swarthy complexion had a wan cast. But he acted cheerful as he hoisted the portmanteau and climbed down into the mud on the right side of the wagon.

Gideon looped the reins over the brake lever and jumped down on the left. Both men walked forward, then halted, the heads of the horses separating them. Gideon couldn't find the words to ask for the forgiveness he wanted so badly.

A light rain pattered on the wagon's canvas top. The left-hand horse stamped, slopping mud on Gideon's faded light-blue trousers. It was Jephtha who broke the strained silence:

"I do appreciate your company all the way up here, Gideon." He rubbed a hand across his mouth. "I'd better be going along—"

"If we can believe those troopers, I don't expect you'll run into any danger from here to the river."

Jephtha grimaced as he eyed the hills. "Why, no. Everyone in Richmond said our boys are sitting in Washington drunk and demoralized, or praying the new hero of western Virginia, that young McClellan, can bring some order out of the shambles of the Division of the Potomac. Lincoln certainly dumped poor McDowell fast enough."

"The night after the retreat from Centreville, the paper said—"

Idle talk. Empty talk. Gideon hated it. There was so much that needed to be said, and he didn't know how to begin.

Jephtha faced him, laying his left hand on the neck of the restless horse. The hand moved back and forth, calming the animal.

"I don't expect we'll see each other again soon. I owe

you my life, just as I owe Davis my freedom. I've turned into such a cussed Yank, I never imagined I'd be thanking two Southerners—even if one is my own son."

Both tried to smile.

Suddenly Jephtha walked around the horses and gripped Gideon's arm.

"You have a lovely wife. I'm happy I was permitted to attend the wedding—even if I did sit there with a guard on either side. Damnedest marriage service I ever saw! All that kneeling those Episcopalians do—a Yankee prisoner and the President of the Confederacy and his wife in the pews—and that poor old cripple, drunk as a lord and wheeling that little platform in the aisle when he gave the bride away. Bizarre—that's the only word for it." He added softly, "But I'm glad I was there."

Gideon looked into his father's eyes. "I am too."

"Davis was damned decent to me. He came up afterward and expressed his regrets about what happened at the Almshouse. I do wish I'd had a chance to speak with your mother alone, though. I wanted to offer something more than what I said in public—worn-out words of condolence. Tell her—tell her I'm genuinely sorry Lamont died."

"Are you?"

"Yes. It would have been better if he'd just been arrested. I know Fan loved him. I know he must have had good qualities or she wouldn't have married him. Tell her also that I don't want her to feel guilty about Lamont's plan. She was deceived."

Gideon nodded in a glum way. "So were we all."

"I'm glad your mother's going back to Lexington. She'll be safer there—"

That irked the younger man:

"You're still positive Richmond will fall, aren't you?"

Jephtha smiled. "There's that Virginia blood. It's what makes some of the Kents so feisty—and you a good cavalryman, I don't doubt."

The smile faded. "Yes, Gideon, I know Richmond will fall. Along with the whole Confederacy. If not next month, then next year. It's inevitable."

"I don't agree with—"

"Listen to me a minute. On the Sunday morning before I rode out to Cub Run in that rented buggy, I ate breakfast with a colleague. British fellow, name of Billy Russell. He's over here for the *London Times*. He went out to Cub Run, too, but I gather he got back safely. Anyway, Russell's a little pompous, but he's a smart fellow. Especially on the subject of warfare. He was in the Crimea for the *Times,* among other places. He gave me his opinions about the war—starting with people. There are five and a half million whites in the South—six and a half if you add in some in the border states that haven't seceded. Balance that against twenty-one million in the North. That alone means the Confederacy can't win. Russell said something else interesting. He predicted this would be a war unlike any other ever seen on the face of the earth before. Not even numerical strength counts as much as the equation of your men against our machines."

"You mean Northern factories."

"Yes. There are other new ingredients, too. Railroads—look at the Bull Run battle. If Johnston hadn't shipped men out of the Valley by rail, the outcome might have been entirely different. The armies have telegraphs now. Communication is much faster. It could decide an engagement. Russell called it war on a titanic scale. The first in history. And all the advantages—except maybe plain courage—are on the side of the North."

Gideon scowled. "I intend to do my best to prove Mr. Russell's judgments are wrong."

"I wouldn't expect you to do anything else." Gideon was astonished to hear admiration in his father's voice.

Silence again. Rain splashed softly in the roadside pools. In the distance, a clatter of hoofs indicated mounted men on the move, unseen in the mist. Gideon was sick of the quibbling about the war. Time was running out.

"Papa—"

"What is it?"

"I want you to know one thing before you go. I—I'm deeply sorry for hurting you in Washington."

Jephtha waved. "It's forgotten. Completely! Don't forget I wouldn't be here if it weren't for you."

"And don't you forget Edward isn't all there is to the South. Nor Grandpa Tunworth either. I don't want you to spend your life thinking every man in the Confederacy's a monster."

Jephtha shook his head. "I won't."

His father turned his head. Rain got in his eyes. At least Gideon assumed so, because Jephtha wiped the corners with the back of his hand.

"I told you before, Gideon. Time changes people. Once I was a zealot like Lamont. Perhaps not quite ready to commit murder for what I believe, but a zealot all the same. Unforgiving of anyone who didn't see eye to eye with me on the slave question. I haven't changed my thinking about the institution, mind you, but I have a different view of some of the people who defend it— or should I say the people who have been forced to defend it? You helped accomplish the change. Davis, too. You know, it's peculiar, our standing here like this—a father and his boy on opposite sides of the quarrel. We share the same blood, but not the same ideas. I don't believe in what you're fighting for and I never will. But I'm proud of you—"

A rueful smile:

"Rebel or not, you're a Kent to the bone."

He sighed.

"Too much has happened for us to ever be close, I expect. But we mustn't hate each other any more. We need to live through this war and prove Mr. Lincoln's prophecy wrong. At least as it applies to our family."

"What prophecy, Papa?"

"The one he appropriated from Saint Mark. 'And if a house be divided against itself, that house cannot stand.' When the war's over, I'd like to see the Kent house still standing. Whole, and healed. But there's one thing even more important—"

Jephtha had tears in his eyes. So did Gideon.

"I don't want this war to destroy you. I gave you life, and Margaret's given you life in another way. Both are too precious to lose."

"I'll come through just fine, Papa."

"I pray so." Jephtha looked at his son. "Because I love you."

The quiet words faded quickly. Something drove Gideon forward then; a bursting relief; a draining of old pain. He took his father in his arms and held him close.

When they drew apart, Jephtha uttered another small, pleased sigh and picked up his portmanteau. Then he put it down again:

"By the way—I know nothing about smuggling money across a hostile border. I suppose it can be arranged—"

"Edward was apparently going to try."

"So am I."

"*What?*"

"One way or another, I'm going to see you receive five thousand in gold from the Ophir money."

Gideon's mouth dropped open.

"If that's not enough, I'll send more. In care of your mother in Lexington. It may take a while, but I promise I'll get it to you. If you're going to survive this damned war, you have to be adequately equipped."

"I don't understand, sir. Why should you send me gold?"

"To buy horses, Lieutenant. Horses! It's the only gift I can give you besides a father's love and a prayer for your forgiveness."

Once more he picked up the portmanteau. The bottom dripped muddy water.

"Now you turn that team around and head back for Richmond. If you stay away from Margaret too long, some other chap's going to steal her."

They laughed and clasped hands.

"God keep you, Gideon. You and your brothers and your mother, too. We'll see each other when this trouble's done."

He leaned forward and kissed his son's cheek. Then he turned and trudged past the junction and on down the road leading north.

iii

Gideon didn't leave immediately. He couldn't.

He climbed up on the seat of the wagon, untied the reins and sat watching the black-clad figure dwindling into the misty landscape of pale greens and gray. There seemed to be a briskness to his father's walk; a vigor entirely new and reassuring.

Jephtha's figure grew smaller and smaller. He walked steadily toward the place where the road wound out of sight between low hills. The words from Saint Mark lingered in Gideon's mind.

"And if a house be divided against itself, that house cannot stand."

Perhaps it was true of America. He hoped it wasn't true of the Confederate States. Despite the victory at Manassas, Davis' policies were already being called into question. The very principle of state sovereignty which had caused the separation from the Union was becoming the basis of outraged protests from governors throughout the South. How dare Mr. Davis insist on additional military levies? The power of centralized authority was the very power against which the South had rebelled—

But a few thoughtful men were already warning that unthinking insistence on states' rights would ultimately undo the Confederacy. Or at least dangerously hamper its ability to fight.

No such philosophic arguments disrupted the North. Lincoln was recouping swiftly and firmly. Speaking to the special session of the Yankee Congress in early July, he'd demanded authorization to call another four hundred thousand men to arms, and spend four hundred millions of dollars to wage war against the cause symbolized by the flag Gideon had finally sent to Miss Nancy Wonderly of White House.

His father was probably correct. Terrible times might lie ahead. The war could be longer and grimmer than anyone had imagined.

But no matter how it came out—and he fervently hoped it would come out in favor of his side—perhaps his father was also correct in saying the Kents needn't be forever split into warring camps. The possibility doubled his reasons for wanting to live through the days ahead.

One reason was Margaret, of course. The other was the sense of family that had never quite left him. Until the windy evening when he went rushing to the Almshouse, he'd never fully realized how wide and deep the river of family blood flowed.

And if a house be divided—

Whatever else happened, perhaps the Kents *could* fight from principle, not hatred. And prove that wrong.

Far in the distance, Jephtha Kent halted. Gideon watched his father's arm rise in a final wave.

He lifted his own hand, waving in return. Then Jephtha disappeared in the murk between the pale green hills.

Gideon snapped the reins over the backs of the horses. He maneuvered the wagon into the crossroads, turned it around and headed south, the sound of his fine, strong voice singing "Lorena" drifting out behind.

CHAPTER XII

The Better Angels

"COWARDICE! ABSOLUTE cowardice and the refusal to obey orders—that's what caused the defeat, gentlemen."

The voice of the young captain in spotless blue carried through the racket of Williard's saloon bar. It reached Michael Boyle where he sat at a small table against the wall, sipping his fifth whiskey of the hot August evening.

Late in the afternoon he'd received a startling and wholly unexpected note. He was waiting for the sender of the note. And growing more sullenly drunk by the moment.

His first couple of whiskeys hadn't cost him a penny. A gregarious, flamboyant young man named Jim Fisk had bought every soldier in the bar two rounds before departing for a dinner engagement. Mr. Fisk was one of the hundreds of businessmen who had come to Washington to vie for a piece of the Federal military budget. Fisk had told Michael he represented the Jordan Marsh store of Boston, and was prepared to make the War Department an attractive offer on badly needed blankets.

The loud-mouthed captain notwithstanding, drinking was certainly preferable to the guard duty for which Michael had been scheduled this evening. Only the note had rescued him; the duty officer recognized an important name when he saw one. Michael had been glad to leave the dispirited encampment out on the grounds of

Georgetown College and walk all the way to Pennsylvania Avenue.

In the past few weeks he'd lost fourteen pounds. He was gaunt in the face and seldom clean shaven. His splendid Zouave uniform was long gone. He'd thrown all of it away except for his trousers and shirt on that Sunday afternoon last month when—

He closed his eyes and tossed off the whiskey, trying not to remember.

A couple of civilians at the bar objected to the captain's remarks. But not loudly enough to discourage him:

"We've heard a lot of damned nonsense about poor leadership. Speaking as an eyewitness—as a man who was *there*—I can tell you the fault doesn't lie with the commanders. Ninety percent of the enlisted men in the Union Army are damned yellow-bellies."

At the far end of the bar a huge, bearded man slammed down his whiskey glass. He stalked to the captain, caught him by the left epaulette and spun him around:

"And I say you're a damned liar, shoulder-straps!"

The captain started to laugh. Then he took the full measure of the big man's size. He replied in a mumble:

"Who the devil are you?"

"Name's Whitman, if that matters. I write a bit for the New York papers. I help in the hospitals, too—"

"So?"

Red-faced, the burly Whitman jerked the captain's epaulette again:

"Don't sneer at me, you son-of-a-bitch. I've knelt by the cots of those poor youngsters shot up at Bull Run. Were *you* with them?"

"Indeed, I was! My regiment was never actually committed to the fighting, but I saw—"

"Oh, you *saw*!" Whitman roared. "You saw, did you, shoulder-straps? Well then, you tell me where all the Union companies have gone to! I'll tell you where—they've gone to their graves because their leaders ran and abandoned them. I've talked to the boys who got back. I know the truth. Blow—brag—put on airs in Willard's parlors—Bull Run was *your* work!"

"Blast your insolence—" the captain began.

"*Yours*!" Whitman jabbed an index finger against the captain's chest. "You and the rest of those incompetents who call themselves officers. If you'd been half as brave as your men—one-tenth!—Bull Run would never have happened!"

Michael was fascinated by the strange, bullying fellow. He was so furious, tears were forming in his eyes.

The officer reached for the hilt of his saber:

"I'd be happy to settle this difference with you outside. Not only happy—I insist."

"I haven't got a weapon, shoulder-straps," Whitman said. "But I'll oblige you."

"A male nurse! Probably fondles the little darlings while he's caring for them—"

The captain's contemptuous aside produced only one laugh. Men were clustering around Whitman and the officer in anticipation of a fight. Slowly, Michael stood up. He threw his whiskey glass on the floor.

The sound of it shattering turned every head. Michael weaved toward the bar, a rail-thin soldier in cast-off blue he'd recovered from a pile of clothing stripped off the Union dead brought back from Bull Run. The little metal harp winked on his forage cap.

He reached the officer. His eyes were watering from the thick cigar smoke. "I'll oblige you, too, Captain. I'll join Mr. Whitman in obliging you right now."

"Private, remember yourself!" the captain warned.

"Fuck you."

Someone clapped. The captain swallowed. He glanced at Michael's cap.

"What's your unit? I intend to report—"

"Go ahead! You go on down to Richmond and report me to Colonel Corcoran of the 69th. You'll find him in prison."

The captain tried to be intimidating: "The New York 69th, is it?"

"Yes—*sir*. The regiment that went up the Henry House Hill right after the Second Wisconsin and Colonel Cameron's Highlanders. We went all the way to the top. We weren't fortunate enough just to observe—"

The words brought it all back; shook him; set hideous images whirling in his head:

The running men stripped to shirt sleeves and weapons.

The shoes left behind because they were too hot to wear.

The shouts of encouragement—some in English, some in Gaelic.

The rattle of musketry—and the deafening thunder of the rebel field pieces sweeping the summit as the first ranks reached it.

The 69th had made three desperate charges against a Confederate battery. At last, beaten, the survivors had fled back down the slope and attempted to reorganize—

Michael's golden-brown eyes glittered in the light of the hanging bar lamps. "Let me ask you, Captain—how many did your regiment lose?"

"None!"

Derisive laughter.

"See here, that's not the point!"

"Yes, it is," Michael said. "We lost thirty-eight dead, fifty-nine wounded, ninety-five missing. Sixteen percent of the regiment. We fought until the retreat to Centreville started and there were no more officers to give orders. Ours were lost. Every other one we saw was *running*."

He took a step forward. Whitman tensed. The captain was sweating.

Michael reached for the captain's epaulette:

"You don't deserve these, Mr. Shoulder-straps—"

A hand fastened on his arm:

"Michael! Good Lord, I didn't expect to find you in the middle of a brawl!"

"This preening prick—" Michael blurted. Abruptly, he recognized the grave, fatigued face of Joshua Rothman.

The captain chose the moment to whirl, dart away and rush for the door. He reddened as curses and jeers followed him.

The eyes of the big bearded hospital orderly grew surprisingly gentle. He extended his hand to Michael:

"I thank you for your offer of help, sir. But I'd have done it myself."

"I know, Mr.—Whitman, is it? I just felt like joining you."

"For that I don't blame you. God bless you, soldier."

The crowd parted respectfully to permit Whitman to return to the drink he'd left at the end of the bar.

ii

Michael Boyle had no stomach for the elegant supper Joshua Rothman had arranged in a private dining room on Willard's second floor. He poured a full goblet of white wine as Rothman dipped into his soup.

"I knew from the papers that you must have been at Manassas," the banker said between swallows. "I don't doubt it was worse than any civilian can imagine."

In his mind, Michael saw the emerald colors fall.

"A lot worse."

He tried to focus his eyes on Rothman's face. "Your note was certainly unexpected, Joshua." A humorless smile. "At least it saved me from guard duty. I never imagined you'd turn up here—"

"You didn't? With the Treasury pleading for loans from any available source? I'm seeing Secretary Chase in the morning."

"But your note said you had something personal to discuss."

"Quite personal—"

Rothman put down his spoon. Dabbed his lips with his napkin.

"Louis."

The mention of the name produced a spontaneous image of Julia's vivid blue eyes. Disgusted with himself, Michael drank more wine.

"What about Louis?"

"He's going ahead with that profiteering scheme."

"Federal Suppliers—"

"Yes."

Michael shook his head as if he were unbearably tired.

Rothman continued, "I assumed your precipitous departure from Kentland and your equally quick disappearance from New York meant you wanted no part of it."

"You're correct."

But not entirely. There was another reason.

"Well—" An embarrassed shrug. "—it took me a bit longer to reach my decision. Perhaps because I'm not as young as you, Michael. And, like most bankers, notoriously conservative. But I've done a good deal of thinking, and my original reaction stands. Louis' plan makes a mockery of the Kent name. He can't be permitted to carry it out. The only way to stop him is to threaten to expose him. Not merely threaten—do it, if necessary."

Abruptly, Michael began to feel quite sober.

"How, Joshua?"

"In the newspapers."

"You don't mean that."

"I do."

"Well, you certainly don't need my permission."

"But I need your corroboration. If I show Louis a draft of an article describing the scheme, it's a standoff. His word versus mine. But you were at Kentland too. You and Israel Hope. I've written Hope a letter but as yet I've received no reply. So you're the only one who can help. You heard Louis. If there are two of us making the charges, I believe I can persuade Benbow and Benbow to release the incorporation papers for Federal Suppliers. Members of the Benbow firm still aren't happy about their involvement."

"Who'd write such an article? You?"

"My first thought was Jephtha. I understand he's back in Washington—"

"Safe," Michael said. "He was caught in the retreat from Bull Run and held prisoner in Richmond for a while. Then he was paroled suddenly, though he won't say how he managed it. He came out to Georgetown to visit me two days ago—" He pondered. "I think Jephtha would do it. Louis is stealing what belongs to his sons. I think he'd do it even though it'd cost him his job."

"It will cost us all something," Rothman admitted. "It will cost my bank the profits from handling a very considerable fortune. It'll cost the Benbows substantial fees and a major share of their business. It'll cost you—"

"Never mind about me."

"No, you must examine the risks, Michael. You'd acquire a powerful enemy."

"Hell—" Michael shrugged; his alcoholic torpor was almost gone. "—I've already got thousands of those on the other side of the Potomac."

"Do you plan to remain in the army?"

"Yes. When my ninety-day enlistment ran out, I signed on again." Another sip of wine. "Suppose Louis refuses to be bluffed. Suppose it's actually necessary to print an article. The *Union* won't do it, much as Theo Payne might like to—"

"Naturally. But someone will publish it. Greeley— someone. I'll see to it."

Quietly Michael asked, "Why are you doing this?"

Rothman covered his eyes a moment. "I thought I explained. Evidently I didn't do it well. I have a very strong feeling for the Kent family, Michael. I believe the family stands for values Louis cares nothing about. You'll probably accuse me of being a sentimental fool—"

"Only sentimental."

"Well, that's good. Because I'm going to say something very presumptuous. I know Louis is Amanda's flesh and blood. But I honestly feel you and I and the Benbows—and Mr. Hope before he resigned—are more representative of the Kents than Amanda's own son."

Michael chuckled. "A slum boy, a Jewish banker, a bunch of Boston lawyers—Joshua, that *is* presumptuous."

"I warned you. Still, I think we have a duty to preserve the family's integrity until such a time as Louis comes to his senses—or there are other Kents who understand their heritage better than the gentleman under discussion."

The banker paused. Then: "Well, Michael? What do you say to my presumption?"

"I applaud it. I'll help you."

"You *must* understand what you're doing. You'll never see a penny of your handsome salary again. You'll have Louis against you as long as you live."

"He can't hurt me."

"Not now. But when the war's over—when you need employment—"

"Joshua, how can a soldier even be sure he'll survive the war? I'll worry about Louis venting his wrath if and when it happens. Now, do you want me to speak to Jephtha, or will you?"

"I think we should do it together. Do you know where he lives?"

"G Street."

"Tomorrow, then, after I've called on Chase—what the devil's so humorous?"

"Us. The presumptuous conspirators—" He raised his goblet. "Here's to us, Joshua. Custodians of the honor of a family to which we don't even belong."

"Do you think it's an unworthy role?"

Remembering Amanda, Michael replied:

"No. It's exactly the right one. I do realize it means starting another war. Smaller than the one occupying the attention of the country, but no less fierce."

Rothman grew thoughtful. "I might be wrong in what I said a moment ago. You could fare better with Louis than I predicted. It's very strange, but you seem to have acquired a strong partisan in his wife."

"Julia?"

"Yes. Ever since you left New York, she's praised you time and again—extravagantly. Before, she all but ignored you. Certainly a curious change, wouldn't you say?"

Michael recalled her face; the taste of her mouth; the feel of her body that night he'd taken her.

Her body. Responding to his—

Perhaps she'd never known how it felt to be loved because of passion instead of marital necessity. He'd damned near—hell, he *had* raped her to prove he wouldn't play her flirtatious games, and now she was— God, it was almost wickedly funny.

Except that he had no desire to laugh just then. The memories roused emotions he'd been struggling against—unsuccessfully—ever since Kentland. Fool that he was, he *cared* for her!

And now Rothman intimated she cared for him a little, too.

Christ! What a ridiculous, impossible situation!

And yet he knew that if he didn't fall in battle, he'd see her again. Somewhere, sometime—dangerous as it was for his peace of mind—he *knew* he'd see her—

His hand jerked involuntarily, knocking over his goblet.

Baffled, Joshua Rothman watched him as he dabbed at the spilled wine, then refilled the goblet and drained it. He was having trouble containing his urge to laugh. He couldn't get over how strangely things worked out for the Almighty's confused and imperfect creatures—

The laughter erupted. He threw his head back, his voice pealing. He kept laughing, louder and louder. Joshua Rothman looked nonplussed, and completely incapable of deciding whether the tears streaming down Michael's cheeks were tears of mirth or misery.

iii

Molly Emerson woke abruptly, wrinkling her nose.

She'd been sleeping close to Jephtha despite the heat of the August night—no, the night was over, she realized. Grayness tinged the windows.

She sniffed again.

A cigar!

Opening one eye, she saw the orange tip brighten, then fade. Jephtha exhaled smoke. He was propped in an awkward position, the back of his head jammed against the wooden headboard.

Still drowsy, she slipped a hand across his stomach. "Can't you sleep?"

The end of the cigar glowed and dimmed again.

"No."

She wondered whether it had anything to do with his meeting the preceding evening. He'd gone out to dine

with two men she'd heard him mention in connection
with the family interests in New York. The men had
called for him in an expensive rented carriage. One of
them, superbly dressed and growing gray, was introduced as Mr. Rothman, a banker from Boston. The
other was a young Irish soldier named Boyle.

After Jephtha had returned about midnight, he'd
rushed straight to his room and spent three hours working on a piece of copy—a news story, she presumed—
before he came to her bed.

"Jephtha?"

"Mmm?"

"What are you thinking about?"

He shifted his head to gaze down at her. Worked his
arm beneath her shoulders, and his hand to her right
breast, letting the fingers rest gently.

"I'm thinking perhaps you and I should get married."

"Married?"

After the shriek of surprise, she tried to sit up.

"Calm down, Molly. Is marriage anything to get so
alarmed about?"

"No, I just—I just don't understand what you're saying—"

"It's perfectly straightforward, woman."

"But you know—you've always known you weren't
under any obligation to marry me just because we—"

"Hush," he interrupted. "I've grown quite fond of
you, Mrs. Emerson. More than fond. I believe I love
you very much."

She caught her breath. His voice had a note of—
elation, that was the only word for it.

"Besides, I think marriage would probably be necessary before I set foot in a pulpit again."

"A *pulpit*! Have you gone mad?"

"I certainly hope not."

"Then—then you've been drinking—"

He opened his mouth. She smelled the cigar, but no alcohol.

"Hiram died the day before yesterday," he said.

Bafflement upon bafflement:

"Hiram?"

"The old black porter at the National. He was also the minister at Grace Redeemer, the African Methodist church up in Negro Hill."

"Oh, yes, I do remember you mentioning that."

"They need a temporary preacher. Hiram was ordained, you know. They want another ordained man to replace him. Finding one will take a while. The church said they'd pay me a dollar or two every week— whatever they can raise. I may need the money."

"Why?"

"I'm going to write an article for Mr. Rothman. It's possible—no, very likely—that as soon as I do, I'll be out of a job."

Molly's head began to ache. All this was too much; incomprehensible. She untangled herself from his hand and once again started to sit up:

"Jephtha Kent, *what is going on*? Why would you lose your job?"

He leaned across and kissed her on the mouth. "I'll explain everything in due time, I promise."

"But—I never thought you had the slightest desire to preach again."

He shrugged, too casually. "Maybe I'm just curious to see whether I can still do it."

She didn't believe it. Something had happened to him since his return from Richmond. Something she didn't understand.

Of course she hadn't missed the distinct improvement in his spirits. He'd spoken with genuine fondness about his son Gideon, who had saved his life and exposed Lamont's plot. She'd attributed his changed mood to thankfulness that he was vindicated, out of the Confederacy's hands—and no longer the enemy of his former wife and eldest son.

But that was only part of it, she sensed now. His capture, imprisonment and parole had affected him more profoundly than she'd ever suspected.

"Do you think you *can* preach again, Jephtha?"

He picked up the cigar stub from the bedside table, puffed, then crushed it out.

"Yes, I do. I couldn't do it a year ago. Not even a month ago. But now I can."

"For so long a time, I—I thought you didn't believe in God any longer."

"Perhaps I didn't. The fault was mine, not His. Life's curious, Molly. Here we are, caught in what will probably be the most devastating war in this nation's history—a war tearing the country apart—and in the midst of that, He showed me the angels."

"Angels?"

"Remember Lincoln's inaugural? 'The better angels of our nature—' I saw them in Gideon. And Fan. They can bring us through this war. They can heal the wounds afterward if we only let them. They were there all along but I didn't see them. Not even when you tried to show them to me—"

He squeezed her shoulder, a smile in his voice:

"You're a wonderful woman, Molly. The good Lord made you a fisher of men, not to mention a saver of string."

She lay against him, her mind brimming with questions. How long had he been pondering his decision? All night? She'd ask him that, and many other things. But not now. She was too happy.

The windows were lightening the bedroom's sultry darkness. At length Jephtha resumed:

"Yes, I believe I'll help Hiram's congregation. Have

to give up my whiskey, I suppose. And stop saying damn and hell in public—"

He laughed, a deep, joyous sound. Somewhere in the street, sharp commands rang out. Horses trotted by. The noises of war. She could ignore them when he laughed.

"We ought to shop for a ring soon, Molly. Oh, yes—and one more thing."

He slipped his arm under her shoulder again, pulling her close.

"I must buy another Testament."

Epilogue

Captain Kent, C.S.A.

Two notable events occurred on Saturday, May 31, 1862. One was private, the other public. Both were to affect the life of Captain Gideon Kent.

After nine hours of labor, Margaret Marble Kent was delivered of a six and a half pound daughter. And General Joseph Johnston suffered a severe wound at Seven Pines, just a few miles east of Richmond.

A vast Union army of invasion—a hundred thousand men and a siege train under the command of General McClellan—lay across the Peninsula, its target the capital. The campfires of the Northern lines could be seen from the city by night.

Gideon Kent's elation over the birth of his first child, and the happy confusion attending the selection of a name, helped him forget for a few hours that Richmond was in mortal danger, the Confederacy's best general out of action and an unpopular replacement serving in his stead. Robert E. Lee's reputation had suffered after his defeats in western Virginia the preceding year. Captain Kent of the First Virginia Regiment of General Stuart's cavalry was not encouraged that the fortunes of the Army of Northern Virginia—and the future of the Confederacy—were now in the hands of the reserved, courtly soldier now being called "Evacuating" Lee.

On Wednesday, the eleventh of June, Gideon was assigned to a special detachment of approximately twelve hundred troopers; portions of the First, Fourth and Ninth Virginia, plus men from the Jeff Davis Legion. He didn't know the detachment's mission when Brigadier Stuart led the horsemen out of Richmond next day, riding his new charger, Star of the East.

Stuart's escort had expanded. It now included a very special soldier named Sweeny. The former minstrel-show performer had been stranded in Richmond at the start of the war. Stuart had maneuvered him out of another unit into his own because of Sweeny's talent on the banjo. Now the general had banjo accompaniment when he rode and sang.

He also had conversation in a bastard combination of German and English. A few days before Seven Pines, he'd taken a flamboyant European dragoon into his retinue; Von Borcke, late of the Royal Prussian Army. The officer had run the blockade in order to join the Confederacy.

Gideon looked smart in his gray uniform as he set out along the Brook Road behind the First Virginia's commander, Colonel Fitzhugh Lee. Colonel Lee permitted his men to decorate their hats much as the brigadier decorated his. Unable to afford an ostrich plume, Gideon settled for a pair of turkey feathers.

He hated to leave Margaret in Richmond when the Yanks were closing in. But he had a job to do. The war had become that for him—a task, not a crusade.

Still, three things buoyed his spirits as he rode.

The first was a tiny lock of hair—more properly, down—snipped from the head of his daughter Eleanor. This he carried in his blouse pocket.

The second was his horse. It was probably a stolen animal. It had certainly been outrageously over-priced by the trader with whom he'd arranged a confidential meeting near Camp Qui Vive last autumn. Nevertheless,

Will-O'-The-Wisp was a splendid roan, and surely part thoroughbred.

Gideon had written a letter to his father to tell him the smuggled bullion had enabled him to buy the horse. He'd paid an exorbitant price to an illegal courier, with no guarantee the letter would ever reach the New York *Union*'s Washington office. He'd received no reply.

The third thing that helped lift his spirits was a flag. It had been sent to him as a token of gratitude by Miss Wonderly of White House. Like the one she'd given Rodney, she had sewn it herself immediately after the new and less confusing battle standard had been approved and adopted in November.

The flag, half the regulation cavalry size, was brilliant red, with white stars on a blue St. Andrew's cross. Gideon carried it neatly folded over his belt near his revolver—a .44-caliber, pin-fire, ten-shot buck-and-ball Le Mat, French-made and mint new. That particular revolver was growing more and more popular with the Confederate soldiers who could afford to buy one. He'd used some of the gold to buy the revolver as a replacement for his Colts. He'd lost one during a hot skirmish at Drainesville in December. The other had been stolen from his tent a month later.

The flag, the horse, the child—they were his talismans; the sum of his hope for survival and victory. He was confident they'd carry him through whatever lay ahead.

As his father had predicted, the war was assuming near-unimaginable dimensions. In March the C. S. *Virginia*—the captured *Merrimack* refitted—had dueled with a queer-looking Northern craft in Hampton Roads. *Monitor* and its Confederate counterpart belonged to a new breed of vessel everyone was talking about. Ironclads, they were called. Experts said the day of the wooden fighting ship had ended at Hampton Roads.

April had driven home the war's mounting human cost. Somewhere in Tennessee—Gideon had only the sketchiest understanding of the geography of the western theater—a gigantic battle centered near a place called Shiloh Meeting House had resulted in casualties almost beyond the mind's capacity to comprehend. Over ten thousand were killed or lost on the Southern side; over thirteen thousand on the other.

Gideon's father-in-law had mixed feelings about the battle. Willard Marble didn't know whether to grieve because a Confederate triumph the first day had become a disaster on the second, or to celebrate because his old protector, Uncle Sam Grant, now a Union general, had been instrumental in the battle's final outcome. Given two reasons to seek the bottle, the Sergeant indulged with a vengeance, and lay in a stupor for five days.

Matt was involved in the war now. Fan's last letter from Lexington had enclosed another from her second son, together with a sketch of black men loading coal aboard a rakish-looking steamer. Matt had scribbled his letter and sketched the dock workers in Nassau, where his ship had put in to fill her holds before undertaking the perilous voyage to Cape Fear. Matt's skipper was running the blockade.

Despite the widening war, Gideon was in a good mood as the special cavalry detachment turned east from the Brook Road. It didn't take much imagination to guess they were going on a reconnaissance mission; probing the strength and strategic position of the Union army led by the general called Little Napoleon. Gideon was confident the mission would succeed. Stuart had proved himself a superior leader. And Gideon had his talismans.

The fine horse.

The brave flag.

The precious lock of hair.

Three days later—Sunday—when the jubilant Brigadier's troopers dashed back into Richmond after riding completely around McClellan's army, there was no roan named Will-O'-The-Wisp among the lathered horses.

The regimental roster listed Captain Gideon Kent as missing in action.

*From Georgia ravaged by Sherman's horde
to the raw railheads and cow towns
of the frontier . . .
from the Western plains
bloodied by the lances
of the Indian wars
to Eastern streets
bloodied by the bombs
of the labor struggle . . .
the Kents battle their own natures,
and each other,
for control of the family's destiny
in*

The Warriors

Volume VI

of

The Kent Family Chronicles

Afterword

Researching The American Bicentennial Series would have been impossible without the help of the Dayton and Montgomery County Public Library, which is under the able direction of Mr. William Chait. When specialized questions have cropped up, his dedicated staff has always been ready to assist in digging for the answers—or to locate obscure but necessary reference works in other parts of the country.

In preparing THE TITANS, I also received generous and invaluable assistance from The Virginia Historical Society, Richmond, and the Archives of the United States Military Academy, West Point. My warmest thanks go to all three institutions—though of course none is in any way responsible for errors of fact or interpretation that may have found their way into this book, or the Series.

It was in a Boston bookshop during a promotion tour for THE SEEKERS that a reader first approached me with a family tree he had drawn up for the Kents. Since then I've seen quite a few others and heard of more. Frequent letters to the publisher have likewise requested a family tree covering the books to date.

You will find one included in this volume.

JOHN JAKES

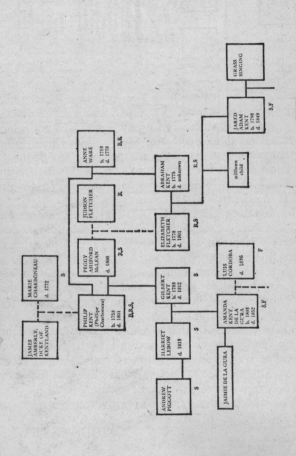

JAMES
AMBERLY,
DUKE OF
KENTLAND

MARIE
CHARBONEAU
d. 1772

B

PHILIP
KENT
(Phillipe
Charboneau)
b. 1753
d. 1801

B,R,S,

PEGGY
ASHFORD
McLEAN
d. 1800

R,S

JUDSON
FLETCHER

R

ANNE
WARE
b. 1753
d. 1778

B,R

ABRAHAM
KENT
b. 1775
d. unknown

R,S

ELIZABETH
FLETCHER
b. 1778
d. 1801

R,S

JARED
ADAM
KENT
b. 1798
d. 1849

GRASS
SINGING

S,F

stillborn
child

GILBERT
KENT
b. 1785
d. 1812

S

HARRIET
LEBOW
d. 1813

S

AMANDA
KENT
DE LA
GURA
b. 1803
d. 1852

LUIS
CORDOBA
d. 1896

F

S,F

ANDREW
PIGGOTT

S

JAIMIE DE LA GURA

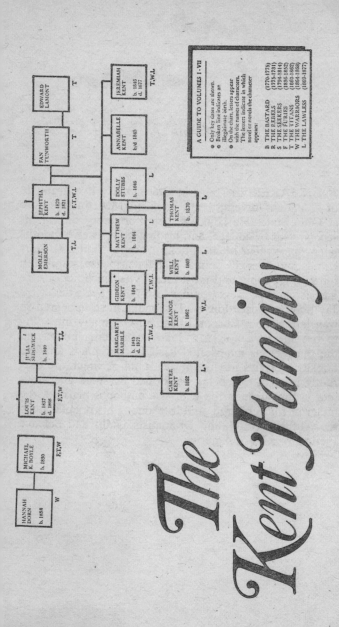

The Kent Family

A GUIDE TO VOLUMES I–VII

- Only key dates are shown.
- Broken line indicates an illegitimate birth.
- On the chart, letters appear with the names of characters. The letters indicate the novel or novels in which the character appears:

B	THE BASTARD	(1770-1775)
R	THE REBELS	(1775-1781)
S	THE SEEKERS	(1794-1814)
F	THE FURIES	(1835-1852)
T	THE TITANS	(1860-1862)
W	THE WARRIORS	(1864-1868)
L	THE LAWLESS	(1869-1877)

HANNAH DORN b. 1858 — W

MICHAEL K. BOYLE b. 1830 — F,T,W

LOUIS KENT b. 1857 d. 1908 — F,T,W

JULIA SEDGWICK b. 1849 — T,L

MARGARET MARBLE b. 1843 d. 1877 — T,W,L

CARTER KENT b. 1862 — L

MOLLY EMERSON — T,L

JEPHTHA KENT b. 1820 d. 1871 — F,T,W,L

FAN TUNWORTH — T

EDWARD LAMONT — T

GIDEON KENT b. 1843 — T,W,L

MATTHEW KENT b. 1844 — L

DOLLY STUBBS b. 1846 — L

ANNABELLE KENT b/d 1845

JEREMIAH KENT b. 1846 d. 1877 — T,W,L

ELEANOR KENT b. 1862 — W,L

WILL KENT b. 1860 — L

THOMAS KENT b. 1870 — L

Poldock

Kirsten Graham

About the Author

JOHN JAKES was born in Chicago. He is a graduate of DePauw University, and took his M.A. in literature at Ohio State. He sold his first short story during his second year of college, and his first book twelve months later. Since then, he has published more than 200 short stories and over 50 books—chiefly suspense, nonfiction for young people and most recently, science fiction. He has also authored six popular historical novels under his Jay Scotland pseudonym. His books have appeared in translation from Europe to Japan. Originally intending to become an actor, Mr. Jakes' continuing interest in the theater has manifested itself in four plays and the books and lyrics for five musicals, all of which are currently in print and being performed by stock and amateur groups around the U.S. The author is married, the father of four children, and lists among his organizations the Authors Guild, the Dramatists Guild and Science Fiction Writers of America.